TANZA

ZAMBIA

LAKE NYASA

MALAWI

•Vila Gonçalo

ZAMBELA
SANCTUARY

M O Ç A M B I Q U E

Moçambique•

MOÇAM-
BIQUE
ISLAND

M O Z A M B I Q U E   C H A N N E L

CABORA
BASSA

Zambeze River

GORONGOSA
NATIONAL
PARK

RHODESIA

•Beira

INDIAN   OCEAN

KRUGER NATIONAL PARK

SOUTH
AFRICA

MOÇAMBIQUE

0   100   200 MILES

•Lourenço Marques

SWAZI-
LAND

J. P. TREMBLAY

Books by

JAMES A. MICHENER

Tales of the South Pacific
The Fires of Spring
Return to Paradise
The Voice of Asia
The Bridges at Toko-Ri
Sayonara
The Floating World
The Bridge at Andau
Hawaii
Report of the County Chairman
Caravans
The Source
Iberia
Presidential Lottery
The Quality of Life
The Drifters

with A. Grove Day
Rascals in Paradise

THE DRIFTERS

The

DRIFTERS

A
Novel
by

JAMES
A.
MICHENER

RANDOM HOUSE
New York

ISBN: 0-394-46200-9 Tr.
ISBN: 0-394-47020-6 Ltd.

Library of Congress Catalog Card Number: 75-117655

Manufactured in the United States of America
by Kingsport Press, Inc., Kingsport, Tenn.

An extract from *The Lusiads of Luis de Camões,*
translated by Leonard Bacon, is reprinted by
permission of The Hispanic Society of America,
New York, 1966, p. 16.

98765432

Designed by Bernard Klein

CONTENTS

J O E

Youth is truth.

No man is so foolish as to desire war more than peace: for in peace sons bury their fathers, but in war fathers bury their sons.—Herodotus

The greatest coup engineered by the university in recent years had been the employment of Dr. Richard Conover, Nobel Prize winner in biology. He added much luster to the faculty, but his principal work continued to focus in Washington, where he was conducting experiments on nerve gases for the Department of Defense. This meant that he was unable to do any actual teaching at the university; his courses were handled by a series of attractive young men who were, on the average, two and one half years older than the university students, four per cent more intelligent, and six per cent better adjusted. Of course, students could sometimes catch a glimpse of Dr. Conover heading for the airport on Sunday afternoon, and this reassured them.

War is good business. Invest your sons.

The university had lost its way and everyone knew it except the Board of Regents, the alumni, the faculty and ninety per cent of the students.

I am a serious student. Please do not spindle, fold or staple me.

He was looking through all the markets to find a Christmas
present for L.B.J. What he had in mind was a set of dominoes.

Goddammit, I wish you'd listen to my main argument.
Thirty years from now the government, the banks, the important businesses, the universities and everything that
counts in this world will be run by today's humanities ma-
jors. The scientists will never run anything except labora-
tories, they never have, they never can. Yet in this university
we spend all our time and money training scientists and we
ignore the humanities people on whom the welfare and
guidance of the world have always depended and will always depend. I say that is stupidity, and if the Board of Regents and the faculty aren't smart enough to stop it, we
must.

Better a certain peace than a hoped-for victory.—Livy

When they conk you on the head with their billysticks,
zap them right back with superlove.

With men, the normal state of nature is not peace but war.—Kant

Political exile has been the last refuge of many noble
minds. In exile Dante Alighieri wrote his finest poetry
and Vladimir Ilyich Ulyanov forged the ideas that
were to paralyze the world. It was in exile from German militarism that Carl Schurz made his scintillating
contributions to American life, and in exile from
Spanish reaction that Duque de Rivas wrote his
notable books. A flood of exiles from Scotland
founded the intellectual excellence of Canada, and
daring adventurers, thrown out of their native islands,
peopled the Pacific. The brilliant minds that conceived the atomic bomb for the United States were
principally Jewish exiles kicked out of Nazi Germany.
For three centuries the United States profited from
the political exiles who fled to our protection. It
took the politicians of this generation to launch a
reverse flow.

Never pick up a girl before one o'clock in the afternoon.
If she's so beautiful, what's she doing out of bed before noon?

If a young man, no matter how insecure, can't make it with the girls
in Torremolinos, he had better resign from the human race.

Zeus picked up Ganymede at the Wilted Swan.

ON his twentieth birthday Joe faced a problem of such complexity that he had to ask for help, and in this way he met Mrs. Rubin.

His confusion had started two years earlier, when against his will he registered for the draft. He told the other fellows in high school, in the awkward sentences that characterized his attempts at communication, 'How does that grab you? Can't order a beer but can go to war.'

He had always been tall for his age, rangy rather than compact, and in the style of his group, had begun to wear his hair rather long at the sides, noticeably so in the back. He had not been good enough in athletics to attract the attention of any college or sufficiently intellectual to win an academic scholarship. About the only thing he had to show after graduating from high school was a wallet-sized piece of white cardboard attesting to the fact that he had registered for the draft and been automatically classified 1-A; his real classification would come later, after he was called for his physical. Upon entering the university he had been required to show his draft card, and the professor in charge seemed gratified that he had one.

On his nineteenth birthday he received an official letter which scared the hell out of him. It was from his draft board and was waiting for him when he got back from chemistry. For ten agonizing minutes he had been afraid to open it. 'I'm not scared of war,' he assured his roommate, a sallow-faced philosophy major from Nevada, 'and I'm not a conscientious objector, but Vietnam bugs me. Jesus, I don't want to crawl through rice paddies.'

When he finally opened the letter he found nothing but a mimeographed statement: 'In view of your enrollment in the university, you are classified 2-S, which you will keep until you graduate. However, you must inform this board of any change in your educational status.' A new card was enclosed, which he had to show to college officials and bartenders.

Even though he had managed good grades as a freshman, his sophomore year was proving difficult. The university he had chosen was no brain-train like Berkeley nor a mod-squad like Stanford; it was one of the numerous solid institutions that dotted California and accounted for that state's superiority in so many fields; where a state like Pennsylvania provided a college education for thirty-one percent of its high school graduates, California educated seventy-three, and this difference had to tell. Joe held his own with the competition, drawing down grades that kept him in college and out of the draft.

It was this latter that engendered his moral crisis. Four ugly events accumulated in a short period of time. They haunted him, could not be dismissed; of itself, each was trivial, a thing young men would have been able to dismiss ten years ago. Now, in the autumn of 1968, they coalesced to form a dreadful incubus.

The first event was accidental. His roommate, who got almost straight *A*s and had done so throughout high school, was visited one day by an older boy named Karl, who had graduated the previous year. He was a big, able fellow who dropped by the room and lounged on the bed with a beer can. 'No matter what they tell you,' he pontificated, 'take three education courses. The wise guys laughed when I dropped out of pre-law and took Elementary Ed . . . Diaper Changing III, they called it. All right, they're in Vietnam. I'm salted away in an elementary school in Anaheim. I'm safe from the draft for the duration.' He lolled back against the pillows, swigged his beer, and repeated his admonition, 'Take education.'

'How do you find teaching?' Joe asked.

'Who gives a goddamn? You report in the morning. The kids are raising hell. You keep them from tearing the place apart. You go home at night.'

'What do you teach them?'

'Nothing.'

'Won't you get fired?'

'I'm big. The kids are afraid of me. So I keep reasonable order.

The principal is so grateful for one quiet room he don't give a damn if I teach 'em anything or not.'

'Sounds pretty awful,' Joe said.

'I'm out of the draft,' the teacher said.

Later, Joe's roommate dragged him along on a visit to the elementary school to see if the principal might have a job for them when they graduated, and they watched children, many of them black, roaring up and down the halls. The principal was a kindly man, about forty, with falling hair. 'Your friend is one of the best teachers we have,' he said enthusiastically. 'If you qualify for the California certificate, we would be most pleased to add you to our staff.'

The second experience was disgusting. One night their door burst open with a bang and Eddie, a burly football player good enough to hold down a scholarship but not quite good enough for the first team, rushed in to announce with obvious triumph, 'By God, I finally got her pregnant! We're gonna get married next week.'

'Maud?'

'Yep. She saw the doctor and it's official. Morning after the wedding I go back to my draft board and pick up that good old 3-A classification . . . and I'm home free.'

Other students came in to congratulate him, and he said expansively, 'Maud and I studied the rhythm system till we had it pinpointed. During the period when she could be knocked up we screwed three, four times a day. You remember how I fell down in the Oregon game? Hell, I was so weary I couldn't stand up. I screwed her twice that morning. Coach gave me all hell, but I think that was the morning I rammed it home. Anyway, she's pregnant and I'm out of the draft.'

One of the men asked, 'You think your 3-A classification will hold?'

'It's the sure one. All you guys ought to get married. Lot of girls over there would be glad to shack up with you. Screw 'em to death. Get 'em pregnant. Tell the government to go to hell.'

'Is it worth it?' someone asked.

'Who gives a good goddamn? When this nonsense passes, get a divorce and go about your business.'

'Would you get a divorce?' Joe asked.

The football player looked at Joe, started to hand him a wisecrack, reconsidered, and said, 'If the girl you got pregnant happened to be someone you loved, you'd be ahead of the game.'

'Yours wasn't?' Joe asked quietly.

'Mine wasn't,' the big man said.

The third experience made a moral confrontation unavoidable. On the floor above was a pitiful jerk named Max who studied every weekend, with never a chance of understanding calculus or Adam Smith. He was a fat boy from Los Angeles with a bad complexion and he wanted to be a doctor, as his mother said, but his professors quickly saw that this was out of the question, so he had shifted to business, but this was also impossible.

'You've got to stay in college!' his parents bellowed. 'You want to disgrace us? You want to fail and go into the army?'

His mother had arranged for him to transfer to education. 'So you can get a job teaching in Los Angeles, like Harry Phillips, and you're safe.' He had switched to education but lacked even the intelligence to pass those courses, and now it appeared that he was to be dismissed from the university, lose his draft deferment, and return to 1-A.

At this crisis Max waddled through the dormitory, looking for someone who would be willing to slip into the examination room and write a critical test for him. 'The questions are easy,' he explained, 'but I just can't organize my thoughts.' When he found no one on the second floor willing to take the risk, he came back to Joe and said, 'Even if you haven't taken the course, Joe, you could answer the questions. I know you could.' It was a pitiful performance, and after the exams were corrected, Max got the bad news. He was out. His deferment was ended. He must go into the army.

His distracted parents came to collect him, and in the privacy of his room, gave him hell, so that he left the dormitory red-eyed and trembling. He broke away from his parents to say goodbye to Joe. 'You were a good friend,' he said. Then, shuddering, he walked toward the car.

The fellows talked about Max a good deal and agreed that if there was ever a man who ought not go to war, it was Max. A pre-med student said, 'How'd you like to have him as your buddy on patrol through a rice paddy?' Another said, 'It's criminal to pick soldiers because they were dumb in college.' But Joe's philosophical roommate offered a correction: 'The crime began when our nation permitted college to serve as an exemption from a service which for others was obligatory.'

When the crowd broke up, Joe and his roommate continued the discussion till well past midnight, and for the first time Joe heard a literate man propound the theory that the whole system was immoral. His roommate argued, 'As you said the other day, for Karl to ruin the lives of his students so that he can escape the draft is an obvious immorality, but it's caused by a greater. The immorality of the United States waging an undeclared war which has never been authorized by Congress.'

'What do you mean?' Joe asked.

'Take that loud-mouthed football player who was boasting he'd knocked up a girl he didn't love in order to escape the draft. That's obviously immoral, but it couldn't have happened unless our democracy had first been degraded. Officials who are elected to represent us allow themselves to be by-passed, then applaud when our President acts illegally.'

'What are you going to do about it?'

'I don't know. But I do know that a man cannot cooperate indefinitely with an immoral situation without becoming contaminated. And I do not intend to contaminate myself.'

He spoke quietly, but with such deep conviction that Joe had to determine for himself how far he would permit the self-contamination of avoiding the draft by hiding in college.

It was the fourth experience that crystallized his attitude, a thing of itself so trivial that to an ordinary man in ordinary times it would not even be remembered. Joe had gone to a bar in the rougher part of town to hear a musical group, and on the way back to the dormitory he happened to pass a crowd of Negroes lounging at a street corner, and one of them in military uniform had said, 'Hiya, Whitey. See you in Vietnam,' and another said, 'Not him. He's college.' Joe laughed, cocked his right thumb and forefinger like a pistol and shot at the soldier, clicking his tongue as he did. The soldier fell back two paces, clutched his heart, and said, 'Damn, he shoot straight.'

That was all. Joe passed on, but the meaningless incident kept reverberating in his mind, day after day—the horrible fact that in this war black men who could not afford to attend university were drafted and white men who had the money were not. It was indecent, immoral, infuriating, and everything said by the leaders of society, men like General Hershey and J. Edgar Hoover, simply exacerbated the basic wrong. Negroes were drafted, white men weren't; the poor were hauled off to war, the rich weren't; the stupid were shot at, the bright boys weren't. And it was all done from an immoral premise in prosecution of a war immorally founded.

Perplexed by these confusions, Joe entered the final month of the year, unaware that his roommate, thanks to his training in philosophy, had arrived at certain important conclusions that Joe would not reach for some weeks to come. Shortly before Christmas a group of students opposed to the war announced a peace rally. It was scheduled for two in the afternoon at the main quadrangle, and by one the campus was crowded with spectators from the town. Special campus police were on hand, with instructions to prevent physical violence. They were supported by regular police, also determined to forestall trouble. When these saw a parade approaching with signs like *Love America or Leave It, U.S.A. All the Way,* and *Back Our Brave Men in Vietnam,* they quietly diverted the marchers from the campus.

Through a bull horn, one of the policemen told these counter-demonstrators, 'The peaceniks have a constitutional right to their say. You can't take those signs on campus.' The signs were confiscated but the marchers were allowed to disperse through the crowd in the quadrangle.

When Joe's roommate looked down from their dormitory and saw the strangers and the two groups of police, he said, 'Things may get tough. I want you to know that what I'm going to do this afternoon isn't done hastily. I've been thinking about it ever since that day we saw Karl teaching in his school.'

He and Joe walked down to the quadrangle, where they parted, because Joe always backed away from public demonstrations. As a freshman he had refused to attend football rallies and he felt the same about campus protests. 'You do your thing,' he told his roommate. 'I'll watch from over here.'

The demonstration proceeded peacefully. Joe, perched on the base of a statue commemorating the founder of the university, listened to the loudspeakers as a wispy little professor of chemistry, Dr. Laurence Rubin, tried to explain that the war was damaging America's posture at home and abroad, but hecklers from the parade kept shouting, 'You wanna surrender?' Rubin had anticipated such

a charge, but when he tried to explain the difference between surrender and planned withdrawal from a non-productive situation,
the hecklers would not allow him to give it, shouting, 'Ending the
war is Nixon's job. Shut up and let him do it.' So Professor Rubin
was driven from the microphone with his basic thesis unstated.

A student with a voice capable of filling the quadrangle grabbed
the microphone and shouted, 'If action is the only thing Washington
can understand, we'll give them action.' Joe noticed that as soon as
this echoed through the loudspeakers, both the campus police and
the regulars moved closer to the platform. The speaker saw them
coming but nevertheless gave a signal, whereupon a group of some
thirty or forty coeds began singing 'Blowin' in the Wind,' a stately
chant of resistance which some of the men in the audience took up.
It was a wintry song, well adapted to this quadrangle with its milling
and undefined groups.

When the song was at its height a group of seven young men
climbed onto the platform, and in view of everyone, lit cigarette
lighters and with studied resolve burned their draft cards. To his
surprise, Joe saw that his quiet roommate was among them, was
indeed their leader in this act of defiance that solemnly separated
them from a society they could no longer respect and whose laws
they would no longer obey.

The sight of smoke curling into the air inflamed the marchers
from the town, and even those spectators who had brought with
them no intention of violence found themselves outraged. Suddenly,
from many quarters, people started rushing at the platform, trying to
pull down the seven card-burners, and this brought the two groups
of police into action, their clubs swinging. To Joe's astonishment,
the police did not use their clubs against the rioters; instead they
reached up, grabbed the protesting students, and beat them as they
dragged them to the ground. Joe's roommate broke loose and started
to run away, but another group of students, infuriated by the card-
burning, blocked his way and began punching him in the face. He
lurched backward into a girl, who screamed. Other girls, not yet
involved but afraid that they might be knocked down, began screaming, and a general melee developed.

Now the police took over, slam-banging their way through the
crowd to arrest the card-burners. Joe's roommate, his head befuddled by the punches he had taken, stumbled toward the police as if
he were attacking them and was greeted by a rain of sickening blows

which knocked him to the pavement. Joe, when he saw him fall, automatically leaped from the safety of his pedestal and ran to help, but the police considered him one more long-haired troublemaker and waded into him.

One club racked him up, another smashed into his gut, and a third cracked across his skull and brought him down in a heap. He said later that he heard this last blow before he felt its piercing message; it was the last thing he did hear, for he collapsed in a lump of meaningless bone and unassociated flesh. He vaguely remembered thinking that his knees had disappeared and his legs had become water. Then he fainted.

———•—•—•———

While his roommate sat in jail awaiting trial, Joe stayed alone in the dormitory grappling with a slowly developing conviction. Customarily such painful assessment comes to a man in his late forties, when he girds himself for a final push, or in his fifties, when he assesses the dark failure in which he is embroiled without chance of escape, but for Joe's generation the time of reappraisal came early, and he faced his alone.

He liked girls and dated several, but so far had found none with whom he would be easy in discussing his present crisis. He was also familiar with certain boys in the dorm, but knew none well enough to burden them with his confusion. There were no professors with whom he would have cared to talk; those who showed understanding were too busy with their own work, and those who were available were clods with whom any meaningful dialogue would be impossible. So he stayed to himself.

The university was on the quarter system, which required a battery of exams prior to Christmas. Joe mustered enough concentration to try Professor Rubin's chemistry exam, but he did so poorly that when history and English III came around, he didn't bother to report to the examination hall. He stayed in his room and tried to face up to the various dilemmas in which he found himself. He did not shave, nor did he report to the dining hall. Late at night he would wander through the dark streets and pick up a hamburger and some coffee, but for the most part he kept to himself, rubbing the knobby bruise on his head and thinking.

A girl from La Jolla dropped off a letter inviting him to drive her home in her car. When he read the message he could visualize her, an attractive kid with neatly combed hair pulled back into a ponytail. It would be fun spending the Christmas vacation with her, but not this year. He went down to the phone. 'That you, Elinor? It was a sweet letter you sent. I'd like to, but I'm all chopped up.' She said, 'I know,' and drove home alone.

For the first week Joe stayed in his silent room within the silent dormitory. Since the dining room was closed, he ate pick-up meals, and had his dinner at a hamburger joint. As the year drew to a close he tried to cast up his situation, and concluded that for him the university was washed up. He could not in honesty remain in what had become for many a draft haven. He rejected refuge in these classrooms when men like Max had to leave for war, or when the Negroes down the back alleys were being conscripted. He refused to compromise any longer with an immoral position.

On the other hand, he could not publicly burn his draft card the way his roommate had done, for he shied away from exhibitionism. To stand in a conspicuous group while girl students were chanting 'The answer is blowing in the wind' would be ridiculous. That was out.

He remembered the rationalization of a chap from San Francisco who had allowed himself to be drafted last spring: 'The only honorable thing to do is join the army and bore from within. When they get me they're gonna get a guy determined to undermine the whole military complex.' On his first weekend in camp he had begun distributing pamphlets urging his fellow soldiers to revolt against their officers, and he followed his own advice. One morning at roll call he started laughing, real loud, and when the sergeant stormed down the line and asked what he thought was so funny, he said, 'The whole silly system, and you most of all.' The sergeant kept his temper and asked what he meant by this, and he said, 'You, you stupid son-of-a-bitch. You tell us to suck in our guts and you couldn't suck in your gut if . . .' The sergeant had poleaxed him, and in the infirmary he was notified of the court-martial which eventually sent him to jail. The fellows in the dormitory had agreed that he had behaved honorably, but for Joe such action would be inappropriate; he did not like to disrupt things, and even were he so inclined, when the fat sergeant arrived to bawl him out, he would feel sorry for him and not want to cause trouble.

But Joe could get angry, and on the last day of the year he did just that. In fact, he flew into a storming rage, cursing and kicking the furniture about his room. The occasion for his rage was deceptively simple: he received a letter. It was of no consequence, just a routine note, wishing him a Merry Xmas, from the girl who had invited him to La Jolla. What evoked his fury was the government cancellation on the letter: *Pray for Peace.*

'That's what's wrong with the whole damned country,' he fumed. 'On our letters we stamp "Pray for Peace," to prove that we're a peace-loving nation. But let one miserable son-of-a-bitch do anything about peace, and they bust him over the head with clubs. What has happened? When those townspeople were in the quadrangle the other day they actually hated . . . they could have killed my roommate . . . because he wanted peace.'

Alone in his room, he remembered a lecture given by one of the young professors: 'The United States is the most militaristic country on earth. Newspapers, television, universities and even the churches are dedicated to warfare and any voice that speaks out against it has to be silenced. You will notice that newspapers refer to anti-war spokesmen as "the so-called peaceniks." Cartoonists depict them as lunatics. Television commentators speak of them as rioters and scum who should be driven from the streets. Our nation feels it has to destroy the peace people because it knows that to keep our country functioning, we must have war. Not for economic reasons, for spiritual ones.'

Joe recalled a conversation he once had with a music major: 'This university has a very good conservatory. Our teachers can put on damned good opera. But do you know how the board of regents judges the department? How good the marching band is? If a hundred and fifty young men and women in military uniform swing onto the football field between halves, and keep step, then the music department gets a generous budget next year . . . and to hell with Beethoven. The regents are right. Do you know why? Because every little town in California demands that its high school have a marching band . . . in military uniform . . . keeping step . . . drilling to John Philip Sousa. The citizens want this because they love the military . . . they love parades. And if this university can't provide music graduates to build marching bands—by God, the small towns will look to some other university . . . and we'll be in trouble. The regents aren't dumb. They know what's important.'

Joe had been so fascinated by this theory of martial music that he had accompanied his friend on an excursion to a small town to watch the marching band which had been trained by a recent graduate from the music department, and things were the way he had described, except that in addition to the band, they had a drill team consisting of little girls thirteen and fourteen dressed in military uniforms and carrying wooden replicas of army rifles, complete with leather slings. Led by an ex-army man in his fifties, the girls went through drills as if they were an infantry company on its way to the Civil War, and when at the end they lined up in one single rank and fired an imitation salute, a cannon went off and everyone cheered.

Wherever Joe looked in his society he found new proof of America's fascination with violence. If he went into town he passed a dismal hall whose weather-beaten clapboard sides carried the sign: *Learn Karate! Destroy Your Assailant!* A crudely drawn picture showed a fearless young man breaking the neck of a colored man who leaped at him from behind a corner. Some years ago the hall had carried a simpler sign: *Learn Judo. Protect Yourself.* But this had attracted few customers, for it was self-defense. With karate you could kill the other man, and this possibility was so enticing that enrollments quadrupled.

On television it was professional football with its planned mayhem that attracted spectators who used to watch baseball, and in the movies it was constant violence, showing dozens dead where one would have made the point. But most of all there was Vietnam, that running sore which contaminated so much. 'We want peace in Vietnam,' Joe reflected as he looked at the letter which had so aroused him, 'but God help Richard Nixon if he tries to do anything about it when he becomes President.' He threw the letter on his table, and its postmark taunted him: *Pray for Peace.*

And so the lonely debate progressed. Late that afternoon he made up his mind. Taking a sheet of college stationery, he sat at his desk for two hours, composing a careful letter which he spent another hour editing and rewriting. He then walked past the karate hall and into the empty town; at the post office he registered the letter and had it stamped *Pray for Peace.* He placed the receipt carefully in his wallet. When he got back to his room he found Dr. Rubin, his chemistry professor, knocking on the door. 'Come in,' Joe said, and the frail little man sat primly on a straight-backed chair.

Placing Joe's examination paper on the table, he said, in a complaining voice, 'Joe, that was a miserable performance.'

'I know. I'm dropping out.'

'No need to,' Rubin said in his nasal whine. He turned back the cover and disclosed the mark, $B-$. For some moments Joe looked at this unmerited grade, trying to decipher why Rubin had awarded it. Then, as if from an unreal distance, he heard Rubin saying, 'I saw you at the peace rally. I saw the policeman club you on the head. I watched you during my exam and learned later that you didn't even report for the others. But I will testify to the guidance people that you earned a $B-$ in my class and that you were too ill to take the later exams. Joe, without falsifying you can claim head damage . . . stay in the university . . .'

'Not any more,' Joe said. From his wallet he extracted the receipt for a letter he had mailed to his draft board and from his desk he produced his work sheets, and when Professor Rubin read them he grew respectful, for it was a letter that he might have written had he been a student:

I have reviewed carefully my position both in the draft and in my nation . . . I have concluded that I can no longer honestly cooperate with a system that is basically immoral nor with a war that is historically wrong . . . I am therefore returning to you in this letter my registration card and my classification card . . . I shall refuse to report any further to your board and I reject herewith my classification of 2-S. I am aware of what I am doing, why I am doing it, and what I can expect in retaliation.

There was more, some of it obviously the work of a man not yet twenty-one, all of it adding up to the picture of a human being reaching a moral decision and announcing himself as willing to abide by any consequences that might follow.

Rubin folded the letter, placed the receipt on top, and handed both back to Joe. 'Things now become quite different,' he said. 'The $B-$ I've given you and the medical excuse I offer could become quite important when you get out of jail and want to gain readmission.'

'You think it'll mean jail?' Joe asked.

'Probably. What you'd better do, Joe, is talk with my wife. She's an expert in this, you know.'

Rubin insisted that Joe accompany him, right then, to the big brick Presbyterian church in the center of town where the Women's Committee for Draft Counseling had been given a narrow, draughty room for their work. At the beginning, church members had been appalled at the suggestion that their church sponsor such a committee, but in his quiet way their minister had insisted that Christians had a right to resist their government if their conscience warned them that the government was wrong. When the members continued their objections, he preached three sermons on the Nuremberg Trials, and concluded, 'The burden of those trials was that conscience has an obligation. If our young people decide that they must exercise that conscience, we must help them do so in legal and constructive ways.' He had refused to allow a vote. 'This is not a matter for voting,' he insisted. 'This is a matter of human conscience. This is the logical extension of the Nuremberg Trials, and this church is going to discharge its duty.' His argument was the more effective in that he himself had been an army chaplain at Guadalcanal.

When Professor Rubin led Joe into the church basement, they found at a messy table a small, wiry woman of forty with a tightly combed look. Nodding brusquely to her husband, she launched a barrage of sentences, leaping nimbly from one subject to the next: 'I'm glad to see you're not a deserter. I suppose you turned in your draft card and you want to know whether to go to jail or run away to Canada. How do I know this? Elementary, my dear Jackson.' She laughed nervously at her little joke, then proceeded: 'In this business we learn to spot deserters three blocks away. The military haircut, the shuffle, the fugitive slink. Your long hair makes you ineligible. As to the draft card, Laurence never brings me anyone who has burned his draft card, because that's a legal problem. But it's got to be something serious, or he wouldn't bother on the day before New Year's. *Voilà!*'

She smiled, not generously, but with the tight lips of a self-conscious college girl who had not entirely matured. Professor Rubin made a brief introduction and left, whereupon she said, 'Young man, we start with the fact that you find yourself in a position that is totally insane. If we do that, the alternatives become a little clearer. The government's position is contradictory, immoral, illegal and, in my opinion, unconstitutional, in that no war has been declared. This means there is no legal base for the actions they will take against you. On the other hand, by turning in your draft card and rejecting the system, you've struck at the heart of a cooperative democracy and you must be punished. Our job is to work out precisely where you stand.

'You can do one of three things. On the second of January you can report to your draft board, ask them to ignore your letter and request reinstatement. This will be granted quickly, because no one wants trouble. In your case, we can certify mental disturbance after having been unlawfully struck on the head. All this I can easily arrange, and I am legally obligated to recommend it.'

When Joe shook his head negatively, she continued: 'Rejecting that, you automatically revert to 1-A status and are stigmatized as legally delinquent. You can be arrested on sight, but until someone presses the issue, you probably won't be, so now you face two options. You can leave the university and try to hide out within the United States. There's an effective underground which will do what it can to help. It operates in all cities . . . finds jobs for men like you . . . gets you clothes . . . gives you food. You would be astonished at the good men and women who are willing to hide you and provide some kind of living for you. But it isn't easy, because the good firms insist upon seeing your draft card, which means that when you're delinquent you can't safely apply for anything but underground work.

'Your third option is to leave the country . . . become a political refugee. But before you jump at this, I am obligated to warn you that even if you go so far as to become a citizen of another country, on the day you set foot back in the United States, you'll be arrested and you'll face a penitentiary term. And don't rely on hopes of a general amnesty, either, because America is very revengeful and doesn't go in for amnesty. At the end of World War II, President Truman initiated the first amnesty board in our history. It reviewed over one hundred thousand cases of draft-dodging and deserting, and in the end it granted amnesty to five thousand. You must face the fact that ultimately you will go to jail.'

Joe took a deep breath and said firmly, 'I can't take back my draft card.'

Mrs. Rubin nodded approvingly. She was always pleased when a young man said 'I can't' rather than 'I won't,' because the former indicated a moral conviction that could not be set aside, whereas the latter implied mere personal preference without a solid footing. The I-won't boys got into trouble; the I-can't, into jail.

The atmosphere in the narrow room was tense, and Mrs. Rubin broke it by saying, 'If you do change your mind and take your draft card back, we can still offer you several attractive ways to beat the system. Lots of girls would be willing to marry you . . . have a baby real quick. Or we can find a minister who will coach you in how to be a conscientious objector. You're not an atheist, are you? Or we have several doctors who will certify psychological disturbances. With that knock on the head we might even manage a straight medical certificate. Or you could confess to gross immorality.'

'Not interested,' Joe said.

At this point Mrs. Rubin began laughing, shyly but with an underlying sense of delight. 'That leaves only one escape. But it's a dilly. I like it because it highlights the insanity in which we find ourselves. If you're really determined to beat the draft, the simple solution is to assemble two like-minded friends and enter into a conspiracy to shoot a bald eagle.'

'What?' Joe gasped.

'Any young man who commits a felony as opposed to a misdemeanor is ineligible to serve in our armed forces. Since murder is a felony, if you commit murder you beat the draft, but this is rather a stiff price to pay for temporary freedom, because you might hang. There are lots of other felonies you wouldn't want to bother with, like treason. The simplest felony on the books is shooting a bald eagle. But who knows where to find a bald eagle? So what you do is to enter into a conspiracy to shoot one, and then you don't even have to bother with finding the damned thing.'

Joe was not a man who laughed much, but the concept of his sneaking into a darkened hallway, knocking three times on a closed door and whispering, 'Let's go for that eagle, gang,' was so appropriate to these times, that he chuckled, and in this more relaxed ambience Mrs. Rubin said, 'So we face up to the fact that you've chosen a difficult course. It would be easier if you could count on some financial aid from your parents. Your father?'

'A born loser.'

'Your mother?'

'She collects Green Stamps.'

He volunteered no more, so Mrs. Rubin dropped the subject. 'In principle what do you propose doing?' she asked.

'At this point I can't say.'

'Legally I'm not allowed to make up your mind for you. But if you care to ask me direct questions, I'll answer them.'

More than three minutes passed—a long time for silence between two people—before Joe said hesitantly, 'I was sickened by the way the police beat up on my roommate. When they hit me it didn't matter too much. That was an accident. But they were gunning for him and they really unloaded.'

Mrs. Rubin said nothing, and after another long pause Joe asked, 'Suppose I did want to get out of the country? Then what?'

Mrs. Rubin took a freshly sharpened pencil and began doodling in orderly patterns. 'You would have two obvious choices, Mexico or Canada. The first is most difficult. Strange language. Strange customs and no sympathy with student radicals. Mexico's not advisable. Canada is good. Lots of people up there understand your problems and sympathize. But it's difficult to get in. Along our western states the Canadian immigration authorities turn back obvious draft dodgers and notify the American police. To make it you've got to hook up with our underground railway out of New York.'

'How would I do that?'

'There's a church on Washington Square in New York—that's in Greenwich Village. You report there and they ship you north.'

Joe said nothing, so Mrs. Rubin concluded: 'I am legally required to advise you to go to jail now, and I so recommend.' She took down a form, carefully noted Joe's name and university address, and wrote: 'I recommend that this young man submit himself now for his jail sentence.'

But when Joe rose to leave she accompanied him to the door, grasping his hand and whispering, 'My personal opinion is that you ought to flee this insanity. Go to Samarkand or Pretoria or Marrakech. Youth's a time for dreaming and adventure, not war. Go to jail when you're forty, because then—who gives a damn?'

On New Year's Day 1969 Joe started his trip into exile, and it was typical of him that he chose not the easy southern route to

if I say so!" ' He continued bellowing in a theatrical
the Pope. Get the hell back to work." '

Joe slept in a flophouse recommended to him by the
the church, and he was so tired that he dropped off to
diately. His neighborhood was a lively one, and during
he saw young people, including many attractive girls,
in the streets, but he could not bring himself to join them.
diate responsibility was to earn enough money to make
for Canada.

last visit to the church his counselor gave him an address
Haven, and told him, 'Report after six in the evening. This
run by Yale men and they attend classes during the day.'

ft New York with the impression that it was probably a
d times larger than he had guessed, a hundred times more
ing. At some future time, when circumstances were more
ial, he would like to test himself against this city, against
ifference and beautiful girls. 'I wonder if I could handle
York?' he asked himself as he headed north.

landed in New Haven at mid-afternoon, and as the woman
ew York had predicted, the underground office was closed, so
rifted about the ugly city. It was a cold day, and the more
ee he drank in order to share the warmth of the restaurants,
more his bladder suffered from the icy wind, and he was most
omfortable, but when the counseling office opened he was more
n repaid.

The counselor was a professor of poetry with an Oxford back-
ound, so Joe concluded that he must have been a Rhodes Scholar.
o protect himself legally, the professor, a young man with enthu-
iastic ideas, advised Joe to surrender and go to jail, but when Joe
efused, the professor leaned back in his chair and said, 'When I
was about your age I went to Europe with hosannas in my ears.
You'll be going as a criminal. *Plus ça change, plus ce n'est pas la
même chose.*'

'I haven't decided yet,' Joe said.

'Good God! Aren't you the lad I was supposed to meet from Alabama?'

'California.'

'My dear fellow, forgive me. We get these urgent messages and
we don't really spend the time we should. There's a deserter being
smuggled through here this evening on his way to Canada, and I

Boston but rather the ice-bound highways of the north, and it did
not occur to him to call his ineffectual parents: his father would
snarl and his mother would cry, and between them they would
say not one relevant thing.

He hitchhiked up California's central valley and at Sacramento
struck east toward Reno. The high passes were covered with snow,
so that at times he could look up on either side and see solid banks
three or four feet above his head. He then cut across bleak and
empty Nevada to Salt Lake City, where he wasted some days getting the feel of the Mormon capital, but his first moments of
grandeur—the excitement he sought, the feel of America—came
later when he crossed the vast and barren wastes of Wyoming.
The road swept eastward in noble curves through mountains and
across limitless plains. He traveled fifty or sixty miles at a clip
without seeing so much as a gasoline station, and the occasional
tiny town looked like a steer strayed from the herd and lost in the
immensity of sky and wasteland.

At the Continental Divide, that chain of mountains separating
the western lands Joe had known from the eastern he was about
to see, a snowstorm overtook him, and as he rode through the night
on a truck bound for Cheyenne, the headlights reflected back
from a million glittering flakes.

'This is some country,' he mumbled approvingly to the truck
driver, who was worried about the road ahead and growled, 'They
shoulda left it with the Indians.'

East of Rawlins the snowdrifts became so deep that the plows
bogged down, forcing a long line of trucks and venturesome private
cars to halt at the crossroads where Route 130 cut in from the
south. Drivers and passengers crowded into a small diner, where
the harassed owner, caught without waitresses, was dishing out
coffee and rolls.

'This is some country,' Joe said to a group huddling about a
heater vent.

'You headed east or west?' one of the men asked.

'East.'

'You not in service?' an older man asked, indicating Joe's hair.

'No.'

What happened next Joe could not reconstruct later, but somehow the men got the idea that he was heading east to report for
induction into the army, and they insisted upon paying for his

coffee and buying him cigarettes. 'Best years I ever spent were in the army,' one of the drivers said.

'They taught me how to keep my nose clean,' another agreed.

An older man broke in to say, 'I spent three wonderful years in Japan.' He laughed. 'From Guadalcanal to Leyte Gulf, I fought the little yellow bastards; from Osaka to Tokyo, I slept with them—and I'd do both all over again.'

'Them Japanese girls A-okay?' a younger man asked.

'The best.'

'Is the country as interesting east of here?' Joe asked.

'Interesting?' the older man snorted. 'There's not an inch of Japan that isn't interesting. You ever hear of Nikko? Son, when you're in Vietnam and get some leave, haul your ass up to Tokyo and catch the train to Nikko. You'll see something.'

'I meant this country. Is it good east of here?'

'This is a beautiful country, from the Golden Gate to Brooklyn Bridge,' one of the drivers said reverently, 'and don't you ever forget it.'

This note of patriotism induced a different mood, and one of the drivers said, 'They're sure gonna cut hell out of that hair when you join the army, son. You'll be better for it.'

The drivers agreed that Joe would profit from the discipline of army life, and as he listened to them extolling its benefits he thought how cowardly he was to allow them to think that he was about to follow in their steps when in fact he was using their hospitality to escape. He swallowed his ignominy and thought: If I told them I was dodging the draft they'd probably stomp me to death.

Ashamed of such duplicity, he left the diner and walked into the storm, where headlights from cars pulling off the road cast strange beams into the snowy night. At times his universe seemed minute, no larger than the circle formed by the flakes, but at other times, when the lights had vanished, it broadened out to an infinite prairie, silent and of enormous dimension. As he stood in the storm, caught within the circle of light, yet thrust outward to the horizon, he gained a sense of the world, that never-known miracle of which he would henceforth be a sentient part.

At the same time he achieved his first appreciation of America, vast and inchoate in the darkness which engulfed it. 'This is a land worth fighting for,' he muttered, feeling no contradiction in being

a man running away from t[...] which he sensed was good. [...] notable patriot he had met in [...] bin, a Jewish housewife perch[...] church, trying to bring some [...] country had fallen into.

———

As soon as he hit New York he [...] where the church he sought looked [...] in California and where the Quaker [...] have been Mrs. Rubin's sister. She [...] available, but that he'd have to be care[...] got to avoid places where the owner m[...] card. And watch out for the older men [...] They're very patriotic and they'll insist [...] . . . in their way. But here's an address th[...] tearing down an old building and they'll b[...] with a strong back.'

He reported to a site near Gramercy Pa[...] huge hole in the ground next to a large privat[...] demolished. The foreman explained: 'The hit[...] want to save the ceilings. Seems they were [...] years ago. Your job is to get them down withou[...] Before Joe could say anything, the foreman th[...] his hands, shouting, 'Remember, if we wanted th[...] ings torn apart we'd use the wrecking ball. We [...] piece.' A little later an assistant came into the room[...] working from a scaffold and whispered, 'If any[...] your union card, you're a private artist saving the[...] museum.'

'What museum?'

'New York Museum of Architecture and Design,' t[...] promptly. 'There ain't none with that name and it'll kee[...] guy busy till next week figurin' it out.'

The work was dusty and back-breaking, but when Jo[...] down for a rest, the assistant said, 'Imagine you're Mich[...] He worked up there twenty years, I saw it in the movies.[...]

assumed that you were he.' He struck himself on the forehead and said, 'Good God! One look at your hair should have satisfied me you hadn't been in the army. I'm going to turn you over to one of our chaps who specializes in draft delinquency. I really don't know the facts.' He called for a student named Jellinek, but got no response, so he looked outside the door to see if the deserter from Alabama had arrived, then sank back into his chair, adjusting his legs beneath him as if he had no bones.

Speaking rapidly and with mounting enthusiasm, he said, 'Since both of our people are late we may as well exchange confidences. If I were you I'd head straight for Europe. Even if I had only ten dollars I'd go. How? Work on a cattle boat. Ensnare a rich widow. God knows how I'd do it, but I'd do it. I'd see the Van Eyck altar-piece at Ghent, the Brueghels at Vienna, the Velázquezes in the Prado. I'd want to see Weimar and Chartres and San Gimignano and Split in Yugoslavia. Do it, young man, no matter the cost. Don't waste these years in hiding in Canada. There's nothing you can learn there that you can't learn hiding in Montana. Go to Europe, educate yourself, and when this madness is over, come back and go to jail. Because if you go into your cell with ideas and visions, the years of imprisonment won't be wasted and you may come out a man of substance.'

'How would I get to Europe . . . with no money, that is?'

'Good God, money is the cheapest thing on this earth, but with you boys, it seems to be the overriding concern.' He leaped from his chair and stormed about the room, scratching his head. Suddenly he stopped and pointed a long finger. 'I know just the place for you. Get to Europe any way you can and drift down the coast of Spain to a place called Torremolinos. All sorts of bars, dance halls. A smart chap can always make a living there.'

'My Spanish isn't too good.'

'In Torremolinos they speak everything else but. How's your Swedish?' He laughed and ran to the door again to check on his missing Alabaman. Finding no one, he returned to his desk and said, 'In Boston you'll find a splendid group of people. They'll give you surprising assistance. There's a girl up there . . . her name is . . . Jellinek will know when he gets here.'

This exhausted what he could tell Joe, so the two wasted the better part of an hour discussing the university situation in California. The professor had a high opinion of the California schools and said he might like to teach there one of these days. 'It's where the action is,' he said, and Joe thought that no matter where he said he came from, someone always said, 'That's where the action is.' It was a phrase without meaning.

'Torremolinos is different,' the professor said nostalgically. 'For young people it's the capital of the world. You'll find more ideas there in a week than you will at Yale in a year. The right kind of ideas, that is. The irrelevant ones.'

When another half hour passed, with the Alabama deserter still missing, the professor suggested, 'We both seem to be stood up. How about having dinner with me?' He took Joe to an Italian restaurant, where six students were waiting, two with their girl friends. 'I've brought along the walking delegate from California,' he said, and it was understood that Joe was a fugitive of one sort or another. No one asked details, because there was a good chance that before the year ended, each of them might be in similar circumstances.

There was much talk of the Vietnam war, much irritation expressed at the tardy rate at which desegregation of education was progressing. There were no Negroes in the group, but no collection of blacks could have defended the Negro cause more ably than these whites. 'The time is coming,' the professor said, 'when Yale has got to face up to the Negro problem. And do you know when that time will be? When we are surrounded on seven sides by a solid black urban population.'

At this point the professor asked, 'Any of you seen Jellinek?'

'He's in jail.'

'Oh my God! What happened?'

'Tried to wreck the draft board.'

'Damned inconsiderate. Our delegate from California is heading for Boston, and Jellinek has the name of our contact there.'

'Gretchen Cole. Plays guitar and sings at the Cast Iron Moth.'

'The same! I met her when I lectured at Radcliffe. Splendid child. She'll get you into Canada.'

'You're smart to be hauling ass out of this rat trap,' one of the students said.

It seemed strange to Joe that a group of young people so able should have become so alienated from American life. No one tried to stop him from fleeing the country; he judged from what the students said that the professor who had encouraged him to accept exile was one of the brighter men at Yale; obviously he was one of the most popular, yet he openly espoused flight as the only honorable alternative.

As the night wore on, the professor took Joe aside and said, 'I just had an idea. It's not a very good one but it might work. Joe, how tough a man are you?'

'How do you mean?'

'Can you defend yourself? I don't mean with your fists. Against heroin? Against the whole complex?'

'I keep my nose clean.'

'I figured. If you do get to Torremolinos and you're broke and the police are breathing down your neck and threatening to throw you out of Spain, there's a name you might look up . . . at your own risk. Write it down. Paxton Fell. He has money.'

When the time came to leave, one of the students took Joe aside and slipped him a handful of bills. The student said, 'Good luck,' and they parted.

———•◆•———

He arrived in Boston at sunset, lean and shaggy and ill-tempered. It took him some time to locate the Cast Iron Moth. He had found the address in the phone book but was quite helpless when it came to spotting the street, for it lay in that maze of alleys off Washington Street and he must have come close to it two or three times without realizing that he was in the vicinity. He had always disliked asking strangers for advice and tried to zero in on his own, without any luck. Finally he had to ask a man where the Moth was, feeling an ass as he pronounced the name, and the man said, 'You just passed it,' and there it was.

Joe decided to spend some of the Yale money on a good meal, so he entered as a customer, but he must have been very transparent, for the doorman said, 'I suppose you want to see Gretchen Cole.'

'I want to eat,' Joe said.

The menu was on the expensive side but offered a good selection of seafood, which Joe had grown accustomed to in the Portuguese restaurants of Southern California. He found the meal better than average and did not begrudge the money spent, and when the entertainment began, it consisted of a rock-and-roll band accompanied by a girl singer. Music was important to Joe, and now he responded to its visceral beat; he also appreciated the animal shoutings of the girl, but this night he was looking for a guitar player, and when the band was replaced by a male trio singing folk songs, only a few of which he knew, he grew restless. Toward midnight the folk singers gave way to a different girl with a sensational bellowing voice, and Joe went out on the sidewalk and asked the doorman, 'When does Gretchen Cole sing?'

'She don't.'

'I came here to meet her.'

'When you came in I asked if that was it and you said you wanted to eat.'

'Why didn't you tell me?'

'You said you wanted to eat. I should drive away business?'

'Will she be in tomorrow?'

'Nope. She don't sing here no more . . . after her accident with the police.'

'Dope?'

'Not her. Something with the police in Chicago, I think it was.'

'How can I find her?'

The doorman drew back, studied Joe, and asked contemptuously, 'You one of them draft dodgers? Borrowin' money from a girl.'

'I want to see her.'

The doorman gave him an address and said, 'Maybe if I was young I wouldn't have any guts, too.'

The next afternoon Joe found out where the official center was and asked if he could speak to Gretchen Cole. A clergyman said, 'She doesn't work here any more.'

'At Yale they told me to look her up.'

'Professor Hartford?' When Joe nodded, the clergyman brightened and said, 'One of the best. If he sent you, Gretchen'll want to see you.' He made a phone call, then handed Joe an address in Brookline, a suburb of Boston. An hour later Joe was walking up to a handsome Colonial-type house set back among trees. He knocked at the door and was met by a girl about his own age. She was not beautiful, but her face was radiant and well scrubbed. She wore her dark brown hair in two braids and her informal clothes looked quite expensive. Joe noticed two things about her: she moved with unusual grace and she was nervous as a hawk.

'Professor Hartford sent you?' she asked. 'Come in.' She led him into a meticulously arranged living room in which nothing looked conspicuously expensive, yet everything seemed right. The floor was covered by a large elliptical rag rug of a type not known in California but most effective when edged with red-maple furniture. Joe was looking at the rug when the girl said, 'My name is Gretchen Cole and I suppose you're heading for Canada.'

'I am.'

'Good!' She became crisp and businesslike, but after a few sentences of instruction she changed completely and became once more unbelievably nervous and insecure.

'You feel all right?' Joe asked.

'Yes . . . yes,' she said, blushing from her collarbone to the top of her forehead. 'Now first thing you must do is get a haircut. You've got to look as square as possible, because if the Canadian border patrols catch even a suspicion that you might be a hippie or a draft dodger, they'll turn you back. You must wear the best clothes you have and see that they're pressed. And when you enter, you must be extremely careful to maintain the illusion that you are merely a tourist. Do not, and I must repeat this, do not under any circumstance request what the Canadians call "landed immigrant status," even though that's what you want. Wait till you reach Montreal and get safely dug in before you open that can of worms.' She gave him several more useful hints, concluding: 'We're sending a batch of you north with a faculty wife from MIT. She'll claim she's a professor of geology leading a field trip. She'll take you in to Montreal, and from there on . . .'

There was an awkward pause, and she blushed again, uncontrollably, so Joe said, 'I thought you were singing at the café.'

It was easy for her to construct the syllogism that had worked its way through his mind: This girl says she sings in public; girl singers don't blush like teenagers; something's wrong. She said, 'I used to sing.'

'You have trouble with the police?'

Now she blushed furiously, pressing her right hand over her face in an attempt to control herself.

Joe said, 'They told me at the café. What was it?'

'Didn't they tell you that, too?' Joe shook his head. Then, with an obvious effort to speak normally, she said brightly, 'I suppose you'll need some money.'

'Nope,' Joe said. 'As a matter of fact, I was about to ask you to dinner.'

'Oh, no!' she cried.

'Feel my head,' he said half-jokingly. 'I had trouble with the police too.' He reached for her hand, but she recoiled. 'Take my word for it,' he concluded lamely.

She showed him to the door, but it was so apparent that she needed counseling more than he that he said impulsively, 'Miss Cole, I don't know what's eating you, but you're going to have dinner with me tonight,' and he grabbed her by the arm.

She tensed up, resisted, then looked at the ground and laughed nervously. 'Do you think I should?'

'You must.'

She got a coat, and he took her into Boston on the bus and they found a corner bar in no way notable, where they had boiled shrimp and beer and much talk of students and politics and Vietnam.

'I work at helping you boys get to Canada,' she said, 'because I approve of your attitudes. We live in a tragic era and must do what we can to humanize it.'

'What happened with you and the police?' he asked bluntly.

She weighed the question for some moments, then said evasively, 'They did to me what they so often do to you fellows.'

'You've got to decompress,' he said.

'I'll learn,' she said. 'But right now I've had this scene. I've really had it.'

They talked like this for some hours, saying nothing consequential but alluding always to the malaise that infected so many of the best young people of this generation. Then, toward ten o'clock, a group of students from Harvard and MIT dropped in and one of them recognized Gretchen. Quickly they surrounded her table, asking about the police incident, and this caused renewed embarrassment. Sympathizing with her reticence, they switched to lesser gossip, and the young man who had first recognized her said, 'We miss you at the Moth. You ought to sing again, Gret.'

'These days are not for singing,' she said, playing with the ends of her braids.

'Maybe not in a formal café. But if we find a guitar, will you sing for us? Come on.'

She gave no assent, but one of the students disappeared and after a while returned with a guitar of sorts, which she strummed with a grimace. 'You expect me to sing with this crate?' she asked.

Joe noticed that she didn't play coy. She did not require to be begged; in fact, she rather wanted to sing, as if she sensed that it would be therapeutic. She made herself comfortable on a high bar stool, crossed her attractive legs to form a kind of lap, and strummed the guitar thoughtfully for some minutes. Other patrons in the bar paid no attention; they were discussing the collapse of the Dallas football team and arguing loudly that the commissioner ought to launch an investigation to see if the professional gamblers had organized a fix, but one contentious fellow reasoned: 'How can you fix a whole football team?' To which his opponent said, 'You don't fix the whole team. You fix one man . . . Don Meredith,' whereupon the bar in general agreed that Don Meredith could not be fixed, to which the first man said, 'Well, he sure looked it against Cleveland.'

Gretchen was now playing very softly, approaching a series of haunting chords in a minor key. Above them she announced the title of her song, 'Child 113,' and the students, knowing what this signified, applauded. In the ensuing silence she struck a commanding sequence of notes, then began a totally strange song, an ancient ballad about a seal swimming in the ocean, with the capacity to turn himself into a man when he comes ashore. With a human nursemaid the seal has had a child and now wants to take his son into the sea, for it is time he learned how to be a seal.

It was a silly ballad, Joe thought, until just at the end when Gretchen dropped her voice and to music of heartbreaking loveliness, sang of the seal's prediction: the woman would forget him, forget her son. She would marry a gunner, who for no logical reason would destroy everything:

> ' "An thu sall marry a proud gunner,
> An a proud gunner I'm sure he'll be,
> An the very first schot that ere he schoots,
> He'll schoot baith my young son and me." '

On this apprehensive note, with the guitar sounding a series of bitter chords, the strange song ended. The students did not applaud, for the ballad struck much too closely to their own experiences: there was an irrational element in life, something that no man could defend against; some damn-fool gunner always waited in the shadows, eager to take inexplicable pot shots at whatever seals swam in the ocean.

Gretchen would sing no more. This ballad had been her total statement, and the students who knew her appreciated the fact that even this had been difficult for her. They complimented her, asked how things were going at Radcliffe, and drifted away, taking the guitar with them. When they were gone, Joe said, 'How are things at Radcliffe?'

'Wretched,' she said, dropping that subject.

He took her home, and at the door, tried to kiss her goodnight, but this she resisted vigorously. However, she did grasp his hand, asking him to wait while she ran upstairs. When she returned she gave him two hundred dollars . . . insisted that he take it . . . insisted that her committee collected funds for this purpose.

'Where shall you be going?' she asked.

'The gang at Yale told me of a place that sounded just about right.'

'Where?'

'Torremolinos.'

On a gray wintry day in Madrid, Joe caught a ride with a group of rollicking German students heading south, and as they crossed the barren plains of La Mancha they spoke of Cervantes and Goya. They were knowledgeable young men, proficient in both English and Spanish, and were headed for the large German colony in Marbella, not far from the Strait of Gibraltar. From their conversation Joe concluded that their families had been enthusiastic supporters of Adolf Hitler and that the relatives they were about to visit in southern Spain were political fugitives. One of the students told Joe, 'If you see a very thin, straight old man who ought to walk with a cane but won't, and if he clicks his heels when you speak to him, that's Uncle Gustav.' From what the boys had to say of Uncle Gustav, he had been one of Hitler's major supporters, but one sardonic fellow added, 'He lives in Spain because he loves the way American tourists call him Baron and curtsy to the Baroness.'

By the time they reached Córdoba, the chill of Madrid had changed to a welcome sunshine. They stopped to see the mosque, and when they stood in the midst of its forest of pillars, stretching in all directions as far as they could see, one of the Germans said, 'You can see more of Islam here than you can in Muslim countries like Algeria or Morocco. I spent last vacation in Marrakech—exciting in some ways but never a mosque like this one.'

Joe liked Córdoba and would have been content to linger a few days, but the Germans were eager to meet up with their friends. So they pushed on, and were soon approaching that extraordinary plateau from whose southern rim they would be able to look down upon the Mediterranean. 'Ah,' cried the driver as they reached the edge of the cliff from which the city of Málaga could first be seen, 'this is Spain!' He pulled the car to the side of the road and pointed out the distant cathedral, the bullring, the esplanade lined with palm trees, the copious harbor, and to the west that chain of marvelous fishing villages which the Phoenicians had known and the Greeks. Costa del Sol, this area was called, and it served as a magnet for young people from around the world.

'That cluster of tall buildings, beyond Málaga,' one of the Germans explained, 'that's your Torremolinos.' He smacked his lips and said, 'Imagine! Right now! Five thousand of the world's most beautiful girls down there, panting for me to arrive.'

'Is it a good spot—Torremolinos?' Joe asked.

'See for yourself!' the excited German said. 'Endless beach. Mountains to cut off the cold winds. It's not a city. It's not a village. It's nothing seen on earth before. I'll tell you what it is—a refuge from the world's insanity, except that it's totally insane.'

They looked down at the panorama, the most exciting in Spain, with its mixture of old Málaga, the blue Mediterranean, the fishing villages and the stark mountains. To see the area from this height, after having traversed the barren upland plains, was to see an invitation to life and music, to wine and seashore. 'If it's as good down there as it looks from up here,' Joe said, 'it's a scene I'd like to make.'

'The only people who know how to enjoy it are the Germans and Swedes,' one of the students said. 'Americans don't fit in easily.'

'Lot of Germans down there?'

'When you get down, look. You'll find whole areas speaking nothing but German. Signs will be in German, too. Or Swedish.'

They took one final survey of the splendid area, then jumped in the car and started the screeching descent, with tires whining protests as the car swerved first to one side, then wildly to the other. At one point the road had to make two complete circles requiring a sequence of tunnels, so that the car seemed as if it were sliding down the flanges of a corkscrew, and as they sped around the curves Joe caught a kaleidoscopic view of ocean, mountain, sky, tunnel, Málaga and, in the distance, Torremolinos. It was a dazzling, stomach-turning approach, and when the curves grew even tighter the Germans began shouting encouragement to the driver; as he approached a curve they would utter a long-drawn *uggggghhhhh*, rising in tone and volume as the car screamed into the bend, its tires about to pop off their rims, then ending in a triumphant *yaaaaahhhhh* as the car teetered, almost toppled over, then regained its direction. When the road reached sea level and straightened out, the driver exultantly jammed the gas pedal to the floor and they roared along at more than ninety, slowing only when the narrow streets of Málaga appeared.

'That's the way to come down a mountain!' the driver shouted, and Joe said, 'Son of the Red Baron.'

They did not stop in Málaga but sped directly westward past the airport, and in a few minutes were entering Torremolinos, with its nest of skyscrapers along the shore, its lovely winding streets leading inland. The Germans roared into the center of town, came to a screaming halt before a newspaper kiosk that featured papers from every city in northern Europe, and told Joe, 'This is it, American. Learn German and you'll love it.'

Joe said, 'I thought Californians were crazy drivers,' and the driver said, 'You drive fast to get places. We do it for fun.' With a burst of speed that not even an American teenager would have attempted, he exploded through the traffic and zoomed westward.

———— •◆•• ————

With a small canvas traveling bag in his left hand, no hat, no topcoat, little money, Joe stood in the roadway and surveyed the scene of his exile, and what struck him immediately in these first minutes of a wintry day was that he saw more beautiful girls than he had ever before seen in one place in his life. They were positively dazzling, and in a short time he would know them all: Swedish blondes down from Stockholm; lean, good-looking German girls on their winter vacation out of Berlin; many French girls from the provinces; handsome college students from England; and a score of petite girls from Belgium.

Across from the newspaper kiosk, there was a bar with a large outdoor area sunk a few feet below the level of the street. It served as a kind of observation patio, and its many tables were crowded with people sitting in the winter sunshine, nursing glasses of beer and watching the passers-by. Hesitantly Joe stepped down from the street, walked among the tables until he found an empty chair, and sat down. Even before the waiter could get to him, a young man of indefinite nationality grabbed the next seat and said in an attractive accent, 'You're new here, I see. An American running away from army service, I suppose. I don't blame you. If I were an American I'd do the same thing.'

'Who are you?' Joe asked brusquely.

'Who cares?' the young man asked. He seemed to be about twenty, well dressed, amiable. Apparently he had money, for he said, 'Can I buy you a drink? First day in town. Next time you pay.'

He uttered a penetrating *pssssttt* and ordered lemonade for himself, a beer for Joe. 'You ever see so many beautiful girls?' he asked as a procession of especially attractive ones passed on the street above. 'For a man, this town is paradise. The secret is this. Every girl you see has flown here on a special excursion rate. They have fifteen days in the sun, then back to the treadmill. Not much time to waste, so they don't want to bother with involved introductions . . .'

'You speak good English,' Joe said.

'Also German and Swedish and French.'

'What do you do?'

'I look after things.'

'How can a guy get a job?'

Over the rim of his lemonade glass the young man assessed Joe, and while he did so, Joe had an opportunity to study the second layer of Torremolinos, for interspersed among the beautiful girls was a less appealing stream of fugitives—the dead-enders, both male and female, who had sought refuge in this Spanish nirvana and were finding life dreary, if not impossible. They were a shabby lot, young people from all countries who had thought that because Spain was warm it had to be cheap. They wore their hair long and their clothes tattered. Some were incredibly dirty and all looked as if they had not bathed for weeks. A considerable number were glassy-eyed, and they passed along the street as if in a trance; they were the ones who had been eating hashish or popping heroin, and their shoulders sagged and they moved mechanically. Unusually effeminate young men walked hand in hand. And there were the unpretty girls, the ones who had flown south in the same great jets that had brought the beauties. You could almost tell what point in their fifteen-day vacations they had reached; during the first four days they were hopeful that life in a swinging town like Torremolinos might be different from what it had been at home; on the ninth day they faced up to the fact that when so many girls concentrated on one place, even some really attractive girls would have trouble finding young men; and by the thirteenth day, knowing things weren't going to be much different from what they had been at home, they surrendered to desperation and walked the streets heavy-shouldered, with disappointment showing in their faces.

And scattered through this variegated mob of Germans, Englishmen, Belgians and Swedes, there moved a few Spaniards—a very few. They were apt to be workmen on their way to fix abused plumbing systems, or entrepreneurs trying to peddle bits of property their uncles owned, or clerks from the various stores. You could spot them by the sardonic looks on their faces, by the uncomprehending glances they occasionally cast at particularly outrageous hippies. It was a foreign world, one they did not understand, nor did they care to, so long as it provided them with a living. They were surprised at times, when they stopped to reflect that all this was happening in Spain, but they no longer worried about it, secure in their belief that the government in Madrid must be aware of the strange things that were happening and would correct them if occasion demanded.

When the young man with the lemonade was satisfied that he understood Joe, he said, 'With you I'd better be honest.'

Joe heard this frightening statement as if through a blanket of fog, for he was still lost in his review of the passers-by, wondering where in the procession he was going to fit. 'What'd you say?' he asked.

'You can call me Jean-Victor,' the young man said. 'Not French. I'll let you guess what. But I've been studying you and I see that you're capable. Quiet but capable. And I've decided that with you

I'd better speak the truth about Torremolinos. If you were a young girl trying to make your living as a prostitute, I'd have to warn you that it couldn't be done, because competition from the amateurs would drive you right out of town. But you being a handsome young man, with a certain physique, attractive hair . . . Do you speak any language other than English?'

'Spanish.'

'That doesn't count.'

'In Spain? It doesn't count?'

'We're not in Spain. Now if you put on your tightest pair of trousers and wander down this main street until you find a bar called the Wilted Swan, and go inside and order a lemonade, within fifteen minutes you'll find somebody who'll take care of your expenses for as long as you care to stay in town.'

Joe said nothing. Rummaging through his wallet, he looked for a scrap of paper, found the name he wanted, and turned to Jean-Victor, asking, 'Inside would I happen to find Paxton Fell?'

'Oh, you know Paxton Fell!' the young man cried ecstatically. 'Splendid! Splendid!' He insisted upon paying for the drinks and chaperoning Joe to meet Fell at the Wilted Swan. They had walked only a couple of short blocks when Joe saw one of the world's great barroom signs, a heraldic shield painted in bright primary colors, in the center of which floated a swan whose neck and wings had wilted into a limp design, with a result so languid and degenerate that he had to stop and laugh.

'That's a great sign,' he said admiringly. 'I'll bet it looks just like Paxton Fell.'

At this the guide slapped his leg and cried, 'Oh, I've got to tell Paxton what you said!' He led Joe through the brass-studded Renaissance doors and into a dark room ornately decorated with objects of French and English origin. He peered carefully from corner to corner, then pointed to a table at which sat four men who appeared to be in their late forties. They were obviously well-to-do, for they were dressed with that austere elegance which only money can sustain, and they spoke in low voices.

Jean-Victor approached the table deferentially, bowed and whispered to the man whose back was to the door. Slowly this gentleman rose, slim and imperious, and when he turned around, Joe saw that he was much more than forty. As if from a considerable height he studied Joe, apparently found him acceptable, and walked slowly toward him, extending a slim, be-ringed hand. 'I am Paxton Fell,' he said quietly. 'And who might you be?'

'Name's Joe. I'm from California. The gang at Yale gave me your name.'

'It must have been Professor Hartford,' Fell said languidly. 'He's very helpful, I understand, when you fellows fall into trouble with the draft.'

Joe nodded and became aware that most of the habitués in the bar, including one table of oddly dressed women, were watching him. On the spur of the moment he extended his hand to Fell and said, 'Professor Hartford sends his best wishes. I'll probably see you around.' And he walked to the door.

'Just a minute!' Fell cried. 'Join us for a drink.'

'Later,' Joe said. 'I've got to find a place to park this gear.'

'We can always help you find a place to stay. Now if you . . .'

Joe looked at his watch, snapped his fingers and said, 'Damn. I told the landlady I'd look at her room at five.'

On the sidewalk he grabbed Jean-Victor by the lapel and asked, 'What the hell are you trying to peddle?'

'You brought up his name. I naturally supposed . . .'

'You let me do the supposing.'

'When I first met you . . . I showed you the pretty girls and you didn't even look.'

'I was looking . . . in my own way.'

'So I put you down for another American on the make. And when you popped up with Fell's name, I was positive.'

'You one of his boys?'

'Me? I wouldn't go near the place. For me it's strictly girls.'

'Then why peddle me?'

'Simple! If I cooperate with Paxton Fell . . . he sees I get a little money.' Since his manhood had been impugned he felt it necessary to establish his character, so he led Joe down into the oldest part of Torremolinos, a story-book fishing area that had kept out the luxury hotels and skyscrapers. He took Joe past a chain of attractive small bars, each with three or four charming girls waiting on stools, and Jean-Victor said, 'In Torremolinos . . . three hundred bars . . . and they all need bar girls.' They came finally to a row of very old fishing sheds that had been converted into slap-dash apartments, at whose doors the Mediterranean knocked with knuckles of sea foam.

'This is the real Torremolinos,' Jean-Victor said, and as he pushed open the door of his flat, Joe saw two large beds, one empty, the other containing a pair of most attractive girls. 'Ingrid and Suzanne,' Jean-Victor said offhandedly. 'My girl is Sandra, from London, but she's out shopping, I suppose.'

'She went to get her hair done,' Ingrid said in excellent English.

'She's always getting her hair done,' Jean-Victor said resignedly. 'Joe's new in town. From California. No money, but I can assure you he likes girls. I tested him. Now you test him.'

'Running away from the draft?' Suzanne asked with a lilting French accent.

'Yes.'

'Any money?'

'Flat broke.'

'Who cares. Tonight we take you to dinner. We must all fight like hell for peace.'

'You mustn't waste your money,' he protested.

The girls did not even bother to reply. In their crowd, if someone had a little bread he shared it; when Joe was in the chips they would expect him to do likewise. Jean-Victor went on to say, 'You can make your bed on the floor. A German left his sleeping bag. It's that tartan thing in the corner. He probably won't be back.'

The girls did take Joe to dinner, at a fish restaurant where a solid meal cost less than a dollar. They told approximately the same stories: they had come to Torremolinos on fifteen-day excursions, had fallen in love with the place, had looked everywhere for jobs, and had finally met Jean-Victor, who allowed them to sleep in his extra bed. He had also found them work in one of the bars he frequented, and since he would accept no money, they bought the food. Ingrid thought she might have to return to Sweden at the end of next month; she had been away a half-year and a young man with a good job in Stockholm wanted to marry her, but Suzanne said, 'I'm staying. This place was meant for me. Tell you what, Joe! We'll treat you to the Arc de Triomphe.'

They walked up the hill that led from the seafront to the center of Torremolinos, and there, on a side street, an old motion-picture hall had been converted into a ballroom consisting of a tiny raised floor, scores of small tables and much standing room. It was dark and lined with velvet, so that the tremendous volume of sound which erupted from the electronic system came forth clean and hard, without reverberating echoes. The lights were stroboscopic, flashing on and off four times a second, but everything was subordinated to the marvelous beauty of the patrons. By the score, girls who had won honor grades at the Sorbonne and Uppsala and Wellesley came through the big doors, peered into the darkness, and were picked off by keen-minded young men who had won equal grades at Tokyo University and Heidelberg. At any table of six you might find four nationalities; languages flowed more freely than the Coca-Cola which most of the dancers were drinking, and always there was the incredible volume of sound, louder than a score of the bands that the parents of these young people had listened to in the 1940s.

'I really dig this music,' Joe said as the hurricane of sound enveloped him in its metallic cocoon. Regardless of which nation the young people had grown up in, they accepted this throbbing music as an integral part of their culture and were at home with it; to them the ear-shattering sounds were as essential as pipes and cymbals had been to the ancient Greeks when they were evolving the theory of aesthetics.

'This is my home,' Ingrid shouted above the noise as they elbowed their way to a table. There Suzanne closed her eyes, leaned her head back, and invited the sound to flow over her. They were scarcely seated before two German students who had met them at their bar approached and ordered some drinks. They spoke good French, which left Joe isolated, but after a while one of the Germans said in fluent English, 'Are you having trouble with the draft?' When Joe nodded, the German clapped him on the shoulder and said, 'Very curious. One of my great-great-grandfathers ran away from Germany to the United States to escape his draft, and now you run away from the United States to Germany to escape yours.' Joe was about to say that he wasn't in Germany, but the young man interrupted, 'Perhaps you know his family? Schweikert in Pennsylvania. One boy was all-American football at Illinois.'

'Before my time,' Joe said.

He walked back alone to Jean-Victor's while the two girls reported to their bar, and he found Sandra waiting. Jean-Victor was out somewhere, but he had told her of the newcomer and she showed him how to spread the tartan sleeping bag. Joe watched her proficiency in handling things, and asked, 'What did you do in London?'

'Nothing. Father's a banker and he's always let me have a little bread. He was keen on camping and taught me how to cope.'

'You been here long?'

'Like the others. Came down for fifteen days. Wept when the airplane arrived to fly me back. Jean-Victor was at the airport and he said, "Why go back?" So I've been here for almost a year.'

'Who is Jean-Victor?'

'Parents are Italian. Lugano—the Italian city at the southern end of Switzerland. His real name's Luigi or Fettucini or something. He finds the French name involves less explanation. Gets a little money from home . . . keeps his hand in many things down here. We're not sure how he makes his bread. Probably selling marijuana. I know he has connections in Tangier. You care for a joint?'

'I'm not big on grass.'

'Neither are we. If there's a good party we pass the stuff—to be sociable. If not, we forget it for weeks.'

Joe unrolled the German sleeping bag and watched as Sandra knowingly adjusted newspapers and old blankets under it to ensure a better bed. 'I slept in this for three weeks before Jean-Victor allowed me in his bed,' she said. 'Of course, he was sleeping with a Belgian girl at the time and I had to wait my turn.' Joe climbed in and almost immediately fell asleep, but he was vaguely aware that when Sandra went to bed she kissed him lightly on the forehead, as a mother might, and sometime toward dawn he was awakened by Ingrid and Suzanne returning from their work. They undressed casually, prepared for bed, and when they saw he was awake, paused to chat. 'It's good to have a man in the room,' Suzanne said.

Joe pointed to where Jean-Victor slept, and she said, 'He's taken. You're for us,' and they knelt down to kiss him goodnight.

'I'm going to like Torremolinos,' he said drowsily.

'We all do,' Ingrid cried happily as she crept into bed. 'My God, this is heaven.'

'Today I'm going to find a job,' Joe said.

II §

BRITTA

The daughter of a lion is also a lion.

When the Germans invaded Norway, I was able to adjust to their occupation. When the British were defeated in our waters, I never doubted that they would someday return to rescue us. When food was cut off, we survived; when fuel was in short supply, we shivered and made do; and even when Germany seemed triumphant on all fronts, we masked our feelings and never lost hope for an eventual victory. But when Knut Hamsun, our great novelist who won the Nobel Prize, turned his back on all that Norway stood for and openly propagandized on behalf of Nazi Germany, we not only lost heart but experienced a lasting shame, as if one of our own family had done this dreadful thing, for if you cannot trust the great writers, on whom you have lavished your highest rewards, who in God's name can you trust?

The permanent temptation of life is to confuse dreams with reality. The permanent defeat of life comes when dreams are surrendered to reality.

What though the spicy breezes
    Blow soft o'er Ceylon's isle;
Though every prospect pleases
    And only man is vile:
In vain with lavish kindness
    The gifts of God are strown;
The heathen in his blindness
    Bows down to wood and stone.
                    —Bishop Heber

For God's sake, give me the young man who has brains
enough to make a fool of himself.—Stevenson

The curtains of the First Act open on a wild and
savage beach on the Island of Ceylon. To the right
and left, some huts of plaited bamboo. In front,
two or three palms overshadowing giant cactus trees,
twisted by the wind. Below, on a rock which overlooks the ocean, the ruins of an ancient Hindu
pagoda. In the distance, the ocean, illuminated by a
blazing sun.
The Pearl Fishers

Your old men shall dream dreams, your young men shall see visions.—Joel

The secret of being tiresome is to tell everything.—Voltaire

Ah, for some retreat
Deep in yonder shining Orient, where my life began to beat, . . .

Larger constellations burning, mellow moons and happy skies,
Breadths of tropic shade and palms in cluster knots of Paradise.

Never comes the trader, never floats an European flag,
Slides the bird o'er lustrous woodland, swings the trailer from the crag;

Droops the heavy-blossom'd bower, hangs the heavy-fruited tree—
Summer isles of Eden lying in dark-purple spheres of sea.
—Tennyson

This Scandinavian flew down from Stockholm four
times each year. No matter what the temperature, he
dressed in his swim suit and went right out to lie on
the sand, whether the sun was out or not. We asked
him about this, and he said, 'I paid a lot of money to
get down here. I'm supposed to be here on the beach
and the sun is supposed to be there in the sky and
if it doesn't know its job, that's not my fault.' And
you know something? He always went home sunburned.

I hear as in a dream
    Drifting among the flowers
Her soft and gentle voice
    Evoking songs of birds.

The light of distant stars
    Permits a view once more
Of those seductive veils
    That shimmer in the breeze.
The Pearl Fishers

*E*VERYTHING I relate in this narrative I either saw for myself or heard about from those involved. For example, the flaxen-haired Norwegian girl of whom I now speak once spent several days enchanting me, like Scheherazade, with tales of her childhood in northern Norway.

Britta Bjørndahl was born more than two hundred miles north of the Arctic Circle on the island of Tromsø. During World War II her father had been a notable patriot. For three perilous years he had resisted the German occupation, hiding out along the fjords and in the mountains to send wireless signals to London or flash-light codes to British ships as they hovered off the Norwegian coast. At the end of the war four nations decorated him, and in the summer of 1957 the entire crew of a British destroyer flew to Tromsø to relive with him the excitement of those gallant days.

The medals had done her father little good; in peace he returned to Tromsø and earned a frugal living as a clerk in a company that shipped fish to Bergen. He married the girl who at much risk to herself had brought him food and magazines during his long years of hiding from the Nazis, and soon they had three children.

Each summer Britta's mother would scan the sky for a certain kind of day, and when it arrived, she would gather the children and lead them to Holger Mogstad's boatyard, so that he might take them in his sailboat into the channel that separated Tromsø from a westward island which protected it from the Atlantic. Britta's father did not accompany them on these trips because he held

Mr. Mogstad in low esteem: 'Dirty mustaches and bad breath,' was all he would say about the boatbuilder, but Britta guessed that their enmity stemmed from the war days, when her father had gone into the forests to fight the Germans while Mr. Mogstad had stayed in Tromsø to build boats for them.

Britta wanted, of course, to side with her father, especially after one evening when she had caught Mr. Mogstad trying to kiss her mother in the sail loft after the cruise was ended; she said nothing about this incident, which she did not fully understand but from which her dislike of Mogstad arose. Nevertheless, she accompanied the others on the yearly cruise because of the miraculous thing they were to see in the channel.

She would sit with the other children in the bow of the sailboat, peering down into the dark ocean while her mother and Mr. Mogstad sat in the stern, triangulating the craft according to landmarks on various headlands, and after many false starts everyone would agree, 'This must be the place,' and they would lean over the side of the boat and gaze into the water.

And gradually, emerging from the shadows like some monster deposited there in primeval time, the outlines of a mighty battleship would slowly take form. If the sun was right, and if the waves were placid, the children would sometimes see the entire ship asleep in its tomb, stretching so far in all directions that it seemed larger than Tromsø itself. It was mysterious, awesome, an overwhelming message from the past, and the children never tired of seeing it, this gigantic warship sunk in their harbor.

Nor did they tire of their mother's recitation of how it had got there. Britta could repeat the story almost as well as her mother, but she loved to hear it from one who had taken part in the sinking of this mighty ship:

'It was in the winter of 1943 when the fate of the whole world was in the balance. England was starving. Russia was about to collapse for want of arms. We Norwegians? We had nothing to eat, for each autumn the Germans took all our crops. Yet we knew there was a chance if each man and woman resisted every day. When you grow up and face difficulties, you must remember your father and mother in the winter of 1943.

'Your father hid in the mountains up there. Others like him had fled to Sweden, and I don't blame them, because the Germans hunted them with dogs and airplanes, so they had to leave Norway.

But your father stayed. He and Mr. Storness the electrician and Mr. Gottheld the chemist—and how they survived, no one will ever know. Do you know why they stayed in the mountains, dodging the Nazi airplanes and killing the police dogs when they got too close? Because they had to send messages to the airplanes in England. Your father had a radio, not a good one, and Mr. Storness cranked it by hand, hour after hour—and do you know what? Every time they sent a message to London, telling the airplanes where to bomb, German headquarters in Tromsø got the message too. Because they could listen on the radio, couldn't they? So as soon as your father started to speak on his radio, the Germans would send out their patrols with dogs, and we would wait to see what they had when they came back.

'What do you suppose your father was telling London? On most days not much. But the wise men in London . . . you remember I told you that Mr. Halverson the banker was one of them? These wise men knew that someday, strange as it might seem to us, the great German battleship *Tirpitz* would sneak into Tromsø harbor, right here, and hide from Allied airplanes until it was time to rush out and destroy all Allied ships. If the *Tirpitz* did enough damage, the Germans might win the war, and you would now be speaking German. And when you grew up you would have to marry Germans. It was as close as that. So we kept watch for the *Tirpitz*.

'For nearly two years . . . can you imagine how long a time that is? For two years your father stayed in the mountains and told London what was happening in Tromsø. If a destroyer hid in our waters, he would tell the airplanes in London, and next day we would have bombs falling on the destroyer, and our houses too, but we didn't care about that because we knew there was still a chance.

'And then one day, in September of 1944, can you guess what appeared around this headland?'

'The *Tirpitz*,' said the children.

'It was so big we could not believe it would fit between the islands. I remember running down to that pier over there and seeing how high it soared into the air. You couldn't believe it. Where the captain stood was much higher than any building in Tromsø, and its guns were so enormous they terrified you even to look at them. We didn't have to be told that if this fierce thing got free in the Atlantic it would sink every Allied ship. It was a hideous weapon to have hiding in your harbor. Look how menacing it is, even when it lies asleep.'

At this point each summer the children would stare down at the enormous hulk and shiver as they saw it reaching out far beneath them, like a monster biding its time until it rose from the waves to destroy all things. When their mother resumed her story she always spoke in a lower voice, but this was the part they cherished, because it involved their parents. 'As soon as the *Tirpitz* arrived, the German commander in Tromsø sent extra policemen to check on anyone who might have a radio. He sent airplanes to fire machine guns at spots in which your father might be hiding. And up the mountainsides went the patrols and the dogs. But what did your father do?'

'He stayed where he was and sent the same message over and over again for five hours,' Britta told the younger children. 'He told the airplanes in London, "*Tirpitz* arrived Tromsø this afternoon. Big hole forward deck. Probably stay here six weeks." '

'When he finished his last message,' Mrs. Bjørndahl said, 'the dogs were almost upon him. That's when Mr. Gottheld was shot. He volunteered to stay behind so that the radio could be saved.' At this point she stopped her story to recall Mr. Gottheld, a small man who had been afraid of storms and dogs and his wife, and everything except Nazis.

'He was shot. They showed us his body in the Shipsgate. And for a while it seemed that his sacrifice had been useless. Because no airplanes came from London. And when we heard no news from your father and Mr. Storness, we supposed they were dead too. Then, in early November, we got a message from London demanding that we advise them by radio as to whether the *Tirpitz* was still here. But with your father missing, how could we reply?

'Late one night in November a brave little boy came to my house and gave me a message that read: "Go to the wife of Storness the electrician and pick up a package which she will have. Bring it this night to the cabin at the head of the fjord, for our radio is broken." It was curfew, of course, extra strict because of the *Tirpitz*, but I slipped past the Germans and went to the Storness home, where Mrs. Storness gave me a small package wrapped in cloth and covered with hog's fat, which was almost impossible to get. I tucked the package in my skirt, like this, and crept out of her house —and what do you think happened?'

It was Britta who answered: 'A police dog came at you. He smelled the hog fat and you rubbed some off on your finger and gave it to him and he went away.'

'I sneaked through the German lines and got into the countryside and walked till morning. Then I hid in the forest and listened to the German planes passing over me, and the next night I got to the head of the fjord and delivered the package. I kissed your father and started right back to Tromsø—and what do you suppose I saw when I was hiding in the woods that third morning?'

Britta supplied the answer: 'You saw a hundred English airplanes fly over your head. And you saw one explosion after another lighting up the sky. And you heard great explosions echoing through the mountains. And when you slipped back through the German lines and went to the seashore where the others stood, you no longer saw the *Tirpitz*.'

———•◦•———

With the reading matter which Mrs. Bjørndahl had smuggled to her future husband hiding in the mountains had been a back issue of the *National Geographic,* picked up from some passing ship, containing a long story about Ceylon, and as Bjørndahl remained in the hills, cold and without food and constantly harassed by the Germans, he kept this magazine with him and in time developed a fixation about Ceylon, for it was everything that northern Norway was not: it had an abundance of fruit which you could pick right off the trees; it had sunshine every day of the year; you didn't have to go about bundled in fur; and above all, it had a languid elegance in its palm trees, its slowly moving elephants and seductive music. If there was one spot on earth where a man could be happy, it would be Ceylon, and Bjørndahl determined that as soon as the war was over—for he trusted implicitly in an Allied victory—he would spend the rest of his life in Ceylon.

He was reinforced in this decision by the peculiar nature of Tromsø. Even in peace Tromsø presented difficulties, for in the summer there was no night and men lived in a kind of never-never land of dreams and fantasies, while in the winter there was no day. In January the sun never rose above the horizon, and the frail light it provided was gray and ghostly. Of the long years he had remained hidden in the hills, hundreds of days were spent in total darkness, and their deep shadow had entered his soul. 'The day the Germans surrender, I head for Ceylon,' he told his partners again and again.

But with the coming of peace came responsibilities. He married the attractive girl who had fed him in the mountains, and now had to support her children—he always spoke of them as 'her children.' His job did not give him time for travel, nor would he have had the funds if it did. His four medals were hung on the wall in a plush-lined box and Ceylon receded into legend. It still existed in its perpetual sunlight beyond some distant horizon, but by the early 1960s he realized that he was not going to see it.

This did not mean that he lost interest. Starting with the magazine his future wife had brought him, he began to collect all things relating to Ceylon. He had maps, bills of lading addressed to Colombo, accounts of nineteenth-century voyages, bits of Singhalese cloth, and above all, a series of airline posters showing vivid scenes around Kandy and Ratnapura. At exciting intervals some traveler who had actually visited Ceylon would pass through Tromsø, and later, in the bar of the Grand Hotel, he would report: 'That chap Bjørndahl knew more about Ceylon than I did, and I was there.'

His family made one concession to Bjørndahl's mania: a small room was set aside for his mementos of the island. Its walls were lined with maps and decorated with the airline posters, but the salient feature was something which had come late, a phonograph on which he played repeatedly such fragments of Georges Bizet's *The Pearl Fishers* as he had been able to collect from random sources. So far he had found one tenor aria, one duet with tenor and baritone, and an extraordinary passage in which the soprano prays to Brahma and Siva for the safety of the fishermen. When he sat in his Ceylon room and played this haunting music, he seemed to be not in Tromsø but in the land of his enchantment.

The tenor passage, technically a cavatina of almost childish simplicity, was one of the lushest compositions of the nineteenth century, a song so sweetly sentimental that modern tenors had grown afraid of it. Britta's father owned it in three versions: by Enrico Caruso, who had loved it; by Beniamino Gigli, who had sung it better than anyone else; and by the incomparable Swede, Jussi Bjørling, whose voice was geared to the sustained notes. During the long winter nights, which encompassed the entire day, the

Bjørndahl children had grown accustomed to the ghostly tenors singing their complaint:

> 'I hear as in a dream
>   Drifting among the flowers
> Her soft and gentle voice
>   Evoking songs of birds.'

The selection that Britta preferred was the one in which the heroine prayed, for whenever the soprano pronounced the names Brahma and Siva, Britta could visualize their statues and the temple in which they stood. Thus Ceylon became almost as real to her as it was to her father, and while she did not share his sentimental craving to see the island, she did understand how it could pre-occupy his imagination. In school she told her teacher, 'I grew up in Ceylon,' and when the teacher made inquiries and found that Britta had never been outside of Tromsø, she put the girl down as a little fibber, especially when Britta insisted that she had been there . . . with her father.

In Tromsø there were many who smiled indulgently at Bjørn-dahl and his dreams; suspicions grew that the long years in the mountains had touched his mind, but one crucial fact remained to silence adverse comment: of all the patriots who had fled into the mountains, including even Storness the electrician and Gottheld the chemist, he was the only one who survived the cold and the Nazis. Many had started with him, but most had been driven into Sweden; Storness had died of malnutrition and Gottheld had been shot.

So Britta never forgot that her father was an authentic hero, and her mother too. This was why she had kept silent when she saw her mother and ugly Mr. Mogstad with his dirty mustaches. It was also why she consented to sail with Mogstad each summer to see the sunken battleship, because when she peered into the silent waters and saw its grisly terror hiding there, she could honestly say, 'My father and mother sank it.'

As she grew older she had to admit what an ineffective man her father had become; the cavatina was a dirge for the opportunities he had lost. Its long-drawn cries were laments for his vanished hopes, and others felt sorry for him, but when Britta looked at him she could say compassionately: 'I am the daughter of heroes.'

———•—•—•———

In her fifteenth summer Britta Bjørndahl was one of the most beautiful girls in Tromsø, an island noted for its handsome women, including those shy Laplanders who in their brightly woven garments came down from their reindeer herds in the north. The reader will understand that Britta did not tell me in so many words, 'I was counted among the beauties in Tromsø,' for she was modest, but I could see for myself. Also, some of the things she told me in our conversations in Spain could have happened only to a girl who was quietly sure of her attractiveness.

That spring, when we talked so often, she was eighteen, not overly tall, superbly proportioned, with large white teeth, a flawless northern complexion and exquisite hair in a pageboy bob, not platinum as is so often found in Finland and northern Norway, nor honey-colored as occurs in the southern areas, but a soft white with a touch of amber champagne. She laughed easily, had passed the stage of embarrassment and was constantly being touched and approved and even kissed by the free-and-easy patrons of the bar in which she worked. The American sailors, who were obviously charmed, referred to her as 'our Viking,' and she did indeed have a quality of composure and robust good nature which must have characterized those daring people. Also, like most educated Scandinavians, she spoke English without a heavy accent but with just enough peculiarity to add to her winsomeness. But when I have said all this, I have missed the essential quality of this lovely girl. She gave the impression of largeness; she was neither tall nor plump, but her shoulders were broad and so were her hips. She walked with assurance and had about her countenance an openness that was disarming and a cleanliness that caused all men to be attracted to her. She was big in spirit.

In this fifteenth summer her mother arranged once more for Mr. Mogstad to take the children out to visit the sunken *Tirpitz*, and although Britta had seen it often, she went along, and when she found below her the shadowy monster she appreciated for the first time the courage it must have taken to oppose this dreadful force, and tears might have come to her eyes, except that she used her fists to push them back. Mr. Mogstad saw this and said a few comforting words, which Britta rejected. When the launch docked and Mrs. Bjørndahl took the other children home, Britta stayed behind to help stow the gear, and as she carried a set of cushions to the sail locker, she suddenly found Mr. Mogstad behind her, grabbing at her and forcing her down onto the floor.

She was so startled she did not cry out, a fact which Mr. Mogstad interpreted as coyness, and before she knew what was happening, he had her mostly undressed and himself as well and was forcing himself upon her. She had discussed sex with her schoolmates and knew a good deal about it, but was quite unprepared for this assault and in a kind of dumb panic allowed him to have his way, not certain what other course might be available to her. It was a messy business, clumsy, frightening and totally disgusting, with Mr. Mogstad's dirty mustaches and fetid breath adding to the ugliness. When it was over, the shipbuilder leered: 'We won't tell anyone, will we?' She was so perplexed by his behavior that she merely looked at him and went home.

Frequently that summer Mr. Mogstad approached her with invitations to the sail locker, and now that she had an opportunity to study him more carefully, she found him to be a fat man in his middle forties even more objectionable than she had thought, with gray teeth and a nervous twitch. He was really quite repulsive and she found it distasteful even to acknowledge his unctuous civilities. As to his invitations for additional sex, which he said he was willing to pay for if she preferred, they were preposterous, and one day she snapped, 'Go away! You're disgusting!'

In mid-July she struck up a serious friendship with a neighbor boy, a good-looking fellow of seventeen named Haakon, and together they located various dark corners where others would not expect to find them. There they had mutually satisfying explorations, so that her memory of her first disgusting experience with sex was pleasantly erased. She found she liked men and the sexual games they made possible, so in August she and Haakon began associating with an eighteen-year-old couple who were more or less living together, and this older pair would sometimes find an available room which the four of them could share in a kind of respectful intimacy. As Britta said one night when they were separating for their various homes, 'The thing I like about sex is that no matter how it starts, you know how it's going to end.' When in the course of time the foursome broke up, Britta started going with the other boy, so that the rooms he had engineered for his first girl he now got for Britta. His name was Gunnar; he had a job; and it seemed likely that one day he and Britta would drift into a standard Tromsø marriage.

As her eighteenth birthday approached, Britta had to go to work, since there was no money in the Bjørndahl household for further education. Her father continued to peck away at his trivial job with the fish exporter and to spend his nights dreaming of Ceylon. Home was still filled with the sound of Beniamino Gigli singing 'I hear as in a dream' or the great Luisa Tetrazzini playing the role of a priestess in the temple of Brahma. Her father loved to tell the children not only of Ceylon but .also of the singers: 'Mr. Gigli, this fine artist, turned out to be a Fascist and said dreadful things about America, where he had earned his living for many years. He was a hateful man, but he could sing. As for poor Miss Tetrazzini, when she was a fat old lady her children hauled her into court and asked the judge to take away all her money because she was spending it so recklessly and they were afraid she wouldn't leave any for them. They said she was nutty, but before the whole court she sang this song, and the judge said that anyone who could sing like that—and remember the words too—was certainly not nutty.'

Mrs. Bjørndahl found Britta a job—in the office of Mr. Holger Mogstad! The first months were a trying time, because Mr. Mogstad tried to maneuver her into corners where he would pinch her and run his hand up her leg. One day he caught her in the storeroom and started to unbutton her blouse, but this so enraged her that she slapped him about the head, saying, 'You silly old man. Behave yourself or I'm going to punch you.' It was an inept statement but it jolted him into accepting the fact that any further thought of an affair with this girl was futile. He took revenge by assigning her unpleasant jobs and by smiling lasciviously whenever Gunnar appeared at the end of the day to walk her home. Once he whispered, 'I'll bet you sleep with him, don't you?' It was most unsavory, but no other jobs were available.

She received her first serious glimpse into the future one night when Gunnar, having engineered it so that his parents would be at the cinema, took her to his home—and as she lay in bed after their enjoyable sex, she thought to herself: How pleasant it will be when we can live together openly. But as she entertained these generous thoughts she happened to look at him, hunched over the table where he kept a short-wave radio, and she realized that he was as preoccupied with his radio as her father was with Ceylon. At this unpropitious moment Gunnar cried, 'Listen, Britt! It's that fellow in Samoa I told you about!' And as he continued to fiddle with the dials she could visualize him decades from now, wasting his days on some trivial job he could not respect, filling his nights with radio. Her apprehension was multiplied when she happened to mention his hobby to her parents, and her father cried, 'I wonder if he could get Ceylon?' Eventually Gunnar tried to do so, and made contact with an Englishman in Kandy, and for several breathless nights Gunnar and Mr. Bjørndahl huddled over the radio, talking with Ceylon; and as the hours passed, strange messages were exchanged, and Mr. Bjørndahl came home at midnight in a kind of exaltation, for Ceylon really existed. But Britta noticed that during this spell of enchantment Gunnar seemed to forget her almost completely, and they did not go to bed together once during the whole month of October.

But a problem even more profound than sex had arisen: in early November, Tromsø entered the tunnel, forcing Britta to question the values of life in Norway. Each year on the twenty-second of September the sun, in its appointed climb up and down the heavens, reached the halfway mark in its descent, and then day and night were of equal length; but swiftly thereafter the sun declined, so that even at midday it remained hidden below the horizon, making the days brief and the nights interminable. As December approached, the people of Tromsø said, 'We are heading into the tunnel,' an appropriate simile, since it conveyed the idea that after a long dark passage the world would once more burst into joyous daylight; but to young people the image was a mournful one, because they could not take comfort from the promise of a distant spring. They could see only the extinction of light and the beginning of that dark interlude which gripped the soul.

In mid-December, when the darkness was deep upon them, Britta's father said philosophically, 'Well, here we go again, plunging into the tunnel.' And in the nights that followed, Britta heard him, hidden away in his small room, playing the imaginary music of Ceylon, and often as she worked in Mr. Mogstad's office she would find herself softly whistling the cavatina from *The Pearl Fishers*, as if her life, too, were existing in a dream, and she would feel herself enmeshed in the futility that had overcome her father, and the world would seem unbearable, and she would whisper, 'I want the sun.'

You must not suppose that Tromsø lay in complete darkness during the whole twenty-four hours of each day; at noontime there would be a soft gray haze which sometimes produced effects of unforgettable beauty, with the forests on the mainland emerging from shadow like the castles of imagination. At mid-afternoon girls who worked along the waterfront would leave their offices for a brief spell as the steamer from Bergen came around the end of the island on its trip north to Kirkenes, which lay beyond the cape. After the steamer had sailed, the girls would wander reluctantly back to work, and by the time the day was ended, their world would be engulfed in darkness. And when they said to each other, 'We have entered the tunnel,' they implied that the big job was to hold on, by any device, until this dreadful night was past.

On the morning of Monday, December 16, Britta was awakened at seven by a positive premonition that this day was to be special—something perhaps related to Gunnar or her job. Looking at the thermometer outside her window, she saw that it stood several degrees below zero and thought: Nothing special about that. The darkness was as black as ever: Nothing special there either. But she did sense a spirit of Christmas in the air, as if Laplanders might be in the streets with their reindeer when she went to work.

To keep alive the spirit of this strange day, she chose her shortest miniskirt, bright red; and to protect her legs, she pulled on heavy-ribbed raw-wool stockings and a pair of white boots made of reindeer skin. Over her embroidered blouse she drew a parka that did afford protection for her face but which reached only a few inches below her hips. Studying herself in the mirror, she whispered, 'Nothing spectacular, but you'll pass.' Calling goodbye to her mother, she left home and started picking her way along icy paths hemmed in by waist-high drifts. Within moments her cheeks were as red as her skirt.

Few towns in the world could have been more attractive than Tromsø on this Arctic morning, for it presented a man-made aurora borealis. Years ago the citizens had decided that they had better do something to offset the drabness of the north, so they agreed that each man would paint his house some individual and brilliant color. Now, when Britta walked to work, she passed blue houses and purple, and cerise and ocher and golden yellow. And each was brightly lit, for electricity was cheap and lights that were turned on in October were left burning till April. Tromsø was a fairyland of color, accentuated by girls like Britta in their bright miniskirts.

As she entered Peter Hansen's Gate, a wide street that led to the harbor, she waved to everyone, then turned left into Storgata, filled with red-cheeked people, their faces shining like lanterns in the perpetual night. She smiled at each one, still convinced that this was to be her lucky day. Then, as she was about to leave Storgata, she came face to face with the plate-glass window of a travel agency displaying a poster showing a life-size Scandinavian girl in a swim suit standing beside an ancient stone windmill overlooking the Mediterranean. Only three words appeared on the poster, but they carried a mighty impact: *Come to Torremolinos.*

At this first moment of confrontation, Britta did not stop to look at the poster, for she did not yet understand that it was the premonition which had awakened her, but in some subtle way it fired her imagination, so that when she looked at Mr. Mogstad she saw a stone windmill, and when she spoke with his secretary the woman became a girl in a bikini standing beside the Mediterranean.

On her way home that evening she studied the poster again, and when she heard her father playing 'I hear as in a dream,' she saw as in a dream: herself standing in sunlight beside a windmill in Spain. On its first appearance the image awakened no particular longing; in fact, her response was intellectual: Of course . . . Torremolinos . . . tower of the mill . . . what a lovely name. But when she went to her father's room and asked to borrow his atlas, she found that the map of Spain did not show Torremolinos. It must be very small, she thought.

Gunnar came to dinner, after which they went to a cinema and from there to the home of a friend, where they popped quickly into bed. Their love-making was fun, mostly because Britta insisted that it be so, but it had little significance, and as Gunnar fell asleep beside her, for he had no radio to play with, she saw on the walls of the darkened room stone windmills and curving beaches of white sand. On her way to work next morning she looked specifically at the poster and at a card beside it: *You too can enjoy sunny Spain for less than you think.* That evening she entered the travel office and tentatively approached the man behind the counter.

He was an eager little chap, quite short for a Norwegian, and wore in his left lapel a large plastic yellow flower. It carried a small personalized banner: *Come to Sunny Italy. Sven Sverdrup Tours, Tromsø, Norway.* Behind him stood an enticing poster which read: *Spend Your Vacation in Sunny Greece.* In the travel offices of northern Norway, sun was the marketable commodity.

In spite of the fact that Britta was obviously no more than seventeen and not apt to be interested in an expensive tour, Mr. Sverdrup hurried up to her as if she had thousands to spend. 'My name is Sven Sverdrup,' he said pleasantly. 'And what does milady desire? A trip to Oslo for the Christmas vacation?'

'I was thinking about Torremolinos,' she said.

Without blinking, he assured her, 'Best winter vacation in the world. I've been there myself. Perfection.'

'How much?'

'You get fifteen glorious sun-filled days. Tromsø, Oslo, Copenhagen, Torremolinos. Look at the accouterments.' This word she did not know, but with it he handed her a brightly colored brochure whose cover contained the same Scandinavian girl, the same swim suit and the same windmill. He opened the pamphlet to show her the hotel she would be occupying in Torremolinos, the swimming pool, the dining facilities. 'Appointments customarily reserved for American millionaires,' he summed up.

'How much?'

'For fifteen days, every single expense, including tips . . . Look here, a mere ninety-five dollars—less than seven hundred kroner.' Before she could react he dropped his voice and said, 'Of course, that's two in a room. If you insist upon a single, the rate is a little higher—one hundred and ten dollars.'

'I'd be willing to share the room,' she said quickly. He had tricked her into the first positive response.

'Why not?' he asked professionally. 'You're young. You're not so stuck in your ways you need a room to yourself.'

'You're right,' she said as she left.

All next day, as she worked among her papers, she thought of Spain. At mid-afternoon, when the boat from Bergen steamed up to the wharf, she remained at her desk, studying the brochure and fixing in her mind the location of the dining room and swimming pool. She also began those calculations which would occupy her during the rest of December: I'd need to have some spending money. She then reviewed her finances, considering a loan from her father (hopeless), a salary advance from Mr. Mogstad (dangerous, because he would agree, provided she join him again in the sail locker), and some kind of new job that would pay her more money (none available, and besides, if she changed jobs she wouldn't be entitled to a vacation till next summer). I'm certainly not going to Spain in the summer, she thought. I'll take the winter when it does you some good.

She began questioning her friends about Spain, and those with acquaintances who had made the trip gave enthusiastic reports. She finally found a woman in the clothing store who had actually made the trip, a large woman in her fifties, but her report was somewhat deflating: 'Some people say a lot more about Spain than other people ought to believe.'

Firmest encouragement came from Mr. Sverdrup and his hymns of praise to the sun. Day after day, as she stopped by his office for additional temptations, he assured her that even if she had to beg or borrow, Spain was a necessity: 'Imagine yourself in the sun, with the blue Mediterranean ten feet away from where you are dining, lulling you to sleep at night with its gentle waves.' After one especially enthusiastic description of what she would be enjoying, she went to Mr. Mogstad's office and said, 'I'd like to ask you a hypothetical question.'

'A what?'

'For instance. If I can get the money together, would it be all right if I took my vacation in January?'

Mr. Mogstad put his right thumb and forefinger to his mustache, smoothing down the two halves. 'January would be a good month for a vacation. But where would you get the money?'

'I've been saving.'

'And where would you go? Oslo?'

'Torremolinos.'

'Spain?' he asked incredulously. 'You'd go to Spain?'

'It's where the young people are gathering,' she said, quoting from the brochure.

Mr. Mogstad bit the ends of his mustache, then said in a low voice, 'But why not go to Oslo? I could come down on business. It wouldn't cost you . . .'

'I'm going to Torremolinos,' she said.

'But if you went to Oslo, we could see the *Kon-Tiki* at Bygdøy.
I'd give you the money.'

That afternoon she returned to the travel office and asked
Mr. Sverdrup, 'Torremolinos . . . what's your very cheapest rate?'

He looked at her carefully, as if weighing whether or not to
take her into his confidence, then said, 'Miss Bjørndahl, ninety-five
dollars is a sensational bargain. But'—and here he led her to a
corner of the office—'we reserve a few seats for clergymen, students, hardship cases . . . The man who owns this agency used to
be a clergyman. He authorizes us . . . well, seventy-five dollars.'

Britta, trying not to show her exultation, asked crisply, 'And
how much would I need for spending money?'

Mr. Sverdrup preened his plastic flower and said, 'You're young
and pretty. You ought to enjoy yourself. Don't try to get by on
less than five dollars a day.'

'That's a hundred and fifty dollars in all. That's a lot of money.'

'It is a lot of money but you have a lot of years to live. Take
my advice. Enrich them with lovely memories of the sun. If you
were my daughter, I'd say, "Go." '

She grasped his hand and said, 'You give good advice.'

———•◆•———

And then something quite unexpected happened. Gunnar had
been spending so much time with Britta's father on the short-wave
talking to Ceylon that she felt he had lost interest in her. Certainly
she no longer cared much for him and had already decided that
whether she got to Spain or not, when Christmas vacation was
over she was going to look around Tromsø for some new young
man. 'To put it bluntly,' she told one of the girls in the office,
'Gunnar bores me.' Then, with a tender display of affection, he
arranged for his aunt to stay with relatives so that he and Britta
could use her quarters, and when they were in bed he said, 'Britta!
Mr. Nordlund's promoted me to general supervisor, so I think we
ought to get married.'

The suddenness of the proposal caught her unprepared, and its
prosaic genesis offended her. As she lay there she could visualize
the long years ahead. Her life would be an endless continuation
of what it had been with her parents, and when she had children,

locked in by the long Tromsø winters, they would develop their own dreams and crystallize them into prisons. It was an unlovely prospect, made more so when Gunnar began reciting the special problems they would face: 'We won't be able to find a house of our own, naturally, but if you continue at Mr. Mogstad's and I get a few more raises at Mr. Nordlund's, we can place our names on the list and maybe after eight or ten years we'll be eligible.'

'In the meantime?' Britta asked.

'We could live either with your parents or mine.' The conversation ended and they drifted into desultory love-making, after which Gunnar fell asleep, convinced that he was now engaged, but Britta stayed awake, thinking that a proposal of marriage ought to be something rather more special than Gunnar's had been, the vision of the future more challenging. When she caught herself humming 'I hear as in a dream,' she stopped angrily and muttered to herself, 'I want no more of dreams,' and she decided then that she would have to tell Gunnar she could not marry him.

Always willing to face the reality of the moment, she shook him several times, and when he was awake, said, 'Gunnar, I don't think we ought to get married.'

'Why not?' he asked like a sleepy child who had not comprehended an adult comment.

'I'm not ready. I think I'm going to Spain.'

'Spain!' He sat up in bed, and with his left hand on her breast, asked, 'What do you mean you're not ready? What about this?'

'I enjoy being in bed with you,' she admitted. 'I enjoy sex. But I don't think we'd make a good family. I'm not ready.'

'What's the matter, Britt?'

She sat up beside him, drawing her knees to her chin and adjusting the covers. 'I think it's because I want to see those places in the sun that you and Father dream about. I don't want to talk to Ceylon or listen to it. I want to see it.'

'Britt! Ceylon's nothing. In Tromsø you have a hundred sailors who have been every place in the world, and they'll tell you the truth. Most places are just as dull as Tromsø.'

She would not be persuaded, and as they sat side by side in bed, completely naked, huddled in the blankets, they argued about life and marriage until passion overtook them again, involving them in wild, wintry love-making, but later, when Britta was dressing to go home, she realized that this was the finish.

'I don't think I'll bother to see you any more,' she said at the door.

'That's a hell of a word to use for Merry Christmas,' Gunnar growled. 'I'm not going to *bother*.'

'It's exactly the word I was looking for.' She closed the door and walked through the starry night to her own bed.

———•◦•———

Her break with Gunnar made it imperative that she get to Torremolinos, and she took a realistic survey of her finances. She had less than forty dollars saved and needed a hundred and fifty—assuming Mr. Sverdrup could get her one of the cheap fares. She asked him about this, and he said, 'That much I can promise you. Now what's the money situation?' When she told him, he said, 'Forty is a long way from a hundred and fifty, but you're young and you must make the effort. This could prove the difference in your life.'

He showed her how, if she worked through the month of January and saved every penny of her salary, she would come close to the necessary figure. Also, he thought that perhaps she could get night work at a shop that was overhauling its shelves after Christmas, but this proved illusory, so he found a substitute: she could type his reports to the central office in Copenhagen, and she did so, night after night.

Shortly after the New Year, Mr. Sverdrup received fresh posters showing vacations in Spain, and as he lifted the old one from the window he asked Britta, 'You want this for your room?' She was tempted to grab it as a memento of a land she had grown to love, but before her hand could reach out she saw the poster as a temptation, the first of many substitutes with which she would line her room as recollections of lost dreams, and she refused. 'No posters for me. I want the real thing.'

It was this stubborn dedication to reality that encouraged Mr. Sverdrup to take her into his complete confidence. Waiting till she reported after work one cold, dismal Monday night, he told her, 'This week, no typing. But I've something I must tell you.' He led her into his back office and sat her on a chair. 'Exactly how much money have you?' he asked. She showed him the results of her frugality, and he said, 'Miss Bjørndahl, you have just enough.'

'No!' she protested. 'I will not go down there as a pauper. I've got to have seventy-five dollars' spending money.'

'You have,' he said.

'How do you add?' she asked.

'This way,' he said. 'I'm not supposed to tell prospective clients this, because naturally we want them to pay full fare. But if you wait to buy your ticket till the very last moment, and if we have any empty spaces on the plane, we'll sell you one of those places for . . . how much do you guess?'

Since her fare had already been dropped from ninety-five dollars to seventy-five, she knew it could not go much lower, so she guessed: 'Sixty-five?'

'You can have the whole thing for twenty-six dollars.'

Britta sat with her hands in her lap and said nothing. This was bound to be a trap . . . a joke. She knew that no one could fly in a jet to Spain, live in a good hotel with all meals paid, and have a top-flight fifteen-day vacation for twenty-six dollars—and she was not going to be made a fool of. So she said nothing.

'Did you hear what I said?' Mr. Sverdrup asked.

'Yes. Twenty-six dollars. What for? The sandwiches?'

'For everything. Plane, hotel, food, tips, buses. Everything for fifteen days.'

'Do you mean it?' she asked quietly.

He was amused at her inability to accept the evidence, then said, 'Britta, in this world there are many people who want to help the young. Our company reasons that since the plane must fly down anyway, and since we've already paid for the hotel for the entire year, it's better to have the vacant spaces filled by young people who can profit from the experience than to operate half-empty. I could have told you this a month ago but I wanted to test you—to see if your desire was strong enough to make you sacrifice.'

Britta was afraid she might cry, so she made no reply.

'So you have enough money,' Mr. Sverdrup said. 'Go home and make your plans. The airplane leaves February 3 at five o'clock in the morning. But . . .'

'I knew there had to be a *but* . . .'

'It's a small one, but it's irritating. As of this day, we have empty seats. I'm sure that tomorrow we'll have empty seats. But if the plane were to fill rapidly—for some unexpected reason—well . . .'

'I'd not be able to go?'

'Not to Spain. But in Copenhagen there will be other planes flying to other places.'

'I want to go to Spain,' she said firmly.

'And I want to get you there. But in everything there is always a negative chance. You may wind up in Greece.'

The days that followed were taut with anxiety. Each morning as she went to work in the darkness Britta would stare at the new poster in the window. At lunch she would leave the waterfront and hurry to the main street, and in the silver haze produced by the sun as it scurried along beneath the horizon, she would look through the door at Mr. Sverdrup and he would nod, signifying there was still a vacancy. In the evening, after work, she would stop by his office and do whatever typing had piled up, refusing money for this service, and each night as she helped him close the office she would hear his reassuring words, 'Copenhagen says "Still a vacancy." '

She got her passport in order, said her goodbyes to Gunnar, who was certain she would be back to marry him, and grew much closer to her father than she had ever been before. Often, late at night, she would go to his small room with its posters and maps and sit with him as he traced explorers' routes across the Indian Ocean, insatiable in his desire to know all things pertaining to his island. And he would play *The Pearl Fishers* as they talked, so that she would hear his voice coming to her through a veil of chanting priests or the songs of Singhalese fishermen, and she developed deep compassion for this taciturn man whom life had treated so shabbily.

When Britta told me later of her departure, she said of her father, 'He was a lot smarter than I suspected. He's the one who first sensed the truth about my going away . . . the real reasons. And he guessed correctly that I hadn't admitted them to myself . . . wasn't even conscious of them.' Her father wanted to broach the subject but remained tongue-tied, as always, and took refuge in lesser topics. 'Things with you and Gunnar finished?' he asked hesitantly. When she nodded, he said, 'Not surprised.' He had known, of course, that like many young people in Tromsø—and throughout Norway for that matter—they had been living together, but this had not bothered him. He supposed that if Gunnar proved a good sort, she would marry him in due course, and if not, it was proper that she find out for herself. 'He seemed limited in spirit,' he said. Then, frightened because this observation had brought him close to fundamental reasons, he shut his mouth and looked down at his maps. After a long pause he said, without looking at her, 'You've a good clean spirit, Britt. Keep it that way.'

She also wanted to talk but was afraid of the deeper proddings that were impelling her toward Spain, so, like her father, she retreated to trivialities: 'It would be disgraceful if I got to the airport and there were no seats. Imagine saying all those goodbyes, then reporting back to work as usual to Mr. Mogstad.'

'What's he like?'

'Miserable.'

'Your mother seems to like him.'

'He's miserable.'

'Perhaps when you come back . . .' The words were those any parent concerned about his daughter's first employment might have said, but to Bjørndahl they were as dangerous as fire, for they brought him face to face with the real question: Would she come back? He looked at his daughter, and without either of them speaking, they acknowledged that she was leaving Tromsø for good . . . was fleeing Norway with a stern resolve never to return. 'I wonder if she knows the reasons?' Bjørndahl asked himself. He longed to speak openly with his daughter, for she pleased him. Even though she had a striking beauty, she was sensible. If she was fleeing Norway, he was sure she had good reasons.

With her mother Britta was punctilious, helping with the meals, washing the dishes afterward and answering questions with unusual courtesy. When Mrs. Bjørndahl asked what had happened with Gunnar, Britta said, 'I'm afraid it's ended.' She gave no details, and Mrs. Bjørndahl closed the conversation by saying, 'He'd have made a good son-in-law. Your father liked him.'

On the second of February, Britta rose with an anxiety that she could not mask, for this day would tell whether there was to be an empty seat on the plane. At ten in the morning Mr. Sverdrup would receive a telegram from Copenhagen summarizing details, so at ten-thirty Britta told Mr. Mogstad that she wished to be absent for a few minutes, and while he carefully parted his mustache, pondering whether to allow her to leave or not, she walked out. At the travel office she found that Mr. Sverdrup had also stepped out, and she asked his assistant if any news had come from Copenhagen, but nothing was known, so she waited in growing apprehension.

Finally Mr. Sverdrup returned, his wax flower bobbing briskly in the pale light. 'Good news!' he cried as soon as he saw Britta. 'As of last night . . . seats. You will fly to Copenhagen in the morning. And if you can't get on the plane to Torremolinos, we'll fit you into one of the others. Morocco, Greece—who knows where you'll be tomorrow night?'

'I'll be in Spain,' Britta said.

Because there was little difference between night and day, the airplane to Copenhagen always left Tromsø at three in the morning, so Britta did not go to bed; she talked with her father for the last time, and he said, 'I'm not going with you to the airport.' She felt very close to her mother and talked with her too, but as she did she heard the ghostly strains of the cavatina, and its desperate longing so tore at her heart that she returned to where her father sat alone, leafing through his books. 'I wish I were going with you,' he said, but what he meant was: 'I wish I'd had the courage to cut loose years ago.'

At the airport she kissed Gunnar perfunctorily, mainly because he had brought along some of his friends and would be embarrassed if she did not make believe they were still lovers. When the time came for her to say goodbye to her mother she experienced a flood of emotion, and in the passing of a second, acknowledged to herself the real reasons why she had fought so desperately to get to Spain. 'I'm leaving Tromsø for good. I can't abide the dull orderliness . . . the years that never change . . . the heavy system of the same old things. I don't want to wait ten years before I begin my life. I want no more of the tunnel.'

Then, to her own surprise, she blurted out the truth to her mother: 'I'll not be coming back . . . not ever. Tell Father.'

Mrs. Bjørndahl grabbed her arm, intending to force an explanation of this extraordinary announcement, but Britta pushed her away and ran to the plane, dashing up the stairs before her mother could reach her.

At Copenhagen there was a two-hour wait as the three planes chartered by the travel agency were loaded. The first, headed for Spain, had large numbers of tourists, and the agency man whom Britta questioned said he thought all the stand-bys would have to fly on the second, which was headed for Morocco. 'It's a great place. You'll like it.' The third plane, also well patronized, was heading for Greece, but on this one, there were definitely no vacancies. So it was either Morocco or Torremolinos, and Britta began to pray.

There were six stand-bys this day, five young girls and a boy from a university in Sweden. They all said they didn't care much where they went so long as there was sun, so Britta proposed: 'If you don't care, and if there's only one seat on the Torremolinos plane, could I have it?'

'We'll go where they send us,' one of the girls said.

'At these prices you can't be selective,' the boy said.

So Britta stood by herself with her fists clenched, and when the travel man came to the stand-bys and said, 'We have two seats for Torremolinos,' she almost knocked him down as she leaped forward, and even when she was strapped in her seat she was afraid to relax, but when the huge SAS jet finally sped down the runway and left the ground, she was at last satisfied that her protracted dream was to be a reality, and disregarding the startled passengers around her, she threw her arms high in the air and shouted, 'It happened!'

———•—•—•———

When the jet landed at Málaga and the two hundred Scandinavian tourists disembarked, a curious thing happened. As they entered the airport they ran into another two hundred whose vacation had ended and who were returning to Scandinavia, and as the two groups passed, there was vibrant excitement showing in one set of faces, dejection in the other, for the first were coming into sunlight, the latter were heading back into the tunnel. Men tourists on their way home masked their faces in stolid acceptance, consoling themselves with the fact that as between modern Sweden and archaic Spain, there was really no choice; any man in his right mind would prefer Sweden with its insurance, its fine hospitals, its even finer schools and its just, democratic government freed from clerical influences. But the young girls, tanned by the wintry sun, did not so deceive themselves; they had loved Spain and wanted to remain, at least till summer reached the northlands, and their faces were often clothed in gloom: 'I don't want to go home.

I don't want to go home!' they seemed to be chanting, like the chorus in some Scandinavian saga.

Britta Bjørndahl's first view of Spain exceeded her expectations: for once the travel posters had not lied. The day was bright and there was a sun, with fleecy clouds drifting in from the Mediterranean and warmth nestling against the mountains to the north. A covey of yellow buses pulled up to the airport entrance, and as the newcomers piled in, they saw the SAS jet refueling, like some huge bird impatient to return to its nest. Britta nodded to it as she went past. 'Go home!' she whispered. 'I shall not be needing you again.'

The trip from Málaga to Torremolinos required less than twenty minutes but it represented a journey from one civilization to another: golf links waiting in the sun, small restaurants with patios open to the sky, glimpses of a Mediterranean more deeply colored than sapphire, and, surprisingly, a cluster of twenty-seven skyscrapers marking the official beginning of the town. The buses sped directly through Torremolinos, turned left toward the sea, and pulled up in a neat convoy before a new seventeen-story hotel called the Northern Lights, whose staff was completely Scandinavian. With the efficiency that came from handling such incoming groups twice each week throughout the year, the blond young men behind the desk distributed numbers and room keys as fast as the tourists entered the lobby and handed them printed cards which explained how to get to their rooms and from there to the dining hall. Within six minutes of having descended from the bus, Britta was carrying her small bag off the elevator onto the sixteenth floor. Pushing open her assigned door, she found a Swedish girl who introduced herself as Sigrid and who said within the first minute of greeting, 'I have to go back on Friday.'

Britta's first question was one she would repeat constantly for the next two weeks: 'Is it possible to find work here?'

'Absolutely impossible. Not a job to be had.'

'But suppose there was,' Britta persisted. 'How would I find it?'

'I started with the manager here. He told me he gets fifty inquiries a week from girls like us. About the best you can do is select some bar and hang around till they know you. If anything's available, they'll tell you.'

'Where are the bars?' Britta asked.

Sigrid laughed and said, 'Go down, turn right, stub your toe and you'll bump into seven. But you have to make up your mind. Swedish, or German, or American?'

'Do they go by nations?'

'Of course. So do the restaurants.'

'Could I get a job as waitress?'

'Not a chance. I tried that too.'

'What about the bars?'

'The Swedish are the cleanest . . . and of course you know the language. But you don't meet men with money . . . or who can give you a job. The German bars are the most fun and you do meet . . .'

'I couldn't work with Germans,' Britta interrupted, and Sigrid, aware that she was Norwegian, said no more.

'The American bars are ugly places and very noisy. I can't stand them, but you do meet men from the military bases and they do have money.'

'Can they find you a job?'

'No. But the money you can scrounge allows you to hang on till you find a job.'

'Then there are jobs?' Britta pressed.

'Darling! More than a hundred Scandinavian girls work in Torremolinos. Not one of them found a job when she came here, but somehow they held on. And now they have good jobs, and I'm eating my heart out with envy to think that they managed and I wasn't able to.'

'Please, how did they manage . . . really?'

'Three ways,' Sigrid said, standing by the window and looking eastward toward Málaga, which lay in sunlight between the mountains and the sea. 'On the weekends Torremolinos gets many Spanish men from business offices in Madrid, and they all hope to find a *sueca* . . . that's what they call us. They have a tradition of being generous with their mistresses . . . give them apartments . . . small allowances . . . and they don't expect it to last forever. Second way is the Germans. They're even freer with their money, but for a Norwegian, I suppose that's out.'

Britta stared straight ahead at the outlines of Málaga, so Sigrid concluded: 'What's left is the way most of the girls manage it. The American soldiers flock down here each weekend—even sailors from Rota. And the big thing in their lives is to set up an apartment with a Swedish girl. They're very generous, because they get paid well, but they're loud and damned near illiterate. I thought about it . . . quite seriously . . . anything to get a foothold in Spain. But in the end I couldn't take it. What would you talk about with an American soldier?' She sighed, then said quietly, 'So on Friday I fly back . . . if I don't jump out this window first.'

Unhappy with this report, Britta said, 'I'm hungry,' so they went down to lunch and were given one of the best tables, and not once during her stay in the Northern Lights did anyone indicate in any prejudicial way that they knew she had made the trip at the cheapest possible fare. To the hotel staff she was another beautiful Norwegian girl who could be used to decorate the hotel and make it look something like the photographs in the advertising brochures, and they knew that if they treated her well, she might in future years return . . . at full rate.

In every respect Britta found the physical aspects of her vacation better than she had expected. The room was larger, the bedding cleaner, the view more spectacular. The food was good, with three courses at every meal, four plates to choose from in each course: one was strictly Scandinavian, with the accent on fish; one was Spanish, with emphasis on spices; one was French, with a new sauce every meal; and one was international and totally bland. Only the indoor swimming pool had a serious weakness: three girls to every man. In sum, the Northern Lights was one of the best tourist values in the world, even at top prices, and at $26.13 for fifteen days it was a miracle.

Yet Britta could not enjoy it, because every morning when she awakened she realized that the time of her departure was one day closer, and this depressed her. She asked the hotel manager if he had any jobs, and he threw up his hands: 'My dear girl! If I had fifty jobs I could fill them.' She also stopped by the SAS offices, but they were fully staffed. 'Girls who get jobs here don't leave,' the office director said. She tried the luxury hotels, one after the other, and found nothing. On Friday she bade her roommate goodbye; Sigrid had tears in her eyes as she left Spain, and that evening her bed was taken by Mette, a delightful girl from Copenhagen, the daughter of a newspaper editor.

Mette had firm ideas about how a vacation should be spent, and on the first night invited Britta to accompany her to the Arc de Triomphe, explaining, 'When two blondes walk in together, a nicer type of boy swings into action, because he has to have a buddy, and to have a buddy you must be at least human. If a blonde goes out alone, she's likely to pick up creeps who operate solitary.'

When they entered the discotheque they made a stir, with confident Mette leading the way, and before midnight she had arranged dates with two American soldiers from the base near Sevilla. The men were young and bright and noisy and had an apartment near the ocean. Mette said she'd like to see it, but Britta felt that this could come later. Before she shacked up with soldiers she would exhaust every possibility of a job; she was convinced that something dramatic would happen to save her from flying back to Tromsø and she would pursue every possibility that might help it to happen.

'I'm not a prude about sex,' she told Mette the next morning when the Danish girl returned to the hotel. 'In a crisis I'll take an apartment from the Americans. But what I really want is a job.'

'You find one,' Mette said, 'and they'll build a statue to you—in Copenhagen harbor, right beside the Little Mermaid.' But later she admitted, 'You were smart to go home last night. They just got drunker and drunker.' But when midnight approached she said, 'I will not spend Saturday night in a hotel room with another girl. Come on, I'll treat you to the Arc de Triomphe.'

At the discotheque Britta saw the two American soldiers, but they were standing at the bar, so glassy-eyed drunk they did not even remember the girls. Nothing happened. The music was tremendously loud and good, and there seemed to be about the same number of young people as the night before, but no men dropped by their table to talk, so about two in the morning Mette in desperation walked to the bar and reminded the almost-unconscious Americans who she was. It was agreed that she would sleep at their place again, whereupon she returned to Britta and said, 'You can come along if you like,' but Britta said, 'No thanks. I don't object to a little sex, but the man has to be awake when it starts.'

She walked home alone, and it was on this night, as the stars were brilliant above the mountains and music came from every bar, that her panic began: 'Oh God! I'm going to miss the whole thing. In nine more days the plane will return and drag me back into the tunnel.' Without realizing what she was doing, she began whistling softly the cavatina from *The Pearl Fishers*, and its languid melody, so appropriate to southern Spain at night, tormented her with its vision of lost paradises. She passed a score of bars crowded with weekend visitors, and twice Spanish gentlemen from Madrid accosted her in gallant hyperbole, and she thought: Don Energetico, one false step and you're going to have a Norwegian mistress on your hands.

When she reached her hotel she could not go in. She could not bear to see that clean Scandinavian lobby, that antiseptic, lonely room with its distant view of Málaga: Oh God, I am so afraid. I am so alone. In the dark night she wanted to weep, but felt that it was beneath her Norwegian dignity to do so. Biting her lip to restrain the tears, she started back toward the center of town, an eighteen-year-old girl determined to find a solution, any solution to her problem.

Nothing happened. She drifted into four different bars and out again before any of the men could talk with her. She went down to the silent beach and walked eastward along it, hundreds of apartments towering above her. 'There must be someone up there,' she said to herself, 'who's as lonely as I am. But how in the hell do you find him?' She kicked the sand and wandered back to the center of town, where some American soldiers wanted to talk with her, but they were drunk. She tried another bar, but it was German, so she walked right out, and in the end she had to go back to her hotel. It was four in the morning and Mette was not home.

'There must be some way,' she told herself repeatedly, falling asleep in a chair with her clothes on.

Each day at noon she surprised the Scandinavians and astonished the Americans and Britons by appearing in her bikini, wearing a loose robe and sandals, headed for the seashore. 'You're not going swimming?' guests asked. 'Why not?' she asked. 'Sun's out.'

On the way to the beach an icy wind whipped at her ankles, tossing her robe aside, so that men could see her excellent legs and beautiful torso. They whistled at her and made sly suggestions, and as she passed them she thought: If you clowns only knew how easy it would be if you had any guts. One proper word. One decent invitation.

Along the windswept beach the municipality maintained a series of low walls constructed of wattle and reed plaited in ancient peasant patterns, and they provided good protection against the wind. Each day, snuggled close to these walls, a few hardy Scandinavians and Germans came to profit from what sun there was, and whenever Britta came among them and threw off her robe, revealing her flaxen hair and handsome body, the sunbathers stopped whatever they were doing and admired her. Invariably some German athlete would ask where she was from, but she found it impossible to talk with him.

Actually, when one was protected from the wind, the beach wasn't bad, and before long she had accumulated the tan she had dreamed of, but occasionally she would look up from the sand and see on the roadway beside the beach English and American ladies in overcoats, and everything would seem contrary and strange.

After lying in whatever sun there might be for an hour or so, Britta would leave the windbreak and dash down to the water's edge. Without testing the ice-cold waves, she would grab a deep breath and run into the sea until the water reached her waist, then plunge beneath it and swim underwater for a few minutes. The water, always colder than she had expected but warmer than it ever was at Tromsø, nearly paralyzed her at first, but the exercise was so invigorating that she found real joy in swimming and gasping and shaking her blond hair free, and after fifteen minutes of this she would run from the sea, dash across the beach and rub herself vigorously with a towel, finding in her ability to withstand the cold a courage to face the disappointments she was encountering in Torremolinos.

Always when she stood drying herself people came up to converse with her, but never did anyone arrive in whom she detected that flash of interest which she might care to pursue and develop. On Friday afternoon, the twelfth day of her vacation, she slipped into her robe, recovered her sandals and walked disconsolately back to the Northern Lights, flicking at imaginary ghosts with her towel. 'Are you having a good time?' the hotel manager asked her. She forced a smile, drew her pouting lip back from her white teeth, and said, 'Wonderful.' Alone in the elevator she growled, 'I could kick this damned building down stone by stone.' When she reached her room, Mette was preparing to join her Americans, and suggested, 'Remember, this is Friday, so maybe there'll be some new men coming down from the base. You want to come along?'

Britta did, desperately, and said, 'Well, if there were only someone new . . .' By the time the girls reached the Americans' apartment the men were already drunk; there was nobody new; Mette's
friend insisted upon going to bed with her immediately; and ten
minutes after Britta had arrived at the party she was walking back
to her hotel, alone.

Saturday was the worst day of her vacation, one that she would
often recall with a sense of terror. It was the thirteenth day, an
ominous fact which she noted when she arose. At lunch she realized
that she had memorized the menu; the food was good, but here it
came marching at her in established order. She looked about her
at the sturdy Scandinavian families, solid middle-class women and
their honest husbands, and she thought of them saving their money
throughout the year for this one glorious vacation in Spain, with
the regiments of food coming at them, and she could visualize
herself in this room twenty years from now.

On the beach that Saturday she was so terribly lonely that she
allowed a German to talk with her for twenty minutes. He was a
most handsome man, blond and well muscled, and he proposed
that they have a drink, but she could see him only as an officer
on the great battleship that lay sunk off her island, and he became
a ghost in a beribboned uniform and she felt sorry for him and sent
him away.

She could not go in to supper, but went into the center of town
and with her own money bought a Chinese dinner, and as she was
eating, a Spanish businessman down from Madrid sat at her table,
speaking excellent English. He volunteered to pay for her dinner,
assuring her that he came often to Torremolinos and would be
happy to know that someone as attractive as Britta was waiting for
him. She studied him as if he were an applicant for a job and was
tempted to pursue the matter, but she knew intuitively that this
was not what she wanted. She was intended for something better
than the weekend mistress of a Madrid businessman, no matter
how charming, so she said, 'Sorry, I'm waiting for my fiancé.' He
knew she was lying; he was sure no young man was going to appear, but he appreciated her courtesy in offering him a plausible
excuse, so he nodded and withdrew. After a decent interval she left.

It was Saturday night and she was stricken with loneliness, made
no less oppressive by the fact that she had brought it upon herself:
she could have stayed with the drunken Americans or she could

have picked up the Spaniard, but she felt that these were not honest options, and she would not delude herself with them. Slowly she walked toward the sounds coming from the Arc de Triomphe, bought a ticket and went in. The music was exciting, reminding her of how much she had enjoyed it on her first visit, but as the night wore on, nothing happened. She met no one and decided to go back to her hotel, but as she left the discotheque she felt someone take her arm. It was the Spanish businessman.

'Your fiancé failed to appear?' he asked graciously.

'Had to work in Málaga,' she replied.

'Then there is nothing to impede you.'

She allowed herself to be led away from the street and toward a public park with many obscure areas. Adroitly and with charm, the Spaniard took her to a protected corner and within two highly proficient minutes had her practically undressed. With lightning speed his trousers were down and he was about to mount her when she came to her senses and pushed him away.

He had anticipated this and covered her with kisses, pulling away her remaining clothes, but now she rebelled. Shoving him so hard he fell to one knee, she recovered her clothing and began adjusting it, but he would have none of this, for he interpreted her hesitancy as natural modesty on the first night and he intended to respect it on the one hand but to override it on the other.

He therefore began kissing her violently as he tugged for her clothes, whispering as he did so, 'What is your name, beloved? Will you stay in Torremolinos if I find you a flat?'

His speech was so ridiculous that she began to laugh, but this infuriated him and he gave her two sharp blows to the head. That did it. With violent thrusts and slaps she drove the poor fellow back, more than a match for him if he cared to pursue the fight. He struck at her ineffectually while she fought to recover her skirt from his left hand. 'Get yourself dressed,' she said contemptuously.

'You a lesbian?' he growled. 'You don't like sex?'

The question was so preposterous that she gave no answer. 'I'm sorry,' she said grudgingly. 'It was your idea.'

'You think of yourself as some cold goddess from the north?' he asked from the shadows.

'Oh, quit it!' she said. A dozen clever comments came to her mind, but she offered none because she knew they would hurt him; other responsible observations occurred to her which would allow him to preserve his dignity, but she was too distracted to bother with them. It had been a mistake, a regrettable accident, and she wanted it to end. 'I'm sorry,' she repeated, resuming her walk to the hotel.

She was not proud of herself. If she had not been so obviously looking for companionship in the Chinese restaurant, the Spaniard would not have approached her; and if she had not lied to him, he would not have accosted her at the discotheque. 'It's time I got out of this town,' she said grimly to herself as she walked through the darkened streets, but no sooner had she said these words than their consequences overwhelmed her: to leave Spain, to surrender her glimpse of another life. In desperation she ran through the streets, and as she did so she came upon a small bar she had not noticed before. From the noise issuing through its open door it had to be American, and when she looked at the sign she recognized the name from a John Wayne movie she had seen in Tromsø, THE ALAMO; it was printed in crude letters along the barrel of a huge wooden revolver. For a moment she listened to the screaming music, the sound of high-pitched voices, and she thought: This is the kind of place you need on lonely Saturday nights.

Hesitantly she entered and slipped into a seat in the corner. The bartender, a tall, slim American with long hair and a beard, waited for her to get settled, then casually walked over to ask what she wished, and she said, 'How about a beer?'

'It's lousy. Refrigerator broke down. But we do have some cold orange.'

He brought her one and stood by her chair for a moment. 'You just in?'

'Yes. Norway.' She said nothing more, so he made some general comment and returned to his work at the bar. He did not come her way again for about an hour, during which time he was quite busy both tending the bar and serving the tables. When he did return he was as noncommittal as before. She asked what part of America he came from, but before he could answer he was called back to the bar.

At two in the morning she was taken in tow by three American sailors from the navy base at Rota, a noisy, generous lot. Since she was blond and Scandinavian, they insisted she was Swedish and wanted to know what she thought about President Eisenhower's famous accusation that Sweden was a degenerate, socialistic, immoral nation where suicide was rampant. 'I'm not Swedish,' she said, 'but I don't believe a foreign statesman in President Eisenhower's position would make such a charge.'

'But you are socialistic, aren't you?' one of the sailors pressed.

'Not that I've noticed,' she replied. And when the sailors became abusive about the Swedes, accusing them of encouraging American military to desert, she tried to counter their arguments, then blurted out, 'What about Vietnam?' The sailors had various answers, and the discussion continued till about four in the morning. They liked the free manner in which she spoke and wanted to know where they could see her the next day, and she said, 'On the beach. Where else?' and they asked in astonishment, 'You mean you go swimming? In February?' and she told them, 'Norwegians are real sea people. Not little boys in sailor suits,' whereupon one of the Americans caught her by the shoulders and gave her a goodbye kiss, crying, 'You're the little Viking I've been looking for.'

Once more she had managed to get through the night.

On the final Sunday afternoon Britta had to admit that her bright dream of Spain had disintegrated. Putting on her bikini, she threw her robe about her shoulders and went down to the beach for the last time. She noticed that the wind was a little less cold, the sun a bit warmer, and she thought: How utterly rotten! On my last day they make things better. After a sunbath that was actually relaxing and imparted a finishing touch of tan, she ran into the icy waters, swam vigorously for twenty minutes, and dashed back to find a visitor standing by her robe.

It was a Scandinavian girl, about twenty, who had come purposely across the beach to speak with her. 'You're a real mermaid,' she said as Britta dressed. 'Stockholm?'

'Norway.'

'I've seen you the last four days . . . from our apartment. I admire the way you take the water.'

They had talked for only a few minutes when Britta voiced her usual question: 'How can a girl find a job here?'

'Not easy. It took me three months.'

'But you did find one?'

'Yes. So do most of the kids who stick it out.'

'How do you live?'

'A very sweet guy let me sleep in his room. He had his own girl. Every night when I went to bed I prayed. I don't know what for, but I prayed. And one day a Belgian businessman came to him and said, "I own a bar here but I have to go back to Antwerp. I'll sell it for what it cost." And it was in that bar that I got my job.'

'Is it . . . decent work?'

'It's not a living but it's better than Stockholm in winter.' She suggested that when Britta was dressed she might want to stop by the apartment for a drink, and Britta said, 'My clothes are up there,' and the Swedish girl looked at the hotel and said, 'That's how I got started. On the tenth floor of the Northern Lights. It seems so long ago.'

'Was it worth it?'

'Every minute. Now I'm going home to get married.'

Britta froze into position, like a Greek statue, one knee bent, sandal in the right hand. Very cautiously she asked, 'But if you're going home . . .'

'I am.'

'Then your job at the bar . . .'

'That's what I came here to speak about.'

Britta went all limp. Her leg dropped and the sandal fell to earth. 'God bless you,' she said. Neither girl spoke, then finally Britta asked, 'What kind of bar is it?'

'Like the rest. Small, dirty, noisy. I'll be content if I never hear a note of music the rest of my life. If my husband comes home with a hi-fi set, I'll throw it in the Baltic.'

Recovering her sandal, Britta experienced a moment of panic and asked abruptly, 'It's not a German bar?'

'Worse. It's American. A joint they call the Alamo.'

'Oh!' Britta cried. 'I know it! I was there last night!' She paused. 'I didn't see you.'

'Some Swedes gave me a farewell party . . .'

'This sounds ridiculous,' Britta whispered, 'but when I was in your bar last night, watching that man run back and forth—tend the bar, wait on tables—I said, "He ought to have a helper," and tonight I was going to go back for one last effort. I was going to tell him, "You need a waitress to help you." You really think I might get the job?'

'Yes. My name's Ingrid. Let's go along and fetch your clothes.'

The remainder of that Sunday, the fourteenth day of her vacation, was one that Britta would never forget, a compound of hope and anxiety. Her hope stemmed from the fact that Ingrid felt sure she could pass her job along to Britta; the anxiety came when the two girls got to the apartment where Ingrid was staying, and found nobody. There were two large beds, and since each was covered with men's and women's clothes intermixed, it was obvious that two couples were occupying the room.

'They'll be back,' Ingrid said reassuringly. 'Probably went somewhere for a drink.'

Britta pointed to one of the beds and asked, 'Is this part of the job?'

'Not necessarily.' Indicating one bed, Ingrid explained, 'The owner has his girl. He's very nice. An Italian boy from Lugano. This bed is mine. The tall bartender you saw used to sleep in a bag on the floor. After a while I asked him to join me, so we put the bag away. If you prefer to use it, I'm sure they won't mind.'

'You mean I can sleep here? On the floor?'

'Everybody else does. But you may also want to take over the bed . . . when I'm gone. He's a very sweet guy . . . gentle . . . confused . . . not like an American at all.'

They waited for the better part of an hour, talking about Spain and Scandinavia, and Ingrid said that the young Swede she was marrying was an architect, and a good one. 'I think we'll be happy. This vacation in Spain . . .'

'How long were you here?'

'Eight months. I tried a Spanish businessman once, but it didn't work out. They have such silly conventions . . . such ridiculous ideas about courtship . . . I was worn out trying to understand what his various tricks meant. All I wanted was a place to stay and enough money to feed myself from Monday through Thursday, but he had this complicated routine and I finally said to hell with it. I hadn't a coin in my purse, but Jean-Victor met me in a bar . . . he's the one who owns the place . . .' She sighed and said, 'It's been a good eight months and I think I'm ready to go home.'

'When are they coming?' Britta pleaded. 'My plane leaves at two tomorrow.'

'They'll be here,' Ingrid reassured her, but night fell and no one came. A real panic overtook Britta and for the first time in many years she actually started to cry. 'I'm sure it'll come to nothing . . . this lovely dream.' She sat on the bed for some time, holding her face in her hands. Then she said with conviction, 'If he won't hire me at the bar I'm going to proposition the first man I see. I will not fly back to Norway.' She grabbed her topcoat and walked resolutely out the door, and Ingrid followed her, saying, 'We'll go to the bar. They'll have to be there.'

They walked up the hill away from the beach, past the myriad bars where other girls who had landed jobs were beginning to congregate, and into the center of town where restaurants of all nations posted on their windows the names of the travel clubs from Copenhagen, Berlin and London whose members could pay for their meals with the dinner chits the clubs issued. Some of the cheaper restaurants displayed as many as twenty-four decalco-manias, but the girls were not interested in dinner, so they went directly to the Alamo, whose violent music they could hear a block away. Inside, the American soldiers and sailors were having the last noisy drink of the weekend before starting back to their bases on the far side of the mountains, and all of them greeted Ingrid with cheers and kisses, for she did much to make their visits happy. The three sailors who had entertained Britta the night before made a series of whirlwind proposals . . . they had an apartment . . . she could use it . . . there was food in the refrigerator . . . and next weekend she could decide whether she wanted to live permanently with any of them. She thought how surprised they would be if they knew how close she was to saying yes; she even studied the three to see which she would choose if she had to. She asked, 'When do you start driving back to Rota?' and they said, 'At midnight,' and she pressed the hand of the least objectionable and said, 'I'll be around to say goodbye.'

But sometime around ten the bartender appeared, tall, long-haired and generally presentable. She restrained herself from running up to him and waited until Ingrid called her over. 'Joe, this is Britta. The Norwegian I've been telling you about.'

Joe looked up from his beer bottles and said, 'I noticed you last night. Think you could run the place?'

'Yes . . . if you'd be patient the first days.'

He smiled and said, 'It isn't the days that are the problems. It's the nights.'

'I am not afraid of nights,' Britta said.

'When did you say you were leaving, Ingrid?'
'The ticket reads Wednesday.'
'Can *you* start work Wednesday?'
'Oh yes!' She had not wanted to sound too eager, but she could not restrain herself.
'I'll have to move her things into the apartment,' Ingrid said.
'Why not?'
'She can use the sleeping bag.'
'Why not?'

When Joe went back to the bar, Britta said, 'I want to move in right now. No, I won't wait till tomorrow, because something might go wrong. He might see another girl who looked better, but if I'm sleeping at the foot of his bed . . .'

'Few girls look better than you,' Ingrid assured her. 'Come along. We'll get your gear.'

Britta walked back to the Northern Lights as if the pavements of Torremolinos were clouds. She wanted to sing and to kiss everyone who passed, and at the hotel she ran up to the Swedish manager and said, 'I've found a job. You said it couldn't be done, but I've found a job.' She took his two hands and danced, then went to the tour desk and announced in a voice that could be heard throughout the lobby, 'You can take my name off tomorrow's list, I'm not flying back to Tromsø.' Mette was not in the room, so Britta left her a hastily scrawled note: 'I found a way to stay here. Hope you do too.'

When they took her clothes to Jean-Victor's apartment, he and Sandra were in bed, and without getting up they welcomed her, told her how to find the sleeping bag with the tartan cover, and directed its placement on the floor. Sandra said, 'You'd better pin a note to it: "This bed belongs to . . ." What's your name?'

'Britta. I'm from a little town in northern Norway.'
'Narvik?' Sandra asked brightly. 'My father fought at Narvik.'
'Even farther north. Tromsø.'
'Daddy was there too. In a destroyer. He says it's wildly beautiful.' Sandra maintained a running comment about her father and the battles he had engaged in off the Norwegian coast. Obviously she liked her father, and Britta said, 'My father was in the mountains signaling your ships,' whereupon Sandra leaped from her bed, naked, and ran to kiss their new guest. 'You'll like it here,' she said warmly.

And in the second week, after Ingrid had returned to Sweden, Britta lay one night in the tartan sleeping bag and heard Jean-Victor and Sandra in their bed and thought of Joe sleeping alone in the big bed, and the arrangement seemed ridiculous, so quietly she crept out of the sleeping bag, walked the short distance to Joe's bed, and shook him gently by the shoulder, saying, 'It's no fun down there,' and he said sleepily, 'Come in here where it's warm,' and the pathway back to Tromsø closed forever.

III §

MONICA

An Englishman is never at home except when he is abroad.

There is a feeling of Eternity in youth which makes us amends for everything. To be young is to be as one of the Immortal Gods.—Hazlitt

Finally we arrived at that mysterious plateau where the rivers begin, and wherever I went I was attended by a thousand birds of colorful plumage. If I tried to cross the swamp I saw before me hundreds upon hundreds of hippopotamuses who lazily moved aside at my approach. And if I went to the dry areas I found myself surrounded by a multitude of wild animals, some of whom I could not even identify, so abundant were the species, and I said, 'This is Africa, the real Africa that will never perish so long as the plateaus are preserved and the men who govern them share their responsibilities one with the other.' For remember that it was a black guide who had brought me to this place, to share its wonders with me.

—Lord Carrington Braham, February 1899

Burn pot, not people.

A great empire and little minds go ill together.—Burke

Hire the morally handicapped. It's more fun.

The blunders of youth are preferable to the success of old age.—Disraeli

For more than eighty years we have been the wards of Great Britain. Today we become the friends of Great Britain and I am certain that it will be as difficult for us to be peaceful friends as it was to be obedient wards. Many Englishmen lie dead in this land, heroic men who fought our fathers to establish empire here; and beside them lie many of my ancestors, who tried to prevent empire from intruding on our ancient ways. Out of those battles we built a mutual respect, upon which we shall operate in the future. In Vwarda there will always be a home for such Englishmen as choose to live with us. In Vwarda there will always be businesses for Englishmen to run, offices for them to fill, jobs for them to perform, because I promise you this, the Negro Republic of Vwarda will never be an anti-white government, for we have learned how fruitful the cooperation of white and black can be.
　　　—Inaugural address of President Hosea M'Bele,
　　　　August 1958

Whom the gods would destroy they first make promising.

It is better to be a young June-bug than an old bird of Paradise.—Mark Twain

　　The stability of England is the security of the modern world.—Emerson

　　　To use bad English is regrettable.
　　　To use bad Scotch is unforgivable.

It is my pleasure to confer upon you this knighthood in honor of the great services you provided our former subjects in British Congo and the creative assistance you gave our newest ally, the Republic of Vwarda, in the critical days when it was designing the patterns under which it would operate.
　　　—Queen Elizabeth, at the investiture
　　　　of Sir Charles Braham, Buckingham
　　　　Palace, December 1958

　　Sex to a young girl is like a bed of flowers to a honeybee. She can sense its existence even though she has not yet seen it.

　　　All empire is no more than power in trust.—Dryden
All government is the same. (Scrawled in the margin of the book)

　　Please behave like decent young ladies and gentlemen. No suicides, no dynamiting, no abortions.—Sign in a Torremolinos hotel

OF the six young people I was to meet that year, the one I was closest to was a dark-haired English girl whose family I had known in the Republic of Vwarda when I was arranging industrial loans during that exciting decade when African Negroes were assuming control of their governments.

At first I did not work directly with the new Negro president of Vwarda, nor even with members of his cabinet, for in that beginning period the new nation had no Negroes sufficiently informed to handle the economics of an international loan. I conducted my discussions principally with Sir Charles Braham, in many ways the archetype of the British colonial servant, in others about as atypical as you could find.

He was archetypal because of his education at a good public school plus later attendance at Oxford, two experiences which imparted that serene mixture of cool superiority and amateurish bumbling which mark the English gentleman. He had been born into one of the historic rural families, which gave him the appreciation of nature so common in the best Englishmen. And he had grown up in an atmosphere of public service, his various uncles having distinguished themselves in places like India and Afghanistan; it was said by the shopkeepers of his home county that 'the Brahams are so incapable of handling their own affairs that the only thing they can be trusted with is public service . . . especially in the colonies.' Sir Charles's father, having started his career in Vwarda when it was known as the British Congo, terminated it in London as cabinet minister specializing in empire problems.

I was not surprised, therefore, when reporting to Sir Charles's office in Vwarda, to find framed behind his desk this motto:

> Not lust of conquest
> but love of order
> is at the basis of Empire.
> —Duff Cooper

With Sir Charles this boast was not pompous; he believed that the duty of empire was to bring order into any part of the world which strove to discard ancient patterns and accept new. In 1948, when the British government proposed that he give up his comfortable job in London and go out to the British Congo to help whip that faltering colony into shape, he never thought of protesting, for this was the kind of challenge a gentleman accepted. As he told his wife on the day of his appointment to the Congo, 'It gives us an opportunity to put into practice what we've been talking about here in London.' He was also mindful of the fact that he would be following in the footsteps of his father, 'and it isn't preposterous to think that perhaps I, too, may be recalled one day to serve in the cabinet, mayn't I?'

His record in Africa had been outstanding and he should have been brought home in 1958, but that was the year the British Congo was scheduled to become Vwarda, and he had been designated by the Queen to supervise the transition, a ticklish job which he performed with such ease and good will that both England and the new nation wanted him to stay on for just a few more years. Government knew that he was not the stuff from which cabinet ministers were made and judged it propitious to leave him in Vwarda, where he served a useful purpose.

Now, in September 1968, when spring was blossoming in heavy splendor, he was ending his twenty-first year of service and had come to think of Vwarda as his homeland and these people as his charges, whether they were, as in the past, the illiterate and savage servants of an empire or, as now, the well-intentioned rulers of a wealthy new republic. He was fond of saying at banquets, 'I was seconded here for a crisis job of four months. I have stayed twenty-one years. Either the crisis was bigger than they thought, or I was smaller.'

He had behaved with a certain grace in those years of change, shifting from his role as representative of the Queen, with all the panoply and prerogative that this conferred, to his present role of paid public employee of the Negro republic. It had not been an easy transition—overlord in be-medaled uniform one day, hired hand in blue serge the next—but he had drawn upon his training as a gentleman and had shown lesser men how easy it was to take orders from Negroes to whom they had been giving orders only the week before. Observers could not detect whether Sir Charles was indeed embittered by this dramatic shift in fortune. He said simply, 'Vwarda is my home and all men are obligated to till their own gardens, aren't they?'

The only petulance Sir Charles ever demonstrated came in his private talks with me. We spent some months together, trying to wrap up the loan which would enable Vwarda to build its hydro-electric dam, and sometimes late at night, when things had gone wrong, he would confide his disappointments. In his huffing, stumbling manner he would growl, 'Thing I object to most is the damned postage stamps. In the old days we had those superb stamps . . . great dignity . . . portrait of the Queen . . . splen-did etching, just that and nothing more . . . subdued color, marvelous design . . . and those simple words . . . British Congo. Now what do we have? These damned tropical birds and animals . . . looks like a bloody zoo . . . and the new name plastered over everything . . . no taste . . . no feeling for dignity and propriety.' Later I found that his real complaint was against the change in name. One night when we had taken on a rather heavy burden of gin at the British Club—formerly the Colonial Club, one of the stuffiest in the empire—he confided: 'Thing I simply cannot understand is why they felt they had to drop that splendid old name British Congo . . . you knew what it was, where it was, what it meant. What does the new name stand for? A bloody river that not one person in a thousand ever heard of. Vwarda!' He snorted with contempt, then quickly apologized: 'I must tell you, though, that these blighters are damned decent to work for . . . and they do pay their bills, first of every month. Fact is, if the truth were known, it's somewhat better working for Vwarda that it was working for the Labour Government in London, what?'

About the Vwarda River, Sir Charles was wrong. It was far from an unknown waterway, because those of us who were inter-ested in geography had always loved this famous river with its unique history. Far to the north, at a swamp imprisoned within a cup of mountains, much rain fell, and depending upon the season of the year and the set of the wind on a particular day, the swamp drained sometimes into River Banga, which debouched into the Congo and thus into the Atlantic; at other times into the Vwarda River, which crossed to eastern Africa and emptied into the Indian Ocean, finally making its way to the Pacific. Thus two drops of water falling from the same cloud and landing in the same spot might ultimately travel to different river systems and enter two different oceans on opposite sides of the world, thousands of miles apart.

In addition to this peculiarity, the Vwarda was notable for its chasms, its waterfalls, and especially its population of hippopotamuses, crocodiles and exotic water birds. It was a great river, one of the world's fascinating waterways, and I thought it an act of genius that the Negroes of the region had named their new republic in its honor.

The atypical part of Sir Charles's character stemmed from the fact that he in no way resembled an English country gentleman. He was a tall man, grossly fat, sloppy in appearance, and with a petulant droop to his mouth that caused it to quiver at moments of excitement, so that he gave the impression of being a crybaby devoid of either resolution or courage. He wore baggy suits, often stained with gravy, and his nails were rarely filed. Worst of all—and this often convinced strangers that they were dealing with a fool—when he talked he bumbled, repeating words and falling back upon the stock phrases of the anti-intellectual British ruling class. He was fond of 'I shouldn't wonder' and 'Mark you,' and often used 'As a matter of fact'—which he pronounced 'mettra fect'—two or three times in a paragraph. He also chewed his words, repeating phrases three or four times at the start of a statement, and I can recall numerous conversations regarding the dam in which he would preface every comment with 'Well now, I mean, yes, it's something we've got to face up to, haven't we?' repeated three or four times. He was partial to rhetorical questions and ended almost every positive statement with one: 'We shouldn't want that to result, should we?' In my early days of work with him I used to answer the questions, and he was always surprised that I had bothered: 'We don't want to clutter up this business with a lot of unnecessary words, do we?'

If one looked merely at the sillier aspects of Sir Charles's deport-
ment during the first stage of a discussion, one would be justified
in concluding that he was a fool, but as negotiations deepened and
his unflagging devotion to humanity and the rights of the Vwarda
Negroes manifested itself, one had to conclude that here was a true
public servant, a gentleman who would have lent dignity to any
government of which he was a part. As I reported to my superiors
in Geneva: 'If Vwarda and the other Negro republics had a couple
of hundred Sir Charles Brahams, it would be safe to invest anywhere in Africa, with the assurance that we would get a fair
break . . . and not a penny more.' Shortly before my arrival in
Vwarda the Queen of England decided to make Charles Braham
a knight in recognition of his services in the Congo, and many
people in Vwarda told me, 'There wasn't a person out here who
asked, "Why him?"—but when he reported to Buckingham Palace,
sloppy, sixty pounds overweight, repeating his words and looking
like someone out of the nineteenth century, people asked, "Did
they get the names mixed up?" '

In early 1959 Lady Emily Braham died, leaving behind a thin,
dark-haired girl of seven. Since I reached Vwarda only at the end
of that year, I never knew Lady Emily; I saw only her photographs in voile and lace at various government functions, a petite
woman ill-mated to the gross man who stood beside her in his ill-
fitted uniforms.

I did, from the first, know the child Monica; indeed I served as
a kind of mother to her, taking care of the various duties that her
mother would have performed had she been alive. My first glimpse
of the child came one hot afternoon when my plane from Geneva
cut in from the Atlantic, flew up the Congo to the Banga, turned
south, passed over the high swamp where the rivers started, picked
up the Vwarda and followed its dramatic course through mountains and veldt, to land at the capital. In those early days there were
few Negro officials in evidence, and I was met by Sir Charles,
stamping around in a heavy blue suit and directing the porters how
and where to take my stuff: 'We don't want him here without any
luggage, do we? Mmmmmm, yes, watch that, eh?' He seemed quite
the fool and I was distressed that it was he with whom I would
have to negotiate.

As he led me to his government car, a highly polished Rolls-
Royce bearing the new seal of Vwarda, I saw peering from a rear

window the small, beautifully formed face of a little girl. When I sat down beside her, she demurely stroked her long dark braids and looked up at me with an impish look in her very dark eyes as she said, 'I expected you to yodel. You're from Switzerland, aren't you?'

'I'm from Indiana, really. I work in Switzerland.'

'Have you learned to yodel?'

'I'm afraid not.'

'Then go back and learn.'

This jolted me and I leaned forward to study the child, but as I did so, Sir Charles said, 'Mustn't mind her. Since her mother's death she's incorrigible.' Monica stuck her tongue out at me, then winked, and to my surprise, uttered a very good yodel which echoed through the Rolls. 'She learned it from the gramophone,' Sir Charles said.

I cabled my maid in Geneva to send me down a carton of those imaginative toys which the Swiss make so well, but when I gave them to Monica, she spurned them, passed them on to the children of her Negro maid, and told me, 'What I'd really like is some dirndl dresses.' When they arrived, I became her favorite uncle.

She loved music, and through the years, as I returned at frequent intervals to inspect the dam we were building along the upper reaches of the Vwarda, I brought her gramophone records of all kinds and through her kept vaguely aware of rock-and-roll, the Merseyside beat and soul. She seemed to need music, and whenever she heard that I was about to leave Europe for Vwarda, she would send me urgent letters, explaining which records she wanted; she loved the Beatles, the Rolling Stones, the Animals and a group called Procol Harum, but she did not care for American styles, except for one particularly violent group called Canned Heat. When she first ordered these records, I tried playing them at home before taking them out to Africa but found I had no capacity for judging whether the strange wild sounds were musical or not. I simply delivered the records and watched as Monica devoured them; I was not then aware of the destructive lyrics that accompanied the music. In my naïveté I supposed that the words were gibberish, unaware of the fact that to the young people they were a call to revolution.

When Monica was sixteen her father asked me if I would supervise her placement in a good English school; he could recommend several which might be inclined to accept her in view of the tradition surrounding his family name, but he could not himself get away from Vwarda to make the choice, so in the European spring of 1968 I found myself touring rural England with a dossier on Monica Braham, including a photograph of a striking child with black eyes and dark hair and the frail beauty of an elf. I was surprised at the first two schools when the headmistresses took one look at the photograph and said, in effect, 'Oh, dear! And she was raised by her father with native servants. This one'll be difficult to handle.' The experienced teachers saw something in the photograph I didn't and refused her a place in their schools.

However, at the school I liked best, St. Procas north of Oxford, the headmistress studied Monica's credentials, which included high marks in various standard examinations, and said, 'I'm not at all sure this is the school for young Monica. She looks a most unsettled sort, but we had her cousin Victoria Braham, and she proved a sturdy child.' St. Procas took her, on speculation as it were, but they were never happy with their decision.

In the late autumn of 1968 an urgent cable from Vwarda begged me to fly to St. Procas to see if I could do anything to keep the school from expelling Monica, so I interrupted some work I was doing on behalf of Ansett Airways in Australia and returned to Europe to find that St. Procas had every reason to expel young Monica. When I reached the school the headmistress said with open hostility, since I was the man who had persuaded her to accept Monica and was therefore responsible for her escapades, 'Your Monica disappeared from school for three days. She seems to have run off with an older man who delivers chocolates to a store in the village. We believe she and this man went to cover in a hotel in Cirencester. I suppose we could assign a detective to the matter and prove her delinquency, but we prefer not to know the details.' She was determined to expel Monica forthwith, but I prevailed upon her to give the child a second chance.

'Child?' the headmistress echoed in astonishment. 'Have you seen her?'

When Monica appeared she seemed a whole epoch older; she was only sixteen, but the braids were gone, the frailty had given way to an appealing maturity, and her face had lost its childish quality. She was a woman, much older than her years, much more cunning than either I or the headmistress. There was an amused smile at the corner of her beautiful lips, as if she knew some vital secret that we did not; but there was nothing coarse or provocative about her. She did not challenge us or defy us to expel her; quite the contrary, she was totally adorable and my first impulse was to take her in my arms and kiss her as I had so often done when arriving or departing from her African home. But a change had overtaken her which would prevent me henceforth from greeting her as a child. She was extremely beautiful and was aware of it.

'Hello, Uncle George,' she said with quiet dignity, extending her hand.

'What've you been up to?' I asked.

'I thought it was time . . .' She did not end the sentence. Shrugging her slim shoulders, she smiled and looked away.

I managed to keep her in St. Procas, but a month later I was called back to the school. The headmistress told me she had found the girls on Monica's hall smoking marijuana, and while there was no substantive proof that Monica had been involved, one of the girls had reported, under pressure it was true, that Monica had bought the marijuana during her expedition to Cirencester, and I was asked to interrogate her about this, because the school was again on the verge of expelling her but wished to be just.

It was a wintry day and I met Monica in a glass-enclosed porch where the younger mistresses of the school met for afternoon tea. One or two of them wandered in as we talked, and I noticed that as soon as they spotted Monica, they backed away in a hurry. I asked my acquired godchild about the marijuana, and I phrased the question so as to let her know that I expected a truthful answer; she might refuse to answer, but if she told me anything, I was certain it would be the truth. 'Marijuana's nothing,' she said contemptuously. 'They get uptight.'

'Did you bring it into the school?'

'I've tried it. All the girls have.'

'Don't you think it's dangerous?'

'Uncle George! It's like a martini for you . . . a gin and bitters for Daddy. If you're a drunk, such drinks are trouble. Taken sensibly, they're nothing.'

'Are you smoking regularly?'

'What's regularly?' she asked, not defiantly but with an impudent interest in my opinion.

'Did you bring it into the school?'

'Ellen brought it in. Marjorie brought it in. I could name six other girls who brought it in.' Then she smiled and added, 'In small quantities.'

'But the large quantity? Who brought that?'

'I think I've about used up St. Procas,' she said, and we left it at that.

'We'll move her to another school next year,' I assured the headmistress.

'We think she'd better move now.'

'But with her father in Africa . . .' I prevailed upon the good lady to keep Monica for the rest of 1968–69, and this was a mistake, because in late February, I was summoned to school, where a distraught headmistress shouted at me, 'Take her out! This day! Out!'

With some difficulty, and with the aid of a fourteen-year-old girl who lived on Monica's hall, I pieced together what had happened. On three days a week the school imported from the city of Oxford a music teacher, a tall, gangling, tousled-haired young man who had studied in Paris and whose classes on the appreciation of Beethoven and Stravinski were, as the girls said, 'super.' He was about twenty-two years old and came from a family of most limited means with whom he still lived. He had attended one of the redbrick universities in the Midlands and had graduated with honors, but the shyness which had always marked him had been erased neither by that university nor by his stay in Paris. He was a big, awkward, likable oaf, and one day in January, Monica boasted to her hallmates, 'I'll bet I could get his pants off in three weeks.'

Bets were made and placed in the keeping of the fourteen-year-old who told me the story: 'The rules were simple. We were to give Monica every assistance . . . even the girls who had bet against her had to help . . . What I mean is, we were to make it easy for her to be alone with him. But the other rule was that at least two girls from the committee . . .'

'What committee?'

'The ones who wrote out the rules.'

'You mean you put this in writing?'

'Sure.' She rummaged among her papers and handed me the typewritten rules: 'It is agreed that Monica cannot simply claim that she had intercourse with Mr. Dankerly. At least two members of the committee must be in a position to see them in bed, or whatever.'

Monica had gone to work on Mr. Dankerly with a professional skill acquired from her earlier bout with the chocolate salesman from Cirencester. She let him know that she considered him the best teacher at St. Procas, also the most understanding and the gentlest. Having said this latter, she told him he was also very manly and she supposed he had played rugger at university. But what attracted her most, she said, was his years of experience in Paris, where, as she phrased it, 'a man must learn all there is to know about love from those French girls.' When she said this she was aware that Mr. Dankerly was breathing deeply, and that night she informed her dormitory, 'The bet's won. I'll have his pants down next Friday.'

On Friday the girls arranged it so that the music room was left unattended. Actually, it was flanked on all sides by sentries plus the designated witnesses, and as one of the latter reported to the group, 'When they were rolling around on the floor you couldn't be dead sure they were making love, but they certainly could have been.'

That night Monica announced calmly that she had won the bet; then she added a bit of information which quite startled the girls, nurtured as they had been on the super-capable love-making of Albert Finney and Richard Burton in their movies: 'Poor fellow, he knew absolutely nothing and I had to show him how to manage.' It was a very sobering end to an escapade.

By Monday, of course, the faculty had got wind of the wager and its successful termination, and by Tuesday morning poor Mr. Dankerly had been fired and Monica had been sequestered in her room till I could fly in from Geneva. The headmistress was livid and said she should not have listened to my blandishments after the Cirencester escapade. 'I'm afraid Monica is a depraved little delinquent, and you'll have your hands full in the years ahead. What do you propose doing with her?'

'I'm sending her back to Africa. On tonight's plane.'

'Good decision. She's not ready for England.'

'Or vice versa.'

I was most gloomy as I drove Monica to the airport to put her aboard the Air Vwarda plane; it was preposterous that so small a nation should presume to have its own airline flying to London and New York, but of course it consisted of only one Pan American plane and crew on lease to Vwarda, as arranged by Sir Charles. By stipulation, one Negro assistant rode in the cockpit, but what he did, no one knew—the pilots and engineers were invariably from Texas.

When the time came for me to bid Monica farewell, I saw that she was peering over my shoulder to see whether any attractive men were flying south, and before I left the airport she had snuggled up to a rugged South African football player who was buying her some sweets for the long trip home.

———•••———

I was not aware of it at the time, but when I shipped Monica back to Vwarda—which she reached after a five-day detour to South Africa with her football player—she was returning to her father's care at a time when that poor man was facing a major crisis. When the March Riots exploded across Vwarda they struck real fear into the hearts of Europeans who had great hopes for the new republic.

When I read about the riots in a Geneva newspaper, I fell prey to the apprehensions of my superiors, who had seventy-two million dollars committed to the Vwarda Dam and now saw it vanishing in the aftermath of the killings. From what I could piece together from the *London Times* and various diplomatic reports which the Swiss foreign office let us see, it became obvious that the March Riots were long overdue and had occurred simply because the Negroes had grown tired of waiting.

Vwarda had now been a sovereign state for eleven years. It had a Negro president, a Negro cabinet and a Negro as chairman of the state bank, but anyone could see that the good jobs were still held by whites, especially jobs commanding substantial salaries. The judges of the supreme court were white, as were the appeals judges. All jobs pertaining to the economic control of the country were in the hands of men like Sir Charles Braham, who had stayed over from the colonial administration. The top general of the army was a Sandhurst man, and the well-paid pilots of the Vwarda jet were Americans. This condition prevailed far down into the hierarchy, and it was not surprising to me that the Negroes had rebelled.

In the first two days of the rioting they killed sixteen white men, burned some warehouses, and issued a series of inflammatory pronouncements. To many in Europe, it seemed as if the great African revolution, which white men feared, had started and must soon spread to neighboring countries like Tanzania, Zambia, the Congo and Swaziland, but this did not happen, and when order was restored my directors ordered me to Vwarda to report on the status of our investments.

When my plane crossed the high swamp in which the Vwarda River found its origin, I felt that I was back in a country of which I was a citizen, for I had worked in its forests so long that I seemed a part of them, and the dark faces that had recently burned and killed were the faces of my brothers. When we landed at the capital I saw the same trees covered with late flowers, the same broad avenues lined by Victorian houses which had once been populated with Englishmen and their finicky wives, the same corrugated-iron shacks that had both depressed and exhilarated me when I first saw them. It was a fine African city, destined to become finer with each passing year as the shacks were replaced by stucco houses. In some ways it was the most primitive of the Negro capitals; in others it was the most representative, for it was a city in growth, a land where a once depressed people made its bid for self-government.

When I arrived, Sir Charles, as I might have guessed, was deep in the jungle inspecting the area where most of the killings had occurred. In his black suit, his tie carefully knotted and tight about his sweating throat, he was plodding along jungle trails, assuring the local chieftains that there was no cause for fear. He, for one, was not alarmed and the great dam to the north was proceeding as usual. 'None of the European engineers have fled,' he told me on the radio, 'because things must go forward. There has been trouble. There have been regrettable assassinations, but all countries have hotheads, and Vwarda will know how to handle ours, won't we?' In that difficult period following the riots, Sir Charles was the typical English colonial servant doing his best to quieten things down. 'We don't want a revolution on our hands, do we?' he told the jungle chiefs. 'Mettra fect, who would be hurt by such folly? Your sons, not mine, and we don't want that, do we?'

From the capital I reported to my superiors in Geneva: 'The

recent events have been termed riots. I would call them a rampage, a blind senseless rampage which has subsided as quickly as it started. In this district the disaffected Negroes made three demands— Negro judges immediately, the nationalization of the diamond diggings, and Negro pilots to fly the Vwarda plane. The government has agreed to do something, and quickly, about the first two demands, but the third has its comic aspects and will be forgotten. When the Negro agitators captured the airport, they surrounded the Boeing jet that was loading for its flight to New York and shouted, "Reginald Huygere must fly it! Reginald Huygere to the controls!" Huygere, a bright young fellow who has had about fifty hours of ground training from the Pan American instructors and who barely knows the fuel system, let alone the controls, stuck his head out the cockpit window and shouted, "Who, me?" And everyone broke up into laughter and the plane took off as scheduled.

'I know you want my harshest appraisal of the riots. They were inevitable. They were justified. They were unimportant. At periodic intervals during the next two decades they will be repeated. And nothing very bad will grow out of them. I judge Vwarda to be where Mexico was in the period from 1910 through 1927, and you well know what a stable country developed out of that revolution. As to the dam, every man and woman in Vwarda knows the nation needs it, and if the sensible elements of the government appeal to us tomorrow for the additional eighteen million dollars, which I figure they need, give it to them. It's as safe here as it would be in Detroit.'

In the days when I was composing this report I saw a good deal of Monica, who was now seventeen. She had had, so far as my records showed, three lovers: the chocolate salesman, Mr. Dankerly the music teacher, and the South African football player. Yet she gave the impression of an unspoiled young woman; her dark charm was extraordinary and her capacity to use other people to her advantage uncanny. Looking at her in her father's house, I concluded that it would have been ridiculous for a child as knowing as this to have been kept in a girls' school. She was at least ready for university, and she knew it.

As I talked with her, she showed for the first time a deep disrespect for her father. 'Old Tremble-chin,' she called him, because of the uncontrollable trembling that overtook the lower part of his face during any crisis. 'Old Tremble-chin is out in the jungle, play-ing the role of British raj. "Chin up, boys," he's saying, while his own chin shakes like a woman's.'

'Your father's a courageous man,' I protested.

'Courageous and stupid,' she said.

'He spent a lot of his time bringing you up.'

'And look at the result.'

Her bitterness was so unexpected that I suggested, 'You feel the guilt of having busted out of school and you're throwing it onto your father.'

'Not at all,' she corrected, lighting a cigarette. 'I'm appalled at the prospect of my dear father, about to be heaved out of Vwarda, doing all sorts of contemptible little things to preserve his position. He'd do anything to hold on . . . another year . . . another month.'

'This has been your father's life. It's natural for him . . .'

Savagely she pointed with her cigarette to a statue that stood on the front lawn. 'Lord Carrington Braham, my grandfather. One of these nights the Negro radicals will come along this street and knock the old man off his pedestal. They should. We ought to get out now, but Father insists upon holding on. Can't you see . . . he lacks dignity.'

'What would you do . . . after a lifetime of service to a nation that still needs you?'

'I know exactly what I'd do. I'd put on my full uniform, all my medals, all the reminders of my grandfather . . . I'll admit the Brahams did good work here and I'm proud of it, but our day is past and to grasp at straws is degenerate.'

'But what would you do?' I repeated.

'In full regalia I'd march into the office of President Hosea M'Bele, throw my contract on his desk, and tell him, "Ram it up your ass." '

I am never able to control my shock at the vocabulary of young people these days and I must have blushed, for Monica wagged her finger under my nose, an act which permitted me to smell the cigarette she was smoking. 'Is that marijuana?' I asked.

'Want a drag?'

'You little fool,' I said with considerable anger. 'What are you trying to do? Live all your life in one year?'

'I'm tired of everything my father stands for,' she said with a kind of languid grace. Falling into a large chair, with her lovely legs hooked over one arm, she lost her previous animosity and said reflectively, as if she were already in her sixties, 'I've seen Vwarda at its best—the end of the old, the beginning of the new—and it's time we Brahams departed. The killing was no problem. Any white man who got his head chopped off did so by sheer accident. And the burning was of little consequence. It can be rebuilt. But the death of the idea . . .' She trailed off into silence, took several deep puffs of her cigarette, and said, 'You know, Uncle George, I very nearly married the chap in South Africa. He was pleasant and we had a marvelous time in bed. You know why I didn't?'

'Because you're only seventeen and couldn't get a license.'

'Because on the race issue they're such bloody fools. They're heading for terrible retribution, and who wants to be part of that?' She took several deep drags on her cigarette, then concluded: 'Father's almost as bad, in his sweet, clumsy way. He knows it's time to get out, but he can't bring himself to leave.' Then, grinding the cigarette into a tray and hiding the remains in her pocket lest her father see them when he returned, she said, 'I'll get out! I will not compound the idiocies of your generation.' And she walked slowly from the room.

———— · ◆ · ————

'You must promise me one thing,' Monica said in early March of 1969 as she tied her father's tie for his climactic interview. 'Tell him, Uncle George. He must not cringe. Father, you're not to beg.'

'I intend to present the case unemotionally and to abide by his decision.'

'What I'm saying is,' she warned, 'don't make an ass of yourself.'

'Monica!' I protested, for Sir Charles was already nervous at the prospect of what he must do and his daughter's unfair assault made him worse.

'I don't want a Braham to grovel,' she snapped. 'And certainly not in Vwarda.'

'I'm not going to grovel,' Sir Charles promised. He was now dressed in his best dark suit, with one ribbon in his lapel buttonhole. It had been given him by the King for meritorious service during the war, but in spite of his finery he looked barely presentable, for March was summer in Vwarda and he was sweating about the face.

His clothes did not fit properly, nor could they have, for his bulk was ill-disposed and made any jacket look too tight. Also, his bottom waggled when he walked. But his worst feature was the lower part of his face, which was already twitching with anxiety. 'Do I look acceptable?' he asked us hopefully.

'You look perfectly awful,' Monica said, and then, to our surprise, placed one of her mother's summery hats on her dark head.

'Where are you going?' Sir Charles asked in a petulant voice, well aware of the answer.

'With you,' she said. 'I'm not going to let you make a damned fool of yourself.' As I was thinking that I'd like nothing better than to give her a sound spanking, she turned on me and said, 'You're not to lie on his behalf. State the facts and that's that.'

'You're not directing this expedition,' I said.

'Oh, but I am! I'm the last of the Brahams in Vwarda and I shall protect Lord Carrington's memory.' She pointed to the statue and said, 'Grandfather would have known how to act on such an occasion.'

The Rolls-Royce was brought to the garden gate and the three of us walked mournfully toward it: Sir Charles sweating and running with little-girl steps; Monica striding purposefully, the weight of a notable family on her shoulders; and I plugging along, a sixty-one-year-old troubleshooter from Geneva by way of Indiana and the University of Virginia. We drove along the gracious residential roads of the capital, across the business section with its three skyscraper hotels, and on out to the edge of town where the presidential palace stood, an august Victorian edifice long occupied by the lesser sons of British noble families sent here to serve as the King's representatives. At the entrance, where Scottish soldiers in kilts had once stood guard, two Negro soldiers saluted briskly and waved us forward. At the stately doors, where generations of Englishmen had come to sign their names in the book, proving that they considered themselves an honorable part of empire, a young Negro graduate from Cambridge greeted us and said, in polished accents, 'President M'Bele is waiting for you,' but when we reached the pompous Salle des Audiences, where European merchants and black natives had once cowered before the majesty of English power, the president was not visible and we stood in a pathetic little cluster waiting for him while the stucco cherubs adorning the high ceiling smiled down at our discomfort.

Finally one of the gilt doors swung open and a smallish black man in his late forties hurried into the room, extended his hand to Sir Charles, and said in Oxford English, 'My oldest friend and counselor, welcome, welcome.' He kissed Monica's hand and said, 'You are even more beautiful than my wife said. She saw you at the tennis.' Then he took my arm, linked his with it, and led us to a more intimate corner of the great room. 'Mr. Fairbanks, we are gratified that your superiors have seen fit to extend the loan.'

'They did so because they want to remain associated with a prosperous country.'

'We shall make it so.'

In appearance President M'Bele was quite undistinguished; he could have been the minister of a rural church in Virginia or the owner of a minor clothing store in Soho. He would have fitted in well in any large American city as the one Negro professor in a community college or as the political reporter for the colored newspaper. In the British government today there must have been two thousand white men who looked and acted much as he did, pecking away at jobs set them by their better-educated superiors, yet because of his education at Oxford he was, in Africa, a precious commodity and he discharged the job conferred upon him by the British when they left rather better than anyone else they could have found, and much better than any white man could have done. Like almost all the new leaders of Africa, he had been trained in law, but since both Oxford and the Sorbonne sponsored a rather broad interpretation of what law was, the Negro lawyers were at least as well qualified to govern as any other group would have been, and infinitely better than the military, who were beginning to shoot them off, one by one.

Seating himself at a large table, he spread his palms downward, leaned forward, and said, 'I suppose you know what this meeting is about?' He paused, and when Sir Charles nodded, the president continued: 'I am afraid, my dear old friend, that the decision is irrevocable. There were the riots, you know. The young hotspurs insist that your job is one which our people can fill.'

At this point Monica gave her father a stern glance, warning him that she expected him to maintain his dignity. Sir Charles started well. 'Excellency,' he said softly, 'I am dispensable. That's been known since independence, hasn't it? We've all known that, haven't we, Monica?' He appealed to his daughter for substantiation, but she stared ahead, convinced that this interview must end in disaster. She would do nothing to speed the moment.

'But the function of the job, Your Excellency! That's something quite different, isn't it? Mettra fect, the function of the job is crucial to the welfare of this nation . . .' He made an involved speech, repeating himself so often that I wondered at the president's patience. Twice M'Bele cast imploring glances at Monica, as if trying to enlist her aid in silencing her father, but she ignored them. Much too late, Sir Charles ended his presentation with a plea: 'So I am not asking preferential treatment for myself, Your Excellency, am I?' This time the question was not supposed to be rhetorical but M'Bele treated it so, and Sir Charles ended lamely on what should have been the main thrust of his argument: 'In five more years Thomas Watallah could well be able to discharge my duties—perhaps even in four years—but certainly not now, Your Excellency.'

Now the president had to speak, and in the mellifluous cadences of his poetic people, overlaid with the best accents England had to offer, he recalled his debt to Sir Charles, and I judged that he did so in order to prevent Sir Charles from reciting these facts: 'My dearest and oldest friend, you of all white men must know how deeply indebted I am. I recall, Sir Charles, when I was a child fresh out of the jungle. I came here to the capital to find it occupied by white men, hostile for the most part, and it was you and your dear wife Emily who educated me, gave me a vision of what a university was like in England, convinced me that I might even qualify for Oxford. You gave my brother a job in your family and kept him there for eighteen years. He told me what an inspiration you were. This young lady should know. My brother was her father when you were absent in the jungle. Sir Charles, if you came here this morning to remind me that I owed my present position to you, I would be the first to acknowledge that debt. Would to God that all white-black relationships had been as fruitful.'

I was dismayed when I saw Sir Charles wipe a tear from his left eye and swipe futilely at a second which ran down his fat right cheek. His chin was beginning to tremble, and I thought: This whole thing is going to fall apart.

The president, hoping to avoid what I feared, reasoned: 'But the forces of history in Congo Africa cannot be stayed. Sir Charles, you must know better than I that in the cities I am beset by radical intellectuals who insist that the top jobs be given to blacks. In the bush I am threatened by the tribesmen who want their members given important positions. In the interests of humanity the white judges must be retained for another ten years. In the interests of national security the two Irish generals must be held onto. So what's left? Jobs like yours which must be transferred quickly to black control . . . to forestall revolution. It's as simple as that, Sir Charles.' He bowed his head, pressed his palms even more firmly against the table, and muttered, 'It's as simple as that, old friend.'

Sir Charles allowed not one second of silence, pouncing upon the president's argument and turning it to his own advantage: 'That's precisely what I am talking about, Your Excellency! I too am afraid of revolution! If the economic measures which I've started are not carried . . .'

'Father.' This harsh, commanding word, uttered by a girl, filled the Salle des Audiences and brought the interview down to fundamentals.

'I promised Monica I'd control myself, Your Excellency, and I shall. But truthfully, Vwarda is my home. For twenty-one years it's been my whole life.' He laughed nervously, his chin twitching insecurely, and made a little joke which pleased him: 'Twenty-one years! I've reached my maturity here. I'm old enough to vote.'

The president smiled and Monica looked as if she might jump out the window. She was about to prod her father again, when he resumed his argument: 'So this is my home. It's my country, too. What can I do if I'm suddenly told, "Your work is ended?" I'm not an old man.'

'It was with that in mind, Sir Charles—and also, I may say frankly, because of your long and devoted service to Vwarda, not forgetting your father, who laid the foundations of this nation in his arguments at Versailles . . .' The president found himself ensnared in a sentence that covered too many points, so he threw up his hands and laughed at himself. 'I talk like a lawyer,' he said, and I thought how lucky Vwarda was to have such a sensible man as its head during these critical years. 'What I was trying to tell you, Sir Charles, was that the cabinet has proposed that you receive pension and a half for the remainder of your life. You'll not be destitute, Sir Charles.'

'It's not money that worries me, Your Excellency. It's Vwarda.

The nation itself. You need me.' His voice trembled, and when he had brought it under control he asked, 'What would I do retired in England?'

President M'Bele was growing impatient. Having anticipated Braham's unhappiness at being fired, he had personally insisted upon pension and a half, and now to have it rejected as irrelevant was irritating. 'We must have your job,' he said firmly. 'I am announcing at noon today that Thomas Watallah is assuming your duties.' He rose to indicate that the interview was over, but Sir Charles had numerous other arguments which he had not yet pressed and which he was sure would sway any thinking man.

'Your Excellency! Just a moment! Have you considered the cotton barter with Egypt? Thomas Watallah simply cannot . . . And the leases on the sulphur drilling . . . There's still that business at the dam . . .'

'Father!' Monica cried with brutal disgust. 'Shut up and make believe you're a man.'

President M'Bele turned back on his way to the door, his dark eyes flashing as he said, sternly, 'You should be ashamed of yourself. He's your father.'

'It's him I'm ashamed of,' she snapped.

'Take him back to England. And be sure you go too. You have both used up your days in Vwarda.' He strode toward the door, but before he could exit, Sir Charles asked pitifully, 'Couldn't I stay on . . . I could work for Thomas and help him over the . . . There are many things I could do . . .'

'It would not be dignified,' M'Bele said, and with the innate dignity of a man who had inched his way from the jungle to Oxford, he left the room.

'You damned fool!' Monica cried, grabbing at her father's arm. 'Let's get out of here.'

'Where will we go?' Sir Charles asked in pitiful confusion, sweat showing along the collar of his shirt.

'Into exile,' Monica said quietly as she led him from the Salle des Audiences. At that moment, though she was only seventeen, she seemed extraordinarily mature, as if she alone among the four who had participated in the interview appreciated what had happened. An old order was passing, new forces with new faces were intruding upon the scene, and it was appropriate that there be entrances and exits. What galled her was that her father was playing his role so poorly.

As we left the presidential palace and walked to the Rolls-Royce, Monica said nothing, but I could see that she was evaluating her father coldly, with the innocence of youth. Later, in their home, she told me of that moment: 'Remember what happened after the president walked out on us? We were left standing in that preposterous Salle des Audiences and I stared up at the ridiculous ceiling with its plaster-of-Paris cherubs, and when I looked back at my father he seemed like one of them—a bare-ass little cherub, devoid of self-respect. I could have wept.' When I asked what Sir Charles had done to earn her contempt, she said, 'He backed the wrong horse . . . empire . . . grandeur of the Queen . . . England expects every man . . . all that immortal claptrap. And when it blew up in his face . . . You know, to tell the truth, I don't blame him getting angry over surrendering his position to Thomas Watallah. Did you ever do business with Thomas? Really, a colossal fart.' She shook her head wearily at her recollection of the man, a conniving, almost illiterate fool who ruined everything he touched and then stole the pieces; Africa was not well served by the smart-alecky young black men who replaced the English, the French and the Belgians.

'It must be deflating for poor Father,' she reflected as we drank beer. 'You persuade yourself you're doing work of humanity . . . indispensable, really . . . whole Congo basin fall into chaos if I leave. And when they kick you out they hand your job to some clown like Thomas Watallah, and things go on about as well as they did when you were in charge.'

She shook her head, recalling the disasters of that interview. 'What really finished me was Father's lack of dignity. That's what gnaws—that a man should waste his life on baubles and at the end cry out, "I've been defrauded." Believe me, at my end I'll not complain.'

'Are you confessing that you've already made wrong choices?'

'We all do. The trick is to accept the consequences when they fall due. I've no respect for your generation, Uncle George, because at the end you chicken out.'

I judged that Monica intended to react differently.

The next three weeks were as difficult as any I had known since that summer of 1948 when my son had stormed out of our home, for then I was shown what the gap between the generations meant, and now it was a headstrong young girl who was repeating the instruction. After the announcement of his dismissal Sir Charles begged me to stay on as a guest while he went about the doleful business of winding up his affairs in Vwarda and deciding what to do with the remainder of his life. He was, as you might guess, disoriented and poorly equipped to deal with Monica's various rebellions and he wanted me to give the girl some guidance.

He chose poorly. I had always been fond of Monica and unable to discipline her. In the years when the great dam was under construction I had often stayed with the Brahams and had pampered her, bringing her whatever gramophone records she wanted and occasional dresses or adornments from London, so it was impossible for me suddenly to turn dictator, not only because I was not inclined that way but also because she would have ignored me had I tried.

What was she like that African autumn of 1969? She was seventeen years old, motherless, with no brothers or sisters to cushion her extravagances and with a father whom she held in contempt. Intellectually she had done well in school, both in Rhodesia, where her father had sent her at the age of nine, and in England, where I had taken her. Morally she had not done so well. She had been kicked out of the Rhodesian school for cursing the mathematics teacher and, as I have told you, she was expelled from the English school for having sexual relations with the music instructor. In each school there had also been instances of shying books off the heads of other students.

She seemed to grow more beautiful each day, her fine English complexion showing white with natural touches of rouge in the cheeks. She had started wearing her jet-black hair in a coil on top of her head. When I asked her why, she said frankly, 'Older men don't like to go with girls who wear their hair schoolgirl style.' And when I asked her why she felt she had to go with older men, she said, 'Because they know what's what and they don't waste time.'

Her beauty lay principally in her dark eyes, which were keenly expressive, almost penetrating, and I could appreciate the complaint of the English headmistress who had told me, on the afternoon of Monica's dismissal, 'I'm afraid none of our teachers, fine girls from average backgrounds, is a match for Miss Monica.' Having met some of the instructors, my guess was that Monica was much keener than any of them. Her thin face, so exquisite when she looked up at you suddenly, peering directly into your eyes, as if she could cope with whatever you wished to say, was often marked by a half-smile that clung to the corner of her mouth; she seemed to be reserving judgment as to whether or not to laugh outright. She weighed less than a hundred pounds and would have given the impression of being skinny had she not been so unusually graceful. Often she reminded me of the impalas that roamed the plains of southern Vwarda, animals of grace and poetry who could leap far into the air and land on their small feet, looking startled at having traversed such distances.

The one new thing about Monica that I noticed in these three weeks when I was trying to tame her was that sometimes she spoke in a deep, husky voice which I had not heard before; it was as if she were a boy entering adolescence, for at other times she would forget the new voice and speak like a girl of seventeen, but when she caught herself doing this she would quickly speak the next sentence in her deep voice. When I asked about this, she said, 'I'm practicing my bedroom voice.'

Like other prematurely developing young girls in the various parts of the world I have worked in, she had discovered, either through experiment or through discussions with older women, that there were several ways in which a girl could with seeming innocence touch a man and get him started thinking. For example, one morning when I was standing at the window, looking out at the statue of Lord Carrington Braham and recalling Monica's prediction that in the next riots the young hotheads would tear the old man down, she came up behind me and ran two fingers down my spine. It produced quite an electric shock, which I am certain she intended, for when I turned to look at her, she was smiling that mischievous half-smile, but it showed not the open joy of a child who has played a clever trick but the calculating wit of a woman who has said to herself, 'Let's see if he's a man or not.'

She also took my arm a good deal, pressing her fingers into the inner turn of my elbow, and when we were seated she was apt to grasp me by the knees. I affected not to know what she was doing, but she would not let me get away with that, for once when I had been lecturing her about the necessity for her focusing upon some one thing she wished to do when she got back to London, she drew back, looked at me provocatively and said, 'Do? I'm going to become the mistress of the first millionaire I meet.' Then, to break the spell, she gave me a brushing kiss, ending up with her lips close to my ear and whispering, 'Sometime it would be fun to give you a real kiss, Uncle George.'

Her father was absent during most of this time, gone into the jungle on his final inspection tour, carrying on as if he were still in charge of Vwarda's economic development. He knew that both President M'Bele and the new Minister of Economics, young Thomas Watallah, would prefer to have him leave, but he felt that it was his duty to inspect each ramification, so he spent the last hot days of March slogging his way into remote areas, perspiring constantly, giving the local chieftains his old brand of encouragement: 'We don't want the new man to find things sloppy, do we?'

At one interval, when he returned home, he asked me suddenly, 'I smelt a strange odor near Monica's room. Tell me, Fairbanks, is she smoking marijuana?'

'Yes.'

'Is it serious? Like heroin?'

'I don't know too much about it. I wouldn't touch it myself, but from what I hear, it's a phase young people go through.'

'Would you speak to her about it? Please? We don't want a drug addict on our hands, do we?'

I asked him why he didn't speak to her, and he said, 'She'd never listen to me in serious affairs. Mettra fect, she doesn't listen to me at all, does she?' And he was off again, this time to the far northeast where the primitive tribes concentrated and where he was held in much affection, for he was the only government official who had ever appeared in their kraals; there was not much likelihood that young Thomas Watallah would ever bother with that part of Vwarda. The new officials being appointed across Africa preferred cities like Paris and New York; it required an Englishman trained in the hard school of colonial service to appreciate that the farthest corner of a realm was still part of that realm.

As Sir Charles had requested, I spoke to Monica about her use of marijuana, and she laughed at me. 'Mary Jane? It's nothing but a pleasant way to relax. Like I said, an evening cocktail but less dangerous to your health.' She was most eager that I try the weed for myself, but this I did not care to do, for the sickly smell that emanated from her room did not attract me. Furthermore, my attention was diverted from marijuana by an extraordinary development which I could not have foreseen. At six o'clock one evening Monica told me hurriedly, 'Dress, Uncle George. We have a guest for dinner.' She would not tell me who it was, but at eight a young, handsome, well-dressed Negro man knocked at our door, and Monica announced, 'Mr. Thomas Watallah, come to dine with the Brahams.' With elaborate courtesy she showed him into the living room, handed him a whiskey, and plied him with questions, whose answers she attended to with a sincerity that obviously pleased the new administrator.

At dinner she directed the conversation so that Watallah could appear at good advantage, and afterward, as he and I stood smoking, she came up quietly behind him and ran her hand down his spine, saying, 'Mr. Watallah, if you have any intelligence, which I know you have, you'll refuse to take this house if the government wants to give it to you. Insist on a new one.' She then led him about, showing him the various things that were wrong, and when they returned from the upstairs it was obvious that they had been kissing.

She told me, 'Uncle George, Mr. Watallah is going to take me to the discotheque. I'll see you later, but don't wait up.'

Six days later President M'Bele summoned me to the presidential residence; I supposed that he wanted to talk about the extension of electricity services to the northeast, a project that Sir Charles had been pressing upon the government and which our company had agreed to finance, but his concern was quite different. 'We've been friends for ten years now,' he said bluntly, 'and you've done many things to help us. Now you must do another. I want you to put Monica Braham on a plane to London. Immediately.'

'Sir Charles is with the tribes in the northeast. I couldn't get in touch . . .'

'Don't get in touch with anyone. Get that girl out of Vwarda. Immediately.'

'Why?'

'Don't you know?'

'Marijuana?'

'No. Watallah.'

'Thomas?'

'Yes. She's been carrying on a flagrant affair with him. Night clubs. Kissing in the cinemas. They've been sleeping together in a little house on Esplanade, and you know he has a wife and two children.'

'I didn't know, Your Excellency.' It has always seemed strange to me how easily one accepts the custom of referring to the head of state as Your Excellency, not because it flatters the recipient, but rather because the governing of any large unit of mankind is a most difficult job deserving of respect. I remember reading about how John F. Kennedy's close cronies were celebrating with him on election night, and it was 'Jack this' and 'Jack that,' but next morning when the results were known, everyone instinctively drew back and spoke to him as 'Mr. President.' It was with no sense of condescension that I referred to this hard-working Negro lawyer as Your Excellency, for he was facing a difficult problem and needed help.

'You know why she's doing it,' he said with some bitterness. 'She's angry that Sir Charles is being sent home. She's even more angry that his place is being taken by young Watallah, who of course is not fitted for the job but who's the best we have at the moment. And she wants to show us up—petty, petty motivation— to show up the government of a supplanting state.' He rose, offered me his hand and said, 'I'll send Thomas to a meeting of economics officials at Addis Ababa. If the truth were known, most of these young men want cabinet positions only so they can travel. I'm told it's the same in Latin America.'

He walked me to the door, his arm in mine, then stopped and held onto me as he said, 'You mustn't come to wrong conclusions about us, Mr. Fairbanks. I doubt that Vwarda or Congo or Zambia or Tanzania—they're the new republics I know best—are any worse off than Angola and Moçambique, which are still ruled by Portuguese white men, or Rhodesia, which is ruled by its own white men. At this given moment we may be worse off, but today is a prelude to tomorrow, and in the long run a self-governing democracy with all citizens enfranchised has got to be best. Don't lose heart. In ten years Thomas Watallah and his crew will probably nationalize the dam, but whom will that hurt, really?'

As if he wished to reassure me of his constructive intentions, he walked with me all the way to my car, concluding: 'But I want Miss Braham out of here at once. For her safety, not mine. You see, Thomas Watallah's wife comes from a tribe which kills women who steal other women's husbands, and she has many relatives in this city. That's why I had to appoint him to the cabinet. The tribesmen would not understand that she's sleeping with Thomas just for the fun of it. They might think she intends stealing him, and this they would not permit.' When I returned to the Braham bungalow I found two men I had not seen before standing on the opposite side of the street . . . not doing anything . . . not going anywhere . . . just standing.

———————•◦•——————

It was a lot easier for President M'Bele to order Monica out of his country than for me to get her out. For one thing, her father was well lost in the eastern jungle and would remain incommunicado for a week, by which time Monica had to be back in England. Naturally I tried to send him messages, but they piled up in the eastern capital, awaiting his return from the frontiers. I tried also to communicate with Sir Charles's relatives in England, and although I got back some disheartening cables, for none of them wanted Monica, the real veto came not from England but from Vwarda, when Monica said flatly, 'I will not go live with those old farts.'

At this I grew angry and said, 'Young lady, do you realize that this marks a turning point in your life? What you and I decide these next two days will determine the kind of person you'll be.'

'You decide?' she asked in disgust. 'Who in hell are you to decide anything?'

'I'm not your father,' I said. 'But I'm an older person who loves you very much . . . who wants to get you safely out of here . . . before they do the job.' I pointed to the two watchers, two very black men from a jungle tribe. 'I suppose you know about them?'

'Thomas told me they might show up. I'm not worried.'

'I am. And on Thursday you board that plane to London and . . .'

'I will not go to London. I will not go to England.'

'Where do you propose going?'

'Where I'd like to go is California.'

'What would you do there?'

'But I haven't the money right now. I may have it later.'

'Why California?'

'There's a place out there you probably never heard of. Haight-Ashbury. The kids say it's sensational.'

'That was a few years ago, Monica. Today it's a savage dump for broken young people. In Haight-Ashbury you'd last a week.' I sat her down and summarized a crop of recent articles I'd read on the collapse of this particular dream, but she refused to listen, saying, 'Mallorca's also good. Or I might try Berlin. They say it swings.'

'Monica! You're seventeen. You're going back to school.'

Rising and taking a position from which she could stare down at me, she said, 'Get it in your noodle, I'm not going back to school.'

She was so firm in her refusal that I had to drop the subject. Pulling her down into a chair beside me, I asked, 'Why the rebellion?' and she said simply, 'Because I despise everything my father stands for. If school and family in England produced him, I want no part of either.'

I started to protest, but she cut me off: 'Did you see the contempt President M'Bele had for him the other morning? Father ought to be the one sent home, not me.'

'Why are you so savage?'

'Because it breaks my heart to see a man who could have been quite fine . . . he could have been, you know. He's wasted his life on such false values.'

'He helped a nation evolve.'

'For all the wrong reasons. Do you know why he's hanging on . . . in spite of the indignities heaped upon him by these Negroes? Because he thinks in the back of his trivial little mind that one of these days the Negroes will have to call England back to govern. And he'll be the governor general, and live in the big house the way his father did.'

That was the first indication I had that the real cause of her irritation was the manner in which the Negroes had treated her father. Her resentment ran deeper than she allowed herself to show, and her curious affair with Thomas Watallah made sense only if seen in this light. When the Negroes struck at her father, they struck at her, and she was prepared to fight back.

The longer we talked in those final days, when I tried to keep her under house arrest pending the arrival of her plane, the more convinced I became that it was the values of her father's wasted life that she was rejecting and not her father himself. 'I love him,' she confessed one night, 'in spite of his fuddy-duddy ways and his little-boy petulance. I'm much more a man than he is.'

She was also much more a woman, for although I tried to keep her safely in the house, which was now guarded by a federal policeman, she managed to slip past each of us—and for what purpose do you suppose? To have dates with Thomas Watallah prior to his departure for Addis Ababa. She went boldly to his office, made him take her to dinner at a public restaurant, accompanied him to the home of a friend and spent the night with him. When he smuggled her back to our place he took me aside and spoke like any man who has grown tired of an affair with an importuning woman: 'Please, convince her to leave me alone. It could be very damaging for both of us.' He was a good-looking young chap, apparently not too bright, but with an ambitious wife who was determined to make him president after M'Bele was shot. He had been gratified, no doubt, that a beautiful granddaughter of Lord Carrington Braham had wanted to sleep with him, but now he found her tedious. 'You will help me, won't you?' he asked as he slipped out a side door.

That was the end of the Thomas Watallah affair, for Monica sensed that he would be relieved to see her board the plane. 'He's as dumb as everyone said,' she told me at breakfast.

'He's smart enough to disengage from you,' I said, hoping to jolt her into facing the facts.

'If they ever make him president, Vwarda is doomed.' She was quite content to see no more of him, but this decision projected us both into a new set of problems. One of the airlines that flew into the capital was Lufthansa, the well-run German outfit, and its crews were popular, for the young men were handsome and well groomed and the stewardesses were trim. They spoke English well and had a historic sense of mission in southern Africa. They were especially well received in centers like Johannesburg and Salisbury, where many white men felt that except for certain regrettable excesses, Adolf Hitler had understood world problems rather more clearly than his contemporaries. In Vwarda the young Germans were, in a sense, idolized by Englishmen who, through following the liberal principles of men like Winston Churchill and Clement Attlee, had lost an empire. Monica, for example, often wore an iron cross suspended from a silver chain, and boys of her group were prone to display swastikas, not because they had Nazi tendencies but because they knew it infuriated their parents, many of whom, like Sir Charles, had fought against the Germans in World War II. When some outrageous idiocy was promulgated by the new Negro republics, and Vwarda produced more than its share, these young Europeans were apt to say among themselves, 'Hitler died before his time.'

Among the German airmen who flew regularly to Vwarda was an assistant pilot named Dietrich, but whether this was his first name or second, I never found out. He was a tall fellow, blond, handsome in bearing, witty in conversation. I had met him at various cocktail parties and identified him as the best of the Germans; he was married and had two little girls, as blond as he and, judging from their photographs, as intelligent. On the afternoon of the day Thomas Watallah brought Monica home at dawn and asked me to tell her that their affair was finished, she slipped out of the house, past the policeman, and into town. At five o'clock she brought Dietrich home with her and we had tea together.

He was most amiable, and we talked of the various countries into which he had flown. He liked Asia and knew the cities in which I had worked, but his principal affection was reserved for Spain: 'It was just about a year ago, I was flying charter from Frankfurt to Málaga. We packed a couple of hundred tourists into the plane and whipped them down to Málaga, and God must have been looking after me, because when time came for take-off our engineer reported a leak in the hydraulic system—couldn't get the wheels up, had to lay over for two days. So I left Málaga and went to a little town where the tourists were going, and I found a paradise. Such a wonderful place!'

He spoke of the beaches and the sun with such enthusiasm that both Monica and I encouraged him to continue; I knew the area he was talking about, for I had visited Torremolinos and was delighted to hear news of old friends whom he had met. But for Monica his description of the crowded, music-filled village provided a kind of enchantment, and from her questions I knew that she had begun to think that perhaps Torremolinos might be the answer.

Although I did my best to keep her in the house that night, she slipped away to meet Dietrich at a bar, spending the night with him somewhere, and when I upbraided her for such wanton and dangerous behavior, she told me, 'Uncle George, you don't seem to realize that for me my father is dead, the old ideas are dead, England is dead, and you're beginning to sound more and more like a ghost.' She elbowed her way past me and went up to her room, where she fell on the bed and slept all day.

Or rather, I supposed that she was sleeping all day. Actually, at about four in the afternoon she slipped out of the house, caught a taxi to the airport and with only a small handbag, boarded the Lufthansa plane for its flight to Germany, from where she and Dietrich dropped down to Torremolinos for a concentrated vacation.

When I found that Monica had, in the words of President M'Bele, 'flown the coop and saved us all a lot of trouble,' I naturally tried to communicate with Sir Charles, and this time I was successful. From a small town deep within the eastern jungle he spoke to me on the telephone: 'What's to do? We can't let her go knocking about Europe, can we?' He had no substantial ideas of his own, but he did ask me, 'Fairbanks, dear fellow, could you pop along to Europe to check up on what's what?'

'Sorry. I've already stayed here too long. I'm due in Afghanistan the beginning of next week.'

———•◆•———

Whenever I recite these events to older people who have no children—or whose daughters are safely married and in their forties—they ask indignantly, 'Why didn't you stop her?'

I respond, 'How could I have stopped a headstrong girl of seventeen who had decided to rebel? When I realized that my power to reason with her was futile, what public agencies could I have called upon for support? And when society applauds the child and condemns the parent, what could an outsider have done?'

My counterquestioning produces bitter argument; the recommendations I receive most frequently are:

'You could have horsewhipped her.'

'You could have locked her in her room.'

'You could have seen she had no money.'

'You could have asked help from the police.'

'You could have thrown her into jail for smoking marijuana.'

'You could have thrown her out of your house.' (This proposal leaves me baffled, for it looks to me as if this was precisely what Monica had accomplished on her own. That's what the argument was about, but apparently a family earns points if it throws a daughter out one day before she decides to leave of her own accord.)

'You could have sat her down and told her what's what.'

'You could have disciplined her.'

'You could have asked some agency to step in and help.' (When I ask, 'What agency in Vwarda did you have in mind? Or London, thousands of miles away?' the response is feeble: 'There must have been someone in authority.' There was, but Monica was not listening to them.)

'You should have persuaded her that her behavior was criminal.'

When younger couples are in the group, they listen to the suggestions from the older people, say nothing, but imperceptibly shake their heads no, rejecting as impractical each of the proposals, and I suspect that such parents have children of their own whom they are trying to guide through these especially difficult times, and have learned that the suggestions so glibly offered do not work . . . not in late March 1969.

I remember one such group in which a man of stern opinion said, 'Simple, I'd cut her off without a penny and throw her out of our home,' and a younger father replied, 'So would I. But what happens three weeks later when she comes back? Broke? Stands on your porch and knocks to be let in? What then?'

'I'd . . .'

'It's your daughter. Seventeen years old. At the door. What in hell would you do?'

'I'd . . .' The self-opinionated older man began to fumble.

'So would I,' the younger father agreed. 'I'd swear at her, and I'd make a whole chain of threats, and I'd tell her she'd not get another penny of spending money from me, and she could damned well get a job, and then do you know what I'd do?'

'You'd open the door,' another young father said.

'You're damned right I would and so would you,' he told the older man.

But the wife of one of the young men said, 'I suppose the best thing a parent can do these days when society refuses to give us any help and when even the schools and churches are powerless,

is to start when the child is in the cradle and try in our own way
to give her a sense of values . . . I'm saying it wrong. I don't mean
give. I mean help her develop her own sense of right and wrong . . .
something she'll want to hold onto because she worked it out . . . I
mean, you should have shown your concern way, way back . . .'

———•◆•———

When Dietrich and Monica reached Torremolinos they checked
into the Brandenburger, an imposing German hotel facing the
Mediterranean, and for six happy days they lived in a warm atmosphere of bierstubes, black bread and schnitzels. The record
player in the Black Forest, as the hotel's night club was called,
played principally German music, but the chief attraction of the
place was conviviality and a lack of pompousness. Only German
was spoken at the scrubbed-wood tables, but when Dietrich explained that Monica did not know that language, well over half
the tourists were able to talk with her in English, and they told
her many interesting stories about Torremolinos. And always there
was someone who in the years before World War I had had a
relative who had lived for a while in the old German colony of
Sudwest Afrika, a land primarily of deserts and uncomfortable
little towns lined with corrugated-iron huts, but captivating in
memory. 'Uncle Peter always said those were the best years of
his life,' one elderly woman told Monica. 'You were lucky to have
known Africa.'

It was March and the sea was much too cold for swimming,
even though Dietrich tried it once when the sun was bright. 'Too
much ice,' he reported, and they spent the rest of their time close
to the hotel, making love two or three times a day and satiating
themselves with the joy they found in each other. It was like a
violent honeymoon made more exciting by the fact that when it
was over they would probably never meet again. One lazy afternoon Monica lay in bed, exhausted, and traced her lover's nose
with her forefinger. 'At last I know what a man is,' she told him.
'I think I know all there is to know, thanks to you, and from here
on I can pick and choose without being too excited by the man-
liness.'

He said, 'There's a lot still to learn. For example,' and he put his powerful hands about her neck, 'can you imagine the circumstances which might drive me to murder you?'

'Of course!' she said, and she told him of her escapade with the music teacher at the school in England. 'When he didn't know exactly what to do, I started to laugh at him and I said something really horrid. No, I won't repeat it. And he grew terribly red in the face and I can understand how at such a time he might want to kill somebody. I wasn't exactly scared. More like I was sorry I'd hurt him. So I wrapped my legs around him and pulled him down and showed him what to do and all the bitterness ran out of his body.'

'But can you imagine the other part?' Dietrich asked. 'Like when I come back from a long flight to Johannesburg . . . I'm exhausted . . . my nerves are exposed . . . like needle points. And you haven't had any sex for nine days and you're waiting for me and I get into bed and I'm quite incompetent.' He pulled down the sheet and touched the various parts of her body, dispassionately, and said, 'You know you're as beautiful as ever . . . several men have tried to make love to you while I was gone . . . and I'm able to show no interest at all . . . the only thing I want is to go to sleep. Do you understand that too?'

'The way you've been these past five days, it's hard to believe,' she said.

'But it happens,' he assured her, and she added this bit of knowledge to her repertoire.

When the time came for him to leave, she rode to the airport with him, watched him board the plane for Germany, then left the field undisturbed by the fact that she would not see him again. Twice they had spoken of his wife and two children and he had confessed that he loved them very much; also, she knew that he did not fly the Lufthansa planes into Spain and that only some unforeseen development would bring him her way again. She smiled, recalling his tall, manly body as the German plane flew overhead, and then she prepared to banish him from her mind; he had taught her all she required to know and for his gentle, laughing instruction she would remain grateful. Waving farewell to the plane as it sped out across the Mediterranean, she thought: After a chocolate salesman and a music teacher and a frightened government official, I needed him. But what now?

She had in her possession at this time one hundred and forty British pounds plus the assurance of a small trust account in

London left by her mother's father. Currency restrictions would prevent her from getting hold of all the yearly dividends from that account, but she would have enough to live on even if her father didn't send her anything from his retirement pension. She did not, therefore, experience any panic as she rode the bus back to the center of Torremolinos, an area she did not yet know, for with Dietrich she had stayed in the German hotel and patronized only the German restaurants.

The bus dropped her off at the newspaper kiosk, from which she wandered naturally to the bar with the sunken patio, and there she found a table which commanded a good view of the passing tourists. It was a sunny afternoon and for the first time she realized what a delightful amalgam of young people inhabited this village. In the first few minutes she saw a score of handsome Swedes, a whole covey of attractive young Frenchmen. Tall Americans shuffled by, and she wondered how such disorganized people could presume to take the place of Britain in the matter of empire; she was not at all impressed with the American girls, most of whom seemed unwashed.

'You English?' a boy asked as he stopped to lean on her table.

'No,' she lied. At this moment she had no desire to talk with her countrymen, so the young fellow passed along to another table.

'Can we join you?' a strange voice inquired, and she looked up to see two Japanese students, extremely neat and well presented. Without preamble, both boys said they had been at school in the United States and were touring Europe before returning home. 'Where are you from?' they asked.

'Vwarda,' she said, confident that this would end the conversation, but she was unacquainted with Japanese.

'Ah, so!' one of the students cried. 'Formerly British Congo. Diamonds, sulphur, tin. How is President M'Bele doing? Will they unite one day with Zambia?'

'How in hell do you know about President M'Bele?' Monica asked, both pleased and surprised.

'My father's firm does much business with Vwarda . . . Tanzania . . . both Congos.'

'What is your father's business?'

'Steel. We provided the lacing rods for the big dam in Vwarda.'

They talked of many things, then asked if they could take her to dinner. 'Can you find another girl?' she asked, and they went

from table to table till they came upon a French girl who was looking for something to do. The four of them traipsed off to a fish
restaurant down near the waterfront, where they sat for many
hours, speaking French and talking about the good parts of the
world.

Toward midnight one of the Japanese said, 'Monica, have you
been to the Arc de Triomphe yet?' and when she shook her head,
he cried, 'Tonight's the night!' and they climbed the hill back to
the center of town, where they bought tickets for the discotheque,
and as soon as Monica stepped into the crowded, noisy room she
felt at home, for the thunderous beat of the music was what she
had missed during her stay with the placid Germans. 'This is the
real thing!' she cried, jumping onto the small floor and starting
one of the dances in which, without the necessity for having a
partner, she entered into various gyrations which dated back to
the oldest temples in Greece and the darkest huts in Africa. Working her body as if it were disjointed, she threw her arms and legs
into angular forms that had little association with ordinary movement, then jerked her head and shoulders in unaccustomed ways,
disregarding the specific rhythms of the electronic orchestra. It
was a strange, passionate performance, and all the young people
who saw her that first night noted her beauty and passed the
word along, 'She's a young chick from Vwarda,' and this exotic
provenance helped establish her on the Torremolinos scene.

She found a room at the Berkeley Square, one of the English
hotels, but was not often in it, for each evening she haunted the
bars until the Arc de Triomphe opened, then reported there for
the dancing, and before long she had attracted a regular group of
followers, young men from different nations who were doing their
best to get into bed with her, and also a few English and American
girls who intuitively sensed that where Monica was, the action
would be. They sat in the discotheque night after night, with the
music so crashingly loud that conversation was impossible, yet
somehow they talked and even conducted serious discussions in a
cryptic shorthand that was incomprehensible to anyone over the
age of twenty-five.

'Well, you know . . .'

'It's a gas . . . like my old man . . . he digs it . . . big.'

'Like I said . . .'

'Look, I buy it. I buy it economy wholesale-size. You know, like what you said.'

'Buster, you play it on a moog, my old man still wouldn't . . . you know.'

'Yeah, but if it keeps 'em happy—why should you sweat?'

'Like you say—who's gonna refute that?'

The preceding was a philosophical debate regarding the existence of a man's soul, with the participants agreeing on an agnostic position as opposed to outright atheism. In such discussions, Monica attracted young intellectuals from the Sorbonne and Oxford, with whom she maintained a rapid bilingual debate, shifting automatically from English to French. Sometimes her group spoke in whole sentences.

One night as the two Japanese students walked back to the hotel with her, she experienced a sense of loss when they told her they were flying home next day. She kissed each of them goodbye, but then had the happy thought, 'Why not stay with me tonight?' and the three quietly entered by a back door and slipped into her room unnoticed.

She undressed quickly and popped into bed, indicating that if they could find room, they were welcome to sleep beside her, so they undressed and slid under the sheets, one on each side, and after a while one of them said, 'I would like to make love to you. Saburo can sleep in the bathroom,' but she said, 'I don't think we'd better make love. Let's just go to sleep.'

In the morning someone reported her to the hotel manager, and he said, stiffly, 'We do not condone this sort of thing, especially with orientals,' and she told him to go to hell, and he asked her to get out . . . immediately, so she yelled for the two Japanese students to join her and they marched out together with her shouting back over her shoulder, 'You can send my clothes to the Arc de Triomphe.'

She was sitting there at four in the afternoon when the hotel maid appeared with her luggage, a small cardboard suitcase bought in Málaga and the handbag with which she had fled Vwarda. 'Where are you going?' a pleasant voice asked, and she looked up to see an attractive young man who said his name was Jean-Victor.

'I've been kicked out of my hotel,' she said.

'Something serious, I hope.'

'No. I allowed two very nice Japanese boys to sleep with me in my bed.'

'Good! A groupie.'

'Wash out your mind.' She laughed and pointed to a chair. 'Where's a decent place to hole up?'

'How old are you?'

'I'm a self-supporting woman,' she said.

'Here comes my girl,' Jean-Victor said. 'Sandra, this is . . . What's your name?'

'Monica . . . Braham.'

'You're the one I read about . . . in the London paper.'

'Me?'

'Yes! Your father's a well-known something or other. He's been asking the police where you were. You ran away from some place in Africa, didn't you?'

'Oh my God! The newspapers. If you knew my father, you'd know he'd get it into the newspapers. Where'd you see it?'

Sandra explained that her father had mailed the clipping out from London, warning her not to do anything foolish like that. 'I wonder what he thinks I've been doing?' she asked in honest perplexity.

'Have you the clipping?' Monica asked.

'It's down at our digs.'

Sandra proposed that since Jean-Victor had work to do in town, she'd take Monica down to the apartment and show her the clipping, so they left the center of town, with Sandra carrying the small handbag and Monica the light suitcase. In no time the two girls realized that they were kindred spirits, and they were in the apartment only a few moments—Monica said it was super—when Sandra said with a display of enthusiasm, 'There's an old sleeping bag in the corner. Why don't you dig in here?'

'Could I?'

'Why not? We often have kids sleeping on the floor.'

'Who's in the other bed?'

'A darling Norwegian girl, whom you'll love, and a perfectly swell American . . . very quiet and well mannered.'

'Look, if you have a foursome going . . .'

'It's not like that . . . not really.' And she pulled the tartan sleeping bag from the corner, spreading it on the floor between the two beds for Monica to test. 'Not bad,' Monica said, and it was symptomatic of these young people that she was accepted into the group, invited to dinner, introduced to the Norwegian girl Britta and the American bartender Joe before anyone thought to ask, 'By the way, have you any money?'

'A small supply from home.'

'You're one of us,' Jean-Victor said, and Monica asked, 'Any of you kids have a joint? So we could sort of celebrate?' Britta and Joe indicated that they did not use marijuana, but Jean-Victor and Sandra said they did and he produced a box of fine cigarettes from Tangier, and when Monica took her first deep puff she said, professionally, 'Lots better than the junk we got in Vwarda.'

IV §

CATO

I am black but comely.—The Song of Solomon, 1:5

Stop it, Mom. How many white boys you know who are as smart as Ralph Bunche or as well behaved as Jackie Robinson?

One of the true mysteries of our civilization is the American businessman who sits before his television set marveling at the football prowess of Leroy Kelly, the basketball genius of Wilt Chamberlain, the baseball magic of Willie Mays and the boxing superiority of Cassius Clay but remains unwilling to give the Negro workman an even break on the grounds that 'all niggers are inferior.'

> The three most important building blocks of American history are black: anthracite, petroleum, slaves.

> Advice to tourists: When you come to Philadelphia in the summer you have two things to look out for: the heat and mortal danger.

> My mother bore me in the southern wild,
> And I am black, but O! my soul is white;
> White as an angel is the English child,
> But I am black as if bereaved of light.
> —Blake

> For 364 days a year the black man puts up with an agony that would drive the white man to suicide. On the 365th day he escapes by staying home drunk and then the social worker reports, 'He was incapacitated, as usual.'

A black man is a pearl in a fair woman's eye, and is as acceptable as lame Vulcan was to Venus.—Robert Burton

At the end of the first week of rioting the Committee to Save the University submitted its list of non-negotiable demands which the Regents would have to accept in toto before serious discussions could begin:

1. Any black student who has completed two years of high school must be admitted without entrance examinations.
2. Any black student who has once been admitted must be graduated.
3. At least twenty per cent of all courses taught in the university must be taught by black instructors whose credentials will be certified by this committee alone.
4. Any professors of courses not covered by the preceding who wish to comment in any way on black history must, prior to their lectures, submit their notes to this committee for approval.
5. The placement office of the university must be headed by a black and at least sixty per cent of his assistants must also be black.

I don't want a separate black nation, but I sure as hell want a piece of the action on my own turf.

The wisest among my race understand that the agitation of questions of social equality is the extremest folly, and that progress in the enjoyment of all the privileges that will come to us must be the result of severe and constant struggle rather than of artificial forcing.—Booker T. Washington

Last year my big problem was identity. This year it's where to get dynamite.

It's a simple question of anatomy. For three hundred years we have been turning the other cheek. From here on out it's gonna deal with eyes and it ain't gonna be an eye for an eye. It's gonna be three eyes for an eye.

Soul is the ability to manipulate adversity so that it becomes tolerable.

For the American Negro one simple phrase summarizes the relevant history of our country: Last hired, first fired.

$\mathcal{T}$o introduce my next young man I wish I could show a photograph, because he occupied a prominent place in one of the crucial pictures of this century. As much as any other it crystallized emotions throughout the United States and, in a sense, the world. When you saw this terrifying photograph, you stopped and began to make an honest assessment of your beliefs and prejudices. When I saw it for the first time, on the front page of a newspaper in Vwarda, my head snapped back and I cried, 'Good God, what are they up to?'

The photograph showed the front of an Episcopalian church in Llanfair, one of the Welsh suburbs of Main Line Philadelphia, standing between Bala-Cynwyd and Bryn Mawr. It was a bright Sunday morning in March at about the time when parishioners should have been filing past their minister to shake his hand. Instead, backing out of the church but looking over their shoulders to be sure of their escape route, came three Negroes carrying submachine guns at the ready. The first was bearded, disheveled and fearsome. The second was tall and emaciated, with a scrawny beard. The third was a good-looking young fellow of about nineteen with a totally inappropriate grin on his face. The caption said that the leader headed a committee which had just presented the Llanfair Episcopal Church with a demand for two million dollars in reparation for past crimes against the Negro. The men were carrying submachine guns because they had been forewarned that if they attempted to present their demands at that particular church they would be ejected.

'Ain't nobody gonna eject nobody,' the bearded leader had shouted as his group burst into the church, and while he read his manifesto from the pulpit, his two henchmen stood with their guns leveled at the heads of the congregation. A newspaper photographer, who had been invited by white parishioners to be on hand to get shots of the Negroes being thrown out, was waiting as the trio backed out of the church, and thus caught a photograph which would win him the Pulitzer Prize.

Unfortunately, when the flashbulb exploded, the second Negro, the tall thin one, became frightened and discharged his machine gun in the air, blasting a hole in the roof and subjecting the invaders to criminal charges. The police had already captured the two bearded men and were confident of finding the third.

The second thing I said that day in Vwarda was, 'Hell, I know those kids!' I checked the names in the caption, and of course one of them was Cato Jackson of Grimsby Street in North Philadelphia. I not only knew him, I also knew his father, Reverend Claypool Jackson, African Church of Our Redeemer, and the reason I knew the Reverend is an interesting comment on our times.

My employers in Geneva are American citizens. Before they launched World Mutual they had established good track records in states like Minnesota and Massachusetts. They elected to charter their new company in Switzerland because restrictions at home had become oppressive and they sought a freer arena in which to operate. They lost much by making this decision, for they would have preferred to work out of New York, but they gained a lot, too.

One thing they lost was personal contact with problems then emerging in the United States. I have found that few men become heads of great companies without at least knowing what the score is. They may react conservatively or liberally, but the facts they know. If they didn't they'd crumble. So our team knew what was happening in America and we wanted to participate . . . in our own way.

One area in which we cultivated a sophisticated interest was race relations. As an international outfit we could ill afford to look down our noses at any group of human beings; one of our most profitable deals had been with a consortium of apparently simple-minded Japanese entrepreneurs who were smart enough to drive a disgraceful bargain with us, and got away with it because they had something we knew we could make a profit on, a new kind of steel. I've already said I was consultant to a Negro republic.

So we were more ready than most to offer our brains and our money to any determined Negroes who might see ways out of the jungle which America had created for them and to which they were still confined. Our group had no special love for Negroes, no illusions that they were better than anyone else. But we did know that they comprised twelve per cent of the American people, and we could find in world history no case of a successful nation which had condemned so high a percentage of its human resources to a life of less than full utility. Even the great slave-holding nations of history had encouraged their slaves to operate at top efficiency; for a democracy based on freedom to do less was unthinkable. So we spent a lot of time looking over the situation in America, seeking that viable situation into which we could pour thirty or forty million dollars in an effort to demonstrate what could be done when Negro and white businessmen cooperated.

We settled on Philadelphia, because this city contained a heavy concentration of Negroes moved up from the south, while its suburbs had a well-educated and generally progressive population. As usual, I was given the job of scouting possibilities, and one after another blew up in my face. In the suburbs white leaders were somewhat bewildered by the problem that had overtaken them; in the city the Negroes were so uninstructed in financial management that I could not even find a point at which to start. It was in this dejected frame of mind that I went one Sunday to the African Church of Our Redeemer simply to hear what kind of religion these leaderless people were consoling themselves with. It was a dismal experience. The minister was the Reverend Claypool Jackson, a benevolent man in his late fifties who, judging from the size and magnificence of his church, ought to have been a leader. Instead he was an obvious Uncle Tom repeating a Green Pastures vision of God and man. He preached in an exaggerated dialect, spending most of his sermon on a highly colored version of Daniel 3, which he called 'the story of the three little Hee-brew chir'n, Shadrach, Meshach and Abednego.' He must have been a lineal descendant of the scribe who had composed this chapter of the Bible, for he was mesmerized by the three poetic names, shouting them again and again. In the Bible, within a space of nineteen verses, the three names are sung out thirteen times, always in the same order, and Reverend Jackson held that what was good enough for the Bible was good enough for him. The church resounded with the names, and whenever he called them out, someone in the congregation would shout, 'Oh, them poor Hee-brew chir'n.'

Reverend Jackson especially liked the passage which dealt with the preparations for throwing the three into the fiery furnace: ' "He commanded that they should heat the furnace seven times more than it was wont to be heated. And he commanded the most mighty men that were in his army to bind Shadrach, Meshach and Abednego, and to cast them into the burning fiery furnace. Then these men were bound in their coats, their hosen and their hats, and their other garments, and were cast into the midst of the burning fiery furnace." ' He came back several times to the hosen.

He droned on and on, bewailing the fate of the three little Hebrew children, but I had no suspicion of what he was leading up to. In his peroration, when the three were saved, he cried exultantly, 'And today we have in our midst a fine gentleman who has come to save us. He sits among us now, all the way from Switzerland, with millions of dollars for stores and churches and schools and maybe even factories. There he sits, a gentleman of great power, and if you elders with the plates approach him politely, I'm sure he's going to give us at least fifty dollars.'

I slumped in my seat, but the elders descended upon me and I could do no less than peel off five tens, which the plate carrier bore in triumph to the front of the church, displaying them to the congregation. There were some hymns, some announcements, a long closing prayer in which I appeared favorably, and the service was over.

I tried to slip out a side door so that I wouldn't have to encounter Reverend Jackson's effusive thanks, which I could see headed my way, but when I reached the escape route I found it barred by a slim, taut, good-looking young Negro boy in his late teens. 'Trying to escape? You couldn't stomach Father's soaring bullshit?'

And that was how I met Cato Jackson.

———•◆•———

In the weeks that followed, Reverend Claypool Jackson became a continuing headache; in any situation he was an unctuous clown who felt no shame at playing the role of plantation Negro buttering up the white man in order to get what he wanted. In my case the problem was aggravated because he knew I had a substantial sum of money to dispense and he had conceived the idea that he alone could give me advice.

What irritated me was that he assumed the role of Negro leader and was ever willing to speak on behalf of the million or more Negroes who lived in Philadelphia. This would have been tolerable had he had an understanding of the Negro community, but of the actual life in the crowded streets he was sweetly innocent. Every shred of advice he gave me was not only irrelevant; it was corrosive.

His huge Gothic church stood on the corner of Grimsby and Sixth. His home was two blocks away at Grimsby and Fourth. Taking these two points as foci of an ellipse covering six or seven blocks in each direction, the church and the manse were centers of an area epitomizing the collapse of city living, so far as Negroes were concerned. Within the preceding twenty-four months in this area six Negro adults had been murdered, seven Negro children under the age of nineteen had been slain, plus three Jewish storekeepers. Sixty-nine per cent of all births had been illegitimate; fourteen adult men made their living pushing heroin to black students attending nearby Classical High, where four teachers had been assaulted in their classrooms and one raped in the cafeteria.

This ellipse of the future was governed principally by Irish and Italian policemen whose sentimental attachment to Catholicism rendered them incapable of comprehending what was happening in the Negro community and insensitive to the aspirations of its residents. Twice the district had been on the verge of explosion, once because a white policeman had shot and killed an eleven-year-old Negro boy, once because Negroes, seeing a white policeman trying to save the life of a Negro boy by breathing into his mouth, thought, naturally, that the policeman was strangling a fallen boy, and so jumped him. In the confusion the boy died and the policeman lost an eye.

As for prostitution, dope addiction, illiteracy, unemployment, theft and the other indices of urban collapse, the district around Reverend Jackson's church was a microcosm; indeed, that was why we had selected this particular area for our experiment. We were convinced that the human population within the ellipse was salvageable. We wanted to help this disoriented group find a solid economic base from which to restructure their community and their homes. To us, Grimsby Street was both a challenge and a promise. We appreciated the special problems of Negroes, and wanted to work with them. We knew that only radical approaches carried any hope for success and were prepared to underwrite them.

I was therefore dismayed when Reverend Jackson insisted that the one good thing I could do to help the Negro population was— guess what? 'Mr. Fairbanks, I feel sure that what we require most is for you to pay off the mortgage on our church.'

I felt numb, but decided to see what was in his mind: 'How much?'

'One hundred and eighty-eight thousand dollars.'

'Why would you have so large a mortgage?'

'When we bought the church . . .'

'What do you mean?'

'God didn't give us this magnificent edifice. We bought it.'

'From whom?'

'From the white folks. When they moved out to the suburbs.'

'How much did you pay for it?'

'Two hundred and fifty thousand dollars.'

'And you've already reduced the mortgage by more than sixty thousand?'

'Yes,' he said proudly. 'Our whole effort—cake sales, rummages, special summer collections—everything we do is aimed toward one great goal. To make God's house stand free of debt.'

I noticed that in his talks with me he did not use the exaggerated dialect of his sermons. He had been to college in the south and had apparently done well.

'What our community needs,' he told me with varying types of supporting data, 'is to have the mortgage on this church paid off so that this great edifice can stand like a beacon, reminding us of the life that Jesus would have us follow.'

'Is the church a leader with the young?' I asked.

'Oh yes! Last summer it was the young people who collected the majority of our funds. If you look at our choir, you'll see it's filled with bright young faces.'

'And the young people in the streets? The ones who beat up teachers at Classical High?'

'Some of them have drifted from the Lord, but when our church grows strong, they'll come back. They respond to a good sermon, just like the others. I'm sure I've made it clear that the major need of the black community in Philadelphia is to have this church stand free of debt. Then it could assert its leadership.'

At each public meeting Reverend Jackson came back to this theme of religious leadership; before an audience his sense of propriety kept him from pressing his own case, and he did not refer to the mortgage, but he always waited to catch me alone, beseeching me to pay off his debt.

Concurrently with the general Negro community, I was undergoing an ambivalent experience in my attempt to invest Geneva funds. On the one hand, there was a small cadre of knowledgeable Negro experts who presented me with sensible plans for workable projects: small-loan banks, Negro industrial centers, merchandising schemes, cooperative apartments for young married workers, and an idea which I liked very much, an insurance company which would specialize in writing policies on unwed mothers so that in case of disaster their children would be assured of an education. After my meetings with such men I would return to my hotel room, alive with enthusiasm, and think: This community has all the intelligence it needs. Tomorrow we'll get started.

But on the other hand, there was Nordness. He was a tall, acidulous, unhappy Minnesotan who had accompanied me from Geneva to act as office manager for the Philadelphia project, and he almost gave me an ulcer, because whenever I reported in the morning, eager to get started on some promising project, Nordness would stalk like a ghost into my office and launch his complaint. It was always the same: 'I was very careful about hiring our master secretary, Mr. Fairbanks. I finally found a Negro who looked much better than the secretary we have in Geneva. But this is his sixth day on the job—and where is he?' On the seventh, eighth and ninth days, Nordness started my mornings by reporting mournfully that the secretary was still absent. Then on the tenth day Nordness smiled his bitter smile and said, 'Well, our man is back. And when I asked him where he had been for four days, what do you suppose he said? "Look, Harry got hisself into a bad scrape, somebody got to help out." Who was Harry? A cousin three times removed.'

It was the opinion of Nordness that any incident relating to family life was an excuse for a Negro employee to abandon his office responsibilities. 'And the family is very broadly defined,' he said dourly. 'The other day it was an automobile accident involving the nephew of the woman to whom a man's uncle was married. The man stayed away two days, and when I asked him how he could justify this, he told me, "We talkin' about a boy. He got to be protected from the bulls." '

If I launched a project in which strict performance was essential, Nordness kept things going well at first, but before long he was in my office protesting that he could not make Negro supervisors enforce consistent standards of production because they identified with any worker who came up with a special problem. One day Nordness asked me, almost tearfully, 'Where the hell do you suppose our treasurer is? I sent a messenger to find out and he came back with this good news: "Miss Catherine say she have to see her aunt in West Philadelphia. She be back start of next week." '

I told Nordness, with some impatience, 'You seem unable to adjust to the Negro community.' Then I threw in a suggestion which I did not intend him to take seriously: 'Maybe you'd be happier back in Geneva.'

'I can leave tonight!' he cried. 'I've been spoiled by working with Germans. With them, you agree upon a system and it gets done.'

I asked, 'Can't you visualize a world in which Germans and Negroes work in their own ways?'

He said, 'Maybe in two hundred years the Negroes will learn to work like Germans. Until then, you can have Philadelphia.' He shrugged his shoulders to indicate that he didn't give a damn what happened to the city, and that night he was on the plane back to Geneva.

So one after another of the hopeful projects Nordness and I had proposed when tackling this problem in the abstract, teetered and fell into the bog of indifference. I wasted a good few million dollars and accomplished little, yet always at my elbow when another enterprise failed would be Reverend Jackson advising me: 'It's like I told you at the beginning, Mr. Fairbanks. What Philadelphia really needs is to have the debt of the church paid off so that it can exercise moral authority and give these good people standards they can adhere to.'

When I work in a new community and drink unfamiliar water I often develop a cold sore on my lip, and if I leave it unattended it grows bothersome. An Austrian chemist has devised a salve which suppresses such sores almost immediately and usually I carry a tube with me, but now I had none, so that evening after a community meeting at Reverend Jackson's ornate church I stopped by a drug-store at the corner of Grimsby and Fifth, halfway between church and manse. When I pushed the door open, an old-fashioned, spring-activated bell alerted the unseen chemist to the fact that someone had entered his shop. On the wall facing me hung a large sign: *Smile, You're on Store Detective,* and photographs explained how an unseen camera took pictures of you, even if the owner wasn't visible. Another sign read: *When You're in Trouble, We Work Double.* A rather grubby table offered a special to Puerto Rican customers: Emulsion Gimenez, with a portrait of a bald-headed doctor in a velvet-collared evening dress of 1905. Agua de Azahar was also featured, and a bold red package labeled *Assassinator! Takes Care of Bedbugs, Roaches and Other Vermin.*

A swinging door from the rear opened and the pharmacist, an elderly man wearing a celluloid badge stating that he was Dr. Gold-stein, moved slowly to greet me. He had heard of the Austrian salve. He didn't have any but he thought he could get some from the wholesale house: 'You come back tomorrow, I'll probably have it.' In cases like this, when I have ordered something which the storekeeper might not be able to sell to anyone else, I always pay in advance, and when I did so, the old man smiled and said, 'This doesn't happen very often here. In my father's shop in Germany it was customary.'

'How is this community for paying bills?' I asked.

He sighed. He was past sixty and this would surely be the last store he would own, so that he had a natural inclination to think kindly of it, but he couldn't: 'It's very difficult. This neighborhood is hell put down on earth to test us.'

'Are the Negroes so tough?' I asked.

'No! They're good people, fundamentally. The hell is worse on them than it is on us. But I don't think a white man—certainly not a Jew . . .' He shrugged his shoulders. 'We'll have to get out. Three times they've broken through that door to get heroin. I don't carry any, so they get mad, smash things up and drink a quart of paregoric, which kills them. Is that civilized?'

I asked about the work habits which had distressed Mr. Nordness so much, and he said, 'I've tried Negro helpers. The black people who buy here used to complain that my assistants were Jewish, which was a just complaint. So I hired three different young men to help me—and what happens? They either steal me blind or don't open the store on my day off. So then I have to fire them—and they charge me with discrimination.'

'What will happen?' I asked.

'Time will happen. I could take you to a dozen homes around here that contain some of the best people in America. Kind, generous, well behaved. You've heard of Leroy Clore? Plays third base for Chicago . . . American League, that is. Well, he lives one block from here, and if he came in right now and said, "Morris, I have to have three hundred dollars," I'd give it to him. I have great hopes that fifteen years from now we'll have lots of Leroy Clores. But from now till then . . . trouble.'

Next day our business meeting was interminable, with Reverend Jackson contending that the failure of our commercial projects proved that we must direct our funds to the churches. The sore on my lip was becoming painful, which made his refrain doubly tedious, and I am afraid I was brusque. He smiled benevolently and said, 'In the end you'll find I'm right. We must build the church so that it is a beacon.' This irritated me so much that I was tempted to say, 'Why not light a fire under the damned thing and make it a real beacon,' but instead I pressed my lip to relieve the pain and assured him we would consider all proposals. I left the meeting in disgust and walked over to Fifth Street to see if Dr. Goldstein had my Austrian salve, but I could not get into the store.

It was surrounded by gaping people, most of them black, who watched as two police cars picked their way through the crowd, lights flashing but with no sirens, for this was a section of Philadelphia in which sirens should be avoided; even a flashing light could attract a crowd too big to handle. The policemen, more than half Negroes, hurried from their cars into what seemed an apartment building, but when I finally edged my way through the crowd I saw that they had entered the pharmacy.

They were too late. Dr. Goldstein lay on the bloody sidewalk, gunned down by assailants whose mission had not yet been determined. Before I could ask any questions, an elderly Jew ran down from a nearby building, crying at the top of his voice, 'I told him a dozen times, "Morris, get out!" We were going to sell the store next month.' He identified himself as Julius Goldstein, registered pharmacist, brother and partner of the dead man.

A white policeman tried to intercept him before he could enter the drugstore, but Goldstein forced his way in, saw the bloodied body of his brother, and began screaming charges against Negroes and the doomed neighborhood. It was a hideous moment, with the Jew accomplishing nothing by his blanket accusations.

'Get him out of here,' the white policeman ordered. Then, seeing me, he cried, 'You, too, out!' A black policeman grabbed me and started shoving, when a young man moved out of the shadows, interposed himself between me and the policeman, and said, 'Cool it, man. He's one of us.' The policeman looked at the young man, nodded in recognition, dropped his hand from my shoulder, and said, 'How you like what happened back there, Cato?'

The young man turned to survey the drugstore and asked, 'You surprised?' The policeman shrugged his shoulders and returned to the store. Now the young man said, 'We met at my father's church. I'm Cato Jackson.'

———— • ◆ ◆ • ————

That night was a revelation. Cato Jackson, more deeply troubled by the murder than he had allowed me to see at the drugstore, walked with me for six hours through the dark neighborhoods of his youth, sharing his confusions and apprehensions. He was a sophomore at the University of Pennsylvania, a year ahead of grade; at the age of fourteen he had been identified by a committee from the university faculty as a brilliant boy and had been given a preparatory scholarship. He was now in the process of fulfilling course requirements leading to specialization in urban affairs, and his grades, if I could believe what he said, were excellent. In one hour he made more sense than his father had made in two months. I shall not try to reproduce our conversation, but here are the major points he made during that long, dark night:

'My father came from South Carolina as an ordained minister, though what that means intellectually, I wouldn't care to say. Here in Philly he opened a storefront church, and as you've seen for yourself he can preach pretty well, so he prospered. By that I mean he gathered about himself a group of loyal followers, and from them he made not only a living for himself but also enough to move his congregation out of the storefront and into a small brick building on South Grimsby—about twenty-two blocks down from where he is now.

'He's always been adroit at collecting money, so before long he had the brick building paid for. Now here comes the bite. Blacks were moving into the neighborhood and whites were moving out. So that big Gothic church you were in the other Sunday was standing mostly idle. No whites, while the little brick building overflowed with blacks. The white congregation, which was very rich, moved out to Llanfair on the Main Line, built a fine new church, then looked around for some way to dispose of the old one.

'Philadelphia Episcopalians are a canny lot. I suppose all Christians are. Anyway, they came up with a deal whereby my old man would pay them two hundred and fifty thousand dollars for their old church. That was the price. It never occurred to them that they'd had a hundred good years in that church . . . that they'd all made good incomes from this neighborhood . . . that they were way ahead of the game and ought to give the church to those who were following. No, they took their profits out to the Main Line, and their businesses, and their taxes, and then, by God, they sold their old church to my father.

'He had twenty thousand dollars he'd saved from collections taken at the brick church. And he was able to sell that property for thirty thousand, and with this he made his down payment. He got a two-hundred-thousand mortgage from the very Christians who had sold him their used-up church, and now he and his flock work twelve months a year to pay the rich people on the Main Line.'

When he said this we were walking over a bridge across the Schuylkill River, and from it we could see the lovely silhouette of Alexander Hamilton Square, named for that noble immigrant from the West Indies whom Cato suspected to have been part Negro, like his countrywoman Joséphine de Beauharnais, whom Napoleon married. Hamilton had labored intelligently and well in Philadelphia and it was appropriate that one of the finest residential squares, overlooking the western river, should honor him.

'When I look at the skyline of this square,' Cato said, 'what do you suppose I see? First, you tell me what you see.'

'I see some very fine old buildings,' I said. 'They're worth preserving . . . if that's what you mean.'

'I don't mean that at all. I mean those highly polished brass name-plates.' He led me around the square so that I could read the names of the organizations that used these distinguished buildings as their

Pennsylvania headquarters: women's clubs, youth groups, church societies, foundations, art leagues, and all those voluntary groups which are so essential to the well-being of a society.

'Every group tax-exempt,' Cato said. 'Every group collects funds from the city and spends them in the suburbs. This square is the spiritual capital of suburbia. There's not one goddamned committee headquartering here that does a shred of good for the city. And it's all exempt from city taxes.'

He led me to other squares where the same condition prevailed: 'In this square sixty per cent of the buildings are tax-exempt, and every one of them operates solely for the benefit of the suburbs. In this square fifty-one per cent tax-exempt. Over here factories shut down, paying no taxes. Wherever you look, the guts torn out of the city and either moved to the suburbs or thrown into tax-exempt status.'

'I take it you're studying this problem at Penn?'

'No! Penn is worst of all. That huge operation in the heart of the city, paying no taxes for the services we blacks have to pay for.'

'But they're giving you an education.'

'Grudgingly.'

We proceeded through the city, and for the first time I saw a major American metropolis through the eyes of an embittered young Negro: 'Even though the rich white Protestants have fled with their wealth, and even though they've sold their used-up churches to people like my father, they won't relinquish control. They use tax exemptions to cripple us. They use the state legislature to prevent us from governing ourselves. They emasculate the city, rob it blind, then throw it at us and say, "Now it's your problem." But they give us no money and no control.'

Two policemen in a prowl car moved slowly past us, properly curious as to why a white man would be walking in that part of the city after midnight. When the occupants—one black, one white—saw my age and Cato's, they assumed we were homosexuals. 'You keep your noses clean,' they warned us.

'One thing Whitey does keep control of when he leaves the city,' Cato said as the car slowly disappeared. 'The police department. They sure as hell keep control of that. You know why?'

When I said no, he did a strange thing. He dropped his university accent and lapsed into an ancient dialect his family had acquired during their stay in the coastal swamps of South Carolina. Geechee, Cato called it, and I found it practically indecipherable, composed as it was of African words, grunts and mocking pronunciations. Fortunately, it was intermixed with what Cato termed 'high middle-period Stepin Fetchit,' and it was this mélange that Cato and his friends used when engaging in put-ons, the art of kidding white folks by expounding in exaggerated form the race phobias they nurtured. Cato was a master of the put-on, and although I cannot reproduce the African words he used and the full fantasy of his illiterate grammar, what he told me that first night came out something like this: 'Yassuh, Mistuh Charley, me 'n mah boys, we gonna ass-emble one night 'n we gonna march wid clubs and knives and ropes right out to Chestnut Hill 'n Llanfair 'n Ardmore 'n all them fancy places 'n we gon' to dem fine'—he pronounced it *fahn*—'residential areas like Jenkintown and Doylestown 'n we gon' murder 'n rape 'n burn all dem people in de suburbs. Yassuh, Mistuh Charley, dat's what we got in mind to do.'

'You murdered one of them a couple of hours ago,' I said, impatient with the put-on.

'Have you seen the district where I live?' he asked soberly.

'I have.'

'Aren't you surprised there haven't been more murders?'

'I shrink from even one.'

The finality of my reply caused him to drop the subject. Abruptly he said, 'You asked me if I got my ideas at Penn. I said no. Would you be interested in seeing where I do get them?' When I nodded, he looked at his watch, a rather good one, and said, 'Let's go.'

He led me far uptown to an extremely dirty street in North Philadelphia, where he looked up and down to be sure no police had trailed us. Satisfied that we were alone, he ducked into an alleyway, then doubled back to the side door of an incredibly filthy apartment house. 'Just for the record,' he said, 'this building is owned by one of the gang that unloaded the church on my father.'

We climbed stairs that no sane man should have trusted and kicked open a door whose latch had not worked for years. The room was dark, but in one corner I could vaguely discern a bed with at least one sleeping form. Cato made a clatter, knocking over a chair and a kitchen utensil of some kind. Finally he found a light, which disclosed an unkempt room with scarred furniture, including a chipped iron bed on which two men were lying.

One was well bearded, naked to the waist and surly. The other, a very tall thin man with a scraggly beard, made no impression on me. When the first climbed out of bed I saw that he was wearing green basketball shorts emblazoned with the most honorable name in the business: Boston Celtics. 'This is Akbar Muhammad,' Cato said. 'He's the professor who taught me.'

Akbar reached for a towel, dipped one end in a pitcher of water, washed his hairy face, and asked, 'Why you come here?'

'This Whitey you ought to know,' Cato said. 'He's the cat from Geneva.'

'With the millions?' Akbar asked.

'The man,' Cato said.

Akbar dropped the towel on the floor, kicked it aside and strode over to greet me. 'I've heard about you,' he said, grasping my hand firmly. 'You make a lot of sense.' He pushed a chair my way and sat down on the end of his bed. 'You find anything worth investing in?'

'No,' I said.

'I didn't think you would.'

'There was another murder tonight,' I said. 'Right near the church where we were meeting.'

'There'll be more.' He reached back and rapped the thin man on the forehead. 'Go get Vilma,' he commanded, and the thin man dressed quickly and left the room.

'Who are you?' I asked.

'You know my name. You're probably asking what it used to be. Eddie Frakus. Detroit. Parents from Mississippi. I graduated Michigan State. Mr. Fairbanks, you might just as well go back to Geneva. It'll be ten years before the blacks of Philadelphia will be able to comprehend your offer.' He paused, stroked his beard with his right hand, then pointed at me with a long finger. 'And by then we'll have changed so much that even men of good faith like you won't offer us the help you offer tonight. No, believe me! The things we'll have to do will alienate you . . . totally. But that won't matter, because then we won't need your help.'

He spoke so forcefully, with such clear comprehension of what he was saying, that I had to like him. I asked, 'Why are you so sure you'll lose me?' and he pointed to a mimeographing machine in the corner. 'Go ahead. Find the message yourself. It'll give you a sense of discovery.' He watched as I walked to the corner and picked up one of the first copies of a document that was to become famous, Akbar Muhammad's bill of charges against the Christian churches of Pennsylvania.

It was a document so inflammatory that I had to wonder if the same man who had just shown himself to be so reasonable had composed it. The preamble was a call to revolution, the first paragraphs a program for black control of the city. The mayor's office, the chief of police, the president of the Board of Education and the director of welfare were all to be black, and the funds to ensure this takeover were to come from contributions made voluntarily by the white churches not only in the city but also in the suburbs to a distance of twenty-five miles. When I was finished with the document, which was well reasoned and persuasive, I realized that it had been calculated to enrage the white reader as no other statement could, for it insulted his prejudices and parodied his most precious beliefs.

Jesus Christ was portrayed as a cheap sentimentalist whose contradictory mouthings had been used by whites to subdue blacks and by blacks as a narcotic to make their perpetual servitude tolerable. Church leaders were depicted as gangsters who had systematically robbed the Negro and kept him in a position from which he could not extricate himself. Church members were proved to be damned fools who sanctimoniously approved what was happening and capitalized upon it. The general taxpaying public was depicted as being in collusion with the churches, to their detriment. The final paragraphs had about them the icy coldness of the November nights before a revolution: 'We therefore demand, in the name of Akbar Muhammad and black humanity, as reparations from the white churches of Philadelphia, an immediate sum of $10,000,000 in cash, to be provided as follows . . .' and the names of forty denominations were listed with specific amounts due from each. 'We likewise demand from the white churches of suburban Philadelphia an immediate sum of $20,000,000 in cash, to be provided as follows . . .' and now came the addresses of about ninety wealthy churches from Paoli on the west to Doylestown on the north. The manifesto was signed 'Akbar Muhammad.'

It was about dawn when I finished reading the challenge, and before I could ask any questions, the thin man returned with a most beautiful young Negro girl, whose relationship to the three men I was never to get straightened out. Apparently she was not the girl of the thin man who had fetched her, but Akbar Muhammad treated her with such indifference, if not contempt, that I doubted she would have been long content with his sponsorship. Young Cato, on the other hand, was painfully careful not to express an interest in her, so I judged that one of the other men must have warned him away, but I could sense that he was deeply affected.

She was like a young forest animal, sleek, innately graceful, fawn-colored and somewhat petulant. Her features were Grecian in their regularity, as if carved from some precious golden marble from North Africa. She was comely, in the words of the Bible, and it required little imagination to see her standing coolly under an Arabian palm while Solomon sang to her.

'You got the labor union material typed?' Akbar Muhammad asked as she joined us.

'Like I tol' you, it's in Paul's room.' Impatiently she left us and climbed to another floor, where I could hear her rummaging about. In a few minutes she returned with a sheaf of papers, which Akbar handed me. They presented his demands on the labor unions of Philadelphia, similar to those planned for the churches but in my opinion more justified.

First he recited the adroit chicanery by which the white unions had forbidden Negroes to learn the basic skills that might have supported them. No Negro could be a bricklayer, an electrician, a plasterer, a roofer, a carpenter, a structural-steel man. 'But I've seen Negro carpenters,' I protested. 'Read on,' Akbar growled.

He then quoted from the rules of the various unions, citing high-flown phrases from constitutions which ensured all honest men a fair entrance to the unions, if only they served their apprenticeship, mastered the basic skills and paid their union dues. Next he cited the actual figures of union membership, after fifteen years of Negro agitation for a fair deal:

Gaye Street				
Electricians	1143 members	2 blacks	43 apprentices	1 black
Petawley				
Bricklayers	219 members	1 black	9 apprentices	1 black
North Philadelphia				
Steel	396 members	2 blacks	11 apprentices	0 black
Bay City				
Carpenters	1823 members	4 blacks	112 apprentices	6 blacks
Grimsby Roofers	81 members	0 blacks	6 apprentices	0 black
Radford Plasterers	366 members	2 blacks	16 apprentices	1 black

The list went on and on, with one very large construction unit having more than four thousand members, of whom seven were Negro. This union was training 218 apprentices, of whom three were black. No one could look at these disparate figures without seeing the oppression that was sanctified by the union movement. What made the figures doubly insane was that this was happening in Philadelphia, where the working population was at least fifty per cent Negro.

'And there's no sign that things will ever be better,' Akbar said coldly. 'At least not until we sock the unions for eight million dollars, which we shall do.'

'Here's the real trouble,' Cato broke in, and as he spoke with rapier efficiency, I got the idea that he was interested more in impressing Vilma than me. 'The one avenue which the Negro has for escaping his ghetto is work. Yet here in Philadelphia his opportunity to work is totally blocked by the unions. And who are the unions? Good Catholics, good Protestants whose churches have condoned this evil state of affairs. And who are these good Catholics and Protestants? Italians, Poles, Germans and white immigrants from the south who fear we'll take their jobs. Can you see the pressure cooker they keep us in? No taxes so that we can run our own city. Nothing but eternal frustration.' He turned to me and asked, 'Now do you understand why these documents are needed?'

I asked Akbar, 'Could we send the man out for some coffee and doughnuts?' I handed the thin fellow five dollars, and later he returned with a fistful of paper bags. 'There ain't any change,' he said. 'I got sandwiches for the men upstairs.'

I sat on the bed and recalled certain experiences I had had in this field. 'You're interested in what a practical-minded white workman thinks about the problem?' They nodded. 'I want to say four things. You'll agree with three of them and thank me for having told you. I can imagine you using them in your speeches later on. You'll despise me for the fourth, and when I leave, it will be with mutual animosity. But here goes.

'First, some years ago I was on the border of India and Tibet, watching a gang build a difficult mountain road. They were using woman-power. Thousands of women at the mountain face quarrying rock by hand. Thousands of other women with little reed baskets carrying large rocks. Thousands of still other women sitting in the roadbed breaking the rocks into pebbles. They laid about two feet of road a day, but that was all right, because they had nothing better to do, until you figured that with proper machinery and direction, a few men could have done in one day what these five thousand women would accomplish in one month. I spoke to the foreman about this, and he said, "But we get the women for almost nothing." He was ruining his whole project because the labor was so cheap. Wherever I went in Asia after that I looked at the work force and found the same thing. In Japanese steel mills before the war they used hundreds of workmen instead of one machine, because they got the workmen cheap, and they also got a cheap product that couldn't compete in the world market. In China they used thousands of workmen where ten would suffice, because they got them cheap, and the results suffered. I concluded that the most expensive product in the world is cheap labor, because it lures you away from rational operations. You pay a man a high wage, you demand a high return, and from high returns you pick up a good profit. So ever since, I've believed in paying a man high wages, then taxing him like hell for the welfare of the state. The thing that appalls me about America's philosophy regarding the Negro workman is that we're doing with him what the government in India was doing with the five thousand women, misusing them because they're cheap. And we hurt ourselves more than we do the Negro. I'd pay every Negro at least five dollars an hour, and then tax hell out of him for schools and public parks.'

Akbar and Cato had followed my reasoning with delight; it was what they had already figured out. 'Man, you see the problem,' Akbar cried enthusiastically. 'The white honkies that keep the brothers out of the labor unions are hurting themselves as much as they hurt us.'

'Second,' I said, 'when I was working with the navy in Guadalcanal—in the bad days, that was—we didn't have enough men to go around. Anyone who could shoot a rifle was needed on patrol, because those Japanese were murder. Henderson airfield posed a difficult problem, because we had to keep it operating to give our planes a place to land and refuel. You know what we did? It still sounds incredible, but we did it. We took Stone Age cannibals from the nearby island of Malaita . . . this is the most backward island on earth, believe me. And we took these men right out of the jungle and put khaki shorts on them and within two weeks we had them driving ten-ton trucks and refueling airplanes. Nothing infuriates me more than the argument of the white American unions that blacks can't learn. If the plantation system of the south still prevailed—with Negro slaves—you can be dead sure that Negroes would be the electricians, the plasterers, the bricklayers. They were in the old days, and they would be now. And they'd be better technicians than the free whites in the neighborhood, because to be so would be a source of pride. So the simple skills you can perform. What about the complicated ones?

'That brings me to the third point. When I was connected with that big dam in Afghanistan, I saw our people take men from the desert, train them for three months, and then turn over to them one of the most complicated of modern machines. It's a big dredge . . . thousands of tons. It goes into swampy land and cuts drainage channels. How does it keep from sinking into the mud? It carries its own highway with it . . . great chunks of steel marsden matting. With a long crane it lays a length of matting, crawls out onto it, then swings the crane around to the back, picks up the matting it has just used and lays it through the swamp ahead. At the end the damned machine is a mile out in the middle of the swamp, marooned on the platform it built for itself. Would you believe that we could teach Afghans from the Stone Age to operate that machine? We did. Today you can teach a capable man almost anything. With less than a year of training, Negroes could man every union job in Philadelphia, and the output would scarcely suffer.'

This theory met with wild agreement. Even the thin man said, 'My brother, he can fix television like you never saw.' Vilma also spoke for the first time. 'The brothers could learn. I know they could learn.'

'What's your last point?' Akbar Muhammad asked.

'The one you won't like,' I said. 'The one thing that prevents the Negro from accomplishing these things when the white man does allow him to try . . .'

'Goddammit!' Akbar shouted, leaping from the bed. 'Don't speak like that! The day is past when you white people are going to *allow* us anything. We're going to take things like jobs. And if you try to stop us, there has got to be blood.' He raged about the room, kicking at discarded mimeographed sheets containing his manifesto. 'If a man like you, who understands the problem . . . if you still speak of allowing us to try our skills . . . goddammit, what hope is there?' He ended with his pugnacious beard a few inches from my nose.

'I'm sorry. I understand.'

'No, you don't understand!' Akbar shouted. 'Damn it, you do *not* understand. I am telling you right now that I expect to be shot down in the streets of Philadelphia . . . before I'm thirty years old. You, tell him!'

The thin man said in a voice I could scarcely hear, 'I expect to be gunned down. But I'm gonna take half a dozen white men down with me.'

'You! Cato! Tell him!'

'I'm positive we'll have to go into the streets to win equality. We realize you have the guns . . . you got us outnumbered . . . I expect to die fighting here in Philadelphia.'

'Wait a minute!' I shouted. 'Akbar, you have a college degree. Cato, you're getting one. There's a place for you in our society.'

'You don't seem to understand. It's no longer enough for me to get a job. I want every black man to have a fair chance. I want the brothers to be free, and I'll die for it.'

Vilma had said nothing while the others uttered their manifestos, but now she did something that was even more dramatic. She crossed the room, yanked open a closed door, and showed me a small arsenal of guns and ammunition. Standing like a black Joan of Arc beside this lethal cache, she said nothing, then closed the door and resumed her place on the bed beside the thin man.

'What was your fourth point?' Akbar asked.

I pointed to the arsenal and said, 'After that it would be anti-climactic.'

'I want to hear it.'

'It'll only make you angry.'

'No angrier than I already am.'

'Here goes. Up till yesterday I had an office manager named Nordness. Brought him with me from Geneva. He quit. Why? He told me that all he got from the Negroes in Philadelphia was ulcers. Because at levels lower than you and Cato, he found no sense of responsibility. If he gave a man a job on Monday, the man took off for three days on Friday. If he opened a branch on the edge of town and staffed it with Negroes, next week it might or might not be open for business. Nordness believed that union leaders were dead right, whether you like it or not, when they said, "Sure the

Negro can learn, but you never know whether he's going to report for duty." So until your inner society is restructured, this dreadful self-condemnation will haunt you . . . and keep you from the good things you want.'

To my surprise, Muhammad listened to my criticism, pursed his lips thoughtfully, and said, 'Nordness was right. We know this—painfully—and only our program will change things . . . I mean, change the character of the black.'

'What program do you have?' I asked, pointing to the two sets of papers, which seemed determined to isolate the Negro further.

'Self-respect,' Muhammad said. 'When blacks are able to organize things their own way . . . do their own thing . . .' He stopped, fumbled for a concept that apparently he had not adequately formed, and said nothing.

'I know what you mean,' I said. 'And I agree. Negroes must erect their own citadels of self-respect. In all things. All men have to do that. But if you think this means you can run a grocery store on Negro principles, or a factory, or an insurance office, and that you can ignore cost efficiency studies or reporting to work regularly and on time . . . You know, Mr. Muhammad, there will not be special rules for you Negroes.'

'There you miss the whole point,' he said eagerly, as if recovering the strands of thought he had lost. 'We are going to establish enterprises whose primary motive will be to instill self-respect in the blacks who run them and patronize them. Competing with white stores in the neighborhood will be secondary.'

'One hundred per cent wrong,' I said flatly. 'The inescapable motive of every store, black or white, is to earn a profit which will enable it to keep functioning. You establish your Negro store and run it as poorly as I see Negro establishments run, and every Negro in your district will patronize the white store, because it'll be a better store.'

'Will you give our committee a hundred thousand to try it our way?'

'I won't give a committee anything. But if knowledgeable men like you and Cato want to try, I'll lend you the money to get started.'

'My job is not running grocery stores,' he said.

'That's why they'll fail,' I said.

'Then you see no hope?'

'On the terms you suggest . . . no.'

'There will be no other terms,' he said, and on this cold note our discussion of economics ended, but another of more significance started.

The thin man had lit a cigarette, but instead of smoking it as one usually did, he inhaled deeply, closed his eyes, kept the smoke in his lungs a very long time, then blew it slowly out. He took two more such puffs and handed the cigarette to Akbar Muhammad, who inhaled even more deeply, for he had powerful lungs, and ejected the smoke in heavy rings that hung round and yellow in the air.

'Drag?' he asked, offering me the cigarette.

'What is it?' I asked.

'A reefer.' When I showed no recognition, he growled, 'Grass, man. Grass.'

'You mean marijuana?'

'What else, man?'

I started to smile, and he asked belligerently what was so funny about grass, and I said, 'It's seven o'clock in the morning. We haven't had breakfast yet,' and the thin man said, 'You got to get through the day,' and Akbar said, 'We're with friends. We've been talking sense. Let's celebrate.'

I started to pass the cigarette on to Cato, but Muhammad grabbed my arm and asked, 'You not partaking?'

'I don't think so.'

He held my arm and said, 'I told you we were celebrating. Smoke.'

'Yeah, man,' the thin fellow said. 'It ain't gonna stone you, one puff.'

I appealed to Cato, who nodded, so I took a cautious drag on the cigarette, tasted the sweetish smoke, found it both inoffensive and unimpressive, and passed the cigarette along to Cato, who took two deep puffs before handing it to Vilma. In this way the cigarette passed around the circle three times, after which the thin man produced a second, which was used in the same way.

In all, I had about six small puffs of the marijuana, which, so far as I could judge, had no effect on me, but the four Negroes inhaled deeply, held the smoke for long intervals, and blew it out slowly, and since they took three or four substantial puffs to each of my token ones, they were affected in whatever way it is that marijuana affects the human consciousness.

So far as I could see, the cigarettes made them more relaxed, pleasanter, a little more inclined to laugh at the contradictory positions in which they found themselves. Put succinctly, they were more agreeable and I found myself liking them more. For example, Akbar Muhammad grew positively congenial, placing his powerful naked arm about me and speaking frankly, as if our earlier conversation had been a testing and not a true exchange of ideas. 'Mr. Fairbanks,' he said confidentially, 'we are going to press our demands in ways that will startle you—that might turn you off—but we'll get the money. One way or another, we'll get the money, because just like you and your friends in Geneva, the white man has a guilty conscience. He knows that what we say is right. He knows he has defrauded us—that he owes us a perpetual debt—and the white man is smart. He acknowledges the truth, and the truth is that we have a right to compensation. We'll get it, and when we do we'll set up our own stores, in our way, and we'll run them according to the best black principles.'

'And they'll go out of business in three years,' I said with no rancor.

'You're right!' he said. 'The first wave will go broke—every goddamned one of them. And we'll learn from our mistakes. And we'll start a second wave. And in them we'll follow all the rules you've been trying to teach me tonight. And those stores will succeed.'

'So why don't you follow the rules the first time?'

'Because we have got to learn,' he said softly. 'And we have got to learn our way—the way every white man on this earth learned anything. Our own way. All it's going to take is time and money. We have the time. You have the money. And the experiment can be most productive for all.'

'You have some busy years ahead,' I said.

'Indeed we do,' he said jovially. 'For we're going to remake a people, and in so doing, we're going to remake a nation.'

Perhaps the marijuana had touched me more deeply than I had suspected, for when he said this I began to laugh, and instead of his getting angry he laughed with me, then asked amiably, 'What's so funny?' and I said, 'Did you know that for some years I was practically an advisor to the Republic of Vwarda? Yes, I've been working rather intimately with the Negro republics. And in the heart of Africa they said precisely what you just said. "We are going to remake the people, and in doing so, we'll remake the nation." '

'What's so funny about that?' he asked, laughing at the joke he did not understand.

'That Negroes in Africa and Negroes in North Philadelphia should be saying the same thing . . . and for the same reasons.'

'What you're really saying,' he suggested, poking me in the ribs and chuckling, 'is that we're both savages.'

'Don't put words in my mouth,' I cautioned, laughing at his audacity.

The thin man lit another cigarette, and we smoked it as before, and again I took only ceremonial puffs.

Akbar Muhammad, dragging deeply on the aromatic weed, said, 'I suppose you're right, in a way. All black people have the same problem—Vwarda on a national scale, us on a local scale. But it isn't a black problem only. It's the problem of all emerging people. When I was at Michigan State we had one great professor. This cat could see right into the heart of the black man. Big Irishman, educated at Notre Dame. Third team in football. He came from Boston, and when he saw sixteen blacks in his class he interrupted his planned lectures and gave five talks on how the Irish established themselves in Massachusetts. You know what he said? For twenty years every Irishman elected to office in that state turned out to be either a crook or a fraud. Every Irish business failed because somebody stole the cash register blind.

'The Protestants had all sorts of jokes about the Irish, and they were true, but they were also irrelevant. Because in time the Irish learned. They began to elect honest politicians. And they learned to hire honest clerks. And after a couple of generations, America found itself with Jack Kennedy. The patience paid off.'

He reached for the cigarette and took four very deep puffs before passing it on to Vilma. 'In their years of discovery and settling down, the Irish had whiskey to console them. We have marijuana.'

'Be sure that it doesn't have you,' I said.

----•◦•----

It was now nearly nine o'clock, and Vilma said, 'It's time for me to go to school.' In the euphoria that had settled over our meeting, this caused general laughter, and Akbar said in broad dialect, 'When teacher ask, "Where you been, chick?" you gonna say, "Smokin' pot wid de New Muslims." '

I asked Cato, 'Are you a New Muslim?' and Akbar intercepted the question: 'He doan know hisse'f yet. He doan know what he is.'

'I'm one,' Vilma said, not belligerently but with a degree of pride. I had not figured out whose girl she was, but now she rose, went to the door, and said, 'Cato, you gonna walk me to school?' He leaped up to join her, then turned and said to me, 'You better come along.'

We left the tenement and walked slowly down Eighth Street toward Classical High, and as we moved through the Negro neighborhoods we saw many children starting off to school, and I wondered how many of them had been puffing at special cigarettes. There was no way of telling, just as no one could have detected that Cato and Vilma were walking in a rarefied atmosphere in which colors were just a little brighter and sounds more persuasive.

In Muhammad's room I had thought it strange when Vilma asked Cato to walk her to school, but now we entered an especially grubby neighborhood not far from Classical and I began to understand, for here several large groups of Negro girls gathered at street corners to abuse Vilma as she walked by.

'Scab!' one girl of sixteen yelled at her.

'You spend all night fucking with Whitey?' another shouted.

Hideous charges were made against her, but she ignored them, moving closer to Cato as we walked. After we had run the gauntlet, I asked, 'What's this all about?' and Cato said, 'She refuses to join their gang.'

'What gang?'

'Boys mostly. They're the ones that do the killing. Thirty-two murders last year by kids under the age of twenty. The girls are the hangers-on. Corner girls, they're called.'

'They sounded pretty tough.'

'They can get very tough,' he said.

We were now at the entrance to Classical High, in years gone by one of the great schools of America, in which the Irish and German and Jewish boys whose parents had come to this country learned the ground rules that governed life in America. In addition to Latin and patiently taught English, those earlier boys had also acquired an insight into how to manipulate the system of which they were now a part. From Classical, young scholars had left to become heads of industries, authors of good books, chiefs of police departments and professors at universities. Quick-moving Irish boys had become quarterbacks at Michigan and Alabama; studious Jewish boys had become philosophers at Harvard. It was a school of noble tradition, one which had played a significant role in the building of this city and this nation. Today its major intellectual problem was coping with the twenty-eight per cent of its students who could not read; its principal disciplinary problem, preventing rape and stabbing in the halls.

As we approached the school, Cato and I were halted by two policemen. 'Don't come any closer,' they warned us.

'Why not?' I asked.

'Crackdown on adult pushers,' they explained, and when they moved on, Cato told me, 'Lots of trouble in this school. Grown men sneak in to sell the kids heroin between classes.'

As we stood on the corner with Vilma, I had a chance to inspect the famous school; spelling was no longer one of its specialties, for signs scrawled across its façade read: *Join Omaga Phi, Danise Love Fillip* and '*All Power to the Madadors,* and farther along—in red— was the ominous *Death to the Madadors.*

'That's the gang that wants Vilma to join,' Cato said. 'The girls' branch is called the Madadoras.'

One of the girl gangs that we had passed now swaggered menacingly by, whispering threats to Vilma as they went. The police stopped them and a woman officer was called over to search them. She took away four switchblade knives, then allowed the girls to enter the school. 'There's been a lot of cutting in this school,' Cato said.

Now a group of four Negro mothers appeared from Grimsby Street, escorting their daughters to school. In a white community such mothers would not, in the first place, have been accompanying fifteen-year-old girls to school, but even if they had been escorting infants, they would have left them at the corner, once the traffic of the streets had been safely passed. Here, however, the mothers brought their daughters directly to the school entrance, where police could protect them, for in recent months there had been fearful assaults on the approaches to this school.

Since it was now time for classes, we delivered Vilma into the area protected by the police. Cato said goodbye to her and we watched as she made it safely to the entrance, but as she disappeared, a group of three girls passed Cato and whispered so that the police could not hear, 'We gonna get that chick. Nobody ain't gonna rat on the Madadoras and live.' I looked at the girls as they went by, attractive fifteen- and sixteen-year-olds who should have been worrying about history class and boys, but who were obsessed by a death feud which seemed a normal aspect of their society.

'It's nothing,' Cato said as we left the school, but I at least was badly shaken. 'You scared?' Cato asked. I shook my head and went back to my hotel for some sleep.

———————

The days that followed were a phantasmagoria. Mornings and afternoons were spent with Reverend Claypool Jackson's committee discussing Negro economic problems as if Negroes in Philadelphia were old-time Germans or Irishmen with a few specialized problems. Never did we come to grips with youthful leaders like Akbar Muhammad and his New Muslims or with the girl gangs that terrorized approaches to high schools. The toll of drugs, murders and despair we glossed over as if it were not important, but in my mind's eye as we talked were the four Negro mothers convoying their daughters to school, insistent that their girls get an education and remain free of the gangs. I was able to accomplish nothing and prepared my return to Geneva.

In the evenings I entered another world—part fear, part hope— with Cato Jackson as my cicerone. I found that he was dating Vilma regularly, but that she was also dating Akbar Muhammad. How she arranged matters, I never understood, but when she was with Cato she was as delightful as she was pretty. She had an ironic sense of humor, and I judged that if she kept away from marijuana she would do superior work in school. We often had dinner together, and one night I asked her if she was planning on college.

'Me? No . . . no.'

I could see that she did not automatically reject the idea, so I asked her reasons, and with some hesitancy she said, 'For me there's no Mister Wister.'

'Who's he?' I asked.

She inclined her lovely brown forehead toward Cato. 'He'll tell you.'

Perhaps because he was embarrassed, Cato lapsed into broad Geechee, saying, 'This cat, Mister Wister, he b'long white folks' church. Time come for them to sell to mah pappy, he the one that say, "Mo' bettah we give them the church. At heart we all one religion." De udders, dey laugh at what he say. So when de big deal concluded, what you think? Go ahead, give a guess. Mister Wister he come to mah pappy and he say, "Reverend Claypool, we done God a grave injustice this day," and mah old man, Uncle Tom to de bitter finish, he say, "Mister Wister, maybe God have His own purpose. We got a respectable home. We got somethin' to work for." But Mister Wister he say, "Reverend Claypool, I gonna send your boy to college." So he fix it up I get into University of Pennsylvania. He pay all my fees. Das what he do, das just what dis good man do.'

I suspected this to be another Cato put-on, but Vilma corroborated the story. Mister Wister they called him, pronouncing his name in one swift sound—'Swister.' He was a Quaker whose wife belonged to the Llanfair congregation that had unloaded their outgrown city church, and out of a sense of guilt he had given Cato the scholarship to his old university, Pennsylvania. Quarterly he stopped by Sixth and Grimsby to see how his protégé was doing, always pleased to find that Cato was able to hold his own with his white competitors.

'A few more men like Wister,' Cato said in ordinary English, 'and we could hack this deal. But his kind is rare.'

Vilma said she had no hopes of finding one for herself, an idea which I ridiculed. I said, 'A bright Negro girl like you could win scholarships to a dozen colleges. They're scouting for you. To tell you the truth, today it's better to be a bright young Negro than it is to be white. Chances are better.'

'Chances for what?' Vilma asked.

'For really doing something. You get yourself a college education, I'll hire you.'

'Doing what?'

'Working as my secretary—executive secretary, that is—lots of responsibility when I'm away on trips. You'd live in Geneva.'

'Is that in France?'

'Switzerland.'

The word was like magic and I could see it take effect. 'I saw Shirley Temple. She's running for Congress or something now. But in this movie she was a little girl in Switzerland. Do they have Alps in Geneva?'

'Right next door.'

'You putting me on?' she asked. 'You'd really hire me?'

'Hundreds of companies are eager to hire you. Don't you think we know as much about your headaches as Akbar Muhammad knows?'

'No,' she said coldly. 'You think you know? Come with me.'

She led us to a part of North Philadelphia that I had never seen or even heard about. It was an alley called Dartmoor Mews, off Sixth Street and not more than five blocks from Classical High. There were low tenement buildings on either side, and it was filthy with garbage. It was completely ugly, except for the beauty of the children who crowded it.

Vilma picked her way around the holes in the pavement, trying to avoid a group of girls who, in spite of Cato's presence, muttered threats at her. She took us to a squat house that had been occupied in the latter years of the last century by an Irish trolley-car conductor; from it he had sent his son to Villanova. Later it had passed into the hands of an Italian bricklayer; from it he had sent his sons to St. Joseph's, and one had gone on to St. Charles Borromeo to become a priest.

'In those days an Irishman could become a conductor,' she said as she led us up an incredible flight of stairs, 'an Italian was allowed to be a bricklayer.' She led us into an apartment which occupied one half of the second floor; four Negro families shared what one Irishman had rented. It was a dreadful hovel, with stained wallpaper and waterlogged flooring. The bathroom was in a shed on the floor below and was used by all the families.

It was scarcely accurate to call Vilma's group a family. It was a hard-working mother surrounded by six children, whom she tried to educate, doing so alone, for her three husbands had been of no help.

Three consolations kept her operating: Vilma and her two younger sisters were going to be beautiful and would be eligible for exciting lives; Reverend Claypool Jackson was an inspiring preacher who brought God into his big church; and television was better than movies. With these three sedatives she could survive the misery of this alley and the insolence of the Jewish welfare worker whom she had to placate if she wanted her monthly relief check.

'Mama, this man says that if I go to college he'll give me a good job in Switzerland.'

'What you talk? College?'

I thought that in this reply one had the story of what happened to too many young Negroes in America. If they suggested college, or if someone suggested it to them, their peers and even their families ridiculed the idea and hammered at their insolence in 'thinking above themselves,' whereas in Irish and Jewish homes, a child capable of going to college was accorded special consideration, for he was the one who might salvage the family. I remember back in Indiana when I returned to our farm home, from which no college student had ever come, and told my parents that the teachers thought I should try to go on with my education, my mother was overcome with visions of what I might become—minister, lawyer were as far as she got—while my father said that it was every boy's right to get the best education he could handle and that he would help me make a go of it if I really thought I had the brain power. But when I assured Vilma's mother that I meant what I said, she drew back, studied me cynically, then smiled in self-satisfaction because she had penetrated my deceit: no white man helped a pretty colored girl unless he wanted to get into bed with her.

'You forget that college stuff . . . get yoursef a job,' the mother said.

'But he says he'll give me a good job . . .'

'He says! He says!'

———— •••• ————

On Friday morning, February 14, 1969, Vilma left her alley home carrying a comic valentine she intended mailing to Cato Jackson, but it had to be hand-delivered by the police, because as she reached the corner of Grimsby and Seventh, one short block from her school, four teenage girls from the Madadoras caught up with her, formed a menacing circle, and demanded that she join them. When she refused, they stabbed her eleven times with switchblade knives. They were easily apprehended, because when she fell to the pavement they stomped her, kicking in her face and rupturing her lower abdomen, which left blood on their shoes.

This was the tenth juvenile gang murder so far that year, the forty-fourth within the past twelve months.

Cato was studying in the University of Pennsylvania library that afternoon when he happened to see a copy of the *Evening Bulletin* bearing photographs of Vilma and the four young girls, none over sixteen, who had stabbed her to death. He gave a horrible cry, which resounded through the quiet library, then rushed into the street and shouted wildly until some students calmed him and took him home. I was there having a last futile meeting with his father, and it fell to me to try to console him.

I was powerless. During his furious rejection of all his father stood for, he told us in savage words of his love for Vilma, and as he ranted I wondered if he had ever told her. I used every kind of logic I could muster up—that he was young, that he could have had no blame for her death, that such things were senseless, that he must not curse all white men, since in this affair they were not involved, but this last reasoning infuriated him. 'You are!' he stormed. 'Who owns that filthy house she lived in? Who refuses to pay taxes to give us better schools? Who allows dope to be peddled right in the school hallways? The whole system is wrong, and you're to blame as much as anyone else, Fairbanks.'

With a bitterness that allowed of no consolation, he stormed out of the handsome stone manse and raged through the streets. I did not see him again, for I left shortly thereafter to check on the Vwarda dam, but that night on television I did see Vilma's mother. She was telling the reporter, a proficient colored girl, 'I never wanted much for Vilma, only for her to be a good girl, to do what her teachers said. I brought her up careful and even walked to school with her before they got the cops to guard the place. What can mothers do in this city if their children can't walk five blocks to school?'

It was two weeks later that Cato Jackson, Akbar Muhammad and his thin, silent companion backed out of the Llanfair Episcopal Church, their guns ready to fire. For the latter two men, it was an act long planned and daring; for Cato, it was a gesture of desperation, a final rejection of the agony he had been experiencing in so many directions and particularly of his father's supine religious solutions to those problems.

The famous photograph was taken at three minutes to twelve, and within two hours the police had identified the three intruders and had raided the headquarters on Eighth Street, uncovering the cache of guns and ammunition that I had seen. Akbar Muhammad and his silent aide were arrested and charged with numerous felonies, but Cato Jackson could not be found. Detectives maintained a watch at the African Church of Our Redeemer, and much was made in the news stories of the fact that Cato was the son of a minister. Reverend Jackson went on television four times to explain that in these difficult times even the most careful parent was not immune to the tragedy that was engulfing our land. Permissiveness, marijuana, agitation over Vietnam, and above all, the confusions regarding race were just as apt to strike at the Negro family as at the white, and he hoped that white parents who had experienced similar problems with their children would remember him in their prayers. The young Negroes of North Philly listened to this rigmarole and told each other, 'Cato smart. They ain't gonna catch Cato Jackson. You know what I heard? He so smart he can't get a degree at Penn because they ain't but three professors in the whole world smart enough to understand what it is he's studyin', and one of them was Einstein and he's dead and the other two are in Russia. You think Cato gonna let the fuzz nab him? No sir, he smart.'

Following the assault on the church, and half-blinded by the photographer's unexpected flashbulbs, Cato, realizing that the affair had gone poorly and that the police would surely be after him, did a bold thing. Instead of fleeing back to North Philadelphia with Akbar Muhammad, who was certain to be caught, he took a wide circle through the Main Line countryside and wound up back in Llanfair, not three blocks from the church. The garage he had chosen to hide in belonged to Mister Wister, and when Cato saw that the rest of the family was preoccupied with telling neighbors what had happened in their church that morning, Cato whistled to Mister Wister and brought him to the garage.

'My goodness! What are you doing here?' he asked.

'I need advice.'

'I'll say you do!'

'What do you think I should do?'

'I take it nobody was hurt. I can't make head or tail of what the women are saying, and since I wasn't there . . .'

'Nobody was touched. But I suppose the police will arrest us all.'

'I should hope so. It was a most stupid gesture and you've most probably ruined your career . . . for the time being.'

Cato was impressed by the way this man, projected into an affair that distressed him, was so easily able to slow down the tempo and to look at facts as they were. He was particularly free from cant, offered no lectures, simply looked at alternatives.

'What you must do is lie low until the excitement subsides. If anyone had been hurt, I would not say what I'm about to say, but the fact is that you were right in asking the church for reparations. They charged your father a disgraceful sum for the old church. They ought to dismiss at least two thirds of the purchase price. As for the other wrongs done in the past, no amount of reparation would compensate for them, but it wouldn't be a bad idea for our churches to make a gesture of conciliation.'

'You think we were right?' Cato asked.

'Assuredly,' Mister Wister said, and he started making plans to smuggle Cato out of the region, much as his great-grandfather had connived to smuggle Negro slaves through Philadelphia in the late 1850s. He kept Cato in the garage that night, then drove him to New York under the guise of a business trip and gave him the address of a Professor Hartford at Yale University, who could be trusted. From there Cato could easily get to Boston, where they would instruct him on how to slip into Canada. When he bade Cato goodbye at Washington Square, on the edge of Greenwich Village, he said, 'You've pretty well ruined yourself at Penn, so that's finished. If I were you I'd enroll in one of the universities in Canada.'

'How about Europe?' Cato asked. 'Lots of blacks find themselves in Europe.'

As was his custom, Mister Wister stopped, considered this new problem, studied various ramifications, and said, 'That might be a good idea, Cato. You might come home an intelligent man. And God knows we need them!' He shook Cato's hand and asked, as a proper Quaker would do, 'What will you be using for money?' When Cato fumbled with his answer, Wister said, 'I earmarked a certain sum for your education. I wouldn't be averse to having you spend it in Europe. Send me your address,' and with that, he got into his car and drove back to Llanfair, where citizens were convincing themselves that the entire congregation had barely escaped death.

The airport bus deposited Cato at the central newspaper kiosk in Torremolinos, and like thousands of other tourists each year, he wandered naturally down into the sunken bar and found a table at which he could catch his breath and from which he could review the enticing world of which he had so unexpectedly become a part. He was struck by two things: the handsomeness of the young people he saw, and the fact that none was black. 'If this is the capital of the world for young people,' he said to himself, 'they sure ain't got many black constituents in the electorate.' He thought this especially strange since Africa lay only a few miles to the south.

He had not yet ordered anything when a clean-cut young man, apparently French, sat down at his table as if they were old friends and asked, 'What brings you here?'

'The scene.'

'Best in Europe. You got a hotel yet?'

'Nope.'

'I get ten per cent if you stay at the Felipe Segundo.' He handed Cato one of the hotel cards and said, 'Near the beach. Heated swimming pool.'

'What's the general pitch. Any jobs?'

'None.'

'Any way to make a buck?'

'You broke?'

'I got some bread . . . but I'm gonna need more.' The free and easy manner in which the two men, having known each other for less than three minutes, discussed finances and opportunities appealed to Cato, so that he became more relaxed with this Frenchman than he could have been with a white man of similar age from America. 'What's your name?'

'Jean-Victor.'

'Were you in the student rebellion at Paris?'

'Not French,' the young man said. 'But about the extra money. Anybody on the way down mention the Wilted Swan?'

'Nope.'

'It's quite a spot. If you're an athletic-looking young blond from Sweden or Germany, you can drift in there and get yourself pretty well fixed up . . . for spending money, that is.'

'I'm not famous for being blond,' Cato said.

'That might make you especially attractive.'

'Are the ground rules rough?'

'Each man looks out for himself.'

Cato slumped in his chair, studied Jean-Victor, and asked, 'That how you make it?'

'Me? I got a girl . . . we live down by the sea.'

'You pushing for the . . . what's its name?'

'The Wilted Swan? No, it's like my deal with the hotel.' He tapped the card which lay on the table before Cato. 'I earn my bread through lots of different commissions. You like to give the Swan a try?'

Cato kicked his suitcase and said, 'Remember? I don't have a place to stay.'

'Park it.' He called the waiter and told him to stash the bag behind the bar. 'Because with the Swan, you can never tell what might happen. Chances are, you won't need a hotel.'

Later, when Cato told me about his meeting with Jean-Victor, I was astonished at Cato's behavior, as if a wholly new young man had emerged in the brief crossing from Philadelphia to Torremolinos, but he justified himself in this manner: Vilma's death— you ever see a sixteen-year-old girl with her face kicked in?—and the business at the Llanfair church . . . the commitment involved in each instance. 'I was torn loose from every mooring and I truly didn't give a goddamn what happened to me. If the white world wanted me to make my bread at the Wilted Swan, that was okay by me.'

So Jean-Victor led Cato down the main drag and after a short while they spotted the notorious swan, so wilted that it seemed about to fall in a heap on the sidewalk. 'Whoever painted that sign, they ought to pay him double,' Cato said.

He was nervous as Jean-Victor led him through the Renaissance doors and into the darkened bar. He stood awkwardly by the door as Jean-Victor scanned the place, then turned back to him, showing disappointment: 'No one I know. Let's have a lemonade.'

They sat at one of the tables in the center of the bar, and gradually Cato became aware that from the surrounding booths a good many faces that he could not fully see were staring at him, and Jean-Victor whispered, 'This is the best table. Everyone can see who you are.' To Cato's surprise, someone rose in one of the booths and walked across the floor to where he sat. It was a woman, in a tweedy suit, and she spoke in rough, manly accents.

'You from the States?' she asked, leaning down on the table.
'Yep.'

'Give 'em hell. Tear 'em apart. If I were young and black I'd
dynamite the subway. I'm in your corner, kid.' She clapped him
on the shoulder and went back to her table.

After a moment a waiter came up to them and said, 'The ladies in
that booth wish to buy you drinks.'

'Chivas Regal,' Jean-Victor ordered promptly. 'Two.' When the
waiter left, he whispered, 'Those dames are loaded. Order the most
expensive drinks there are.'

'What's Chivas Regal?'

'If you don't like, I'll drink it.'

They sat for the better part of an hour, during which several men
stopped by the table to speak with Jean-Victor, who seemed to
know everyone in Torremolinos, and each of the men wished Cato
a good time during his vacation. Finally Jean-Victor said, 'We'd
better get you a place to sleep. Fellow I was looking for isn't
coming, apparently.'

'Who?'

'Chap from Boston named Paxton Fell. Lots of money. Exquisite
taste. He has a swank place on a mountain back of town. Extra
rooms . . . you know.'

'Not exactly,' Cato said frankly. 'I'm a new boy in town. What
do I have to do to get one of Mr. Fell's rooms?'

Jean-Victor raised his palms upward and leaned forward till his
face was quite close to Cato's. 'To tell you the truth, I don't know.
I've arranged for several young men to take accommodations
at Fell's apartment, and I know they live there for nothing and get
a little spending money to boot. But what happens when the lights
go out . . . who does what to who . . . I really don't know.'

'Sounds adventurous,' Cato said.

'Judge for yourself,' Jean-Victor replied, pointing over Cato's
shoulder.

Through the brass-studded doors had come a gentleman, perhaps
in his early sixties, very tall, very slim, very well dressed. His shoes,
Cato noted, were brown, with extra-heavy soles and the kind of
sewing that men paid real money for. 'I dig those shoes,' Cato whispered.

'Mr. Fell!' Jean-Victor cried. 'Join us.'

Slowly the newcomer surveyed the bar, peering into the various booths and nodding gravely to those who greeted him. Apparently he found nothing more interesting than this table, so with a kind of genteel reluctance, looking elsewhere as he did so, he sat down. Then slowly he turned to face Cato, and after appraising him, said, 'We find very few Negroes in Torremolinos.'

'I saw that on the street.'

'So we are especially gracious in our welcome to those who do come.' He paused for Cato to say something, then said petulantly, 'Come, come. That's a cue for you to explain how you got here.'

Cato was about to mumble something, not knowing what he ought to say, when the tweed-suited woman who had paid for the drinks moved boldly across the room, ignoring Mr. Fell and grabbing Cato by the shoulder.

'My God!' she cried in a shout of triumph. 'It's him!' She slammed onto the table a newspaper clipping of the widely publicized photograph, with Cato, his machine gun at the ready, looking over his shoulder and backing out of the church. 'You're that one, aren't you?'

Everyone in the Wilted Swan gathered about the table while Jean-Victor and Mr. Fell scrabbled for the photograph. Finally Fell gained possession of it, held it up to the light, and compared it to Cato. 'My word!' he finally said. 'An authentic folk hero!' Then, to Cato's astonishment, he leaned across the table and kissed Cato twice. 'You were a genius,' he said admiringly, 'to pick the Episcopalians. Laura here is an Episcopalian'—he indicated the tweedy woman—'and they're all filthy rich. To take money from them is like being an ecclesiastical Robin Hood. You amazing boy! Did you have to flee the country?'

'Tell me about it!' Laura said, ordering drinks for everyone. 'This is so exciting, I feel like singing "La Marseillaise." ' In a loud, clear whistle she offered a few bars of that revolutionary song, then asked, 'Did you gouge any money from the skinflints?'

While the free drinks were circulating, Jean-Victor grabbed off two whiskeys, downed them rapidly, and as he left, whispered in Paxton Fell's ear, 'You will remember that I brought him to you.'

The discussion continued for an hour and a half, at the end of which Laura invited everyone to her place for dinner. She lived in a castle west of Torremolinos, furnished with antiques she had found in rural farmhouses on her excursions through the mountains. The atmosphere of each room had been so tastefully re-created in the old style that one expected Don Quixote to come marching in for his dinner. The chairs were lumbering old master-pieces in oak, no two alike, and the dining table was thirty feet long and eight wide, made of planking hand-hewn more than four cen-turies ago. The fireplace was enormous and burned logs cut in eight-foot lengths, requiring two men to heft them, and the lights were so constructed that the electric bulbs were invisible. En-crusted candles guttered in the drafts which moved though the castle.

'Come in!' Laura shouted, alerting her servants, and while her guests found places about the table, she spread the notorious photo-graph before them and demanded that Cato explain what it was all about, and as he looked around the circle of faces, he imagined that these self-indulgent expatriates seriously wanted to understand the revolutionary forces that were sweeping their homeland.

———————

By the time dinner ended, at one-thirty in the morning, Paxton Fell was satisfied that in Cato Jackson he had found a literate, well-mannered young man of extreme vitality and charm. He looked upon this exotic Negro as other Caucasian men look upon pretty Chinese girls, as a challenge, and when the guests started to depart he took Cato by the arm and said, 'Jean-Victor told me you had not chosen a place to stay. I have ample room.' And he led Cato to his Mercedes-Benz convertible, a car with many special features, and when Cato had sunk into its ample leather he reminded Fell, 'My bag is still at that bar in town.'

'Forget it!' Fell said. 'I'm sure I can find some extra pajamas and a toothbrush. We'll get your luggage in the morning.'

With considerable skill he drove the Mercedes down from Laura's castle and onto the main shore road, where cars from all nations were screaming along at seventy and eighty miles an hour; a good many people were killed in Torremolinos and the surround-ing villages each year, for the most daring drivers in the world frequented the broad, sweeping roads and insisted upon testing their cars and their nerves. Fell drove at eighty, then slowly ap-plied the brakes and turned left up a steep hill that led to an area called Rancho de Santo Domingo, a private domain guarded by a stucco wall, uniformed security patrols and German police dogs.

Inside the walls Cato saw a series of spectacular mansions, one challenging the other, and at the edge of the settlement was Paxton Fell's house.

It was low and neat, whereas the others had been somewhat opulent, but it was apparent that a fortune must have been spent on the landscaping and the touches of exquisite decoration. 'I want you to get your first glimpse of the place from the terrace,' Fell said, leading Cato to a garden overlooking the Mediterranean, which lay far below. There was a partial moon, which cast arrows of shimmering light across the water, and in the distance, not far from the shores of Africa, a dimly lit British freighter plowed its way slowly toward Alicante to pick up a cargo of oranges.

'This is to be your home,' Fell said, leading Cato inside. The large room into which they stepped was a refreshing change from the castle, for it contained not one extravagant note, except perhaps three magnificent bovedas that occupied most of the ceiling.

Cato had never before seen these Spanish domes, which were constructed of bricks laid in overlapping circles, each round projecting inward from the preceding, until at last, in some mysterious way which the workmen would not explain, a final group of bricks was set in place, closing the opening at the top and locking the whole together. During the month he lived at Paxton Fell's, he never ceased to wonder at these lovely bovedas, for they formed a kind of heaven, their inverted domes lacking only stars and a moon.

When Cato was telling me, some time later, about his arrival in Torremolinos and how he had made his acquaintance with Paxton Fell, I asked him frankly, 'What did you have to do to earn your money?'

He told a bizarre story. 'I was interested, too, because I didn't know any more than you did. First night, nothing. Second night, nothing, and I was beginning to get worried. Nothing but the best food you ever tasted, prepared by two Spanish cooks, both men. And of course, each afternoon we went to the Wilted Swan and sat at one of the tables till nearly midnight, when we had dinner. I think Fell wanted to show me off . . . like he wanted the others to see he could still attract a live one.

'Third night we had Laura and her gang in for dinner. It was outstanding. Lot of noise, lot of wild chatter. When I go to bed Paxton Fell comes into the room with me and I think: Here it comes. And you won't believe what he wanted! For me to get undressed and stand in a white marble niche where there should have been a statue but they hadn't got around to it yet. He had rigged a special spotlight to shine on me, and as I stood there, he said, "Like a Greek statue . . . like a great masterpiece from Mycenae." He kept repeating this, and then he did the damnedest thing you ever heard of.

'From his coat pocket he took a feather—a feather carved from pure silver. Where in hell he found it, I'll never know. And he came over to the niche where I was standing and with this damned feather he tickled my balls until I got an erection. Then he stood back and gave me some more jazz about the Greek statue and the Mycenae bit. Then he came up again and tickled some more, and finally he said with great conviction, "Oh, Cato! With that instrument you are going to make a score of girls supremely happy." And that was it.'

'You mean, that was his bit?'

'With me, it was. Now he did have some friends—all men—and he insisted upon showing me off to them, and one of them got so excited when he saw me standing in the niche that he busted into my room later that night and crawled into bed with me and gave me a sensational blow job. And another night Fell brought in Laura and her gang of women and they admired me for half an hour, and it was then I figured I better get to hell out of there.'

———◆———

When Cato decided to quit Paxton Fell's pleasure dome, he encountered no recriminations from his sybaritic host. 'You're a splendid young American,' Fell said approvingly as they dined together the last night. 'You have a brilliant future—if you stay away from machine guns—and it's been a privilege knowing you.' In the morning Fell drove him into town in the Mercedes and said, in parting, 'Remember, you'll always be welcome on the hill. If you care to stop by now and then, you can leave word at the Wilted Swan.' He bowed deeply, then drove off, and before the car had disappeared around the first bend, it was doing seventy.

Once more Cato stowed his gear with the bartender—this time with four pairs of expensive shoes given him by Fell—so that he could tour the town to find lodgings, but the spirit of Torremolinos had so infected him that before taking action he decided to rest awhile, and he lounged at the bar, inspecting the new batch of tourists. It was now April and livelier groups were arriving, including many who were determined to swim no matter how cold the sea. As he sat in the sun, the only Negro within the area, he contemplated his position and found it rather promising: In a pinch I can always live at Fell's . . . and pick up spending money too. His crowd thinks any black man who can use a fork exotic, so if I need additional cash I can get it from his friends. The fat guy who got into bed with me . . . the other one from Chicago . . . or the guy with the poodle. On the other hand, I'm sure I could get some kind of job at the castle. Those rich dames really dig the black boy. They like to have him around—sort of a toy, dangerous but fun. Cato, you got it made. What I mean, you got a safety valve.

Even in his thoughts he fell into Geechee: I judge Mister Wister gonna keep sendin' that long green. He got a evil conscience—not for hisself, for dem udder ofays—'n he good for bread, man, he good for bread.' He shook his head in incredulity at the prospect of Mister Wister's sending him a regular check, then smiled at the security this gave him. Course, I can't go home till that warrant for my arrest cools off. Maybe one year, maybe two. So I'm stuck in Spain, and there couldn't be a better place. No, there could not be a better place for exile.

He leaned back and let the warming sun hit him in the face. When he opened his eyes he saw a squad of beautiful Scandinavian girls passing, and he said softly to himself, 'Man, this is livin'.' But the sight of the girls forced him back to a contemplation of his real problem, and he thought: I have a feeling homosexuality is not for me. I just don't dig it—they wanna make horses' asses of themselves . . . For me, straight is better—maybe not better, but it keeps things a little cleaner. What I really need is to find me a chick for the long haul. If I'm gonna be here a year, I better find me a chick who's gonna be here a year too.

He knew it was inevitable that the girl would have to be white; there were no black ones. No problem. In Torremolinos to be black was an asset, because it made you unique. Girls were on the make; they were in exile, too, and some of them would also be looking for the long haul, and that kind of white girl had a built-in curiosity about black men. I calculate it's gonna be easier to get me a chick here than it would be in Philadelphia, he thought. Content with this generalization, he snapped his fingers: But the problem's the same the whole world over. How you gonna find one with money? I can support me, but I sure as hell can't support the chick too. He then took refuge in a saying he had learned in North Philadelphia: 'A man don't have to be dumb. He can look around. He can take his time.'

Satisfied with these tentative conclusions, he left the sunken bar and started walking idly about the town. When he passed the Northern Lights he was tempted to go into the bar to see what was happening, but he refrained for a good reason: Stay clear of that joint. Them Swedes is gorgeous and they go for black boys, but they're all down here cheap tourist rates and there ain't a ruble in the lot. Farewell, Northern Lights.

At the Brandenburger he saw a large group of attractive girls, probably down on a special tour from West Berlin, and he was tempted to join them, for they were obviously interested when they saw him standing by the hotel entrance and he knew from others that German girls liked blacks, perhaps as a means of outraging their parents, but he was afraid of them. Yes, he was afraid of what they would have done to him in 1941 had he been a black in Germany. They were enticing people, the Germans, and the young girls were luscious, but they were not for him.

He liked the French hotels. He liked the strangeness of the language, the men who spoke like Charles Boyer, the classy girls who always seemed to have a ribbon or a hemline that was provocative. He could go for a French girl but he had heard that they brought even less money than the Swedes. He therefore lounged in the sunlight before the French hotels, admired the women he saw, then continued on.

By the time he completed his circuit of the town, he had thus formulated four working principles: no more men, no impecunious Swedes, no Germans under any circumstances, and probably no Frenchwomen. He feared he might be narrowing his field unwisely, but he felt that he had time. With the cushion of safety provided by the regular checks from Mister Wister, he could afford to drift for a couple of weeks. He'd start dropping by the Arc de Triomphe in the evening to see what the action was providing.

In this mood he saw ahead of him the street sign of a bar he had not noticed before: a huge wooden revolver, Texas style, with the words THE ALAMO. That's all I need, he thought ruefully. A Texas bar. Them Ku Kluxers. He was about to pass by when he happened to spot through the open door one of the most beautiful blondes he had ever seen. She looked like a Swede—not too tall, not too heavy. She had champagne-colored hair, worn naturally, so that it bounced about her lovely round face. Her eyes, her teeth, her complexion, the formation of her body were all perfection, and he stopped in admiration: A boy could bury hisse'f in that all night and wake up in the mornin' screamin' for more.

He stood at the bar door for some moments, simply looking at the Scandinavian. She appeared to be working in the place, for she moved among the American soldiers, shoving drinks, and they all seemed to know her, for the bolder ones made grabs at her legs as she passed. Such advances she repelled with solid swipes of a towel and a hearty laugh.

'You can come in, you know,' a tall bearded American said. 'Always providing you got money.' The man extended his hand and said, 'Name's Joe. I run the place. Come on in and have a beer on the owner. He waters the stuff.' He led Cato into the small drinking area and introduced him to six or seven of the soldiers. 'They come down here from Sevilla,' he explained. 'The girls are mostly Americans.'

'The Swede?' Cato asked, sipping his beer.

'Norwegian. Name's Britta. Come on over, Britt.'

She interrupted her duties and walked trimly over to the two men, extending her hand to Cato and saying, 'Hello, my name's Britta.'

'And from the looks of things—you're his girl?'

'I am . . . in a way of speaking.'

'I could cut my throat. Son,' he said, turning to Joe, 'you are to be congratulated. In fact, you can even be jubilated. Can I buy you both a beer?'

'Today, no. You're the guest,' Joe said. 'But we'll mark it on the book.'

'And when we do that,' Britta warned, 'we never forget. The handsome black American . . . owes us two beers.' She smiled at him in her frank uncomplicated way and moved on.

'So far, she's the winner,' Cato said admiringly.

'When the circuit is completed, she's still the winner,' Joe said.

They were still talking amiably when one of the soldiers suddenly jumped up and shouted, 'My God! That's the guy who shot up all those people in the Philadelphia church!'

A group formed about Cato, plying him with questions about the massacre at Llanfair. The comments were inquisitive rather than accusatory, and one fellow said, 'Is it true there were corpses up and down the aisle?' And in the corner another whispered, 'I don't want no jigaboo shootin' up my church.'

'Wait a minute!' Cato protested, but he was powerless to stem the tide of admiring yet fearful comment. The GIs, respectful of anyone who could handle a gun, treated him with caution, one telling the other, 'I read about it. You saw the pictures. Hundreds dead. Somebody told me he was hiding in Torremolinos.'

'Knock it off!' Joe yelled, banging on the bar. 'I read the stories too. This guy and his committee simply asked for some money. Some shots were fired. But nobody was hit. As a matter of fact, later on, the church did turn over some money . . . voluntarily.'

'But isn't there a warrant out for his arrest?'

'There is,' Cato said.

'Hope you beat the rap,' a girl called from a corner, and the excitement subsided.

But now Cato was a member of the group. He had bucked the Establishment. His picture had been in the paper as a young revolutionary. The fuzz was after him, and that made him automatically one of them. Britta put a stack of rock-and-roll records on the machine and the great good sounds of youth began to fill the bar, the ear-splitting sounds that few people over the age of twenty-five could tolerate, and through the terrifying crescendo of noise which he liked so much, Cato could hear two GIs explaining to a new arrival, 'He's the one who shot hell out of that Episcopalian church in Philadelphia. You saw the photos.' But above the noise and the chatter of aimless conversation Cato remained preoccupied with the rhythmic movements of Britta as she placed bottles of Coca-Cola on the various tables.

———•◦•———

He returned to the bar each day, mesmerized by this Norwegian girl. Both Britta and Joe realized that he was infatuated with her, and one evening Joe said, 'Why don't you two have dinner? I'll tend bar.'

So Cato invited her to select a restaurant, and she chose a small Swedish place that served good food and they talked aimlessly, and finally he took her hand and said, 'You know I'm bowled over by you,' and she laughed and told him in her lilting accent, 'But I'm Joe's girl.' He said, 'But suppose you weren't Joe's girl? Could I . . .' and she said, 'You're handsome and you're intelligent. I think any girl would like to know you,' and he said, 'But you are Joe's girl?' and she nodded.

When they returned to the bar Cato told Joe, 'I've been making wild love to your girl,' and Joe said, pointing to the soldiers who were waiting for Britta, 'Get in line, buddy.' Then he added, 'That girl in the corner said she'd like to meet you . . . about the church,' and he led Cato to a corner table, where he said, 'Cato Jackson, this is Monica Braham. Ask her where she's from, you won't believe the answer.' With that he left them.

Later, in this same bar, seated at this very table, Cato told me, 'I came into that room in love with Britta. Of that there can be no question, because she was the best-looking girl I'd ever seen. But when Joe left me standing there, looking down at Monica Braham, all the muscles seemed to run out of my legs, because this was a girl so special . . . something was eating her . . . we blacks have a sense about people in trouble . . . and when she asked, in that cool knowing way of hers, "Shooting up any churches lately?" I knew she intended to hurt me—that her future questions would be even tougher, uglier. So I sat down and said, "Where you from?" and she said, "Vwarda," expecting me to go into a big Africa bit. Now I knew all about Vwarda. In North Philadelphia you hear one hell of a lot about Vwarda this and Vwarda that—you'd think it was the new Athens—but I said, "Where's that?" and she smiled at me real cool and said, "As if you didn't know, you cunning bastard." '

Monica and Cato stayed in the bar till four in the morning. With the echoes of the music still ringing in their ears, they walked arm in arm down the hill to the sea front and she took him into the apartment, where he saw the two big beds, and she explained that one belonged to Jean-Victor—'The Pimp? I met him'—and the other to Joe, and when she said that Britta shared the latter bed, it seemed as if the Norwegian name had come from another world, one that he had known decades ago.

Then she indicated the tartan sleeping bag and said, 'This is where I live,' and they stood there for an electric moment, after which she said quietly, 'I'm sure you'll get into the bag with me sooner or later. We might as well make it sooner.' And she proceeded to strip, and when she stood before him, slim and pale, as beautiful as the Greek statuary that Paxton Fell spoke about, Cato knew that she was the most compelling girl he would ever meet. He leaped at her, thrust her into the sleeping bag and joined her in the wildest love-making of his imagination, at the end of which they both fell asleep, exhausted.

When Jean-Victor came in with Sandra toward five, he looked down at the floor and asked casually, 'Who'd she bring home with her tonight?' but when Britta and Joe returned after closing the bar, Britta looked at the sleeping bag, smiled and said quietly, 'It was bound to happen.'

V §

YIGAL

A man who changes his country is like a dog who changes his bark . . . not to be trusted.

On the basis of fact alone, you could deduce the theory that wherever you have x number of Jews, you will have x plus 2 committees.

I have never understood this adulation of Moses. I calculate that in the forty years he wandered about the desert, not knowing his ass from his elbow, he could have accomplished great things. For example, if he had led his people just thirty yards a day in the right direction, he would have landed them not in Israel but in England, and all this confusion would have been avoided.

God is not dead. He simply refuses to get involved.

The other night I brought my girl friend home to meet my parents. They liked her but they couldn't stand me.

Every man over forty is a scoundrel.—Shaw

Following World War I, the countries of Europe absorbed a million five hundred thousand refugees. Following the Greek-Turkish war, Greece absorbed a million four hundred thousand refugees thrown out of Turkey. Following World War II, the countries of Europe had to adjust to thirteen million refugees. Following the India-Pakistan war, the two sides absorbed upwards of fifteen million refugees. But in the wake of the Arab-Israel war, the Arab countries proved themselves totally incapable of absorbing a few hundred thousand refugees, for which they were themselves largely to blame.

A rose-red city—'half as old as Time.'—Reverend John William Burgon

In this country we get stuck with taxes, but in the old country we used to get stuck with bayonets.

The use of a university is to make young gentlemen as unlike their fathers as possible.—Woodrow Wilson

Worse than war is the fear of war.—Seneca

One of the historical highlights of this century has been the stubborn insistence by the Arab nations that they did not lose the Six-Day War. By girding their loins, adhering to a simplistic interpretation of facts, and bolstering up each other's flagging resolve, they accomplished a miracle. They simply announced to themselves and to the world, 'It was an Arab victory,' and as a result they were obliged to attend no peace conference and make no adjustments. They accomplished in the world of will what they could never have accomplished in the world of battle, and their victory was the greater because it was spiritual and not physical. We had better all accommodate ourselves to what has become a fact: the Arabs won the Six-Day War and must be dealt with as victors.

It was the saying of Bion that though the boys throw stones at frogs in sport, yet the frogs do not die in sport but in earnest.—Plutarch

Look after the other man's belly and your own soul.

The Arabs can lose every war, if only they win the last one. The Jews have gained nothing if they win all the wars but lose the last one.

Everyone complains of his memory, and no one complains of his judgment.—La Rochefoucauld

If you insist upon booking passage on the *Titanic*, there's no point in going steerage.

History tailgates.

EACH year, in various nations around the world, a select group of young people nearing the age of twenty-one is faced with a dilemma, which though gratifying, is nevertheless most perplexing. They must sit down, judge alternatives and make a choice that will determine their future. The choice, once made, is irrevocable, and if wrongly made, can produce unhappy consequences that will permanently damage them.

Of course, the above could be said of every human being in the world: sometime around the age of twenty-one he or she will make a series of crucial choices which will delimit the future, but usually one is not aware of this. The young people of whom I speak are painfully aware of what they are doing, because in one brief moment of time they must select the nationality to which they will owe allegiance for the rest of their lives.

Because of accidents of place of birth—or the peculiar decisions of their parents at that time—they find themselves legally entitled to two or even three different passports. In the years of their childhood they may travel one year on a British passport, for example, the next on an Italian, as convenience dictates. But at the age of twenty-one they must make up their minds and state formally, 'From this date on I shall be a British subject,' or a German, or an American.

I have known several such multiple-passport people, the most dramatic being a lovely Swedish girl living in the unlikely kingdom of Tonga in the South Pacific. Her parents were both Swedish, so she was entitled to a Swedish passport. She had been born in

London, so she could claim British citizenship. She had lived in Tonga most of her life, and was eligible for Tongan citizenship. And when, some years after her birth, her father became an Australian, she was included in the legal maneuvering and came away with a passport from that country.

I met her when she was twenty, a beautiful, fair-skinned young lady living among the dark Tongans and exciting the imagination of all young men who passed through her island. She talked with me often about which of the four passports she should choose when she became twenty-one; I advised the Australian, since she would presumably live within the influence of that nation, but in the end she surprised me by opting for Tonga, and her reasoning introduced me for the first time to what later came to be known as 'the disengaged generation.' She said, 'I don't want to belong to any large nation with large plans. I don't want the responsibility of either England or Australia. Let them solve their problems in their own ways, without involving me. I don't want to be a Swede with the schizoid problem of living next to Russia, so that I must insult America, yet trying to be a free nation, so that I must defend myself against Russia. I want to be a Tongan. Nobody hates us. Nobody envies us. Any of the great powers can invade us by mailing a penny postcard, addressed Chief of Police, Nuku'alofa.' And damned if she didn't drop all her other passports and keep the Tongan.

Psychologically, the most interesting case was that of a young man whose history I followed from birth—indeed, from before birth. Thanks to a curious set of circumstances, he was legally entitled to two passports—United States and Israel—and as he matured he grew increasingly aware that one day he would be required to state which of these two nations he would elect as his permanent home.

It happened this way. Many years ago, when I was still working for Minneapolis Mutual, peddling funds throughout the midwest, I spent one campaign in Detroit, where I wasted two weeks trying to sell an investment program to one of the merchandising experts at General Motors. He was an extraordinary man, an Odessa Jew named Marcus Melnikoff; around the automobile industry he was called with some affection 'Mark, our mad Russian,' it being more fashionable in Detroit to be known as a renegade communist than as a Jew. He was a genius in the management of ideas and men but was having much difficulty with his daughter, a pretty senior at Vassar with headstrong ideas and numerous admirers from Yale and Amherst.

I remember Melnikoff's interrupting me one afternoon in 1949 when I was trying to explain the merits of Minneapolis Mutual: 'You're lucky your kid's a son. Don't never have daughters. Zowie, what a headache!' Seeking to ingratiate myself, I asked why, and he exploded: 'Because they grow up and want to get married. Last summer, a tennis bum. Never earned a kopek in his life. Last autumn, an exchange student from Indonesia. Where the hell is Indonesia? This winter an assistant professor at Mount Holyoke with radical ideas. My wife keeps asking, "Why can't you settle on some nice, respectable Jewish boy?" '

Several days later, when I dropped by to see Melnikoff at his home in Grosse Pointe, I found him awaiting a visit from his rabbi. 'It's embarrassing to have that goddamned Rabbi Fineshriber park his Ford in our driveway,' he growled. At first I thought the make of the car was the problem, since his job at General Motors was to fight Ford, but he explained, 'When the social committee was meeting to determine whether my wife and I were educated enough to be permitted entrance into Grosse Pointe, our sponsors passed us off as fugitive Russian scientists. That idea seemed rather exciting, so we were admitted, but there has always been a distrustful faction which suspects we're Jewish. Now this goddamned Rabbi Fineshriber begins driving up, and everyone knows.' I was startled at such a statement and was about to question him, when I realized that he was making fun of the system he had outsmarted.

When Rabbi Fineshriber arrived, he turned out to be a plump, jovial man of about fifty, as extroverted in religion as Melnikoff was in salesmanship. He felt no embarrassment at having me overhear what he had come to say and welcomed my questions, so we had a pleasant drink together, waiting for the arrival of Mrs. Melnikoff, an ebullient woman in her middle fifties. When she joined us, she warned that the rabbi would have to go over his admonitions a second time when Doris came back from playing indoor tennis with her latest admirer. 'Non-Jewish, naturally,' Mrs. Melnikoff said wryly.

Rabbi Fineshriber said, 'I oppose heartily your plan for taking Doris to Israel. She'll meet Jewish young men . . . some with great potential. But there's a danger. Word will circulate very quickly concerning your purpose in coming to Israel. They'll hear about your husband's fortune. The suitors will begin to gather, and I want you to promise me this. Whenever one of them proposes, as they will, Doris must say rapturously, "Oh, David! All my life I've wanted to live in Israel." When he hears that she intends to live there instead of bringing him to the United States, you'll see his interest evaporate. I said evaporate. It vanishes.' He waved his hands violently back and forth across his face to indicate total abolishment.

I asked, 'You mean the Israeli young men see American girls principally as passports?'

'For a gentile, you express yourself very well,' he replied. 'And with a girl as pretty as Doris, the urge to get to America and her fortune will be . . . well, accentuated.'

Now Doris returned from her tennis, a tall, attractive, dark-haired girl in her early twenties. It seemed ridiculous for Rabbi Fineshriber and her mother to be worrying themselves about getting her a husband, for I judged she could have pretty nearly anyone she wished. Melnikoff must have guessed my thoughts, for he said, 'Mr. Fairbanks may think it strange that with a girl like Doris we should be so concerned about her marrying a Jewish boy.' I noticed that Doris showed no embarrassment at such discussion before a relative stranger; apparently it had occurred before. 'But when you've been a boy in Odessa, you see Jewish-gentile relationships in a different way. I support the idea of taking this long-legged colt to Israel for some training.' He leaned forward and slapped his daughter on the knee.

'So what you are to do, Doris,' the rabbi instructed her, 'is to say, as soon as the boy proposes, "Thank God, I've always wanted to live in Israel." ' He snapped his fingers in an afterthought: 'Even better, say, "I've always wanted to live on a kibbutz." That will really scare hell out of them.'

There was much discussion of Israel, which Rabbi Fineshriber knew favorably from having led three pilgrimages of his synagogue members there. He liked it, understood why Jews might want to settle there, and hoped to return often in the years ahead. But as a practical man who also knew Detroit and its surroundings, he preferred the United States and felt that a Jew had about as good a chance in Michigan as he did anywhere in the world. He especially wanted Doris Melnikoff not to make a fool of herself; three times in the last year she had come close to doing so with unworthy gentile men, and he saw no reason why, having escaped that nonsense, she should now fall into an equally bad Jewish trap. As I left, still unsuccessful in my attempt to peddle mutual funds, I heard the rabbi saying, 'Doris, if you really want yourself a nice Jewish boy, why don't you inspect my sister's son? Thick glasses, failing grades at Stanford, thirty pounds overweight and vaguely addicted to Karl Marx.' In Boston I had once known an Irish priest who talked with his parishioners in this same joshing way.

Doris Melnikoff did go to Israel, she did fall in love with a nice Jewish boy, and she did tell him, 'All my life I've wanted to live on a kibbutz.' The hell of it was, he replied with great emotion, 'I'm so relieved. I was afraid you'd want me to go to America and work with your father.' He was Yochanan Zmora, a scientist teaching at the technical school in Haifa. When he took Doris to see that marvelous city, perched on a hill at the edge of the Mediterranean, with the Crusader city of Acre to the north and timeless Megiddo, the scene of Armageddon, to the southeast, she knew that this was what she had always hoped for, and on the spur of the moment she married him to share in the excitement of building a new land.

I was with her father in Detroit when Mrs. Melnikoff's cable reached him. 'My God! Married to a Jew named Zmora and living in Haifa?' He looked it up in the Bible and got it confused with Jaffa, so that for the whole time his wife remained in Israel, buying furniture for the newlyweds, he imagined her and Doris in a much different part of the country. By cable he employed a private detective in Tel Aviv to find out who this Yochanan Zmora was, and the man reported: 'Reputation excellent. Professional ability excellent. Personal appearance excellent. Born an English citizen under name of John Clifton, Canterbury, Kent, England. Honors in science at Cambridge. Emigrated to Palestine in 1946. Assumed Hebrew name Yochanan Zmora in 1947. I find no adverse report on this man except that he tends toward the left in Israeli politics.'

Melnikoff showed me the cable and asked where he should fly to, Jaffa or Canterbury? I asked him why he didn't stay in Detroit and wait for further information from his wife, but he snapped, 'I didn't make a million dollars staying in Detroit. I have one rule. When there's trouble, fly there. It never does any good, but it impresses hell out of the boss.' Against my judgment he flew to London, hired a Rolls-Royce, and tootled down to Canterbury, where he met the senior Cliftons, a nervous, thin-lipped pair who were appalled by his obstreperous Russian mannerisms. He was relieved, however, to find them as disturbed about their son as he was about his daughter, and when he asked, pointing at Mrs. Clifton with his teacup, 'Frankly, what can you do about headstrong children these days?' he won the Cliftons' sympathy. Mr. Clifton was a precise and pettifogging lawyer; in a burst of enthusiasm he invited Melnikoff to his club, a dreadful place with dark ceilings, dark walls, dark chairs and dark drapes. Melnikoff said, 'This is very attractive,' and Clifton said, 'Yes, well . . . mmmm, yes. It costs rather more than one would normally wish to pay for frivolity. But it is rather nice, isn't it?' After two inconclusive days Melnikoff flew back to Detroit, and when I tried to reopen our discussion about his investing with us, he growled, 'Get the hell out of here. Who has time to invest money with his daughter in Jaffa?'

Two years later my phone in Minneapolis jangled and the voice of Marcus Melnikoff shouted, 'Come down immediately. Business.' As he drove me in to Detroit from the airport he ordered, 'Set me up a fund—one hundred thousand dollars—favor of my grandson.' When I asked what name, he frowned and said, 'Now we face the problem. When we heard that Doris was pregnant, Rebecca flew to Israel and brought her home. We insisted the kid be born under the American flag—ensure him an American passport. We talked Rabbi Fineshriber into registering him as Bruce Clifton, using his father's legal name in England. Of course, in Israel he had to be registered as Yigal Zmora.'

'This all sounds silly,' I said. 'What name shall I use?'

'Not so silly,' Melnikoff said gravely. 'If you had been a Jew in Russia, trying to escape—a matter not of preference but of life— you'd have appreciated it if some loving grandfather had thoughtfully arranged for you to have two names . . . two passports. When he grows up, let him choose. United States or Israel. In the meantime, use the name Bruce Clifton. I'm sure he's going to be an American.'

Thus the boy grew up with two names, two personalities, two homelands. His father, now Dr. Zmora and dean at Israel's well-regarded scientific university in Haifa, intended Yigal to be an Israeli citizen, finding his place in the national life; but Grandfather Melnikoff, his Russian enthusiasm intensifying with the years, intended Bruce to be a good American, to attend an American university, and to make his way in American society. The struggle never became overt; certainly from what I heard, it did not scar the boy. He spent most of the year with his parents in Haifa, but each summer he flew to Detroit so that he would be familiar with that home. Dr. Zmora and Grandfather Melnikoff competed for his affections in permissible ways, and although at that time I had not yet seen the boy, I was told that he was becoming an admirable young fellow.

It is strange that I never met him on my visits to Detroit, for I continued to sell funds to his grandfather. After I transferred over to World Mutual, I also spent some time in Haifa conducting feasibility studies of Israel's oil business, in the course of which I came to know Dr. Zmora and his wife Doris rather well, since he represented the Israeli government in our discussions. Under his tutelage I became familiar with Haifa and was always gratified when, after work in areas like Sweden or Afghanistan, I once more approached this city of steps, this very ancient seaport that had known the Prophet Elijah, the armies of the Pharaohs, the chariots of King Solomon, the violence of the Crusaders. Haifa became one of my favorite cities, for in its harbor I could see Carthaginian longboats and Roman triremes bringing legions to subdue Jerusalem. With the Zmoras as guides, I went as far east as Lake Galilee, which carried connotations of a graver sort.

And all the while I was vaguely aware of a boy growing up with this weight of history bearing down upon him ten months of the year, but with the vigor and allure of industrial Michigan attracting him the other two. Once as I trekked over the Galilean hills with his parents I asked Doris if she ever regretted having chosen Israel, and she cried, 'Oh no! For me the ordinary events of life form the adventure. Marriage, having children, seeing how the world around you develops. That's what's important. So I'd have been just as happy living in Detroit, but no more so. In Israel, however . . . well, you do get something extra.'

'And your son?'

'He'll make up his own mind,' Dr. Zmora said as he looked across the historic battleground where Saladin had driven away the Crusaders.

———•◆•———

In the spring of 1956 World Mutual sent me to Haifa to make an actual investment in the new oil refinery, and naturally I cabled Yochanan Zmora to meet me at the airport, for I would be conducting my negotiations with him, and as I stepped out the door of the El Al plane I saw, waiting on the tarmac below, Doris Melnikoff, her husband, and a charming little boy of five wearing English-style shorts and a *kova tembel,* the little white beanie favored by young men in Israel; it was supposed to remind them of the improvised hats worn by freedom fighters in the 1948 War of Independence.

When his parents ran to meet me, asking what news I brought from Detroit, the child stood aloof and waited till the greetings were completed. Then he marched politely forward, extended his hand, and said, 'At this end of the airline I am Yigal, at the other end Bruce.' I shook hands with him and returned his bow, and thus we launched a warm acquaintance, marked by periodic letters from Haifa to Geneva. Written first in large capitals, then with constantly improving conciseness, they came from Yigal bearing requests that I bring him, on my next flight, those important little things which he could not obtain in Israel.

Later I would receive similar letters from Vwarda, but those would come from a spoiled and impulsive girl who expected any man she knew to bring her whatever she requested; it would never occur to her to enclose money to pay for things she ordered. In Yigal's letters there was always a money order, signed by him and not by his father. I could visualize his parents telling him, 'If you want something, save your money, go to the post office, and send the check to Mr. Fairbanks in Geneva.'

What did he order? 'I see in a report from Berlin that the Japanese have invented a new-style radio tube. Can you please to bring me four? Don't mail them, because then I have to pay duty.' When he was older he asked for popular music from the Phillips catalogue in Amsterdam and a circular slide rule. At another time he wanted to know if I could find him a copy of a new atlas just published in Moscow, but first he needed to know the price. When I reported that it was an adult publication and cost more than twenty dollars, he canceled his order, but on my next trip I brought it along as my present to a fine young fellow. When I handed him the package, big and flat, he knew of course what it was and tears filled his eyes. He kept his hands at his sides and would not take it.

When I tried to force it on him, he said, 'I was unfair. I made you get it for me.' I thought this over for a moment, then said, 'Yes, you did put the idea in my head. But I brought it to you not for that reason but because your grandfather told me you were becoming a good geographer.'

'Did he say that?' Yigal asked gravely.

'Yes. When I was in Detroit.'

'Well,' the boy said reflectively, 'when we were in the hills of Mount Tabor he did get lost and I showed him the way back.'

'So it's a legitimate gift,' I said, and he rubbed his fists into his reddened eyes and accepted it.

By the time he reached fourth grade in the Haifa schools, it was recognized that his IQ stood well above 150, but his teachers found in him none of that excessive shyness which often marks the boy of high intelligence. Both his English father and his American mother had no-nonsense ideas for his upbringing. He was expected to behave, but was encouraged to participate in family conversation. Topics from English, American or Israeli history were discussed, as were his problems in school. The moral obligations of the individual were constantly explored, as were art and religion. The Zmoras found it difficult to take seriously the oppressive theology then popular in Israel and took no pains to hide their contempt for the ridiculous behavior of the orthodox rabbis.

Dr. Zmora and his wife also saw to it that Yigal got knocked about by children his own age. They encouraged him to play with groups of tough young immigrants from Morocco and Iran and dismissed any complaints he might have about rough handling. They were pleased when he organized some of these immigrant boys to build radio sets in their basement, and they put up the funds when he wanted to buy a tent so that half his friends could camp out on the Galilean hills and communicate by short wave with the other half remaining in the city. They were amused when military police came to their house to report, 'Your son is jamming our radio frequencies.' The police were astonished when the culprit turned out to be a boy of nine.

Yigal loved Haifa. It was a city of vivid contrast: a knockabout waterfront with ships from all parts of the world, a crowded commercial area that had been the focus of merchants for thousands of years, and the magnificent highland of Mount Carmel with its famous Catholic churches and its heavy concentration of refugees from Germany. What pleased him most, however, was the historical quality of the region: a few miles away stood caves which anyone could climb into and which had been inhabited for fifteen thousand years. In their dark recesses he could see steps that the ancients might have carved. There were also lost cities, mentioned in the Bible as having been of some importance, and a marvelous subterranean burial ground with some of the coffins still in place and accumulations of dust in which you could find flasks of Egyptian glass.

The people of Haifa were just as interesting as the land. One day Dr. Zmora showed Yigal a newsstand with papers in eleven different languages; among the families who visited their home it was customary to meet people who spoke seven or eight languages; most spoke at least three. Food of all kinds was available, and among the older people national dress from many parts of the world was still worn, so that a boy growing up in this city was made aware that the earth contained many people who were unlike himself.

Yigal was not a big child; in fact, he was somewhat undersized, but he had such good coordination that he was not at a disadvantage with his playmates. In running up and down the myriad flights of stairs that characterized Haifa, he was quicker than they, a wiry little fellow with dark eyes and light complexion. He loved games that required a combination of speed and endurance, for he could move quickly and thus neutralize the larger boys who had the advantage of greater force.

It was natural, therefore, that he would like soccer and be good at it. 'That boy could make himself into a terrific forward,' friends of the family had said in Canterbury one summer when the Zmoras were visiting their English family. In Haifa his skill was also appreciated, and before he was ten he was playing with boys considerably older, for he contributed to team play, and while he did not have what sportswriters refer to as 'a lust for the jugular,' he did have a strong desire to win and ideas as to how this could be accomplished. 'When you kick him the ball,' a teammate told me, 'he's good at passing it back.' No boy could give another higher praise, and when teams were being formed he was chosen promptly. This habit of associating with older boys would play a major role in his life.

His main interest, however, was not sport but electronics. When he was nine I brought him a Heathkit from the States, which he assembled into a first-class radio receiver, and when the components which he ordered from Europe were hooked in, he had a system of professional quality with which he talked to all parts of the world. Once when I brought him some special gear from Germany, he threw out the stuff it was replacing and within a few minutes had the new set assembled. I nodded my approval and started to leave, but he caught my arm. 'Wait! Didn't you guess what I had in mind?' He adjusted the verniers on his dials and within minutes was speaking with an amateur in Detroit; this young man called Marcus Melnikoff on the phone, and soon Yigal and I were talking to him.

He became so proficient in electronics that when he was fifteen his older associates, who were now discharging their military service in the Israeli army, enlisted his aid whenever signal corps problems arose, and in a short time he was more skilled than they in using and maintaining military communications. On one of the high hills in Mount Carmel there was a barracks which Yigal frequented; there, with his friends, he tore down government radios and relay stations, reassembling them with such improvements as he judged they needed, and in the summer he accompanied some of his buddies on their maneuvers, handling their communications for them. He had, of course, taught himself Morse Code, but his major contribution came from his knowledge of what made the new developments in electronics work.

His parents were aware of both his intellectual interest in science and his personal involvement with the military, and since like all Israeli boys he faced three years of military service, they judged that it might help if he identified his field of specialty early and perfected himself in it. They were not therefore alarmed when they discovered that they had in their home a premature soldier, 'our para-trooper,' they called him, but the joke was so cerebral that they stopped trying to explain it to their friends. When I visited the oil project in late 1966, Doris pulled the joke on me, and I said, 'He looks too young to jump,' and her husband said with a grimace, 'I told you to forget that would-be witticism,' so in self-defense she told me the whole story of her para-military son, and I asked, 'Aren't you afraid?' and she said, 'Fear is an aspect of twentieth-century life. Aren't you afraid?' and when I reflected on the various things I saw around the world—famine in India, black-white revolt in America, reassessment in Vwarda—I had to admit that I was.

'Not excessively,' I said. 'I still retain hope.'

'So do we,' Doris said, and when her wiry, confident son of fifteen joined us, I could see that he felt the same way.

———•◆◆•——

So much for Yigal Zmora. What of Bruce Clifton?

In the summer of 1956 Jewish friends of Marcus Melnikoff had warned him that from what they had heard in Washington, there was bound to be war between Israel and the Arab states. 'Better get your daughter out,' they advised.

He had sent urgent letters to Haifa, warning Doris that she must bring her family to Detroit until the future was secure, but this she would not hear of: 'If as you say, war does come, Yochanan will be needed in the scientific branch, and for me to desert him in order to find safety in America would be unthinkable. So put such foolishness out of your mind.'

Melnikoff had wired back insisting that the boy, at least, be flown to Detroit, to which Doris replied, 'I know Yigal very well, and if we forced him to flee Israel in time of crisis, he might be emotionally scarred. But that's beside the point, because I don't think a team of horses could drag him away right now. You see, his gang is playing at soldier and they've laid plans as to what they must do if trouble strikes.'

When Melnikoff received this letter he showed it to me and snorted, 'Good God, that boy's five years old. They must be out of their minds.' He conscripted me to drive him to the airport, and without any luggage, flew off to Israel. Two hours after his arrival he had persuaded the Zmoras to let him take Yigal to America until the crisis passed. Six hours after that he and Bruce were on their way back across the Atlantic, and I was waiting for them at the airport when they arrived.

Bruce came down the steps first, a slim, well-behaved boy of five wearing a *kova tembel* to proclaim his citizenship. Recognizing me, he walked gravely forward and bowed. 'We had a splendid trip,' he said in a clipped British tone.

In spite of his age and small size, his grandparents enrolled him in the Grosse Pointe school as a first-grader, and he adjusted easily to American ways. When, in late October, war did erupt as Grandfather Melnikoff had predicted, the family tried to keep knowledge of the matter from Bruce, but that was impossible. On television and in conversation with his friends at school he followed the course of the war with an almost adult concern, and was quietly gratified when his nation triumphed. After the re-election of President Eisenhower, whom his grandparents had supported with substantial contributions, he asked, 'Now can I go home?' It was decided that he had better finish that year in the Grosse Pointe schools, for, as Melnikoff told me, 'It's not likely they have any schools as good as this in Israel.'

As a matter of fact, in later years it was this problem of schooling which caused the most serious friction between the two portions of the Melnikoff family. Grandfather Melnikoff felt that since he had the money, and the entrée, Bruce ought to be educated in America, but Doris insisted that her son attend school with his peers in Haifa. When the argument was laid before the boy he solved it in a surprising manner: he told his grandfather, 'I like America, but compared to Haifa, your schools are so very bad I'd imperil my education.' When Melnikoff flew to Haifa to look into the matter, he found that Bruce was right; he had been lucky enough to gain entrance to the Reali School, one of the best in the world, where Israeli boys of ten got an education about equal to what boys of eighteen were getting in America. 'Of course,' I pointed out to Melnikoff when he discussed the comparison with me, 'in America nearly every child goes to high school. In Israel about one out of twenty-five makes it. Reali ought to be superior. It doesn't have to bother with the clods.'

But in 1965, when Bruce was fourteen, Grandfather Melnikoff would listen to no further argument; he insisted that Bruce attend school in the United States and enlisted my support to convince his parents. On my next trip to Haifa, I told them, 'Marcus is right. American law demands that when a child like Yigal is born with dual citizenship . . .'

'The child can opt for whichever citizenship he wants . . . at age twenty-one,' Doris said. 'I looked it up.'

'Apparently you didn't look far enough,' I proceeded, 'because what you say is only partly true. The child does elect at age twenty-one, but he is eligible to do so only if he has had five years of schooling within the United States.'

'Is that correct?'

'I'm not positive about the exact number of years required—that's what your father told me.'

'Father gets crazy ideas. We'd better check into this,' she said.

We drove to Tel Aviv, where an official at the American embassy had the exact law on his desk: 'Any child born overseas . . .'

Doris interrupted joyfully. 'That doesn't apply to us. Yigal was born in Detroit and that makes him a citizen.'

The clerk confirmed this: 'Any child physically born in the United States, regardless of the citizenship of his parents, is irrevocably an American citizen.'

Having heard this, Doris would bother with no more arguments, and we returned to Haifa. But when she reported her findings to her father in Detroit, he wrote her a thoughtful letter, sending me a copy in Geneva:

Dear Doris,

You and the bright young man in the embassy read the law one way, I read it another. Since you're a college graduate, you're probably right. But I went to a much tougher college than you, the offices of the Russian secret police, and they taught me something. So I went to the office of the United States Immigration Service and I looked at their book, and it says there that children like Bruce have to have five years of their education in the United States if they want to claim full-fledged citizenship when they're twenty-one. Now maybe this doesn't apply to Bruce. Maybe I'm being unduly cautious. Maybe if I consulted the top lawyers here at Pontiac they'd agree with you and tell me I was being needlessly prudent.

But I am not consulting high-priced lawyers. I am consulting all the Jews who fled Odessa after the pogroms, all the dispossessed who rotted in prison camps after the last war, all the Jews who are still trying to get out of Russia. They are the real experts in nationality law and they cry out to me, 'Melnikoff, if there's any way on God's earth to safeguard the passport of your grandson, do it.' I can still remember the heavenly joy that filled our house in Odessa when we finally got that blue slip of paper, and I remember the terror that possessed us when we found that your Grandfather Menachem's name did not appear. Bravely he sent us on by ourselves, to prosper in a land he would never see. In the next pogrom he was murdered.

I want Bruce to get his schooling now . . . immediately . . . the next plane maybe . . . so that when some damned fool in 1975 makes out our blue slip, his name will be on it.

Love from your father,
Marcus Melnikoff

The appeal was too strong for the Zmoras to resist; Dr. Zmora conceded, 'I suppose Yigal ought to know America as well as he knows the Galilee. Perhaps his future does lie there.' So the boy was loaded onto an El Al plane and shuttled back to Grosse Pointe.

Luckily, the Melnikoffs located a private school which had too few boys to field a football team and which therefore specialized in soccer. Bruce was the youngest member of the team and in many ways the best. At fourteen, a small boy with the reflexes of a coiled spring, he helped his school defeat teams from much larger institutions and was thus brought into the mainstream of both his school and his new country. When one of the Detroit newspapers carried his picture as all-state forward—there being practically no schools in the state which played soccer—it was a kind of confirmation. Bruce Clifton was well on his way to becoming an American.

School had one curious effect on him. His fellow pupils were mostly gentile, and for the first time he began to understand what it meant to be a Jew, for as he told his roommate, a gentile from Grosse Pointe, 'In Haifa everybody's Jewish. It never occurs to you that there could be anything else—except of course Arabs, and they're just as Jewish as we are. The Arab-Jewish trouble is more political than racial.'

But the fact that he was a soccer star did not mean he was exempt from the normal prejudice of an American private school. He learned that the school had a quota and that he was lucky his grandfather had influence so that he, Bruce, could occupy one of the cherished Jewish spots. He was also warned that certain of the colleges he might want to attend had de facto quotas. 'They don't put it in the catalogue, you understand,' one of the other Jewish boys explained, 'but they just won't take too many Jews. I suppose they can't.'

'That's no problem to me.' Bruce laughed. 'Where I'm going to college my father is dean and everybody's Jewish.'

But there were other problems, inescapable ones. When the school had a dance, Jewish students invited Jewish partners and stayed somewhat to themselves. Also, Bruce had great difficulty keeping his mouth shut where the excellence of the school was concerned. He was apt to say, 'At the Reali in Haifa we studied this kind of foolishness when we were ten.' He made the comment so often that teachers got wind of his ridiculous boasting and cautioned him about it, whereupon he wrote to Haifa for the course outlines he had studied at age ten and proved that what he had said was right. Israeli schools were at least three years ahead of American ones, but at this point Mr. Melnikoff took his grandson aside and said, 'A sensible man never brags about two things. How lovable his first wife was and how good his last school was. Shut up.'

So then Bruce turned to discussions of military life in Israel and told how girls little older than the ones in this school were soldiers and how he had trained with one of the army units and had been in charge of their communications.

'I think he's smoking hash,' one of the soccer players said after an especially exciting yarn about being three days in the Negev desert, but at that same moment Bruce was telling his grandfather, 'I find these American boys awfully young alongside the kids I knew in Haifa. You know the difference? They can't do anything. They're city kids. Put them ten miles out in the country, they'd be lost.'

Nevertheless, Bruce Clifton found himself becoming each day more American, and he was not entirely unhappy with the change. His grandfather took him to the Pontiac proving grounds, where even though he was too young to have a driver's license, he was permitted to try out the new models and roar them at eighty miles an hour over simulated highways. His grandfather told his business associates, 'It's pretty clear the boy's decided to live here the rest of his life. He should, because this is where he belongs.'

But Bruce was far from making a decision. Each summer he flew back to Israel, and as soon as he saw the sun-swept hills of the Galilee, or accompanied his older friends on their maneuvers in the Negev, he felt himself drawn tremendously toward the Jewish state. His two younger sisters also attracted him to Israel; he liked the way they fitted in, their lack of pretense or affectation. Young men in Israel were not much different from young men around the world, but the young women were something quite new and he found he liked them much more than their American prototypes.

'You haven't met any first-class American girls yet,' his mother argued. 'Wait till you go to college and see what they have waiting for you at Vassar and Smith.'

'I'm going to look into that when I get back this year,' he had told her in the late summer of 1965, but the next year proved no more conclusive than the preceding one. He still found no American girls he liked; he still bored his friends by telling them how much better the school in Haifa was; and he still outraged them with his accounts of military maneuvers in the desert. The only thing that changed was that his grandfather installed in their home in Grosse Pointe a sensational radio station with a retractable antenna, and when his schoolmates saw how proficient Bruce was with the equipment, and how he knew operators across the world, they began to wonder if perhaps he had been telling the truth about his experience with the military.

Then came his excursion to the Red City, and everything was changed.

———— •••• ————

Children in Haifa sang a song which struck terror in the hearts of their parents. It was called 'Ballad of the Red City' and told of a midnight expedition in the Negev. When Doris Zmora first heard her son Yigal singing this song quietly, whispering the words,

> 'I am a man.
> I am going to the Red City.
> I am marching boldly to the east . . .'

she cried, 'Yigal! You must never sing that song again. Never!'

He laughed at her fears, and two days later was caught singing the provocative song again. This time his mother summoned his father, and Dr. Zmora said, 'Your mother's right. Don't get that song into your blood.'

'Why not?'

'Because it leads to death. Meaningless death. And any death that has no meaning is a terrible thing.'

'I'm not afraid.'

'It's not terrible to the one who dies . . . only to those who are left behind.'

But Yigal kept singing the song to himself, as did many other young people throughout Israel, and one morning in the summer of 1966 he was waiting in his yard in Haifa when a black automobile drove slowly past, carrying two young men, one of whom nodded gravely to Yigal as the car passed on. Without creating suspicion, Yigal slowly finished what he was doing, went indoors, grabbed a jacket, and wandered aimlessly down the street. His young sister Shoshana met him on her way home and noticed the jacket, thinking it strange that he should be carrying it on so hot a day. She turned to look in the direction her brother had gone and saw him jump into a black car that had apparently been waiting for him, but when she got home she said nothing. However, when Yigal did not show up for dinner, the truth came to her like a light flashing in the darkness.

'He's gone to the Red City!' she cried. 'I know it!' There was an exultation in her voice that terrified her parents, for they knew that she had guessed right.

At that moment Yigal and his friends were approaching the historic city of Beersheba, at the northern end of the Negev. Without slowing down, they sped through the section of that city where the camel market was held each Thursday and entered upon the stony desert that separated them from their goal.

When they were well into the Negev they turned east over a road that one of the young men had scouted the previous summer, and after a while, as they had anticipated, it ran out, so they cut across the desert itself, driving without lights and speaking only in whispers. To the north there was a good road, leading more or less to where they wanted to go, but similar adventurers had learned at grievous expense not to use that road, for it led to death.

Finally they halted the car, descended, and began to walk purposefully to the east, so that before long they had left Israel and had entered the Jordanian sector of the Wadi Arabah, that great and desolate depression which cuts south to the gulf. They moved swiftly across the emptiness, for they would be most vulnerable if enemy rifle fire were to catch them there, and in time they lost themselves in the safety of low rambling hills.

Now they had to depend upon the excellence of their maps, for a wrong turn might throw them either into enemy arms and certain death or into some cul-de-sac from which they would be unable to reach the Red City. Their maps were good, and toward two in the morning they checked off the various signs which assured them that they were on the way to the city.

They now instituted a rule of total silence, and the two older boys produced revolvers, which they held before them as they crept through the grass. They had proceeded in this manner for about an hour when they faced a steep, rugged slope festooned with boulders, any one of which might be hiding an Arab guard. It was on this slope, when Jewish boys suddenly came upon a waiting patrol, that most lives were lost, for it was understood by both sides that infiltrators trying to reach the Red City would be shot on sight, and would in turn shoot down any guards who tried to stop them. Sixteen Israeli boys had been killed in the last two years playing this appalling game; more than three hundred had negotiated the perilous terrain, whispering to themselves as they crept along,

> 'I am a man.
> I am going to the Red City.
> I am marching boldly to the east . . .'

At the end of a tiring climb this particular trio reached a small plateau, and in the dusky moonlight they could see that some yards ahead it terminated in what would probably be a steep cliff leading down to a valley below. With his revolver the boy in the lead indicated how he proposed to guide them across this plateau, and silently they fell in line behind him.

Wriggling like snakes across a desert, they crept through the shadowy darkness, and as they came to the edge of the cliff they caught their breath, for below them unfolded one of the supreme sights of the world—the ancient rose-red city of Petra, its towers and promenades shining in the dark night like dusky stars of immortal radiance.

'Oh!' Yigal gasped.

They lay there for some fifteen minutes, drinking in the grandeur of this city, carved into the face of the cliff years before the birth of Christ. It was deserted now, a red metropolis that once had housed a half million people, but its ghosts still lingered, for in the pale moonlight the three Jews could see the vast temples, the curious treasury, the seats of administration and all the other appurtenances of power which the builders had once enjoyed. It had been like no other city on earth, for none of its buildings had stood free . . . by itself. All had been carved from standing rock, so that the back of each continued to be that living rock. It was a city eternally coming into being, never completed. In the age of St. Paul it had commanded all the territory north to Damascus, but it had perished for lack of water. So dry did the atmosphere become that erosion had damaged none of the buildings; they stood as they had two thousand years ago, filling the night with majesty.

'I have seen the Red City,' one of the young men said, and with these words he constituted himself a Jew apart. Many sang of making the perilous journey to Petra but only a few risked it, for if they were detected at any point of the way, dogs were set upon them and they were tracked down and shot.

'I have been to the Red City,' Yigal whispered in the night, but as he did so, a pair of Arab guards patrolling the heights against just such an incursion approached. Closer and closer they came, on a course that would require them to step upon the huddled Jews. Yigal saw with horror that his two friends had their revolvers ready to fire, but at the last minute the Arabs turned aside to look down into the city below.

'Nothing here,' one said, and they passed on. When they were well out of hearing, the leader waved his revolver in the dim light and they started back down the slope, crossed the Wadi Arabah and found their car in the Negev.

There was no jubilation on the ride north, for each knew how close he had come to death. They did not conceive of themselves as heroes who had accomplished an Odyssean voyage, but they did think of themselves as Jews who were compressed on all sides by avowed enemies and who felt an uncontrollable urge to visit a forbidden city which had become for them a symbol with meaning so vast that it could not be expressed in words.

By the time Yigal reached home, his family had agreed, after much passionate discussion, that no one was to refer to his absence. The car dropped him at his home about three in the afternoon and he sauntered nonchalantly into the house. His mother greeted him casually and his two sisters were studious in their indifference. At supper his father spoke only of the university, but when Yigal had gone to bed and was nearly asleep he heard his door creaking open. It was Ruth, the older of his sisters, and she whispered, 'What was it like?'

'It's there,' he said, and she kissed him fervently on the cheek.

That winter, when he was again Bruce Clifton at his school in Detroit, some of his more daring classmates began experimenting with marijuana. They were conspiratorial about it and invited him to join them. 'It's exciting!' they assured him. 'Boy, you see visions like you never saw before. And sex! Stand back, Errol Flynn, because here I come!' When he indicated that he wished no part of their frolic, they asked, 'You chicken?'

Then June 1967 erupted, and when the stories filtered back to Detroit, there was no further question of his being chicken.

————•◆•————

By mid-May it had become apparent to Bruce that the Middle East was not going to escape war.

He and his grandparents had followed the collapse of civilized relationships with a kind of horror; they could not believe that U Thant would dare to behave as he did; they could not believe that Gamal Abdel Nasser would take the risks he was taking. 'He must know,' Bruce said at dinner the night the Gulf of Aqaba was closed to Israeli shipping, 'that our army can defeat his at any time.'

'How can you feel so confident?' his grandfather asked.

'I've seen our army.'

The regular junior-year examinations, coming as they did when Egyptian pressure was at its height, were an ordeal; Bruce had the subject matter well mastered, but he could not attend to abstract questions when the real questions of life and death were being decided in his homeland. On the morning that he left his grand-father's house to take the examination in mathematics, the radio carried reports from Damascus, boasting that the Syrians were go-ing to cut right through Israel, slaughter everyone they encoun-tered, and push the remnants of the nation into the sea. The Syrian spokesman specifically said, 'We shall bomb Haifa from the face of the earth.'

When the exam was over, the last in the agonizing series, Bruce took one of his classmates aside, a Jewish girl, and said, 'At six o'clock tonight—now remember, at six, no sooner—I want you to call my grandfather and tell him that I stopped by your place after school to discuss the exams. You must convince him that I am there having dinner with you.'

'You want me to lie for you?'

'You must.'

'Where will you be?'

Bruce looked about him, then said quietly, 'Can I trust you?'

'You know you can.'

'I'll be in Israel.'

The girl stiffened as if an electric shock had coursed through her. In a flash she comprehended everything and realized that she was being asked to become a conspirator for a noble cause. She said nothing as Bruce explained that in his family, people kept their passports up to date and that when he came to America each autumn he had a round-trip plane ticket. From a leatherette folder he produced the two imposing documents and satisfied her that he was telling the truth.

'I'm driving to the airport right now, catching a plane to New York, and at seven I'll be in the air for Israel. My grandfather's a smart old geezer, and if he doesn't hear from me, he just might guess what I'm doing, because he's as worried about Israel as I am. I figure he'll be getting suspicious about six o'clock, and I don't want him telephoning the airport police in New York.'

So the plot was laid, and although his co-conspirator was not a pretty girl, nor one that he had ever dated, he kissed her, and she asked, 'Are you going to join the army?' and he said, 'Most of my friends are in the army and I help them with the radio bit.' He kissed her again, jumped into his Pontiac convertible, and sped off to the Detroit air terminal. At seven, as he had predicted, he was flying out of New York bound for Israel.

He landed mid-morning on Friday, June 2, to find his homeland caught up in what he later described in a letter to his grandfather as 'a terrible reality. No one panicked. No one made empty boasts. But everyone knew the dreadful threats that had come from Radio Damascus. What stupefied me was that King Hussein, on whom we relied for some kind of balance, had joined the chorus and was shouting stupid things. We knew it was to be war, and we knew that if we lost we would be slaughtered. They told us so. So we decided not to lose.'

He caught a *cherut*—a private car operating as a taxi on a set run—and drove north to Haifa, where his parents were both astonished and relieved to see him; they approved of what he had done and said that at such times a family ought to be together. 'I was prepared to see them, and their quiet courage,' he wrote to his grandfather, 'and I was prepared for the tense excitement that gripped Haifa, but I was totally unprepared for what happened when I met my two sisters, for suddenly it dawned on me that when Radio Damascus cried that everyone in Haifa was to be slaughtered, it was Ruth and Shoshana they meant, and without being able to control myself, I burst into tears.'

He had arrived in Israel on Friday, the day of worship, and although his family avoided synagogues, on this night Dr. Zmora said, 'I think we might go to *shul*,' and they went as a group. Later that evening Yigal established contact with his older friends who were in the army reserve. He had gone into the center of Haifa to that public square where the Carmelit, the underground funicular, starts its climb up to the top of Mount Carmel, and at the open-air café he met three of his gang. They were delighted to see him, but the air of hushed expectancy which gripped the whole city operated there, too, and they kept their voices low lest their neighbors at the other tables think them afraid or excited.

'It's got to be war,' they told him.

'Why aren't you at the front?' he asked.

'The front? Everywhere's the front. They haven't called us yet because there isn't room to absorb us. We're waiting.'

June nights in Haifa can be exquisite, with the dark whisper of cedars on the hills and the echo of the sea along the waterfront. Lovers climb hand in hand up the long flights of stairs, while the babel of many languages lends a counterpoint to the fundamental Hebrew which most speak. But on this Friday night the city was trebly beautiful, for people on the edge of doom were trebly attentive to one another.

Then, without sirens or horns, ordinary passenger cars began circulating through the city, both in the alleys by the waterfront and on the broad boulevards of Carmel. The driver was often a girl, never in uniform, and the men she drove were in civilian dress too. The car would stop, motor running, and the men would move out quickly, but never at a run lest they excite panic. They would go from door to door, almost in silence, knock once or twice, and nod to the man who had been anticipating their call. Oftentimes not a word was spoken, just the knowing nod, the grim smile of recognition, the closing door and the messenger on his way back to the car, which would then carry him to another quarter of the city. Israel was moving quietly, without a single word on the radio or in the streets, into total mobilization.

It was about nine o'clock that lovely spring evening when one of the cars pulled into the plaza where Yigal was drinking orange soda with his friends. They saw it coming and could guess its import as soon as they spotted the girl driver. She pulled beside the curb, and four men sifted through the crowd. When one of them reached Yigal's table, there was a flash of recognition, but neither the messenger nor the civilian soldiers spoke. The man simply looked at them and nodded. When he was gone the young men quietly rose and walked unostentatiously from the plaza, except that as they went, one of them turned back to Yigal and asked, without speaking a word, if he wanted to come along, and he did want to, very much, and he rose as casually as if he were going to a movie and followed them into the darkness.

Mobilization plans for this particular unit called for them to requisition one of the *cheruts* and twenty gallons of gasoline from a dealer at the edge of town, and to motor down to the desert capital at Beersheba. They were to leave immediately, without goodbyes, and would find that the necessary gear had been assembled in the south. From there they would pretty surely head westward into the Sinai, for their specialty was foot-soldier support for heavy tanks, the kind of operation in which communications were vital.

As they drove south that clear, still night Yigal thought: The difference between an American and an Israeli is that my grandparents are wailing in Detroit, asking, 'Why has he done this thing?' while my parents in Haifa, when they find I've gone, will ask, 'What else could he have done?'

It was not yet dawn when their car reached Beersheba, to fall in line behind a thousand others that had assembled from all parts of the nation, and the military depot to which they reported was so agitated that Yigal's unauthorized presence was not noticed; after all, he was not much younger than many of the troops, and his civilian appearance corresponded to theirs, for it was a civilian nation that was girding for war. When it became apparent that their unit was not going to accomplish much that night, they fell asleep in the car, a bunch of casual young men who might have been waiting for a soccer game.

By noon on June 3 the unit was more or less formed up, and the officer in charge, a civilian-dressed major known to everyone as the Sabra, for he had been born in Israel and spoke only Hebrew, looked into Yigal's car and asked, 'Who's this?' and Yigal's friends explained, 'He's a communications nut. He can fix anything.' The Sabra studied him and asked, 'You acquainted with our gear?'

When Yigal nodded, the major said, 'We could use him,' and in this haphazard way Yigal Zmora went to war.

By midnight on June 3 the unit had moved, by commandeered taxicabs, to a point within two miles of the Egyptian border, but this measure was misleading, for the part of Egypt which touched Israel in this region was merely the Sinai, that vast and empty wasteland which ought to have served, throughout history, as a natural buffer between Egypt and her neighbors to the east but which never did. Instead of forming a wall, it formed a garish, terrifying highway which for the past four thousand years had consumed camels and armies and which in recent decades had developed an appetite for tanks and airplanes.

During the long, hot day of June 4 Yigal and his companions waited; they cleaned their guns and he fiddled with the radio gear, unable to test it properly because of the enforced silence. He did monitor messages coming from the Sinai, and although they were in code, he deduced that there must be considerable tank movement in the area. 'I wonder what it's like facing a tank?' he asked his buddies. 'We'll find out,' they said stoically, 'because those tanks of ours aren't going to hang around protecting us. When the flag drops, they're off to Cairo.'

It was known generally among the foot soldiers that once the war began, they were on their own, because victory depended not on their safety but on the speed with which the tanks could slash into Egypt. 'We'll be at the Suez Canal two days after war begins,' one of Yigal's companions predicted. 'We're going to move so fast . . . well, you keep that radio going so they can keep track of where we are. Because we're on our own.'

The unit had some trucks geared for desert warfare, but not enough. They also had some taxicabs with extra tires and racks for gasoline cans, but not enough of them either. 'You couldn't claim we were a flashy unit,' Yigal's friend said. 'The good gear is up front, where it's needed. But you know what I think? I feel absolutely confident that before nightfall of the first day we'll be riding in Egyptian equipment.'

In the hot afternoon they asked Yigal what the United States was like, and he said, 'Not bad. Big roads. Air conditioning. I liked it, but the schools are sort of sloppy. You don't learn much . . . not if you've been to a good school in Israel first.' None of his listeners had been to high school, so they couldn't judge.

'You think you might like to live there . . . permanently, I mean?'

'You could do a lot worse.'

'The girls?'

'Funny thing. Something I never realized before. But when you're in the United States, people expect you to be a Jew. Over here—who gives a damn, except maybe the Egyptians, and only some of them. My parents almost never go to synagogue. But in the United States . . . You were asking about girls. Every girl is either Jewish or not Jewish. Big deal. Besides, any soccer player in Israel could make one of their teams.'

Night fell and there was silence. From the Sinai, not a sound. Pale light showed nothing moving, and the men fell asleep, but toward morning there was a steady sound of airplanes. Everyone prepared for an attack from the Egyptians, but none came, and shortly before dawn the word was passed, 'Move out,' and the motley collection of cars and trucks revved up and started westward toward the border, but they had gone only two miles when they were ordered to pull off the road, and they sat in dust, amazed and somehow terrified, as a convoy of tanks sped past with every apparent intention of crossing the border ahead. Even when the young soldiers saw these monsters standing only a few feet away, they were awed by the tremendous power, but when they heard them rushing past, collapsing the world with noise, they understood for the first time what war might be.

'Form up!' the officers of the ground units shouted, but when the column started moving again, everything was different. Two minutes ago it was mobilization; now it was war.

It was daylight when they reached the border and halted, which seemed a ridiculous thing to do, for obviously the tanks had already penetrated deep into Egyptian territory, but final orders were missing, so they waited, and soon they saw a stream of planes overhead and at first took them to be Egyptian. 'Hit the ditch!' the officers yelled, but before Yigal could leave the communications truck, someone else shouted, 'Israelis! Israelis!' and the men cheered.

They waited at the border for about two hours, during which they heard nothing and saw nothing, but at eight in the morning a motorcyclist roared up with instructions that would turn them loose, and for the second time Yigal had a taste of what war could be, for the messenger was a girl—about twenty, very broad shoulders—and somehow she seemed more a human being than the men, and when she wheeled in the dust and sped back toward Beersheba, Yigal found himself shouting, 'Good luck!' It was as if she were going into battle, not he.

'On to Cairo!' someone yelled, and everyone took up the cry. The motley convoy swung into action and at maximum speed crossed the border and entered that vast desolation in which God had once handed down to the children of Israel His commandments on tablets of stone.

From the speed at which the convoy traveled, Yigal supposed they were trying to reach Cairo by nightfall, with no expectation of encountering hostile Egyptians, for throttles were jammed to the floorboards and no account was taken of bumps or dangers in the road. They had penetrated about forty miles before the war became a reality; ahead of them, flaming fitfully like a dying torch, stood a burned-out Egyptian tank. The men cheered as they sped past, and Yigal was surprised to note that no one even so much as fired a shot at the tank.

But by mid-afternoon the situation changed considerably. For one thing, the terrain was much rougher. For another, an Egyptian aircraft appeared in a wild and futile strafing attempt. 'That pilot must be drunk,' one of Yigal's companions said. 'I could fly a plane better than that, and I've never been in one.'

'Look! He wasn't drunk. He was scared.' Another soldier pointed to the horizon where two swift Israeli jets appeared from the other side of low mountains. With hideous speed they swept through the sky and closed upon the bewildered Egyptian. It wasn't a fight, merely a shooting exercise, with first one, then the other Israeli plane running at the doomed Egyptian, who dodged and twisted before exploding in the air. Yigal and the men cheered.

It was about dusk, at the close of an unimpeded dash across the Sinai, when the column approached the western mountains and located a cleft named on the maps Qarash Pass. At a signal the trucks halted and the soldiers dismounted to look at the terrain ahead. Like all men, they experienced the delusion which mountains create: 'If we could just get to the top of that ridge, we could see all the way to the Suez.' Attainment of the ridge became an end in itself.

The Sabra gathered his lieutenants about him and said, 'Common sense says there's got to be Egyptian tanks hidden away in there.' His subordinates nodded. 'But I think we ought to push through.' Again his assistants agreed. He hesitated, walked slowly from one group of men to the next, looking into their faces. In civilian life he was an insurance adjuster, but as an army man he had fought in the Sinai in 1956 and he knew that Israel's principal weapon was mobility backed up by the courage of her men.

'We go,' he said quietly. No one cried, 'On to Cairo.' For them it was into a nest of dark hills on which the sun would set just as they reached the deepest point.

'We go,' the subordinates said, and they all returned to their vehicles and left the flatlands behind them.

When they were well into the narrow defile, where retreat was impossible, Egyptians opened fire from three sides and unlimbered six tanks that had been hidden among the rocks, thus escaping the probing eyes of the Israeli air force. A frightened Israeli lieutenant rushed up to Yigal and shouted, 'Send a message. We're surrounded.'

Before Yigal could operate his radio, an Egyptian shell roared through the truck, destroying most of his equipment and ripping off the head of the lieutenant. Yigal's first action in the battle of the Sinai was to push away the gaping torso whose open neck was spewing blood over what was left of the radio.

As night fell, the trapped Israelis had fourteen useless vehicles, two mounted guns and one hundred and twenty men. They were surrounded by six tanks, a large number of emplaced guns and more than six hundred enemy soldiers. Continuing salvos killed off about thirty of the Israelis before any damage had been done to the Egyptians. At midnight the Sabra gathered his officers under a truck, trying to decide what to do. Yigal heard them talking gravely about alternatives, and he sensed that they anticipated a. disaster. The Sabra left the conclave and came to him, asking how soon the radio would be working, and Yigal said, 'The big one, never. The smaller one, pretty soon,' and the Sabra said, 'You told me you could provide radio communication,' and Yigal said, 'Look at the equipment,' and the major snapped, 'Well, get it working.'

About three in the morning, with the Egyptians still shooting into the stalled trucks, Yigal had the receiving elements of his radio in shape, and the officers gathered to hear reports on world-wide news programs and thus learned of the mighty victory that

Israel had won that day. They could scarcely believe what they heard: six hundred enemy aircraft destroyed; tank units poised to attack the Suez; great battles at Jerusalem and in Golan Heights; the skies empty of enemy aircraft.

'My God,' one of the officers said solemnly. 'We're in a position to win.'

'The other units, not us,' the Sabra pointed out, and as if to underscore the correctness of this analysis, the Egyptians sent another flurry of shells into the trucks.

'They don't know they've lost,' the Sabra said, 'and when morning comes they'll chop us up. Our planes will never find those tanks. How's that goddamned radio?'

Yigal could do nothing with the sending apparatus, but over the receiver there continued to come a constant stream of reports that exhilarated all who heard them. In Jerusalem the leaders of the government were openly hailing a victory of enormous proportions, with more likely to follow the next day. In the darkness the men cheered, then speculated soberly upon their own ridiculous position: about to be wiped out at the moment of national triumph.

So just before dawn the Sabra assembled his ninety survivors and told them, 'We're going to knock off those tanks one by one. We're going to drive every Egyptian out of this pass. And we're not going to lose one Israeli doing it.'

They surrendered any hope of miraculous intervention from the outside; if the air force hadn't sighted the Egyptian tanks yesterday, they wouldn't see them today, and if the radio could not send messages of location, no help could be expected. 'We destroy those tanks,' the Sabra said, and before light broke across the timeless hills the Israelis scattered into eleven assault parties. Yigal and four of his friends from Haifa would remain in the shattered radio truck, trying to establish some kind of contact with the victorious Israeli forces. They would be at the center of the perimeter, but they would not be protected. 'You stay here and work,' the Sabra said, and Yigal nodded: 'I'll get it fixed . . . somehow.'

The Sabra asked, 'How old are you?'

'Sixteen.'

'You're sure you know about radio?'

'I can fix it.'

'If you get through, tell them Qarash Pass. Give these coordinates. Six Egyptian tanks dug in behind the hills. But there won't be six very long.'

It was a morning of heroic action, with the scattered Israeli forces swooping down on first one Egyptian tank, then another, usually with no success, for turrets would turn to confront them from whatever quarter they came. Yigal, watching now and then from the radio truck, saw two of the tanks lumber forward a few yards, unloose incredible bursts of gunfire at unseen attackers, then retreat to their established positions. From time to time one of the tanks would lob shells at the stalled trucks, setting one or another afire, but apparently the Egyptian commanders judged that the trucks were empty, because during long periods there was no shelling.

In frustration Yigal fought to bring some kind of order into his ruined equipment and became oblivious to the fighting in the valley, but in mid-morning he heard the four men in his truck cheering, and looked up in time to see one of the Egyptian tanks exploding in a fiery ball. A detachment had gotten to it with thermite charges.

But in the excitement of this local victory, one of the men in the truck threw something out, and when this was seen by the Egyptian command they realized that the truck was occupied and deduced that it must be the communications center. They directed their guns to wipe it out, but when the tanks concentrated on this problem they left their flanks unprotected and two more went up in flames.

This infuriated the Egyptians and they sent two commando units in to destroy the truck. One of Yigal's friends shouted, 'Here they come!' In one swift glance Yigal saw that no Israeli unit was close enough to interdict the assailants, and that he and his four companions must hold them off during at least the first two assaults. He grabbed a machine gun, with which he was not too familiar, and threw himself under the truck.

The Egyptians were not well led, but they were brave and came forward with resolution. In the brief moment before the fight began Yigal wondered if they had heard over their radio that the war was lost, that they were an enclave without hope—one that must soon be discovered by the Israelis and destroyed. He guessed not, because they began their attack as if they were part of a larger victory.

Yigal and his men drove off the first attack, inflicting enough casualties to make the Egyptians withdraw and call in more supporting fire, but when the tanks disclosed their positions, one or another of the Israeli units swooped down and silenced them. The firing ceased and the Egyptian commandos returned for a second try.

This time they fired low, trying to get their shots underneath the truck, and they succeeded, for in the first salvo they killed the man to Yigal's left. Instinctively Yigal reached for the dead man's gun in case his own jammed, and by firing rapidly and with good effect, the four surviving Israelis drove their attackers back.

This gave the Sabra time to double back from his assault on the tanks, and he interposed his well-trained men between the commandos and their escape route. With terrible, crackling efficiency the Israelis picked off every one of the attackers—killed every man in the unit. Then the Sabra ran to the truck and asked, 'You all right?'

'One dead.'

'Can you fix the radio?'

'Give me half an hour,' Yigal said.

'You got it. We'll keep you covered,' and he returned to fighting tanks.

Yigal and his men climbed back into the truck, ignoring the shells that whistled past. With a zeal that he had never before known, Yigal went patiently over each item of his remaining equipment: 'This is all right. This is good. This is functioning. This is getting current.' He worked without fear, without anxiety, and finally he decided that if he changed one set of tubes the system would have to work. 'Signal that we've got it fixed,' he told one of his helpers, but before he could test the gear a cry went up.

'There goes another tank!' Yigal stopped long enough to look out the shattered back door and see a fireball exploding more brightly than the morning sun. It was then that he fitted the whole together, tested it, and sent the message that electrified the high command and the people of Israel when they heard it: 'Qarash Pass. We are surrounded by six enemy tanks and have destroyed four of them.'

When planes finally arrived, wiping out the remnants of the Egyptian position, the battered Israelis gathered at the radio truck to direct the fire of the aircraft, and after the planes had sped eastward to their home bases at Beersheba and Haifa, and when it was known that an armored column was sweeping north to bring relief, the tired Sabra sat with his men and said, 'Learn from this. If you ever command tanks, don't dig them in to fixed positions. Tanks are nothing unless they're kept moving. Because if you leave them static, a determined team can destroy them every time.'

----•◆•----

When exultation swept Israel, Yigal took no part in the celebration. During the first days he was idolized as 'the boy radio operator of Qarash,' but this passed when it was realized that in her time of crisis Israel had produced a thousand heroes.

In the beautiful summer months, when investigation proved how superior the enemy armament had been and how numerous his army, the miraculous nature of Israel's escape was appreciated, and people caught themselves whispering to each other, as parades of captured Russian weapons passed through the streets, 'Thank God, we were so lucky.'

Doris Zmora wrote to her parents in Detroit, with a carbon copy to the Cliftons in Canterbury:

In these days of reappraisal, I am constantly reminded of Biblical criticism—especially the revisionist theories of German scholars. Two thousand years from now, when critics look back on our June days, they will write ponderous essays explaining that when we said we were faced by a hundred million enemies we didn't mean a hundred million, for we were using the word *million* symbolically. What we really meant was that we faced a hundred hundred. And when they read that our few defeated their many in only six days they will explain that we didn't mean six days. We were speaking euphemistically, with a day representing a season, so that the war really lasted three summers and three winters. But I can tell you, from having been here with all my senses and with fears for my son who was at the front when he should have been in school, that we did really defend ourselves against a hundred million aggressors and we did really force them to surrender in six days.

Yigal wasted no time with such thoughts. He found it exhilarating to see the new maps which depicted vastly extended borders— 'About where they should always have been,' some said. 'Much too extended,' the cautious warned—but he found that what the people he knew really wanted was peace. His friends had expected a peace conference by August; by early September it became apparent that peace would not be attained easily . . . if at all.

None yearned for it more than Yigal, who now felt that because of his dual citizenship, he had to evaluate the situation prudently. In Detroit he could rely on peace—not guaranteed and not immune to civil disturbance, but nevertheless a kind of peace. In Israel he knew none, and the difference disturbed him: 'At Qarash I found I wasn't a coward. But I don't think a man ought to live on the edge of Qarash the rest of his life. It was a great experience, serving under the Sabra, but one not to be repeated.'

By September, when the time came for him to fly back to Detroit to finish the American part of his education, he was quite content to bid Israel farewell, and during the last picnic in the hills overlooking the Sea of Galilee, he left his sisters and wandered by himself to a high point from which he could survey one of the most impressive sights in the world, beloved by Romans in their day, and by the band of Jesus, and by the Arabs who had followed. Each of these groups had found and left a desert, but the Jews had made it a flowering paradise in which he now sat down to grapple with the big concepts of history.

Maybe the phrase means something, he thought. Push us into the sea! Maybe if the Arabs hold on . . . refuse to parley with us . . . bide their time . . . He hesitated, unwilling to continue this line of reasoning, but the summation came of itself: Maybe it will be like the Crusades. Maybe the Arabs will hoard their strength for two hundred years, and then, slowly, like a glacier, push us into the sea, erasing everything that went before. He began to see how this might be possible, for he was perched on one of the hills used by Saladin in his mighty thrust against the Crusaders, the push that eventually drove them into the sea: If I were a young Arab, I'd plot ways by which this could be accomplished—it would become an obsession with me . . . He snapped his fingers with the joy of intellectual discovery, even though this particular discovery could bring him no personal joy: And I'd operate not from reason, nor from need, but rather in the spirit of a game. I would oppose Jews just for the hell of it. He paused to digest his thoughts: I'd make it the national pastime—year after year through the decades.

He realized that such a commitment presupposed a renewal of

the Six-Day War: It's going to happen all over again—Haifa under the bombs . . . tanks crossing the Sinai. The Sabra will become an old man lecturing the new tank commanders—'Never dig your tanks in to fixed positions.' What a hell of a life. He saw, however, one gleam of hope: If somehow both sides could sponsor conciliation . . . honestly . . . get down to rock bottom and settle these grievances. Shaking his head mournfully, looking regretfully at the Galilee, in which the Jews had accomplished so much and the others so little, he concluded: Not in my lifetime . . . the bitterness is too great. For the next two hundred years this isn't going to be a good place to live. But then, with the inextinguishable hope of youth, he thought: Unless we can get together.

With this tentative conclusion, which he chose not to discuss with his sisters, for they did not have American citizenship, he returned to Detroit, where he entered a special hell which kept him in agitation throughout the academic year of 1967–1968. On the one hand, sentimental Jews made a hero of him—none worse than his grandfather, who moved among his acquaintances, saying, 'You kept telling me that because Jews don't go out for football they can't fight. You hear about my grandson . . . sixteen years old'— but what was worse, he had to listen to inept jokes about the futility of the Egyptians; intuitively he knew that this was not a constructive approach to the problem. The Egyptians he had faced at Qarash may have been poorly led, but they were not cowards, nor were they jokes; they were men faced with problems which permitted no solution.

In the first days of school Bruce tried to explain what had really happened at Qarash—the bravery of the Egyptians, how they had chopped up the Israeli trucks, how foot soldiers had moved in and killed his buddy under the truck—but no one cared to listen. The war was a joke in which Egyptians were the clowns.

More serious, however, was his growing awareness that a surprising number of well-educated Jews in the Detroit area were turning against Israel and finding it fashionable to parade pro-Arab sentiments. He first encountered this phenomenon when a young Jewish leader from the University of Michigan conducted a seminar in Grosse Pointe during which he charged that Israel was no different from Hitler Germany and that Arabs were morally justified in opposing what had to be seen as American imperialism. Bruce considered the first charge preposterous and the second unfounded, but even in his own school three of the top Jewish students announced that they were pro-Arab; when he asked them if they understood what such a statement implied, they brushed him off: 'It's in the interest of American Jews to see that Israel is absorbed by its neighbors.' This pronouncement gained wide currency, and one of the Jewish boys was invited to address the local Rotary Club to explain it.

Intellectual Jews took special umbrage at the conspicuous figure of General Dayan. Whereas some of Bruce's friends made Dayan a popular hero—anyone could get a quick laugh by wearing an eye patch and declaiming, 'General Westmoreland, President Johnson sent me to help clean up the war in Vietnam. I can spare you six days'—those who were leading the philosophical attack on Israel pointed to Dayan as evidence of the new Jewish imperialism. Bruce wondered if they knew what they were talking about, and one night when he and his grandfather attended a meeting at which this line was peddled by a clever Jewish writer from New York, Bruce stood in the audience and asked, 'Are you prepared to sponsor the slaughter of two million Jews in Israel?' and the speaker laughed and said, 'Young man, you've been listening to fairy stories,' and Bruce shouted, 'I've been listening to Radio Damascus,' and the speaker brushed him off airily with, 'All people engage in hyperbole, just as you're doing now,' and the audience had laughed comfortably at having had this ghost laid to rest.

Bruce was not trained in psychology, so he could not analyze what impelled some of the Jewish intellectuals to adopt this unexpected posture, but he did know enough to dissect the next phenomenon for what it was worth. Grosse Pointe allowed no Negroes, but nearby Detroit contained many, and wealthy householders in Grosse Pointe listened with approval as their Negro servants began to express violently anti-Jewish sentiments. It was rather exciting to hear one's maid say, 'Adolf Hitler was right. Them Jews, they run everything. They the enemy of all good people.' White matrons were tempted to encourage the Negroes, and nodded gravely when the latter said, 'Blacks ain't never gonna have a chance in this here country till we take care of them Jews that's holdin' us down.'

At Bruce's school it was customary to enroll four Negroes each year, basketball players if possible, and since the process of selection was meticulous, boys of more than average ability were enlisted.

Prior to the Six-Day War, these Negroes had usually found common ground with boys like Bruce, but in the strange backlash that
followed the war, they began to stay aloof from the Jews, especially from Bruce, who was reported to be an Israeli. There was
much talk of, 'Them poor Arab refugees. Maybe we gonna have to
go over there and set them free.'

In February the school invited to its forum one of the Arab
representatives at the United Nations, and he gave an excellent account of himself. He had a few jokes against the slothfulness of his
people, a few titillating views of Islam as an exotic and lovely religion, and a series of soft-sell persuasions calculated to instill a
partiality for his side. In short, he was doing, for the first time,
what able Israeli diplomats had been doing at similar forums for the
past twenty years. He created a sensation, and after the meeting,
conducted an informal session with the students, at which the four
Negro students asked a series of probing questions. He told them
frankly, 'The future of your race in Africa is to align yourselves
with Islam. The future of your people in this country is to do the
same.' After he had left the campus two of the Negro athletes announced that they had become Muslims, and one snarled at the end
of history class, 'We gonna push you right off that land you stole.'

It was in this rapidly shifting climate that Bruce Clifton graduated with high grades, and this raised a new set of problems, for his
proud grandfather launched a series of campaigns which resulted
in his getting offers of scholarships to the University of Michigan
and Cal Tech. To his grandfather's astonishment, Bruce said, 'I'm not
going to college in America. I've enrolled at the Technion in Haifa.'

'You must be out of your mind!' his grandfather shouted. 'Do
you realize how tough it is to get into Michigan? Or Cal Tech?
Like getting into heaven.'

'I want a good education,' Bruce said. 'At the Technion . . .'

'Just because your father works there. Bruce, it's a high school
compared with a place like Michigan . . . or Cal Tech.'

'In the fields I'm interested in, it happens to be better than either
of them.'

'Insularity,' Melnikoff stormed. 'That's what's wrong with Israel.
Goddamned insularity.'

But Bruce would not even consider the application forms when
his grandfather placed them before him. 'I'm going to the
Technion,' he said stubbornly, but one night his grandmother came

to his room and said, 'Bruce, when a boy has a grandfather who has a lot of money—who has to write a will whether he wants to or not—with such a grandfather a young boy shouldn't be obstreperous.' Bruce looked at her stonily, and she continued, 'So you'll be a good boy, please, and tell him you'll go to Michigan or maybe California. I hear they're both very nice.'

Bruce explained that he needed to know Israel better, that he wanted to reestablish association with the boys he had grown up with, and that nothing could keep him from returning there. The next morning he scribbled a hasty note to his grandfather, enlisted a friend to drive him to the airport, and boarded a plane to Israel, but when he found that it stopped at London, he decided on the spur of the moment to break his journey and visit his other grandparents in Canterbury.

On the third day of his visit, Bruce was astonished by something his Grandfather Clifton told him. He had always regarded the Cliftons as strange and unimportant people, deriving this interpretation from comments made at odd times by Grandfather Melnikoff —'They're downright stuffy' and 'As a lawyer he's pettifogging'— but on this day Grandfather Clifton said, 'Son, I want you to lunch with me at my club. Time you understood British ways.' And he took Bruce to his dark and somber club, where everyone looked to be over sixty, even those in their thirties, and he showed Bruce how to order dishes that were the mainstay of the menu: beef with Yorkshire pudding and trifle. When the bowl containing the latter was passed, Bruce took a modest helping, whereupon his grandfather grabbed the serving spoon and piled the riches on his grandson's plate. 'Boys always like trifle,' he said. 'I did. Your father, too.'

When the dessert was finished—one of the best Bruce had ever tasted, with its curious combination of flavors: sherry, custard, raspberry—Grandfather Clifton led the way to a dark-paneled room, where he asked the servingman to fetch a briefcase crammed with papers. When these were delivered he said, 'Bruce, I've been watching your progress carefully. You're a remarkable boy . . . one of the few. You've proved you have that glorious trio: character, courage, intelligence. Your parents gave you the character. Courage you developed yourself. God gave you the brains. What you going to do with 'em?'

'Science, I think.'

'No, I mean which country?'

'Oh . . . I've been wondering about that.'

'I know. How are you inclining?'

Bruce took a deep breath and said, 'This sounds arrogant, but since you're the first person who's asked me point-blank . . . What I mean is, since you're the first person who's discussed it in an intelligent way . . . Well, to put it bluntly—when I'm in Israel, I prefer the United States, and when I'm in Detroit, I prefer Haifa.'

'Precisely,' Mr. Clifton said in crisp, sardonic tones. 'Just about what I'd do. But human values rarely balance. Which way do the scales tip?'

'If they tip, I'm not clever enough to detect it.'

'Good. I hope you're telling the truth, because it makes my task easier.'

'What task?'

'I hope that Israel and America are in balance. Because you're not confined to those two, Bruce. You're also an English citizen.'

'I'm what!'

'When you were born I was much impressed with the thoughtfulness of your Grandfather Melnikoff—ensuring that you would be entitled to an American passport. I thought about this for two weeks, satisfied myself that he was right, and had you registered as a British subject.'

'How?'

'Because I had always taken careful steps to ensure that your father retained his British papers—no matter his great concern about Israel, no matter his dedication to Jewish causes. Legally I kept him a resident of Canterbury.' He paused, shuffled among his papers, found what he was seeking, and handed it to Bruce. 'You, too, are a citizen of this city. This birth certificate proves it. This next paper is an application for a British passport. We'll get the photographs this afternoon and the passport tomorrow.'

Before Bruce could respond to this startling news, Grandfather Clifton produced two other sets of papers, one an application to Cambridge University, the other an application to the best science college within that university. 'If you want to spend your life working on the practical application of science,' he said, 'attend the

Technion with your father in Haifa. If you want to build bridges, enroll in one of the American universities. But if you want to be a scientist—if you want to judge the field as a whole and make what contribution your brain entitles you to make—go to Cambridge.'

While Bruce held the papers in his lap, Clifton took out yet another document, the passbook of a Canterbury bank. In it, starting back in 1952, the bank had entered from time to time notations of small savings which Clifton had set aside for the education of his grandson. The total was now over two thousand pounds, meticulously saved from the small fees accruing to a lawyer practicing in the provinces. 'I did not want you subservient to your Grandfather Melnikoff,' he explained. 'He's a wonderful man, and if you were a race horse he would train you prudently. But you're an intelligence —a sensitive brain with enormous capacity—and I don't think Melnikoff could ever appreciate that.'

The amount of love represented by these papers was so great that Bruce was silent, recalling his flying visits to Canterbury. He had never been gracious to his grandfather, had never given him the slightest shred of love or encouragement. Canterbury had always been a forced stop between the two real poles of his life and never a vital thing of itself.

'If I had not come here to see you,' he asked in a low voice, 'what would you have done with these papers?'

'I'd have waited. I was confident that an intelligent boy faced with your choices would ultimately want dispassionate counsel.'

They said no more for a long time, then Bruce asked, 'In which country is it best to be a Jew?'

'The worst is France.'

'Worse than Germany?'

'Yes. Because France practices the most virulent anti-Semitism but is not aware of it. True Frenchmen—those who love their country—can never forgive the Jews for having forced the Dreyfus issue. Made their public institutions undress in public, as it were.

'Second worst is Russia. It has always been pitifully confused about its attitude to Jews—love one day, pogroms the next. Every wise Jew should study three events. German Nazism. French Dreyfusism. And particularly the Russian experiment with Birobizhan. Look it up. It's on the Amur River in Siberia.'

'Those aren't the countries I have to choose among.'

'It's no fun being a Jew in England. It's not easy to be one in

Israel, with the rabbis running everything and compounding all the errors of Europe. But in the United States, I think it would be most difficult to retain your identity. Because Americans want so desperately to absorb the Jews.'

'What would you do . . . if you were me?'

'I'd use this bankbook to free myself of Melnikoff. He loves you, but love is never protection against exploitation. I'd enroll at Cambridge . . . get loose from your father's intellectual influence. I'd study diligently, and when I graduated I'd try some new country like Australia, or maybe Kenya. They'll need all the intelligence they can find. They'll also need some Jews to keep them in balance.' He hesitated, then concluded, 'But right now, the photographers. Tomorrow, London for your British passport.'

And it was on this passport—this precious dark blue document which for a hundred years had taken the organizers, the producers and the arrangers around the world in security—that Bruce Clifton flew out of London for Israel.

———•◆•———

In the fall of 1968, when he was only seventeen years old, Yigal entered the Technion in Haifa, a scientific university which had the capacity to give a first-class education but which was obviously going to fail in his case. The trouble was not the difficulty of instruction, for he found the beginning courses too easy, but his inability to focus on education when other problems were usurping his attention.

He kept comparing Israel with the United States, to the detriment of each, and he began seriously to think that he ought to transfer to Cambridge and become a British subject. What he had seen of the islands he liked; Grandfather Clifton's quiet approach seemed more congenial the more he thought about it.

From a distance, he found America and Grandfather Melnikoff too boisterous on the one hand and too trivial on the other. He could not imagine the boys and girls of his Grosse Pointe school facing up to invasion the way his friends in Israel had done. (This was an error commonly made when assessing the capacity of American young people; already it had proved disastrous to Adolf Hitler and the Chinese communists. One day it might prove equally so for the calculators in the Kremlin.) And he found the role of the Jew in America, now made more complicated by Negro animosity, distasteful.

On the other hand, life in Israel had a built-in tension that frightened him. He was not a coward, a fact of which he had given ample proof, but he did seek peace in which to develop ideas which were beginning to evolve. Curiously, they did not involve science directly but were rather those soaring contemplations of justice and equity which harass the best young men of all nations. Yigal Zmora was quite incapacitated by the confusion he had brought upon himself, and by the beginning of 1969 it was apparent to his father, dean of the Technion, that his son had better drop out for the remainder of that academic term.

Doris Zmora agreed. She told her husband, 'When a boy's been through what Yigal's seen, he needs time to recuperate. I can't tell which is worse, the Six-Day War or Grandfather Melnikoff.'

'I'm afraid it was Grandfather Clifton who disturbed the tranquillity,' her husband said. 'My father has that devilish trick of asking important questions.'

They decided that Yigal should work the rest of the year, but when Grandfather Clifton heard of the plan he interceded: 'Let the boy stay in Canterbury till school opens again. He should do some reading and some thinking.'

This appealed to Yigal, and he flew to Britain, much against Grandfather Melnikoff's advice, and dug into that great sequence of books from which young people have been gaining their insights in this century: Gibbon, Spengler, Marx, Dostoevsky, Flaubert, Max Weber, Keynes, Charles Beard. His most fruitful experience, however, was his running conversation with his grandfather, for Lawyer Clifton had a sweet simplicity of manner that allowed him to become eighteen years old again, and he discussed Bruce's reading at precisely the level which the boy could understand.

It was a great winter, with formal parties at which Bruce met the few young Jews of the Canterbury area, and he might have continued with this life if one day he had not seen, in the display window of a travel agency, the same poster advertising Torremolinos that had created such havoc in the mind of a Norwegian girl in Tromsø some months earlier. He was walking home from the library, thinking of nothing in particular, when he saw this near-naked girl standing beside a windmill on a Mediterranean beach, and she seemed so real that he could have touched her, and all of a sudden he realized that what had gone wrong was neither Israel nor the Technion but the simple fact that he was eighteen years old, and though he had ventured to the Red City and had helped stand off six enemy tanks, he had never been really involved with a girl.

'I want to spend my vacation in southern Spain,' he announced that night at supper. His grandparents considered this for a moment, then nodded.

'It's time you occupied yourself with something frivolous,' Grandfather Clifton said, 'and I hear that the south of Spain is very nice,' and the next day when he went to inquire about plane tickets and reduced rates at hotels, he saw the Torremolinos poster and recalled how he had felt at eighteen. He said nothing, paid for the tickets, and handed them to his grandson. When the boy was gone, Lawyer Clifton did not share his suspicions with his wife, but two days later, when she was returning home from shopping, she, too, saw the girl by the windmill, and that night she said, 'I should think the call of Torremolinos must have been very powerful. Probably better than meddling around in Canterbury.'

———— • ————

British airlines offered a series of preposterously favorable excursions to Torremolinos. You could fly from London to Málaga, get free lodging at a good hotel for two weeks, receive a set of meal tickets entitling you to food at the best restaurants, then catch a plane back to London—all for something like $71. On Bruce's plane a group of sixteen girls had taken passage, and two were named Pamela. (On such trips it was not uncommon for five or six girls to be named Pam, for this name had been popular after the war.) These two were differentiated by their friends as Mini-Pam, sporting the briefest red miniskirt the police would allow, and Fat-Pam, clearly on the pudgy side, but with an amiable disposition that kept her attractive.

They were hardly over the English Channel when Mini-Pam plumped herself down beside Bruce and started telling him about her plans for Torremolinos. 'They're putting us up in this swell place called Berkeley Square. My girl friend stayed there last year and she said the management let you get away with anything so long as you didn't annoy the guests. I'm going to find myself a lover and snuggle down for thirteen days of glorious love-making.'

Bruce was only vaguely aware of what she was saying, for he was obsessed by her slim, bare legs, nestled close to his and visible to the thigh. He became painfully conscious of his hands and could find no place to put them, for they were attracted like steel filings to the magnet of her legs, but he was afraid to touch them. His mouth went dry, and when she turned to ask him a question, her bright young eyes staring at him and her breasts pushing against his arm, he could only gulp.

Not getting an answer to her question, she rambled on: 'There'll be French boys and German and a lot of real horny American soldiers. If a girl plays her cards right, she can find a date in Torremolinos, no matter what the others say.' Bruce started to ask her what the others had said, but the words formed clumsily in his mouth, so after taking a deep breath he placed his hand high above her knee. She shivered, closed her eyes, and whispered, 'That feels good. Let's move to the back seat. No! You stay here for a minute. I'll go back for a drink. After a while you follow me.'

When he reached the rear seat he found that she had covered herself with a blanket, as if about to take a nap, and when he sat beside her she took his hand and placed it at the top of her leg, covering everything with the blanket. 'Isn't that good?' she asked.

When she saw he was able to say nothing, she giggled. 'I picked up this trick from a naughty joke.' And she told him about the big Texan who was flying on Japan Air Lines and went to the washroom. After he returned, the stewardess handed him a letter.

Honored Traveler,
    When you came from the washroom you forgot to close your zipper and you are completely exposed. I have a plan! I will put a blanket over you as if you were sleeping and you can fix it. I pray you are not embarrassed.

                                                            Your Stewardess
P.S. I love you.

Bruce chuckled, and within a few minutes Pam was practically undressed and had begun to unfasten most of Bruce's buttons, too, and as the plane droned eastward they came as close to having sexual intercourse as a couple could in those awkward seats. Then she found a way to pull out the dividing partition, and with an admirable contortion, so manipulated her body that sex was not only possible but well-nigh inescapable.

Fat-Pam, watching approvingly from the front of the plane, alerted the others as to what Mini-Pam was up to, and the fifteen English girls took furtive peeks at what their companion was accomplishing. 'He's cute,' one of the girls whispered. 'I wouldn't mind being back there with him.'

'There they go!' another cried, and a dozen girls watched with varying degrees of envy as Bruce stiffened, then fell back inertly against his headrest. Soon thereafter Mini-Pam walked the few steps to the washroom, and when she returned to the cabin she caught Fat-Pam's eye and smiled. Making the sign of victory, she sank back into her seat beside her companion and wakened him. 'What's your name?' she asked.

'Bruce.'

'That's a keen name, Bruce. When we get to Torremolinos and find a proper bed . . .' She ran her fingers in an arpeggio from his throat to his knees, then suggested, 'You ought to button up, Bruce. But this is only the beginning.'

When they reached Torremolinos she insisted that he join her group at the Berkeley Square, and before his bags were unpacked she was in his room, undressed and in bed. 'Do you think me too bold?' she asked with the covers primly drawn against her throat. 'It's just that we haven't much time, have we?'

They enjoyed four tempestuous days together, but they might just as well have been in Brighton for all that Spain mattered. Then, in a maneuver that Bruce could not understand, for it was incredible that she should have found time to meet another man while so totally engaged with him, she moved out of the Berkeley Square and into the flat of a German businessman.

Bruce, left unexpectedly alone, rather relished the opportunity for digesting what had happened so far. While Mini-Pam was still with him they had taken their meals with various members of the English group, and he was appalled at the bleakness of their lives. They had read nothing, contemplated nothing, seen nothing. In Spain for the better part of a week, they had not gone to Málaga or to the inland towns, preferring to hang around their English hotel and two or three English bars. They were overly eager to meet men, and most did, but out of the whole lot no girl met anyone with whom she might logically expect to develop a continuing interest.

'It's a vacation!' Mini-Pam had cried, flicking at him with her napkin. 'Who wants to talk or read books or bother with deep ideas on vacation?'

Then one morning she was back at the Berkeley Square, as beautiful and as provocative as ever. She had surprising news. 'I'm off to Palma on the afternoon plane. A very nice English gentleman I met in a bar.' She didn't think she would be going back to England, and one of the girls was to break the news to her Mum. She came to Bruce's room and stood in the sunlight, her exquisite bare legs set off by the brief red miniskirt. 'Will you remember me?' she asked. 'When you're a professor or a member of Parliament or something big? That first time on the plane? God, almost broke my back.' She whirled, caught him by the hands and pulled him onto the bed. 'You'll remember this . . . always,' she whispered, and within the space of a few farewell minutes she lavished upon him an explosive love that no man could forget.

'Goodbye,' she called from the door. 'You were precious, and one day I'll see your picture on the telly.'

For two nights his room was empty, but on the third Fat-Pam sat on the end of his bed and said, 'You're deep. You're a real gentleman, Bruce. I watched you and Mini-Pam, and you treated her with respect.' She sat there a long time, talking of her life in London and its tragically circumscribed potential. 'I'll never amount to much,' she said. 'I'm cut out to be a housewife, that's about all. But I'll be a good mother. My children will grow up without a lot of crazy ideas, because I know what love is. It's giving yourself to the other person—your husband, or your children, or your minister when he's trying to do a good thing. My view of life is quite different from Mini-Pam's. I would never use people. Of course, maybe I have to be that way because I'm not beautiful like her, and when a girl isn't beautiful, there's only so much she can get away with.'

'You're very attractive,' Bruce said. 'You lose two stone, you'd be a knocker, just like Mini-Pam.'

'You think so? You think that if I put my mind to it?' She halted this line of daydreaming, for she knew how futile it was, then said, 'You read books and things, don't you? Ordinarily, you'd never look at a girl like me . . . or like Mini-Pam either, would you? But this is a vacation.'

Bruce, standing by the window where Mini-Pam had often stood in the sunlight, her slim legs forming a provocative arch, suddenly saw Fat-Pam as a human being, a rather plump young woman from the poorer section of London on what might prove to be her only holiday in Europe. With a mixture of kindness and condescension he said, 'Why don't you move in here?' and she replied, not ashamed of the joy she derived from his words, 'Could I?' and he said grandiloquently, 'Why not?'

It was an invitation bearing consequences he could not have foreseen, for Fat-Pam was one of those rare human beings in whom all segments of personality were at peace and who lived solely for the purpose of conveying that peace to others. She possessed a graciousness—nay, a nobility—of manner that Bruce had never encountered before: his two grandfathers were ambitious men; his mother and father were kept tense on the sensations of history; Mini-Pam devoured. But this girl was an eighteen-year-old shop assistant with an insight so profound that it gave Bruce a new concept of humanity. When she made love, it was as if she absorbed him into the timeless bosom of the universe, beyond human beings and pettiness of any kind.

She thought only of him. 'You must go on to university,' she said. 'You have something important to contribute. Lor, it would be a crime to waste it.'

He said, 'You use words in an interesting way,' and she said, 'I go to the cinema a lot. I listen to the way Richard Burton and Laurence Harvey speak. I always say you don't have to be a slob if you don't want to be.'

'Where'd you get your ideas? Your mother?'

'She ran off. Drinking too much. She stole money from all the neighbors and ran off.'

'Your father?'

'He never had any ideas. He wasn't a bad man, but he was weak. I earn more money now than he ever did. I didn't really blame my mother for running away. It isn't easy for a woman never to have a new dress.'

'But your sensible approach? Where did it come from?'

'We had a very good minister . . . for a while. He was consumptive, and I'm sure he knew he was dying. He wanted to tell us all he knew, but only the important things. I used to look at my mother, and my father, and then at him. I was about ten—maybe eleven—and I thought: There's one hell of a difference between strong men and pitiful men. Of course, my father could have punched him in the nose. In that way my father was strong. But between him and the minister there was a gulf so enormous . . .' She paused, passed a pudgy hand over her face and concluded, 'I decided then and there that I would be strong—in the good meaning of the word.'

The longer Bruce shared his room with this generous girl, the more surely he knew that the English system was wrong. Fat-Pam in her bucolic way, Mini-Pam in her mercurial—both were alike cut off from what in another country would have been normal attainment. A dead and heavy hand bore down upon them; call it tradition, class consciousness, an unimaginative education, whatever it was it exacted a grievous toll. In Israel the two Pams would have served in the army and acquired a functional education. They would not escape being dragged into lives of maximum service. Of course, Mini-Pam on maneuvers in the Negev would have been just as boy-hungry as in London; there were many girls in Haifa and Tel Aviv like her, but after they had slept with their quota and brought their cravings into balance, they found logical places and were none the worse for it.

In America the two Pamelas would probably try college. Mini-Pam would bust out the first year, probably because of marijuana, but Fat-Pam would persevere and develop her intelligence and be in a position one day to make a creative contribution, probably in a field she had not now even heard of.

And yet he liked this group of English girls—brave, brash, uneducated but gallant in a Churchillian sort of way. As a matter of fact, he thought, any group that produces even one Fat-Pam deserves respect.

When the day came for the airplane to fly the girls back to London, Fat-Pam kept Bruce in bed beside her until the last possible moment. With her forefinger she drew designs on his naked body, as if constructing a map of one-time happiness which she would want to remember in the years ahead. She said, 'There's a boy who wants to marry me. He's a lot like my father, I suppose, and no good can possibly come of it, but I imagine I'll find no better. I shall look to see what happens to you, Bruce. Promise me one thing. You won't give in cheaply? You see, if I go down, what's lost? But if you go down . . .'

She burst into tears and leaned against him, crying for some minutes. 'Oh God, I wish it had been different. I wish I knew something. I wish I had been to school.' She lay silent for some time, then slowly drew him onto her in a long, slow, rhythmic ritual of love, as if the innards of the earth were involved.

When they parted, she said a strange thing: 'People like you and me draw strength from one another.' And she was gone, a plump girl on her only vacation prior to the establishment of a home which, because of lack of funds and an equal partner, would be perpetually on the verge of disaster.

————— · ◆ ◆ · —————

When the distraction of the two Pamelas had passed, Yigal found time to explore Torremolinos. He liked the German area and stopped several times at the Brandenburger for sandwiches. The vast collection of skyscrapers at the eastern end of town surprised him, but he was mainly attracted by the endless beach, along which local businessmen were constructing temporary restaurants for the summer and a variegated array of umbrella parks and bathhouses for the swimmers. It was cheap, ugly, crowded, noisy, exciting—and he liked it.

He was not happy with the Berkeley Square. It was too English in a Spanish setting, and although the constant supply of attractive English girls brought in by each new plane was titillating, he felt obliged to see rather more of Spain than this narrow base permitted.

So he started wandering about the old fishing village, looking for something Mediterranean and finding nothing, for he did not know where to look. Eventually he came upon the Swedish area, where shops contained signs only in Scandinavian. He stopped to survey the Northern Lights and imagined each of its many rooms with a Swedish girl waiting inside. Wouldn't that be heaven? he thought, but the only Swedes who made their appearance while he waited were a rather fat Danish couple arguing about how many kroner the husband had wasted buying a sweater.

He passed along the narrow streets, crowded with May visitors, and at least half the people he met were adventuresome girls from various parts of Europe. This town is better than the poster promised, he thought, and it was while laying plans as to how best to meet a cross section of these girls that he saw down one of the alleys a garish signboard: a huge Texas revolver bearing the name THE ALAMO.

If it's as lousy as the movie was, it's just what I need, he thought, hurrying through the crowd.

As he looked through the half-open door he saw something that would remain with him the rest of his life: a Scandinavian girl in a miniskirt, with straw-blond hair, limpid complexion and saucy eyes. At that moment she was serving beer, but she saw him in the street and smiled, her white teeth forming a beautiful arch over her lower lip. In the passing of a second he knew that she combined the compelling allure of Mini-Pam and the sweet, stable womanliness of Fat-Pam.

Like a man voluntarily placing himself into a cell for a lifetime of imprisonment, he entered the small bar.

He waited until she finished serving her tables, then caught her wrist and asked, with a boldness he did not know he possessed, 'What's your name?'

'Britta. What's yours?'

'Yigal. I'm from Israel.'

She turned to a table occupied by American soldiers and announced, 'Fellows, this is Yigal from Israel,' and with a purposeful shove in the middle of his back she projected him over to the Americans and resumed her duties.

The young soldiers were much interested in Israel and how it had managed to win the Six-Day War. 'Them Egyptians weren't the pushovers the papers said, was they?' a soldier from the south asked.

'You bet they weren't. Individually they were very brave. Their leaders . . .' He held his fingers to his nose.

'Can you go on knocking them off every ten years?'

'No. In time they'll learn. Then it'll be your problem as well as ours.'

'Oh no! No more Vietnams.'

They were talking in this way, feeling one another out, when Britta returned with a beer for Yigal, and when she placed it before him he had a chance to look into her eyes, and it seemed as if an earthquake had hit him in the gut. 'Who's the girl?' he asked when she had gone.

'Get in line, like we tell all the guys. She's a Norwegian. And she's even sweeter than she looks. And she belongs to the bartender.'

'Married?'

'Just about.' The speaker shrugged his shoulders, watched Britta for a few moments, then asked, 'Class, eh?'

Among the soldiers was a Jew from Atlanta, Georgia, and certain things that Yigal said reminded him of several photographs which had appeared in the Jewish press, and after studying the newcomer for some minutes and listening more acutely to what he was saying, this Georgian slammed his right palm noisily onto the table and cried, 'I know who you are! Hey, gang, you know who this is? This is the kid who held up those six Egyptian tanks at that pass.'

Everyone stopped talking to look at the Israeli, a frail young man of only eighteen, and from the embarrassed manner in which he reacted, it was apparent that he was indeed the hero of Qarash. A multitude of questions flew at him, and he spent some time making diagrams on the table top with mugs and ashtrays.

'You mean less than a hundred Jews held off six tanks? And destroyed four of them?'

'They were dug into fixed positions,' Yigal explained.

'Hey, Britta!' one of the soldiers yelled. 'Come here. Did you know you were serving a bloody hero?'

Britta came to the table, listened to the account of what this boy had done, then stooped and kissed him on the forehead. 'You fought for all of us,' she said. 'I know. My father did the same.'

At a table by the door, watching with detached calm, sat an American, who now rose slowly, like a coil expanding, and came to where Yigal sat. He was a black man, young, handsome, bearded, snappily dressed. Standing over Yigal, he poked at him with a forefinger and asked, 'You the cat that blew up the tanks?'

'I was the cat hiding in a communications truck . . . scared shitless.'

'But you were there? Qarash, that is?'

'I was there.'

'Man, I would like to shake your hand. My name's Cato. I hang out here, so we'll be seeing a lot of each other.'

He drew up a chair and pummeled Yigal with a rapid-fire series of questions: How were so few able to stand off so many? What kind of guns did the Jews have? Why didn't the tanks simply rev up and crush the whole operation? How did the Sabra get his men fired up enough so they would tackle a tank?

It was long after supper when the conversation broke up. Through it all, Yigal had managed to keep one eye on Britta, and he was more certain than ever that here was the girl who would command his affection . . . for many years to come. He was therefore not listening attentively when Cato asked, 'Where you staying?' Not getting an answer, the Negro asked, 'Hero, where you sleepin'?'

'Matter of fact, I'm looking for a place.'

'You just found one, hero. We got a sleeping bag at our place, and you're welcome to it.'

'Where is your place?' Yigal asked.

'Best part of the neighborhood. Down by the water.'

'Can I rent a room . . . or something? Who owns it?'

'Some French cat. He and his chick are in Morocco . . . buying up marijuana. I'm using his bed. Plenty of room. And a free sleeping bag.'

Intuitively Yigal liked this Negro, and since he wanted to know more about what made such men function, he wanted to join him, but an innate sense of honesty required him to level with the stranger. 'Actually, you know, I'm not really an Israeli. Well, that is, I am, but I also have an American passport. I went to school in Detroit.'

'Hey! You did! What's with them Detroit cats? That big riot, what happened?'

'I was in Israel at the time. Later, of course, I heard the white man's side. But when you're Jewish . . .'

'I dig you, Yigal. I dig you real good. Let's go down and see the room.'

When they reached the apartment, Cato pushed open the door and disclosed the two beds. Before Yigal could ask any questions, he said, 'It's all clean. No gang-bang or stuff like that. Over here the boss's bed. I'm using it while he's in Morocco. That one belongs to Joe . . . you'll meet him later. And over there in the corner, the sleeping bag. It's yours.'

'Can I help to pay . . .'

'You damned well can! I keep records, and we split up the cost of the beer and the food and whatever else we use.'

'I meant the rent.'

'No rent.'

Further discussion was halted by the arrival of an exquisite dark-haired English girl, very slight in build and most incisive in manner. She banged open the door, threw her packages about the floor, and dropped onto the bed which the Negro had said was his. Kicking off her shoes, she cried, 'I'm exhausted. Pour me a gin, Cato. Who's your friend?'

'This is Yigal. The Israeli cat who shot up the Egyptian tanks in that pass.'

'Are you . . .' The girl on the bed pointed at him with a slender hand, then squealed with delight and cried, 'Welcome to the sleeping bag! We could use somebody like you. Keep these goddamned Africans in their place.'

Cato laughed at her and said, 'Monica Braham. Degenerate daughter of a degenerate English nobleman.'

They all drank gin for some time, after which Yigal said he'd better go fetch his gear, but they insisted that he stay with them tonight and get it in the morning. So they talked till about two in the morning, about England and Vwarda and Detroit and all the soaring problems of youth. Before they went to sleep Cato and Monica had a couple of marijuana cigarettes but showed no displeasure when Yigal said he didn't care for any.

About four in the morning he was wakened in his sleeping bag by a noise. With intuitive prudence he made no sound, anxious to see what was happening, and in the shadowy light, he discerned that another couple had entered and were preparing to climb into the other bed. With natural curiosity he watched them undress, and when the girl stood naked only a few feet from where he lay, he recognized, with a deep stab of pain, that it was Britta, the Norwegian girl from the bar.

He was so dismayed that he must have gasped, for he heard her whisper, 'Joe! I think there's somebody in the sleeping bag.'

A tall man came over, lit a match, and studied the sleeping form. 'Probably some kid somebody brought home from the bar.'

Britta stooped down to peer more closely. 'It's that boy from Israel! Cato must have brought him.'

'The one who held up the tanks?'

'Yes. I'm sure it's he.'

The match went out. The two forms withdrew. And Yigal opened his eyes again, just in time to see Britta climb into the bed.

VI §

GRETCHEN

Sappho is a Greek dike.

It would be a sad day in American legal history when our courts refused protection under the law to the unwashed, unshod, unkempt, untrimmed and un-inhibited.

Frodo is not dead. He is hiding out in Chicago until Mayor Daley leaves.

I have listened to a dozen families deplore the indifference of their children, praying that they might show an interest in something. But as soon as children display any interest in political movements, the parents choke up and charge them with radicalism. What the parents really want is for their children to be interested in what they were interested in thirty years ago.

Hire the handicapped. It's a real gas watching them work.

Nostalgia isn't what it used to be.

No phrase of the young is more revolutionary than that odd cry 'Zap them right back with super-love.' If this became a widespread tactic, it could demoral-ize society as presently constructed. If a southern sheriff puts his police dogs on a group of blacks, and they sing spirituals of forgiveness and pray for him with obvious love, they are going to accomplish mir-acles. If a college girl can accept being beaten by clubs and can then kiss the hands of her assailants and offer them her love, it's going to knock hell out of their program. Christ devised this tactic two thousand years ago, and with it he helped bring down the Roman Empire.

The latest peace feeler from Hanoi has just been arrested in Central Park.

The Youth of a Nation are the Trustees of Posterity.—Disraeli

I love America most when I am caught up in its politics . . . in the grubby battles whereby contending social groups try to hack out their unjust portion of the spoils. I like to see Catholics battling for a little more money for their schools, Jews fighting for a better relationship between Washington and Jerusalem, gasoline companies trying to defeat government supervision, and the developer of a new drug doing his damnedest to slip it past the health inspectors. To me, a place like Newark, where old Protestants surrendered to new Italians who will not surrender an inch to new Negroes, is more interesting than the battleground at Troy, for this is real warfare, in my terms, in my day. That's why I enjoyed the Democratic convention at Chicago so much. You could stare at your television and see the dinosaurs of the west plodding slowly toward the volcano of extinction without being in the least aware of their march. It gave me more catharsis than the fall of the House of Atreus, because public suicide is inevitably thrilling, as the Japanese learned long ago.

> She's taen out her little pen-knife,
> And twinnd the sweet babe o its life.
>
> As she was going to the church
> She saw a sweet babe in the porch.
>
> 'O sweet babe, and thou were mine,
> I wad cleed thee in the silk so fine.'
>
> 'O mother dear, when I was thine,
> You did na prove to me sae kind.'
> —Child 20

Each day more of them die and more of us are born.

IN late 1967 our head office in Geneva sent me to Boston to look into the possibility of our financing a rather large nest of apartment houses under contemplation for the Fenway Park region, and in the discussions I was thrown into daily contact with a formidable Boston financier, Frederick Cole. I found him aloof but capable; in most of our negotiation it was him against me, his judgment of facts against mine, and rarely have I met a man to whom I could present additional data with the assurance that he would inspect them fairly and adjust his former position if required. This is an unusual aptitude, for most of us, when we lock ourselves into a position, utilize additional data merely as additions to our fortifications. Cole could reason.

At the end of one difficult session, when the difference between our assessments amounted to more than eight million dollars, and he was coldly defending his figure, I sought to terminate that part of the discussion on an amicable note, so I said, 'It's odd to find an Irishman with the first name Frederick.' He laughed and said, 'Not Irish, German. When my great-great-grandfather came over here after the Revolution of 1848 his name was Kohl, but he was afraid Bostonians might think he was Jewish, so he changed it to Cole, and then everybody thought he was Irish, which in those days was worse.' I laughed, and in his icy way he asked if I would care to have dinner with him that night, so on the spur of the moment it was arranged.

I had assumed that he meant us to drop into some restaurant, but his plans were quite different. He called his wife, told her he was bringing me along and that we'd eat whatever was available. We caught a cab and drove out Huntington Avenue to the more expensive section of Brookline, where we pulled into a garage set among trees and carefully tended shrubs. The white clapboard house had been occupied during the last century by a famous professor at Harvard and had passed through his family to Mrs. Cole, who was apparently of distinguished lineage.

The three of us had barely sat down to a casually prepared meal of beef and potatoes, with New England touches such as spiced crab apple and quince jam on hot rolls, when we were unexpectedly joined by the Coles' daughter, who was attending Radcliffe College nearby. She was tall, tanned, and with long brown hair which she wore in two braids. Her tweed suit was what we call 'country expensive' and her manner was patrician in the best Boston sense of that word. She was extremely quick in her appreciation of situations and knew without being told why I was there. I was not surprised, therefore, when her father said, as she disappeared to wash up, 'Gretchen's only nineteen and already has her B.A. summa cum laude from Radcliffe. She's entering the graduate school in January.'

'That is,' her mother said, 'if we can wean her away from this Senator McCarthy nonsense.'

Gretchen now returned and we had an enjoyable meal, with her making us laugh at stories about how uninstructed most of the kids were at the McCarthy headquarters. 'They really expect politics to be either 1810 with torchlight parades or 2010 with super intellects reaching super decisions. They have no idea of the grubbiness of 1967, and very little taste for it.'

But it was not the politics of that first night with the Coles that I remember so vividly. After dinner Gretchen was about to run off to a meeting at Harvard—had to be there, she was the lady co-chairman—when her father said, 'Gretchen, you look tired. Why don't you relax for half an hour and sing to us?' Apparently she had inherited her father's gift of common sense, for she stopped, weighed the proposal for a moment, nodded her head briskly, and said, 'That's a damned good idea. I've been working all day.'

She threw aside her coat, went to a cupboard and returned with a rather large guitar, which when I first saw it, seemed a trifle too much for her to handle. However, she sat on a low stool, tossed her head so that her brown braids fell out of the way, and said quietly, 'Child 243.' I was about to ask what this meant when she strummed her guitar twice and started to play a gentle melody, after which she sang in a good, clear voice the ancient story of a young woman who marries a ship-carpenter after being assured that her betrothed has died in a foreign land. Four years later, when she and the carpenter have three children, the lover returns:

> ' "I might have had a king's daughter,
>   And fain she would have married me;
> But I've forsaken all her crowns of gold,
>   And all for the sake, love, of thee.
>
> ' "For my husband is a carpenter,
>   And a young ship-carpenter is he,
> And by him I have a little son,
>   Or else, love, I'd go along with thee." '

The lady deserts her husband, flees with her first love, only to discover that he is no longer human but has become a daemon. Gretchen's voice grew delicate and foreboding as she concluded:

> ' "He strack the tap-mast wi his hand,
>   The fore-mast wi his knee,
> And he brake that gallant ship in twain,
>   And sank her in the sea." '

'What was the name of the song?' I asked.

'Child 243,' she said, then laughed. 'That's the identification we use. Actually, it's "The Daemon Lover." The Child number came from an old-time friend of our family.'

Mrs. Cole explained that during the latter years of the last century, in a house not far from where we sat, a famous Harvard professor, Francis James Child, had collected historic ballads which were then disappearing from memory. He had spent nearly fifty years at this task, assembling every known variation of each ballad. Shortly before his death he published his findings in ten large volumes containing the life history of 305 classic ballads.

'The amusing thing,' Mrs. Cole said, 'is that dear Professor Child used to leave Boston each spring to tramp over England and Scotland, searching for his precious ballads. He really spent all his money and energy on the task. But about the same time an English scholar was spending his vacations and his money tramping around the mountains of Kentucky and Tennessee, collecting precisely the same ballads. Because, as you know, the first English settlers who hid themselves away in our southern mountains brought the ballads with them. Quite often our Kentucky mountaineers preserved them in a purer form than the English did.'

'Mrs. Cole knows so much about this,' her husband explained, 'because Professor Child taught her mother to sing many of the ballads. Right in this room. Gretchen learned them from her grandmother, so the strain is fairly pure.'

'Could I see one of the volumes?' I asked.

'Unfortunately, they're quite valuable now,' Cole said, 'and our family has never owned a set. Gretchen studies her material at the library. Darling, sing us 173.'

I don't know enough about ballads to say which one is the king. Later I was to hear Gretchen and her friends sing many manly ones about brave knights and doughty sea captains, and some of these old songs were most stirring; but I am quite certain what the queen of the ballads is. It has got to be Child 173. From the first moment that Gretchen strummed her guitar with a set of ominous chords, I was captivated by the story of Mary Hamilton, a country girl who came to Edinburgh to serve as one of four girls named Mary who were maids to Mary, Queen of Scots. Unfortunately, Queen Mary's husband fell in love with this one and got her pregnant. The tragedy begins with one of the greatest single stanzas of English popular poetry:

> Word is to the kitchen gane,
>   And word is to the ha,
> And word is up to Madame the Queen,
>   And that is warst of a',
> That Mary Hamilton has born a bairn,
>   To the hichest Stewart of a'.

When I studied this admirable ballad later, I concluded that the progression of those first three lines, the way in which rumor is depicted flying about the palace—gone, to, up—was folk poetry at its best. The entire misery of the ballad is foretold in those breathless lines, and when I heard Gretchen Cole sing them the first time, she imparted a wonderful sense of history to them. Mary Hamilton was a real girl, involved in a total scandal; here was a beginning that could end only upon the scaffold, and such compelling situations are the stuff of poetry.

When Gretchen came to the last verse, as great in its sad way as the first, she sang in a low, heartbreaking manner she had learned from her grandmother, who had got it from the professor; I have never heard a conclusion to a popular song that I have found as totally satisfying as this, perhaps because when I hear it I recall the silence that always filled the room when Gretchen Cole finished singing it:

> ' "Yestreen the queen had four Maries,
>   This night she'll hae but three;
>   There was Mary Beaton, and Mary Seaton,
>   And Mary Carmichael, and me." '

The first two lines are essence of tragedy, sparely portrayed; the last two, with their beautiful sequence of real names, bring the tragedy down to earth and remind us that it was a real girl who was hanged.

I was therefore startled when Mrs. Cole told me, 'Whenever my mother sang 173 she would tell us children the true story of Mary Hamilton, as Professor Child had told it to her, and it would make us shiver with fear.'

'Grandmother told me the story when I was young,' Gretchen broke in, 'and even today when I reach the last verse tears come to my eyes. Sometimes people tell me, "You get such emotion into the last verse." I don't tell them it's because Grandmother put it there with her story about the real Mary Hamilton.'

'Who was she?'

Mrs. Cole replied, 'Court documents from Queen Elizabeth's time show that when Mary of Scotland was young and in France she really did have four beautiful attendants, each named Mary. But it wasn't one of them who was hanged. It was a beautiful Scottish adventuress who went to Leningrad a century later . . . in the time of Peter the Great. Somehow she got to court, and some accounts say she became Peter's mistress. At any rate, she had an illegitimate child whom she wrapped in a napkin and threw in a well. She was condemned to death, not because Peter wanted it but because he had recently issued a proclamation decreeing death to women who slew their illegitimate children.

'The beheading was a notable affair, with Mary Hamilton dressed handsomely in her finest silks. When her head rolled in the street, the Czar picked it up, kissed it twice, then delivered a funeral oration. Then he kissed it again and threw it back into the gutter.'

———•◦•———

In early 1968, after hard negotiation, Frederick Cole and I reached an agreement on the Fenway Park project, and to celebrate he invited me back to Brookline for a champagne dinner, to which I brought a special gift that I had picked up in London, but when we sat down to dinner I was much disappointed to find that Gretchen was not to join us. 'She's in New Hampshire heading one of the McCarthy offices,' her mother said with some disgust. 'She took the slogan "Be Clean for Gene" quite seriously and has hired a barber to give male volunteers free haircuts.'

When I said that I thought it rather refreshing to find young people concerned about politics, Mrs. Cole said, 'Oh, I don't mind that at all. Frederick and I are Republicans, of course, and I'm sure you are too, and I admit it seems strange to have our daughter working so hard for a Democrat. But we can adjust to that. What disturbs me is the fact that she's dropped out of graduate school. Didn't even attend her first classes. I think that's a pity.'

'She's young,' Cole said. 'A year's more maturity will be good for her.'

So that night I was not able to make my presentation, but when Gretchen came back to Boston after the thrilling McCarthy performance in New Hampshire, the family invited me over again, and I found young Gretchen, now twenty, even more refreshing and provocative than before. She was filled with stories about the New Hampshire primary: 'President Johnson is definitely through. We're all going out to Wisconsin . . . the whole team . . . you ought to see our spirit. I assure you, we're going to change politics in this country. No one will ever again be able to start anything like the Vietnam war.'

'You ought to de-escalate a little yourself,' Mr. Cole said. 'Mr. Fairbanks has a present for you.'

She now became a little girl, excited at the prospect of a gift, and when I showed her a rather large and heavy box, she clasped her fingertips to her mouth and tried to guess what it might be. I am fairly sure she could not have known what it was, for even when she removed the wrapping to uncover the heavy cardboard box inside, she was obviously perplexed. Opening the lid, she encountered wads of tissue paper and cried, 'What is it? You're driving me frantic.'

When the tissue was pulled away she saw the ten handsome volumes of Professor Child's *The English and Scottish Popular Ballads, 1882–1898,* bound in heavy leather by some former London owner. She had nothing to say. These books were not only one of the major accomplishments of American scholarship; they were also the work of a man who had been her grandmother's neighbor, the inspiration of all the young balladeers in America and England who sang the haunting poetry he had rescued. This was more than a set of ten books; it was a basic testament for Gretchen's generation.

Choosing one of the volumes at random, she leafed through the pages she knew so well from library study, and cried, 'Here's the one I shall sing as my thank-you letter,' and she brought her guitar into the living room and handed me Volume IV, opened to the last page: 'Child 113. "The Great Silkie of Sule Skerrie." '

'It's quite a name,' I said.

'A silkie is a seal.' When I shrugged my shoulders, she said, 'A seal that swims in the water. When he comes on land he's transformed into a man. This seal has had a baby boy by a nursemaid he seduced. He has come to see how his son is doing.

    ' "An it sall come to pass on a simmer's day,
      When the sin shines het on evera stane,
      That I will tak my little young son,
      An teach him for to swim the faem." '

The music that accompanied these strange words was a haunting thing; you could hear the whisper of the cold Scottish sea and the mysteriousness of a time when seals and men interchanged their being. It was the kind of ballad that young people of this generation loved, for it had both the simplicity they longed for and the beauty they respected. I was reflecting on such matters while Gretchen played a minor-key transitional passage on her guitar. She then began the final verse of her song, and I was astonished at its content, quite unlike anything I had heard previously in the ballads. The seal is telling the nursemaid that after he takes his son from land and teaches him to be a good seal, the nurse will find a good life of her own with the gold that he has given her.

> ' "An thu sall marry a proud gunner,
> An a proud gunner I'm sure he'll be,
> An the very first schot that ere he schoots,
> He'll schoot baith my young son and me." '

It was as if this very old ballad had foreseen the sense of tragedy that was to overtake the young people of this generation in the United States. There was nothing in the preceding verses of the ballad that prepared one for the seal's presentiment of his death at the hands of the arbitrary gunner; it burst upon the listener with a kind of divine irrationality. I have often had a similar sense of broken sequences when discussing the draft with young men like Joe or race relations with Cato. Intuitively they perceived aspects of the future that I could not.

In succeeding months, while I worked in Boston getting the project started, I saw a good deal of the Coles, and although Gretchen was often absent working for Senator McCarthy, whenever she was in the area she kept me advised as to what was happening. I found she was a much better singer than I had supposed when I bought her the ten volumes; she sang in coffeehouses and occasionally with groups in set concerts attended by collegians from the Boston area, and whereas the others specialized in songs of protest until you would think that revolution was just around the corner, she kept to the Child ballads and was unquestionably the star of whatever concert she appeared in.

She still wore her hair in braids, preferred low-heeled brown shoes and simple dresses. She had a clear complexion which required little makeup and sufficient beauty to attract attention. Her manner was clean and unaffected; she neither mimicked the illiterate mountain accent then so popular with entertainers nor vulgarized her songs with topical allusions or sex. She kept severely to the Child text, as if the old professor might drop in at any time to check on what was being done to his handiwork. Also, as she told me one night, 'The further back you go in selecting your words, the more likely you are to be right.' I asked her what she meant by this, and she showed me one of her volumes. For Child 12, which was perhaps the most popular of the 305—it dealt with Lord Randal, who was poisoned by his sweetheart—there were fifteen distinct versions, including a fine one edited by Sir Walter Scott, and she said, 'If I used the latest, you'd find it had been all gimmicked up with touches that were supposed to improve it. You go back to the earliest version and you always find it stark and harsh and very close to human emotions. I think that's why the kids dig them so much.'

In time I came to know some of the Child ballads rather well, but the highlight of any performance came when Gretchen announced in her soft voice, 'I shall now sing Child 173,' for then the audience would cheer; in the Boston area it was known that her rendition of 'Mary Hamilton' was tops. But I preferred Child 113, that haunting ballad of the seal's premonition of death. She did not sing this at every concert, for sometimes the mood of the audience was not right, but sometimes late at night when the crowd was composed mostly of young men worried about the war in Vietnam, she would sing this song, and the strange ending would stupefy the men, as if this clever girl from Radcliffe had penetrated their minds and dredged up the things they had really been thinking about:

> ' "An the very first schot that ere he schoots,
>   He'll schoot baith my young son and me." '

I first became aware that Gretchen Cole might be in trouble one afternoon when she burst into my office near Fenway Park and asked, 'Can you let me have two hundred dollars . . . now?'

Her request was so abrupt and in a sense irrational, for her family was better than well-to-do, that I asked, 'What's it for?'

She looked at me impatiently and asked, 'Do you really want to know?' When I nodded, she said, 'Well, it's not for an abortion, which I'm sure you thought it would be. And I'm not running away from home.'

'That takes care of the interesting reasons,' I said.

'But you still want to know?' she asked with some irritation.

'For two hundred dollars, yes.'

'It won't please you,' she said, and she left my office, stood in the hall and whistled. Soon she was joined by two young men, as miserable a pair as I had ever seen outside the television newsreels. The first was tall, very skinny, hirsute, unpressed and downright dirty. The second was stocky, close-cropped and mad at the world. They seemed about Gretchen's age but lacked her assurance. In fact, the only hopeful thing I noticed about them was that their teeth were white and very straight, as if parents had taken them regularly to the orthodontist.

'This is Harry from Phoenix and Carl from New Orleans. They need one hundred dollars each.'

'What for?' I asked, suspecting that she had been right when she said I wouldn't want to know.

Very evenly she replied, 'They have to get over the border . . . to Canada. Harry has to escape the draft. Carl's already in . . . he's deserting.'

When she said this, a whole constellation of objections flashed before my mind, in a sequence she must have encountered before: First he's thinking, 'These damned punks, taking money from a girl.' Then he thinks, 'The army would do them a lot of good. I ought to call the police.' Then he thinks, 'I could get into a lot of trouble if I gave that kid from Phoenix money to escape the draft. Even worse if I helped the other one desert. They could arrest me for giving counsel and comfort.' And finally he thinks: 'I don't want any part of this.'

Soberly I asked Gretchen. 'You know that what you're doing is illegal?'

'And necessary.'

Turning to the young men, I asked, 'Why do you feel you have to run away?' They shrugged their shoulders as if to say, 'Look, man, we can't go through all that jazz again. Either give us the two hundred or don't, but for Christ's sake, lay off the sermons.'

I said, 'I don't want to know your names. I don't want to know anything about this. I'll lend you the two hundred, Gretchen, but I want my secretary to hand it to you—personally—in front of witnesses.' I showed the two fugitives the door and they left. When they were well out of sight I called my secretary and said, 'Miss Cole wants to borrow two hundred dollars. Will you please get it from the cashier?'

'Your personal account?'

'Naturally.' When she left, Gretchen said, 'You're pretty cautious, aren't you?' and I said, 'Look, young lady. I work out of Geneva in a dozen different countries. A lot of people would just love to catch me playing the black market or smuggling currency or running dope . . . or helping young punks evade military service. If that's your bag, all right. It's not mine.' I summoned two draftsmen, ostensibly to review a segment of their work. I wanted them there when my secretary returned to my office with the two hundred. They could watch me hand it to Gretchen and hear me say, 'Here's two hundred till next Friday. Don't waste it.'

Later that afternoon she returned to my office and thanked me. 'It was a real crisis,' she said. 'Those two poor kids had one more day before they'd be in real trouble. By this time tomorrow they'll be safe over the border.'

Her tone was so conspiratorial that I asked, 'Do you do this sort of thing all the time?' and she countered, 'Why do you suppose I sing so much in the cafés? Every penny I earn goes to helping kids escape the draft. My allowance, too.'

'But why?'

'Because we're trapped in a cruel, unreasonable situation. Last year about twenty of us Radcliffe girls took a course with Harvard juniors. We soon learned that if we pulled down the top grades, the boys would be left with the low ones, which would mean they'd lose their deferments and be grabbed by the army. So I organized the girls. We agreed to play dumb . . . allow the boys to carry off the top grades. But after our first exam the professor called us in and said, "I know what you girls are doing. You're a lot more intelligent than your exams show. Cut it out." When we tried to explain about the draft, he interrupted: "Before class started I had decided to drop each girl two grades and lift each boy one. So please write your most brilliant papers, get an education and let me protect the boys." Only *C* I ever got. I cherish it.'

I took her to dinner and listened as she outlined the corrupt tricks she used in helping boys beat the draft: drugs that induced high temperatures prior to physicals, other drugs that simulated heart murmurs, fake medical reports, forged educational documents, and an underground railroad such as slaves had used in the 1850s, leading from New York to New Haven to Boston to Montreal. One of her classmates at Radcliffe, daughter of a minister, specialized in teaching young atheists how to be conscientious objectors with the aid of fake documents from fake clergymen. A miasma of corruption had sprouted from the Vietnam war, and Gretchen Cole found herself at the middle of it.

'I know it's filthy—smuggling able-bodied young Tarzans over the border into Canada—but nothing we do compares with the greater crime of waging an undeclared war that kills off young Americans and leaves people like you and Father free to go ahead with your normal business enterprises. That two hundred dollars was not a loan, Mr. Fairbanks. It was a tax.'

We went from dinner to a club where she was singing, and as I saw her seated beneath the lights, her large guitar masking her body, her braids about her shoulders, I thought that here was a girl of crystal purity; she was like a woodland spring on a winter's day, running clear and cold, without one molded leaf along the edge. When she sang the old ballads she seemed to bring them from some deep and protected reservoir of human experience, almost as if she were a priestess responsible for the preservation of things which the race had found to be good. She was no ordinary girl, this one. She was an authentic, a compelling combination of intelligence, character and morality. It was proper that she should restrict herself to the pure old ballads, uncontaminated by modernisms introduced to make them more palatable, for they expressed her personality and conveyed to her youthful listeners the ideas she wished to communicate.

'I shall now sing Child 286,' she announced before offering a ballad I had not heard before. Like the times, it was awkward, illpolished and infuriating. It told of Sir Walter Raleigh's action when his ship *The Golden Vanity* runs unexpectedly upon a superior Turkish galleon. When it looks as if Raleigh must lose his ship, he finds help in a surprising quarter:

> 'Then up starts our little cabin-boy,
>   Saying, "Master, what will you give me if I do them destroy?"
> "I will give you gold, I will give you store,
>   You shall have my daughter when I return on shore,
>   If ye sink them in the Low Lands Low." '

The enterprising boy swims underwater to the Turkish enemy, bores holes in her flanks and sinks her, but when he swims back to

The Golden Vanity, Sir Walter suffers a change of heart, finding
it repugnant to give his gold and his daughter to a mere cabinboy.

‘ "I'll not take you up," the master he cried;
   "I'll not take you up," the master replied;
   "I will kill you, I will shoot you, I will send you with the tide,
      I will sink you in the Low Lands Low."

'The boy he swam around all by the starboard-side;
   They laid him on the deck, and it's there he soon died;
   Then they sewed him up in an old cow's-hide,
   And they threw him overboard, to go down with the tide,
      And they sunk him in the Low Lands Low.'

When Gretchen finished the song, applause showed the crowd's
approval, for Raleigh's crass immorality reminded the young listeners of the unjust world they faced, and as the night wore on,
with professional groups taking over to sing the songs then popular, I sat alone and reflected on how little I knew of the music I
had been taking to Monica and Yigal on their gift records and
what a powerful influence it was having upon this generation.

It was ironic: children of the affluent classes sitting in Haifa
cellars or Vwarda bungalows and listening to laments about
murderers, bank robbers, bums, revolutionaries and motorcycle
Robin Hoods, all chanted by unshaven young men in dungarees
who earned a million dollars a year. The songs I heard that winter
in Boston were an invitation to rebellion, and for the first time I
realized that if able young people like Gretchen had been nurtured
on these songs over the past ten years—the most formative of their
lives—things in the adult world were bound to be changed.

The discovery was so new to me that one night I stopped listening to the music and paid attention only to the words that were
being sung by a well-known soloist; in one normal group of four
songs he recommended a jail break, the blowing up of a bank, the
seduction of two fourteen-year-old girls, and an extended heroin
binge. It was a powerful brew that such singers concocted, and I
could understand how Gretchen, weaned on such sentiments plus
her old ballads that recounted similar stories of their day, had
decided that she must support draft dodgers and army deserters.

I was relieved, therefore, when she took the stand to offer a simple love song: Child 84. It told the story of Barbara Allan, who with icy heart rejected the love of a young man:

> 'He sent his men down through the town,
>   To the place where she was dwelling:
> "O haste and come to my master dear,
>   Gin ye be Barbara Allan."
>
> 'Oh hooly, hooly rose she up,
>   To the place where he was lying,
> And when she drew the curtain by,
>   "Young man, I think you're dying." '

I laughed at the incongruity of this line, but the solemn young people around me stared as if I had committed a sacrilege, so I put my hand over my mouth and listened.

It occurred to me, as she ended this lament, that I had never seen her with young men except in a group, and I wondered why an attractive girl, with so many talents, did not have a young man for herself. It was almost as if she were the heroine of one of her ballads: cold-hearted Barbara Allan, or perhaps the young girl in love with a daemon.

As I sat speculating on these matters, Gretchen joined me, and while we were finishing our drinks—she took ginger ale—a professor from Harvard stopped at our table to say, 'Thanks, Gret, for helping those two boys. They told me before they started north.' She nodded, and for some time that was the last I knew of either her or her problems, because on the next day I received a cable from Sir Charles Braham in Vwarda, asking me to locate a school in England that might enroll his daughter. I flew off to discharge that pleasant obligation.

───·•·───

In March, Gretchen drove west with her troupe of students to help Senator McCarthy in the Wisconsin primary, and it was while working at the Milwaukee headquarters that she heard an older woman tell a group of volunteers, 'If the Senator does get the nomination, he ought to appoint someone like Gretchen Cole to head a nationwide committee of Young Republicans for McCarthy,' and one of the college students cried back, 'Committee hell, she should be in the cabinet,' and the older woman explained, 'Heading a committee now is how you get into the cabinet then.'

At any rate, in Wisconsin they took her seriously, and on the night when President Johnson announced that he was withdrawing from the Presidential race, the young people had a noisy celebration, for they deservedly felt that at last they had influenced national politics. 'Johnson knew what he was doing,' excited young men said. 'We were going to take his pants off in this primary . . . Oregon and California, too.' Toward morning, when the crowd had thinned out, two young men from Berkeley took Gretchen aside and warned, 'The real test comes in California. Bobby Kennedy will want to make a strong showing, now that Gene has flushed Johnson out. The Kennedys will pour money into our state like it was water.'

'Do you think Gene will have to take California to stay alive?' she asked.

'Definitely. You better move your whole gang out . . . and fast. Can you get hold of any real money?'

'No, but I can find kids who'll do the work.'

'Be there.'

So in late April, Gretchen and fifteen other girls from the prestigious colleges of the east got hold of some cars and drove cross-country to Sacramento, where they hooked up with the Californians who were backing McCarthy, but in this campaign they were faced by a new element. Bobby Kennedy was a most attractive young man, with ideas they could subscribe to, and whereas it had been easy to oppose President Johnson when it looked as if he were the one that McCarthy had to defeat, it was not so clear-cut when Kennedy was the enemy. In fact, two of the girls switched their allegiance when they came in contact with the Kennedy charisma.

Consequently, many of the young people around Gretchen experienced ambivalent feelings when Kennedy defeated McCarthy in California. They had begun to suspect that McCarthy might not be able to go the whole distance, that in the end powerful forces would conspire to deny him the nomination, and they were prepared to have some drab and ordinary politician steal the prize. They were therefore relieved when Kennedy loomed as an alternative. 'I could accept Kennedy,' many of the young people reasoned, consoling themselves in advance for what boded to be a McCarthy debacle.

Not Gretchen Cole. She had the gift for single-minded commitment which one often found in New England, especially among women of good education. By a process of hard thinking she had reached the conclusion a year before, when others had barely heard of McCarthy, that he was the quiet man who could bring sense into the maelstrom of our times, and with rare single-mindedness, had clung to that position; when McCarthy won in New Hampshire and Wisconsin she felt confirmed in her early judgment, and was so heartened that she could now absorb the temporary setback in California. Bobby Kennedy impressed her as a fine young senator but never could she think of him as the moral equivalent of Eugene McCarthy.

After the defeat she stayed in California to work with various McCarthy groups, making preparations for the big push at the Chicago convention, and she was at the Los Angeles headquarters, now quiet and nearly empty, early that Wednesday morning when a confused Arab got it into his head that he could solve his region's problems by shooting one of the men best calculated to decipher them. Gretchen was at a desk, working over a list of names, when a boy from Brigham Young University burst into the room, shouting, 'They've shot Kennedy!'

Others crowded into the headquarters from the street, and till well past midnight there was pandemonium as one rumor after another flashed through the room. A portable radio was produced and the long vigil began. A man who knew Kennedy, and who had been at the scene of the attempted assassination, came on the air to reassure everyone: 'Bobby Kennedy will be playing touch football again,' and the McCarthy supporters cheered, but on the Wednesday evening broadcast, a brain specialist from New York, diagnosing the case from three thousand miles away, warned, 'With the kind of brain damage reported from Los Angeles, if he does survive, it can only be as a vegetable,' and the horror of the situation deepened.

It was two o'clock Thursday morning when the desolate word came: 'Senator Kennedy has died.'

A sense of terrible despair settled over the McCarthy camp, for the irrational, against which they had fought, had once more triumphed, bearing with it an indefinable premonition of collapse on all fronts. The honorable alternative, if McCarthy had to lose, had been snatched away. Gretchen stayed at her desk, her head lowered over a pile of address cards, and it seemed as if something vital had been drained from her, something to do with idealism and the hope for a saner world.

She stayed in California, watching on television the Mass for the dead at St. Patrick's in New York, and that night the McCarthy volunteers gathered with some college students who had worked for Kennedy. They went to a beer parlor at one of the distant edges of Los Angeles, where they would be left alone, and in bleak misery reviewed the situation. The young man from Brigham Young said, with some prescience, 'It looks to me as if the Kennedy people will not rally behind McCarthy, so the whole thing goes down the drain,' but a clever chap from the University of Virginia argued, 'What we've got to do is everyone get behind Teddy Kennedy right now. Listen to me, with him we can stampede the nomination at Chicago. And he can go on to win.'

'I would not want Teddy Kennedy,' Gretchen said.

'Why not?' the Virginian demanded.

'Because I know him, and he's too young. In 1972 or 1976 I'll support him—1968, no.'

They inspected one fruitless possibility after another, always with a deepening sense of gloom, and finally one of the Kennedy men said, 'Gretchen, you have tears in your eyes!' She lowered her head. They pressed her to explain, and she said quietly, 'A very good man has been taken from us. He wasn't my man, but he was a hope. And when that happens, tears happen.' No one spoke, for she had said what they all felt. The man from Virginia blew his nose, then said very brightly, snapping his fingers, 'Didn't someone tell me you were a singer, Gretchen?'

'She's great,' one of the McCarthy people said. 'The ballads.'

'By God,' the Virginian cried, 'this is the night for a ballad. Haunted moors and lovers on horseback. Come on.'

Gretchen explained that she could not sing without a guitar, and a vigorous effort was made to find one, without success. She smiled, shrugged her shoulders, and said, 'It's quite useless,' but one of the McCarthy people said, 'I think it's important, Gretchen. You don't need a guitar.'

A place was made for her, and she looked into the faces of the leaderless Kennedy people, the faces of the McCarthy cohorts who sensed defeat, and she said, quietly, 'Child 181.'

'There could be no better,' a girl from Wisconsin said.

And Gretchen began, in her clear, steady voice, that great lament for the Earl of Murray. It was one of the powerful death songs, the equal of 'McCrimmon's Lament' or the slow movement of the *Eroica* or the funeral procession of Siegfried winding through the forest, except that it was so rough and so much of the earth that it seemed to speak of a real man whose death could ill be spared, whereas the others were songs to death in the abstract.

'Ye Highlands, and ye Lawlands,
  Oh where have you been?
They have slain the Earl of Murray,
  And they layd him on the green.

'He was a braw gallant,
  And he rid at the ring;
And the bonny Earl of Murray,
  Oh he might have been a king!

'He was a braw gallant,
  And he playd at the ba;
And the bonny Earl of Murray
  Was the flower amang them a'.

'Oh lang will his lady
  Look oer the castle Down,
Eer she see the Earl of Murray
  Come sounding thro the town!'

As her voice died to a whisper, the young people sat in silence; more than anything that had happened since the assassination, this timeless lament for the fair one who might have been king summarized their grief. Something good and powerful had been stolen from American life, and its absence left a harrowing gap.

———•◆•———

When Gretchen returned to Boston her manner became even more grave than before, and her parents were distressed that she felt the assassination of young Kennedy so bitterly. She did not care to discuss the matter with them, but one night at dinner she did say, 'Now it's imperative that we nominate McCarthy. I'm going to Chicago and we'll need all the money we can get our hands on.' And she looked steadily at her father, until he asked, 'What are you suggesting?' and she said, 'Next year when I'm twenty-one I begin my allowance from grandfather's estate. Could you . . .'

'Give you an advance? No! One of the most immoral things in the world is to anticipate an inheritance.' He threw down his napkin, the sign among Boston bankers that a particular line of inquiry is blocked.

'Father!' she pleaded, but he said, 'Fools and people of no responsibility borrow against inheritances. I'm sure there are scoundrels in Boston who would lend on prospects—at twenty-five per cent—but we don't patronize them. Not in this family.'

She realized that this possibility was closed. On her twenty-first birthday she would have control of the allowance; until then she was a minor, subject to her father's supervision, and it was understood within the family that she would accept this. 'All right,' she said, 'will you give me five hundred dollars?'

'Yes,' Cole said. He was a Nixon man himself and disliked Senator McCarthy almost as much as he did Governor Rockefeller, but like many parents, he sensed the good that might result from his daughter's commitment to ideas, misdirected though they might be at the moment. He gave her the money, and with it she went to Chicago with her committee of enthusiasts.

Her experience there was the kind of thing that Dante drew upon in his later years when reflecting upon his travels out of Florence. She spent her money to rent rooms at the Hilton Hotel on the floor above the McCarthy headquarters, and here she provided sleeping quarters for the college students who had worked with her in New Hampshire, Wisconsin and California. They were an attractive lot, clean in appearance and dedicated in manner. With the collapse of the Teddy Kennedy balloon on the Democratic side and the nomination of Richard Nixon on the Republican, it seemed so apparent to the McCarthy people that their man had to be nominated in order to provide the voters with a choice, that young people like Gretchen convinced themselves McCarthy stood a real chance of winning the nomination and, after that, the Presidency.

'Look at it straight,' a law student from Duke University reasoned. Gretchen liked him better than the others because he not only had a keen mind but also a guitar on which he played Kentucky versions of the ballads she had learned from the English sources. He had grown up in eastern Tennessee and had won a scholarship to Davidson, then a graduate grant from Duke law school. He seemed the best type of southerner, prudent yet excitable when fine ideas were in the air. 'Nixon will be a formidable opponent. He's a top campaigner, but he's stuck with the Johnson attitude on Vietnam and will never get us out. The voters will see this, and what they'll want is a clear-cut choice, and the only one with guts enough to present this is McCarthy.'

On the Friday and Saturday prior to the convention, the McCarthy people were filled with hope, but when the committee reports started coming out and the disposition of the delegates became clear, a sense of panic began to infect the rooms occupied by the college students, and when the parade of violence, indifference and old-line political thuggery filled the screens of the rented television sets, the young people were assailed by a feeling of tragic disbelief. It couldn't happen . . . the gallant senator who had led the fight for more than a year . . . he couldn't be coldly thrust aside . . . the votes he had won in Pennsylvania couldn't be stolen from him.

On Wednesday night, blocked off from the convention by cordons of police and impotent to accomplish anything in a cause that was swirling around in eddies like the refuse in a toilet bowl, Gretchen and the law student from Duke left their hotel and crossed Michigan Boulevard to mingle with the demonstrators in Grant Park, facing the lake. What they had in mind when they did so, neither could have explained, but they moved inside the police barricades to be where the action was.

In the pale light provided by park lights, flares and headlights from police cars, they saw thousands of other aimless young people, most of them less properly dressed than they, and through the crowd there seemed to move a visible sense of frustration and anger. Bitter phrases were being hurled, and Gretchen was not surprised when some helmeted police broke line to swing at some especially obstreperous students. 'They probably deserved it,' she said to her escort.

'I don't know,' he said, pausing beside a hydrant to watch the scuffle. 'I'm constitutionally opposed to police action. You see a lot of it in the south, and it's always wrong.'

This particular disturbance was quickly settled. The students retreated and the policemen re-formed their lines, with no damage done to either side, but across a large open space Gretchen saw the shadowy outlines of another confrontation that didn't seem to be ending so simply. She and the law student ran across the grass to see what was happening, but some National Guardsmen in helmets and with rifles at the ready—boys not yet twenty brandishing heavy rifles—ordered them back, so that they were able to catch only spasmodic glimpses of what must have been something more than a mere scuffle.

'What's going on?' the law student asked one of the Guard officers.

'I don't know, but you better be glad you're over here.'

'Any shooting?'

'No. Just some head-banging.' He had no sooner said this than a group of policemen began running away from the melee and to-ward the National Guardsmen, who drew back to let them through. They were carrying the inert body of a policeman whose face was smeared with blood.

'Get back, goddammit,' they shouted as they tried to break a path through the spectators that had formed behind Gretchen. She saw one agitated policeman swing his club, not viciously but rather like a conductor's baton, clearing the way before him. He struck one young man slightly, and the fellow snarled, 'Pigs,' whereupon a policeman behind the first gave the protester a sharp crack across the head. 'Pigs, pigs!' others shouted, but by now the policemen had reached an ambulance and were off. The young man who had been struck leaned against a tree, rubbing his head, and Gretchen asked him, 'You hurt?' and he said, 'No. Just them pigs comin' through like they owned the place.'

Gretchen and the Duke law student left that part of the park and joined a large crowd surrounding six young men and a girl whose faces were quite bloodied, but no one could explain how it had happened. No ambulance came, but a young doctor who had been in the crowd asked for handkerchiefs—clean ones only—and he was staunching the flow of blood and telling the crowd, 'You ought to get this one to a hospital.' The girl had a big gash across her forehead.

'She was hit by the butt of a gun,' an older woman said. 'She wasn't doin' nothin', but the soldiers came through.'

'Was there any firing?' the Duke man asked.

'No. No. In fairness you'd have to say it was an accident. She just happened to be in the way.'

Wherever they moved, something had happened some minutes before, but they saw nothing. A lot of bodies were laid out upon the grass, but no one was dead, and as soon as ambulances were able to penetrate the crowd, the wounded were hauled away. Among the wounded there were no police, but one newspaper cameraman sat on a curb, his equipment smashed and his head laid open, and he told Gretchen, 'The swine. The swine.' She asked who, and he simply repeated, 'The swine.' He looked as if he were going to faint, so she stayed with him while the law student tried to flag down an ambulance, but soldiers guarding it mistook him for a rioter and jabbed at him with their gun butts. Fortunately, he was able to leap backward and avoid damage, but when he returned to Gretchen he said, 'We better get out of here. They're playing for keeps.' She said they couldn't leave the cameraman, who was now unconscious, so the law student tried again to attract attention, and this time a squad of policemen came over to the fallen man.

'Goddamned newspaperman,' one of them snarled, but the officer in charge said, 'Get him to a hospital. And take his camera along.' He blew his whistle several times until a patrol car came screaming up, but the two policemen detailed to lift the unconscious man into the car included the one who had cursed, and he grabbed the photographer's shoulders and pitched the inert body headfirst into the wagon.

'What are you doing?' Gretchen cried, running up to the patrol car.

Suddenly the policeman whirled about, his nerves frazzled by this night, and grabbed Gretchen by her dress, jerking her to him. 'You keep your fucking mouth shut if you don't want to lose all your teeth.' He looked about to see whose girl she was, then shoved her with great force at the Duke man. 'Get her to hell out of here,' he stormed, jumping aboard the patrol car and waving his club as it made its way through the crowd.

'I think that's good advice,' the young man said, and he led a startled Gretchen out of the park and back to her hotel room.

What happened next is difficult to say. Police reports, submitted later, insisted that from the floor of the Hilton Hotel where Gretchen and her college students had rooms, some men had dropped paper bags containing human excrement on the heads of police standing guard below. Gretchen's committee denied this. What is certain is that a cadre of inflamed police stormed through the floor, kicking open doors, hauling kids out of bed, and thrashing them unmercifully with clubs, brass knuckles and bare fists.

Without speaking a word, four policemen rushed into Gretchen's room, upended her bed, and began beating her with clubs as she lay on the floor. One kicked at her but struck only her pillow; another beat her about the head with his fists. She saw none of them, too startled to appreciate what was happening, but as they rushed from her room to assault another, she heard one of them mutter in a voice of black rage and frustration, 'Next time stay in college, you smart shits.'

Gretchen was not hurt, not even bruised, for the police clubs had become entangled in her bedclothes, and the man who had tried to punch her in the head had been highly inefficient, but when she ran into the hall she saw something she would never forget. The law student from Duke had been dragged out of his room and under the hall lights, which had aided his assailants, and been clubbed until his head and face were masses of clotted blood. His jaw was broken and hung at an ugly angle, and he had been beaten so viciously across his left shoulder that his collarbone was broken too. He took four steps toward Gretchen, and collapsed.

As Gretchen knelt to cradle his battered head, she looked into the room from which he had been dragged. The police had kicked in the television tube, so that the picture was no longer visible, but the radio part was still functioning and a voice from the convention hall was announcing: 'We can now say with certainty that the lonely crusade led by Senator Eugene McCarthy has come to nothing. He could buck President Johnson in New Hampshire and the late Senator Kennedy in California, but in Chicago he was powerless against the machine.'

———•◆•———

The battered Duke law student did Gretchen an unwitting disservice which radically changed her life. When she stopped by the hospital to check on his injuries, lingering to commiserate with him over the disaster of the Democratic party, she compared him to herself, and laughed: 'We're like two medieval Crusaders who set forth in polished armor to accomplish wonders in the Holy Land. Thieves set upon us before we got to our ship. We're a pair of fools.'

'This battle's lost,' he said through his wired jaws. 'But they'll have to come back to us. Because we were right.'

'Do you have enough money to get home?'

'Yes. But there's one thing you could do for me. Did you look in my room today?'

'A shambles.'

He groaned, shrugged his painful shoulders and said, 'I suppose they wrecked the guitar.'

'I didn't see one.'

'Those pigs.'

'Don't use that word. That's for children.'

'After what they did last night?'

'Don't use it.'

'There's a chance they missed the guitar. It was in the closet. On top. If it's there, take it home with you and you can send it to me later. It's a real Kentucky swinger.'

When she got back to the hotel she went to his disheveled room, which the hotel was having photographed for the insurance company, and looked in the closet, and there, safely tucked away, was the rather large, carefully polished old-style guitar. She struck a few chords and was pleased with the sound.

Gretchen had never traveled with a guitar, for she thought it needlessly conspicuous, the sort of thing that girls on the make liked to do. She was therefore not happy at the commission the Duke student had given her, but when she thought of his painful condition, she deemed it a small favor that he had asked.

But her intuition was correct. When she and her friends reached the town of Patrick Henry, east of Chicago, two policemen stopped them and forced their car onto the shoulder of the high-way, then muttered with satisfaction when they saw the guitar. 'This has got to be one of them,' they said. 'You come with us.'

They yanked Gretchen out and threw her into their patrol car. One of the men strode back and grabbed the offending guitar, slamming it into the back seat of their car. 'You,' they growled at the boy who was driving, 'get this crowd the hell out of here.'

'What are you doing with her?' the driver shouted.

The older of the policemen whipped about, rushed over to the car and said in tones of frustration and overflowing anger, 'Look, you snot-nosed kids, we've taken all we can from you. One more crack . . . just one . . . and I'm gonna tear you apart. Now you drive the hell out of here . . . fast.'

The driver, an honors student in English literature from Yale, had also had as much as he could take, so he calmly reached into the glove compartment, took out a pad of paper and proceeded to write down the policemen's badge numbers and the license of the prowl car. Then, with studied care, he shifted the gears lever on the floor of his car and pulled away.

The policeman, red-faced because he had not thought of something dramatic with which to startle the young punks, returned to his car in a rage, slammed it into gear, and tore through the streets to police headquarters, where he yanked Gretchen onto the sidewalk and into a red-brick building. Thrusting her before an overweight desk sergeant, he growled, 'Book her,' and when this perfunctory job was completed he hauled her along a corridor and threw her into an empty room, tossing the guitar in behind her. Within a few minutes the room was filled with four policemen and one plain-clothes detective.

'She's the one who hit the policeman in the face with a brick,' the arresting officer said, reading from a teletype message. 'Braids, guitar, good-looking clothes. That's her. We'll ship her back to Chicago.'

Of the five men in the room, two would say nothing during the interrogation, the man in plain clothes and the younger of the two officers who had arrested her. The others referred to him as Woiczinsky. He seemed quiet, strong and apparently new at the job.

Her three questioners were men of distinctive appearance. The arresting officer was burly and red in the face. The second man was tall and spoke in a soft voice. The third was short, thin, very quick and birdlike. 'Red Face, Soft Voice, Bird Man,' Gretchen repeated to herself as the questioning proceeded.

Bird Man wanted to know what she had been doing in Chicago . . . why she thought it all right to assault policemen? He was concerned about her smoking marijuana and the fact that heroin had been found in her room. 'Why does a pretty girl like you fool around with that stuff?' he asked several times.

Red Face used a more startling tactic—leaping at her and shouting close to her ear, 'Why do you smart college kids think you can go around hitting policemen in the face with bricks?'

Gretchen was unable to speak. Not yet recovered from the shock of Chicago, she was incapable of comprehending what was happening to her now. She could only stand silent.

It was Soft Voice who started the real trouble. Very quietly he asked the others, 'How do we know she ain't smugglin' heroin right now?' His question was greeted with silence, so he added, 'I mean, how would we know? If she's a junkie?'

Bird Man moved very close and asked, 'You a junkie? You a hophead?'

When she remained silent, Red Face took over and shouted, 'We spoke to you. You better answer. Why are you a junkie?'

It was now that Gretchen realized: They aren't going to beat me. If he were going to strike me, he would have done it then. I can stand their abuse . . . if they don't beat me. She guessed, from the careful manner in which the men refrained from touching her, that they had received careful orders: Don't rough up the prisoners . . . especially girls. And she guessed, too, from the way in which her three interrogators looked from time to time at the plain-clothes man, that he was there to enforce the edict.

Now Soft Voice resumed his argument: 'How can we be sure she ain't smugglin' heroin? Remember that chick had it hidden in her guitar?' He looked at the plain-clothes man, who nodded, whereupon Soft Voice took the guitar, shook it, stuck his fingers into the center hole, looked at it from various angles, and then in a sudden move which made Gretchen gasp, swung it over his head and smashed it into scattered pieces.

'Now you better talk,' Red Face said menacingly, 'or we're gonna smash you in exactly the same way.'

'No heroin here,' Soft Voice reported as he kicked among the wooden fragments. 'She probably has it hidden.' Again there was silence in the room, and Soft Voice repeated almost in a whisper, 'She probably hid it.' This time there was a much longer silence, which Gretchen could not understand. She was watching the plain-clothes man, who slowly nodded his head.

'Strip!' Red Face shouted into her face. 'I said strip!'

Gretchen, bewildered by a sudden flood of lights and by the menacing faces, made a gesture of incomprehension, so Soft Voice moved closer and said, admonishingly, 'He told you to strip. To take off your clothes. We want to see where you hid the heroin.'

'I can't,' Gretchen tried to say, but she was so terrified that no sounds came.

'You sensitive or something?' Red Face yelled. 'You sleep with that gang of punks in the car. You screw with them every night. Probably gang-bang. And now you're sensitive. Lady . . .'

Bird Man moved in and said, 'Lady, you're under arrest. You face a whole string of charges. And you are gonna strip. Now!'

Gretchen was so bewildered, she couldn't move or talk, whereupon Soft Voice came closer to her, holding a heavy leather strap. 'I'm gonna count to six, and if you haven't started taking off your clothes, I am gonna beat the livin' shit out of you. Get goin'.' He started counting in a menacing whisper, 'One, two, three,' and although Gretchen was certain he was not going to strike her, her assurance was diminished by the fact that the man was an obvious psychopath. Of the five, he was the one who might beat her, so in a terrified daze she began unbuttoning her dress. 'That's better,' Soft Voice said reassuringly. 'We won't need the strap.'

'Everything off,' Red Face commanded. 'Yes, every goddamned thing. You smart college girls think it's all right to screw with anybody. New morality, you call it. Well, we're gonna see some of that new morality.'

Someone giggled, and Soft Voice said, 'The purpose is we want to see where you have the heroin hidden.'

When Gretchen stood in her panties and bra she hesitated, whereupon Soft Voice screamed at her with a violence that shattered, 'Everything!' He grabbed the leather strap again and swung it viciously under her nose. She wavered, and he brought it with terrifying force onto the floor, an inch from her left foot. 'You strip, goddamn you! Now!'

Trembling, Gretchen unfastened her bra and let it fall away. She was vaguely aware that each of the five men leaned forward. No one spoke, and she rolled down her panties. In the long silence someone sighed, then Soft Voice asked in an insinuating whisper, 'How would you like that in your Christmas stocking, Woiczinsky?' The men laughed nervously, then Red Face asked in real perplexity, 'Lady, why does a dish like you fool around with politics? Why don't you get yourself some nice young fellow and crawl into bed and have a lot of children?'

'You got a boyfriend?' Soft Voice asked. 'I mean a special one? One you go to bed with regular?'

'Do you like it in bed?' Bird Man asked. 'I mean, do you have real fun when he climbs aboard?'

Gretchen clenched her fists and tried not to faint, but even though she did summon up what little strength she had left, she was ill-prepared for what happened next. 'Bend over,' Soft Voice said. When she remained motionless under the lights, he repeated gently, 'You must bend over now.' When she still made no move, he brought the strap down beside her foot and screamed, 'Bend over, you fucking whore!'

'We want to see where you got the heroin hidden,' Bird Man said quietly, and for the first time one of the men touched her. Bird Man lifted a metal ruler, placed it gently on her head, and delicately pushed upon it until Gretchen's forehead was nearly touching the floor. Soft Voice swung one of the bright lamps about until it focused on her rear, then said approvingly, 'Target for tonight. How you like them apples, Woiczinsky?'

Who approached next, Gretchen could not say, but while Bird Man's gentle steel ruler kept her head lowered, someone took a pencil and poked at the openings of her body. 'No heroin here,' Soft Voice reported.

The men stepped away, and slowly Gretchen resumed an upright position. Looking with anguished eyes at the shadowy circle, she uttered her only words: 'You are really pigs.'

From the darkness Woiczinsky leaped at her, struck her violently across the head with his fist, and knocked her sprawling into a corner.

'You stupid shit!' the plain-clothes man shouted. 'Get him out of here.'

Red Face and Bird Man hustled the young policeman from the room while Soft Voice came to the corner and probed Gretchen with the toe of his shoe. 'She's not hurt,' he told the man in mufti, who threw Gretchen her clothes and said, 'Get dressed, you slut.'

Appalled, and only now becoming aware of what had happened to her, Gretchen huddled in the corner, trying to sort out her clothes. Her bra was missing and she clumped ineffectively about the room to find it. She was engaged in this futile process when she heard voices in the corridor. They came closer, and someone pushed open the door. With a relief she could not express, she saw that it was the driver of her car, the English major from Yale. He had consulted a lawyer, who had summoned the mayor. These three now entered the room to see Gretchen standing naked among her scattered clothes.

'What in hell happened here?' the lawyer demanded.

'Now, now!' the mayor said consolingly. 'There's nobody hurt.' He looked at Gretchen and asked, 'You weren't sexually ravaged, were you?'

When Gretchen shook her head no, the lawyer said, 'There's a lot of ways a girl can be sexually molested.'

'But there's only one that counts,' the mayor said. While Gretchen was getting into her clothes he inspected her face and asked, 'Nothing broken, is there?' When he had satisfied himself that no real damage had been done, he said to Gretchen, 'A mistake, an unfortunate case of mistaken identity. You weren't hurt in any way, were you?'

Gretchen understood the question, understood its implications. She was being asked to hush up an incident that everyone regretted and whose ventilation could only bring trouble, to her as well as to the others. It was a real temptation for her to say that nothing happened, but when she was about to assent she happened to look at the floor and saw the shattered pieces of the guitar. People in authority who would willfully smash a guitar because it was the symbol of things they could not comprehend deserved no protection.

'Yes,' she said quietly, fully aware of what she was doing, 'I was assaulted . . . brutally . . . by Patrolman Woiczinsky.'

'Maggidorf!' the mayor shouted. When the plain-clothes man entered the room, the mayor yelled, 'This girl says that Nick Woiczinsky assaulted her.'

'Woiczinsky!' the detective gasped. 'He's in Gary. Been there all day. Picking up that kid on the murder rap.' He called for the three other policemen, who assured the mayor that Nick Woiczinsky had left that morning for Gary and wouldn't be back for some hours.

'Where do you think I heard the name?' Gretchen asked with

stubborn force. She turned to the lawyer, who shrugged his shoulders.

'Best thing for you kids to do,' the lawyer advised, 'is to get back in your car and drive east.' When Gretchen started to protest, he warned her, 'Otherwise you can be arrested for bringing false charges against the police. Clearly, Patrolman Woiczinsky couldn't have assaulted you, because he wasn't in town today.'

When Gretchen rejected this infamous collusion, the lawyer smiled at her, undisturbed. Shrugging his shoulders, he said, 'Lady, if these four fine officers testify that Nicholas Woiczinsky wasn't in town today . . .'

When the lawyer said this, the English major stepped forward, about to speak, but Gretchen sensed what he was going to say and she stopped him. 'I think we'd better go,' she said quietly.

'That's a good girl,' the mayor said reassuringly. 'I'm sure you weren't hurt, and I'm sure this can all be forgotten. These last few days . . . Chicago . . . it's been very difficult . . . for all of us.'

When they were well out of town, headed east, Gretchen asked the driver, 'You were going to say that you could identify Woiczinsky, weren't you?'

'I took the number of his badge,' the driver said.

'Good.' She sat in silence, then repeated the word, 'Good. When we get to Cleveland I want you to drive me to the Associated Press. Because I have taken enough.'

———•◆•———

When the story splashed across headlines, Gretchen heard reverberations from three sources—social Boston, academic Cambridge, agonized family—and she was prepared for none of them.

In Boston, older circles were incensed, not at the Patrick Henry police, 'who were only doing their duty,' but at Gretchen for having paraded her indecencies in public. One woman reasoned: 'These students have got to learn that policemen are given billy-clubs and guns to enforce order, and if one persists in breaking order by protests and demonstrations, one must expect to get clubbed around a little bit.' Another summarized Boston opinion by pointing out: 'All sensible persons are aware that now and then women get raped, but one never runs to the newspapers. It's an accident a family must accept in silence.' The graver question, however, was, 'What was a nice girl like her doing in a city like Chicago anyway?' There were also muttered doubts as to the propriety of her having driven across country with a young man she barely knew, 'even if he did come from Yale.' And when both the mayor of Patrick Henry and his chief of police swore that Nicholas Woiczinsky had not been in town that day, thus proving Gretchen's story to have been a fabrication, opinion solidified: 'One more radical young person was caught in her own trap.'

In the Cambridge universities, reactions were quite different. Students from Harvard and MIT, along with girls from Radcliffe, were prepared to accept Gretchen's story precisely as told; most knew friends who had undergone unsavory experiences with the police or National Guard, and when stories began appearing as to how Mayor Daley's force had manhandled the press, who were not demonstrating, credence was lent to Gretchen's report. Among the various faculties she became something of a heroine, with the younger professors saying, 'You acted on behalf of the entire civilized community.' A Harvard law professor told her, 'Press your charges. Citizens are not obliged to accept such indignities.' He volunteered to represent her free of charge if the case came to trial. But what alarmed her was the violence of the reactions among her liberal friends. Negroes told her, 'Now you see what we've been talking about. Now you know why there has got to be gunfighting in the streets.' An action committee from Harvard met with her and said, 'After Chicago, there has got to be overt resistance. Buildings are going to burn.' In her agitated condition she felt powerless to combat such threats.

It was the reaction of her parents that perplexed her most. They were, of course, outraged that their daughter had been mistreated and they defended her stubbornly; but they were also ashamed that a child of theirs had allowed herself to get into such a mess, and she caught them saying things that betrayed their suspicion that it was the police who were telling the truth. 'Where there's smoke there's fire' seemed to be their attitude. And that she should have paraded her discomfiture in the Cleveland press, with stories of being stripped naked and abused by five leering men, passed their comprehension. 'I should have thought you'd have wanted to keep it a secret,' her mother said one afternoon, dabbing at her eyes, and when Gretchen replied that the Harvard law professor was going to support her in civil action against the city of Patrick Henry, her mother quite lost her balance.

At this point Frederick Cole showed himself to be the stalwart man I had known in our negotiations. 'If our daughter has suffered what she says took place in that police station,' he told the family circle, 'we are going to defend her all the way. Not only for herself, but for all other young people who might find themselves in similar situations.'

'You mean . . . fight it all over again in the headlines?' his wife asked. 'That would be too much. Gretchen, tell him to stop.'

In compromise, Mr. Cole asked one of the Brookline detectives to try to unravel what had really happened. He left for Patrick Henry in early October, worked two weeks, and returned with disquieting news. At a conclave attended by Gretchen, her parents and the corporation lawyers, he reported: 'I've checked all the records, and they seem to be quite clear. Chicago police had broadcast a valid warrant for your arrest on suspicion of assault against one of the policemen. Four Chicago witnesses place you in Grant Park on the night of the assault. Two witnesses identify you from photographs as the girl with the guitar who hit the policeman in the face with a brick . . . or a stone . . . or something.'

'I didn't have a guitar in Chicago,' Gretchen protested.

'The police have a photograph of you with a guitar,' the detective said, and presented a picture which showed her carrying the guitar of the boy from Duke whose jaw had been broken.

'But that's not my guitar,' she protested again, and as she spoke she looked at the faces of her family, at her family lawyers, and each was impassive, because everyone knew that Gretchen had a guitar.

'Now as to Patrick Henry, the testimony is overwhelming— almost irrefutable, I'd say—that Patrolman Nicholas Woiczinsky was not on duty that day in Patrick Henry. Also, the mayor and the lawyer, Hallinan, have given sworn depositions that when they got to the police station you were fully clothed and that nothing had happened. I got the strong feeling that if you dare to go back to Patrick Henry, you're going to find yourself in jail, either for the proven assault in Chicago or on the charge of bringing false witness against the local police.'

'But what about the driver of our car? He saw Woiczinsky. He saw me in the police station.'

The detective coughed and said, 'I didn't want to bring this up, but I have three depositions here. The first shows that the police have run a check on that young man and he has a conviction in the state of Connecticut . . . on what charge do you suppose? Marijuana. Now as for these next two'—and here he slipped a pair of legal papers to Gretchen—'you may prefer keeping them to yourself. I haven't shown them to your parents.'

Gretchen saw that the first related to the Blue-and-Gray Motel at the Breezewood Interchange of the Pennsylvania Turnpike, whose night clerk had deposed that on the night of Thursday, August 29, Gretchen Cole of Brookline, Massachusetts, and Randolph Pepperdine of New Haven, Connecticut, had registered together. The second deposition came from the maid, one Claribelle Foster of Somerset, Pennsylvania, who swore that the two had shared the same room. 'The marijuana charge would blast the young man's testimony right out of court,' the detective warned, 'and these could make you look awful bad. Take my advice, tuck those papers away and forget the whole affair.'

This Gretchen was tempted to do, but something within her made surrender impossible, so without thinking of the consequences, she threw the depositions before her father and cried, 'They're lies. We did check in at the motel together . . . along with the other kids. They'll testify I shared my room with two other girls.'

But as soon as she said this she saw with dismay that only one person in the room accepted her story. To the others it was incomprehensible that a college student should be right and the mayor of a city wrong. She was a young person, mixed up with strange philosophies and stranger people, and nothing that was charged against her was improbable. In a kind of dumb fury she looked from one stern face to the next, realizing that in them she was seeing the jury that would listen to her case in Patrick Henry, and the dreadful futility of her position bore down upon her. The very people who should have been defending her had become her accusers.

For the first time her father spoke. He was the one who believed. 'I spent the last week checking up on the four young people who shared that car with you, and I'm convinced that what you say is true.' Gretchen looked at him with the compassionate love that a young woman can sometimes feel for her father when she suddenly sees him as a man who has had to fight against the world, and she waited for him to tell the family lawyers to proceed, but instead she heard him say, 'But there's absolutely nothing we can do. With their fabric of interlocking lies, they've got us boxed in.'

'What do you mean?' she cried.

'That there are times when a conspiracy makes the individual helpless.'

'Now wait a minute, Mr. Cole!' the detective protested. 'If you think that I'm so dumb I can't spot a conspiracy . . .'

'Of course it's a conspiracy,' Cole said evenly. 'I've seen Randolph Pepperdine's notebook and he took down Woiczinsky's name and number. You don't make up things like that.'

'The boy's a marijuana addict.'

'He's nothing of the sort, and you know it. But the fact remains that if the mayor of Patrick Henry and his chief of police and the lawyer, Hallinan, act in collusion on their stories, there's nothing we can do.'

Gretchen was stunned by this conclusion. In consternation she pointed to the depositions lying on the table, and cried, 'I suppose you believe them, too?'

Mr. Cole placed his arm about his daughter and said, 'I think I know what happened at the motel. Do you think your mother and I would believe depositions like that?'

Gretchen looked at the lawyers, at her red-eyed mother, at the obdurate detective. In her frustration she bowed to the latter and said, 'The people of Brookline should feel secure with you protecting them.' Then she fled from the room, and when she was gone her mother dropped her head on the table and muttered, 'Thank God, it's not to go any further.'

———— ·•·•·• ————

The balance of 1968 was a trying period for the Coles. Gretchen, after the session with the detective and the quashing of her lawsuit, continued living at home but found it impossible to speak with her parents. Mrs. Cole attempted a conciliation, with assurances such as: 'We are on your side, dear, no matter what you did in Chicago.' Gretchen dismissed her as a fool, which she was not.

Mr. Cole did his best to understand the torments his daughter was suffering; at one point he wrote to me in Geneva:

> You told me when I saw you in London that you were helping an Englishman in Vwarda get his daughter back on an even keel. I wish to God you could do the same for me. That adorable child you saw with pigtails and a guitar has suffered a shattering experience which has left her bedazed, and I find myself standing helplessly by. I have tried repeatedly to assure her of my understanding and sympathy, but to no avail. I went to great pains and some manipulation to prevent her from engaging in a lawsuit against venal public officials, intending only to help her, but my efforts have blown up in my face. You said once you had a son. Is raising a boy any easier?

He made many overtures to his daughter, admitting that he was misguided in persuading her to drop her charges against the police, but he was powerless to regain her respect, and they lived as enemies in the house where she had learned to sing.

Her fellow students, aware of what was happening, asked her how she could bear to stay in the same house, and she explained, 'I'm not twenty-one till January. But with the first income from my inheritance . . . goodbye to Brookline forever.'

By late October it was apparent that she could not concentrate on her graduate work at Radcliffe, nor could she get excited about the election, since she was convinced that either Nixon or Humphrey would find himself locked into old concepts of government. She winced whenever either of them referred to law and order, and by mid-November she stopped even the pretense of attending classes.

At the beginning of December some law students at Harvard tried to get her to head a committee backing Justice Abe Fortas in the Congressional fight over his appointment as Chief Justice, but she could generate no enthusiasm. Still, the law fascinated her and she wondered if perhaps the young radicals were not right when they preached: 'Whenever society insults you, zap it right back with super-love.' Setting aside all other matters, she spent a day composing a careful letter, which she sent registered:

Brookline, Massachusetts
December 10, 1968

Patrolman Nicholas Woiczinsky
Police Department
Patrick Henry, Indiana

Dear Officer Woiczinsky,

I am the young woman whom your fellow officers humiliated last August at your police headquarters, the one with the guitar whom you arrested falsely as we were driving through Indiana.

I have often recalled that day, and I remember that during the time I was in that room you said nothing and did nothing to add to my dismay. It occurs to me now that you were ashamed of the whole procedure.

I also am ashamed. I am ashamed that my spirit broke and that I called you pigs. It was a hateful word, one I should not have used. You were right to react as you did, and I forgive you for having knocked me across the room. I might have done the same had I been in your position, and I now wish to apologize.

You may wonder why I did not press charges, as I threatened to do. The sworn statements of your mayor, your chief of police, the lawyer and Officer Maggidorf convinced my parents and their lawyers that I was a liar. They were also convinced that you were not in Patrick Henry that day. I wish you had not been, for you were better than the others. Please stay that way.

Yours respectfully,
Gretchen Cole

The next day she was summoned by her senior professor, who asked, 'Are you as disorganized as you appear?' When she nodded, he suggested, 'Why don't you drop out this semester? Go to Florida . . . Virgin Islands . . . some place completely new and try to get things in focus?' He seemed the first adult who appreciated her problem.

'I may do that,' she said. 'After the New Year.'

'Why delay?'

'In January I'll be twenty-one.'

He took off his glasses. 'Are you only twenty? With your outstanding record?' He looked at her undergraduate marks and then at some appended notes. 'Didn't you use to sing in one of the cafés?' When she nodded, he said, 'Go back. Forget studies for the rest of the year.'

'What do you think I ought to do when I resume?' she asked.

'You can go in almost any direction,' he said. 'You have an inclination toward politics?'

'I don't think so. I thought I might like to . . . well . . . find some earlier period in history when values were in flux . . . Hundred Years' War maybe . . . '

'And write about it?'

'Yes.'

'Absolutely splendid! A first-rate challenge! A first-rate relevancy!' Gretchen smiled at his enthusiasm; it was so good to hear an adult agree with something rather than bring up a score of objections as to why the proposal could not work. 'How's your Latin?'

'Eight years of *A*.'

'German?'

'I read it.'

'French?'

'Not so good.'

'Then it's very simple.' He rose and walked about his study. 'My God, I wish the other problems that reach this office were so simple. You're a brilliant girl. One of the ablest undergraduates I've had. Go to Besançon—that's in France, near the Swiss border—enroll in the American Institute. Brush up your French. Then come back prepared for some real work.' He consulted a catalogue on foreign study and found the name he wanted. 'Karl Ditschmann. Splendid fellow . . . Alsatian . . . taught at Michigan and Middlebury . . . tell him I sent you and that you're not to worry about grades. Just browse . . . walk in the hills . . . imagine you're back in the year 1360 . . . the first part of the war is over . . . Crécy and Poitiers are past . . . the Black Death is gone . . . everyone's sighing with relief . . . so imagine the terror when fighting erupts again . . . Agincourt and the Peasants' Rebellion lie ahead.' He prowled the small room and said, 'Get the feeling of France in your bones. The rioting peasants are coming down this valley—this valley here at your feet—and they storm past. Supposing you comprehended— you just might be able to write something relevant to our days.'

He imbued her with his enthusiasm, and she took down the name of the institute at Besançon, but as she was leaving, he said, 'Maybe even more important is to sing again,' and she asked, 'Have you ever seen a guitar kicked to pieces? It affects singing, you know.'

So for the last weeks of 1968 she lay about the house, read in desultory fashion about the Hundred Years' War, and kept to herself. Boys from Harvard and Amherst and MIT who had known her stopped by occasionally to talk, but she drew back from them as if they were leprous. Once when four of them were with her she saw their faces change into that circle of policemen at Patrick Henry.

The Cast Iron Moth asked her to sing, both at Thanksgiving and at Christmas, but she could not bring herself to do so. She did not even sing when she was by herself at home. The only thing that retained her interest was committee work in helping draft evaders slip into Canada; one tall Californian to whom she had given money aroused her from her lethargy, for he seemed a gentle person, aware of the confusions that had overtaken her, but when he tried to kiss her goodnight in thanks for what she had done, she shied away from him.

On January 10, her birthday, she marched into the office of her family's lawyer and informed him that she wished one quarter of her yearly income. She said further that she would advise him by letter at the beginning of each quarter where future checks should be mailed. When he started to explain what she ought to do with the money, she cut him short: 'I shall be here to pick it up to-morrow at nine.'

'This time you must be careful of your companions . . .'

She looked at him with contempt. His had been one of the strongest voices advising against her lawsuit. He had spoken first and had set the pattern for the group's acceptance of the charges against her. She thought of a dozen clever things she ought to tell this cautious old man, but she knew that communication would be impossible, so she controlled her anger and withdrew from his office. He followed her into the hall to ask, 'Where did you say the subsequent payments were to be sent?' and she could not forbear replying, 'Perhaps Nepal. Maybe Marrakech. I don't know yet myself, but I'll keep you advised.' On her way home she laughed as she thought of him poring over his atlas, trying to locate Nepal and Marrakech. She couldn't have helped him; they were names that some of the kids at the café had dropped.

On January 11 she picked up her first check, went to the bank, transferred it into a fistful of traveler's checks, went to the Air France office to collect her flight ticket, and that afternoon informed her mother, 'I'm flying to France on the eight o'clock plane.'

'When?'

'Tonight. You can tell Father.' She would divulge no more of her plans.

Mrs. Cole immediately telephoned her husband, who rushed home in a taxi to demand, 'What's this?'

'I'm going to France,' she said. 'When I'm settled I'll tell you what I plan to do.'

'How can you go to France?' her father cried.

'Very simply. I catch a cab, go out to the airport, and board the plane.'

'But we can't give you the money . . . your university fees will be wasted . . .'

'I don't need you, Father,' she said coldly. 'In October I needed you badly.'

'You mean about the Patrick Henry business?' her mother asked. 'Darling, we've forgiven you . . . no matter what happened out there . . . we've forgotten.'

'I haven't,' she said, and she would not allow them to accompany her to the plane.

Besançon was ideally constructed for the purpose of helping a confused American girl regain her balance. Set beside a river and within a cup of hills, it had always stood on the frontier. Julius Caesar had used it as one of his capitals, and Roman legions, weary of pursuing barbarians in the north, always returned with relief to the security of Besançon. Later it had been the frontier between Germans and French, and its rows of stolid stone houses had often given sanctuary. It was not a beautiful city, but it was stable and courageous, and Gretchen appreciated its stalwart quality.

Dr. Ditschmann was a burly, cabbage-eating scholar who each day muttered a prayer of thanks for his good luck in getting back to civilization after those long years of exile in Michigan and Vermont. He had been chosen by a consortium of American universities to head a graduate seminar which they conducted in loose affiliation with the University of Besançon, one of Europe's principal centers for language study. Ditschmann delighted in his work, finding the European academic life refreshing after his long absence. He understood young Americans and provided an anchor for troubled ones like Gretchen, because he appreciated the contradictions that assailed them. 'Today it is more difficult to be a thoughtful American than it was two thousand years ago to be a thoughtful Roman,' he said, and his American wife, a no-nonsense young woman from Vermont with a bizarre New England sense of humor, agreed: 'I'm always amazed when I find an American who can manage her back buttons.' The Ditschmanns liked to run off on short trips to Switzerland, Germany or Italy and take students with them to savor new lands.

Ditschmann approved Gretchen's idea of burrowing into the earth to establish contact with the motives that had animated the Hundred Years' War. 'Today you be the peasant and I'll be the knight,' he would propose, 'and I have come riding by to ravish your daughter,' and his wife would add, 'A hell of a lot of ravishing you would accomplish. You couldn't even catch her.' He interrupted his work to drive along country roads to places like Cravant and Agincourt, where battles had been fought, and to Orléans, where Jeanne d'Arc had entered the wars, but by mid-April it was obvious to both Gretchen and the Ditschmanns that she was not finding the combination of values she sought. Her French had improved, but her involvement in the wars had practically vanished.

'Are you disappointed in me?' she asked as the Ditschmanns drove her back from Troyes, where one of the treaties had been signed.

'Not at all,' he said. 'It's the good minds that find difficulty in committing themselves. A lesser girl would have felt obligated to plod ahead. You inspect for twelve weeks . . . find a host of weaknesses . . . in yourself or in the subject . . . you're well advised to chuck it.'

Mrs. Ditschmann asked, 'What decided you?'

'Jeanne d'Arc. She's too amorphous. She absorbs the landscape and I'm not equipped to deal with her. I need a more solid footing . . . among the peasants.'

So it was agreed that she would quit Besançon, but she had to stay around until her next check arrived. Of course, when she sent her address to the bank, they passed it along to her father, who found that it was only a few miles from Geneva to Besançon. He sent me a cable asking if I could meet him there to discuss matters with his daughter, but I was in Afghanistan and my secretary did not forward the cable, for she expected me back in

Geneva momentarily. I arrived during the last week in April and immediately wired Cole that I would proceed to Besançon, for I was eager to discover what had happened to Gretchen.

I am partial to that mountainous region of France, for if modern history has passed it by, so has progress, and it is always pleasant to see old manners being maintained on old farms. Linguists claimed that the best French in the empire was spoken in Besançon, so it was reasonable for the American universities to locate their institute here. When I reached it, however, I found that Dr. Ditschmann and his wife had taken some students on a field trip to the oft-besieged city of Belfort. They would return in time for dinner. In the meantime, his secretary told me, Mr. Frederick Cole of Boston was arriving on the evening plane, but when I asked if I could see Miss Cole, the secretary mumbled that Dr. Ditschmann would explain when he returned, so I concluded that Gretchen must have accompanied them to Belfort.

I retired to my room knowing nothing of her problem, except that she still had one, because her father was not the kind of man to take an airplane to Besançon, or Washington either, unless something grave had transpired. As I recalled a remark of Gretchen's, 'Father's not apt to run if he can walk, nor fly if he can dog-trot,' the phone rang to announce that Cole was waiting for me in his room.

In Boston I had respected this man; in Besançon I liked him, for he showed himself to be a compassionate human being, much disturbed over the welfare of his daughter. 'I didn't advise you earlier that she was so close,' he explained, 'because I didn't know where she was. That's right. She rejected us completely. It was our fault, but once we'd made the mistake, she would permit no amends. How do you think we learned where she was? Through the bank. How pitiful.'

'Why did she leave?' I asked.

The terseness of his reply startled me. 'Ugly external reasons. Worse internal ones.'

'What triggered it?'

'She was, as you know, interested in McCarthy's campaign. At the Chicago convention a series of miserable things happened— what, we don't know for sure. On the trip home her car was stopped by small-town police who gave her . . .' He hesitated, looked down at his knotted fingers, then said, 'They gave her what newspapers call a working-over. Extremely rough for a girl . . . for anyone. She became outraged—had every right to—and launched a public complaint . . . through the Cleveland papers, if you please. Mrs. Cole and I panicked. Purely to protect Gretchen, we took steps to hush things up, and Gret felt that we had abandoned her. Mrs. Cole said some inappropriate things, and I must have looked quite wishy-washy. That's when the internal trouble started. She rejected us. Terminated her education. Went into a blue funk . . . or worse . . . and here I am.'

He sank into a chair, poured himself a half-glass of whiskey and pushed the bottle to me. 'There was also some nonsense about a law student from Duke and a marijuana case at Yale. What happened, we really don't know.'

I tried to digest this mélange of information, but could make no sense of it, for through it all I saw the stalwart figure of Gretchen Cole as I had known her, shy but self-assured, and with a sense of dignity that no police or no law student from Duke could undermine. 'You must have it wrong,' I protested. 'I got to know Gretchen fairly well when I was in Boston. No, let me put it this way. That English girl from Vwarda that I told you about . . . now if you said that she had raised hell in Chicago, I'd ask, "So what's new?" Not Gretchen.'

'That's why I wanted you to come here to talk with her . . . because you do know her.'

'I'm most eager to find out what happened,' I assured him.

At seven that evening we took a taxi to the institute to see Gretchen, but in the reception room we were met by the secretary, who advised us that Dr. Ditschmann and his wife would be down to see us shortly. Mr. Cole shrugged his shoulders and looked at me as if to say, 'What's the poor girl done now?'

His speculation ended when Dr. Ditschmann came in with his American wife. He was rosy-cheeked and ebullient, the kind of man you would expect to find running a gymnasium in rural Germany. She was a sharp-eyed girl, much younger than he but with the same infectious enthusiasm. It was apparent they enjoyed their work and would feel no hesitancy about telling Mr. Cole what had happened to his daughter. However, the interview started wrong.

'My good friend Cole!' Ditschmann cried as he hurried across the room and grasped my hand.

'I'm her father,' Cole said stiffly.

Ditschmann stopped, studied us, and said to me, 'I'd have thought you were Cole. You look more European. Gretchen's very continental, you know. Wonderful with languages.' Without embarrassment he turned and shook Cole's hand. 'You have a most superior daughter.'

'A delightful girl,' Mrs. Ditschmann agreed.

'Then she's not in trouble?' I asked.

'Gretchen? Heavens, no. I wish all our young people . . .'

'Could we see her?' Cole asked abruptly.

Dr. Ditschmann turned to him in some surprise. 'See her? Hasn't she told you?'

'She tells us nothing,' Cole said quietly.

'My dear man!' Ditschmann said. 'Sit down. Please.'

Mrs. Ditschmann pulled up a chair and took Mr. Cole by his two hands. 'You mean . . . she hasn't written to you about her plans?'

'No,' Cole said, withdrawing his hands. 'She has not.'

The Ditschmanns looked at each other, and he cocked his head in an Alsatian mannerism as if to say, 'She must have had a damned good reason.' Aloud he said, 'Then you aren't aware that Gretchen is no longer with us? Hasn't been for two weeks?'

'Where is she?'

'I don't really know,' Ditschmann said. Turning to his wife, he asked, 'Did she leave any clue with you as to where she might be on'—he consulted his Swiss watch for the date—'on May 5?'

'No,' Mrs. Ditschmann said without visible concern. 'I think the group was going to look at the Loire Valley . . . then maybe the Côte d'Azur.'

'No need to get excited,' Ditschmann said reassuringly. Again turning to his wife, he asked, 'Who was in the group?'

She reflected for a moment, then ticked them off: 'Wasn't there the boy from Denmark? How about the German girl? The American girl, yes. And some other boy. He wasn't associated with the institute.'

'You mean you don't even know . . .'

'Mr. Cole,' Ditschmann explained patiently, 'we have many young people here. From all parts of the world. They come, they go, some of the finest human beings on this earth. Your daughter is with three or four of them right now. Where, I don't know. Somewhere in Europe. In due course she'll let us know.'

'I'm perplexed,' Cole said. 'Our daughter enrolls here . . . and you don't even know where she is. Somewhere in Europe. With three or four other young people equally irresponsible.'

'Mr. Cole,' Mrs. Ditschmann corrected, 'Gretchen is not irresponsible. She is, if anything, one of the stablest students we've had. She has absorbed all we have to offer and is intelligent enough to know it. Where is she now? She's looking.'

'For what?' Cole asked.

'Ideas,' Dr. Ditschmann said. 'She came here with a plan . . . to write something about the Hundred Years' War. Upon inspecting it *in situ*, she found it wasn't her thing, as they say. She had the guts to drop it. Just drop it. And now she's looking for something else.'

'What?' Cole repeated.

'I told you. An idea. She's looking through France for an idea big enough to absorb her interest and her talent for the next dozen years. Such ideas are very difficult to find. We must all wish her luck.'

'This is most distressing,' Cole mumbled. 'An educational institution which doesn't even know where its children . . .'

Dr. Ditschmann smiled. 'We don't think of twenty-one-year-old girls with IQs of 170 as children. As a matter of fact, your daughter was probably never a child. At this moment I'd say she's right where she ought to be.'

'Where?' Cole insisted.

'In a yellow pop-top . . . knocking around Europe . . . with a bunch of bright-eyed young people.'

'What is a yellow pop-top?' Cole asked, trying to control his temper.

Dr. Ditschmann deferred to his wife, and she explained, 'Volkswagen of Germany has produced this new idea in station wagons. Very popular with young people. Provides an ingenious arrangement of sleeping bunks plus a roof that can be swung upward to give extra space and a view of the scenery.'

'Sleeping bunks?' Cole repeated as if a chasm separated him from the Ditschmanns.

'When Gretchen decided to quit the institute,' Dr. Ditschmann explained—'With our full blessing,' his wife interpolated—'she had just received a rather large check from Boston. From you, no doubt. So she had this happy idea of buying a pop-top. My wife helped her pick it out.'

'We encouraged her,' Mrs. Ditschmann corrected. 'You see, from the first day when pop-tops became available, Karl and I have wanted one. It would be great for taking students camping, so I guess you could say that in abetting Gretchen we were sublimating our own desires. Anyway, she had her heart set on a yellow pop-top. No other color would do. The dealer had this groovy red one . . .'

At her use of the word *groovy* Mr. Cole winced, and I was afraid that the interview would end in disaster, but Mrs. Ditschmann ignored him: 'So our dealer here in Besançon telephoned Belfort, where they had a bright yellow one, and we drove up to inspect it, and when Gretchen saw it shining in the sun, she ran up and kissed it and said, "I've been with dark things too long." She bought it on the spot, paid cash, and the next day drove south.' She hesitated, then added, 'With our blessing, Mr. Cole. With our complete blessing.'

'Where is she now?' Mr. Cole asked quietly.

'We haven't a clue,' Dr. Ditschmann said.

'Knocking about Europe?' Cole asked sardonically. 'With boys you don't even know?'

Dr. Ditschmann sighed, leaned back in his chair, and said, 'Your generation has got to face facts, Mr. Cole. From what I saw of Gretchen, there was only one thing wrong with her. Something very harsh had happened to her. I don't know what, but it probably had something to do with sex. Her overwhelming responsibility right now must be to bring that experience, whatever it was, back into balance. My wife and I were powerless to help. I suppose you were powerless too. Only people her own age can do her any good. As a matter of fact, only boys her own age. You better pray to God she meets them.'

I expected Cole to bristle at this. But to my surprise he relaxed and listened, almost with approval, as Mrs. Ditschmann said, 'You have a marvelous daughter, Mr. Cole. Sensitive, totally lovely. Karl and I would be proud if we had such a girl. But if we did, we're certain she wouldn't behave as we would want her to . . . as I behaved at Smith a generation ago. It's all changed . . . in most ways for the better. Look at him.' Students were now moving through the room on their way to the dining hall, and she pointed to a roundish young man with a fantastic head of hair and a bedraggled mustache that looked like a kitten's toy at the end of day. 'He'll probably be conductor of the Boston Symphony before you die. And that one. He would be shocked if I told him he was going to be a banker in Denver. And that girl with the awful trousers . . . she could be a senator . . . not a state senator . . . United States. Whether you and I like it or not, Mr. Cole, these young people who are searching . . . exploring . . . rejecting . . . they're going to run this world.'

'These amiable drifters?' Cole asked with an unexpected warmth.

'What alternative is there?' Dr. Ditschmann asked. 'Take that fellow over there,' and he indicated a Negro boy with a ferocious African hairdo. 'You'd better be prepared for the day when your daughter brings him home as her husband. He's a brilliant boy . . . and very likable.'

Cole looked at the Negro, smiled, and asked quietly, 'You're speaking allegorically, of course?'

'Not necessarily,' Ditschmann parried.

Then Cole did a most surprising thing. He left us, went over to the Negro, and said, 'Could you have dinner with us tonight? Excuse me, I'm Gretchen Cole's father.'

'Sure. What do you hear from Gret?'

'I was hoping you'd tell me.'

'She had this big thing about the Loire Valley. I wanted to go along, but I have to pass third-year French or lose my scholarship at Stanford.'

Cole put his arm around the boy's shoulders and brought him back to us. 'Dr. Ditschmann, can you and your wife dine with us tonight?' When the educators nodded, Cole said, 'There must be a country-style restaurant in the area. Let's make a night of it.'

We found a cab and drove out to the edge of Besançon, where an Alsatian-type restaurant served red cabbage, seven varieties of knackwurst and a dark, sour bread. As we sat down to our pitchers of beer, Cole said, 'In Boston I serve as chairman of St. Peter's School. It's rather proper. I'm fascinated, Dr. Ditschmann, by your approach to education. Students coming and going on their own, you not giving a damn, young men like this prospering under the system. You'd be a breath of fresh air at St. Peter's . . . if you'd ever care to try.'

He then turned to the Negro and asked, 'How did Gretchen get along in Besançon?'

'A winner . . . all the way.'

'Was she happy?'

'No. Very uptight.' The young man hesitated, then added, 'I was about the eighth boy in line who tried to kiss her. She was very tense. We expected her to bust loose sooner than she did.'

'You approved her going?'

'We all did,' the young man said. 'It was time for her to move on.'

Later, after we had deposited the Ditschmanns and their Arkansas scholar at the institute, Cole and I were driving back to our hotel when he broke into a robust laugh. 'I hope I'm alive on the day that boy with the fantastic hair takes over the Boston Symphony. Can you imagine our Friday audience?' He then dropped his face into his hands and asked quietly, 'And can you imagine flying to Europe to help your daughter and not even being able to determine where she is?'

———·•••·———

By the time the yellow pop-top pulled into Avignon, Gretchen had only one passenger. The Danish boy had dropped off when they left the Loire Valley; Elsa and Fleurette had stayed as far as Bergerac and had then doubled back to the institute. That left only Anton, a tall, somber Czechoslovakian expatriate whose pressing problem was whether or not he should return to Prague to help combat the Russian occupiers. He was indebted to Gretchen for the understanding manner in which she helped him analyze his alternatives, and he agreed with her that what he ought to do was stay in western Europe for two more years, complete his education, then trust his luck in Prague.

'But if the amnesty is withdrawn by then? Suppose I can't get back?'

'Second best would be to come to Canada,' she said. 'I think there's a great future there.'

He asked if she would drive to the bridge at Avignon; as a child he had sung about it with his sisters, so they drove along the Rhône till they came to the humpbacked bridge which lived in the affection of so many children, and he hummed the old nursery song and tears came into his eyes and he told Gretchen that his sisters were fine girls, that missing them would be the most difficult burden of exile. He asked if he could kiss her goodbye, and she stood like a pillar of ice as he touched her cheek. He said he would never forget her generosity.

'I hadn't a penny,' he said, 'and you were so generous. If I come to Canada, I will repay you. That's a solemn promise.' He clicked his heels on the bridge at Avignon, bowed, and started hitchhiking back to Besançon.

Now she was alone, an attractive girl of twenty-one with a yellow pop-top of her own, on her way across southern France to the great cities of Italy. She had bought a Muirhead for Italy and on its front map had designed her trip to Milan, Florence, Siena, Orvieto and Rome. She looked forward to the cathedrals with their frescoed chapels and to the public squares with their Michelangelos and Verrocchios. She felt reasonably sure that somewhere within the Italian culture she would find a subject capable of absorbing her interest and replacing the Hundred Years' War, which had proved abortive. She rather hoped that it might be something in the history of Siena, perhaps the emergence of the city-state, so in her bleak hotel room at Avignon she spread out the map of Siena and tried to imagine what it had been like in the middle 1300s.

That night she took the Muirhead with her to dinner, and all during her meal she kept her attention on Siena, ignoring the admiring attention of various Frenchmen who openly speculated on why she was dining alone. One stopped at the table to ask if he might buy her some champagne, and when she smiled at him and said no, she involuntarily thought: How attractive he is! When she left the dining room and passed the airlines office in the corner of the lobby, she happened to see a brightly colored poster advertising Torremolinos in Spain, and said, half-aloud, 'Who was it who mentioned that place? Maybe I don't need cathedrals and chapels right now.' The office was closed, but in the morning it was staffed by a pert young girl with whom Gretchen talked in French.

'Torremolinos!' the girl cried. 'Ah, if you have the time . . . the money . . . my God, don't miss it.'

'I was heading for Italy,' Gretchen said hesitantly.

'Italy can wait,' the girl cried with infectious enthusiasm. On the spur of the moment she shut down her office and made

Gretchen join her at the café for a glass of wine, even though most of the hotel guests were still having their breakfast. 'Torremolinos is an obligation,' the girl told her as they sat in the bright spring air that filled the sidewalk. 'Once a year my company flies us somewhere . . . so we'll be able to talk intelligently. They made a big mistake when they took me to Torremolinos. It's the only place I recommend, and since it's a short trip, we don't make much money on it. The boss asked me, "Can't you bring yourself to like Crete?" and I told him, "I'll like Crete when I'm as old as you are and need the relaxation." '

'I'm afraid I'm wasting your time on me,' Gretchen said. 'I'm not flying. I have my own car.'

'Who gives a damn?' the girl asked. 'You say the word, I'll drive down with you. To hell with this job if I can get back to Torremolinos.'

'Is it that much fun?' Gretchen asked.

'In Torremolinos there are few disappointments,' the girl said, 'because there's music and the beach and young people who have lost the calendar. For God's sake, don't go to Italy. Not if you have a car of your own and a figure like yours.'

Gretchen insisted upon paying for the drinks, but the girl would not allow her, saying, 'This is my charity for the day.' But Gretchen left the hotel firmly determined to plow ahead to Italy, and when the porter had finished stowing her luggage in the pop-top, she stopped by the travel office to thank the girl again. 'I'm afraid it's got to be Italy.'

The French girl shrugged her shoulders and said, 'When we're both sixty and have married millionaires and meet at some restaurant in Paris, you'll confess, "What a horse's ass I was that morning in Avignon!" ' and they both laughed.

Gretchen drove out of town, but when she came to the fork in the road where the highway to Aix and Nice swings left toward Italy and the road to Nîmes and Perpignan turns right toward Spain, she found herself inexplicably bringing her car hard right, crying aloud as she did, 'Italy can wait. They're singing in Torremolinos and they need me!'

* * *

At four o'clock in the afternoon of May 3, 1969, the habitués lounging at the tables of the café that faced the central kiosk in

Torremolinos stopped staring at the passing tourists long enough to watch as a dusty yellow pop-top with a French license pulled into the center of town, driven by an attractive young woman traveling alone. Everyone asked, 'Wonder what a kid like that's doing by herself?' and most of the men followed with the reflection, 'Some lucky guy is gonna latch onto a good thing with that one.' They watched as the girl parked the station wagon, descended, idly looked about the town, gave no sign of having seen the bar or wanting to enter it if she did, bought an armful of French and German newspapers, climbed back into the pop-top, and drove away.

'She'll be back,' one American college student observed to another, 'and she'll be worth knowing.' Then, seeing that her car was halted at a traffic light, he ran to it and asked congenially, 'Anything I can do to help?'

'Yes. Where's the camping?'

'There is none. You look along the beach. Fine your own place.'

'Is the beach in that direction?'

'Yep.'

'Thanks.'

When he got back to the bar he told everyone, 'American. Expensive clothes. No other luggage in the pop-top. She must be traveling alone. She's going to park along the beach. Her newspapers were French and German, so she must be a college kid . . . maybe from somewhere in Europe.' The listeners took note of the fact that she had no boyfriend and would be parking along the beach. Everyone intended looking into the matter.

<hr/>

Gretchen followed the road to the beach, and when she saw that broad sweep of sand reaching all the way to Málaga, she understood why the tourist-agency girl in Avignon had been so enthusiastic. She drove slowly eastward until she came to the big German hotel, the Brandenburger, and the inviting shore that fronted it. 'This is where I dig in,' she said to herself. She searched the beach until she found a small, flat area into which she could back her pop-top so that through the big rear window she could look out upon the Mediterranean and through the windshield at the German hotel and the mountains behind. It was a clever choice, and by the time she had the car and its contents arranged, the sun had begun to set, and as darkness crept swiftly across the sea and the mountains, she experienced a sensation of pervasive well-being.

In the days that followed, the German residents of the hotel proved an amiable lot. At first they seemed merely curious as to why a girl like her was camping alone. When they found she spoke German they took a personal interest in her, invited her to the hotel bierstube, talked with her hour after hour about German and American politics. They were particularly interested in what had happened at the Chicago convention, and Gretchen caught the idea that with their background of Hitler, they saw portents which Americans missed. They urged her to take meals with them and persuaded the manager to let her use the hotel toilet.

'When you need a bath,' one housewife from Hamburg assured her, 'you come to our floor. When we were younger Willi and I used to camp.'

Not even in France had she met people she liked more than these stolid, well-behaved Germans, and as she lay alone at night, stretched out in the pop-top, she reflected that she too was German, that she was restoring contact with her genetic roots, and what she saw she liked. Several young men tried to date her, but she was still so unnerved by her experience with the police that she felt no inclination to play games with men. One especially good-looking fellow from Stuttgart once insisted upon walking her back to the pop-top, and when he saw the two beds waiting side by side he said, 'If no one's using it, that second one . . .' but she had no desire to wrestle in her own car with a man in whom she could feel no interest.

At the end of the second week she experienced a desire to see some Americans, so she edged the pop-top slowly out of its resting place and drove in to town, parking the car in the big area beside the post office. Climbing down and unlimbering her legs, she started exploring the various shops and the wild variety of restaurants. In one back alley she saw a sign which captured her fancy: a wooden revolver, and on it, the words THE ALAMO.

Just what I need! she thought. Texas talk. She pushed open the door to find a very small room containing not a single Texan; the girl tending bar was obviously Scandinavian, but at one table in the corner lounged a group of American men who could not have been out of their teens. When she sat down, two of them slouched over to ask, 'You American? What you doing here?' They explained that they were soldiers from the American base near Sevilla and invited her to join them. When she did she was appalled at the youthfulness of their conversation—really, they were interested only in baseball and bullfighting—but when she made inquiries, she found that none of them had been to college and only half had finished high school. They did show interest, however, when a Negro entered the bar accompanied by a most attractive young girl whom Gretchen guessed to be English.

'Pssst,' one of the young soldiers whispered, 'that's the spade who shot up that church in Philadelphia . . . murdered all those Episcopalians . . . you read about it?'

Indeed she had. The Paris *Herald Tribune* had been full of the story last March and she had discussed it with black students at the institute. They had justified both the incident and the philosophy that lay behind it, but she had not been able to agree with them, for she believed that if Negroes insisted upon armed confrontation, they would get it . . . to everyone's loss. She looked at the newcomer with interest and asked one of the soldiers, 'Could I meet him?' and the boy replied, 'Why not? He comes here every day.' He called the Negro to the table and said, 'Cato, want you to meet my good friend from America—what's your name?'

'Gretchen Cole.'

'Cato Jackson.' He looked around for his girl friend, but she was behind the bar helping the Scandinavian girl.

'These young men tell me you were involved in the Philadelphia incident.'

'I was,' he replied evenly, never certain what attitude a white interrogator might display.

The discussion was protracted, with several of the soldiers surprising Gretchen by making sharp and telling points, and with Cato demonstrating a mature intelligence. She gained the impression that he was putting her on with some of his comments. But she liked him and hoped she might have an opportunity to see him again soon. But when she drove back to her camping spot she found a German businessman, a Herr Kleinschmidt from Berlin, waiting for her with good news: 'You spoke the other night about guitars . . . said you might like to buy a Spanish one. Well, I found out where they make them and tomorrow I'll take you.'

It was a mountain village in the high sierra north of Málaga. The road leading into it was treacherous, but by driving slowly Gretchen negotiated the pop-top into a town square that might have been used as a hideout by El Cid. She was captivated by the antique quality of the place and wondered what she would find in the craftsman's shop to which the German led her. The owner was an old Spaniard with four teeth and a sheepskin jacket. On racks above his head he kept a store of old wood from which, when the humidity was right, he fashioned country guitars, big strong instruments with heavy bridges and stout heads into which the old-style wooden keys were well fitted. For his strings he used natural gut, and when Gretchen took one of his instruments and struck a chord, it reverberated with gratifying overtones.

'A good guitar,' the workman said in Spanish.

They discussed the price, the German businessman acting as interpreter, and at first Gretchen felt that it was too high. 'But this is a good guitar,' the man insisted, and Gretchen, playing a series of rapid chords in which each stood clear of itself with a hard, true sound, had to grant, 'I've rarely heard better. I'll take it.'

'But first I must polish it,' the man said, and Gretchen told him she'd wait. But he explained that the polishing would take two days, so she asked her German guide, 'Is there any way you could get back to Torremolinos?' and he found that a bus left at four, so she said, 'I can get along without Spanish. You know, this guitar is worth waiting for.' So the German went down the mountain.

When the bus disappeared toward Málaga, she was alone, as totally alone as she had ever been, and she walked about the impoverished village looking for a good place to park the pop-top, and after a while she found a spot past which a mountain stream ran, and she drove the car there and parked it so that her head was almost directly above the running water, but when she had been in the pop-top for a while and dusk had not yet come, she felt an uncontrollable urge to sing, so she returned to the craftsman's shop and asked if she could borrow one of his other guitars, and he gave her one and she walked through the streets with it and children followed her and older men, too, for they had nothing better to do, and when she reached the pop-top she sat on a rock beside the stream and began playing the old ballads.

In time an old man from the village asked for the guitar, and with it he sang mournful flamenco, and a woman took it to sing flamenco of a wilder type. Then they returned the guitar and asked her to sing again, and the inconsolable loneliness of youth fell upon her and she sang the lament for the long-dead Earl of Murray, and although the peasants could understand not a word she was saying, they knew that in her song some good thing had perished, and they sorrowed with her:

> 'He was a braw gallant,
>   And he playd at the ba;
> And the bonny Earl of Murray
>   Was the flower amang them a'.'

For two days she stayed in the village, watching as the craftsman finished polishing her guitar, and with each new application of oil he would rub it for an hour or more, handing it to her from time to time so that she could test its growing voice. 'It's getting sweeter,' he told her. 'By this time next year it will sing like a dove.' She understood.

But at night, when her singing with the borrowed guitar was ended and the peasants were gone home to their beds, she would lie in the pop-top and listen to the whispering of the mountain stream and confess how lonely she was. There seemed to be not a person in the world with whom she could communicate, and she wondered if this was to be the course of her life. She had known many fine young men, some more concerned about the American society than she, but she had met none in whom she could express a continuing interest. She wondered if there was some latent deficiency in her character which the ugly experience in Patrick Henry had merely brought to the surface. Like any sensible person she preferred not to believe that frightening thesis. There's nothing wrong with me, she insisted to herself.

But toward morning on the second night, when roosters were preparing to rise, she could no longer fool herself that she was going to fall asleep, so she rose and in the quietness of the pop-top took down the borrowed guitar and played meaningless chords to herself, and after a long while she began singing:

> ' "Yestreen the queen had four Maries,
>   This night she'll hae but three;
> There was Mary Beaton, and Mary Seaton,
>   And Mary Carmichael, and me." '

And as she sang she wondered if that was not really the essence of life, to serve at the source of power, to do what had to be done, and if the gallows became the logical end of your behavior, to accept it . . . but above all else, to participate, to be at the center of life as a participant.

Slowly she became aware that villagers had gathered about her car; they had been watching her through the night, and now, seeing that she was awake, they had moved closer to discover what kind of girl this strange, lonely American was.

VII §

TORREMOLINOS

Times were good in Torremolinos—but when weren't they?

Debauched? Yes. Degenerate? No. I don't think you can
call a man degenerate if he likes boys *and* girls.

> After a lifetime of travel he settled here on the
> Costa del Sol and told us there were five rules for
> successful travel. Never eat in any restaurant called
> Mom's. Never play poker with anyone called Doc.
> Get your laundry done at every opportunity. Never
> refuse sex. And order any dish containing wild rice.

> God is great but grass is gentler.

He set up this marvelous bar right near the beach, but he
made one unfortunate mistake. He sold sixty per cent of the
bar to each of seven different people and skedaddled to
Tangier with the money. His mistake lay in coming back.

He lived for five years over a bar in Torremolinos,
writing his great novel on Spain. He gave me two
chapters to read, and I realized he was a little mixed
up when I discovered that he was calling his Andalu-
sian matador Leopold Kupferberg.

> 'You visit sixteen countries in seventeen days
> but you fly real low over eight others.'

Margaret kept such a close watch on Justin, doing her damnedest to keep him off the bottle, that the only time he had a real chance to get loaded was on the nights she let him out of the house to attend the Torremolinos chapter of Alcoholics Anonymous.

If within the old man there is not a young man, then he is but one of the devil's angels.—Thoreau

Wandering through Torremolinos by night is like touring a sewer in a glass-bottom boat.

I heard her myself. She told the Swedes, 'I don't give a damn what you do so long as you don't frighten the horses.'

To be seventy years young is sometimes far more cheerful and hopeful than to be forty years old.—Oliver Wendell Holmes

He that has a beautiful wife or a castle on the frontier must be prepared for war.

The guide told my mother that it took at least one hour to see the Prado, but she said they also had to see the Escorial and she would give him two dollars extra if he could cover the Prado in half an hour.

Torremolinos . . . where the only people not on a trip are the tourists.

Each year, just before Easter, the Spanish police make a sweep of all the bars and joints and clean out every hippie who looks like Jesus Christ. You'd be astonished at how many they find who look like him.

Switzerland is very nice, but I'm homesick for California. I like to see the air I breathe.

SOMETIMES even Greek shipping tycoons run out of money. Several times I have mentioned that nest of skyscrapers which clustered at the eastern end of Torremolinos like some gigantic Indian pueblo transported to the Mediterranean. The complex had been conceived by a consortium of Greek shipowners and had been launched in their grandiloquent style. When completed, it would consist of thirty-one individual buildings, each seventeen stories high, for a total of 527 stories, or 3,162 apartments. And since each apartment would contain four single beds, the Greeks were building from scratch, as it were, a city for a population of 12,648.

Unfortunately, in the summer of 1968, after they had completed eighteen of the buildings, with thirteen others in various stages of construction from mere holes in the ground to buildings without roofs, they ran out of money and had either to abandon the project or to look around Europe for additional capital. Their search threw them into the orbit of World Mutual, so that I spent May, June and July of 1968 in Torremolinos, looking over the possibilities of our bailing them out, but they were a difficult lot to do business with, and no matter how carefully I reviewed their perilous position and explained the degree of control World Mutual would insist upon if we were to provide the missing money —about twenty-six million dollars, I calculated, if furnishings and landscaping were counted in—they gagged at the prospect of surrendering any rights. All they wanted was the money, at the cheap rate of interest, and on this rock our negotiations foundered.

They had struggled along through the latter part of 1968 under-financed and handicapped at every turn, but early in 1969 it became obvious that they must either get additional money immediately or lose the project. Now they came to Geneva, begging us to succor them on any terms we could offer. Unluckily, they came at a time when we were so deeply involved in Australia, Philadelphia and Vwarda, and facing such unexpected demands for our long-range projects in Portugal, that we could not answer them quickly. Of course, this worked to our advantage, for the Torremolinos situation was degenerating swiftly, and the Greeks suspected we were delaying only to embarrass them.

At any rate, in 1968 we had offered them the cash on favorable terms; now we stalled, but in mid-April, when our position had strengthened, our directors told me, 'Go down to Torremolinos and buy out the Greeks. Get rid of them. Write your own terms.'

So on May 5 I flew to Málaga and jumped into a Rolls-Royce in which the unsuspecting Greeks waited for me, and as we approached Torremolinos we could see the eighteen completed towers plus the jagged beginnings of other buildings on which work had been halted for nearly two years.

'A magnificent project,' one of the Greeks told me with nervous enthusiasm. I said nothing, and they led me to a luxurious penthouse which they had reserved for me on one of the seventeenth floors, and when I saw that splendid panorama, looking far past Málaga to the east and almost to Gibraltar in the west, with beaches of shimmering beauty, I could not suppress a gasp, for this was surely one of the most compelling sights in Europe, a vision of the new tourism when cities of more than twelve thousand could be constructed from scratch for the pampering of travelers from South America, Africa and the Antipodes.

Seven nervous Greeks waited apprehensively for me to say something, so I smiled and reviewed in my mind the study which I carried in my briefcase; it had been prepared for my guidance by the experts in Geneva:

We therefore conclude that the Greek consortium has got itself bogged down in a complex of 31 buildings whose final cost will have to be about $57,000,000, or about $18,000 an apartment. They have already spent about $30,000,000, which means that they need an additional $27,000,000 to finish the project. Our only interest is to buy them out completely. We should offer them for openers about $17,000,000 for their entire rights, but we should be prepared to go to about $25,000,000. We calculate, from our current sampling in Congo and Rhodesia, that we can sell off the 3,162 apartments at about $30,000 per apartment, for a total intake of $90,000,000. If we could buy out the Greeks at about $20,000,000, and invest no more than $26,000,000 additional funds, this would represent a good profit.

'You've built a masterpiece,' I conceded, adding quickly, 'And World Mutual proposes to take the project off your hands in its entirety—land, buildings, furnishings—for seventeen million dollars.' There was a gasp, and one of the men started to speak, but I said quickly, 'As to a loan, no possibility . . . none at all.'

'We'll go to Gianni Agnelli,' one of the men blustered.

'No possibility in Italy, either.'

We had a knock-down confrontation, after which the Greeks had to accept the reality that the possibility of a loan no longer existed. They could either sell to us or throw the project into bankruptcy and recover only a fraction of what we offered. Having surrendered on the loan, they whispered among themselves, after which their spokesman said, hesitantly, 'Your offer of seventeen million dollars . . .'

'Is negotiable,' I said with complete frankness.

Collectively they sighed. I knew from the study that at seventeen million dollars they would lose substantially; our people had no desire to strafe them and were prepared to escalate to some figure that represented a reasonably fair shake. But what figure? Deciding this would require time and tricky footwork.

So the shipping men left me alone in the luxurious penthouse, and as they retreated to the elevator I realized that this was going to be a protracted negotiation. I suspected that I would be in Spain for at least a month, and the prospect did not distress me, for after the hectic pace I had been keeping—Philadelphia, Vwarda, Afghanistan—I could profit from some prolonged sunbathing.

When I unpacked my bags I found the four large boxes of Bircher *muesli* I had brought with me. They would last about four weeks if I rationed myself prudently, and at the end of that regimen I would be back in condition, for there is no better breakfast in the world than *muesli*. To have a dish of it with cold milk and slices of juicy Valencia orange is the best possible way to start the day; after any long spell of eating greasy Afghan food or heavy American, I take *muesli* not only for breakfast, but for lunch as well. I eat a small dinner at night and in no time I'm back in shape. My weight has kept at about 170 since I moved to Switzerland, and much of the credit for this goes to *muesli*.

What is it? A combination of roasted whole wheat and millet mixed with shredded dried apples, apricots, raisins, hazelnuts and almonds, the principal ingredient being unmilled oat flakes. I get hungry thinking about it and thank the Swiss doctor who invented it. In my Spanish penthouse I poured myself a dish, had it for lunch, then lay down for a nap.

———— ·•••· ————

Negotiations with the Greeks dragged along as I had predicted. They knew they were in a hopeless position but were reluctant to surrender. In one sense it would have been easy for them to scrape together the missing twenty-seven million; all they had to do was sell off some of the ships on which they had made their money originally, but to do this would have been insane. If they lost their ships, they would be losing their life's blood, and they were not stupid.

But what they could not yet bring themselves to face was the collapse of their dreamlike city on the shores of the Mediterranean, so I wandered contentedly about the town and gave them time, knowing that when they read the weekly statements of loss, they would be psychologically prepared to accept our terms. They had to have cash to keep their various shipping companies operating, and the only way they could get it was to unload the buildings to World Mutual. We could wait; they couldn't.

On my self-enforced diet of Bircher *muesli* I lost weight, restored my energy, and felt ravenously hungry every afternoon at four o'clock. While the Greeks were agonizing over what figure they would accept for their skyscrapers, I agonized over which of the Torremolinos restaurants to patronize that night. Because of its international clientele the town had a plethora of good places: a superb smorgasbord, a fine German restaurant at the Brandenburger, an Indian-curry place that was better than any in New York, six or seven top Chinese restaurants, a French one good enough to rate at least one star in Michelin, and a wonderful old Spanish dive called, naturally, El Caballo Blanco. It was a pleasure to contemplate these restaurants when one was famished, and I ate better in Torremolinos than in most of the other places in which I worked. Often as I left the penthouse on my way to an evening meal, I said a little prayer: Thank God, I'm not in Afghanistan or Marrakech.'

Nevertheless, my enforced idleness began to pall, for my talks with the Greeks occupied me only a few minutes a day: 'Yes, we'd consider going three million more . . . with certain considerations even four . . . definitely not six.' As the probable length of my stay increased, I began to look around for something to divert me; a man can read Simenon only so many hours a day and the hundred-odd night clubs and bars grow tiring when one is over sixty. It was in such a mood that I wandered down one of the alleys at about ten o'clock one night and saw above me a preposterous sign: a huge wooden revolver, crudely carved, along whose barrel were the words THE ALAMO. Loud noises were coming from it, punctuated by raucous profanity in Brooklynese, and I thought it would be fun to see what the Americans were up to. The door was open and I walked into an extremely small room with three tables and a shabby davenport along one side. The walls were decorated with a variety of nineteenth-century pictures of the old west, now fly-specked and torn loose at the corners. The serving bar was short, crowded at the left-hand end by a record player and a huge stack of disks; at the right, by cases of a bilious-colored orange drink.

And there was something more! Behind the bar stood a Scandinavian girl of seventeen or eighteen with a countenance so beautiful and so unaffected that I had to stop in my survey of the joint to marvel at the perfection of her blond hair and cool complexion. She caught me looking at her and smiled, cocking her head delightfully to one side and disclosing her white teeth. Using only gestures, she asked if I wanted a beer, and when I nodded, she poured me one, left the bar and brought it to me. I could then see her miniskirt and shapely legs, and I found myself asking, 'Swedish?'

'Norwegian,' she said simply, and for a reason I could not have explained to myself, except that she was obviously such a delightful human being, I quoted from a famous old barroom ballad:

'Ten thousand Swedes
Crept through the weeds
Pursued by one Norwegian.'

'Ssssshhhhh!' she cried, putting her finger to her lips in mock horror. 'That's how fights start. Where'd you learn that?'

' "The Siege of Copenhagen." Everyone knows it:

> 'We all took snuff
> But not enough
> At the Siege of Copenhagen.'

'You recite that to a patriotic Swede and he'll knock your head off,' she warned.

'I don't recite it to Swedes.'

She sat down with me for a few minutes, rose to go back to the bar, changed her mind when a tall American with a heavy beard came to take over, and resumed her seat with me. We talked of many things, for she was a girl with a most probing concern about the world. She asked me particularly if I had ever visited Ceylon. I said no, and she began to hum a piece of music that I had known since childhood. As she hummed the music, I sang the English words:

> 'I hear as in a dream
> Drifting among the flowers
> Her soft and gentle voice
> Evoking songs of birds.'

'You know it!' she cried with pleasure. 'I'll bet that when you were a boy you had a Caruso record . . .' She stopped abruptly, studied me, and said, 'You are very much like my father. You poor man. I feel so sorry for you.' She took my right hand in hers, kissed it and disappeared, but not before I saw that she was close to crying.

Later in the evening she came back and we began the first of our probing conversations. She struck me then, as she does now when I recall her, as one of the most vital persons I had ever met. All her senses seemed to work overtime, hauling into her brain observations which she weighed, judged and filed away. In her evaluation of herself she was harsh: 'Mr. Fairbanks, if I'd had a first-class brain, do you think I'd have dropped out of education at seventeen? I'd have gone on to become a doctor . . . or a'—she hesitated, casting about for the precise word and ending her sentence with one I had least expected—'or a philosopher.'

'You can go back,' I said. 'At eighteen your education's just beginning.'

'Yes, but what I also lack is a first-class imagination. I have no originality . . . I'm not an artist.'

'Why can't you just be an educated person?'

'I'd want to make a contribution . . . something constructive.'

I should not have said what I did, but I asked, 'You expect to make one in a Torremolinos bar?'

She did not flinch. 'I'm like all the other serious ones down here. I am really trying to find myself.'

'And so far?'

'I'm satisfied with one conclusion. I was not meant to live away from sunlight. I work in here till about four o'clock in the morning . . . night after night. The fellows don't bother me. The American soldiers like to grab at my legs, but who cares, it's a job. But at noon next morning, when the sun is high, I'm on the beach. An hour's sunshine and I'm rebuilt. That I've learned.'

'And after that?'

'I'll keep my looks till I'm thirty.'

'Long after that,' I assured her.

'You don't know me,' she corrected. 'My God, how I like to eat. So if I do last till thirty . . . well, that means I have twelve good years to look around. That's a hundred and forty-four months. I'm not stupid. In a hundred and forty-four months I'll find something.' She paused, exchanged pleasantries with some of the soldiers, then said, 'But nothing I shall discover in those months will be bigger than what I've already discovered. That I live by the sun. If they sent a commission from Oslo, saying, "Britta Bjørndahl, you have been elected prime ministress of Norway," I'd tell them, "Move the capital to Málaga and I'll accept." Since they would be reluctant to do that, I have given up all hope of becoming prime ministress.'

'Marriage?'

'There's a neat question.' She pondered it for some time, then said, 'I like men. I'm not like some girls who crumple if they don't have a man around. But I like them. However, if my luck shall be that I'm not to find . . . I could live without them . . . that is, without them on a permanent basis.'

'Have you found anyone here?'

With a nod of her blond head she indicated the tall fellow behind the bar. Her gesture was not deprecatory, but on the other hand, it wasn't marked with excitement, either. I had asked if she had a man for herself, and she had replied, in effect, 'Well, yes, you might say. That's him.'

It was in this way that I first took studied notice of the bartender. He was a tall, lean chap, well built and well mannered. He wore his hair in what the younger generation called 'the Jesus bit' or 'the Kahlil Gibran thing'—that is, his hair came almost to his shoulders and a flowing beard covered his face. He wore tight faded-blue Levis and Texas boots. He was a commanding figure, most gentle in speech and behavior, and he ran a good bar. Britta told me he was an American draft dodger, like so many of the others I would meet in Torremolinos.

Intuitively I liked the young bartender, and was about to say so when she said abruptly, 'You must forgive my emotionalism when you were singing the song. 'What do you think of *Les Pêcheurs de perles* . . . as an opera, that is?'

'I've seen it only once. It's about the same as *Norma* and *Lakmé*. A native priestess falls in love, with a European in *Lakmé*, a Roman in *Norma*, and an Indian of some sort in *Pêcheurs*. Of course, there's a high priest who sings bass and in the end the girl dies. It's no better than the others, no worse.'

'I mean the music.'

'Well . . . that's another matter. *Pêcheurs* is certainly the poorest of the three. But what you must remember is that Bizet was writing it when he was only twenty-four. It's a lovely, youthful opera, and at your age you ought to like it.'

'But I don't,' she said. 'I think it's a real bore. I just wondered what you thought.'

'But you were singing it,' I said, and she told me of the frozen years her father had wasted dreaming of Ceylon and of how his fixation had influenced her. 'I'd really like to see the place,' she said. 'If some young fellow—and he wouldn't have to be so young either—if he walked in this bar and said he was going to Ceylon, I'd go along with him tomorrow morning, no questions asked.'

'You really have cut loose, haven't you?'

'I'll never go back to Norway. I've saved seventeen dollars, which is all I have in the world. Yet I'd go to Ceylon without thinking twice . . . so long as it had sun.'

It was in discussions like this, as I sat in the Alamo nursing my beer, that I came to understand the new breed of young women who drifted about Europe and whose most attractive representatives congregated in Torremolinos. They were intelligent; they were beautiful; they were grimly determined not to be sucked back into routine; and they were a challenge to all who met them. Since they were a new force in history and a new experience for me, I have often pondered how best to describe them; no device could be better than a sample of the notes which were tacked onto the bulletin board at the Alamo, and at a hundred other spots throughout Torremolinos:

> Swedish girl nineteen wishes to see
> southern Italy. Can drive. Will share
> expenses. Go group or single. Ask the
> bartender details.

> English girl seventeen, good
> driver, absolutely must get
> to Amsterdam. Has eleven
> dollars. Will accept any
> offer.

> California girl eighteen has new Peugeot.
> Heading Vienna. Will accept partner if he
> can drive and pay his share expenses. For
> details see bartender.

I chose these three notices because I happened to meet each of the girls involved, and any young man in his right mind would have journeyed to the moon with any one of them. It was an exciting time in Torremolinos.

———•◆•———

In these first days when Britta Bjørndahl talked with me of Tromsø, I had not of course spoken with Joe; I had only seen him behind the bar, nor was I then aware that four other young people whom I had known in the past were in town. I supposed that Gretchen Cole was touring somewhere in southern France, and that Cato Jackson was hiding out in Newark or Detroit. I had no idea that Yigal Zmora had quit his father's university at Haifa, nor that he had visited his English grandparents in Canterbury. As for Monica Braham, the last I heard of her was her flight from Vwarda in the cockpit of a Lufthansa plane. She could be anywhere; Buenos Aires or Hong Kong were logical possibilities.

During my first two visits to the Alamo, I did not happen to run into any of the four. I discovered later that Cato, Monica and Yigal had borrowed a car and were in the mountains on a tour of those three historic cities Ronda, Antequera and Granada. Gretchen, of course, was still cooped up alone in her pop-top.

But on my third visit I did meet Joe. In fact, I took him and Britta to dinner at a Chinese restaurant and we talked for about two hours. At first I was antagonized by his hairdo, and by the fact that he was a self-proclaimed draft dodger; I had served in the navy in World War II and had never known of a single draft evader among my acquaintances, and I felt ill at ease sitting with one.

'No comparison of the two cases,' Joe said when I raised the question. 'Your war . . . you had a visible enemy . . . everyone recognized him . . .'

I was surprised at how well and how sparingly he used the language, and as the evening wore on I listened with attention as he made one sensible point after another. 'How did you become a rebel?' I asked.

With his long fingers he fluffed out his beard and said, 'This doesn't make me a rebel. The fact that I can't cooperate with a ridiculous draft doesn't make me a revolutionary. What I want most of all . . . is go back to college . . . get a degree.'

'To do what?'

This stumped him. He chewed on his lower lip for some moments, shifted in his chair and said quietly, 'I don't know. I really don't know.'

'What's eating you?'

'Well, when you haven't done anything yet—don't even have a degree—wouldn't it be pretentious to sound off with big ideas about what you're going to accomplish?'

'But you do have ideas . . . back in your head?'

'I do.'

'Like what?'

He saw that I was badgering him into making a statement for which he was not yet emotionally prepared, but this did not irritate him, for he also saw that I was willing to talk with him about important matters, so he looked up at the ceiling and said, 'On the night of January 4 there was a blizzard in Wyoming. I was caught in the middle of it.' He paused, looked down at me and asked, 'You ever in a blizzard?'

'Not in Wyoming.'

'I stood out in the road . . . all the cars were stranded . . . and the world seemed to have two faces. More drawn in and tiny than you could imagine. The whole world was a tight circle drawn about you by the snowflakes. But it was also much vaster than I had realized, reaching out in all directions so far that it met itself coming back. I experienced the same sensation driving down here from Madrid . . . over those empty plains. The hugeness of the distance and the closeness of the part where you happened to be standing.'

'Leading to what?' I asked.

'Speculations,' he said, and it was apparent that he intended to drop the question. Britta said something about having been in lots of blizzards, endless ones, in fact, but Joe was staring into my eyes. 'Speculations,' he had said, and I had not a clue as to where those speculations would lead him but I suspected that here was a young man who had conceived an image of the world, and to have attained this was the beginning of constructive thought. Our mutual respect dated from that moment.

In the days that followed, while the nervous Greeks surveyed their crumbling empire and postponed decision, I often sat at the bar while Joe served drinks and kept the phonograph going, and in broken sentences amid the interruptions he related the history of his flight. He doubted that he would return to the United States, for he had no inclination to be a hero nor any taste for jail. He wondered what he ought to do about an education, because he was saving little money in Torremolinos and knew no foreign languages in which to study at European universities.

The more I talked with him about important matters the more I grew to like him; I had invited him to dinner the first night because he was attached to Britta, but now I was inviting Britta because she was associated with him. In our talks I tried to find out something about his parents, but he forestalled me. Of his mother he said simply, 'Grotesque,' of his father, 'Pathetic,' and he would say no more.

He was an archetype of the young man of promise who is a

natural loner. He was generous with his money and insisted upon taking Britta and me to dinner when he had a little saved; he was helpful with the forlorn drifters who kept pestering him at the bar, asking for handouts or leads to jobs; and he was gentle with girls, especially with Britta; definitely he was not the savage-animal type that young men in long hair and leather jackets are supposed to be. He was an appealing human being, perplexed by his society and his relationship to it, and bewildered as to what he ought to do next. But in his confusion he was developing character, and if he ever found his way out of his present dilemma, he could, I felt sure, become a notable man.

There was a shock in store for me, because one night after we had dined at the smorgasbord, and I had sat mesmerized by the amount of food he and Britta could eat, plates piled high four times, he suggested, 'I'm providing identification papers for an American girl who's trying to cash personal checks. I left them at the apartment. Care to see where we live?' We left the center of Torremolinos and walked slowly down the hill to the old fishing village, where we passed a collection of low cottages, stopping at one which overlooked the Mediterranean. 'Good location,' I said as Joe pushed the door open and turned on the light.

He explained that he and Britta were occupying the place while the owner was in Morocco lining up a regular supply of grass, so I was more or less prepared for what I saw: a couple of beds and a little furniture, but when I saw the wall decoration I burst into laughter. Over the bed to the left hung a very large, well-printed poster which showed a benevolent yet monitory Pope Paul, his gentle eyes smiling and his forefinger wagging. Below in bold print stood the words:

THE PILL IS A NO-NO.

Over the other bed, on which Joe and Britta threw their things, hung the famous poster of W. C. Fields in black-rimmed top hat, evening coat and white bricklayer's gloves, holding a poker hand and looking balefully at some scoundrel on his right. Between these two figures, the Pope and the Clown, the young people of this generation existed.

The noise of my laughter wakened two sleepers in the bed below the Pope. Drowsily they pulled down the cover that had been hiding them, and I saw their faces—one very white, the other quite black. 'Good God!' I shouted. 'I know them!'

They sat up in bed, obviously nude but clutching the sheets about their throats. It seems ridiculous for me to say so, but they looked like two angels on some super-cute Christmas card. Even Britta and Joe burst into laughter as I stood there in amazement.

At this point sleepy Monica cried, 'Uncle George,' and started to come over to greet me, but becoming aware that she was wearing nothing, yelled, 'Throw me a robe!' Britta did so, and when Monica had slipped into it she ran across the room and gave me an enthusiastic kiss. 'How did you get here?' she cried.

'How long have you known him?' I countered, pointing to Cato, who was pulling on a pair of pants.

'Ages . . . simply ages,' Monica said. Cato shook hands with me and said, 'Philadelphia seems a long way off.'

'How did you meet?' I asked, pleased to see two young people in whom I had taken more than a passing interest.

'At the bar,' Cato said. 'The Arc de Triomphe. This is a town for swingin' cats.'

'Let's celebrate!' Monica cried, and she opened a closet in which the owner of the apartment had left some of his trade goods, and within a few minutes she had rolled a huge marijuana cigarette, which Cato lighted for her. We sat on the two beds, and the cigarette passed slowly from hand to hand as we talked of past experiences. I was sitting next to Britta, and was surprised when she took a puff and handed it to me. I passed it quickly to Cato.

'Come on, Uncle George!' Monica cried. 'Give it a try. It'll make you feel twenty years younger.'

'I already do,' I said.

We sat thus for some hours, talking about Vwarda and Philadelphia. I told Cato, 'You know, she's not an ordinary girl.'

'Sir, you are belaboring the obvious,' he said primly, pinching Monica's leg.

'And she's not from an ordinary family. The Queen of England knighted her father with the words "Sir Charles Braham, architect of Vwarda's freedom." He was.'

I noticed that of the four smokers, it was Monica who kept the cigarettes longest and puffed most deeply from them. She offered little to the conversation, and in time it became obvious that she had become bored. Finally she made an extra large cigarette for herself and puffed it deeply for some minutes, then astounded us all by saying, 'When you get really stoned and have sex, it can go on forever. You feel as if God was plowing a field. Come on, Cato, get high. You weren't worth a damn in Granada.'

Cato took no offense, but when Monica tried to force the cigarette on him, he passed it along to Joe. Monica studied him with contempt, and I was afraid that a scene might develop, so I looked for the door, but she changed her mind, threw her arms about his neck, and said, 'So smoke up, baby. I'm going to bed right now, and so is Britta. Uncle George, you can run along. We have work to do.'

She threw off her robe, jumped into bed, and cried, 'Turn off that damned light, please!' Before I left the room she was asleep, and as Britta showed me to the door she whispered, 'Monica talks more than she acts.'

As I was leaving I saw at my feet a tartan sleeping bag, and asked, 'Which one sleeps down here?' and Cato said, 'A real good kid. He stayed in Granada an extra day. You'll meet him at the bar.'

———— • ▪ • ————

The Greeks, with a tenacity I had to admire, continued to flush out unsuspected sources of money, hoping to collect enough to enable them to proceed with the skyscrapers without surrendering ownership to World Mutual. I was kept aware of their efforts by reports from various money centers that had turned them down; one night they came back to me and asked if I would lend them eleven million at a good rate of interest. They tried to convince me that they had somehow got together sixteen of the missing twenty-seven million, but I told them flatly that my company was not interested in lending money. What we insisted upon was ownership of the project. There were no bad feelings. They accepted my answer in good spirits and retreated to do some more scrounging.

'We'll see you again next week,' they said, so once more I was left to myself with nothing to do. I took long walks, sunned myself in my penthouse, read Thomas Mann, and stopped by the bar to talk with the young people.

It was delightful to see Cato and Monica again, for these were surely two of the most appealing members of the younger generation. In a way they were like young animals, for they responded automatically and with amusing verve to whatever stimuli reached them. As I talked with them I found Monica even more self-oriented than she had been in Vwarda; she really did not give a damn about the opinions of anyone but herself. She was an uninhibited spirit, forthright in manner and prepared to accept the consequences of whatever she did. Certain American soldiers from southern states, attracted by her crystalline beauty, which they considered a monopoly of southern belles, tried to dissuade her from living with Cato Jackson. They not only offered themselves as replacements but let her know that the American contingent would approve if she ditched Cato and took a white man.

She replied in a way she knew would infuriate them: 'I've had four lovers so far, two black, two white, and if any of you gentlemen think you can offer in bed what the black gentlemen do, file your credentials with the bartender.'

When I asked her about Sir Charles, she said, 'The old dear! He put the police on my trail and for a while I had a hell of a time. I think he's growing roses in Sussex.'

Several members of the British colony in Torremolinos, having known Sir Charles in Africa, had sought to establish overseer relations with his daughter. Hearing that she hung out at the American bar, two of these ladies came to the Alamo one afternoon to extend an invitation to Monica, but when she saw them approaching, she asked me to send them away, then fled upstairs to the washroom. But before I could say anything, Britta told them frankly, 'She's in the john, but she'll be down soon,' so I was left to entertain them.

'We have a lovely clubhouse on the hill,' the women assured me. 'Monica would find it delightful . . . garden . . . good English food . . . meeting old friends from India and Africa . . . it's really rather choice, and on Fridays we have formal meetings with the liveliest discussion.'

I said I was sure that Monica would want to know about this, and after a long wait I told Britta, 'Better fetch her,' and Monica came down reluctantly, planting one foot solidly before the other and glowering at me as she drew her thumb across her throat.

'We've come to invite you to our British Club,' one of the ladies said.

Because of her menacing appearance, I expected Monica to be

extremely rude; instead she was all charm. 'It's so frightfully good of you,' she said with schoolgirl politeness. 'Of course I remember when you were stationed in Rhodesia. Of course I'd like nothing better than joining you at the club. But there's one problem.'

'I'm sure there couldn't be any problem,' one of the ladies said.

'You don't know my husband,' Monica said. 'He is a very big problem. As a matter of fact, he's sitting on the end stool at the bar.' As the astonished women looked at where Cato was perched with his head propped on his hand and his elbow cocked against a case of orange drink, Monica called, 'Come here, darling,' and Cato ambled over.

With that hilarious cunning I had noticed in Philadelphia, Cato immediately grasped the situation and lapsed into his most obnoxious Stepin Fetchit. 'I sure am pleased to meet wid you ladies.' Here he sniffed two or three times like a heroin user, jerked his head twice, and said, 'I always say, any frien' of Miss Monica's is a frien' of mine.' He paused and smiled vacuously at each of the women, making himself look a complete idiot. Sniffing a couple of more times, he gave Monica a tremendous whack across the behind. 'I don't want you hangin' around this bar all night. Get home. Get some work done.' And with this he shuffled back to his stool.

'He's the son of a chieftain,' Monica said with embarrassment. 'His father wanted him to go to Oxford but . . . well, you can see.' She paused, doing her tragic-queen bit, then said quietly, 'It would be quite impossible. If he'd known you were British he'd have given you a speech on imperialism.'

The ladies withdrew, and when they were well out of hearing I said, 'I ought to wallop you,' and she said, 'Life is too goddamned short.'

Cato was profiting in many ways from his stay in Europe. He had updated his wardrobe so that except for his color he was indistinguishable from the better-dressed Frenchmen and Germans. He listened to the observations of others and was acquiring an insight into European and African problems; most of all, he ingratiated himself with people of the most diverse quality.

Apart from the occasional southern soldier who wanted to steal Monica, he got along fine with Americans from the deep south, outraging them one time with his frank statements of belief, enchanting them the next with his assurances that in the next generation there would be many blacks like him, willing to talk seriously, willing to make necessary concessions to keep the ball game going. He loved to talk with Europeans who sought information about America; with them he was brutally frank, feeding their animosities at one moment, appalling them with his challenges the next. I got the feeling that he was trying out his powers, finding how far he could go with people and what led to success in debate. I had no idea what he had in mind, but I was sure that he was slowly generating a picture of himself and deciding what he could accomplish with that picture.

Often he infuriated me. He had now picked up about six good accents: gutter Philadelphia, deep-south Geechee, University of Pennsylvania high society; debonair French, grandee Spanish, and what can only be called put-on—the flamboyantly funny and aggravating speech with which he kidded anyone who asked questions that probed too deeply into his Negro consciousness. He could really be most exasperating.

But no matter how irritated I became with Cato, and he could be infuriating, one aspect of his behavior commanded my respect: in his relations with Monica he took pains always to be decent. Many young men who conduct affairs with girls better positioned than they, feel driven to compensate by giving the girls a difficult time; not Cato. Or a man who goes with a girl who has more money than he, often needs to affirm his manhood by treating her meanly; not Cato. That she was the daughter of a titled Englishman did not impel him to humiliate her, and the fact that she was white did not make it necessary for him to denigrate her in public. He remained a normal, sex-driven, amiable young man, and I found much fun in being with him and his girl.

For example, one night an American newspaperman, learning that the young fellow who had shot up the Llanfair church was in town, sought him out at the Alamo, and while the regular customers sat in an admiring circle, interviewed Cato, who perversely adopted the role of a pansy Negro gone French. His answers were hilarious and we had to control ourselves to keep from giving him away.

The newspaperman asked gravely, 'Do you see the black revolution as sweeping all parts of America?'

With ultra precision Cato replied, 'So far I have been permitted to visit only Philadelphia and New York, with an occasional visit to the brothers in Newark, but couriers reach me continuously from the provinces, and piecing together what they tell me . . .' He shrugged his shoulders in a gesture of defeat and said, 'California is totally lost . . . lost . . . lost. Those filthy Mexicans with their goddamned grapes have stolen the play from us. You could explode seven tons of TNT in the middle of Watts, and it wouldn't make that much difference.' He snapped his fingers. 'Those goddamned Mexicans horning in.'

When the reporter tried to zero in on just what the revolution was trying to accomplish, Cato cut him short: 'What I said about California applies even more strongly, I fear, to New York.' One of the soldiers started to laugh at the 'I fear,' but his friends muzzled him. 'In New York it's the goddamned Puerto Ricans. They're taking the play completely away from us. If you're a Puerto Rican, you get the headlines. If you're black, who cares? But in places like Birmingham and Tupelo we rate. So from what my friends tell me, we've written off California and New York. Let the spics have them. But you can tell your white readers this. When we strike our blow we are really going to strike.'

By now we could see that the reporter realized he was dealing with a put-on, but he kept at Cato, obviously hoping to get some usable quotes on how Negroes felt about Spanish-speaking people. Again Cato cut him short: 'What's this Whitey word Negroes? Who's Negro? I'm no Negro. That's a filthy imperialist word dreamed up by Bible-spouting white folks and kept alive by the captive press. You ought to be ashamed of yourself, using a word like that in what I thought was to be a friendly interview.' He ranted in a French accent and so confused the reporter that the discussion fell apart.

At the end, the reporter took Monica aside and asked her, 'Does he always kid around like this?' and she confided, 'No. He's usually quite coherent, but his wife is having a baby.' 'I didn't know he was married,' the newsman said. 'Yes, to a very fine Spanish girl. Her family thought he was Moroccan . . . very dark. Now they've found out. They're applying dreadful pressure on the poor girl, and Mr. Jackson's afraid she'll lose the baby.' The reporter hesitated, looked at his notes and said, 'Wait a minute! Three months ago he was in Philadelphia. Hadn't even seen Spain.' 'I know,' Monica said stiffly. 'That's the real tragedy of this affair. The father of the baby is a Finnish businessman. Mr. Jackson married her to save her good name.' The reporter played it straight, saying to

Cato as he left, 'I hope your wife comes through all right,' and Cato, suspecting that Monica had been up to some nonsense, replied almost instantaneously, 'Thank God, they have transfusions these days.' It was a great closing line for an interview with a revolutionary.

On this occasion Cato had a surprise for me, too, because when the reporter left, he and Monica came to sit at my table, and he said, 'Guess who's going to come through that door at midnight.'

When I said they'd have to give me a clue, Monica said, 'The kid who uses the sleeping bag. The one we said was in Granada.'

'When he told us he knew you,' Cato said, 'it was a real gasser.'

Shortly before midnight the door opened, and in the entrance stood Yigal Zmora in hiking shorts, blue knit shirt and Israeli idiot cap. '*Shalom!*' he cried as he came to greet me. Spreading his arms to indicate the bar and its occupants, he said, 'This is the way to study engineering!' It was obvious that the American soldiers respected him as 'that kid from Qarash.'

When I asked how he had met the others, Cato interrupted, 'Same way I did. Stumbled into this joint for a drink, caught a glimpse of Britta, and fell in love with her.'

I happened to be looking at Yigal when these joking words were spoken, and when I saw the deep and automatic blush that confused him—red surging up into his ears—I realized that Cato had made a joke which to Yigal was not funny, nor would it ever be. He stared down at my beer mug while Britta served drinks at another table, and during the rest of that night he seemed afraid to look at her.

In speaking of Torremolinos, I have used phrases like 'We were talking at the bar' or 'Someone said to me at the Alamo,' but these words must be understood in a special way, because during every minute of its operation this bar, like all others in Torremolinos, was filled with a deafening cacophony of sound.

When the bar opened at eleven in the morning Joe would start a stack of records and until he closed at four the next morning, they would grind on, each giving the effect of being louder than its predecessor. If, by accident, a disk recorded at moderate volume did find its way onto the machine, someone in the bar was sure to yell, 'Turn that goddamned volume up.'

We therefore had to talk above this Niagara of noise. It was constant and immutable, as if the young people of the world were afraid to be alone with mere thoughts. What did this cascade consist of? At first I could not have said. I had been trained in classical music, with a strong predilection toward Beethoven and Stravinsky. Two of the best concerts I had the good fortune to attend were a Toscanini performance in Boston at which he played the *Leonore Overture No. 3*, the *Fifth* and the *Ninth*, and that popular gala, often repeated at the Moscow ballet, in which they danced *The Firebird, The Rite of Spring* and *Petrouchka*. I knew most of Verdi by heart and had played recordings of *Carmen* and *Faust* so often that I could have conducted them.

I loved music. In my youth I had enjoyed the songs then popular, not so avidly as some of my companions, but enough to remember the major successes of men like Duke Ellington, Louis Armstrong and Jimmy Lunceford. I was never much taken with vocalists, but I did like Sarah Vaughn and Ella Fitzgerald. Of the composers, Harold Arlen was my favorite, but I also liked some of the finest Rodgers and Hart inventions. My education had ended with *Pal Joey*.

I was not able to study or comprehend the musical explosion after the war. It did not repel me—no music could do that—but it had shot off in new directions I did not care to follow. About the only songs I remembered from this bleak and noisy period were 'Nel Blu Dipinto del Blu' and 'Rock around the Clock.' The first captivated me, as it did the whole world, for I understood what the author was trying to say; it was a fresh, authentic cry from a man imprisoned on earth in a job he did not like and surrounded by people who bored him: it was a real *cri de coeur*. 'Rock around the Clock' I first heard at a skating rink under my hotel window in Austria; the proprietor had a stack of records three feet high, but it seemed that every third selection was this noisy, throbbing thing whose title I could not decode. Finally I went down to his establishment, where red-cheeked young Austrians were twirling over the ice, and asked him, 'What's that piece of music?'

' "Rrrruck around ze Cllllluck," ' he told me.

This left me still bewildered, so I asked if I might see the record when he was through this spinning, and he showed it to me with some pride. 'From London,' he said. 'Very popular.' The tune, having been hammered incessantly into my brain, was my introduction to rock-and-roll, and I predicted, 'This can never last.'

I was, therefore, not well prepared for the music in which I was immersed at the Alamo. I heard only compulsive noise. Sometimes, when none of the young people I knew were present, I would sit in a kind of stupor trying to decipher what the music and its mumbled lyrics signified, but always I threw in the towel without having learned anything. At such times it was comforting to leave the noise and wander down the beach for a beer at the Brandenburger, where sensible German folk songs were featured. It was good to hear music with a tune and words with meaning.

Then one day as I sat in the Alamo waiting for Monica and Cato, doing nothing and with my mind at rest, a miracle happened. In order to explain it, I must explain how I learned French.

When I chucked my job with Minneapolis Mutual and moved over to World Mutual, it became obvious that if I wanted to function in Geneva, I would have to learn French. Fortunately for me, at about this time the French government awakened to the fact that French was no longer the premier intellectual language of the world, having been replaced by English, German and Russian, in that order. Therefore, a crash program was initiated at the University of Besançon, where, as I have said, a pure French was spoken, and I came along just as these experts had decided on a daring new technique and were looking for older people on whom to try it.

I was introduced to Madame Trenet, a small, intense gray-haired woman of about fifty-five. My English-speaking intercessor told me, 'Madame Trenet guarantees to have you speaking French within two weeks. She won't say a word of English to you, but she asks me to tell you this. It's a matter of breaking the sound barrier. You must have faith that the day will come when the sounds will fall into place—they will become not a jumble, but French. Everything she does will be directed toward that mysterious moment when the sound barrier falls away and you understand, somehow or other, what she's saying.'

This sounded most recondite to me, and I hoped that he and Madame Trenet knew what they were doing. Within the first ten minutes I learned that she did.

She sat me in a chair in my hotel room and placed a watch on the table between us. She then, so help me God, launched into a lecture in French on the rivers of France. She gave me not a single clue in English as to what she was doing, but with a most compelling sense of drama—*joie de vivre,* suspense and intonation, her hands and face contributing all the time—she told me her feelings about the great French rivers and the landscape through which they passed.

How did I know that was what she was talking about? I heard the words *Loire, Rhin, Rhône, Garonne* and *Seine.* I missed completely whatever it was she told me about the last four, but when speaking of the Loire she used the word *chateaux,* and as she spoke of certain magnificent buildings she had known as a little girl, her face became diffused with memory, and the spaciousness of what she had seen was transmitted to me, and for a brief second the French words, which I could not possibly comprehend, conveyed a message which was as clear and visible as a newspaper headline. Out of sixty minutes that first session, I heard about three seconds' worth of French, but I heard it with an intensity I remember to this day.

On the second day Madame Trenet lectured me on the French cinema: Fernandel, Raimu, Brigitte Bardot, René Claire. In the middle of her discourse, when I was catching nothing, she happened to mention a name I knew, Arletty, and on the spur of the moment I cried, '*Oui,* Les Enfants du Paradis.' A lovely smile came over her face and she asked, '*Vous connaissez?*' and I said, '*Oui.*'

Now for my money, *Les Enfants du Paradis* is the finest motion picture ever made, a long glowing account of what happened in and around Les Funambules, a vaudeville theater in Paris at the time of the 1848 revolution. It introduced Jean-Louis Barrault to the world, and many critics cherish the scene in which, through miming, he solves a police problem. I know a philosopher in New York who divides the world into two parts, those who have seen *Les Enfants* and those who haven't; he categorizes the former group according to which character in the movie they prefer. I gave myself away when I confessed that among the glittering roles, I have felt closest to that stupid young man, his heart on fire with love for Arletty, who stands in the courtyard below her window making romantic and poetic love to her while the more practical-minded man-about-town—a wretch if there ever was one—has slipped into her bedroom and, unseen from the courtyard below, is about to haul her into the hay. One of my bosses, an austere, clean-living man, told me that he imagined himself as the baron who is murdered in the Turkish bath.

At any rate, on our second day of French, Madame Trenet and I discussed *Les Enfants du Paradis,* and she was so eloquent in her response to this notable film, and so gratified that I shared her high opinion of it, that we spoke for some fifteen minutes on the subject. She would not permit me to give my impressions in English, so I had to do with '*le premier film du monde en mon opinion*' and '*cette grande scène dans la nuit entre les trois amoreux.*' Where had my French words come from? Opera librettos, I suppose.

Her third lecture concerned French painting; her fourth, the grandeurs of the French theater; her fifth, French foreign policy; and in the middle of the last, when she was speaking of Bismarck and Thiers, the miracle that she sought took place: suddenly the random sounds she had been making for five days fell into orderly place and I perceived each sound as a word or part of a word. I suppose a light of recognition must have flashed across my face, for Madame Trenet halted her discourse on the perfidy of Bismarck and said in French, 'Good, now we can start learning the language.'

She gave me a list of two hundred short words—*en, avec, de, sur, sous, mais*—that I was to memorize, and another list of about eighty phrases and sentences which comprised the bulk of casual conversation; these I was to start using immediately, and I was to introduce them to every possible situation, even if I had to distort what it was I had wanted to say. Finally she showed me how to get along with only three tenses—present and future, and a past in which the verb remained the same and only the participle changed—so that to this day I never say in French *I saw* but only *I have seen: J'ai vu. J'ai acheté. J'ai pensé.*

Sixteen days after my first meeting with Madame Trenet, I gave a short talk in French to a Geneva club on winter in Minnesota. I was not a fluent success but I was understood, and from that moment I spoke French with assurance if not accuracy.

There was one additional feature of her method; at the end of the first week she told me, in French, 'Here is a dictionary. Do not use it. But sit down and make out a list of the words that are important in your business . . . in English. The things you really want to talk about. Look up their French equivalents and memorize them. Then throw the dictionary away, because we have found that if you read French and guess at the meanings of words, you'll do a little better in the long run than if you look up each word as you go along. What's important, you'll enjoy remembering it more.'

So as I said, one day I was sitting in the Alamo wasting time, and as I half-listened to the awful noise coming from the record player, I mysteriously heard, for the first time, the actual music and the words. The sound barrier was broken. What a moment before had been mere noise, now became a succession of individual sounds, powerful and with profound meaning. It was a song like 'Nel Blu Dipinto del Blu,' a cry from the heart, and the words were such as I might have uttered, for the husky voice of a troubled man lamented: 'Someone left the cake out in the rain . . .' I asked Joe to play the record again, and since the bar was doing little business, he did so, and thus I began my investigation of the revolution that music had sponsored while I was attending to other things.

Coming to the bar now became not an escape from the temporizing Greeks—who had still failed to collect enough money to save their skyscrapers—but an adventure in sound. I listened to the records, watched the reactions of young people, and entered a world much more powerful than the world of marijuana, more persuasive than that of LSD.

When I finally heard the music, I was struck by how varied it was: what I had once lumped together as noise, now separated into a wider variety of sound than what I had known in my youth, and I began slowly to pick out selections in each category that seemed to me to have musical merit; with each discovery I moved closer to the world which the young people around me were inhabiting. Music thus became a passport to a terra incognita, and now as I look back upon those idle days in Torremolinos, they seem among the more productive of my life.

I found that I liked best the raucous visceral music of the groups with odd names like Chicago Transit Authority, Canned Heat, The Animals, and especially one called Cream. I understood what the pulsating guitars were trying to say, and although the words of the songs seemed not to matter, I did learn to appreciate full sound and pulsating beat.

The next category was so good, by any standards, that I was surprised at myself for not having discovered it earlier. These songs were the lineal descendants of the ones I had enjoyed as a college student, and cynics who ask, 'Where are the lyrics today?' obviously never listen to the present crop. There was one in particular, about a group of young musicians trying to keep their heads above water in California:

Busted, disgusted/Agents can't be trusted . . .

I don't see how you could distill more of youth into six words. I grew very fond of this song—since the Alamo was open seventeen hours a day, it was inevitable that any given number would come up at least six or seven times, the popular ones, up to twenty—and every time its deep-throated, lovely guitar chords echoed through the bar, I anticipated the blending of the youthful voices as they sang their complaint. When I asked Joe what the name of the song was, he said condescendingly, ' "Creeque Alley," ' as if everyone knew that. I thought he must have made a mistake, so I looked at the jacket, and there it was, 'Creeque Alley.' Some of the other titles were worse.

In this group of singable songs I discovered such delightful compositions as 'Up—Up and Away,' 'Go Where You Wanna Go,' 'Little Green Apples' and 'Dedicated to the One I Love,' but after I had heard them for a while I found myself hungry for that solid hammering of the more or less wordless songs featured by Cream and The Animals. I remember how pleased I was when I found one that combined the best of both styles, a thundering guitar-and-organ bit with great lyrics, 'The House of the Rising Sun,' but when I commented on it, Joe told me, 'It's an old New Orleans song. Older than you are.' Well, it was enjoying a lively reprise.

I was surprised to find myself looking forward to records by two girl shouters; as a college student I hadn't much cared for such music, but now it seemed in tune with the times. Aretha Franklin was quite popular with the habitués, and I grew to appreciate her heavy, sensual grumblings, but it was Janis Joplin who won my heart. Her protest 'Women Is Losers' seemed both timely and universal. Sometimes when she belted it out I would see older men in the bar nodding their heads; that had been their experience too. I liked almost everything Miss Joplin did, in a fascinated sort of way. Her raucous voice was the antithesis of music but it was contemporary and compelling.

There were also what one might call occasional nuggets, songs tucked away in albums that were otherwise useless, but carrying a wallop that was immediately recognized: 'By the Time I Get to Phoenix,' 'Spanish Eyes' and 'Gentle on My Mind.' Of course, anyone who listened carefully could enjoy nonsense bits like the one which was very popular that spring, 'Harper Valley P.T.A.,' but at the end of a couple of weeks of intensive listening, I found that there were two types that I truly liked, as much as I had liked any of the music of my youth: songs like 'MacArthur Park,' which told about the cake melting in the rain, and the deep gutsy hammering of the guitar-and-drum groups.

But as I listened to this flood of music, I began to hear things in it that had escaped me in my first excitement over its excellence. I was disturbed that almost universally—even in songs recorded in England—the singers felt they had to imitate illiterate southern crackers. I took the trouble to find out where some of the singers had been raised, and they came from a wide variety of northern sites, not to mention England, but when they got before the microphone they lapsed into the snarl of a southern cotton-chopper angry at the world. The literate man or the educated woman had no place in modern music.

I was also impressed by the fact that so many of the songs glorified gangsters, hoodlums, dead-enders and degenerates. Bonnie and Clyde, Pretty Boy Floyd, the fugitive on his way to Phoenix, the boy in the death house trying to get a last word to his girl, the girl ridden by dope, and the young outcasts daring the pigs to sic 'em were the heroes of this generation, and I often wondered what the effect was going to be of this constant incitation to revolution.

I had been listening for some time before I caught on to the fact that so many of the songs glorified the results of taking drugs: marijuana, LSD and heroin appeared to be the new religion, and I wondered how a child of thirteen who played such records constantly could come away with anything but a determination to try drugs at the earliest opportunity.

As for sex, it was rather fun trying to decipher what new procedures the latest songs were advocating; music sponsored an underground which spread the word as to what the lyrics of the latest song intended. This was a youthful folly which reminded me of some children I had known in Boston while working there. They were enchanted by a new television series called *Batman*, in which an ostensibly normal young man from a wealthy family who lived in a mansion on the edge of town was, in reality—a phrase much used in such circumstances—Batman, the avenger of evil. Every little boy and girl I talked with was convinced that only he or she knew that the fine young man was Batman, and when the children whispered to me, 'You know, he's Batman,' they were honoring me with one of their most precious secrets. They knew and I didn't; the young people in the Alamo behaved exactly the same, except that their knowledge was more heady.

Depressed somewhat by these thoughts, I was sitting in the bar one day when Joe dug deep in his pile of records and came up with 'Michael from Mountains,' a song so crystal-pure and simple, so beautifully sung by a girl with a natural voice, that I felt exalted by the good feeling it produced. What was it? Only an unpretentious song about a young girl who watches a strange boy from the mountains and the things he can do with nature. She has a premonition that one day in the distant future she may know him very well. It was one of the realest songs I had ever heard, something that Schubert might have written. I asked Joe to play it again, but the singer had got into only a few bars when one of the soldiers protested, 'Hell, that's an oldie,' so Joe switched to something newer. The song had been written the year before.

———•——•——•———

On my walks down the beach to the center of town I regularly passed the Brandenburger and occasionally stopped in for a drink of German beer. In doing so, I became vaguely aware of a yellow Volkswagen camper that stayed parked along the sea front, and one afternoon as I was leaving the bierstube, I happened to catch the Volkswagen in a new light and saw that a portion of its top opened up to admit air and sunlight, and the idea struck me: That's what they must mean when they use the name pop-top. I walked over to the bus to see if anyone was inside. No one was, and when I peered through the curtained doorway to see how the interior was arranged, a German tourist from the Brandenburger left his table on the lawn and walked across the sand.

'You look for something?' he asked abruptly. He had a Prussian haircut and spoke English.

'I just wanted to see . . .'

'The car is not yours,' he said in reprimand.

'I know it isn't,' I fumbled. 'But I was just wondering . . .'

'Better you leave it alone,' he said. 'The owner not like it if you . . .'

'I'm just looking at it. See here, is it your car?'

'No. But I watch it when the owner's gone. So please move along.'

It has always amazed me, in my work around the world, how Germans can make other people feel morally inferior. Like a prospective thief I left the Volkswagen and continued my way to the Alamo, where I found Britta arguing with the American soldiers over something they had said.

'What's the matter with you nuts?' she demanded, standing over their table.

'President Eisenhower himself said it,' one of the soldiers insisted.

'Then he didn't know what he was talking about,' she snapped.

'Isn't there a very high rate of suicide in Sweden? Isn't the country morally degenerate?'

'I'm not a Swede!' she said defensively.

'Isn't Norway just as bad?' the soldier asked.

'Where do you get such ideas?' she asked, dismayed.

'President Eisenhower said so, in a speech.'

She turned to me and asked, 'Who tells them such nonsense? That Sweden is degenerate?'

'Don't you publish sex books?' the soldier pressed. 'With colored illustrations?'

'That's Denmark,' she snapped, heading back toward the bar.

But another American repeated, 'Isn't it true you have a lot of suicides?'

Britta threw her cloth to the floor and turned on her tormentors. Lately she had been badgered at least once a day about Sweden's high rate of suicide. She now came to me and asked pleadingly, 'Explain to these barbarians that Sweden is a civilized place.'

'We know it's civilized,' the first soldier said. 'What we want to know is why it's so degenerate.'

I knew that many Americans accepted this judgment, so I suggested that they take out pieces of paper and jot down some numbers which had impressed me years ago and which, more than any other evidence I had ever heard, kept me from making damn-fool statements about other nations and other cultures.

'I remember the report very well,' I said. 'It came out about 1950 and showed that Sicily had more murders per capita than anywhere else in the world. Everybody got into the act and wrote essays about how the Sicilians were natural criminals. Some fanciful theories were developed and widely circulated. Sicilians were shown to be the worst people in the world, and we had the figures to prove it.

'A couple of years later another research team made a similar study about suicides in Sweden. Very high. Definite proof that Sweden had more suicides than any other nation, and again we had a whole raft of ingenious theories about why Sweden was so corrupt. It had to do with socialism and lack of individual challenge, and that's where President Eisenhower got into the act. In a speech he proved that Sweden was pretty degenerate.

'At that point we had figures showing that Sicilians killed one another and that Swedes killed themselves. So some bright young man compared these figures and found that the percentages were almost identical. On this clue he assembled all the available statistics, and I think you'd be interested in what he found.

'Draw three columns. Label one *Country*, the second *Murders*, the third *Suicides*.'

When the soldiers had done this, I recited some index figures which I vaguely remembered; whether any particular one was accurate, I couldn't say, but I will guarantee the relationships. When finished, the tables looked like this:

Country	Murders	Suicides
Sicily	22	0
United States	16	6
England	11	11
Germany	6	16
Sweden	0	22

'What it means,' I concluded, 'is that in all societies we find a constant index of violence, but how that violence manifests itself is determined by local custom. In Sicily a man cannot survive in his society if he refuses to murder the man who betrays his sister. His aunts and uncles, the corner café, the pool hall insist that he murder the man and thus restore his family's good name. In Sweden such a course would be unthinkable. You stay home and brood about it, and when winter comes with its interminable nights you kill not the other fellow but yourself.'

Monica, who had just wandered in, looked over my shoulder as I pointed to the figures. 'Good old England!' she cried. 'Always on an even keel.'

'You're right,' I agreed. 'When murders and suicides balance, it indicates a healthy population.'

'There's one mistake,' Joe said from the bar. 'I think you'll find that today in many parts of the United States our murder rate approaches Sicily's, and in other parts our suicide rate is close to Sweden's. We're the violent country, not Sicily.'

'That's only because we're so diverse,' I said. Somewhere I'd seen recent figures which proved that murders with gunfire were greater in Texas than in Sicily, while in Vermont suicides were frequent. 'There's probably some geographical factor operating in these figures,' I said. 'In the north you commit suicide. In the south, murder.'

'Good!' Britta cried to her soldier critics. 'While I go out back and cut my throat, you Dixie men can shoot each other. But don't give me any more of that stuff about Sweden.'

Her soldier opponent was not so easily deflated. 'That takes care of the suicides, but what about the degenerate part? Don't they teach sex in schools?'

Britta looked as if she was mulling over three or four arguments with which to refute him, but apparently she decided to discard them, certain they would accomplish nothing. Instead she smiled at the soldier and said, 'Yes, they do teach us about sex. And that eighth-grade course is a real knee-slapper.' But even this riposte did not satisfy her, for she told the soldiers, 'You clowns remind me of what happened in Tromsø. We were so far north of the Arctic Circle that tourists who got off the boat expected to see polar bears in the streets. We tried telling them that Tromsø was a civilized place, but they still wanted to see polar bears. So what did we do? One of the stores bought a stuffed polar bear and put it on the sidewalk and told the tourists, "We shot it at city hall last winter," and they went away satisfied. You know what I got behind the bar? A polar bear.'

Turning to me, she said, 'Tell them about skid row.'

The soldiers looked at me, so I repeated a story I had told her: 'Friend of mine conducted surveys of skid row in Boston, New York, Philadelphia and Chicago. Found them very similar, but one fact stood out. Of the men who were lost in skid row—the real down-and-outers—ninety-two per cent were Irish and Catholic. Negroes aren't found there. They stay with the mob and work things out. Quakers and Jews don't wind up on skid row, either.

It's a phenomenon that grows out of heavy drinking and the delayed marriages in Irish communities. My friend found that almost ninety per cent of skid-row men had never experienced a sustained relationship with a woman. This isn't a condemnation of the Irish or the Catholic. It simply means that this is the social disease to which they're susceptible.'

'In Sweden it's suicides,' Britta called from the bar. 'What is it in Dixie?'

It was night when I started back to my penthouse, and as I approached the Brandenburger, I noticed again the yellow Volkswagen from which the German had dismissed me earlier in the day. It now showed a light, and from the aperture in the roof came the sound of someone playing a musical instrument, so on the spur of the moment I turned aside, went to the station wagon, and knocked on the door. A girl responded in German, 'Who's there?'

As I started to mumble some explanation, the door opened and I saw standing in the dim light a handsome young woman in shorts holding a guitar. It was Gretchen Cole, and at the same time that I recognized her, she realized who I was, tossed the guitar on the bed, and threw herself into my arms.

'Oh,' she cried with her face against my shirt, 'am I glad to see you!'

Continuing to hold her by her shoulders, I pushed her back, looked at her grave, familiar face, and asked, 'How'd you get down here?'

'You wouldn't believe it.'

'I've been to Besançon. Yes, with your father.'

'How'd he know I was in Besançon?'

'The bank. Newspapers never know. Neither do private detectives. Banks always do, because we have to write for money.'

'I wonder where I'll be writing from next time?' She laughed at the sententiousness of this question.

'What happened to you after I left Boston?' I asked.

'Didn't Father tell you?'

'He said . . .'

'Yes?' she asked sternly. 'What did he say?' She sat on her bed and indicated that I was to take the folding chair, but before I could do so, there was heavy knocking on the door and a voice asking in German, 'Are you all right, Fräulein?'

Gretchen pushed open the door and replied to the crop-headed

German who had accosted me before, 'Everything's all right, Herr Kleinschmidt. This is my uncle.'

Herr Kleinschmidt stared at me menacingly and said, 'We think a great deal of this young lady.'

'So do we all,' I said.

When he retreated into the night, Gretchen turned to me with a faint smile. 'They've been so good to me at the German hotel.' Suddenly she jumped from her bed, ran to the door, and called, 'Herr Kleinschmidt! Wait a minute!'

She reached down, grabbed my hand, and pulled me out after her. We ran a few steps to where the German waited. 'Let's go over to the bierstube and have a brew.' Linking one arm in his, the other in mine, she led the way to the Branderburger, where we found a table and sat drinking German beer while various patrons who had gotten to know Gretchen stopped by to speak with her. Only then did I realize that Gretchen had brought me here so that she could delay talking about herself; the social ease that she was displaying with her German friends bore no relationship to the uncertainty she seemed to feel about herself.

After a half hour of forced camaraderie, an exhibition directed at me, I felt sure, we walked back to the pop-top, and when we were inside I said, 'Now tell me what happened,' and in a sudden flood of self-revelation she told me of Chicago. I noticed that even at this distance, nine months after the events in the Patrick Henry police station, she did not have those ugly incidents under control; they still possessed her on their terms, so when she was finished with her narrative, I took her two hands and said, 'Gretchen, I've met a delightful group of young people at a bar in town . . . three of them I knew before. Anyway, you and I are going there. Yes, right now.' When she started to protest the lateness of the hour, I said, 'It's important that you meet them . . . that you break out of the misery . . .'

'Who says I'm miserable?' She jerked her hands away and said defiantly, 'I have all those friends at the hotel.'

'I say you're miserable. Come along.'

I dragged her from the pop-top, but again she broke away. 'I have to lock up,' she said, and as we started back into town she called to someone on the lawn of the German hotel, 'Look after the Volkswagen while I'm gone,' and in German a deep voice replied, 'We'll keep an eye on it.'

When we had progressed about halfway to town, she asked, 'Where are we going?' and I said, 'Just a small bar . . . an American one,' and she said, 'Oh, you mean the Alamo. I've been there.' She said this not disparagingly but with a certain lilt of expectancy, so I said, 'Maybe you've already met my friends,' and she said, 'I saw a good many American soldiers from the base at Sevilla, but the only person I remember was a young black.'

'Named Cato Jackson?' I asked.

'The one who shot up the church . . . yes.'

I started to say that he hadn't really shot up the church, but she interrupted me, 'I'd enjoy seeing him again. He had something to contribute,' and I said, 'The others are equally good,' and she grabbed my arm and began walking faster, exactly as a young woman should who hears that she is about to meet interesting people her own age.

When we reached the bar, Cato and Monica were missing, but the other three were lounging about; it was nearly one o'clock in the morning and business was not lively, for only one table of soldiers remained. I introduced Gretchen to Britta, and the two girls liked each other immediately. Britta then took Gretchen to meet Yigal, who was English-proper, but when they came to Joe, he nodded rather formally and said, 'We had dinner together in Boston.' She looked at him carefully, and it was obvious that she could not differentiate him from the many long-haired draft evaders she had helped get to Canada, but when he added, 'I told you that night I was heading for Torremolinos,' she cried, 'Of course! That's where I heard the name!'

About two in the morning the door banged open and Cato slammed his way in with Monica on his arm. They had been drinking heavily and probably smoking pot, for their eyes were dilated and extra bright.

'What news!' Cato cried. 'Paxton Fell invites us all up on the hill tomorrow night for a real gas. We're all to go, and he's sending a car down to pick us up.'

He then saw Gretchen and came over to her. 'I know you! You're that chick from Boston. You're all right.' He brought Monica up and introduced her, and as the conversation began to flow in broad and easy forms, I appreciated how much Cato added to any group. He was a catalyst.

It was Britta, however, who comprehended why I had brought

Gretchen to the bar. She said, 'But if you have your own pop-top, and it's parked on the beach . . . well, why don't you park it outside our house . . . you could use our bath.'

The idea seemed so sensible that the group adopted it as official policy and insisted that it be implemented at once. 'You want to close up the bar?' Joe asked one of the soldiers, who agreed.

'Target for tonight,' Cato cried. 'One pop-top.' At his use of the phrase *target for tonight*, which the police at Patrick Henry had used so offensively, Gretchen shuddered, and on the noisy hike back to her car she kept close to me.

When the gang saw the yellow pop-top they cheered, and lights started to go on in various rooms throughout the Brandenburger. 'It's all right,' Cato shouted. 'Just a friendly gang-rape.'

'You all right, Fräulein?' a hoarse voice cried in German.

'Everything's fine,' Gretchen called back as Yigal started the car. 'I'm moving to a new location.'

'Oh, Fräulein!' several voices protested.

'I'll be back,' she promised, but within a few minutes Herr Kleinschmidt was among us in his night clothes, carrying a flashlight.

'You sure you're all right?' he asked solicitously, and after we had piled into the Volkswagen he remained on the beach, his flashlight glowing.

———•◆•———

As we approached Jean-Victor's apartment I found something I had not noticed on my previous visit: beside the house stood a small open space into which the pop-top could be backed, and when this was done Gretchen had a better camping place than she had enjoyed at the beach, for she was protected on each side and had the convenience of a bathroom a few steps away.

But when the pop-top was tucked away, Cato studied the sleeping arrangements and asked, 'Which of us fellows shares the bed with you?' And she replied, with no sense of humor, 'That's my prerogative,' and Cato said, 'If I knew what that word meant, I'd know whether I'd been insulted or not,' and she said, 'You were.'

When we moved indoors and Gretchen saw the posters of the Pope and W. C. Fields she burst into laughter, and I think it was then that she first felt that with this group she was going to have fun. She took Britta by the hand and said, 'You had a great idea.' Then, with her Boston frankness, she pointed to the bed guarded over by the Pope and asked, 'You girls sleep here?' and Monica broke in to say, 'You have the wrong idea,' and by some gesture which I didn't catch she indicated that she and Cato shared the Papal bed while Joe and Britta kept to the one guarded over by Fields.

It was then that Gretchen saw the tartan sleeping bag by the door. 'Is that where you bunk?' she asked Yigal, and he nodded, whereupon Monica said, 'You see, Gretchen, it would be so much more convenient if Yigal slept with you,' and Gretchen said, 'Convenient for Yigal but not necessarily for me.' Monica interpreted this as a challenge, and recalling her schooldays, she proposed a similar bet. 'I'll wager you five British pounds that one of these three men is sleeping with you in that pop-top within thirty days.' 'If I had five pounds,' Gretchen said, 'you'd lose.'

It was in the succeeding days that life in Torremolinos stabilized itself. Inside the apartment Joe and Britta kept to their bed, Cato and Monica to theirs. Yigal found that he didn't mind sleeping on the floor, and although he continued deeply in love with Britta, there was nothing he could do about it. Once or twice at the Arc de Triomphe he found a girl, generally from France, eager to share the sleeping bag with him, so that on the following morning the newcomer would meet with Britta and Monica and Gretchen and compare notes, using a wild variety of languages to do so, but none of his attachments lasted, a fact about which Monica teased him: 'What's wrong? You the original One-Time Charley? Girl never comes back for a replay?'

'I'm looking,' he said.

Monica knew well what he was looking for, but about this delicate subject she did not joke. Like all of us, she respected Yigal and approved of his sober approach; if he was infatuated with Britta, he was handling himself well.

Gretchen posed a different problem. By her manner she warned young men that she was not interested in their approaches, and if someone did try to pick her up in a restaurant or bar, she denied him permission to walk home with her, so that there would be no problem of keeping hopeful lovers out of the pop-top. With the three men in the apartment she was proper, more inclined to listen than to talk. She would sit on one of the beds for hours and encourage Cato or Yigal to tell her of his experiences. Joe, of course, said little, and she made no serious effort to pierce his reserve.

I wondered then, as I have often wondered since, why at my age I bothered with this curious group. At the time I reasoned that it was because the recalcitrant Greeks were keeping me imprisoned in Torremolinos: If it weren't for the Greeks, I'd be out of here in a shot. But looking back on the matter, I doubt that I would have. Certainly the fact that later in the summer I dug up excuses to visit them in various places betrayed a desire on my part to keep close—to see what would happen to them.

But deeper than that was the unspoken feeling that at my age of sixty-one, this would be the last young group I would ever associate with; my own son was lost to me through bitter misunderstandings and I felt the need of comprehending what the youth of this age were up to. I saw in them the only hope for the future, the vitality of our society, and I approved of much they were attempting. When I thought of the dreadful loneliness I had known as a young wanderer through Europe—how fearful a place Antwerp could be for a young man from the University of Virginia who judged himself shy and unprepared—I much preferred the present mode which enabled a chap like Yigal to go to the Arc de Triomphe and find himself any number of lively young ladies prepared to make love in Belgian, Dutch, Italian or Danish, with sometimes no words needed in any language. This was preferable.

As for the young people, I discovered one afternoon at the bar what they thought of my presence. I was in the back room helping check a delivery of orange soda when I heard a soldier ask Monica, 'Why do you bother with that old geezer?' and she said, 'Fairbanks? He's a harmless old fart.' From the serving counter Britta said, 'He's dreadfully square but he doesn't hurt anybody.' Cato volunteered, 'You've got to say this for him. Not once has he mentioned the depression,' to which Monica added, 'We put up with him because . . . well, you have a feeling that if somebody had got to him early enough, he could have been saved.'

So that was it. The new generation was so convinced of its values that it judged us older people not by our standards but by their own. I was a flop, but if they had got to me forty years ago I might have been redeemed. This attitude angered me, because although I saw their manifest weaknesses, I never felt that if they had had my education they might have been saved. They needed desperately some of the things I had acquired; surely Joe's problems would have been simpler had he seen history as I did, and Cato would never have invaded the church had he acquired my attitudes toward social change, but never in my arrogance did I believe that I could have saved these two young fellows—or Monica or Gretchen either—by training them in my pattern. It was this arrogance of youth, this precious insolence that set them apart. I think now that even if the Greek shipowners had settled their finances promptly, I would have remained in Torremolinos that spring, for there is nothing in the world more promising than the unfolding of youth, and I was privileged to witness it, even if the youth I was watching did consider me a harmless old fart.

They had several reasons for considering me a square. I kept asking questions about their music, and irritated them when I pointed out that their musicians seemed deficient in skills. 'They simply don't know how to end a composition. Listen to how many of your records trail off with the crude device of repeating the last phrase while the engineer turns down the volume. Listen to the inept manner in which you transpose from one key to the next. Where's the modulation that makes a song palatable?'

'We want it to be crude,' Monica said as Yigal applauded. 'The old tricks of da-da, dum-dum, dee-dee and you're off in a new key are for the birds. You want a shift? Shift.'

They were also irritated, I think, because I refused to adopt their terminology and call them kids. Even Gretchen used this juvenile description: 'Hi, Uncle George. You know where the kids went to dinner?' Or, 'The kids are throwing a picnic in the hills. Want to come along?'

I pointed out that young people their age were not kids, but I noticed that her group used the word even for people in their thirties, so long as the men had long hair and the women wore sandals. They insisted upon being kids—the gang, the mob, the girls, the boys—as if growing up were an ugly thing and responsibility something to be deferred as long as possible.

But mostly they thought me square because I would not join them in their marijuana. Cato and his black friends in Philadelphia had forced me to smoke that morning, and I had frequently sat with the group while they shared a round, but if they asked me, I never refrained from telling them that I disapproved. 'You one of them cats who think that grass leads to heroin?' Cato asked me late one night.

'Yes.'

This caused an explosion, with Monica and Britta especially vocative in citing studies which proved that marijuana was neither habit-forming nor escalatory.

'Do you reject such studies?' Monica demanded.

'Yes, because they refer only to chemical and physiological facts. I'm thinking of the psychological.'

'Meaning what?' Cato asked with contempt.

It was not contempt for me, because he had worked with me long enough in the Philadelphia slums to know that I was not an automatic do-gooder. 'Meaning that marijuana itself may not be escalatory, but the milieu in which it's smoked is. The general social atmosphere of this room, for example.'

'Leads to heroin?' Gretchen asked.

'Unquestionably,' I said.

'You mean,' Joe asked slowly, 'that you expect one of us to move on to LSD?'

'I do.'

'But why?' he asked. 'We've proved it isn't habit-forming.'

'But Torremolinos is. You stay in this room long enough, or in this town . . .'

Monica got up and came to where I was sitting. She carried a fat lighted cigarette, which she handed to Britta, then asked me, 'You think one of us in this room is going to try heroin?'

'Without question.'

'You're wrong,' she said contemptuously. 'Because we're all going to try it.'

For a moment no one spoke, then Gretchen said, 'All but one,' and Britta added, 'Make that two.'

Monica turned to survey the room and said brightly, 'Uncle George, it looks like I'll have to make another bet. Everyone in this room will try heroin before the year's out. And I'm including you, you dirty old man.'

———•◦•———

Paxton Fell sent his Mercedes-Benz plus an English limousine to pick up his guests. Of course, the two cars couldn't enter the alley leading to the Alamo, but a liveried chauffeur did walk down to the bar to announce that the cars were waiting in the public square. Joe threw his keys to one of the soldiers and we set forth.

It was a gala evening. Only Cato was familiar with Fell's establishment, so that when we saw the graceful bovedas, creating the illusion of an endless heaven, we cheered. Monica cried, 'This is the way to spend money . . . if you have it,' and Fell's other guests applauded.

Laura, who owned the castle at the water's edge, was among them, no longer in tweeds. She wore an elaborate evening gown, as did an assortment of princesses from various defunct royal houses. An ex-Nazi general was in attendance; everyone called him 'My General' and bowed. There were also two barons, garnering their own bows, and an English baronet who had never heard of Sir Charles Braham, or Vwarda either, for that matter.

Among the five young people who were seeing this austere pleasure palace for the first time, reactions were varied. Monica took one swift survey of the statues and adopted the place as her own. Throwing herself into a deep chair, she accepted a Scotch-and-soda and told one of the barons, 'It's rather homey . . . with just a touch of . . .' She shrugged her shoulders and smiled.

Britta was impressed by the expensiveness of everything, but she was determined not to show it. With quick glances she made appraisals of all the furnishings and the guests; she recoiled from the Nazi general but accepted the others with a kind of Viking superiority. She did not sit down, but moved slowly from one vantage point to another, apparently unaware of the magnificent pictures she was creating with her Nordic beauty set against this southern stone.

Joe was dumfounded. Since that first meeting with Fell on the afternoon of his arrival in Torremolinos, he had often speculated on what life with the aging sybarite would be like, but his imagination had produced nothing like this. He was repelled, yet fascinated by the luxury, the sensuous perfection of the place. 'Living here would be easy,' he whispered to me as we looked out across the garden to where cargo ships were sailing toward the coast of Africa.

Yigal was not affected. He had seen more luxurious homes in Grosse Pointe, more stunning views from the hills in Haifa. To him the Nazi general was merely a military man who had lost his war, while the barons seemed less imposing than the presidents of the motor companies in Detroit. He was not even impressed when the general sought him out and said in good English, 'So you are the brave young Jew who fought the tanks at Qarash!' They talked amiably for some minutes, during which Yigal said that when the Egyptians found good leadership they were going to be formidable, to which the German responded, 'In the past it was the English and the Germans who monopolized stalwart leadership. Landed gentlemen, you know. But in the last war the Russians showed us how a group of peasants—lower-class stock, if you will—could also master the tricks . . . by sheer force of courage. You Jews did the same in Sinai. But what has the Egyptian to offer, I ask you? What tradition to rely upon? I've been there, Nasser invited me down. And what straw did I find to build my bricks? None. The country has neither gentlemen nor an educated lower class. You Jews are safe for another forty years.' He bowed and passed on.

It was Gretchen who sensed most accurately the quality of this extraordinary room. 'When do the revels begin?' she whispered in the first moments. With growing distaste she inspected the furnishings and the posturings of the guests. One of the rewarding aspects of growing up in Boston was that one acquired unconsciously a sense of what was proper and distinguished, and when measured against this austere norm, much of the nonsense that one encountered elsewhere fell into place. She knew intuitively that several of the women who surrounded Laura did so because they were dependent on her wealth. She also guessed that the two handsome young Germans with broad shoulders would not be interested in either her or Britta . . . not while Paxton Fell was watching. And she knew without being told that Cato had once lived in this house as those two young men were now living, and that he was being brought back as a kind of exhibition, the way Radcliffe College brought back graduates who had written books or done well in New York. 'Is this what the young people around here aspire to?' she asked me in a low voice.

'You don't. And Britta doesn't. And surely Joe doesn't. Yigal? Look at him fending off the barons.'

'Did you ever have this as your ideal, Uncle George?'

'The luxuriousness, yes. The sense of delightful depravity, yes. I've thought about it, but never strongly enough to inspire action.'

'You're a fraud! You find this as ridiculous as I do.'

Paxton Fell had imported from one of the mountain villages a group of singers, who now appeared in rough country costume, accompanied by a guitarist, and the lights playing upon the bovedas were extinguished and the guests lowered their voices as the singers took over. They were a lively lot and gave a good performance, but while they rested, I had an idea that turned out well. I said, 'You know, Mr. Fell, one of your young ladies has talent with the guitar.'

This occasioned much chatter, during which I projected Gretchen into the area where the singers were collected, and after much urging from the guests, she took the guitar, asked for a high chair, and played a few proficient notes. The guitarist applauded, which encouraged her to play an intricate number for him alone; he seemed to be honestly impressed by her skill. Then he took the guitar to show her what he could do. After some flashy passages, he returned the guitar, and she strummed softly, saying in a quiet voice, 'Child 209.'

I was apparently the only one in the audience who knew what this signified, for most of Fell's guests were either European or too old to understand what had been happening in American music. Cato knew nothing of the ballads, and while Joe had heard Gretchen sing once in Boston, he knew little of her music. And even I did not know what she was about to sing, for I knew only two of the Child numbers, 173 and 113.

Gretchen had chosen wisely, for 'Geordie' dealt with a young wife whose husband has been caught poaching sixteen of the king's royal deer, and for this crime, must hang. She has come to the judge to plead for her husband's life, and her words convey powerful emotion:

> ' "I have seven children in the north,
>   And they seem very bonnie,
>   And I could bear them a' over again
>   For to win the life o Geordie." '

The judge looks over his shoulder, can find no reason for clemency, and Geordie hangs.

Gretchen sang with such a combination of intensity and authority that the crowd fell silent; the diverse group had to listen because the strongly played guitar commanded their attention and her lovely voice their interest, but none attended to her words with more obvious appreciation than the Spanish singers, who could understand none of them, except that in some curious rural way they understood them all. When she finished, the musicians clustered about, asking many questions, which Britta translated.

The guests applauded and demanded more songs, so in the interval of noise and chatter I went to Gretchen and suggested that she sing either 'Mary Hamilton' or that noble song about the seal, but she placed her hand on my arm and said, 'You would not waste the best on such an audience,' and she launched instead into a rowdy Scottish ballad I had not heard before. She told us the Child number, but I forget what it was.

The song was well chosen. It contained a rollicking chorus which Gretchen tried to teach the guests, but they could not catch its intricacies and mangled it at the end of every verse. The villagers, on the other hand, seemed to understand its broken rhythms and nonsense words instantly, so that they tore into it with admirable gusto whenever Gretchen pointed the fingerboard of her guitar at them and belted out the first words:

> 'With his tooran nooran non ton nee,
> Right ton nooran fol the doo-a-dee,
> Right ton nooran nooran nee,
> With his tooran nooran-eye-do.'

We got a pretty good idea of what his tooran nooran was supposed to be from some of the lusty verses Gretchen sang with a high-school innocence; they dealt with a supposed beggar who stops by a farmhouse near Aberdeen, seduces the oldest daughter in the middle of the night, and disappears with her before morning. Seven years later he returns as a beggar once more, and the good wife castigates him for having stolen her daughter, whereupon he throws aside his tattered garments and discloses himself as a prince. The rowdy verses dealt with what transpired prior to the flight:

> 'The lassie then she did get up to bar the kitchen-door,
> And there she met the jolly beggar, standing naked on the floor.

> 'He gript the lassie by the middle jimp, laid her against the wa,
> "O kind sir," she said, "be civil, for ye will wake my dadda."

> 'He never minded what she said, but carried on his stroke,
> Till he got his job done, then he began to joke.'

This ballad was a notable success, and the guests demanded more, but Gretchen had sung enough. Returning the guitar to its owner, she thanked the musicians for their support and wandered into another part of the marble room. Several aging gentlemen tried to engage her in conversation, but she drew away.

Paxton Fell served his dinner at twenty-three minutes past one in the morning, not unusually late for a Spanish meal, and as the night progressed, his customary guests, one by one, began to show signs of drunkenness. Since none had jobs and would be able to sleep as late as they wished, not rising till three or four in the afternoon, they were prepared to drink enormously; amounts that would have put an ordinary man under the table seemed to affect them little, but by three in the morning they had consumed so much, and so uninterruptedly, that even they began showing signs of collapse. When incapacity overcame them, they quietly moved away from the table and fell asleep in some chair, or stretched out along the edge of a carpet. There was no boisterousness, only the sound of the musicians playing in the background and the subdued chatter of voices around the big table.

During this part of the night I lost sight of the six young people; they were with the two young Germans somewhere else in the lavish quarters, so that I was left with the older group, and as I watched them gliding gracefully toward oblivion, continuing to drink when they had no further need or desire for alcohol, I reflected that every age produces its drop-outs, every nation. The percentage remains constant; it is only the manifestation that varies.

The people around Paxton Fell had dropped out of normal competition as surely as the most bearded young man from Oklahoma who despised Tulsa and believed that he had found a superior alternative in Haight-Ashbury. These elders had despised Berlin and Brussels; they were expatriates from London and Paris; they used cocktails the way the younger group used marijuana, and with identical effect. The Nazi general had been forced into exile; had he stayed in Germany he would have been executed by a Russian court-martial. The others had abandoned their societies willingly and had dropped out from their normal responsibilities. Only their good fortune in having had wealthy uncles and indulgent fathers permitted them to live as they did. Even now Laura, speaking in her rough voice, was telling some amusing incident that had happened on the plains of West Texas . . . how far away it seemed, how impossible those bitter winters in Dalhart.

But it was not only this conspicuous group of expatriates that I compared with the drop-outs of the younger generation; it was also those sturdy, cautious types I had known as a boy in Indiana. Of a hundred average young people I had grown up with, a good forty had dropped out from all reasonable competition by the time they were twenty-five. Some, of course, had become town drunks or obvious wastrels; a few had stolen money and gone to jail; one or two of the girls had become prostitutes of a more or less genteel type, slipping into hotel rooms or staying with businessmen when their wives were absent on summer vacations. It was not these inevitable drop-outs that I referred to in my estimate of forty per cent; it was, rather, that constant group of Americans who avoid difficult tasks and grab onto the first job offered, clinging to it like frightened leeches for the remainder of their unproductive lives. It was the girls who marry the first man who asks them, building families without meaning or inspiration, producing the next cycle of drop-outs. It was the adults who surrender young and make a virtue of their unproductivity, the miserable teachers who learn one book and recite it for the next forty years, the pathetic ministers who build a lifetime of futility on one moment of inspiration entertained at the age of nineteen. These were the drop-outs that concerned me most.

Paxton Fell's group, now amiably incapacitated and waiting the dawn, did little harm to themselves or society, just as the wilder young people we saw passing through Torremolinos accomplished little that was reprehensible; it was the great silent minority that aspired to nothing and achieved less that worried me. There must have been, that night when the guests were falling asleep around the table, a hundred thousand or more young college students throughout the United States who were gradually dropping out from any meaningful role in their society—but they were not people like Cato Jackson, who had taken a stand, however mis-guided, at the church at Llanfair; they were not the brilliant young girls like Gretchen Cole, who had tasted the core of a system and found it unpalatable; they were not young men like Joe, who found his nation conducting itself immorally and could no longer support it; nor were they men like Yigal Zmora, who saw the contradictions of two societies so clearly that he was incapable of bringing them into balance—not yet, not at eighteen, but perhaps later, if he maintained his questioning.

I liked the young drop-outs I was with in Torremolinos, and when the last of Paxton Fell's older group had quietly fallen asleep or had retired to unaccustomed partners in unaccustomed beds, I looked for my companions. I found them clustered together in a far corner of the garage. They were with the rustic musicians, and Gretchen was singing softly her ballad of the silkie, that overwhelming song of a man trapped in inescapable contradictions. Britta stood with the villagers, interpreting roughly the words Gretchen was singing, and I thought how appropriate that was, for the song must have originated with the ancient Norse invaders who had stormed the coasts of Scotland.

I was surprised at how easily they understood this rather difficult song, for when Britta explained to them that the seal had taken back his son and predicted that the boy's mother would marry a huntsman who would one day shoot both the seal and her son, the villagers nodded. To them such outcomes seemed logical.

———

It was Britta who suggested that Gretchen bring her guitar to the Alamo and offer regular programs as respite from the incessant records. 'I know the customers would appreciate the music. Remember those Spaniards the other night. And they couldn't even understand the words.' Since Jean-Victor was still absent in Morocco buying marijuana, the only one who had to be consulted was Joe, and when he heard of the proposal he said, 'Why not?'

I was present at Gretchen's first appearance. Some of the soldiers grumbled at this type of interruption to the usual records, but after the first strong chords on her Spanish guitar they paid attention, and before many days had passed they were making their requests by yelling out the Child numbers.

This was made easier when one of the soldiers stole the paperback reprints of Professor Child's volumes and donated them to the bar. On each inside cover was stamped: *This book is the property of Morón Air Base,* but in my opinion the books were doing more good in Torremolinos that they would have at the air base; at any rate, whatever I know about the Child ballads I learned thumbing these volumes while Gretchen sang in the Alamo.

Which ballads did the soldiers prefer? They never tired of 'Barbara Allen' and would yell 'Child 84' four or five times a day. 'She just sang it,' one of the men would tell a newcomer, who would yell, 'Well, let her sing it again.' I think the young men relished the idea of a faithless girl dying of a broken heart, for when Gretchen sang this perennial favorite, I would see the soldiers nodding complacently.

'Mary Hamilton' had no charm for them; apparently her tragedy was one that older people related to. But they loved 'The Twa Sisters,' with its haunting refrain 'Binnorie, o binnorie!' This ballad related events that developed when a young man courted an older sister but ran away with a younger; again the soldiers could identify with such an impasse, for all of them, apparently, had at one time or other wooed one girl while keeping an eye on another.

They also liked Child 12 very much, the account of a gallant knight who was poisoned by the girl he was proposing to marry. To watch the nods of approval when Gretchen sang this ballad, one would have concluded that such poisonings were commonplace and that the soldiers had been lucky to escape. But the song that seemed to strike the most responsive chord was 'The Prickly Bush,' for its moist sentiment reflected their own sense of morality:

> ' "Oh, the prickly bush, the prickly bush,
>   It pricked my heart full sore;
> If ever I get out of the prickly bush,
>   I'll never get in any more." '

The singing of the ballads had one consequence that I should have anticipated but didn't. When Gretchen placed herself on the high chair, twisted her left foot around a rung and crossed her right knee over, she formed a most appealing picture, and with her braided hair about her shoulders and her bright eyes flashing, it was not surprising that many of the casuals who drifted into the bar should have been attracted to her. In fact, barely a day passed without some man asking her to dinner, or to a drive down to Marbella, or a swim; but she rebuffed all invitations with an iciness that frightened or perplexed them. Habitués, having repeatedly tried to lure Gretchen to their flats, passed the word that she was frigid, or a lesbian, or a weirdo. Interesting speculations circulated, with the men occasionally bringing Joe or Cato into their seminars.

'What's with Miss Boston?' they asked.

'She's okay,' Cato reported.

'What goes on in the yellow pop-top?'

'She sleeps there,' Joe said.

'I know that. But with who?'

'With herself. And you lay off. When she sends out the message that she needs a companion, you'll be the last to get an invitation.'

'What bugs me,' one of the Americans said, 'is that in a place like Torremolinos, where girls go nuts looking for dates, this one is no-no.'

'Maybe she feels no-no,' Cato suggested.

'There you're wrong. Because I look at her when she sings, and those songs come from the heart. She lives them.'

'All you look at is her legs,' Cato said.

'How else would you know what a girl's thinking?' the soldier asked.

And then Clive flew in from London, and the music changed, and for two weeks the Alamo was bewitched, for Clive brought with him such a compelling sense of this day, this generation, that everyone had to listen.

I was sitting in the bar one afternoon, waiting for instructions from Geneva as to what I must do next with the fractious Greeks, when a soldier who was gazing aimlessly into the alley suddenly leaped from his chair and shouted, 'It's Clive!'

I looked into the alley and saw standing there, with sunlight on his face, a most unusual-looking young man. He was in his early twenties, tall and slim in a soft, effeminate way. He wore his hair long, and had a beard much like Christ's, above which peered the biggest, most limpid eyes I had ever seen in a man. He was dressed London style, in a velvet jacket that was obviously expensive; and around his neck he wore a heavy Renaissance chain from which dangled a large flat metal disk on which had been engraved the copy of a Verrocchio head. He created an impression of a young faun, lacking only horns and a wreath of olive.

The American soldiers jumped toward the door, shouting, 'It's our boy!' They reached out, grabbed him by the arms, and hauled him into the bar. He responded by kissing each one on the cheek and saying to those he remembered from previous visits, 'Dear boy, it's ripping to have you back.'

'You're the one who was away,' one soldier said.

'Darling boy,' Clive protested, 'I am never far from here. Sink of Torremolinos, Mecca of the world, I bow three times,' and carefully handing me an article he was holding, he threw himself prone upon the floor, knocking his head thrice against the boards. 'I am overjoyed to be here,' he said from his reclining position, blowing kisses to everyone, 'and the good things I've brought you! Oh, oh!'

I now had time to notice that he had handed me a large flat carpetbag, purple in color, with two leather handles. It was about twenty-six inches long, thirteen high and not more than six inches thick, but it was heavy. Before he recovered it from me he moved about the bar, embracing all his old friends and pausing to inspect the three girls. 'You are a glorious addition,' he told Britta. Kissing Monica on the cheek, he said, 'Ah, that English complexion! Tend it with Pond's cream or it'll go to hell.' He tried to kiss Gretchen too, but she drew back in such a way as to indicate that she did not intend to participate in such nonsense. To her surprise, he grabbed her left hand, pressed it passionately to his lips, and cried, 'You can always tell a lady. She keeps her knees together.' Before Gretchen could protest, he was standing before me, saying, 'And now, my good man, you can hand back the jewels, s'il vous plaît.'

As the Americans gathered around him, he cleared a place on the bar for his carpetbag and carefully unzipped the edges. Throwing back the top, he revealed two stacks of gramophone records with jackets in the current mode: weird montages, an extremely austere photograph of an eggplant titled in copperplate *Aubergine*, an 1877 grainy photograph of a public execution in Belgrade, and a series of vignettes of the American west, including the scalping of a white woman in voluminous petticoats. Records by two English rock-and-roll groups predominated: Octopus, Homing Pigeons. The records looked as if they had never been played.

'What shall I start with?' he asked his audience. 'Yesterday these gems were in London, untouched by human hands. Today we offer them to the swine.' He nodded to the soldiers. 'I think the biggest news . . . the really shattering thing that has set music back on its ear . . . this.'

He dug among his records and came up with one enclosed in a jacket that showed a gangster accompanied by three screwball types standing under a bare tree in a western clearing. Looking at the forbidding photograph, I could not guess what the music inside contained, but Clive explained: 'It's a surprising departure for Dylan. A savage attack upon the church . . . a blistering rejection of Catholicism.'

'What!' one of the soldiers cried. 'Must be terrific,' and it was through his response, plus that of his friends, that I became aware of how vitally interested this group was in what was happening in their music. What Bob Dylan was doing in his latest record was more important to them than new army regulations or editorials in the *New York Times*. Music counted; other aspects of culture were in the hands of the Establishment or were controlled by old people like me, but this music belonged to them, and the fact that it outraged the stabler regiments of society made it doubly precious.

'God, I'd like to hear what Dylan has to say,' a soldier said as he watched Clive take the record from its jacket; the young Englishman behaved like a priest conducting a religious ritual. Only the tips of his fingers touched the edge of the record so as not to mar it. Gently he placed the record on the turntable, adjusted the dials to high volume, and leaned back to hear the revolutionary music which he and his friends found so rewarding.

It was a strange record, in which every phrase had a recondite meaning. When Dylan, in his nasal tones, addressed himself to his landlord, who apparently was about to evict him, Clive said, 'Of course he means God,' and when Dylan challenged God not to underestimate him, in return for which he would not underestimate God, the soldiers understood. The lonesome hobo in the next song was mankind defrauded by the religion it had accepted. The wicked messenger, Clive explained, was the body of priests in all religions who misguide and thieve from the faithful; I found this a particularly savage thing, filled with youthful contempt. Tom Paine, bitterly disappointed with organized religion, was the hero of one song; a disillusioned St. Augustine, of another.

I found most of the songs jejune, the type of thinking one should have completed in college bull sessions—freshman year, not senior—but there was one that seemed better than the rest; it dealt with a 'poor immigrant who eats but is not satisfied,' and it displayed a deep and timeless religious spirit. When the record ended and the Americans had had an opportunity to digest its radical message, I judged from the remarks they made that Dylan's interpretation of modern religion was more significant to them than any encyclical of the Pope's. In succeeding days they asked Clive to play the record repeatedly, for it seemed to speak directly to them.

The actual music of the Dylan record was not impressive—mostly guitar and drum—but Clive's next two finds got down to the hard core of modern statement. A London group called Octopus offered a driving number called 'I Get All Hung Up,' in which a singer shouted that phrase forty-seven times, with only a few alternating clauses, illiterate and frantic, which did nothing to explain why he was hung up. The song exerted a powerful effect upon its advocates, who told me, 'That's the best side Octopus has ever done.' When I asked why the endless repetition of a single idea was commendable, they told me, 'You miss the whole point. It's that combination in the background.' When the record played again, which it did no less than once every fifteen minutes, I listened to the supporting music and heard an electric organ that produced a mournful wail appropriate to the words of the song and two electric guitars that sounded like musical machine guns. The third instrument I could not identify, so one of the soldiers enlightened me: 'It's a mouth organ . . . played very close to the mike.' I listened more closely but was not able to confirm that intelligence.

But the combination of these instruments, plus the nasal, wailing voice singing in the accents of a South Carolina Negro—even though the singer had never been outside London—was so different and so commanding that I began to understand why the young people appreciated it so much. Did I? It had been recorded at such tremendous volume that all I heard, really, was a vast blur of noise.

When I said this to Monica, she clapped her hand over her mouth and said, 'You idiot! You haven't caught that wonderful twisting of the sound—like the arms of an octopus? Where do you think the group got its name?' So I listened again as she explained how the two guitars and the organ constantly intertwined while the shrill, staccato mouth organ carried the tune forward. It was a thin musical contribution, but at last I understood it.

'You'll like Homing Pigeons,' she assured me. 'They're for squares.' And when Clive put on their new record I agreed, for I could hear the words and they made sense.

Who was Clive? I never heard his last name, but he came from London and apparently belonged to a good family, for Monica had

known him previously. 'His father and Sir Charles did things together,' she told me, 'although whether it was in school or university I've never understood.'

At sixteen Clive had been a brief sensation in a musical group that
had offered a series of new sounds; what they were I did not learn,
but I did see a photograph of him at that period dressed in Ed-
wardian clothes and seated at a harpsichord with twin keyboards,
which must have been an innovation for rock-and-roll. When he
was eighteen his group had lost its popularity and at twenty he was
a used-up elder statesman. Now at twenty-three he was writing
songs for others—very good songs, I was to discover—and to keep
his imagination fresh he toured the centers of inspiration: Mallorca, Torremolinos, Antibes, Marrakech. On such trips he carried
only a small handbag plus his purple carpetbag containing the
latest records from London and New York.

Arriving at one of his stops, he would seek out some bar or café
with a record player, and there he would ensconce himself, at no
pay, and report upon what was happening in the music world,
playing his disks at their maximum noise-level and infusing the
area with reverberating echoes of whatever new sound had come
along within the past six months. The highlight of any such visit
came when he placed on the turntable one of his own compositions,
and now in the Alamo the time had come for him to uncover what
he had been up to since his last visit.

'I've done two songs,' he explained. 'One for Procol Harum.'
This turned out to be a London group with a fine reputation. 'And
the other for Homing Pigeons.' He played the latter first, and I
was unprepared for either its content or style, for musically it
derived straight from Mozart and poetically from Homer and Sappho.

> Ancient days, ancient days!
>   I sailed among the Isles of Greece
> Peddling handsome slaves to rich wine merchants,
>   Peddling slaves and seeking peace.
>
> Ancient days, ancient days!
>   I traveled to the mainland city
> Selling little girls to fat bankers and trustees,
>   Selling girls and seeking pity.

Ancient days, ancient days!
How terrible the setting of the sun,
For with tumult gone I had to lie alone,
Peddling slaves
Selling girls
Smuggling pearls
Robbing graves
And in my sleeplessness, face up to what I'd done.

The Homing Pigeons had given Clive's composition the right touch; basically they played with an eighteenth-century lyricism, but in unrhythmic lines like 'Selling little girls to fat bankers and trustees,' they gave it an awkward, hammering quality that made it quite modern. I was surprised at how attentively the soldiers listened to Clive's song; without saying so, he had launched an attack upon the Establishment, and this they approved.

At about two in the morning Clive said, 'It's been a long day. I'm getting tired. Is the sleeping bag still there?'

'Yigal's using it.'

'So be it. What's available?'

Britta answered, 'You could sleep in the pop-top.'

'Wait a minute!' Gretchen protested. 'I do my own inviting.'

'What I meant was,' Britta explained, her cheeks flushed, 'was that Yigal and Clive could sleep in the pop-top and you could take over the sleeping bag.'

'Now that's a sensible idea,' Gretchen said, and with no more planning than that, off they went to bed.

———•••———

On one point I was mistaken about Clive. His effeminate mannerisms had led me to think he might be homosexual; certainly the soldiers who were meeting him for the first time thought so, because I heard comments of a fairly purplish hue, but one of the Americans who had been at the army base for three years offered a correction.

'You cats have this boy Clive all wrong. He shared my flat during one trip, and he had so many girls running in and out that the Guardia Civil came around to see if we were running a whorehouse. When they saw Clive, a skinny hundred and forty pounds, one of the Guardia asked me, "What's his secret?" '

The soldier was right. With Gretchen sleeping indoors, Clive and Yigal had the pop-top to themselves, and they arranged the bunks so that four could sleep conveniently and from their pillows survey the sea. It was thus an ideal spot for entertaining young ladies, who later drifted indoors for coffee and bathroom facilities. Whenever I visited the apartment it was populated by girls who seemed prettier than the ones I had seen before. Clive was favorably known along the coast, and some of his guests drove long distances to talk with him about music and to share the bed they had enjoyed on his previous visits. He was a pied piper, attracting the best youth in Hamelin, but before long I saw that whereas he might be sleeping with various young ladies who sought him out, he was interested primarily in Gretchen.

I was present when the infatuation started. (Don't ask me how a young man could entertain four different girls in a pop-top during one week and at the same time be infatuated with the owner of the bed he was using; the young people didn't think it strange.) It was on the third day of his stand in Torremolinos and we were all in the Alamo, where he was playing his records: 'I have one just over from the States that's absolutely delicious,' he shouted. 'You'll love it, and you'll be astonished when I tell you who's done it. Johnny Cash. Yes, the hillbilly. Listen!' It was a rollicking song about a southern gambler who had named his son Sue and then abandoned him. Father and son meet in a Gatlinburg saloon, where all hell breaks loose. It was, as Clive had said, a song everyone would like, and as he replayed it, I kept thinking that in America the new music was discovering what the automobile makers and the cigarette companies already knew: that in the modern world, with its crowded and dirty mechanical cities, romance can live only in the open spaces of the south and west. Sue meets his baleful old man in Gatlinburg; the soldier dreams of his girl in Galveston; the lineman comes from Wichita and the absconding guitar player is on his way to Phoenix. You can look at a dozen automobile advertisements on television, and you'll get the idea that every American car is driven on dirt roads in the far west. Same with cigarette smokers. You never see them in a city, always beside some cool stream or herding white-faced Herefords beyond the mesa. The open spaces, the goodness of rural life represented what was desirable in American culture; the cities were abominations to be forgotten.

I was contemplating all this when a group of Americans and Swedes entered the bar, listened for a while to Clive's records, then told Joe, 'We thought the girl was to sing at five.' When they looked at Clive accusingly, Joe said, 'She's gonna sing,' and he explained to Clive that in recent weeks Gretchen had been playing the guitar and singing ballads.

'Marvelous!' Clive shouted above his music. 'Simply ripping.' He lifted the needle and gently returned the record to its cover, then sought out Gretchen and said, 'I hadn't a clue, old dear, not a clue.'

'I like your music better,' she said, but after a chair was produced and she had tuned her guitar, I could see Clive widen his eyes when she struck the first professional notes. He looked at me and nodded vigorously, as if to say, 'This one knows.'

'Child 81,' she announced, and soon she was singing the saucy account of how high-born Lady Barnard met Little Musgrave in church one Sunday morning and propositioned him with blandishments that even a young man intent on worship could not withstand:

> ' "I have a hall in Mulberry,
>   It stands baith strong and tight;
> If you will go to there with me,
>   I'll lye with you all night." '

Little Musgrave went home with the lady and was caught in bed by her husband, Lord Barnard, who proceeded to hack him to pieces.

Gretchen sang the ballad with a bewitching charm, and Clive, who knew a good singer when he heard one, said, when the applause had died down, 'Most elegant. You sing like a Scottish girl . . . with real boggy coloring.'

I suggested that she sing 'Mary Hamilton,' at which the Swedes clapped loudly, for the song was well known in their country. Clive, surprisingly, did not know this famous ballad, but even on first hearing he appreciated the unusual beauty of the opening and closing stanzas. 'Exquisite!' he cried, and for the rest of his stay it was he who saw to it that Gretchen was called to the high chair at intervals to sing, and it was he who led the applause when she did.

He borrowed the Child volumes and studied them, asking Gretchen her opinion on which the good numbers were. Like her, he found the lament for the Bonny Earl of Murray among the finest, but it was 'The Great Silkie of Sule Skerrie' that showed him how delicate an interpreter she could be.

'You must come to England!' he cried. 'The record companies would flip over what you're doing . . . absolutely flip.'

Gretchen had no ambition to make recordings; professionalism of that sort had never appealed to her and she would have been embarrassed to find her photograph on the jacket of a record, but she did enjoy talking music with Clive and they were together a good deal in those sun-filled days of mid-spring, but more than talk she did not care to do.

One day Clive asked me, 'What's wrong with Gret?' and I said, 'Maybe she finds it distasteful that you keep the pop-top filled with other young ladies . . . her pop-top, that is.'

'Oh!' With his autonomic charm, he laughed at me and said, 'Really, girls these days aren't put off by that. Those kids in the car . . . who worries about them, truthfully?'

'I mean . . .' I tried to say something relevant about love's being a permanent thing that did not fluctuate too much with contemporary style, that any self-respecting girl would object to being courted by a man who was living with another girl—with a string of them, to be exact—but my words sounded so old-fashioned that when Clive poked me and said, 'Really, old chap . . .' I shut my mouth.

'Fact is,' he said, 'it's not me at all that puts her off. Something quite ugly disturbs her. When she sings she's a different girl—all poetry and zest for horses riding over the moor. She'd be great as one of the Brontë sisters. But when she puts down the guitar the dream evaporates. You can see it vanish in the last three chords.'

Clive's presence in Torremolinos had a consequence of which he remained unaware. He and Monica had been talking about old acquaintances in England for the better part of an afternoon, when Yigal came to my table and said, 'I left Canterbury much impressed with England. I liked those girls at the English hotel and was beginning to think I might become an Englishman. Now I'm beginning to have doubts.'

'Why?'

'I've been watching Clive and Monica. What I mean is, I've been listening. They use such an exaggerated vocabulary . . . such an inflated one. Everything's hideous or excruciating or delicious or simply awful.'

'Don't get put off by style,' I said. 'American vocabulary is just as bad in its way.'

'I don't mean anything trivial,' Yigal said. 'Fundamentally, I'm a Russian Jew. When I look at the sun, I want to see the sun as big as it is, and no bigger. I want to live in a prosaic world of known causes and effects. Great Britain is excellent if you're Clive or Monica, if you can construct your own fairy-tale world, but it would be hell for an ordinary Russian Jew who doesn't see things as horrible or devastating or simply gorgeous.'

'Your reaction surprises me,' I protested. 'You're making a serious judgment on irrelevant grounds.'

'They may be fundamental,' he said. 'Israel and America are pragmatic . . . we see things as they are . . . grapple with them as best we can. I'm that kind of person.'

'What did you think of Churchill?' I asked.

'Very inflated, from what I read. The theatrics weren't necessary, not really. He had to use them because he was speaking to Clive and Monica. It's their world, not mine,' and in the days that followed, I could see that he was evaluating his three passports.

Clive exerted other influences on all of us who came in contact with him. For example, he was addicted to picnics, but only in the French style. 'We're going up into the mountains tomorrow,' he would announce, and Joe would arrange for one of the soldiers to mind the bar till dusk.

Clive's picnics were an artful combination of the crudest country food plus whatever *haute cuisine* he could obtain by cajolery rather than a large outlay of money, and when he opened the baskets in some mountain glen, with Spanish mountains looking down upon us with their faces crisscrossed by the trails that smugglers had been using for the past five hundred years, we were never sure what we would find inside, but of one thing we were certain: each participant would receive his own small ramekin containing some delicious concoction. 'I abhor picnics that consist of sandwiches,' he said, and would allow none to be made while he was in charge.

One afternoon, as we sat on a hill overlooking Gibraltar, with the shores of Africa outlined in the distance and shepherds gathering their flocks ahead of us, he suddenly cried, 'Tomorrow let the bombs fall on Gibraltar. Today, by God, we had a feast.'

At his picnics he always invited Gretchen to sing, and he would sit near her and whisper the words to himself, and it would be spring and the sea would be gray-blue and hawks would wheel overhead and we could hear the bleating of newborn lambs above the soft words that Gretchen sang:

> 'O hooly, hooly rose she up,
>   To the place where he was lying,
> And when she drew the curtain by,
>   "Young man, I think you're dying." '

———•••———

One day, because of an especially long session with the Greeks, I did not reach the Alamo until mid-afternoon, and I found an unusual woman waiting for me. Why do I term her unusual? For one thing, she did not seem excited about having made it to Torremolinos, and for a good-looking young woman of twenty-six, that was exceptional. She was a spare, intense person with sharp eyes and a dedicated manner of speech, as if she had only a few days in which to accomplish a mission of some magnitude. But what alerted me most was a silly thing—her insistence upon using her full name, something rarely done in Torremolinos where I never did learn Joe's last name, or Clive's, or the names of any of the pretty girls who climbed in and out of the pop-top.

'I am Susan Eltregon,' she said, shaking hands with me in a businesslike manner. 'I was told I might find Cato Jackson here.' When I nodded, she said, 'And Gretchen Cole.'

'She sings here at five.'

'Is there any way I could see them now?'

'They come and go. They're in town, I'm sure, but I haven't seen them today.'

'And who are you?'

'George Fairbanks. World Mutual.'

At my mention of the Geneva firm, she tensed. I was sure she had heard of us and that what she had heard was unpleasant to her, but she betrayed nothing except this intuitive loathing. 'Can I wait?' she asked.

'It's a bar,' I said. I didn't like her and I suspected she knew it, but she sat down at my table. When I asked, 'What brings you to Torremolinos?' she reflected on the question for some time, then decided that I would probably ask around till I found out. 'Haymakers,' she said.

I had heard of this group only from stories which had appeared in the *Paris Herald Tribune*, but my frown must have told her that I had read some such material, for before I could respond, she said, 'We are everything the stories say.' She clipped her words, giving them emphasis, and for some reason I could not have explained I said, 'That's an expensive outfit you're wearing,' and she snapped, 'Revolutionaries do not have to be paupers,' and I growled, 'They rarely are.'

For some moments she looked at me coldly, then said, 'I have no quarrel with you, Mr. Fairbanks . . . except that when reason rules, outfits like yours will be liquidated first. You are a group of international bloodsuckers and you must go.'

'Right now I'm engaged in a deal in which we're trying to suck some blood, and I'm getting nowhere. Would you care to help me?'

'I am here to see Cato Jackson and Gretchen Cole.'

'How could you possibly be interested in them?'

'You mean how could Haymakers be interested? Jackson and Cole are Haymakers. They do not realize it yet, but they are Haymakers.'

'They will be surprised when you tell them.'

'Their experiences have made it inevitable. All they need is the awakening.'

'They're a pair of born daydreamers, eh? And you're here to awaken them?'

'Events awaken them. I am here to point out the events.'

'Are you an officer in Haymakers?' I asked.

'We don't bother with such frivolity,' she snapped.

The Haymakers had taken their unusual name for three reasons. It carried the image of a roundhouse blow that would knock out the Establishment. It also had the connotation of clever people taking advantage of the current situation—making hay while the sun shone. And, finally, it bespoke rural life and avoided the stigma of being a city movement, which it was.

The Haymakers, most of them under thirty, were committed to the total destruction of American society, nothing less. Their program was simple: move into every disturbed situation, exacerbate it, allow it no time to stabilize, sponsor anarchy, and rely upon the resulting turmoil to radicalize the young people. When a sufficient cadre of able young people had been converted into dedicated revolutionaries, large mass movements would be initiated to tear down the social structure: banks would be discredited, the National Guard immobilized, universities destroyed, and the usefulness of social agencies like newspapers and television stations neutralized.

When total disruption had been achieved, the Haymakers planned to move into the chaos and—with their directed cadres— immobilize the police, the army, the school systems and the municipal governments. If at that late and disorganized date resistance was met, there would have to be fighting in the streets, but even if such fighting did not develop, the old-fashioned holders of power would still have to be liquidated. One of the recurring phrases used by the Haymakers was, 'He's a Kerensky and he must go.'

If such a program were to succeed, potentially disaffected persons of ability—like Gretchen Cole, who had tangled with the police, and Cato Jackson, who had lugged guns into a white church —had to be conscripted; Cato was doubly inviting as a target since he was also a Negro, and one of the basic tenets of the Haymakers was that Negro dissent must be converted into revolution.

In order to enlist Gretchen and Cato in this revolution, Susan Eltregon had been dispatched from St. Louis, where the Haymakers were currently headquartering. She was the daughter of a druggist in Denver; she used the phrase, 'I used to be the daughter of a pair of reactionaries in Colorado,' as if she had, by an act of will, dissociated herself from them shortly after the moment of birth. Her parents had saved money to send her to college in Montana, but that experience had been a shattering one; she found the college unbelievably dull and the professors pathetic. With a group of students from states like California and Massachusetts, she had started a committee for the overhaul of the curriculum, the method of choosing the faculty and all systems of grading and discipline. This placed her athwart the purposes of the school, which longed for peace and the opportunity to graduate students who would become teachers and bookkeepers, so at the end of her freshman year Susan was asked not to return.

She ignored the suggestion, moved into a rooming house at the edge of the campus, drew about her a group of similarly inclined drop-outs and began a program of harassment that ended with a campus-wide rebellion against the athletic coach and the burning of a science hall. Montana police invaded the rooming house, but

Susan and her friends were gone, leaving behind what luggage they had. 'The pigs drove us out,' they reported in New York.

Prior to Susan's arrival in New York, the Haymakers had established a precarious foothold in that city. Their organizing leader was an assistant professor at one of the local colleges; because of his irritating attempts to improve the curriculum of his institution and to force the admission of blacks and Puerto Ricans, regardless of high school grades, he had been denied a permanent appointment to the faculty. He then launched a wild series of confrontations to protect his employment, and although he failed, he did radicalize seven undergraduates, who dropped out of college to work with him, and this formed the nucleus of the movement. But its real force—its tremendous capacity for capitalizing on disturbances and enlisting young people who were offended by them—developed only with the arrival of a group of former students from the midwest.

These were tough, hard-nosed revolutionaries who had matured in cities like Chicago, Detroit, Terre Haute and Gary. They found no hope for the United States as it now existed and were determined to tear it down. Susan Eltregon found a place in this leadership group, for she understood their derivations and approved their commitments. One of the midwest leaders had proposed as the rallying cry of the movement, 'Everyone in authority must go,' and it was the latter concept that now motivated the group.

The Haymakers enrolled many brilliant young people, and in the St. Louis office these plotters and planners kept track of any incident across the nation calculated to produce disaffected students or workmen who could be approached. It was a girl drop-out from Smith College who in the course of clipping newspapers for the Haymakers spotted the names of Cato Jackson and Gretchen Cole. Operatives in the Philadelphia and Boston areas were asked to track them down, and first reports were disappointing: 'Gretchen Cole has disappeared from the University of Besançon. Whereabouts unknown.'—'Jackson flew the coop. Believed to be in Detroit.'

But after further investigation, the Boston people found that Gretchen had sent a postcard to a girl at Radcliffe, telling her, 'You ought to come over here.' And a Mr. Wister of Philadelphia, who was supplying Cato Jackson with funds, disclosed that the young man had asked that his check be sent to Torremolinos.

'You must go to Torremolinos,' the high command in St. Louis ordered Susan. 'There's an army base of some kind near there. You might do some real good, even if you didn't find Jackson and the Cole girl.'

So Susan underwent the indignity of writing to her parents in Denver for money: 'I think that if I go to Europe and see the Netherlands, if I see where grandfather came from and what life is like in his country, I may find myself. At any rate, it will not hurt to try and it may do some good.'

She received seven hundred dollars, which was more than she needed, since a twenty-one-day round-trip excursion from St. Louis to Málaga cost only $340, for which she also received the free use of an automobile while in Spain. When she told me this, I asked where she was keeping the car, and she was about to tell me when a group of soldiers from Sevilla slammed their way into the bar. They were in civilian clothes, of course, and Susan asked me, 'Are they soldiers?' When I nodded, she left me and moved to their table. Two of them were black and she paid most attention to them, buying drinks and asking them how they liked the military. I caught only snatches of her conversation, but she seemed to be asking about black attitudes in the army and what they planned to do when they returned home. At one point I heard her comment on race troubles in Detroit and Los Angeles, but the two soldiers merely stared at her. By some strange mechanism she conveyed to the men the idea that she was not interested in sex.

When Gretchen reported for her stint of singing, Susan Eltregon left the soldiers and returned to my table. 'She is an attractive girl,' she said approvingly. 'Did the experience with the police . . .' She fumbled for the right word, failed to find it, and sat back to listen. She found the ballads exciting, and whispered, 'They were real revolutionaries in those days. Listen to those words!'

At the end of the program Susan went up to Gretchen and said, 'I have come from St. Louis to talk with you.'

'Why me?'

With that forthright beginning, Susan launched into a vigorous delineation of what the Haymakers were endeavoring to accomplish: the overthrow of the United States. I was surprised that she should divulge her plans so openly to Gretchen; that she should feel no compunction about discussing them in front of me was astonishing. She explained this: 'Mr. Fairbanks is against us anyway. It is good for him to know that his days are numbered. As soon as we take power he and his kind are doomed.' She said this looking right at me.

Her arguments with Gretchen were persuasive: 'You have seen the American police system at its worst. No,' she corrected herself, 'I have seen it at its worst—repressing general freedom. What you saw was personal aggression. But with your knowledge you become very valuable to the movement—to the revolution, that is. A girl like you—with that guitar, that voice . . . You know, of course, you are a very special person. Your background, too. You could move across the United States and do a vast amount of good. Young people would listen to you. What we must have is charismatic leadership bringing the people to us. The hard-core brains we have, the guns we have.'

I was interested to see how Gretchen would respond; she listened attentively, followed all arguments with her fingers making diagrams of them as Susan spoke, and treated the discussion as if it were a seminar at Radcliffe. Ideas were being presented to her, and some of them might have merit; she would accord them the dignity of attention. From the sympathetic manner in which she assented to many of the points Susan Eltregon was making, I was afraid at first that she was being persuaded, but when the emissary from the revolution paused, Gretchen said, 'Let's suppose I accept your data but disagree with your conclusions.'

'How could you?'

'Easy. I agree that the police can be abominable. I don't agree that you solve the problem by eliminating them.'

'How else? If the entire system is rotten, what else can you do but tear it down?'

'You amend it. The system has always had to be amended.'

'You mean gradualism?' Miss Eltregon asked contemptuously.

'Precisely.' Now Gretchen leaned forward, and with a barrage of convictions I never knew she had, began arguing Socratically and with much self-control for the kind of ebb and flow in politics that had characterized the English-speaking peoples for the past seven hundred years. The soldiers stopped to listen.

Susan Eltregon was no pushover. During long nights in Montana and blazing hot afternoons in St. Louis she had acquired a social philosophy which sustained her theories of revolution, and she gave a good account of herself: 'The state as we know it must be destroyed by the constant pressure of anarchy, and it is the responsibility of each of us to add to that anarchy now so that we can witness the evolution of a new society tomorrow.' I noticed that when she spoke she never used contractions: invariably she said *it is* and not *it's*. For her, life was intense and single-tracked, and as the twilight fell and the alley darkened, I could see that she was irritated with Gretchen, who listened attentively, judged, and argued back. At no point did Gretchen's eyes brighten with the thrill of discovery when Miss Eltregon made some telling point, for she had heard all these arguments years before in dormitory bull sessions; now she listened respectfully and evaluated, and when Susan finished any line of reasoning, Gretchen smiled, agreed with such data as were irrefutable, and began arguing back. It was obvious that Susan was not going to enroll Gretchen in the revolution.

The discussion ended unexpectedly. Miss Eltregon, who had done her homework, said, 'But did not your own father—a representative of the worst of what we have been talking about—did he not force you to drop your suit against the police?'

'He did.'

'Well?'

'Father's confused. That doesn't mean he's to be liquidated.'

'You believe that the corrupt things he stands for . . .'

Gretchen smiled. 'I don't think Father stands for much . . . except honesty in business relations . . . and the Republican party.'

'And you fail to see that it is men like him who are destroying the country?'

Again Gretchen smiled. 'I think you have drops in your eyes, Miss Eltregon. You see things bigger than they are.'

'It is only that . . .'

'No,' Gretchen interrupted. 'The fault isn't with me. It's with you. Your trouble is that you didn't go to a tough university. One that knocked some sense into you . . . made you think.'

Susan's eyes flashed. She started to make some kind of personal response, but her training with the Haymakers had proved that that wasn't fruitful. Controlling herself, she said, 'For this generation, Miss Cole, the streets are the university.'

'You're right,' Gretchen agreed generously. 'That's where I was educated.' She accented the word I. 'But when I got my education I was able to weigh it against the full range of history. And it came out as something quite different from what you say.'

'You are hopeless,' Miss Eltregon said.

'No. I'm educated.'

The impasse was broken by the arrival of Cato Jackson and Monica, for as soon as Susan saw him she dropped Gretchen and started asking him a series of questions, which he answered with an enthusiasm that Monica encouraged. 'Revolution?' Cato asked. 'It's bound to come.'

'Agreed,' Monica cried. 'Those bloody Dutch in Amsterdam with their queen who owns half the oil in the world.'

'What the blacks must do,' Miss Eltregon said, trying to get back on the track, 'is unite with the laboring classes . . .'

'There you dead right!' Cato cried a little more loudly than necessary and shifting into Geechee. 'We gonna get all the black labor union members . . . how many you think we got?'

'What we have to do first,' Monica said, 'is get them tin workers in Bolivia . . . Cato, you know them tin workers in Bogotá.'

This occasioned a protracted discussion as to where Bogotá was, with one of the soldiers settling the argument: 'Look, I was stationed in Venezuela and I know for a fact it's in Ecuador.' When this location was agreed upon, Cato said, 'Man, we gonna slap them white oppressors, unnnnnh, unh!'

Miss Eltregon, trying to keep the conversation rational, asked, 'Have you heard of the Haymakers?'

'Yeah, das a punch Cassius Clay use,' Cato said.

'Sounds like a cocktail with pineapple juice and a bunch of muck,' Monica suggested.

Miss Eltregon was sharp enough to know that the couple might be putting her on, but she proceeded as if that were not the case. 'The Haymakers are the spearhead of the revolution,' she said.

'Man!' Cato cried enthusiastically. 'Das what we need! My friend Akbar Muhammad, he gonna decimate the town.'

'Your friend who?'

'Akbar Muhammad. He lead the New Muslims in Philly.'

I could see Miss Eltregon taking mental note of the name, searching her memory. 'Was he with you when you shot up the church?' she asked.

'He gonna be with me when we shoot up the world.'

'What would really pay off,' Monica interrupted, 'would be an attack on the House of Commons.'

Miss Eltregon ignored this and tried to bring the discussion back to some kind of sanity, but Cato said, 'You hit the House of Commons and the U.S. Senate the same afternoon, man, you gonna attract attention.'

'There's a time difference,' Monica said, and Miss Eltregon's head jerked.

'What the hell you mean by that?' Cato demanded. 'Don't you suppose I know there's a time difference? Like in the movies. Sidney Poitier say to Paul Newman, "Synchronize our watches." If we smart enough to blow up the whole government, don't you think we smart enough to synchronize our watches?' In disgust he added, 'London seven hours behind Washington.'

This provoked a flood of expertise, particularly from the soldiers, who were trained in such matters. They argued on behalf of time differences varying from London ahead by eight to London behind by seven. Miss Eltregon did not lose her composure; in fact, as I was to learn later, she was ahead of us all, for when Monica went on to propose that they bomb the Chamber of Deputies as well, provided they could synchronize their watches with Paris, I watched as Miss Eltregon studied Monica's eyes. It must have been then that she first caught on that Monica was taking drugs.

Cato said, 'Man, we get them firecrackers all goin' off at the same time, we really gonna have a revolution.' But when he had said this he grew moody and spoke directly to Miss Eltregon: 'In my bones I feel when the smoke clear . . . well, the brother gonna be on the bottom of the pile like before. How you answer that, lady?'

Miss Eltregon did not understand the question and asked Cato to repeat. He said, 'You gonna give the brother the same old end of the stick, eh, lady?'

Instead of trying to answer the question, Miss Eltregon studied Cato's eyes and apparently decided that he, too, was under the influence of something, for she abandoned any further attempt at serious discussion and said with as much cheeriness as she ever mustered, 'Let us all go out to dinner.' She indicated that Monica and I were included.

With shrewd judgment she picked from the soldiers the one Negro who was inclined to listen to the Haymaker message, and the six of us left the bar to find a restaurant, but she had something more special in mind. Leading us to the car which the airline had provided for three weeks, she drove us out of Torremolinos until we reached a side road leading to the sea. Before long we were at the gateway to a small castle, where Cato cried, 'Hell, I know this place, Laura lives here.'

'She does,' Miss Eltregon agreed. 'Friends in St. Louis sent me.'

Laura, wearing a long Moroccan caftan decorated with chains of beaten silver, met us at the door. She led us into the medieval dining room, where Paxton Fell stood tall and trim in his lamé evening jacket. Laura had six additional guests, three of them Americans, who applauded when she announced: 'This is Susan Eltregon, from St. Louis. She's one of those clever Harvesters who are going to lead the revolution.'

'What are you people up to?' one of the Americans asked.

Miss Eltregon replied forcefully, 'We have decided that life in America is intolerable.'

'Of course it is,' the American agreed.

'So intolerable that we must eliminate the whole filthy mess. We shall sustain anarchy wherever it breaks out . . . create it when it does not.'

'Splendid tactics,' Laura agreed.

'Where do you live in the States?' I asked her.

'Texas.'

'I shouldn't think Texas would approve such a plan.'

'Texas is beyond redemption,' she said abruptly, dismissing me and turning to Susan. 'Now tell us, dear child, what progress are you making?'

'We have cadres in all major cities. Good nuclei in most universities. We find encouraging response from the blacks.' Here she placed her hand on that of the Negro soldier she had recruited.

'Splendid,' Laura cried. 'This is the most heartening news I've heard in a long time.' Turning to Gretchen and Monica, she said, 'I'm sure you girls have joined up. It's such a sensible movement.'

'It's for America and I'm English,' Monica said, 'but I'm so excited about it, I plan to take care of central Africa . . . You know, Congo, Vwarda, Bolivia.'

'Bolivia is in South America,' one of the European guests pointed out.

'I know that,' Monica said petulantly. 'I'm going there to organize the tin workers . . . in Bogotá.'

This occasioned the same kind of digression which had disrupted Miss Eltregon's earlier presentation, and she intended to permit no repetition. She started speaking firmly and with a clear voice, continuing until she had captured everyone's attention. Certainly her message made me listen, and I sat astounded at her willingness to share it with us: 'The Haymakers are preparing many far-sighted moves against the day of revolution, but most of our work is being done for us by the doomed society as it thrashes about, trying to save itself. Each improvisation it adopts makes our position stronger and more inevitable. You will, I feel sure, see a sharp decline in the stock market as our corrupt economic system stumbles to its knees. Companies like yours, Mr. Fairbanks, will simply go to the wall. They will vanish. The entire force of history will drive President Nixon to enlarging his war in Vietnam, and when this happens you will see students across the nation rise in protest. Middle America will demand that the students be disciplined, so we can look forward to bloodshed, and this will further radicalize our youth. Now if at that moment, which I assure you is inescapable, a cadre of devoted men and women who comprehend the historical forces operating is in position to provide leadership . . . well, you can see for yourselves what can be accomplished.'

'It sounds perfectly thrilling!' Laura cried. 'I do wish I were younger!'

'Our success depends upon the courage of the young people we enlist,' Miss Eltregon said, looking directly at the Negro soldier. 'If we can rely on them to blow up, at the crucial moment, ten or twelve cross-country airliners, a handful of electrical relay stations, certain crucial radio and television antennae . . . do you visualize what might be accomplished? If hordes of students are ready to confront the police at the same time? And especially if our gallant blacks take to the streets at that moment?' She paused, then concluded: 'I think you can see that America is up for grabs. It can be captured if we are sufficiently devoted.'

Laura clapped her hands and turned to Gretchen. 'What role have they given you in this marvelous development?'

'Me?' Gretchen asked. 'To me it's a bunch of nonsense.'

'What do you mean?' Laura cried. 'We captured Russia with a handful of devoted humanitarians. We can surely do the same in the United States.'

Gretchen reflected on this for a moment, then asked, 'But if you live here in Spain on funds you receive from Texas, why would you sponsor a revolution that would wipe out those funds?'

'Darling,' Laura explained as she motioned for more drinks, 'no sensible person keeps his funds in Texas. We keep them in Switzerland.'

———•◆•———

If in speaking of Torremolinos I have dealt principally with the incandescent young people at the Arc de Triomphe, and the polished sybarites at Paxton Fell's, and the American soldiers at the Alamo, and the delectable Swedish girls at the Northern Lights, I have not been ignorant of the underground that operated throughout the year.

For some reason which no one understood, the Spanish police—one of the toughest and most efficient in Europe—allowed the resort a freedom known nowhere else in Spain. German Nazis held formal meetings, although not in public places. French, Belgium and Norwegian quislings lived in safe refuge. Drugs flowed in and out of the town on regular delivery routes, and through the alleys there was a constant passage of young people either hopelessly filthy or degenerate beyond redemption. They lived in hovels or slept along the beach, and were prepared for any kind of abnormality. Americans contributed substantial numbers to this drifting population—girls from good colleges and young men whose parents believed they were at some European university—but the majority were German, French and Scandinavian.

Sometimes they were a brutal lot. Each year in Torremolinos there would be four or five unsolved murders: customarily the victims were from the underground. A Belgian bar girl would be found along the beach with her throat cut, and her parents in Liège would cable: 'Bury the body and send the bill to us.' For several years they had considered her dead, anyway. But occasionally the drifters would invade some settled area, or murder someone respectable who had a hotel room, and then the police would try to identify the guilty, but with a large eligible population to choose from, their task would be hopeless. Most of the murders went unsolved.

One morning in late May the group living in Jean-Victor's apartment had a sampling of this violence. When Joe and Britta returned at five in the morning, after having closed the Alamo and taken some breakfast, they found on the doorstep of their apartment the body of a boy not yet twenty, his head split in half by a cleaver of some kind which had struck him between the eyes. When they first kneeled over him his limbs were still warm, and they started to call for help, thinking that if they could get him to a hospital he might be saved, but when they saw the gaping head, Britta said, 'That's that,' and went inside to ask Gretchen and the others if they had heard anything, and Joe went to the pop-top, where Clive and Yigal were in bed with two Swedish girls, who disappeared as soon as they learned what had happened.

'Get the police immediately,' Gretchen advised as soon as she saw the body, and Yigal went in search of them.

When the police came they shrugged their shoulders and placed the murder as the latest in a long list. They were disposed to believe the young people when Monica insisted that three of them had been asleep in the apartment and two in the car without having heard a thing. The police asked if the body could have been dragged from some other place, and Britta said, 'As Joe and I were coming home we did see two men disappearing down there,' and the police looked down the empty street.

———•◆•———

Each spring, as the flood tide of tourism began to sweep in, crowding Torremolinos with vacationers from all parts of the world, police took steps to clean the place up. They marched through the town, apprehending any man who wore a Jesus haircut, any girl who looked as if she had not bathed within the last three months.

'Out,' they said.

'But where . . .'

'Out.'

'Where can we go?'

'Out by nightfall . . . or spend the summer in jail.'

Then the mournful exodus would begin. Lucky ones would slip across the Mediterranean to Morocco. Others would disappear into the mountains of Spain and lie low until September, when the flood of tourists would subside. Those who had airplane tickets would hitchhike their way in to Málaga airport, and a scruffy lot they looked when standing beside scrubbed Scandinavians on their way back to Copenhagen. A few, unable to find an alternative, would go to jail.

Clive was the first of the group to be nabbed. 'Out of Spain by nightfall,' the police said. Expecting protest, they growled, 'With that haircut you're not welcome.'

'All right! I have my ticket to Tangier.'

'Use it.' In their records they saw that he had been in the pop-top on the morning of the murder, and said, 'You know you're still under suspicion for murder.' He maintained a grave demeanor and said he hoped they would soon catch the real culprit. Gravely they nodded and made a small concession: 'You can have till tomorrow night.'

'I'll be gone,' he promised. But then he had to smile, adding, 'And next October I'll be back.' The policemen nodded and said, 'Next October it will be all right.'

I went with the others when they accompanied him to the airport. It was the riffraff of Europe, in shaggy hairdo and tattered dress, that he was joining. Some of the most disreputable were guarded by policemen whose job it was to see that this or that particular visitor got aboard the plane and stayed there. Others were accompanied by girl friends with whom they had been living through the winter and whom they would probably never see again; such departures were apt to be tearful, like those at any airport. In the coming months Torremolinos would look more orderly than it had during the winter, and I suspected that winter was better. The world cleans up too many places for the benefit of tourists, builds too many Potemkin villages.

Clive left us with no rancor. 'I've stayed beyond my schedule as it is,' he said, looking at Gretchen as he spoke. 'We'll be meeting somewhere . . . spin a few disks together.' He kissed the three young men, embraced Britta and Monica, and shook hands with Gretchen. When he reached me he said, 'If you could join me for a year, you'd catch the hang of our music.' He shook my hand and disappeared into the mob, a frail young fellow carrying only a purple carpetbag and a shaving kit.

Before our group could work its way back to the pop-top, we were stopped by a policeman, who took Joe by the arm and said, 'Tomorrow . . . out!'

'What have I done?' Joe protested.

'Out.' From this curt decision, reached in the flash of a moment and occasioned only by Joe's haircut, there could be no appeal. The policeman noted in his book: *Bar El Alamo. Fuera.*

The young people were despondent. There was not only the question of who would care for Jean-Victor's bar if Joe had to leave so abruptly, but also the problem of how Joe would live, for he had saved little money. Yigal and Cato were reluctant to see him go, and Britta was most unhappy, for the amiable life she had devised for herself would now go smash.

Cato was driving the pop-top in silence, with none of us having any good ideas, when Gretchen snapped her fingers. Apparently she had been doing sums in her head and was now satisfied with her financial prospects, for she said, 'Why don't we all leave Torremolinos? I mean it. We could rig up two additional bunks in here . . . You could do that, couldn't you, Yigal? And we'd go to Italy.'

'Using what for money?' Joe asked.

'I am hiring you, this instant, to drive the pop-top and care for the luggage.' She placed her hand on his arm and said, 'Please say yes. We need you.'

Joe tugged at his beard, could think of no better prospect, and said yes.

Now Gretchen became excited. 'I know that Cato and Yigal get money from the States. You told me so. And you have some, don't you, Monica?' The three nodded, and Gretchen said, 'So you'd have no problems.' Instinctively, all of us except Cato turned to look at Britta, who blushed deeply. 'How about you, Britt?' Gretchen asked.

'Broke,' she said.

This provoked silence, which ended when Gretchen said quietly, 'You're the dearest friend I've ever had. You're not broke.'

From this impulsive beginning the six young people constructed an intricate program for touring Europe together, and by the time we reached the outskirts of Torremolinos, Yigal and Joe had decided what was required to build two more bunks into the pop-top, so when we entered the town we drove directly to the large hardware store near the post office, where the men purchased a variety of bolts, springs and canvas strips.

I was about to leave them there, for I had to keep an appointment with the Greek shipowners at one of the Chinese restaurants, but as I started to walk away, Joe stopped me and said, 'With me and Britta leaving, somebody will have to tend bar till Jean-Victor gets back. Will you find someone, Mr. Fairbanks?' And he tossed me the keys.

———•—•—•———

If Susan Eltregon had no luck in enlisting either Gretchen or Cato, she did establish good contacts with the Negro enlisted man; he was to meet her in St. Louis as soon as he left the service and would in the meantime distribute Haymaker literature at the army base.

Her big success, however, came with Monica Braham. After prudent observation, Susan had satisfied herself as to Monica's character and potentialities, so on the last night before their forced departure, when the gang was sitting in the bar lamenting with old friends whom they would no longer see, Susan suggested that they pop along to Laura's for farewell drinks. I said I couldn't join them because I had to find someone to run the bar, and this caused Susan no disappointment.

Joe assured me, 'I've cabled Morocco. Jean-Victor'll be here within a couple of days.'

'Peddling marijuana?'

'Guy has to make a buck.'

'What about Britta? Who takes her place?'

Joe looked around. 'Who?' he repeated, waving his right arm toward the center of Torremolinos. 'There must be five thousand girls out there looking for a job. Pick one.'

'How?'

'One with good legs. This is a bar.'

When he was gone I made the capital mistake of confiding to the soldiers my responsibility for finding a reliable bar girl, and within fifteen minutes, parading before me was the most lethal collection of doxies I had ever seen. There were girls from Australia with missing front teeth, tramps from Paris, weather-beaten blondes from Stockholm, Fräuleins who could speak no English. At one point I was tempted to remind them that I was staffing a bar, not an abattoir; instead I chickened out and said, 'I'll let you know tomorrow.' But as to what I would do tomorrow, I had no idea.

I kept the place open till about three o'clock, at which time, un-like the younger crowd, I was getting sleepy, but I was not destined for bed, because when I was about to lock the door Joe ran up, shouting, 'Fairbanks! We need your help.'

'What's happened?'

'Monica!'

'What'd she do?'

'Look!'

Down the alley came Monica, stark naked and surrounded by a mob of cheering night people. Behind her, in jockey shorts and nothing else, came Cato, holding a broom over her head as if he were an Egyptian slave protecting her from the sun. She was lost in a drugged trance, blowing kisses left and right as if she were royalty, and in my first horrified sight of the procession, I could think only of those lurid Sunday supplements in boyhood Indiana; they had taught me whatever I knew about sex. I had cherished one picture in which a near-naked Queen of Sheba approached King Solomon, attended by palm-waving blacks—and Monica looked like such a queen.

'She won't listen,' Joe cried with urgency. 'The cops are bound to get her.'

I ran to where she was about to turn a corner that would take her into the heart of the town, with policemen on the various corners. 'Monica!' I shouted.

She turned toward my familiar voice, looked at me with uncom-prehending eyes, regally pushed me aside, and moved on toward the police. I grabbed Cato and shouted, 'What's going on?' but he, too, looked through me, shoved me aside with his elbow, and fol-lowed the white queen, being careful to keep his broom over her head.

'What's happened?' I yelled to Joe.

'That fucking Eltregon,' he shouted.

Without trying to figure out what he meant, I ripped off my shirt, ran ahead, and wrapped it around Monica. At the same time I pulled her away from the main thoroughfare, but not before a policeman two blocks away had spotted the confusion, if not its cause. He started running toward us, so I passed Monica along to Joe, who lifted her off the ground and retreated with her down the alley. This left me with no shirt at three o'clock in the morning in the middle of Torremolinos, so I darted into a narrow hiding space near the bar and waited until the policeman had run past me. Then I came out, and ran right into an American woman and her husband.

'Aren't you ashamed of yourself?' she asked as I looked about for something to take the place of my shirt. 'At your age?'

From another hiding place Cato appeared, and when I joined up with him, hoping to ascertain what had happened, I found him in a stupor, unable to give me any answers, let alone logical ones; but soon Gretchen and Yigal ran up, yelling, 'Where's Monica?'

I grabbed Gretchen's arm and asked, 'What happened?' and she said, 'That damned Susan Eltregon. Saw a chance to get her hooks into Monica. Fed her some LSD. Laura and her gang have been using it.'

'Joe has Monica in tow,' I said.

Yigal now led us through the alleys to the big plaza at the post office, and there Joe stood, with a nearly naked Monica locked in his arms.

When Gretchen reached them she asked, 'What did you do with the car?' They were clearly unable to answer coherently, so she told me, 'They undressed in the living room at Laura's and ran onto the beach. Laura's gang thought it very funny, but first thing you know, they had climbed into the pop-top and were roaring off toward town. I yelled at them to stop, but Laura said, "What can happen?" and I said, "They can get killed!" and she said, "The car's insured, isn't it?" I suppose it's cracked up against a telephone pole somewhere.'

We found the car in an unlikely place. Cato had driven it into the lobby at the Northern Lights, where the Swedish manager was holding the key. Slowly we collected the group, but when we got everyone back to the car and Gretchen had paid for the damage to the hotel, Monica and Cato were still unaware of what had happened or of the condition they were in.

'It's so magnificent!' Monica assured me. 'You see colors . . . so brilliant . . . they embrace the world.' She collapsed into unconsciousness, and I asked with some apprehension, 'What should we do?' and Joe, who had handled LSD cases at the bar, said, 'Put her to bed.'

We did so, and I asked Gretchen, 'Why did Miss Eltregon give them LSD?' and Gretchen said, 'She knew that Monica was taking something. She felt that if she encouraged her she might get a leverage to make Cato join the Haymakers.'

After we had tucked the pair into bed we sat in the apartment, discussing how near they had come to being arrested, and Gretchen said, 'Before we go to Italy, I think we ought to find some quiet place away from pot and LSD and sort of unwind.' She looked at me as if I would know such a place, and the thought occurred that they would enjoy what I had always considered the gentlest, loveliest part of Europe, that remote and undiscovered southern end of Portugal called Algarve.

When I told them of the sweeping beaches, the almond-covered hills and the small forgotten towns with Crusader castles—and especially when I mentioned the cheapest prices in Europe—their eyes widened and they agreed that this was what they were looking for. 'Algarve,' I told them as dawn began to break, 'is a more beautiful Torremolinos, two hundred years ago,' and they decided to head for it.

At eight in the morning, when Monica and Cato had recovered from the effects of the LSD, the six young people piled into the yellow pop-top. Joe was at the wheel, for he was now the official chauffeur, and the others were tucked away in various imaginative positions. The regular bunks that came with the car were stowed, while the improvised ones were secured to the ceiling by ropes and pulleys. Considering all the gear—the books, the cans of Spanish food, the bottles of wine—I doubt that even a pussycat could have jammed into that vehicle. Joe sounded the horn. Gretchen leaned out to shout goodbye to the neighbors who had been so kind to her, and old women stood in their doorways to wave farewell.

At the top of the hill a policeman halted the pop-top, checked to see that Joe and his Jesus beard were leaving town, and waved the car on its way.

VIII §

ALGARVE

A Spaniard is a Portuguese with brains;
a Portuguese is a Spaniard with character.

There isn't very much in Spain, or Portugal either, to get excited
about if you've already seen Disneyland and Knott's Berry Farm.

Nature is seldom wrong, custom always.—Lady Mary Wortley Montagu

If I did not have a mirror, nor a memory, I would think I
was fifteen years old.—Jane Digby, at age 44, when
about to marry an Arab sheik

The best way to change society is to replace it one man at a time.

Children are amused by games; the lower classes diverted
by bullfights; gentlemen are entertained by noble discourse.

Oui, c'est elle!
C'est le déesse plus charmante et plus belle!
Oui, c'est elle, c'est la déesse
Qui descend parmi nous!
Son voile se soulève
Et la foule est à genoux!
—Les Pêcheurs de Perles

I think society must protect the right of the university professor to free speech, but when someone comes up with the
theory that condemns a whole race of people—and it's just a
theory with no proof—then I think the professor should not be
allowed to wrap himself in the robes of academic freedom. He
ought to be dragged right down into the marketplace, and if
his theory is wrong he should have his teeth kicked in. Of
course, I'm referring to Dr. Shillington's thesis that Italians are
inherently defective in moral codes and intuitively mafiosi.

Never refuse him anything he asks. Observe a certain amount of reserve and delicacy before him. Keep up the honeymoon romance whether at home or in the desert. At the same time do not make prudish bothers, which only disgust and are not true modesty. Never permit anyone to speak disrespectfully of him before you, and if anyone does, no matter how difficult, leave the room. Never permit anyone to tell you anything about him, especially of his conduct with regard to other women. Always keep his heart up when he has made a failure.—Isabel Arundel's memorandum to herself on the eve of her marriage to Richard Burton

Hieronymus Bosch is a fink. He paints
the Establishment that is to be.

A bachelor is a man who comes to work from a different direction
every day.

'Last night I lay in a weel-made bed,
    Wi silken hangings round me;
But now I'll lie in a farmer's barn,
    Wi the gypsies all around me.'
                            —Child 200

My mother always told me: 'Son, you can't buy happiness!'
She never told me I couldn't rent it.

Be considerate. Look at it from her point of view. No man can
be considered really old who has $500,000,000.

People who live in grass houses shouldn't get stoned.

When I'm lonely, dear white heart,
    Black the night or wild the sea,
By love's light my foot finds
    The old pathway to thee.
                    —'Eriskay Love Lilt'

Chicken Little was right.

$\mathcal{T}$HE trip from Spain to Portugal would exert a critical influence on two of the travelers.

Joe, at the wheel of the pop-top, saw for the first time the desecration that Spain had promoted along that stretch of shoreline reaching westward from Málaga to Gibraltar. As he picked his way through the traffic that jammed it, he was forced to look at what had happened to the small towns which had made this one of the most pleasant roads in Europe.

From Torremolinos to Fuengirola a concrete forest had grown up, a plethora of high-rise apartments crowding the waterfront, a jungle of shacks and hot-dog stands inland where the money was being made. What little open land he did see was being converted into golf courses.

And it was ugly, ugly beyond the operation of chance. It looked as if Spain had invited to its southeast corner a convocation of the world's worst architects and given them a commission: 'Transform this beach into an apogee of ugliness.' Prize money would have to be divided, for if the German architects created monstrosities, the Spaniards did worse. It was ironic—builders who had lived in Stockholm all their lives, seeing the beauty which northern architects had devised, moved into Fuengirola and erected slums, devoid of beauty or congeniality.

'Pretty grim,' Joe said as they drove toward Marbella and saw the beehive hotels under construction; these were American and had been lifted from downtown Los Angeles—the poorer section, that is.

What depressed him was that the open plazas, which had once made these towns attractive, giving them a sense of occupation by fishermen who worked for a living, were being filled in by concrete: stores, junk shops, apartment houses that could never be appealing. The rhythm of life that had once characterized the sea front had been destroyed beyond recall.

'Where's Spain?' Joe asked with some dismay as he stared at the ugly apartments sprouting on the once-empty road from Marbella to Estepona, and with this question he put his finger on the worst feature of this desecration: the buildings which destroyed the landscape were being erected not for Spaniards but for Belgians and Germans and Swedes, who in their native cities built good-looking homes. When the concrete strip was completed, it would be populated not by Spaniards who sought the sea but by wealthy northerners who would use the area only as their playground. Few families would be raised in this ugliness and those that were would not speak Spanish.

'Looks to me like a sell-out,' Joe said, pushing the pop-top toward Gibraltar, and as he drove, his mind conjured up pieces of landscape he remembered from his trip across America, and he began to formulate an attitude toward the uses to which the earth should be put. As yet he had no substantial understanding of how things ought to be, but in the swirling snowstorm that had smothered him at the crossroads in Wyoming he had seen emergent patterns of land left open, structures that conformed to such land as was used, a fertile symbiosis between necessity and beauty, and above all, an obligation to help people move and concentrate intelligently.

He said to Gretchen, riding beside him, 'If a relatively few Europeans . . . wrecking this region, I mean . . . well, if they can ruin a whole area.' He paused, attended to his driving, then concluded, 'Imagine what we'll be able to ruin in America when we really put our mind to it.'

It was a gloomy thought and he found no solace in Gretchen's suggestion: 'Maybe by then the world will have more sense.' He shook his head and told her, 'Don't you believe it.'

He stayed depressed all the way to the approaches to Gibraltar. His passengers would have enjoyed visiting the Rock, but some nonsense between the Spanish and British governments prevented this, so they parked at the barrier which halted traffic and climbed out to view the impressive bastion, lying only a few hundred yards away.

'Why can't we see it?' Cato asked.

'Governments,' Monica said. 'Any time you meet something totally stupid, the answer has got to be "governments." '

'Whose?' Cato asked.

'Mine,' Monica snapped. 'One good thing you can say about the British. They're impartial. If they screw up Vwarda and Gibraltar, they also screw up Wales and Ireland.'

In some irritation they returned to the car and started the long drive up the coast to Cádiz. In some ways it was even more mournful, for this road left the areas occupied by the Germans and Swedes to traverse purely Spanish operations, and the difference was conspicuous, because in the stretch just completed, the northerners had created ugliness backed up by adequate funds, and there was in the tall buildings such as the ones the Greeks had built at Torremolinos a certain professionalism, but on the far side of Gibraltar, foreign money had not yet penetrated, and Spanish entrepreneurs were attempting garish projects without adequate resources.

'Instant slums,' Joe said bitterly as he inspected one collection of miserable buildings after another.

Yigal, remembering the good things in Grosse Pointe and Haifa, said, 'Looks as if every time a Spanish architect gets near the ocean he goes crazy.'

'Isn't this still the Mediterranean?' Cato asked.

'Atlantic,' Yigal said. He was always amazed that Americans, who presumed to rule the world, knew so little about it.

'You'd think,' Joe said despondently, 'that somebody would blow a whistle and shout, "If you have to do it, let's do it right." '

'Who'd listen?' Monica asked, and for the rest of that day's trip none of the passengers spoke of Spain's despoliation of her natural beauty.

But Joe, who had it constantly before him as he drove, became involved in trying to differentiate between the good and the bad, and the latter was so preponderant that when he did spot some construction that bespoke human beings solving human problems, he remembered it with affection.

That night, as they pulled up beside the great and muddy Guadalquivir to convert the pop-top into a dormitory, he said to

Yigal, 'Do they do things as badly as this in Israel?' and the Jew said, 'We have so little land, we have to respect it.'

For a long time—as insects buzzed about the screens, retreating when Monica sprayed them with a buzz-bomb, shouting, 'Back, you black little bastards!' at which Cato growled, 'Watch out what you sayin', girl!'—Joe reflected on what Yigal had said. When you have a little land, you have to treasure it. But the fact was, as Joe saw clearly for the first time, everyone has only a little land and no one is caring for it.

He could not sleep, so he left the pop-top to walk beside the river, and after a while Gretchen joined him and they talked of Spain and the desolation he had seen that day, and she said, 'In college we had several lectures on Spanish history, and the point was made that Spain had a tradition of ruining her land . . . something about sheep and contempt for agriculture. A heritage from the Moors, I seem to recall. Upland Spain was ruined four hundred years ago. Now the wreckers are moving to the seacoast.'

'Aren't we doing the same . . . in America, I mean?'

'As Monica says, "If a government can make mistakes, it will." '

'But we have an opposite tradition,' Joe said. He remembered how his hometown had agitated to get forest land put into the national reserve. The leaders of the community had flown to Washington. Then he said, wryly, 'While we were fighting on our side of the forest to save it, on the other side ranchers were fighting to destroy it.'

'In Spain the ranchers win,' she said.

Next morning they drove to Sevilla to see that stark cathedral. They camped that night in a vineyard, after which they drove slowly to La Rábida to see the beach from which Columbus had set forth to discover America. To the surprise of the others, it was Britta who seemed most deeply affected; she lingered on the beach, staring westward. At dawn next morning Joe drove the pop-top to the bank of the Río Guadiana, which separates Spain from Portugal, and the girls held their breath as he inched the car onto a ramshackle ferry that had seemed about to sink even when empty. 'Ave Maria, gratia plena,' Monica intoned as she boarded the frail thing.

'My God!' Cato shouted. 'Look!' And down the unpaved slope leading to the ferry came a huge truck loaded with pipe.

'You going to bring that on board?' Britta asked the ferryman in Spanish.

'Why not?' He signaled the driver to come forward cautiously, and when the front wheels reached the ferry, the boat sank about two feet and water sloshed aboard, but the truck kept coming until the rear wheels hit the ferry, at which point the gunwales were only a few inches above water.

'Just fine!' the ferryman called cheerily.

'What'd he say?' Yigal asked, and when Britta translated the optimistic news, Monica said, 'Wow,' and crossed herself.

It was an exciting introduction to Portugal, this perilous transit of a muddy river on a ramshackle ferryboat. On the Portuguese side there was amiable confusion, with all work stopping while the customs crew gathered to inspect the pop-top. The chief climbed in and asked Gretchen to show him where they all slept.

One of the young Portuguese pointed first at Joe and Gretchen, then at the bed, asking without words if they shared it, but before anyone could answer, the chief rebuked the young man. In Spanish, Britta started to converse with the chief, who looked at her sternly, answering in French: 'We never speak Spanish here. We can, but we don't.' He found a map, which he handed to Gretchen with peasant gallantry. His stubby forefinger traced the roads of Portugal for her, coming to stop at an inconspicuous village on a road well back from the ocean. 'Alte of the four mountains. Alte of the rushing river. You are fine young people and I hope you will do me a favor. Drive up to see Alte. Because I want you to know Portugal at its best.'

He shook hands with each of the six and wished them a pleasant sojourn in his country. An assistant handed Joe the car papers, properly stamped, and as the pop-top started to leave the customs shed the chief turned his attention to the Spanish driver of the truck, and Britta heard him growl in Spanish, 'And what the hell are you going to do with those pipes?'

The introduction to the new country was a revelation. Because Portugal stood so far behind Spain on any social or economic index—it was really an eighteenth-century land—the modern excesses that had ruined the coast of Spain had not yet penetrated here, and one saw how beautiful mountain land could be when it fell gently to meet clean, uncluttered beaches. The towns of Portugal were neat and ancient and feudalistic. Along the edges of the Atlantic there were no skyscrapers, and such foreign millionaires as had slipped into the area to build had been forced to do so unostentatiously, so that from the winding highway the traveler could not even see the new buildings.

But it was the land itself that captivated Joe. The hills were covered with low trees so beautiful in formation that he stopped the car and persuaded Britta to ask what they were. She tried Spanish, but the man she was speaking to refused to use that language, even though she suspected he understood. 'Almonds,' he said in French. 'You should have been here in January when they bloomed. You could smell them for miles.'

There were oranges, too, and old oaks and evergreens, but most of all there was a wealth of small farms, their fields marked off by walls of rock, their homes built low against the ground and looking as if they had grown from the soil and not been built upon it. 'This is pretty special,' Joe said, and the more he saw of the land, and its visible signs of having been tended and loved throughout the centuries, the more he enjoyed Portugal. 'I feel as if I'd been here before,' he said. 'It's like coming home.'

Slowly he drove through that magic area of forest and hill and ocean called Algarve. He suspected that this was one of the choice spots in the world, a locale fortunate of itself, but also fortunately ignored by history and development. Here there was no Málaga airport bringing thousands of money-spending tourists every day. If you wanted to visit Algarve, you had to spend time and ingenuity, not merely money.

'Let's have lunch at Albufeira,' he said, looking at the map. 'It's on the ocean. Afterward we can go back into the hills to see what Alte has to show.' The others agreed with this, so they proceeded— with many stops to view the long, empty beaches—to that curious town on the waterfront where the streets wind in and out of tunnels which carry them through low hills. At one minute they were on a crest . . . two turns to the left and they were directly under where they had been a moment before. Monica was delighted with the fairy-tale quality of the town and cried, 'It's so marvelously different from Torremolinos.' But Joe noticed, as he told me later, that when the time came to eat, she intuitively smelled out the one bar grubby enough to have fitted into the Torremolinos scene.

Inside, an angular, pasty-faced English expatriate known as Churchill lounged in a corner, and with a telepathy that was uncanny, he and Monica recognized each other, not by name but by condition.

'Hullo,' he mumbled as if not fully awake. 'You're English, I see.'

'Name's Monica. How's the food here?'

'Bloody dreadful.'

'And the beer?'

'Acceptable, if you're buying.'

'I am, if you tell us something about the place.' She directed Cato to move some tables together, and said to Churchill, 'Join us.'

He said he wasn't hungry, but he sat with them as he nursed a beer and gave them his evaluation of Algarve: 'Consider it a British colony. We're smart. We know where the bargains are.' With a bony finger he pointed at tourists crossing the square. 'Those two are English. So are the other three. Hell, they're all English. It's bloody dreadful.'

When the waiter brought two greasy menus, Churchill pitched them onto the floor and told the man, in lively Portuguese, 'Go across the street and fetch us six portions of *caldeirada de peixe*.'

'What did you order?' Britta asked.

'You get it, you eat it,' he said rudely. He was about forty, extremely thin, un-barbered, aquiline-faced, sloppily dressed, with dirty tennis shoes, and seemed too bored with his exile to be either witty or truly sardonic. But he was informed, and when Joe said, 'We thought we'd take a look at Alte,' he clasped his hairy hands about his stubbled chin and said, 'God must have lent you His compass. I congratulate you on choosing the best spot in Algarve.'

While he was expatiating on the region, and sipping the dark beer of Portugal, the waiter returned with a tray containing three huge tureens, placing one before each of the girls. 'What is it?' Britta asked. Taking her spoon, Churchill dredged the bottom of the tureen and brought up some shellfish and a baby octopus. Lifting them high in the air, he splashed them back into the tureen. 'Seafood,' he growled, 'of majestic quality.'

Britta, unruffled by his behavior, smiled gently and asked, 'Aren't you having any?' and he replied, 'A bite or two from yours,' whereupon he dipped in, catching a small octopus, which he lifted into the air, allowing it to dribble into his mouth, one tentacle sliding down over his chin. With a loud sucking noise he drew the errant tentacle into his mouth, chewed it sloppily, swallowed it, and said, 'Best dish in Portugal.' He thrust his spoon into Monica's tureen, then Gretchen's, stealing an octopus from each.

The meal was a good introduction to Portugal: hot garlic bread, green wine, and an abundance of potatoes and onions in the *caldeirada*. Britta kept score on the kinds of fish in her helping: eel, shellfish, perch, sardines, squid, and best of all, the baby octopus, sweet and chewy and very marine-like in taste. 'This is good,' she told Churchill, and again he growled, 'Majestic quality. I told you it would be.'

It was late afternoon before they left Albufeira. They drove some distance into the hills before finding a road which led to Alte. After several miles of moderately steep climbing, they reached a turn from which they could look down upon a village so compact that it could be encompassed in a single glance. Perched on the side of a cascade which tumbled down a narrow canyon, Alte was surrounded by four hills; it was a doll's village, and as attractive as any they had ever seen.

It was dusk and drovers were returning from the hills, leading their horses. 'I'm going to like this place,' Joe said.

The second person whose life was affected by the trip to Portugal was Britta, for when the time came on that first night out of Torremolinos to arrange the pop-top for sleeping, she faced up to something that had been troubling her for the past few weeks. The pop-top, as modified, offered six sleeping spaces, and how they were distributed became important. The factory had built in four sleeping spaces: a double bed along the length of the car, spacious and comfortable; one jammed in along the front seats, soft but small; and a hammock suspended from the roof, neither comfortable nor large. The additional pair that Yigal and Cato had contrived were separate bunks cantilevered from the sides; they were large but not very soft.

Going to bed thus became a tactical problem similar to the one faced by the man who first canned herring: who would lie next to whom? Arrangements had to begin with the double bed, for what happened there would determine the rest, and Gretchen, as owner of the car, solved this firmly and in a manner which invited no discussion.

'Joe has to drive and he needs a good night's rest. He gets the big bed. Cato is tall, so he sleeps with Joe. Monica is the shortest, so she takes the catty-corner bed up front, and Yigal is short enough to use the hammock. That leaves the new beds for Britt and me.' Monica started to speak, but Gretchen cut her short: 'And if anyone just has to have sex, you can borrow the big bed during the afternoon.' She nodded slightly toward Monica and Britta.

It was this that forced Britta to make a decision. She had now been away from home four months, and as she climbed awkwardly into the bed assigned her, stepping over Joe as she did, it occurred to her that the restrictions of the pop-top were providential. She had known for some time that her affair with Joe had about run its course.

What is there in it for either of us? she thought as she lay in the unfamiliar bed. He's a good guy . . . but where will it lead?

She was not thinking of the fact that Joe had no money to support her, nor any immediate likelihood of earning any. Nor was she worried about the improbability of his ever marrying her; she enjoyed sex on her own terms and liked men enough to live with them on her own responsibility. She intended one day to marry, if, in the term used so often by girls her age, 'things worked out.' By this she meant that she would have to meet the right man, under the right circumstances and with the right promise for a productive future. If, as the young people also said, 'things didn't work out,' she would not be averse to living according to the pattern of the past four months.

She had found Joe to be the considerate, just man she expected when she first climbed into his bed. They had had a good time together, and if her future affairs proved half as rewarding, she would have no complaints. 'In strict honesty,' she whispered to herself as she lay, sleepless, directly above the man she was preparing to read out of her life, 'I suppose there won't be marriage. Just a succession of Joes. I'm lucky in small things but not big ones. Well, it won't be unbearable.'

Why had she reached these gloomy conclusions? I am able to summarize her reasoning that night because when we next met she reviewed her situation with me and said, 'I decided then that no substantial good would ever develop for Joe and me. It was fun in bed, but what concern did we really have for each other? We weren't going to make a home, or have children, or work for the same goals—so what was the purpose?'

'Are home and children your goals?' I asked in some surprise.

'Not necessarily. But meaning is. I want my life . . .' She hesitated, then started laughing at her pomposity. 'The real reason, Mr. Fairbanks, is that with Joe, there would be no possibility of our going to Ceylon. Joe is not a man of the sun. He's like my father. He'll find a dark corner somewhere and fight his battles with a kind of dull stubbornness.'

She told me much more, of course, and from it I derived the portrait of a self-directed young woman, an Ibsen heroine from the north country, sure of herself inwardly but confused in her outward relationships. Had a young man of even minimum accomplishment come on the scene at that time, inviting her to Ceylon or Hong Kong, she would have left us in six minutes, the time it would take to pack her bag. Sex and emotional involvement played no profound role in her life, but she did insist that both be meaningful over the long haul, and if, when the man got her to Ceylon, she found either it or him to be of little value, she would drop him in the instant and be off for Lima or Wellington, if either city promised a more fulfilling life.

I never ascertained what, in her mind, comprised the fulfilling life. It wasn't sex, or marriage, or an established home, or an assured income, or any of the things girls were perturbed about when I was a young man. When I asked her for definitions one afternoon, she said simply, 'The word is *decency*. I want all parts of my life to add up to something decent.'

So in her hammock that first night, in an olive field beside the Guadalquivir, she decided that the sleeping arrangement which Gretchen had laid out would be permanent. The affair with Joe was ended.

After their visit to Sevilla, when they were preparing the pop-top for the ferry that would carry them into Portugal next morning, Britta said, as they sat about the campfire, 'I liked La Rábida. I think it means more for a Norwegian to stand at the spot where Columbus started than it does for you others.'

'Why?' Gretchen asked.

'It proves so much about Viking history. We discovered America hundreds of years before Columbus, everybody knows that. But we did nothing with it. We were brave but we lacked ideas. I often wonder what the Vikings told their people when they returned home. I suppose they said, "There's land out there," and the kings said, "So what?" and that was that. We even forgot we'd been to America. But Columbus came home filled with ideas . . . his journey amounted to something . . . not because of his bravery, because of his ideas.'

When no one reacted to her theory, she lay back, looking at the heavens. 'It'll probably be the same with America. I think your men will get to the moon next month. But it won't mean very much, because Americans are the Vikings of this age. Brave but stupid. You lack ideas . . . and there goes the moon. A hundred years from now somebody like the Japanese will follow you and take with them a tremendous vision, and they'll be the ones who really discover the moon.'

Again no one spoke, but Britta surprised them by taking the hands of Gretchen and Cato and kissing them. 'It's quite honorable to be Vikings. Stupid, self-centered, without philosophy . . . but very brave. In the end it's the brave who show the way.'

Without knowing it, she had touched a nerve so raw, so harshly painful that Cato leaped to his feet and threw his picnic plate into the fire, his knife and fork ricocheting through the embers. 'That goddamned moon!' he exploded. 'I try to tell you cats and you won't listen. You, goddammit, you!' And he pointed his finger at Gretchen. 'Today you had the nerve to ask me if I wasn't oversensitive? Who the hell do you think you are, some grand lady from Boston who says like a judge, "Too much emotion"?'

'What are you talking about?' Gretchen asked.

'That fucking moon! That's what I'm talking about. And the brothers.'

'Cato,' Gretchen said, 'you're making no sense.'

'You're not listening. In a decade when America watches her cities go to hell—her blacks deteriorate, her schools fall apart—the only thing we do well is build highways. And what do we do then? We say to the cities and railroads and the blacks, "Not a nickel for you," but we go on spending—like a hophead on Friday night—twenty-six billion dollars to put a man on the moon.'

'Priorities are always difficult,' Gretchen said defensively.

'I'm not speaking of priorities,' Cato snapped. 'Haven't you ever seen one of those television shots of the space center? Or the aircraft company that builds the gismos? Or any goddamned thing connected with the space program? The President comes in smiling. He's met by a committee of sixteen, also smiling. And they go through the installation . . . thousands of desks . . . each one with a man smiling . . . and . . .'

He stopped, and in the flickering shadows of the fire, stared at each of us and concluded, 'Not a lousy one of you knows what I'm talking about, do you?'

'What's your point?' Joe asked.

'In all those faces you don't see one black. This whole program . . . billions of dollars . . . spent on something from which the blacks are excluded. The people who need help most right now . . .' His voice had risen to a shout and seemed quite out of place in the quietness of southern Spain. Kicking at the fire, he said, 'It's not ridiculous to think that the United States decided to apply all of its riches to the space program because that was the one thing they could isolate—out of the thousand things they could have spent their money on—in which the blacks could not participate. It wasn't easy to dream up the moon shot, but President Kennedy did it. Just like he did everything else to downgrade the blacks. Worst friend we ever had. Nixon's twice as good, because you know where he stands.'

It was Britta who broke the spell of bitterness. She said, 'We Vikings made one wrong choice after another and we vanished from history, leaving nothing behind us. If white America does the same, she'll vanish too.'

She spoke with such tenseness that when it came time for bed, Gretchen took her aside and whispered, 'Britt, if you want to sleep with Joe we'll arrange it somehow,' and Britta said, 'Oh, no! I've decided not to use his bed any longer.'

'Does he know?'

'How could he? I just found out myself.'

But as Gretchen was preparing to climb into her bunk, Joe grabbed her wrist and pulled her down beside him on the formal bed. In a low whisper he said, 'I think you ought to let Cato and Monica have the bed. They're miserable the way they are,' and Gretchen asked, 'What about you and Britt?' and Joe said very softly, 'We've pretty well had it. I mean, you were a smart gal to arrange the beds this way. I don't think Britta and I . . .' His voice trailed off, and Gretchen whispered, 'We'll keep things the way they are.' And in the morning they passed over into Portugal.

———————

Not far from the center of Alte was a wooded plaza bounded on the east by the tumbling cascade. It was a place of extraordinary beauty, for its rude simplicity, its tiny bandstand and brick-lined footpaths made it more like a large outdoor room than a public place, while the noisy water, rushing over boulders, provided a constant music, whether the band was in attendance or not.

The plaza was presided over by a rude statue of the town's only native son to have achieved importance. In classical stone features marked by a long beard, Candido Guerreiro looked down upon the plaza he had loved; in his day it had had no paving. On a plaque below the tip of his beard was engraved:

> A MEMORIA DO GRANDE POETA ALTENSE
> 'Because I was born at the foot of the four mountains
> Where the waters go singing by . . . '

One judged these to be the opening lines of his apostrophe to Alte; I heard them sung once to a tune more pitiful than a dirge, and concluded that if the old poet had lived a joyous life near this plaza, he had failed to catch that fact in his words.

It was not permitted to park the pop-top in the plaza. A pipe dropping down from one of the four mountains had been led underground to the mouth of a stone fountain set into the same wall which held the poet, and to this fountain came all the women of Alte, lugging great clay pots which they filled with water. Thus the plaza was not only a place of recreation; it was also the essential center of the town, for this was the only water supply.

Gretchen asked a policeman where they might park, and he found them a wooded spot almost on the edge of the cascade, so that they lived within the sound of its music. Later, each of the six would tell me, at different times, 'No matter where we go . . . I'll remember Alte as the best part of the trip.'

One reason they would remember it with such affection was the band. On Friday, Saturday and Sunday nights musicians with time-battered instruments collected at the bandstand to give concerts. Since there was no television in the town, no cinema and only a few radios, this constituted the only source of entertainment, and at such times the plaza was jammed with people.

'Where do they all come from?' Gretchen asked, and she began making inquiries, and found that at least half the listeners had come from the surrounding countryside. 'I don't know whether I understood or not,' she told the group one night as they were cooking their supper beside the waterfall, 'but I'm sure they said that some of the women walk fourteen or fifteen miles.'

'One way?' Britta asked.

'Fourteen here, fourteen back.'

Yigal whistled. Then, on Saturday night, they understood. When they reached the plaza for the band concert they found that the chairs which the townsmen brought with them were kept clear of a central paved area. When the band struck up a noisy number, the young country folk began dancing, and before long the plaza was a beautiful display of motion, swaying peasant dresses and the nodding of weathered faces as the old watched approvingly.

The steps were complicated but not difficult, and after the group had watched for some minutes, Yigal caught Gretchen's hands and pulled her into the dancing area. He had learned folk dancing in Israel, and his performance drew applause from the Portuguese, while Gretchen, through her love for music, had a good sense of rhythm and made a fair stab at following the steps. When the next number began, Cato asked Britta to dance, and they made a striking pair, for she knew the old Norwegian dances and easily adapted them to Alte, and Cato jitterbugged—and the Portuguese loudly showed their approval.

At the third dance the alcalde of the town asked Gretchen to accompany him, and in this way the solid introduction of the six young people into local life began. They were so young, so appealing in their directness that the working people of the town adopted them. They were invited to meals of brutal simplicity and overflowing generosity. They went to church with the townspeople, made tours with the local doctor, gave picnics in the hills, and each day climbed to the spot from which they could look down and see the whole town like a microcosm of an age long vanished. They lived, during those weeks, as people had lived in Europe five hundred years ago, and in return for the hospitality extended them, gave their own concerts on the nights when the band didn't play.

Gretchen would bring her guitar, and sitting on a bench between the fountain and the poet, would play old ballads, which could have come, every one of them, from the daily life of these people. This fact was brought home to her on the first Thursday night as she was singing, for she saw along the edge of the crowd a very thin, gaunt-faced peasant woman who could have been in her seventies, except that she was accompanied by a most beautiful daughter of about sixteen or seventeen. They were barefooted and stood apart, listening to the music with obvious delight. The old woman kept time with her hands and seemed always about to burst into song.

As Gretchen wondered who the newcomers might be, a woman from the neighborhood moved close and said, 'There's one I told you about. She walked fourteen miles.' So between songs Gretchen went to the woman and shook her hand, seeing to her astonishment that she was only in her forties. Gretchen spoke to the daughter also—in French, which the girl could not understand—and they stood thus for a while until someone came who could interpret.

'Yes, my daughter and I live in the mountains . . .

'Yes, we have walked fourteen miles . . .

'Yes, we have shoes but we save them for the dancing . . .

'Yes, I have a husband, but he works too hard to bother with music . . .

'Yes, in the mountains it's known that you are here.'

They were in the audience for the Friday concert, and on Saturday night the girl appeared in a lovely peasant costume, with ribbed stockings and high-heeled shoes. She was obviously the most beautiful girl among the peasants, a fact in which her mother took unashamed pride. Several Portuguese men asked her to dance, and toward the middle of the evening Yigal went to her, bowed and extended his hands. She looked at her mother, who frowned, but Yigal was already leading her to the dance.

They made a good pair, even though she was slightly taller than he, and now Joe asked to dance with her, then Cato. She told them her name was Maria Concepciāo, and Gretchen later found that she could neither read nor write.

On Sunday night, after the last band concert, Maria and her mother carefully wrapped up their shoes and her good dress and started barefoot back to their mountain, but Gretchen interposed and said she would drive them home. The idea was so startling that

Maria and her mother could not fully comprehend it until Joe appeared with the pop-top. Cato and Monica stayed behind, to make love in the woods, but the other four piled in with the two Portuguese and they set off for the twisting mountain roads.

It was late when they reached Maria Concepção's home, and the shock her father experienced at seeing his women coming home in a private car was only surpassed by the astonishment of the young people when they saw how these Portuguese lived. They had a one-room hut built of rocks, with an earthern floor, one window and an open fireplace that threw smoke into the room. Their bed was a paillasse resting upon boards a few inches from the floor; it seemed to Gretchen and Britta that the girl must sleep there with her parents.

The room was bare except for a rickety table and one small cupboard, obviously the place in which the three inhabitants kept their clothes, their eating utensils and whatever few possessions they had. It was remarkable that from such mean, almost nonexistent accommodations, Maria Concepção could have appeared so beautifully dressed at the dance. Gretchen watched as the girl carefully placed her precious clothes in the cupboard, but Britta, who knew something of poverty, looked away, for in her eyes there were tears.

Maria and her parents extended the full hospitality of their home. Having no chairs, they gestured to the low bed as a seating place for their guests. Having no tea, they poured out small portions of the world's rawest red wine. Having no cakes, they passed small pieces of bread and hard cheese. Having no common language, they talked as one does in such circumstances, with gestures and smiles and shakes of the head, but Gretchen did get through to the two women the fact that next Thursday she and Joe would drive up to bring them into town. The three Portuguese nodded passively, as if this were something beyond their comprehension or control.

On Thursday Gretchen drove into the mountains to fetch Maria Concepção, and of course Yigal went along. At the informal concerts, when Gretchen played, Yigal and Maria sat together. They did so at the Friday band concert too, and at the Saturday dance they appeared first in the middle of the floor. On the long ride home Yigal sat with Maria, and although they could not speak a word to each other, they held hands and communicated a universe of thoughts. When they reached the hut, Gretchen and Britta produced bottles of wine and little baskets of refreshment, which the father and mother accepted with humility and gratitude.

'Some of the best meals I've had,' Gretchen told me later, 'were in that hut. For the rest of my life I'll like wine and cheese.' On what would prove to be the last visit to the hut, Gretchen happened to see the father scowl, and thought: He isn't angry. He's unhappy. But as she looked back over her shoulder she saw that Yigal was kissing Maria.

Two days later the village priest stopped by the pop-top as the group was at lunch. Obviously he wanted to tell them something, but first he joined them in some rough food. Later he said in French, 'Maria Concepciáo and her parents have asked that you not drive into the mountains any more.'

'Why not?' Gretchen asked. 'Aren't they coming to the dance?'

'They're coming,' the priest said haltingly. 'Yes, they're coming.' He chewed on an end of salted beef, then said, 'But they want to come on foot.' He hesitated again, then added, 'And go back the same way.'

'Is it something I did?' Yigal asked bluntly.

'Are you the young man who kissed her? No, it wasn't anything you did . . . although I suppose it was you, really.'

This made no sense to any of them, and Britta said in her good Spanish, 'Father, you're not helping us to understand.'

'I don't understand myself,' he apologized. 'I went to the university.'

This was even more incomprehensible, so Gretchen suggested, 'Father, tell us in your own way. Maria Concepciáo's family doesn't want to ride with us any longer. Why?'

'That's the nub of the matter.' He took Yigal's hands and said, 'Obviously they love you. You've been so helpful . . . so generous. Obviously Maria Concepciáo is fond of you, young fellow. She likes to be kissed, and so she should. But in the hills of Portugal a family and a girl have only one chance at life. If they make even the slightest mistake, like riding to the dance in an expensive automobile . . .' He inspected the pop-top and said to Gretchen, 'The townspeople tell me you all sleep in this little car.' When Gretchen nodded, he looked at her left hand, then at Britta's. 'And you're not even married. Well, I'm sure it's no harm, but you're allowed to do these things. A girl from the mountains isn't.'

'She's done nothing wrong, never . . .' Yigal protested.

'But she has ridden back and forth instead of walking. She's at the age when she must find a husband, or remain barren the rest of her life. One little thing . . . anything like appearing too haughty . . .' He looked at each of the six separately and nodded his tired head. 'That's the word I've been seeking . . . haughty. If it is said of her, "She's the kind who has to have an automobile . . ." Well, it could kill her chances of catching a husband. It could be terrible and cruel . . . the effect on her.'

He looked at Britta, who had made a favorable impression, and said, 'You're Swedish. You'll understand what I'm saying.'

Gretchen asked in French, 'So it's not Yigal? It's me?'

'It's you.' The priest nodded. 'You represent a flashy way of life. You scare the people, and if the young men of the region ever get the idea fixed in their minds that Maria Concepciāo is going to grow up like you . . . well, to put it simply, she'd not catch a husband.' He stopped, wiped his forehead, and said with some anxiety, 'You don't understand. But with us a girl has only one chance.'

Gretchen grew angry. 'Chance?' she echoed. 'You mean that if she's a good girl and walks barefooted fourteen miles and has one dress . . . you mean that maybe she'll earn the right to live like a pig in a room with no furniture . . . for the rest of her life?'

'I mean just that,' the priest said.

'It would be better if she rode with us, and went with us to Lisboa, and let happen what will.'

'For you, and for this one'—and here he placed his hand on Britta's arm—'but not for Maria Concepciāo. Her ordained life is here.'

No one spoke, and after a while the priest rose and shook hands all around. He told Gretchen that one night he had heard her playing the guitar and she was good; then he added, 'But when Maria Concepciāo and her mother come this week, allow them to stay in the shadows. At the dancing, young man, you must not dance with her ever again, for if you do, you will be altering her life in a manner that cannot be corrected.' He bowed and left.

Then an unpredictable thing happened. Yigal grabbed Joe by the throat and said bitterly, 'You big loudmouth.' Now if there was one thing Joe wasn't, it was a loudmouth, and no one could understand Yigal's point, but he continued: 'You keep telling us how much more beautiful Portugal is than Spain, how much better they run things over here. Well, there's a hell of a lot more to running a nation than saving the shoreline. There's also people. And in Spain I saw people who were living . . . who were getting out of their mountain hovels.'

'In Torremolinos you never saw a Spaniard,' Joe said defensively.

'You're right. Why do you suppose I went up in the mountains. To see for myself. In back of Ronda, in back of Granada. I can tell you how the Spaniards live, because I was there . . . in the houses with them. And they live damned poorly, some of them, but they live, and if some priest tried to tell a family that their girl shouldn't dance, they'd kick him in the balls.'

'So you like the girl,' Joe said.

As abruptly as he had started, Yigal stopped. 'I'm sorry,' he said, shaking Joe's hand. 'But there's a hell of a lot about landscape you don't understand. There really is.'

Maria Concepção and her mother were not mentioned again. That Thursday night they appeared, barefooted, to hear the music, but spoke to none of the foreigners. On Saturday night Maria appeared in her shoes and dress, looking radiant as a young aspen tree in the hills, but none of the strangers spoke to her, so after a while the local men started asking her to dance.

———•••———

While music filled the plaza at Alte, I was cooped up in Geneva. Negotiations with the Greek shipowners had ended in a surprise: by some miracle they were able to collect almost enough money to save their Torremolinos property. All they needed from us was a loan of three million dollars, and this our board decided to grant, assured that by the end of 1970 the Greeks would have to go broke, whereupon we could pick up the apartments for even less money than we had been prepared to offer this year. Pinpoint negotiations—what our New York lawyers called the nitty-gritty—took longer than expected, but the day came when the work was done and I found myself with a couple of empty weeks prior to my July vacation.

On my desk lay two postcards from Algarve. One showed a hillside near Albufeira covered with almond blossoms. The message, written neatly on the back, read: 'This is the kind of snow I like,' and it was signed 'Britta.' The other showed one of the typical colored chimneys of Algarve, with its customary stork. Its message read: 'This son-of-a-bitch better stay away from us,' and it was sighed 'Monica and Cato.'

The cards made me homesick, for I had been going to Algarve since 1954 and I liked the area. I liked its cleanliness, its antique quality, its unparalleled beaches and its good peasant food.

How had I become involved in Algarve? Through the idiosyncrasy of a man called Martin Rorimer. It's not necessary to remember his name because I won't be mentioning him again, but toward the end of World War II he was on army duty at the edge of a glacier in Alaska, and one wintry afternoon as he watched the sun disappear he had what he called 'my big idea.'

It was simple. He visualized a future when hundreds of thousands of people like himself would be wanting a quiet sunny place near the sea. 'Land along the sea,' he said to himself. 'That's the secret.'

Many people, maybe once or twice in their lives, entertain big ideas, but few act upon them. He did. As soon as he was demobilized he converted all his savings into cash, borrowed what he could from friends, and convinced his mother to let him have his inheritance ahead of time. What did he do with it? He went back to all the places he had visited over the past fifteen years and bought whatever ends and scraps of land he could find along any seashore. When the great hunger that he had foreseen materialized, he had oceanfront land to sell.

He made his most conspicuous success in Hawaii (bought at $4,000 an acre, sold at $167,000) and in St. Thomas in the Virgin Islands (bought at $3,000, sold at $139,000). He also bought along the Mediterranean, in southern France, at Acapulco, in the wooded country north of Seattle, and on the Costa Brava in Spain. His most daring venture was the purchase of six hundred choice acres along the southern coast of Turkey; he was convinced that by 1975 it would be worth a fortune.

When his purchases were completed, Rorimer flew to Geneva with a proposition that World Mutual take over the management of all his holdings. We agreed, because he controlled half a dozen sites we wanted to build on, and I had the pleasure of flying about the world with him to see what he had picked up, for in the early days whenever he sold a parcel in Hawaii for a profit he reinvested most of it in oceanfronts in places like Australia or Japan.

But the land he preferred lay in that unknown part of Portugal called Algarve. When he first mentioned it, one day in Barcelona, I had not even heard of it, but when I flew with him to Faro, I understood the sleeping grandeur of this area and its potential in a world becoming each day more crowded.

Sitting in Geneva now, I began to think about going to Algarve, but whether to see its white beaches and chimney pots or the young people I knew were there, I could not say. I contemplated flying down to check on a hotel we were building. In an abrupt aside, I thought: But I wouldn't know where they were camping. I then rationalized that since Algarve was not large, residents would surely know the whereabouts of anything as conspicuous as a yellow pop-top.

In the end it was a small thing that decided me. As I sat there idly, I picked up Britta's postcard, and I visualized her expressive, lovely face and its abundant vitality. Suddenly it was important that I know what she and the others were up to, so I grabbed a shaving kit, jammed it into the briefcase containing records on our Algarve holdings, and was on my way to the airport.

Clothes? I got into quite an argument over this some years ago. An American couple heard me explaining that I traveled light because I kept six or seven caches of wardrobe in various crossroad cities throughout the world—Tokyo and Rome, to name two—and I flew into these cities as I might move from a townhouse to a farm in the suburbs. The husband snorted, 'Preposterous,' and when I assured him that quite a few men did this, his wife said, 'You must be joking.' We were in Bombay at the time and I asked where they were headed, and he said, 'Bangkok.'

'What hotel?'

'Erawan.'

'Good. When you check in, ask the bell captain to show you the room where they keep such luggage. Mine will be there.' I hope they checked.

It was my habit, acquired when I first traveled the Orient, to fly empty-handed into Hong Kong and then hurry to Jimmy Yen's, where I would order seven or eight suits and a dozen hand-made shirts for less than two hundred dollars. Jimmy supplied his customers with cardboard suitcases, and off we would go with lettering on our cases proclaiming: *I am well dressed. I buy my clothes from Jimmy Yen, Kowloon, Hong Kong.* Because I had to visit Algarve so frequently on land problems, I kept a Jimmy Yen suitcase packed with suits and shirts in Faro.

Where were the young people? I asked at various spots, but no one had seen them, and it looked as if my flight might have been useless. However, in the course of my inquiry two different men said, 'There's an Englishman named Churchill of all things. Hangs out at a bar in Albufeira. He'd know.' On this chance I borrowed the company car and drove to Albufeira, rummaging through the bars until I came to one on the square. In the corner sat a tall, unkempt, tennis-shoed man, with his elbows on the table, his unshaven chin propped on bony knuckles. He was extremely gray in the face, like a lizard, and his manner was listless.

'You Churchill?' I asked. He nodded his head about a quarter of an inch, staring at me from his basilisk eyes. 'Could you tell me if a group of six young people . . . one of them's a young Negro . . .' Again he nodded his head almost imperceptibly. 'Are they in Albufeira?' I asked. He shook his head slightly. 'Alte,' he said, as if the very name of the town were repugnant.

I found him quite objectionable and was about to leave when he whined, 'Aren't you having a beer? It's very good, you know.' I ordered two, and as he sipped his he described the six drifters I was seeking.

'The Norwegian girl . . . steady as an ox . . . real Viking princess. Your black boy is quite jittery. Never at ease in his relationship with Monica. Did you know she was the daughter of Sir Charles Braham? Quite an English lady, but I'll bet she's the gutter type at heart. As for the Jew? I don't much care for Jews. Too bright. Yours is like all the rest. The Boston girl? There's a deep one. She's wasting her time with that crowd.' He studied me carefully, and I felt that if anyone happened to ask about me, he would be able to provide a comparable thumbnail sketch. 'Oh, yes. I didn't mention Joe. He keeps to himself. He's a lot like me.'

I stared at him, aghast at the comparison. 'How do I reach Alte?' I asked. 'Up to the Silves road and turn right.' He did not bother to rise when I left.

When I reached the lower level of the town I stopped at a bar to ask if anyone knew where the Americans were staying, and at my first words the men lounging there understood what I wanted. 'Up there!' they cried with visible delight, and three of them climbed into my car with me, for they had learned that if they did odd jobs to help the Americans, there would be wine and perhaps guitar-playing.

They led me up a cobbled street to a plaza where women were lugging jugs of water. In the trees beyond, they showed me the pop-top. Britta, lounging in a chair outside the Volkswagen, saw me first. 'It's Uncle George!' she shouted, and in a moment bodies were tumbling out of the car and Cato was pumping my hand and yelling, 'You old fart! You couldn't stay away!'

I pointed to my three guides, and Cato growled, 'The three hungriest men in Portugal,' but he did produce wine and cheese— and we held a reunion beside the tumbling water.

———•◆•———

It was not surprising that Churchill should have been able to judge Monica so accurately, because on the days when Gretchen drove the pop-top into Albufeira for marketing or the pleasure of seeing the ocean, the English girl, with her uncanny skill in seeking out the lowest common denominator, had struck up an acquaintance with Churchill and had begun to buy 'spots' for him, eating them under his tutelage.

A spot was a small square of rice paper, about an inch and a half on the side. In the middle it contained a gray-looking discoloration. Churchill stored his spots in his wallet, so the corners were dogeared, and if you were a beginner you tore the paper in half and chewed only half a spot, swallowing it slowly, before progressing to a full spot, which was a more serious affair. As one chewed, there was no discernible taste.

On her first try Monica, as might be expected, swallowed a whole spot, and one with a larger discolored area than usual, but Churchill was experienced in handling such people, so Monica enjoyed an exhilarating experience on this her second adventure with lysergic acid diethylamide tartrate 25, known to her peers as LSD-25.

To take her trip required about seven hours, and during the latter half of that time the other five young people searched for her, and grew increasingly apprehensive when they could not find her. It was Cato who first thought of the English fellow at the bar, and sure enough, when he and Britta went there to make inquiries, the waiter said in broken English, 'She come here. Now his room I think.' When Cato flashed a jealous anger, the waiter laughed. 'Not pom-pom. Sssttt!' he said, and he shot an imaginary hypodermic into his arm.

For five escudos the waiter showed them where Churchill lived; it was on the third floor of a very old house overlooking the ocean, and as they reached the door to his room they could hear Monica moaning and laughing inside, with Churchill's whining voice assuring her, 'It's going splendidly. Everything is all right.' When Cato pushed the door open, Britta entered first, and saw Monica lying mostly undressed on an unmade bed, her head rolling backward off a pomade-stained pillow, her eyes much dilated and apparently crowded with abnormal visions.

'What the hell are you doing?' Cato shouted, to which Churchill merely said, 'Sssssssh. Mustn't waken her abruptly, must we?'

'You son-of-a-bitch!' Cato shouted, lunging at the reedy Englishman, who quietly stepped aside. 'Don't be an utter ass,' he said. 'She's coming out of her trip and needs quiet.'

So Cato and Britta sat on the floor and watched as Monica slowly returned to near-normal reactions. 'It was so spacious,' she moaned repeatedly. She offered no other description of her trip; it was merely spacious in a majestic sort of way.

'You'd better tell the others we've found her,' Cato suggested to Britta. After she left, he started dressing Monica, who oscillated between a normal control of her senses and a reversion to her trip. When she finally realized where she was and with whom, she gave Churchill a kiss, crying, 'You dear, dear boy! Ten times better than you said.' And her first words to Cato set the pattern to which she would stubbornly return during the rest of her stay in Portugal: 'Cato, you've got to try it! The colors . . . the sensations . . . God, to have sex at the height of a trip . . . Cato, we must!'

When they got her into the pop-top and back in Alte, where the air was fresher, her head cleared and she said rationally, 'It isolates and expands the senses. Of course, you still have only five, but each one seems twice as important as the others. I remember looking at the uneven plaster on the wall. Slight bumps became mountains. One broken area became the Alps, each speck of plaster a peak by itself. I heard Churchill saying, "It's going beautifully." I heard the words. I understood them. And I was aware that I understood them. You know, you're aware the whole time. You're aware of everything.' She paused, remembering the effect of Churchill's words, then said, 'Only three words! But they formed the noblest oration I ever heard. It was as if he were the real Churchill, with Hitler and Mussolini thrown in . . . a fantastic orator. It took him about fifteen minutes to say "It's going beautifully," but all the time the multitudes were cheering. God, how they cheered.'

She returned to her intense proselytizing. 'Kids, you've just got to try it. Really, that first time in Torremolinos with the dike . . . that was nothing. But to take it seriously . . . with Churchill there to steer you . . . a real spot with a place to lie down sensibly. It was the greatest experience I've ever had. I'll tell you, it was twenty times better than good sex.'

She insisted that Britta and Gretchen accompany her on her next trip, but they begged off. Yigal also declined, and Joe said, 'You must be nuts.' She did, however, persuade Cato to join her, so three days later they walked and hitchhiked into town, with the understanding that we'd pick them up about ten hours later.

When Britta took us to Churchill's grimy room, we found Monica and Cato naked in bed, with Churchill leering over them. 'This is one trip they'll never forget,' he assured us, and when they returned to Alte their report substantiated his prediction: 'Have you ever wondered what sex would be like, strung out for twenty-four hours at peak perfection?' Monica asked, and Cato replied, 'It ain't bad.'

So the pressure of the proselytizing continued, with Britta under fire one day, Yigal the next. When Monica insisted one morning that Britta try LSD, because it would expand her mind, the Norwegian girl replied, 'My mind expands every morning when I get up and see that sun. You wouldn't understand. You've never been in Tromsø through the winter.'

Yigal was more harsh. 'I'm having trouble with calculus. I sure as hell don't want to muddle up what little brains I've got,' and Monica cried, 'You're just being chicken, chicken, chicken,' and Yigal stared at her, but Joe said, 'I don't think you have the right word, Monica. Not for this little bantam rooster.'

In irritation Monica turned to me and asked, 'You worked in Asia, Uncle George, where they know about expanding the mind. What do you think?'

'I can't understand why anyone would take such risks with an unproved drug,' I said, but again Joe cut in: 'Because she's a damned fool.' This occasioned much discussion, with Monica claiming, 'It's a new development of the human race. Hell, Uncle George, you couldn't be expected to understand. It wasn't even discovered till 1938. Nobody tried it till 1943.'

'How do you know?' Joe asked.

'Churchill told me. He makes it for the whole Algarve. Gets his chemicals from Switzerland. But the point is, it's a new experience and you can't dismiss it until you've tried it.'

To my surprise, this reasoning took root in the one mind that I would have judged least likely to be receptive. One morning Gretchen came to me as I was talking with Joe near the stone poet, and said, 'Uncle George, I seek a favor. You're to watch over me while I try LSD.'

'Are you out of your mind?' Joe asked.

'No, but I want to be. I suspect Monica's right. This is a vision of the future. It could be a whole new pattern of life.' She looked down at her hands and said, 'God knows I don't approve of the pattern I have.'

'You think LSD offers a solution?' I asked.

'I don't think anything. But I'd like to see for myself.' Again she looked down at her hands. 'What I need is a vision of the world—a consistent vision in which things fall into place. I can't devise it by myself.' She fought to choke back a catch in her throat. 'By myself, I simply can't do it.'

'LSD won't do it either,' Joe warned.

'But it might.'

She was so insistent that I finally consented to drive her into Albufeira, where we found Churchill, gray and pasty as ever, his thin hair plastered down on either side of his forehead. Gretchen said, 'Monica sent me. She said you'd supervise . . .'

'This morning I'm busy.'

'I'm sorry,' Gretchen said, and her disappointment was so obvious that Churchill took my arm and said, 'But if he's willing to stay with you, no problem.'

'I know nothing about LSD,' I protested.

'You don't need to know anything. Just sit with the subject and reassure her from time to time. You see, the imagery becomes quite involuted, and a point of reference is required.'

He convinced Gretchen of this theory, clinching it when he said, 'Anyway, you'll be taking only half a spot, I shouldn't wonder.'

He led us to his third-floor room, and as I stared out at the ocean he took from his wallet one of his spots, held it against the light to see how much LSD it probably contained, tore it neatly in half and handed one portion to Gretchen, with the command, 'Allow the rice paper to dissolve in your mouth, then swallow it.' And he was gone.

As Gretchen held the fragile paper in her hand, I tried one last time to dissuade her from tampering with her mind. 'You don't need it,' I assured her, but she repeated the refrain that people my age were hearing throughout the world: 'How can I tell until I've tried it for myself?' I grew impatient with such reasoning from a girl of her ability, and growled, 'Doesn't education teach you that some things are to be taken on the wisdom of the race? Suppose you were pregnant and wanted to use thalidomide to relax your tensions, and I told you, "From the horrible consequences we've seen in Germany we know that thalidomide ought not to be used by pregnant women." Would you, in spite of the evidence, feel that you had to prove the facts again for yourself?'

Like the intelligent person she was, she paused, looked at the paper, and analyzed what I had said. From the way her eyes narrowed, I judged that she was agreeing with my argument, and I expected her to tear the paper up. Instead she shivered and said quietly, 'You can't even guess how miserable I am. If LSD holds even a remote possibility of providing an answer . . .' Defiantly she popped the paper into her mouth.

She kept it there for about a minute, during which she told me, 'At least it doesn't taste bad.' I saw her swallow and expected some kind of quick reaction, but none came. She remained totally normal, and for nearly an hour we talked about the camping trip from Torremolinos to Portugal.

Then, suddenly, she was asleep. For about an hour she lay inert, and I could not help seeing what a lovely, well-proportioned girl she was. She lacked the conspicuous signs of beauty but possessed such a harmony of appearance and liveliness and personality, you knew that in her late forties she would be more beautiful than any of the young lovelies now surrounding her, for she would mature with all components of her being commensurate with one another. She was one of those young women to whom good things ought to happen.

At the beginning of the third hour she began to twitch slightly, and moaned, 'It's so magnificent,' and a kind of kinesthetic movement took control of her body, as if great waves were passing slowly through the room, affecting first her head, then her shoulders, then her torso, and finally her feet. Quite obviously she was in the grip of a force she could not control, and would not for the next four or five hours. Remembering my instructions, I assured her, 'It's going splendidly.'

Apparently, I was close to the truth, for she continued to mutter phrases like 'magnificent,' 'so gentle,' and 'the colors, the colors,' and these words lulled me into a kind of relaxed dozing. From what I could see so far, LSD was generally beneficent and I began to wonder if my presence was needed.

'Acccchhhhh!' came a scream from the bed. I leaped out of my chair to see Gretchen torn by some wrenching force that literally jerked her head in one direction, her torso in the opposite. She went into a wild convulsion, screaming only the horrible 'Acccchhhhh!'

I tried to pin her shoulders to the mattress, and in this way we struggled for some time until the passion diminished, whereupon she went limp, sobbing quietly to herself and shivering in great contractions that tensed her body in reverse waves from her toes up to her head. During this time she said nothing. Even though I was terrified, I tried to reassure her, but she did not hear.

In this cycle, repeated three times, the next two hours passed and my apprehension grew, but as the fifth hour began, she subsided again into her benevolent sleep and entertained once more the visions which had given her so much pleasure before, and I judged that the crisis had passed and that she would remain quiescent for the remainder of the trip. I was glad that I had been there for the bad hours and wondered what she might have done in the grip of those great passions had she been alone.

The room was quiet. Suddenly she uttered a scream much more terrible than before, then went into convulsions that racked her body and against which I was powerless. It was hideous to see their effect upon her: face distorted, shoulders jerking, arms and legs thrashing, and over all, the screams of a girl in torment.

It was now that I began to sweat—rivulets running from my armpits, ugly and sickening in their smell—as I wrestled with the sleeping girl. Try as I might, I could not hold her on the bed, for alternately her head or her feet would slide off to the floor, twitching and writhing as if they had separate lives of their own. Her clothes became torn, and at one frightful moment I began to laugh hysterically, I suppose because all I could think of was that she looked like one of the debauched Egyptian whores in the banquet scene of a Cecil B. DeMille movie.

Now for the first time she uttered the word *death*. She said it first in a low, croaking voice, then with increased terror, until the little room seemed filled with the presence of Death himself, come personally to take her. She pleaded, writhed to escape him, begged me for help, aware of my name and the fact that I was with her. Her face became ashen-gray, and for some moments she went into a catatonic trance which I interpreted as death, or its near approach.

'Gretchen!' I shouted, slapping her about the face to bring her back to life. I was now sweating all over; my hands were wet and slipped away as I grabbed at her shoulders to shake her.

'Death!' she cried repeatedly, adding a pathetic plea, 'Uncle George, don't let me die.'

Whatever I did was useless, and with anguish I watched her come close to dying; her breathing seemed to stop, her extremities grew rigid. I found a glass, filled it with cold water, and threw it in her face, but this had no effect except to make her hair look stringy and snakelike. Her mouth fell open and her tongue protruded, and she looked hideous.

Anguished, helpless, I went to the head of the stairs and started yelling for Churchill, cursing him, holding him to blame for this disaster, but of course he did not reply. He was selling his spots in Faro and other seaports along the coast.

When I returned to the bed, Gretchen had surrendered to a passive state which in some ways was more terrifying to me than the active, for now she moaned that she was beset by snakes crawling across her body, their cold heads twisting under her armpits and down her flanks. The glorious motion that had seduced her so pleasantly at first had degenerated into snakes, whose writhings induced new cries of terror.

'God, God, take them away!' she pleaded. Her forehead was covered with perspiration that glowed in the darkened room and she continued to quiver as the snakes attacked her.

'Kill them!' she pleaded, and once when I went to the bed to try to quieten her, she clutched my hand and begged me to find a broom. There would be one in the corner. I must use it to drive away the snakes.

With the sixth hour, death returned. From the bed came horrible screams and contortions which so sickened me that I had to turn away, but Gretchen, fearing that I might abandon her, crawled off the bed to grab at my legs and plead with me to stay. When her hands found the reassurance she needed in the hard leather of my shoes, she collapsed on the floor, and I was powerless to get her back into bed. She remained there, a quivering mass.

I cannot accurately describe the next half hour, for it was a damnable hell, with moaning voices, sobbing throats, a dozen arms clutching at me. Looking back, of course, I realize that Gretchen was not about to die; she was merely in the grip of some powerful delusion, but at the time it was the most terrifying experience I had ever had to suffer through. My panic was increased when she returned to the long-drawn 'Acccccchhhhh!'—but after she had uttered this cry a dozen times or so, she began to relax and the gentle waves that had passed over her body at the beginning of the trip returned, bringing with them the expansive colors and the protracted sounds.

She spent the seventh hour sleeping, the first half on the floor, the second half in bed, for now when I tried to hoist her up, she cooperated and clung to me for a moment. 'Thank God you were here,' she whispered, and lapsed into the final unconsciousness from which she would emerge a human being once more.

———•◦•———

Gretchen was never able to tell the others of her trip. Apparently the terrors had been so destructive that she considered herself fortunate to have survived them, and now banished recollection from her mind. But when Monica and Cato kept pestering the others to try the acid—they even propositioned me to join them—Gretchen was infuriated when they approached Joe. Placing her hand on Joe's arm, she said, 'If I saw things as clearly as you do, Joe, I wouldn't need any mind-expanding,' to which Monica replied, 'But how can he tell what the world's like until he sees it for real?' and Gretchen said, 'What I saw, I didn't need to see,' and Monica goaded her, 'Were you afraid?' and Gretchen replied, 'No. I accepted what I saw and made my peace with it. It's buried. And I'm content to leave it buried.' To this, Monica said, 'Until the day it explodes and destroys you,' and Gretchen said, 'I think that's what life is—keeping things in balance, delaying the explosion a little longer. When it finally comes . . . it's death.' To Joe, she said, 'You'd be insane to try it. You don't need it.'

'Are you implying that I do?' Monica demanded.

'We're all different,' Gretchen said. 'Maybe you can handle it. I can't.'

'You suggesting Joe can't?' Monica asked. 'Big man like him?'

'If you ask me bluntly, I do have doubts that Joe could handle it. He has such an intense personality it might blow him to hell.' She paused and stood back and studied Joe, then said, 'Sometimes it's the big strong ones that destroy themselves. You don't need to prove anything, Joe.'

So Monica and Cato turned to Yigal, asking how he could comprehend the inner structure of science if he failed to perceive it in its LSD forms. 'Believe me when I say this,' Monica insisted, 'the new discoveries in science will come from men who use LSD. They'll see relationships you clods will never dream of. Look, if an ignoramus like me can look at a fragment of broken concrete and see every molecule . . . each of them standing alone by itself . . .' She shrugged her shoulders at his obstinacy.

But when Monica and Cato renewed their pressures on Britta, they encountered a vigorous and final reaction. For several days she fended them off with polite refusals, but when they argued with her one morning in the plaza that she would never understand sex unless she participated in the act while under the influence of LSD, she became angrier than we had ever seen her; she raised her arms against them and said, 'Goddammit, you lay off me. You're just like my father and the gramophone records.'

This was such a startling statement that we all stared at her. She was leaning against the statue as she said, 'I take my beliefs from that experience, and none of you can change them, so don't try, Monica.'

'What beliefs?' Monica asked mildly. It always surprised me how these young people could come to the edge of a fight and retreat without damaged egos. It was a marvelous attribute, which we lose as we grow older. If Britta had spoken so harshly to me, I'd have been subdued for three days, but little Monica blithely said, 'Okay, let's hear her pitch.'

'I told Mr. Fairbanks about how my father had an obsession about an opera,' Britta said. '*Pêcheurs de Perles*. It's involved and has to do with Ceylon, but accept the fact that when I was a little girl he used to play its arias incessantly. He really loved them. They were a part of him.

'He knew them only on old records made by Italian singers. Caruso, Tetrazzini, Gigli. Good, but Italian. So with the first pay-check I got from Mr. Mogstad—I worked for him, the jerk—I sent away to Oslo to get an Angel recording of the complete opera. It was the most money I'd spent up to then—bringing him the opera he loved wrapped in glassine paper. He had tears in his eyes when he took it. He put the first record on his machine as if it were a jewel—you know, not touching the edges.

'Then the damnedest thing happened. When he heard the voices singing in French—the way the opera was written—he grew quite angry and shouted, "What are they doing?" I'll never forget one passage. The priestess is asking the gods to protect the fishermen. In the Italian record, to save money they didn't use a chorus, just the soprano's voice with a violin representing the chorus. In the new record, of course, they used a full chorus, and the effect was stunning, but he cried, "What are they doing back there?" And you know, he played that wonderful opera only once. The French voices, the real music, a live chorus—they were too much for him.

'He wanted to imagine the opera as it had been on his first old records—wispy voices singing in Italian. I realized then that if he ever did get to Ceylon . . . it would destroy him. He'd expect it to be like the colored photographs he'd seen years ago when he was hiding in the mountains. Real Ceylon would kill him.'

'Meaning what?' Monica asked.

'What you seek, Monica, is a vision of the world . . . not the world.'

'And you?'

'I want the world exactly as it is. If God wrote it in French, I don't want it in Portuguese.' She laughed at the pretentiousness of what she had just said and told us about an experience in Tromsø.

'In the winters we had constant snow. On the whole island you wouldn't see one patch of earth or highway. All covered. So much snow fell that our plows piled it up along the sides of the road, maybe eight feet deep. Our roads became canals cut down through the snow—a kind of safety wall on each side, so that nothing bad could happen to you unless you crashed into somebody at an inter-section. Late at night we kids used to look for a mad taxi driver named Skaanevik. We'd give him what money we had and pile in for a drive across the island to the airport. Why did we do this? Because Skaanevik was the craziest driver in Norway. He'd get his taxi up to fifty miles an hour and go roaring down one of these roads protected by snow walls on each side. To turn a corner, he'd slam on the brakes—and we'd ricochet off the walls for a hundred yards, side to side. What could happen to us? When he came to an intersection he'd flash his lights off and on, and anyone on the side road would stop and the driver would say to his passengers, "We'd better wait. Skaanevik may be driving." And we'd go roaring through, lurching from side to side and bouncing off the walls. It was marvelous, with the stars overhead and wind blowing through the pine trees.'

'So what?' Monica asked.

'So I'm not afraid,' Britta said. 'I was the one who told Skaanevik, "Go faster." But I want the thrills to be real ones . . . made out of this earth . . . with me in control. I don't want dreams. So you lay off.'

Monica propositioned her no more.

———•••———

I tried to be judicious in what I said about marijuana and LSD to the young people, because I did not want to be a fraud. As a former fund salesman, and now an international investor, I had often found myself skating on the far edges of truth and had been forced to develop what the English call 'a nice regard for honesty.' I refused to tell young people what I did not believe myself, and in my reactions to drugs I was on tricky ground.

When I first started working out of Geneva, I was sent to Cambodia to sell mutual funds to Americans employed on a dam being built by Morrison-Knudsen of Idaho, and in my spare time I hung around the Bijou Hotel in Phnom Penh, where a covey of American newspapermen had assembled to report on Cambodia's independence from France. I found the city a new experience, a blend of tedium and challenge. For whole weeks there would be nothing to do except watch the thin-hipped girls in their *sampots;* at intervals bizarre events would remind you that you were in an oriental city, where the rules were different.

I became good friends with the newspapermen, who were also affected by the tedium and exhilarated by the adventure. We visited Buddhist shrines, walked morning rounds with the saffron-robed monks begging rice, went upland to the brooding temples at Angkor, and picked our way into the dives.

In Phnom Penh two rivers meet, the muddy Mekong and the smaller Tonle-Sap, and near their confluence stood several rows of low grass-covered huts. Coolies and sweepers occupied these quarters, and you could tell which families were making money by the fact that over their grass roofs they had placed squares of corrugated iron, the sign of affluence throughout Southeast Asia.

One evening, when the flies were heavy in the Bijou, a Denver newspaperman about twenty-five said, 'Let's go down to the waterfront,' and all who heard him understood what he meant. About seven of us said, 'Why not?' and we hired four rickshaws and set out. I was wedged in with the Denver man, and on the way he told me, 'I figured it would be silly to be stuck in Phnom Penh and not try it.' I agreed and so, apparently, did the others.

Our rickshaws pulled up beside the Mekong at a hut with a corrugated roof. In the door stood a very thin Cambodian or Chinese —we couldn't tell which—nodding to us pleasantly. He ushered us in and asked in French, 'Have any of you smoked opium before?' We all said no, and he assured us, 'It's no great thing. I will show.'

He had two smoking rooms, each big enough to accommodate six, and we divided into two groups, the Denver man staying with me. The traditional idea of inert bodies stretched out on narrow bunks, which most of us imagined as the opium bit, did not apply. We sat in chairs, and a serving man brought us lighted pipes, which exuded a dense but not copious smoke with a distinctive heavy odor that was not unpleasant.

We inhaled slowly, expecting, I am sure, to be knocked flat by the power of the opium, but nothing much happened, at least not in my room. I was aware that the smoke was more penetrating and lingering than that of ordinary tobacco, but nothing more. My senses did not reel, nor did I see visions, nor did I experience that lethargy which is supposed to be the hallmark of the opium user.

I can speak of these things with a certain authority because all of us made careful observations during the session and compared notes when we returned to the Bijou. We concluded that if opium were the menace writers claimed, its effects were cunningly concealed. As newsmen and people who worked in various parts of the world, we would have felt cheated had we been denied this opportunity to judge the phenomenon at first hand.

For six of the seven that was that. The Denver man wanted to investigate a little more thoroughly, so he discovered the location of a posh establishment in the residential area of the city and invited me to accompany him. I told him, 'No more opium for me,' and he said, 'Who's urging? Just wait for me while I see how this thing really works.'

So a rickshaw took us to an ornate structure that could have been a whorehouse in 1880 Denver, for it had the same red plush and mirrors, the same kind of relaxed indifference in the waiting salon. The owner, this time definitely Chinese, spoke with us in good English, and my friend explained that he was an American reporter who would like to see the place and then have a pipe or two in one of the good rooms. The proprietor bowed.

This time we did see the reclining couches and the nearly unconscious men drifting on clouds of their own making. They had retreated from reality and from all responsibility. 'Regulars,' the Chinese told us. He had a larger establishment, perhaps a dozen rooms, with not a woman in any of them, and I received then the impression which I still hold, that narcotics and sex are not good companions, in spite of recent propaganda to the contrary. We ended in a small, well-decorated room, where the Denver man said, 'I'm going to smoke till something happens.'

While he was so occupied, I returned to the salon, where I talked with the owner about his business. He told me he received his opium from China . . . no trouble . . . the French had approved the trade in their day and now the Cambodians continued. It was his opinion that few Phnom Penh citizens were damaged by the drug. 'Most of my customers are older men who have finished with their work and their women. For them, life is over. If they depart relaxed . . . it makes it just a little better.'

After an hour of such discussion, broken by the arrival and departure of obviously well-to-do men in their fifties, we were interrupted by a servant. He whispered something to the host, who broke into laughter. 'Your friend is vomiting,' he said, and a little while later the Denver newspaperman returned to the salon, very pale and much embarrassed. 'Opium will never sweep the world,' he said.

Two weeks later, however, he insisted that we visit another establishment to sniff heroin, and I remember that from this we did derive a sensation of power, and of fear. Two of the time-killing

Americans even tried injecting small amounts of heroin into their arms, and they reported a definite bang. 'Frightening,' the Denver man said. 'I'd never meddle with any of that stuff a second time.' Later that year, when I was doing some work in Tokyo, I roomed with him for three weeks. He was engaged in a tempestuous love affair with a Ginza night-club dancer named Hiroko-san; they had known each other for about three years, and during his absence in Phnom Penh she had started taking injections of helipon, a heroin derivative much used in Japan.

I remember that each Thursday, why that day, I never understood, she would get high on helipon—two ampules shot into her left arm—and then storm into our room, even if I was in bed, and pull all his dress shirts into the middle of the floor and jump on them with her high-heeled shoes, after which she would pour hair tonic over the pile, cursing him in Japanese and English as she did so. When he returned after work he would find her curled up on the ruined shirts, sobbing in remorse. There would be a passionate reconciliation, which always ended with her emptying her purse of helipon ampules and crushing them with her shoe . . . right in the middle of his dress shirts. 'I never take helipon again!' she would promise, but next Thursday she would be back with an armful.

I followed her antics with a kind of detached amusement until the Thursday she dragged out my shirts, too, and crushed her ampules into them. I announced, 'Hiroko-san has got to go,' but the Denver man said, 'More better you go. I think I can straighten her out.' Since I had only a limited number of dress shirts, I decided to scram.

The point I'm trying to make is this. If I were a young man working in the Orient and intending to do so for some years, I would want to know the basic facts about opium and its derivatives. I had spent time with about two dozen American newsmen specializing in East Asia for our journals, and most of them at one time or other, when stranded in places like Bangkok or Saigon, had experimented with opium, but only the Denver man had ever gone back for a second try. Not one of my friends had become even remotely addicted. They had more sense than to punish themselves voluntarily with such a hateful burden.

On balance, I think I would have missed a significant part of that mysterious procession of the Orient—Buddhism, the great temples, the bamboo trees at dusk, the gongs, the warlords, the buzzing new machinery—if I had not taken a cursory look at opium too. Use it? I could not imagine myself doing so even if I lived in Phnom Penh for a hundred years. And actually puncture my arm to inject a foreign substance into my bloodstream? Impossible. I even use alcohol sparingly, because I feel no desire to enhance my capacity for sensation; I already experience things too deeply. Also, I have always had a special loathing for anything that might contaminate my blood, for I have seen too many friends die of leukemia or blood poisoning not to respect my blood, whose delicate balances had better not be disturbed. It has always perplexed me that our young people, who have been so judicious in opposing the pollution of rivers, should be so indifferent to the contamination of their own bloodstreams, which I would suppose to be of at least equal importance to them.

So, because I had circumspectly investigated the drug culture of the Orient, I found it impossible to condemn with an old man's moralizing those of the younger generation who were investigating theirs. But never did I feel inclined to tell them, 'I experimented, with no ill effects. Go ahead.' Because the game they play is much rougher than mine had been.

When I tried opium and heroin in Phnom Penh, there was no likelihood that I would continue living in that city, or in any other where drugs would always be easily available if I happened to develop a craving. Nor would I have friends who were pestering me to continue with the habit if I wanted to retain my membership in their group.

But the young people today do live in such a society. The drugs are available. Their friends do proselytize. Their problem is thus more acute than mine had been, and when the unknown factor of LSD is added, more dangerous. I therefore tried to avoid dogmatism, which explains why, when Monica asked my opinion on LSD, I had replied, 'I can't understand . . .'

But that was before I had witnessed its effect on Gretchen. Even now I cannot erase from my memory that small room, with her writhing on the bed and crawling across the floor. That experience convinced me that sensible people ought to stay clear of the drug, and now I had no hesitancy in warning Monica of its dangers. She laughed at my fears. 'My trips have been stunning,' she said.

Since the young people were inviting my comment on their behavior, I had to crystallize my thinking on the matter. What did

I believe about drugs? My reactions were divided into three categories: heroin, LSD, marijuana. To understand my total rejection of the first, we must go back to Tokyo, where pretty Hiroko-san continued to put on her helipon act. It continued to be amusing until that Thursday when the Denver man shouted in the hall, 'Fairbanks, for God's sake, help me!' I ran to his room, where Hiroko-san, loaded with the drug, had piled his shirts in the middle of the floor, doused them with hair oil, danced the broken ampules into them, then thrown herself upon the heap and with a razor severed her throat. To me, heroin would always be the sight of Hiroko-san's blood on the white shirts.

Looking back upon a fair number of cases, I never met anyone who took heroin for any extended period whose life was not ruined. There may be people who have broken the habit and returned to productive lives, but I didn't know them. The penalty heroin exacted was so devastating that anyone who carelessly stumbled into its use was condemning himself to misery; those who knowingly entrapped others ought to be jailed. I would rather lose my left arm than risk the terrors of heroin, and when the young people asked me, I said so.

When LSD first appeared on the medical horizon, I heard hopes that it was to be the cure for certain specific types of mental derangement, but this did not eventuate, and its widespread abuse by young people, with devastating effect on many of them, convinced me that it should be left strictly alone. Monica and Cato might seem to be able to handle it with what appeared to be minimal effects, but it could have destroyed Gretchen. I myself would not touch LSD, principally because I would be afraid of its impact on my nervous system, but also because my mind was already so expanded with ideas and music and the joy of nature that if it were further expanded by LSD, it would probably burst.

Marijuana raised problems which were especially difficult, because we had so few hard facts about the drug, even though it had been used for more than two thousand years. I had now watched at close hand many marijuana users, and the effects did not seem destructive, but two nagging questions persisted: Did marijuana escalate to more dangerous drugs? Did it induce a general lassitude which destroyed will? Medical testimony appeared strong that cannabis was not of itself addictive, and I had found no user who admitted that he had picked up a craving that could be satiated only by stronger drugs. But it was obvious to me that the social milieu in which it was smoked did encourage further experimentation. Monica smoked grass in Vwarda, preached the doctrine in Torremolinos, and actively looked for LSD in Albufeira, principally because she was in an *ambiente* which enhanced her mood. What I am trying to say is: Marijuana itself might not lead to LSD, but the gang with whom one smoked it, might.

As to the question of lassitude, I was something of an expert. I had worked in seven countries where the use of marijuana was so common as to be almost a national habit, and I was disgusted by the society these countries had produced. Where were the libraries, the child-care centers, the elementary education, the highways, the committees on social justice? I saw only lethargy, both in individuals and in the society as a whole, and I concluded that marijuana was antithetical to the good life. It did destroy will.

I was not much impressed with the argument that marijuana was to the young what a martini was to the adult, for this was a false analogy masking a discrepancy: the milieu of martini-drinking neither led to heroin nor induced an anti-social lethargy. In other words, the martini drinker could still function constructively, even though he might be damaging himself personally. As for the repeated argument that taking opium did not prevent Thomas De Quincy from writing well, I had never been excited by his results.

———•—•—•———

The young people had said they were coming into Albufeira for a lunch of *caldeirada*, so I went to the bar to meet them, and as I waited, Churchill started the gramophone. I wasn't aware of it at the moment, but he was preparing to show me up for a fool.

Since this bar was not a port of call for Clive and his purple carpetbag, it had none of the new records I had grown to like in Torremolinos, which meant that the things Churchill played were outdated and unfamiliar. I didn't appreciate them until, as I was listening with one ear, I heard that crisp, hammering sound which pleased me, and I asked, 'What's the record?' and he said, ' "Sergeant Pepper," ' and I asked, 'Who's he?' and he looked down at me with that weary contempt which only an Oxford man who is pushing LSD in Algarve can muster. 'It's the Beatles,' he said.

At Torremolinos I must surely have heard records by this famous group, but in those days I had not known enough about popular music to identify them. Now I listened with extra care to a sardonic number in which cellos sobbed and violins played nineteenth-century obbligatos while a girl from an English middle-class family ran away at dawn to live with a gentleman from the motor trade. It was devastating.

'I didn't know the Beatles would use a cello,' I said, and he looked at me with a cold expression. 'My good man, they use anything.' Then he said, 'I don't suppose you've heard this either,' and he turned to a savage number in which a callow young man reflects upon the suicide of a member of the House of Lords . . . or something like that. His own alternative is to turn on with acid, but this doesn't accomplish much either, for in the end the world collapses in an atomic explosion. It was a powerful statement, bleak as a desert, and I suspected I would like it when I knew it better.

'That's pretty rugged,' I said.

'It was big news two years ago,' he replied contemptuously. 'In Portugal we get everything late.' I asked if he was a Portuguese national, and he said, 'Do you think I'm insane?'

I was pondering an appropriate reply, when I heard one of the most delightful songs I'd come upon in the last dozen years. It began with the tremulous voice of a young boy reciting nonsense images: tangerine trees, marmalade skies, marshmallow pies. Normally I detest such songs, finding them mock-childhood, but this one carried a stamp of authenticity, as if the boy had actually seen these visions.

The song then moved to a more serious level, for the singer meets a girl with kaleidoscope eyes; not only was this conceit a most happy one, for it reminded me of those dizzy, dainty girls with fluttering eyes who had befuddled me when I was young, but it was accompanied by music that made the image leap with vitality. This boy had truly met such a girl.

The fairy-tale mood was broken by three sharp raps on a drum, whereupon a chorus of voices—the full contingent of Beatles, I supposed—broke into a rapturous cry consisting of the girl's strange name, repeated several times: Lucy in the Sky with Diamonds. That's what her name was, and its effect upon me was mesmerizing, and I said, 'A century and a half ago John Keats described that kind of phenomenon with words almost as strange.'

'You like it?' Churchill asked, with the only show of pleasantness I was to see him display.

'It summarizes our age,' I said, for it captured the fine, free-moving form of the young people I had seen in Europe and Asia.

'It does indeed,' Churchill said benignly. He asked again if I really liked it, and when I nodded, he said cryptically, 'Then you must visit the room one day.' I saw no connection between my liking a popular song and visiting his room, but before I could pursue the matter, the six young people arrived and we ordered our fish stew from across the square.

'Listen to what your Mr. Fairbanks has chosen as his favorite song,' Churchill said maliciously. When the strains of 'Lucy in the Sky' sounded through the bar my companions broke into rancous laughter, and Gretchen said, 'I'll never understand you, Uncle George,' but Monica said, with an evil little leer, 'I knew you were a dirty old man!' When I asked what this meant, the young people teased me but made no attempt to explain. Churchill played the number twice again; apparently my group knew it well, for they chanted the words. I was about to insist upon a clarification when Monica said, 'I'd love to know the things you do when you're alone, you filthy old devil,' and the waiter from across the way appeared with our seven tureens of *caldeirada*, from which Churchill exacted his usual tax of baby octopus.

During the meal I forgot the song, but Monica, who ate little, finished first and put the record on again. 'You still don't know what it is?' she asked.

'No.'

'The name! The name! "Lucy in the Sky with Diamonds." Are you stupid?' I must have looked quite blank, for she said, 'LSD. It's the national anthem of LSD.'

I grunted. I had completely missed the point of the song. Listening anew, I could not believe that the Beatles had played a trick on me, but Monica's interpretation of the words proved that it was indeed an evocation of an epoch, but not in the sense that I had thought. Churchill, having wearily disposed of his last octopus, said, 'That song did more to awaken the young people of the world to the wonders of LSD than any other one thing.'

'Your theme song?' I asked, angry at having been made a fool.

'Indeed. It's helped my trade enormously.'

I was irritated with the lunch. Even the fish stew began to taste ordinary and no longer could I find pleasure in my new-found song. When Monica replayed it, her eyes closed in adolescent ecstasy, I was disgusted. Why? Because popular music, which ought to be a major and beautiful force in our society, was being perverted for the corruption of youth.

Reacting automatically, I strode to the record machine, jerked away the tone arm, grabbed the record, and smashed it across my knee.

The young people were aghast at my behavior, and Monica, her eyes opened by the rude interruption, cried, 'Uncle George! What in hell are you doing?' But Churchill explained unctuously, 'Forgive him. He's an old man in a new world.'

———•••———

Reading Portuguese is quite simple. If you can read Spanish you can decipher Portuguese. But speaking it? That's something else.

When I'm in Geneva and one of my associates is heading for Portugal and he says, 'I'll get along because I speak Spanish,' I no longer argue with him. I simply hand him the name of that bleak headland where Prince Henry the Navigator trained his captains for their conquest of Africa and ask him how he would pronounce it: *Sagres*. After he has made his guess, I say 'That's how a Spaniard would say it, but the Portuguese say *Shagrzh* in one compressed syllable. The rule,' I advise him, 'is to drop as many vowels as possible and insert as many h's.'

So when Gretchen told me one morning, with some excitement, 'Join us! We're going on an expedition to Silves,' I told her, 'If you want to find your way, better pronounce it *Shilvzh*.'

Her excitement was caused by the discovery that Silves, the ancient capital of Algarve, contained a Crusader castle in good repair. It had been built, she told me, by Muslims in the tenth century. When I asked her how it had become a Crusader fortress, and in Portugal, her eyes lit up with the old enthusiasm I had noted when I first met her in Boston.

I was pleased to see this. When the Hundred Years' War had proved disappointing she was left without any central intellectual interest, and I had hoped that some new subject in Spain would enlist her attention, but none did. Now, hearing of Silves and the

Crusades, her enthusiasm was rekindled and there was a possibility that this might prove to be the subject on which she would concentrate.

It was a strange bit of history she told me. In one of the early Crusades a group of knights from England and Germany, more devout than brave, discovered to their relief that they did not have to sail all the way to the Holy Land to battle the infidel. There happened to be some Moors in Portugal, ensconced in castles which could be easily reached from the sea, and which, if captured, would control farmlands that might prove productive.

So this band of reluctant conquerors hove their fleet to just south of Lisboa, where some castles showed on the horizon, and it was not until they had burned the buildings and slaughtered the inhabitants that they found the latter were Christians. The Moors, one of the survivors gasped, lived farther south.

Accordingly, the mob dropped down the coast to burn some more castles, finding that these belonged to Norsemen who had conquered the Moors a good hundred years earlier. 'The enemy,' their survivors explained, 'live beyond the turn of Portugal, on the southern coast.'

So the gallant brawlers sailed even farther south, turned Cabo de São Vicente and arrived at a shore from which they could see the real enemy in the Moorish castle of Silves. With fire in their hearts, they stormed ashore, devastated the land lying between the beach and the castle, and laid siege to the infidel stronghold. It was a bloody, protracted affair and after many weeks the Christians won. For them that was the end of the Crusade. They dug themselves in, appropriated surrounding lands, and terrified the seacoast for a hundred miles.

'They were,' the locals said, 'the first Englishmen to settle in Algarve, great robbers who set the pattern for all who followed.' The shield of Silves shows the ancient castle guarded by two bearded Crusaders and two murderous Moors in headcloths. Residents argue as to which are the more fearsome.

We drove to Silves on the high inland road, catching glimpses of the ocean on our left, and I was impressed with the manner in which Gretchen turned her whole attention to what she was seeing: 'If we were in a Crusader ship out there . . . right now . . . we'd see this road and know it led to some settlement.' Once she asked Joe to halt the pop-top so she could inspect the land. 'If you

were an English countryman, would you try to grow things here?'
Nothing was too trivial for her inspection; she wanted to remember what flowers grew along the road and what birds accompanied them. She became an English Crusader captain eight
hundred years ago.

From the high road the first glimpse of Silves was a summary of
history, for at the northern edge of the city rose the dark brown
walls of a many-turreted Moorish castle, from whose eastern end,
without a break in architecture, sprang a Gothic cathedral, each
building leaning upon the other. The city itself, perched beside a
mountain stream, looked clean, with nineteenth-century buildings
in pastel colors interlocking with stone edifices seven and eight
hundred years old. It was, like other cities in Algarve, still small
enough to be encompassed in a single glance.

Gretchen launched an imaginative debate as to what the Christians and Moors must have thought in those centuries when warfare
preoccupied them. Cato grumbled, 'Just like the Russians and the
Americans . . . irrelevant.' But Britta corrected him. 'If you think
communism is irrelevant, you haven't lived on its flank.' What she
meant by this we did not stop to inquire.

Joe said, 'It's hard to imagine religion as such a force . . . one
whole civilization at war with another,' but Yigal said, 'You haven't
been following Ireland . . . and they're all Christians.' Gretchen
asked, 'Are the Muslims today as much preoccupied with the Jews
as they were with the Crusaders in this period?' She indicated the
distant castle, and Yigal replied, 'When you live in Israel today,
you hear the word "Crusades" every day.'

'How?'

'The Arabs are convinced that since they were once able to
resist the Crusaders for two hundred years and push them into the
sea, they'll do the same with us. For an Arab in Syria, a Crusader
castle is a very hopeful image.'

When we reached the castle we found a complete structure—
with gardens, orchards, water supply and huge roadways—atop
the ramparts. The fortress looked much as it must have when the
Moors occupied it, and all of us gained from it a sense of history.
I remember Cato standing with me at the foot of a tower which
the Crusaders had destroyed in their siege and then rebuilt. 'You
know,' he said reflectively, 'I'm beginning to suspect my old man
was right. Maybe religion is a lot more important than I thought.'

I was about to reply, but he had quickly moved away to study another tower; he had made a remark on which he wished no interrogation.

When we had finished with the castle, and the strange cathedral which grew out of it, we drove southward about seven miles to the beach, where Gretchen got out and waded into the Atlantic, trying to imagine what it must have been like to be a Crusader storming ashore to attack an unknown land.

'Who'll march with me back to the castle?' she asked, and Cato volunteered, for he, too, was much taken with this castle and wanted to see it as it emerged into sight. So the two set forth and hiked the seven miles, studying each aspect of the landscape as they went, seeing it as a marauder would. The rest of us stopped in bars, bought European papers, and listened to what music was available; occasionally we overtook the hikers, and I thought that if Gretchen ever did write about the Crusaders in Portugal, she would at least know the terrain.

We rejoined them at the castle and walked once more about the spacious ramparts; now we were Christians who had successfully stormed the fortress, and as we walked Cato said, 'You know, that's just what a bunch of Englishmen and Germans would do. Build a cathedral over there.' He was much taken, I remember, with the subtle manner in which the cathedral had been made a part of the castle.

On our way home in the late afternoon Gretchen asked again that we halt for a final look at Silves, nestling on its hill, and as we sat beneath old almond trees Britta suggested that Gretchen sing, and the guitar was hauled out and we joined in some of the ballads we had learned. At one pause I said, 'It's strange that you don't know the best folk song ever written.' Gretchen turned inquisitively and asked, 'What?' and I said, ' "Eriskay Love Lilt." '

'Never heard of it,' she said, so I sang the song from the Outer Islands of Scotland; it must have been current when the Crusaders gathered to storm the castle at Silves, a plaintive sea-song of extreme simplicity:

> 'Vair me o rovan o
>   Vair me o rovan ee,
> Vair me o-ruo-ho,
>   Sad am I without thee.'

There was no bombast in the song, no wayside murders or be-trayals; there was simply the timeless complaint of an island woman whose lover has gone to sea. The melody had been judged by experts to be one of the purest ever devised, a sequence of plain full notes. Certainly it was one of the gentlest and longest-remem-bered.

'Where did you learn it?' Gretchen asked.

'In World War II. I was stationed for a while on a Scottish island called Barra . . . so small, a ship could hardly land there. Nearby was another island called Eriskay. One tenth as large. The song was found on that island many years ago.'

Gretchen tried to pick out the melody, then the accompaniment, and as dusk began to gather about the castle, for it was now nearly nine at night, we tried the old song:

> 'When I'm lonely, dear white heart,
>   Black the night or wild the sea,
> By love's light my foot finds
>   The old pathway to thee.'

As we sang we could visualize Moors and Christians inhabiting this valley, sending their fishing boats out to sea and returning at dusk.

———•–•–•·———

The expedition to Silves had an unhappy ending. When we reached Alte, and were about to drive down the mountainside, Britta gave a cry—and we turned to see what had happened.

One of the papers we had bought was from Sweden, the first Britta had seen in a long time, and on an inside page she found this cryptic notice:

Tromsø. The Norwegian government announced today that this Arc-tic city, whose central areas were gutted by fire last week, will be given a grant for rebuilding, so that the industrial life of the city can continue as in the past.

The fire, of unknown origin, burned out a large section of the city, including more than 47 major businesses and many private homes. Famous waterfront establishments long connected with Arctic exploration were lost, but townspeople pledge a prompt restoration of the devastated areas.

And, suddenly, all of us were involved with a remote city we had never seen, and as Britta tried to deduce paragraphs from words, imagining a conflagration even worse than the real one, we caught glimpses of what had been lost.

'Mr. Mogstad had his business in one of the old buildings. Poor man.'

'The other day you said he was a jerk,' Cato remembered.

'He was, and now he's a poor jerk.'

We tried to think of ways that Britta could acquire specific information, and Gretchen had a good idea: 'Tomorrow we'll find an SAS office. They'll have the back Scandinavian papers.'

'What could we do tonight?' Joe asked. He was hovering over Britta, trying to assure her that things could not be as bad as she was supposing, but she pointed to a Swedish word and said, 'Devastated. That's what it says.'

Monica said, 'Why not telephone?' and we hurried down to Albufeira, where the operator at the principal hotel tried to call Tromsø but could get only the airfield at Bardufoss, not far away. We listened as Britta spoke in a language that none of us understood. She indicated to us that the man at the airport was putting a call through on the bullhorn, asking if there was anyone in the waiting room from Tromsø, and we heard Britta pronouncing names: 'Britta Bjørndahl. Holger Mogstad. Gunnar Lindblad. Britta Bjørnsdahl.' There was a long pause, during which she began to cry, and in her tears we could see Tromsø quite clearly. She said thank you and put the receiver back on the hook. She had fought to escape Tromsø, and it had followed her to Portugal.

We went to the bar patronized by Churchill and were gratified to see that he was absent. Gloomily we drank our beer as Britta told us what had happened. A fire along the waterfront had leaped from one building to the next, until half the commercial section of the town was ablaze. Historic buildings from which Amundsen had departed for the North and South Poles were lost. The ship chandlers who had outfitted Fridtjof Nansen's *Fram* were burned out, and Otto Sverdrup's old firm was gone. Mr. Mogstad's boatyard was a total loss, and Tromsø was devastated.

'How much is left?' Joe asked.

'Most of the residential sections,' Britta said. 'I suppose our place escaped.'

When she said 'our place,' she bit her lip, for she had told us repeatedly that it was hers no longer, and this led us to a midnight discussion of what the values of life were, and it was Britta who said, 'I suppose I'm stuck with the damned place. I didn't know I loved my parents so much.'

They asked me what I thought, and I said, 'I've been much impressed with how sensible you people are in your relations with one another. You're way ahead of where my generation was at twenty. You wouldn't believe how stupid we were about sex and jobs. Your way is better.

'But the neat trick in life is not to negotiate the years from seventeen to twenty-five. Anyone can do that, and apparently it's a lot easier than I once thought. The problem is to build something that will sustain you from thirty-five to sixty. Finding some kind of work that gives you pleasure. Finding someone of the opposite sex you can live with through the tough years. Finding a way to rear children. Most of all, keeping your sanity and your dedication.'

Gretchen wanted to know what I considered the criteria, and I said, 'About fifteen years ago, when I looked at the rat race, I opted out. I'll never be president of World Mutual, because I wanted to travel . . . do things my way. I decided then that if a man can live to sixty without being in jail or the booby hatch, he's got it licked. Everything else is inconsequential.'

'You mean that?' Joe asked.

'I do.' No one said anything, so after a while I added, 'I think it's great the way you young people can live together . . . the freedom you have. But I see no evidence yet that you are even one step closer to solving the big problems. Like what work? What girl? What town? What commitment? You're not ahead of where I was at your age. Maybe you're behind, because I was sustained by certain illusions.'

Cato said, 'I don't like to bring this up, but aren't you divorced? Isn't your son in jail somewhere?'

'Yes.'

'So you didn't handle the big ones very well, either.'

'No. But even the act of failing has been fun. I'm sixty-one. I'm not in jail. I'm not nuts. So I figure I'm ahead of the game.'

'You don't think we will be?' Cato asked.

'I see no indication of it yet . . . except for one thing. You do have a certain zest. And that could be important.'

Britta now felt the full weight of what had happened in her homeland, and she slumped to the table, her head upon her forearms. Gretchen tried to comfort her, saying, 'Ease up, Britt,' and she looked up to say, 'Isn't it strange, how a fire in Tromsø can singe you?'

And I said, 'I remember one day in Torremolinos when I saw one of those hippie communes, and everybody was twenty and no one had any obligations, and it was wonderful. But a bizarre question assailed me: "With what ritual will you bury your dead?" Life requires certain rites of passage. They can't be avoided. I've never cared much for the old rituals, but they've been serviceable. I wonder what ones you'll devise.'

The answer came unexpectedly. Churchill came into the bar, and Monica said to him, 'Cato and I would like two damned good dots. Let's go over to your place.'

When Gretchen started to ask if this was wise, Monica said, 'When you've got hold of something you know is super, don't back away.'

And she and Cato disappeared.

Next morning, when I was in Faro packing my briefcase for my return to Geneva, the six young people at Alte were awakened early. A tall blond German about thirty years old banged on the door of their car shortly after dawn, having been led to the spot by Churchill, who in open daylight looked positively ghastly.

When Cato, who slept nearest the door, stuck his head out, the German said in good English, 'I must speak with you,' and Cato asked, 'What have I done?' and the German said, 'With all of you . . . all six.'

'Up, up!' Churchill called through the screen at the top. 'Look how they sleep, Detlev.' When the German climbed up to peer inside, he was face to face with Britta. 'You're pretty,' he said approvingly.

When the young people had gathered in various strange costumes about the door of the pop-top, with women from the village stopping on their way to the fountain to stare, Churchill said, 'This is

Detlev, from Düsseldorf. He has something most interesting to propose.'

'How'd you get up here?' Cato asked, and the German pointed with some pride to a large Mercedes-Benz station wagon, practically a truck, painted battleship-gray and parked under trees beyond the plaza. 'That's mine,' he said. 'Ours, if things work out well.'

'What things?' Cato asked.

Here Churchill became the entrepreneur. 'Detlev's done it three times, so it's not problematical. When he says he's going there, he goes.'

'Where?' Cato pressed.

'Well, the dear fellow bought this—this van, you might call it— in Düsseldorf and he's going to drive it to Nepal—Nepal, mind you—and sell it for a huge profit. That's how he makes his living.'

'What's that got to do with us?'

'For only one hundred dollars each—just enough to pay for your food and the gasoline—Detlev will carry you to Nepal.'

The invitation was greeted with silence. It was too early in the morning for the group to bring into focus the possibility of a trip across Europe, the Near East and the heartland of Asia to the mountain kingdom of Nepal. Monica was the only one who spoke: 'I hear the grass in Nepal is marvelous.'

'It is!' Detlev said with flashing excitement. He was a rugged, handsome fellow who looked like what a college in New Mexico would hire to play football. 'In Katmandu you'll find more swingers . . . The Russian's hotel, you really must see it if you want to be in the scene.'

'When are you leaving?' Monica asked.

'In two hours.'

'There's a fascinating group going with him,' Churchill broke in. 'I met them all last night.' And he ticked them off on his long fingers: 'There's a boy from Australia, a boy from Texas, two girls from Belgium and two from Canada.'

'Isn't that a full load?' Gretchen asked.

'No,' Detlev said. 'We all carry camping gear. You sleep under the van, along the road, in old churches.'

'Are you going?' Gretchen asked Churchill.

'No, no, darling girl. I'm interested solely as a friend. You see,

Detlev brings down my supplies from Switzerland. And on his return from Nepal he brings me many interesting things.'

'So if any of you are looking for a really great trip,' Detlev said, 'it's only a hundred dollars. But we do leave from Albufeira in two hours . . . sharp.' He went to Britta, who had not spoken during the discussion. 'You interested?'

'I'm Norwegian,' she said, dismissing him.

'You interested?' he asked Yigal, who said, 'I'm Jewish.'

Gretchen had the pop-top to care for; Joe was interested but had no money; Cato was interested but had to stay near Albufeira till his check arrived from Mister Wister. Monica was interested. 'I'd like to see Nepal,' she said.

'Have you the money?' Detlev asked.

'I have.' There was an electric silence, broken when she added with a nervous laugh, 'But I'd better stay with the gang.'

'There are four girls with us,' Detlev assured her.

'There are two here. And they're nicer,' she replied. Detlev shrugged his shoulders, nodded crisply to each of the six and told them, 'You're missing a good trip.'

'You're also missing a great trip,' Britta said, tapping the pop-top.

'Of that I'm sure, my beautiful Norwegian.' He blew her a kiss and strode back to his Mercedes.

I arrived at Alte two hours later to find the pop-top in confusion. 'Oh, Uncle George!' Gretchen cried as I appeared to make my farewells. 'Monica's run away. Did you see her along the road as you drove up?'

'I came the back way . . . from Faro. Where'd she go?'

'To Nepal.' Before I could catch my breath, she handed me a slip of paper written in a schoolgirl scrawl: 'I have the $100, so I'm off. Monica.'

'What's it mean?' They told me, and I quickly said, 'We must stop her.' For I visualized her at age seventeen drifting across the roof of Asia, sleeping in the bug-infested tearooms I had known in Afghanistan, and I repeated, with some force, 'We must stop her.'

I told the two girls to wait in the plaza till we returned, and not to panic. Then I jumped into the pop-top with the three young men and we roared off down the mountain road to Albufeira. Hastily scanning the principal squares, we found nothing, so we stopped at Churchill's bar, and he told us blandly, 'Yes, the dear girl made the right decision.' He looked at my watch, having none of his own, and said, 'She's forty minutes on her way to Nepal . . . with a swinging bunch of people . . . so don't you worry.'

I wanted to push him in the face and demand which way they had gone, but Joe, who studied maps when he drove, said, 'They're bound to go through Loulé,' so we jumped back into the pop-top and thundered off in that direction.

Ordinarily Joe was a careful driver, but now he whipped the Volkswagen around curves and up inclines at a violent pace, and none of us cautioned him to slow down, for we were determined to overtake the Mercedes and drag Monica back to sanity. 'That German may prove tough,' Yigal warned. 'That is, if we ever catch up with him.'

'He won't be driving fast,' Joe predicted, and he was right, for on the mountain road north of Loulé, we spotted the gray Mercedes far above us, making a turn with caution. 'On the first day of a long trip you don't drive too fast,' Joe said.

It took us some time to overtake the Mercedes, and when we did, the occupants figured out who we were and Detlev swung the van in such a way as to prevent our passing him. We drove in this manner for some distance, and Yigal said, 'This is going to get rough,' and Joe said, 'Let it.'

'Don't try to pass on those outside curves,' I warned, for there was a steep drop into the valley below. Joe reassured me by saying, 'I'm willing to stay right here for the next fifty miles. The son-of-a-bitch has to stop sometime.'

Monica now appeared at the rear window, waving at us to go back, and I was shocked at how frail and small she seemed when seen from such a distance. The impression was heightened when the two men with her turned to glare at us, their faces looming large and menacing. 'A Texan and an Australian,' Cato muttered. 'Just our luck.' From the apparent size of these two passengers, and remembering how big Detlev was, the opposition in the Mercedes could prove formidable. I had a feeling that Cato wasn't going to be much help in a rowdy affair, and Yigal was quite small. Joe, I supposed, was redoubtable. At least he showed no signs of turning back or any indication of fear when the men in the Mercedes made threatening gestures.

Suddenly, in a move which surprised those of us in the pop-top as much as it did the three men in the Mercedes, Joe swung out along the edge of the road, whipped past the startled German, and pulled the pop-top across the highway so that the Mercedes had to grind to a halt.

'What the hell?' came a roar from the Mercedes as a very tall Texan stormed out onto the road. 'You trying to kill us all?'

'Trying to stop you,' Joe said, getting out of the car. 'We're taking the English girl back with us.'

'You are like hell!' the Australian cried, uncoiling a wiry frame and stepping onto the roadway. He had obviously been necking with Monica in the back, for his left cheek was covered with lipstick, and he had no intention of surrendering anything that promised so much pleasure on the long trip across Asia.

Joe remained calm and said, 'She'd better come now.'

'You touch her,' the Australian said, 'and down you go.'

'Then here we go,' Joe said, taking a swipe at the Australian. He only brushed the man's jaw, but even this was enough to drive the thin fellow backward.

Before I knew what was happening, the mountain road was filled with flying fists, knees aimed at groins, elbows cutting across throats. Each of the three men from the Mercedes was taller than any one on our side and it looked as if our three would quickly go down in a heap, but this did not happen, for Joe was a valiant man, Cato was more adept than I had expected, and Yigal was phenomenal. With a courage I would not have anticipated, even though I knew of his exploits at Qarash, he slipped in and out of the fray, landing as many sharp blows as he could. When Detlev turned to tackle him seriously, I expected Yigal to run. Instead he stood up to the big German and slugged it out for several exchanges before falling on one knee.

But it was obvious that the other side must win, for the Texan and the Australian were concentrating on Joe and giving him a real thrashing. At this moment I remembered the many movies I had seen in which, during a life-and-death struggle between two men, the girl stands immobile, helping neither. I had always been offended by such scenes, so now I felt obligated to behave otherwise. I therefore moved rapidly to Joe's side to give him what help I could, but the Texan saw me coming, and to my astonishment, rammed his head into my belly, knocking me flat on my can. 'Stay out of this, you old fool!' he growled, giving me a departing kick in the side.

I was outraged. I had expected at least the honor of a fist to the jaw. To be butted and kicked was humiliating. I felt the blood rush to my head, and in my fury I looked for some stone with which I might clout him, but I found none—and he was already back at his job of pummeling Joe.

I then saw in the grove that edged the highway a large and rather lethal branch which had been pruned from an old olive tree. It was hardly an ideal weapon, for it was too big, but I knew that if I could get it swinging I could avenge myself. Wincing with pain from the kick, I scrambled down into the orchard, grabbed the branch, and returned to the battle.

Wielding it with all the force I could command, I brought it around in a circle and caught the unsuspecting Texan in the soft corner where his neck joined his shoulder. He went down in a lump, and Cato jumped on him, straddling him like a fallen steer and thumping him until he passed out.

I now turned to where the Australian was giving Yigal a bad time, and with a wide sweep of my branch, held a few feet off the ground, caught him in the back of the knees and quite deflated him, whereupon I clubbed him again while he was down, and Yigal finished him off.

Detlev, seeing me approach with my shillelagh and aware that Joe, though battered, was far from finished, surrendered. 'Take the tramp,' he growled.

'That's what we intended to do,' Cato said grimly, climbing into the Mercedes and grabbing Monica by the arm.

'Some heroes,' the German said. 'Using an old man with a club.'

'Anything to finish the job,' Cato said, jerking Monica toward the pop-top.

'What about him?' Detlev asked, indicating the Texan, who was still unconscious.

Joe replied, and the prudence of his answer surprised me: 'He's not dead, so he's your pigeon. And I wouldn't go to the police, because so help me, if you do, I'll tell them you kidnapped a girl seventeen . . .'

'She came of her own will. Churchill will testify.'

'And I'll add that you smuggle LSD and heroin into Portugal . . . regularly.' As Joe said this he stood toe to toe with the German. When there was no reply, Joe quietly raised his right hand and gently brushed his adversary aside. 'I'm going to turn around and go back to Alte. And no interference from any of you. Get in your car and drive to Nepal.'

He swung the pop-top into a tight arc, and with the outer wheels almost dropping off into the valley below, headed back toward where Gretchen and Britta were waiting.

———•◦•———

As we approached Alte an embarrassing thing happened. When we first started back, we had sounded like a bunch of junior-high basketball players returning from their first game on an unfamiliar court.

'Wow, did you clobber that Texan!' Cato kept saying to Joe.

Joe told Yigal, 'You're not afraid to mix it up. I thought that Australian would break you in half.'

'He would have,' Cato shouted, 'except the old man cut him down with that club. I doubt if his knees ever work again.'

Through the warriors' discussion, Monica sat like Helen of Troy, bemused by the whole affair. 'I thought I was on my way to Nepal,' she said.

'With those apes?' Cato asked. 'They'd have ditched you in Turkey.'

I participated in the self-congratulation, and was expressing my admiration for Joe's performance, when everything snapped. The tension of the morning overtook me and I became an elderly man, appalled in retrospect by the brawling in which I had been involved. It would be disgraceful under any circumstances to clobber an unsuspecting opponent over the head with a cudgel, but to do so at my age was unforgivable. My side hurt and I began to tremble. I folded my hands tightly across my stomach, but I could not halt the quivering.

Monica was the first to see it. Leaning over and giving me a kiss, she said, 'Don't take it so hard, Uncle George.'

'What's the matter?' Cato asked.

'Look. He's shaking.'

'Were you hurt?' Yigal asked. 'I saw him give you one hell of a kick.'

'I'm scared,' I said. 'Scared at what might have happened.' This they understood. They were scared, too, but as young men they could control their fears. I couldn't.

When we rejoined the two girls, everyone insisted that I put off flying to Geneva, and when Britta made me take off my shirt and saw the large blue spot where the Texan had kicked me, she put me to bed and from a neighboring house borrowed some hot water. A Portuguese woman, hearing that someone was ill, came with knowing hands and fixed a kind of poultice for me, and I am ashamed to say that I fell asleep and remained that way for some hours.

I was awakened by the same words that had greeted my arrival at Alte that morning: 'Monica's run away.' A village boy had seen her catching a ride in to Albufeira, and as soon as I heard that name, I understood what had happened. And I knew exactly where she would be.

We drove into town and I deposited the others at the bar while I went off alone to Churchill's room. The door was locked, but I kicked it open, hurting my side again as I did so, and there inside was what I knew I would find: Monica in bed with Churchill.

'Get dressed and we'll go,' I said.

'Old blabbermouth,' she muttered from the bed.

'I figured this out by myself. I'll keep it to myself.'

'She's a free woman . . .' Churchill began.

'Shut up,' I barked, 'or I'll kick the living shit out of you. And she knows I can do it.'

He started to say something, and for the second time that day, blood rushed to my head. Even though my side ached, I said, 'One more word, Churchill, and I will really . . .' I had no idea of how to end the threat, but said no more.

Monica dressed, slowly and insolently, walking close to me several times while she was still naked, and as I led her down the stairs, she asked, 'How did you know I would be here?'

'Because you wanted to hurt us . . . not only Cato . . . all of us. By rescuing you from the German, we proved how much we loved you . . . and you wanted to hurt us.'

'You're stupid,' she said, 'but you aren't dumb. Did you tell the others?'

'No need to. Each one of them interprets your absence in his own way . . . because they too love you.'

She took my arm for the last flight and said, 'You really were scared coming home, weren't you?'

'Aren't you ever scared?'

'Never.'

Why did I bother with Monica? Her behavior in Algarve had been so incorrigible that I would have been justified in dropping her. I refrained for two reasons. She was, in a sense, my daughter. She had no mother, and at various crucial times in her life her father had abandoned her, leaving her guidance to me, and would probably do so again. I had worked hard to bring her to some kind of stability, and in doing so, had come to love her as my child. I appreciated the rare qualities she possessed and believed that if I could help her past the chaotic teens and into the more responsible twenties, she might attain some kind of balance to serve for the remainder of her life. I was encouraged to persist because of my failure with my own son.

My second reason was quite different. I remembered that unbroken chain of eccentric women which proper England had presented the world for its entertainment and, at times, enlightenment. There has been no nation so strict in its proprieties as England, nor so calculated to produce outrageous women. There was a good chance that Monica, if she gained control of herself, would find a place in that difficult company.

At seventeen she was no worse than Lady Mary Wortley Montagu, who had set Europe on its ear with her flagrant behavior and salty tongue. And her willingness to set out for Nepal did not begin to match the similar propensity of Isabel Burton, a proper young lady who conceived a grand passion for the translator of the *Arabian Nights,* following him wherever his exotic fancy beckoned. Isabel was a strange woman; for thirty years she watched her husband patiently writing his masterpiece, *The Scented Garden,* intended as an evocation of all that was erudite and pornographic in the east; when he died on the eve of publishing his great book, she sat alone in a room and burned the only copy of the manuscript, page after page, through more than two thousand, convinced that she was doing a righteous act, since the writing contained passages which she considered 'not nice.'

They were a doughty tribe, the female eccentrics of England,

and if Monica lived long enough, perhaps she would take her place among them. I was even able to overlook her sexual escapades when I compared them to the notable records set by Jane Digby.

Jane was a handsome young lady born in 1807, granddaughter of an earl. At sixteen she was married off to an English lord. At twenty she took her first official lover, a clerk in the British Museum. At twenty-one she negotiated a passionate affair with a cousin, who was promptly displaced by an Austrian prince, with whom she eloped to Paris, bearing him a child. At twenty-four, discarded by the prince, she served briefly as Honoré de Balzac's mistress, abandoning him to become the kept lady of the King of Bavaria, and before long, of his son as well. In order to keep so handy a young woman available to his court, the king married her off to a Bavarian baron, who unfortunately took her to Sicily, where she met an adventurous Greek count who made her his mistress on sight. She had now borne five children to a variety of gentlemen, but at the age of thirty-four she decided to settle down. Accordingly, she divorced her Bavarian and married the Greek, with whom she started a happy domestic life.

On an unlucky day she happened to meet a wildly romantic Albanian brigand more than sixty years old, and after a protracted interlude with him, which rocked Athenian society, broke loose and scuttled off to Damascus, where she underwent an instantaneous conversion to desert life, which she found congenial. Although now in her forties, she struck up a liaison with a young sheik to whom she made the extraordinary proposal that he divorce his wife, give up his harem of a dozen beauties, and rely upon her to replace both. Understandably he refused, so at forty-seven she launched into a vigorous affair with an older sheik and crossed the desert with him as a member of his caravan.

Her free spirit had so captivated the younger sheik that in her absence he did divorce his Muslim wife and he did get rid of his harem. Under those circumstances Jane married him and they lived happily ever after. In her late sixties she was riding by his side in tribal warfare, and at seventy-two she was coursing in camel caravans over the desert, avowing that her sexual appetites were as vital as ever and her attractiveness to men undiminished. At seventy-four, however, she began to slow down somewhat and complained that she could spend no more than a morning in the saddle. At the end of that year, having successfully avoided the plague of cholera that was sweeping Syria, she was struck down by the humiliating disease of dysentery and died of it.

Her devoted husband, whom the niggardly press of Victorian England called 'a dirty little black Bedouin shaykh,' followed her casket to the grave, riding her favorite black mare.

If ever I was tempted to be harsh in my judgment of Monica, I was restrained by the thought of Jane Digby, granddaughter of an earl, Lady Ellenborough, Baroness Venningen, Countess Theotokoy, mistress of two kings—father and son—inspiration of Balzac, companion to an Albanian brigand, and beloved wife of Sheik Abdul Medjudel of Damascus.

I returned Monica to the group and as usual no one questioned where she had been.

'I think you ought to get out of here right away,' I said. 'The German might come back.'

'I don't want to see him again,' Yigal said.

'Where can we go?' Britta asked.

'Somewhere over there,' Joe said, pushing his hands toward the west.

'I know!' Gretchen said. 'We'll go back toward Silves. I've been wanting to see the castle again.'

So it was agreed that they would set out at once for Silves, and after that, to whatever areas came to mind, but Gretchen interposed a caveat. 'I will not leave without saying goodbye to the people at Alte.'

'That's where the German will head if he doubles back.'

'I don't care. Those people did so much for us. To leave in silence would be criminal.'

So we drove back to Alte, and I think all of us were apprehensive lest we confront the ominous gray Mercedes, but it did not appear. The young people said their farewells, some tearful, to the mountain people, and Gretchen entrusted one woman with ten American dollars for Maria Concepção when she next came to the dance.

They then accompanied me to my car as I headed back to Faro. 'If we don't see you again,' Joe said, 'you're one hell of a man with a club.'

'Where will you be going?' Britta asked.

'I must get back to Geneva. Because the first two weeks in July, I always go to Pamplona.'

Gretchen snapped her fingers. 'Isn't that where Hemingway went? *The Sun Also Rises?*' When I nodded, she said excitedly, 'Did you say July?'

'Seven days from now.'

'My God! We could go over to Silves tonight . . . then up to Lisboa . . . then . . .'

Britta asked, 'Where will you be in Pamplona?'

'Bar Vasca,' I said, and as I drove down the hill I could see them in my rear-view mirror, unfolding maps.

IX

THE TECH REP

I do not love war, but I love the courage
with which the average man faces up to war.

The world is but a place of shadows. The guest
pauses for but a few nights and departs confused,
never knowing for sure where he has been. Beyond
the horizon he feels certain he will find a better city,
a fairer prospect, a more sonorous group of singing
companions. But when his camels are tethered he will
find himself engaged with still yet another set of
shadows.

Our country is wherever we are well off.—Cicero

This is the door where you get books about America when you
want to go to college, and this is the window where you
throw the bomb when we have the next demonstration.

Jungle, desert, tundra, icecap, the long wastes of the sea . . .
these are the mansions of the lonely spirit.

In ancient Baghdad there was a wise man who had
read Somerset Maugham, and when he saw death
stalking the marketplace he said, 'I'm not so stupid
as to try hiding out in Samarra. I'm going to lay low
in a little village on the other end of the Bridge of
San Luis Rey.'

The President is going on a twelve-day tour
to visit some friendly nations. What will
he do the other eleven days?

Never was a patriot yet, but was a fool.—Dryden

Lasca used to ride
On a mouse-gray mustang close to my side,
With a blue *serape* and bright-belled spur;
I laughed with joy as I looked at her!
Little she knew of books or creeds;
An *Ave Maria* sufficed her needs;
Little she cared, save to be at my side,
To ride with me, and ever to ride . . .
—Frank Desprez

For my part, I travel not to go anywhere, but to go. I travel for travel's sake. The great affair is to move.—Stevenson

A steady patriot of the world alone,
The friend of every nation but his own.
—Canning

Last time I saw Harry, I think he was on the sauce. It was in a Jersey City diner and he insisted upon paying his compliments to the chef for some extra fine waffles.

There was movement at the station, for the word had passed around
That the colt from old Regret had got away,
And had joined the wild bush horses—he was worth a thousand pound
So all the cracks had gathered for the fray.
—Banjo Patterson

Go on smoking. Who needs two lungs?

We can never be certain of our courage until we have faced danger.
—La Rochefoucauld

Girl Scouts wear green berets.

Show me a man who keeps his two feet on the ground
and I'll show you a man who can't get his pants off.

A good man must have trained the army for seven years before it is fit to go to war. To lead an un-trained multitude into battle is equivalent to throw-ing it away.—Confucius

Courage is the thing. All goes if courage goes.—Barrie

They sleep perpetually on small islands that we may sleep peacefully at home.

IT was now the first of July, so naturally my thoughts turned to Afghanistan, and as I closed my desk in Geneva, I could visualize the great plateau with camel caravans drifting down from the Russian border, the crowded bazaars, vines laden with the best melons in the world, dirty tearooms where men on their haunches endeavored to make one cup last for three hours while discussing those inconsequential things which had preoccupied nomads for the last five thousand years.

It was a land of men, undisciplined men cast in an ancient mold, and no matter where I happened to be working, if someone uttered the word Afghanistan, I wanted immediately to set forth. I wanted to see Kabul again, and the soaring Hindu Kush, and the caravans coming home at night through the city gates of Herat or Mazar-i-Sharif. I had worked in Afghanistan on three different occasions, trying to put together investment opportunities for World Mutual, but had accomplished nothing, primarily because the Russians invariably offered a better deal. Of all the countries of the world in which I have worked, Afghanistan is the one I would always want to go back to.

But when I thought of Afghanistan on that first of July, it was for none of these reasons. I saw not mountains and caravans, but a man, a ruggedly built man, forty-four years old, black hair, quiet gray eyes, five feet ten, with a slight cleft to his chin and a somber, determined manner. I saw him not on the desert, where he had spent much of his time these past two years, but in a rented house in Kabul near the slap-dash airport. The house was unforgettable in that every item within it was in place. In the bathroom, for example, the two toothbrushes—green for morning, red for night-time—hung precisely by the mirrored cabinet, inside of which stood a row of bottles, each in its designated position: one for after-shave lotion, one for mouthwash, one for dysentery pills, et cetera. His bathrobe hung from a special hook, his towels were piled neatly in three sizes, his Sears, Roebuck scales stood in polished chrome by the door, his back-scratcher by the tub.

It was the same throughout the rest of the house. His dressing room contained neat piles of handkerchiefs, white shirts, jockey shorts; his closet displayed rows of suits and tan shoes. It was by no means the house of a fastidious or effeminate man; it was the house of a meticulous one, who wanted things just so, with a minimum of confusion. His rack of guns, well used, was conspicuous in the hallway, and spread on the floor of his study lay an enormous tiger skin, the head snarling with immense white teeth.

———•◆•———

This was the home of Harvey Holt, legal citizen of Wyoming, divorced, graduate of the Colorado Agricultural and Mechanical College, and field expert on radar, on loan to the government of Afghanistan from the Union Communications Company of New York. More briefly, Harvey Holt was a tech rep.

Whatever financial good luck I've had in my later years has sprung primarily from the fact that I've worked with tech reps, those tough, difficult men who serve at the frontiers of modern industry. If I were required to operate in a dangerous terrain, I would rather have as my companion a good tech rep than any other type of man. I could depend on him.

What is a tech rep? Look at it this way. Pan American Airways has a handful of outmoded propeller planes it can no longer use on long hauls in competition with jets. So it unloads them cheap to some small country which is just beginning its own airline and needs short-haul planes . . . say, Burma. To sweeten the deal, Pan American arranges with Lockheed, who made the prop plane, to send along a team of six technical representatives to explain to the Burmese how to operate the old planes.

This team works in Burma for seven months, penetrating to every airfield at which the planes land. When necessary, the men live in grass huts, ford rivers, fight off jungle animals, raise hell in Rangoon when they are lucky enough to be stationed at the capital, and very shortly know more about Burma than the experts, for there is no part of the Burma experience in which they do not involve themselves. Usually they even learn to speak a rough Burmese. But their principal job remains the same: 'Keep those planes flying!' If they have to make a needed spare part in a local machine shop, they make it. And at the same time they are teaching the Burmese to take over.

At the end of the seven months, five of the tech reps return to the United States for their next assignment. The sixth man stays on in Burma, caring for all the Lockheeds in the country. Alone, he settles into a strange and sometimes wonderful life, with an apartment in Rangoon, a hangout in Mandalay, a bar in Myitkyina where he leaves a change of clothing, and a hut up in the mountains at the far end of the line. He often takes a Burmese mistress, or two or three at different airfields, and after he's been in Rangoon for any length of time he is apt to argue bitterly against our State Department men, or the Foreign Office types from London, for he has become Burmese and defends their interests. He is much more sympathetic to their problems than to those of his own country.

The years pass, and he remains in Burma, servicing Lockheeds. He can handle not only the flying problems which develop, but also the maintenance, the servicing of brakes, the overhaul of radios and the replacement of the hydraulic system. His technical knowledge is formidable. At times he keeps the whole Burmese fleet of aircraft operable; without him the planes could not fly. And he functions in any weather, at any altitude, in any emergency. If one word were used to describe him, it would have to be 'competent.' He can do things. He can keep aircraft flying, and if a pilot were to conk out, he could fly the plane himself.

In the remote areas of the world, I have known hundreds of tech reps—aviation, heavy tractors, communications, x-ray technicians, Coca-Cola bottlers, General Motors maintenance—and they always have four characteristics.

First, they are intelligent. Most of them quit education before acquiring their college degrees, but they know much more than the average college graduate. And they continue their education throughout their lives. If Lockheed discovers a better way to do something, the tech rep in Burma will study the report in his jungle hut until he knows every nuance of the innovation, knows it perhaps better than the man who dreamed it up. Or if Lockheed overlooks something it should have been attending to, some tech rep in Burma or Pakistan will invent a device that will do the trick. Their knowledge is pragmatic, but profound.

Second, they are difficult to manage. Left alone in the Burmese jungle, they operate beautifully. Bring them back to California, where they have to attend parties given by the head of engineering, and they fall apart. In civilization they tend to be drunks, lechers, malcontents and irresponsibles. On the frontier they are powerfully organized. Putting it another way, they are the darlings of the technical staff, the despair of the personnel men. Within two weeks of bringing a tech rep back to headquarters, the man in charge of the home office can be depended upon to shout, 'Get that miserable son-of-a-bitch out of here.' But if you send a man to Burma who is not psychologically suited to be a tech rep, even worse trouble develops, and the same boss, reading the reports from the Burmese government, will growl, 'Get that poor jerk out of there and send them a real man.' So the difficult, untamed, competent tech rep is flown out on the next plane, and there is no more trouble in Burma. Thus the tech rep is a continuation of a fundamental strain in American life. He is the lineal descendant of the gifted wagon maker who could not get along in the settled civilization of Lancaster, Pennsylvania, but who was invaluable on the frontier at Santa Fe.

Third, practically every tech rep I have known has had trouble with women. He loves them . . . invariably he loves them in a tough, manly sort of way. But he cannot live with them. They baffle him, confuse him, tear him to shreds with their feminine inconsistencies. If you summoned one hundred tech reps to a convention in Bombay, you would find that at least eighty of them were divorced, some more than once. But in the bars, when the convention meetings were over, you would not find them complaining about their former wives. They would speak most often from deep confusion: 'I don't know what happened. She couldn't stand life away from home, I guess.' You would hear no recriminations: 'After all, I was scheduled to be in Formosa for seventeen months. There was no place for her, so I left her in Amarillo and never saw her again.' But you would also hear some hilarious stories: 'I met this cute chick in Kowloon and set her up with a millinery shop in Hong Kong. A business partnership. I put twelve thousand dollars into the deal, and I had been in Hokkaido for exactly two months, when she sold the place and ran off with the twelve thousand . . . and a newspaperman from the *Chicago Tribune.*'

But no amount of disillusion or ill treatment is sufficient to turn a tech rep away from women. I have never known a misogynist among them. They bounce from one disaster to the next with a kind of animal joy, and the man whose former Chinese mistress runs off with twelve thousand dollars one day, is lending his new Japanese mistress fourteen thousand the next. The scars of love these men bear are not all psychological; many have been cut with knives or broken bottles. Two that I knew had been shot at by their unstable wives. One had been fed ever-increasing doses of poison until he protested, 'This oatmeal is either sour or poisoned, and I bought the goddamned stuff yesterday.' But at the trial he refused to testify against his wife. When it developed that three of her earlier husbands had died mysteriously—all having been partial to oatmeal—he said simply, 'Sometimes a guy gets out just in time.' He told me this in a hut in northern Thailand, where his Siamese mistress had learned how to make oatmeal from boxes of the cereal he scrounged from the United States army base outside Bangkok.

Fourth, every tech rep I have ever known was a nut about high-fidelity music systems and spent much money on equipment. No matter where they pitched their tents, no matter how far into the jungle or how remote from the capital city of the nation they served, the tech reps insisted upon having good sound, and to get it, they went to extraordinary lengths. Because the supply of electricity varied so much from country to country, any tech rep who had to depend upon the local system had to provide his own voltage regulators, transformers, capacitors and safety switches. To bring a fluctuating 220 Burmese volts down to the smooth 110 which American equipment required, the tech rep would often need half a Jeep-load of gear, and this he would gladly lug from one base to the next, content to spend time and money on the project just so long as the end result was sound of high quality. In his assembling of units he was most catholic, for he used Leak speakers from England, Tandberg recorders from Sweden, Sony amplifiers from Japan, Dual turntables from Germany, and McIntosh preamplifiers from the United States. To collect this complicated gear from so many different sources required an ingenuity of its own, and one of the first things a tech rep did on reporting to a new country was to ascertain how he could promote the various components he needed. Pilots from Scandinavian Airlines System could be relied upon to bring the Tandbergs, German technicians working in the country usually could get hold of the fine turntables produced in the Ruhr, and sooner or later each tech rep established relations with someone in the United States embassy who would import McIntosh or Fisher gear. It was not unusual for older tech reps to spend two or three thousand dollars for an assembly.

What kind of music did they play on their super-machines? A surprising number played only classical music, with Vivaldi and Mozart the favorites. Others preferred ultra-sweet waltzes from the period when they were first courting, and these men would often sit staring into space as they recalled the love affairs and marriages that had begun so marvelously only to end in such hell. The majority, however, had large collections of those anonymous records which fill the catalogues: *Music for a Rainy Day, Music for Lovers, Music for the Hours before Dawn.* I remember one man in Greece who had *Bing Crosby's Greatest Hits*, Volume I. He also had *Greatest Hits* by twenty-nine other singers, most of whom I had never heard of.

Regardless of what style of music the individual tech rep preferred, you could be certain that he would have in his collection of records a healthy sampling of those made by Enoch Light. I understand that Light is not too well known in the United States, but overseas he is a hero, for he has made a series of records intended for men like the tech reps. These records feature the best popular songs, some from way back, like 'What Is This Thing Called Love?' and 'Tea for Two,' played so that you can hear the melody, but with the instruments of the orchestra separated to an exaggerated degree. I have sat for hours in remote outposts in Sumatra or Turkey as some tech rep played his Enoch Light records: 'I want you to listen to the way that rasp comes in a half a note higher on the left channel.' If I were writing an opera about the tech reps, I would ask Enoch Light to score the music, and I would provide for things like kettle drums, bongos and flutes, some on the extreme left-hand side of the orchestra, others on the extreme right, and never would any sound come from the middle. That would be true tech-rep music.

After I had been working with the tech reps for some years, one of them showed me an article by a German psychiatrist who argued that men turn to the reassurance of high-fidelity systems only when they find they cannot control the society about them, especially the women. This head-shrinker claimed that a man who has made a mess of his association with a wife or mistress finds spiritual consolation in being able to turn a little dial and thus make a great, intricate system respond. Even the slightest turn produces results. Even the dreariest man can feel himself a master of his fate when he can reduce Beethoven to a whisper or increase Bing Crosby to a greater-then-human roar. Imagine! He does all this with the twist of a wrist, so obviously he cannot be a complete jerk. The German psychologist concluded that no man who was truly normal would need to bother with such mechanical feeding of his ego. Then, lest his meaning be obscure, he added, 'No man whose relations with women are satisfactory would need to construct a high-fidelity music system which he could dominate!' I had a copy of the essay made and showed it to several tech reps who had intricate systems, and they laughed at the analysis, but I noticed that each of them was divorced.

I have a splendid system in Geneva.

———————•◦•———————

I have said that the tech reps were responsible for my financial security. It happened this way. When I got out of the navy in 1945 I kicked around for a while in various jobs—Texas, Connecticut, California—but like a lot of other guys I found that routine work tasted like ashes after the significance of war, so I finally drifted into selling mutual funds for an outfit in Minneapolis, and this gave me some freedom to move about. I became moderately good at the job because I truly believed in saving, and this helped me to convince others. I simply showed them my own account and signed them up.

Word of my hard work reached other companies and I got several flattering offers, but stood pat. Then in 1954 World Mutual was formed and our Minneapolis outfit was among the first to join. Now I found myself with a world-wide market, and after my first trip overseas I knew this type of work was for me. I volunteered for all the out-of-the-way countries that no other salesmen wanted because I knew things they didn't know. Americans on the frontier in Indonesia, Cambodia or Afghanistan earn good money, so there is lots around if you can get to it. And whereas a busy man in Brussels won't give you time to make a sales pitch, men in remote outposts are eager to hear what you want to say. And when the Germans, Belgians, Yugoslavs and Swedes see their American counterparts saving all this money and making a profit on it, they want to get aboard too, so that sometimes you can sit in a fly-specked office and simply fill in the forms; they do the selling themselves.

Well, anyway, it was in these outposts that I first met the tech reps, and when I saw how they were throwing away their money, I became a specialist in selling them common sense. World Mutual published a lot of pretty fancy manuals on salesmanship but none included the kind of pitch I used.

'Listen, you stupid horse's ass! You threw away twenty thousand dollars last year on booze and Singapore whores—and what did it get you? A bad dose of clap. So I'm not arguing any more. I'm signing you up for fifteen thousand dollars.'

'Who says?'

'I already said. Sign here.'

As a result, every Christmas I get a dozen letters from remote places, and every one thanks me for having made some tech rep save his money.

One of the first of this group to invest with me was the especially difficult man I found working in Turkey—Harvey Holt. I was forty-six at the time and he was twenty-eight, a former marine captain whose wife was in the process of taking him to the cleaner's. Bitter, tough, capable, he was then serving his first overseas stint as a tech rep for United Communications of New York, which had recently installed an airport communications system for Turkey. Other members of the original team had returned to the States, leaving Holt in charge of all the installations in the country.

He was required to keep an apartment at headquarters in Ankara but spent most of his time at Yesilkoy airport near Constantinople, where the big four-engined planes flew in to refuel for the Asia run.

Holt was not an easy man to know, for he found it difficult to speak, and when he did he said little about himself. It was only when it became necessary for him to designate a beneficiary for his World Mutual shares that I discovered he had been divorced, for he said gravely, 'Make it to Lora Kate. Where the kid is concerned, she's great.' I could have helped him save more of his money except that he insisted upon sending his young son a larger check each month than the court had ordered. He saw the boy once every five or six years, and once he told me, 'I'd like him to spend a year with me, but where's the school?'

Holt himself had known good schooling and had profited from it. At Laramie High, in eastern Wyoming, he had run into an excellent physics teacher who had taught him advanced electronics in an after-school club, so that when at seventeen Holt had lied about his age in order to join the marines, they grabbed at him and made him a communications specialist. At Iwo Jima he had hugged the beach, running the radio which controlled the landing; and at Okinawa, had picked up several decorations for bravery.

When World War II ended he was nineteen, preparing to land in the first assault wave on Japan. His character was already formed and would change little in later years: taciturn, fearless, competent. The last word was the key: 'I respect people who can do things.' As might have been expected, when the Korean War broke out he volunteered to rejoin the marines, even though his unit was not scheduled for call-up, and it was while serving north of Seoul that he learned of his divorce. A week later he made captain, so the two incidents seemed to balance out.

After Turkey, I met up with Holt in a variety of exotic places: Sumatra, Thailand, the western desert of Australia, and most memorable of all, Afghanistan, where I had last seen him in his meticulous house, the tiger rug upon the floor, a fantastic hi-fi set playing 'A String of Pearls,' in the kitchen a pretty secretary from the Iraqi embassy helping to prepare the evening meal, and facing you as you entered the door, a sign which visitors never forgot:

You are now in

KABUL, AFGHANISTAN
34°30′ North   69°13′ East

If you fly along this latitude in an easterly direction, you will
look down on Malakand, Sian, Suchow, Hiroshima, Santa Barbara, Prescott, Little Rock, Wilmington, N.C., Fez, Limassol
Homs, Herat, Kabul.

If you fly along this longitude starting north, you will look
down on Tashkent, Petropavlovsk, North Pole, Medicine Hat,
Great Falls, Tucson, Guaymas, South Pole, Kerguélen Island,
Bhuj, Kabul.

Harvey Holt insisted upon knowing where he was.

———•◦•———

I have heard the fanciful argument that it is the tech rep who
enables the United States to live well. That is, there are literally
thousands of American businesses which do no better than break
even on their sales to customers in the United States. Their degree
of profit is determined by how much they sell abroad. And they
cannot sell abroad unless they provide technically trained experts
who will keep the product in working condition.

Let's take these ideas one at a time. A refrigerator company I
know—or it could be an automobile manufacturer or a firm making
communications devices—has a market in the United States for a
hundred thousand units. But because of competition, cost of materials and wage scales, this company cannot make a penny on a
production this small. Therefore, at very little extra cost in overhead or planning, and at reduced costs for raw materials and labor,
it makes up a second hundred thousand and disposes of them
abroad. Suddenly the operation becomes profitable and everyone is
better off—the American consumer, the American workingman,
the American shipping company, the American investor and the

foreign consumer, who gets a good product for one tenth of what he would have to pay if someone tried to provide it locally.

Forget the fact that in order to enable the foreigner to buy the refrigerator, we give him the money through foreign aid. A man or a nation must do something with its money. And besides, ninety cents out of every dollar comes right back to us—so who's losing? I think you might be astonished if you knew how many things you buy are made possible because the profit in their manufacture has been insured by sales abroad.

Where does the tech rep come in? I remember back in the 1950s when we had this foreign field pretty much to ourselves . . . well, we and the British. Then the smart Japanese began to cut in, but frankly, in those years their product wasn't very substantial— machines didn't stand up; parts were hard to get . . . and how many workmen in Pakistan spoke Japanese?

It was the Germans—the West Germans, that is—and the Swedes and especially the Swiss who changed all this. First of all they made good machines—no better than what we and the British were making, but very good. Where was the difference? They assured any buyer in a backward country, 'If this machine breaks down on Monday—and machines do break down, as you know from your experience with the Americans—you cable us and we will put one of our men on an airplane within two hours and he will be with you Tuesday night to solve your problems.' And they did it. They showed us a completely new approach to industrial relations. They must have spent a million dollars on air travel, but they made ten million from it, because word got around, 'You buy from the Germans and they keep the stuff running.'

The Americans? Well, in those years our boys were pretty high-handed. They had sold a good product, and if it broke down, it was because the gooks didn't know how to handle it. In our own time we'd send somebody out with further explanations. We were very arrogant.

The British? This was sad. They knew that the workmanship in their factories was the best in the world, their business ethics the highest, their field men the most honorable in their representations —so if some bloody idiot in Burma or Pakistan had fouled the works, they could jolly well unfoul them or wait till somebody happened to be coming out from London on a P. and O. steamer. I well remember one English technician with whom I worked on a project in Hyderabad. An Indian workman had found that he could not coax a screw into place with a proper screwdriver, so he was tapping it lightly with a hammer. 'My God!' the Englishman cried in disgust as he grabbed the hammer, then brandished it before the startled workman's eyes. 'Don't you know what they call this?' he demanded with icy sarcasm. 'An American screwdriver.' He then gave the workman a short lecture on the decline of responsible craftsmanship in the world and warned him never again to drive a screw into an English machine with a hammer. Only Americans did that. At the hotel, later, he told me with real sorrow of the pain he felt as he watched the steady decline of responsible workmanship. 'No wonder the bloody machine breaks down. Driving a screw with a hammer!'

Meanwhile, the Germans, the Swedes and the Swiss were flying in to keep their machinery functioning, and if they found an Indian driving home a screw with a hammer, they suggested to their home offices that perhaps this particular screw ought to be replaced with something better, that a man could fasten with a hammer.

Any idea I ever had that American products had to be superior because of some divine right of American industry vanished when I watched these Germans. They not only made excellent products, they also knew how to keep their customers happy, and after we had begun to lose markets all over the world, we devised our own peculiar solution to the problem. We would not fly experts out from New York. We would have our experts living on the scene. If Germany could provide help within two days, we'd provide it within two hours.

It was in this way that our tough, lonely tech reps became a functioning part of the American system. If a household in Des Moines, Iowa, sleeps securely because some American soldier is standing guard along the DEW line, that same household buys many of its goods at bargain prices because some American technician in Sumatra or Peru is helping to keep his company viable. The frontier is never where we think it is, but able men had better be guarding that frontier.

———•◦•———

Take the time Harvey Holt was left in central Sumatra to maintain the communications system UniCom had installed for the Indonesian government. He was stationed temporarily at Simpang

Tiga, the airfield near Pakanbaru, trying to clear up some trouble that had shown up in a relay station perched on a small hill that lifted its head above the jungle. Temperature 100°, humidity 100 per cent. Normal gear had rusted in the first two months and had to be replaced with stainless steel.

When Holt organized a safari to take him from Pakanbaru into the hill station, some of the old Sumatra hands warned him, 'Better take along a professional hunter.' He said, 'I have my guns,' so they shrugged their shoulders and watched apprehensively as he set off.

At dusk on the first day the gang heard a terrifying scream, and turned in time to see the last man in line having his face torn off by a tiger that must have measured ten feet from nose to hind paws. You see, most people who watch a tiger in a zoo see only the enormous teeth, and say, 'He could bite a man in half.' That isn't it. What the tiger does is creep up on its prey from behind. You simply cannot hear a tiger approaching. Then, with an overwhelming leap, the tiger throws its right paw forward and around its victim's face, while the left paw digs into the left shoulder and the throat. With the first enormous swipe the tiger rips away the target's face and eyes, simply wipes them out. With the second, he cuts the windpipe and the big blood vessels in the shoulder. With his teeth, of course, he bites into the neck, but that isn't necessary for it is the mighty sweep of the claws that kills. Within thirty seconds after the claws hit, the target is dead, and this night the tiger had dragged the workman into the jungle before Holt could get back with his rifle.

It was dusk, since tigers prefer hunting as darkness falls. So on the spur of the moment Holt decided what must be done. He gathered the workers into camp and told them to keep a fire burning. He would go after the tiger. They warned him that no man could track a tiger at night, and he said, 'I'm not going to track him.'

He lit off by himself, picked up the trail of blood in the fading light, and followed the rough path along which the tiger had dragged the dead workman. When the bloody trail disappeared into thick jungle, Holt ignored it and kept to the path he had been on. Finally he came to a small clearing where jungle grass replaced the heavy trees. Here, in the last remaining moments of light, he surveyed the area and chose a tree whose branches formed twin forks about twelve feet above the ground.

Sweating like a pig, his hands cut by the rough bark of the tree, he climbed into this crude platform, braced himself, and took the precaution of using his belt to lash his knees to one of the limbs, so that even if he fell asleep he could not topple. Then he waited.

He kept his gun in his right hand, a strong flashlight in his left, and in the hours before midnight he listened to the wild night sounds that welled up from the Sumatran jungle. He heard pigs and night birds and insects. He judged that one almost silent movement in a tree close to his must have been a snake, but there were no poisonous ones in this region, so he paid no attention.

The sound he wanted to hear, the contented growl of a well-fed tiger picking its way home after a satisfactory feast, he did not hear that night, so at dawn he unfastened his knees, climbed down from the tree and slept for several hours in its shade, satisfied that the tiger would be sleeping too. The bad time came in the afternoon, when he became aware of the insects that were exploring him. The heat was unbearable. Sweat ran in alleyways down his back like a flood leaving a city. He had no water and could not risk searching for any, because aloft he saw vultures wheeling in for their share of the dead man, and this proved that the tiger had left that scene and was wandering somewhere in the jungle.

Holt was convinced that the tiger, having eaten his fill, would not again attack the work party but would leave the jungle depths and come along this trail to the opening and cross it to follow the trail on the other side. He judged that it would make its journey across the open space shortly after midnight.

How did Holt know this? Wherever he was stationed, he made it a point to learn as much about the terrain and the people as possible. He had an insatiable curiosity, plus the capacity to absorb and digest evidence. From his first days in Sumatra, when the various communication centers and relays were being built, he had been fascinated by tigers, and although he had never shot one, he appreciated what would be required to do so. He was as certain of his opinions on tigers as he was on his judgment of radio tubes: 'If you have your hideout higher than twelve feet, branches get in your line of sight. Lower, and the tiger can catch you when he leaps at the light.'

So at dusk Holt climbed back into his perch twelve feet above the ground—tired, sweaty, bitten by insects and ashen-mouthed from thirst. It was a long six hours to midnight and twice he dozed, but the belt-lashing kept him steady.

At midnight the now familiar sounds assailed him, but his ear was attuned for that one signal which escaped him. There was no tiger. At two in the morning a new sound developed, but it was some lesser animal preoccupied with its own problems. At four there still was no tiger and Holt grew heavy with sleep, but at five-thirty, just before dawn, he heard a savage rumbling, as if a satisfied tiger were talking to himself, and as the sound grew closer Holt began to sweat anew.

It was the beast, the most terrifying of all killers, and he was going to pass close to the tree, as Holt had predicted. The jungle night was so dense that not even the shadow cast by a star was visible, so the trick was to wait until the tiger approached the clearing, then, with the gun barrel and the flashlight in the left hand, to blind the beast with a sudden burst of light. For a moment the tiger would halt, confused by this unexpected confrontation, and in that moment you had to fire directly into the animal's heart, destroying his power. If you missed, a wounded tiger was on your trail and would never surrender until he died from loss of blood or tracked you down and killed you.

Holt fired and missed. Had he come prepared for shooting from a tree, he would have had a device to hold the flashlight, leaving his hands free to manage the gun. Or he would have had a helper to direct the light. As it was, when the light came on he was as terrified as the tiger, for directly below him reared this enormous beast, striped and monstrous with tooth and claw. When the flashlight touched the metal of the gun barrel it began to slip, and in trying to clutch it more firmly, Holt's left hand trembled, then lost control, and the shot went wild. Immediately he steadied the light and the gun and fired again, but the tiger had now leaped forward and the bullet ripped into its left shoulder. The force was great enough to drive the animal backward in mid-flight, but it struck no vital spot, and Holt heard the enraged beast thrashing among the lesser trees and bushes as it took refuge in the jungle.

Holt never said what his thoughts were at that critical moment, but I can deduce them from what he did. Although dawn was not quite upon him, he unfastened his belt, methodically ran it through the loops of his pants, tucked his troublemaking flashlight away, and carefully climbed down out of the tree. He then moved slowly about the trunk of the tree, keeping it always at his back, keeping his face toward the source from which the tiger's raging came. He hoped that the animal would attack him, but he knew that with the coming of dawn the great beast would judge that it had better retreat for the moment to lick its wounds, returning to the man later.

In the first pale light of morning Holt saw the bloody trail that he must follow. It never occurred to him that he had an option. The rule of every settlement in Sumatra or Malaya or Burma or India where tigers prowl was clear-cut: 'If you wound a tiger, you track him down and kill him. If you don't, he'll wipe out entire villages.'

All day Harvey Holt patiently tracked the wounded beast, growing ever more cautious, for he knew that as the tiger recovered from the shock of having been hit with a heavy bullet, his cunning would recover, too, and his rage for revenge increase. It was near noon when Holt realized that the tiger had gone over from the one pursued to the one pursuing.

That hot afternoon, with no food and no chance to stop by a stream lest the tiger leap upon him, was a hellish time for Holt. Of this he spoke to me once or twice in later years: 'How did I know he was still there? I sensed he was there. But of course he had the advantage. He could hear me!'

When twilight approached, Holt had his first sense of panic. If he did not encounter the beast in the few remaining minutes of light, what could he possibly do in the darkness? Would the tiger not just go off and disappear into the deep jungle? How could Holt track him then?

Any fear that the tiger might leave him was misguided, for when night forced Holt into another tree, the beast followed him and filled the empty spaces of the night with terrifying roars. He knew that in the morning the man would have to descend to those waiting teeth and extended claws. All night the animal thrashed and roared, but what made the scene diabolical was that on those occasions when Holt flashed his light, hoping for a shot at the beast, trees or brush would intervene, so that Holt could see the striped body but could not fire, because branches would deflect the bullet. And the tiger would move on like a malevolent ghost.

Now hunger attacked, and thirst. Twice Holt felt as if he simply must leap out of the tree to seek water; he even tested his knees against the belt to see if he could break it. I judge from scraps I picked up from Holt in later years that he must have been delirious part of the time, or at least assailed by sounds and images he could not control, but whatever precipitate action he might have contemplated was held in check by the snarling presence of the tiger. And so the night passed.

With dawn the tiger would present a clear target to the hunter, so he withdrew, and once more Holt methodically threaded his belt through his trouser loops, tucked his flashlight away, and climbed down to the hellish job that still faced him. All morning the man and the beast moved in purposeful circles, each trying to come upon the other in a position of advantage. Holt had two heavy bullets in his rifle. The tiger had two sets of claws, made doubly perilous by the sharp flashes of pain that coursed down his left side. No sun penetrated the heavy cover of branch and vine beneath which they moved. Once Holt had to drop to his knees beside a leaf-filled stream to drink, for he was perishing, but he had taken only a few disciplined sips when he sensed a movement behind him, and he had to get moving again.

At high noon the humidity of the jungle became intolerable. Holt once asked me: 'How could a man who was dying of thirst sweat so much?' Twice in this period he seems to have come close to fainting, but the threat of what moved behind the leafy façade kept him alert.

And then, toward mid-afternoon when the savage heat had abated a bit, Holt came to a second stream, and his loss of liquids had been so great that he could no longer restrain himself from falling on his stomach for a long drink. As he did so, the tiger, who had been counting on just this moment, knowing in his animal cunning that a man who moved so much and sweated so much would have to drink, sped from his cover near the stream, took three giant leaps, and came down with his great claws extended and his teeth ready, only to look into the barrel of a heavy rifle that had been swung at the last moment into position.

There was a shattering sound, then another. Without panic Holt fired directly into the chest of the flying tiger, and his hands were so steady that the second bullet struck almost precisely where the first had gone, shattering the great animal's bone structure and exploding its heart.

The claws, as if animated by a will of their own, slashed wildly at Holt, but missed. The massive face, rimmed with whiskers and striped fury, lunged so close to Holt's that he could feel the teeth brush his shoulder. The body, already quivering in death, fell across his, so that the gushing blood stained his clothes. And from the trees above, numerous birds and monkeys chattered of the amazing thing they had witnessed.

————•◆•————

As you have probably guessed, Harvey Holt loved hi-fi systems. He appreciated music for itself, but since he was also an electronics expert, he enjoyed the beautiful technicality of high fidelity. He built so many sets for others that sometimes an incoming shipment of mail, which had lain for weeks at some major distributing point, would contain half a dozen components that he had ordered for friends in whatever country he was then serving.

His own set, which I often listened to in Afghanistan, was a masterpiece costing well over three thousand dollars. He had a Marantz console from America, four omni-speakers from London, a specially constructed Mirachord turntable from Germany, a Roberts tape recorder with extra features added in Japan, and all sorts of sophisticated gear from Sweden and France. He had something like twenty-seven dials he could play with, so that his set could operate at a whisper or with the force of a hurricane. He preferred that his friends not touch the set—it was too complicated for anyone but an expert—but he was happy to demonstrate it for hours, if anyone was interested.

Holt was not a man whom many people liked. Respected, yes. Liked, no. But he did one thing which endeared him to all the music fans in his area. He would assemble from many sources the finest records available. Classical, rock-and-roll, country, soul— you name it. He preferred to use records that had been played only once or twice, and since a lot of men overseas imported excellent disks from Sam Goody or that outfit in Copenhagen, it was fairly easy to put together a representative sampling of any type of music.

Holt would then transcribe these records onto tape of high quality—say, twenty-nine of the best hot jazz numbers or the chamber music of Bach, including the six Brandenburg concerti— until he had a concert of a given type of music that would run a couple of hours. He was so skilled at this and his equipment was so precise that in the end he would have a tape rather better than any which the professional companies were making. He would then process it through his various machines and make half a dozen copies for his friends. The result would be music so flawless that life in the forgotten outposts would be a little more tolerable.

His own tastes were specific. He respected classical music, and sometimes when he was making a tape of Beethoven's nine symphonies or Verdi's *Requiem* for the local prime minister, he would admit grudgingly, 'Not too bad.' But he kept none of these tapes for himself. The raucous music of recent years he understood not at all, yet curiously enough, he enjoyed making transcriptions of it for the younger tech reps, for it presented a technical challenge: 'A record like that . . . pure noise . . . it sort of tests your equipment. Listen to how this gear picks up those bass notes and separates them.'

Spanish music, Mexican, oriental, Russian, Portuguese and everything in those genres he dismissed as 'gook spook.' I remember once when an aficionado asked him to make a tape from some valuable flamenco records. Holt listened to one minute of the first record, then growled, 'I'll do the gook spook but I'll be damned if I'll listen to it.' And he made the whole transcription electrically, in complete silence, without once permitting the offending noise to echo in his quarters. Grand opera was also gook spook, but oratorios or Masses for the dead, like the Verdi *Requiem*, were not. 'That's religious,' he said reverently.

What Holt liked was American popular music from the 1930s and 40s, those memorable years when the great bands crisscrossed the nation, playing in sumptuous ballrooms or over the midnight radio. By dint of careful search, he had assembled the finest records of that period and had constructed from them various tapes which evoked this classic period of American jazz, but after a while I noticed that whatever the program, he invariably slipped in three instrumental numbers which apparently summarized the epoch for him: 'A String of Pearls,' with Glenn Miller; 'In the Mood,' with Tex Beneke leading the old Miller band; and 'Take the A Train,' with Duke Ellington. Once, in Burma, I tried to quiz him on these pieces, but he responded only to my question about 'A String of Pearls.' 'Probably the best piece of music ever written' was all he said, but from other hints he dropped, I gathered that he liked these numbers because they recalled the days when he was a youth just beginning to date girls.

'It was great,' he told me once. 'You've got a Ford. A couple of couples. You drive fifty miles in to Cheyenne to hear Glenn Miller at the Crystal Ballroom or even a hundred and twenty into Denver to hear Charley Barnett at Elitch's Gardens. The lights would . . .' His voice trailed off. 'There's nothing like it now. Nothing.'

In the music he liked, Holt had excellent taste—no sobbing violins, no cheap echo chambers. He went for the hard, clean sound of American jazz and brought to the attention of his friends odd bits of music they might otherwise have missed. He was most partial to a razzmatazz outfit called The Empire City Six, who played a set of variations on 'The Battle Hymn of the Republic,' stepping up the pitch six different times until the room was shaking with glorious noise. He also introduced us to a strange piece of music which I had never heard of but which apparently meant a great deal to him. Louis Armstrong and Duke Ellington had collaborated on it, whiskey voice and heartbreak piano. 'Duke's Place,' it was called, and once Holt confided, 'It reminds me of all the lonely cafés I've eaten in.' It haunts me even now when Harvey plays it, an irritating, inconsequential piece of music that ought not to have the power of evocation it has: down at Duke's Place where we spent those aching, empty hours of our youth.

I can recall a dozen times in recent years when I have been visiting far corners of the earth, without comforts or good food or clean music. It was sweaty, lonely work, and even the fact that I was picking up good commissions made it no easier to take. Then I would hit the town where Harvey Holt was working and he would take me to his immaculate quarters, with the two toothbrushes hung just so, the latest copy of *Time*, some cold Tuborg in the refrigerator and a local girl preparing meat and potatoes in the kitchen, and I would sink into a rattan chair and Harvey would thread onto his machine one of his favorite tapes, but he would have picked it so that selections I liked were included, and I would sit back and hear the sounds I had once loved so well: 'Boogie Woogie,' with Artie Shaw; or 'Two O'Clock Jump,' with Harry James; or 'Muskrat Ramble,' with the Dukes of Dixieland. I sometimes had the feeling that it was Harvey Holt's well-disciplined world that saved my sanity.

It was not easy to talk with Holt. To the longest question, he would reply only with a grunt. Also, it was difficult to identify the places he talked about, since he never referred to cities or nations, only to the airports at which he had installed UniCom systems: 'It was when I was at Yesilkoy putting in the Big Rally II.' This meant that he had been working at the airport for Constantinople, installing a communications system of the second degree of complexity. I never knew where the name Big Rally came from, but there were four of them, and only the largest airports like Kennedy and Orly had Big Rally IV. With this you got radar, side bands, closed-circuit television and half a dozen relay stations about the country, all of which Harvey Holt could keep operating when he was left behind as the tech rep.

'Best job I ever had was Don Muang,' he told me once. Bangkok had come early in his career and he had spent two happy years in Siam. By then the pain of his divorce was wearing off and he was beginning to adjust to his well-organized bachelor's life. 'Don Muang was good.' It was also Kai Tak, not Hong Kong; Kemajoran, not Djakarta; and Dum-Dum, not Calcutta. You also had to be attentive when occasionally he used real names, for on the few occasions that he referred to cities and nations, he kept to the names he had learned in school. Thus it was Constantinople, Persia, Siam, and to hell with innovations like Istanbul, Iran and Thailand.

There was another subject for which Holt used a specialized vocabulary: the general area of life itself, the passions, triumphs and despairs that overtake the average man. For here he related all value judgments to Spencer Tracy and Humphrey Bogart. Like the haunting jazz of the thirties, the chain of excellent movies made by these two men pretty well summarized the life experience for Holt, as the following bits of conversation show.

The son of the Pan American agent in New Delhi cringes before a bully at the international school: 'You remember how Spencer Tracy made Freddy Bartholomew face up to life on that ship.'

A Japanese politician with a notable reputation proves to be a fraud: 'It's exactly like Spencer Tracy proving the facts about Miss Hepburn's husband.' Invariably he referred to lean and lovely Katharine Hepburn in the formal style, and once when an embassy wife in Indonesia gossiped about her, Holt rose and left the room.

Two men court the same secretary from the French embassy in Constantinople: 'You saw what happened when Humphrey Bogart and William Holden were both in love with Audrey Hepburn.'

This other Hepburn he always referred to as Audrey. For him there was only one Miss Hepburn, the actress.

An assistant faces a difficult job transporting a heavy piece of equipment to an outpost: 'You saw how Humphrey Bogart and Raymond Massey took their ship to Murmansk.'

An installation runs considerably over budget: 'Exactly what Spencer Tracy faced when he was trying to get Elizabeth Taylor married.'

A difficult job can be completed only by the exercise of indomitable will: 'Your problem is the same one Spencer Tracy faced when he was determined to catch that fish.'

An Indonesian government official has to make a crucial decision: 'You have to stick with it all the way, just like Humphrey Bogart when he was writing the truth about Rod Steiger and the fight racket.'

The agricultural attaché in the American embassy makes a damned fool of himself over a Hong Kong party girl: 'Who can explain these things? Look at the way Humphrey Bogart kept coming back to Ava Gardner after he had made her a great actress.' This one stumped me, as did many of his references. When I asked what picture he was referring to, he said, impatiently, 'You know. The one where a voice sang "Que Será, Será" in the background.'

He lived an intense emotional life which appeared, at casual inspection, to have been structured upon the films made by these two actors. Actually, it was the other way around; American life in those years was so clear-cut, the national values so well agreed upon, that films mirrored the consensus-type of life Holt led. Instead of his aping Tracy and Bogart, they were copying him. Art thus followed life, which is the preferred sequence; today art, especially popular music, invents new patterns which students follow in enthralled obedience.

Because Tracy and Bogart summarized the best that America was producing in those middle decades, Holt remembered almost every picture they had made and considered it appropriate that they had never appeared in the same film. 'They wouldn't have fitted,' he said when I asked about this. 'Completely different men.' He did not say, 'Their styles were different.' He said that as men they would have clashed, for he saw them not as actors but as living men who happened to be thrust into evocative situations.

Bogart represented the man Harvey Holt felt he was; Tracy, the gentleman he would have liked to be. At his frontier stations he had ample opportunity to watch his favorites in their best films, for construction firms provided their men with five films a week, and the oldies from 1940 to 1960 predominated. Once, when a woman dressmaker in Hong Kong had to go out of business because a Yugoslavian adventurer had stolen her cash, Holt sat morosely listening to Glenn Miller tapes and reflecting the matter. 'I keep thinking of the way Humphrey Bogart saved that newspaper for old Ethel Barrymore. A woman in business ought to have someone she can rely on.'

I said that Holt remembered almost every film made by his heroes, but when he told me they had never worked on the same picture, I was bothered, for I seemed to remember a still photograph showing them together in a movie about a prison riot. When I asked about this, Holt growled, 'Impossible. They'd destroy each other,' but I could not get that old photo out of my mind, so I wrote to a film magazine and received confirmation: they had played together in Tracy's first film but never thereafter. I forwarded the letter to Holt in Burma, and he wrote back: 'Must have been a terrible picture. I'd like to see it someday.'

Whenever Holt returned to the States for leave or instruction on new machines, he would hole up in a motel and sit before the television night after night, looking at the old movies. He was pleased that the people at home were able to enjoy the same old films that he had been enjoying in places like Chengmai and Kandahar. It was after one such visit home that Holt interrupted my sales pitch in Sumatra to say, 'Over in Pakanbaru the English people are showing a movie. I saw it years ago and again on television in Seattle. You ought to see it.'

We drove forty miles into the steaming town, where an English engineering firm had provided a coconut shed with an improvised screen and a flickering projection machine. Since there was only one projector, we had to sit around in pale electric light drinking gin while the projectionist changed reels. I sat next to a rubber expert from Germany and behind a Swiss who was trying to sell the Sumatrans a complicated machine for making glass. There were about fifty of us, come from all over central Sumatra, but none enjoyed the night's movie so much as Harvey Holt.

Perhaps enjoy is not the word. He lived each moment of the film with terrible intensity, giving me the impression that for him this was something more than another in the distinguished chain of Bogart movies. I had not seen it before nor even heard of it, and in subsequent weeks when I spoke of my experience in other camps I found no tech rep who had heard of it either. It was excellent. Bogart was a film writer in Hollywood, accused of murder and trusted only by Gloria Grahame. As the first spasmodic reels unfolded, you got the idea that it was just another murder mystery and that Miss Grahame was certain to save Bogart from the electric chair or gas chamber or whatever it was that California used. In the long intervals between reels we discussed this probable development with the German rubber man, who said approvingly, 'It takes the Americans or the French to put together a really good *policier*.' I asked if he thought Bogart had been involved in the murder of the young woman, and he said, 'Never. Not in an American film. In a French film, yes.'

This type of opinion held through the first four intermissions, but I noticed that Holt did not react to the guesses. He was the only one present who knew how the film came out, and he took quiet satisfaction in eavesdropping on our wrong guesses, for during the fifth intermission the German and I confessed that we had been mistaken. This was something more than a mere *policier*. It was a character study of the film writer in conflict with the likable girl who was befriending him. 'I have the curious feeling,' the German whispered as we looked out toward the jungles that encroached upon Pakanbaru, 'that Mr. Bogart is not going to get the girl this time. He's truly psychopathic . . . something like your friend Holt.'

And in the last reel Bogart did become the archetype of a tech rep—lonely, embattled, obstinate, totally incapable of understanding a woman—so that in the final shot he stalked off-camera, a defeated, bitter man taking his battle to some other terrain populated with other actors whom he would be incapable of understanding or adjusting to. It was a shocking end, and when the watery lights came on, and the night sounds of the jungle closed in upon us, a sense of loneliness pervaded the coconut shed. When the German said goodnight he added, 'Sometimes we get surprises, even in American films.'

On the long drive back to Holt's camp I said, 'I didn't catch the name of that movie.'

'*In a Lonely Place*,' he said. He rarely used the names of movies. In future conversations this would be spoken of as 'that time when Humphrey Bogart kicked away the love of Gloria Grahame.' He thought that Bogart should have received an Oscar for this film. 'Miss Grahame, too, for that matter, but she got one that time when she was Dick Powell's wife.' This missed me, but before I could query him, he added reflectively, 'Funny, Powell was a screenwriter too. I guess Miss Grahame goes for screenwriters.'

On the impulse of the moment I asked, 'When you tracked down the tiger, did you imagine yourself to be Humphrey Bogart?' He turned away from the steering wheel and looked at me in astonishment, saying nothing. I pointed to the road and he returned to his driving. After some minutes of silence he said, 'So far as I know, Humphrey Bogart was never in Sumatra.' Later he added, 'Miss Grahame . . . in some of those last scenes . . . she looked like Lora Kate.' I supposed that Bogart in his domestic chaos had looked a good deal like Harvey Holt, but I kept my mouth shut, and when we got back to the camp out of which Holt was working, he asked, 'You like to hear some music?'

He threaded his machine with a tape he had built up patiently through several years, one that held all the songs and ballads of the golden age when the great bands carried frail and beautiful girls with them, some with surprising voices, and we sat in the darkness of the jungle as those wispy voices came to us from Frank Dailey's Meadowbrook, Glen Island Casino and Station WOR, laden with lush sentiment: 'That Old Black Magic,' 'Falling in Love with Love,' as sung by Sarah Vaughan, Ella Fitzgerald's 'Love for Sale,' and 'Night and Day,' sung by three different soloists. When 'Green Eyes' unexpectedly appeared, Holt apologized for the Spanish intrusion. 'Normally I don't go in for this gook spook, but this one was a great favorite of Lora Kate's.'

'Where'd you meet her?'

'College. Colorado Aggies at Fort Collins. Grew up in Fort Morgan.'

'What happened?'

The tape had come to one of the songs that Holt liked most, 'Sentimental Journey.' 'I heard this for the first time in camp on Iwo Jima. I was a kid eighteen. I wondered if I would ever know any beautiful women like the ones I had seen singing with the big bands. You know, Helen Forrest and Martha Tilton. Or Bea Wain, for that matter.' He hesitated. 'It wasn't that I was afraid of being killed. I'd seen so many men get it that I knew this was pure chance. Like Humphrey Bogart when he was fighting Sydney Greenstreet for the statue.'

He rewound and reversed the tape so that he could hear 'Sentimental Journey' again, and said nothing till it played through, heavy with the longing of old nights. When the tape passed on to 'I've Got You Under My Skin,' he turned down the volume and said, 'So when I got home safe and saw this really terrific girl in chemistry . . . we got married . . . I wanted to work overseas . . . to hell with Wyoming and Colorado . . .' He laughed. 'You ever try to make a woman from Fort Morgan, Colorado, happy at Yesilkoy?'

We played music till dawn: 'Just One of Those Things,' 'I'll Never Smile Again,' 'Symphony.' When Ella Fitzgerald sang 'I've Got You Under My Skin,' Holt repeated the tape three times, and as we went to bed he said, 'I've never been much with the black people, but they sure can sing.'

Holt got good pay. When you were a tech rep you could pick up extra money if you volunteered for what they called hazardous duty. Holt always did, for although he was instinctively afraid of the towers on which communications were based, he had schooled himself to climb them.

'I was stationed at Gago Coutinho . . .'

'You lost me.'

'Moçambique,' he said impatiently. 'Coutinho flew the Atlantic years ahead of Lindbergh. We had finished putting in a Big Rally II and the others had gone back home. This typhoon was blowing across the Indian Ocean—heading away from us but still with a powerful sting in its tail. Snapped off the top of our tower four miles outside of Gago Coutinho—but not all the way off. One girder refused to break loose . . . kept the steel mass hanging there . . . thrashing hell out of what was left. So somebody had to climb up there and cut it away. You face these things. It's like Humphrey Bogart driving that truck when he left Ann Sheridan's restaurant.'

Later, when I was surveying Moçambique for an industrial

project we had in mind, the Portuguese weatherman at Gago Coutinho told me what had happened that night. 'Such winds. Maybe ninety miles an hour. One stubborn girder refused to let loose. We could see it with binoculars. The manager of the station yelled, "Somebody has got to go up there and cut that junk loose." You could hear it crashing against the tower. If it hit a man it would crush him in an instant, so the manager kept yelling for volunteers, but he certainly made no move of his own and none of the Portuguese or the natives wanted any of it. He looked at me and said, "You're the weatherman. It's as much your tower as anybody else's." But I walked away. Then Harvey Holt drove up, and when the manager began yelling at him, he said, "Get me a torch," and the manager, who had worked in England, started yelling to all of us to find a flashlight, but Holt said, "Acetylene." And believe it or not, he climbed that tower in that storm with that mass of steel slamming against the struts. We could see him from down here . . . the white, flickering light at a great height . . . a ghost . . . a ghost.'

Holt lashed himself to the girder, whose twisted top refused to break loose, and with his torch began cutting through the contorted metal, but as he worked, the rest of the top, thrown about by the gale as if it were balsa wood, kept crashing into the pylon, so that he had constantly to withdraw his hands and feet lest they be crushed by the steel. He worked for nearly half an hour in this way, cutting a little whenever a lull in the wind permitted but most of the time dodging the flying steel.

When the girder was almost cut away, a savage arm of the typhoon roared inland from the ocean and carried away not only the flapping top but also the girders below, including the one to which Holt had lashed himself. The weatherman told me, 'We watched in terror as the top part plunged to the earth, wiping out wires and wooden buildings. We thought Holt was on this portion, but his girder must have been very tough, for again it refused to break, although all the others did. So for at least ten minutes this new length of steel flapped back and forth in the gale . . . with Holt lashed to part of it. We were sure he would be either crushed or thrown loose.'

'I hung on,' Holt said later.

When the invading gale retreated, having done its damage, Holt gingerly unfastened the lashings which had saved him, reached out and climbed from the flapping steel onto the lower reaches of the tower, from which he calmly proceeded to cut away the girder. When I asked him how, through all that tossing, he had managed to hold onto the acetylene torch, he said, 'If your job is to cut steel, you sure as hell don't drop your torch.'

The highlight of Holt's life had been his service with the marines, and the apex of this service had been not Iwo Jima or Okinawa or Korea, at each of which he had won decorations, but rather his boot training at Parris Island, where he fell into the hands of a drill sergeant named Schumpeter. 'He took me a boy and sent me out a man,' Holt said. Obviously he worshiped Schumpeter the way he did Humphrey Bogart and Spencer Tracy, but he rarely said much about him except that he owed Schumpeter both his life and his scale of values.

During the early years when I was becoming acquainted with Holt, I supposed that in the training at Parris Island, Schumpeter had interceded in some accident to save him, but that was not what Holt meant. The salvation had been spiritual and had come through the iron drilling Schumpeter had given in the fundamentals of man-to-man warfare. 'A lot of fellows older than I was thought they knew it all,' Holt said cryptically. 'A fat belly like Schumpeter couldn't tell them anything. They're dead.'

'What was it he told you?'

'Lots of things . . . useful things . . . like special ways to care for a gun . . . or use a bayonet.' Holt refused to talk of his war experiences, but he did add this: 'Any good drill sergeant could teach you that, of course. What Schumpeter added was a philosophy of war. To him it was two things. Something you damned well better win. And something you had damned well better live through.'

Several times I tried to press Holt on these points, but he refused to say anything except that Schumpeter may have been a fat belly, as the others said, but when the marines shipped him out to Okinawa for having slugged an officer, he performed on the battlefield even better than he had in the drill hall. 'A lot of man with a lot of belly,' Holt said grimly. 'He was no loudmouth.'

It was by chance one night in Baghdad that I learned about Holt at war. A marine colonel on detached duty with the Iraqi army happened to sit next to me at the bar of our hotel and we got to talking about one thing and another, and when he heard that I did a lot of work with tech reps, he said, 'You ever run into a fabulous guy named Harvey Holt?'

Turned out he had been Holt's platoon lieutenant on Okinawa. 'Just turned eighteen, with stars in his eyes. He was sort of beautiful, so straightforward and gung ho, but he damned near drove me nuts. Every time I gave an order, he'd say, "Sergeant Schumpeter told us to do it this way," until I demanded that he be ticketed to some other outfit. The captain called us in and said he was sure we could get this straightened out, but I said I was sick to my gut of hearing about Sergeant Schumpeter, so the captain asked Holt, "What about this, son?" and Holt said, "All I know is that on Iwo Jima, I did things the way he said and I'm alive. The smart alecks are dead." The captain repeated that he felt sure I would be able to bring Holt into line, so I said, "Isn't Schumpeter that loudmouth who was broken last month because he slugged the officer at Parris Island?" and when we looked into it, we found that he had been sent to Okinawa as punishment.

'Well, Holt went all apeshit running around the island till he found Schumpeter, and that afternoon the Japs struck, as you probably read. It was one hell of a go, and right at the point where they hit us hardest were Holt and Schumpeter, a two-man army. It was really something to see . . . sort of beautiful. I was about a hundred yards behind them, totally pinned down. It was murder that afternoon . . . murder. And these two characters stayed there inside the three walls of a shattered hut and you would have thought they were Napoleon and Ulysses S. Grant. They made not one false move. Christ, they even sortied at one point, right into a machine gun that couldn't be swung around in time to hit them. I'm convinced the Japs thought there were at least fifty men in that hut. It was really sort of poetic, like the way Homer might have described a couple of Greeks, say, Achilles and Ajax—a young boy and a busted sergeant with a huge gut.'

The colonel began laughing, and I said it was funny to think of Harvey Holt as a Greek, but he said, 'I wasn't laughing about that. It was Schumpeter. That night after he and Holt rejoined us and everybody was telling them what a hell of a show they had put on and they ought to get a Silver Star or something, some Japs took a position from which they could bang-bang right into us, and I asked for volunteers to gun them from the rear—not too difficult a job—and I happened to see Schumpeter making himself real small in a corner, and after the team had gone out I said half-jokingly, "Schumpeter, you look scared," and Holt barked at me, "Of course he is. You would be too." I turned to this bright-faced kid and started to ask him who . . .

'He broke in very fast and said, "In boot camp Schumpeter taught us that a man has only so many chances each day, and when they're used up, lie low. He also taught us that a man is a horse's ass ever to get mixed up with the troubles of another outfit. He'll have enough pain with his own. This isn't his outfit and he's afraid to try to get back. Because today he's used up his chances."

'I suppose these days the smart boys would construct some fantastic theory about Holt and Schumpeter to prove their relationship was latent homosexuality. Anyway, Holt appealed over the captain's head and got transferred to Schumpeter's outfit, where—as he probably told you—he won all sorts of medals.'

'He told me nothing.'

'Back there I said a two-man army. It was really a one-man army, with Schumpeter doing the coaching. Holt was one of the real heroes of Okinawa. They gave him a battlefield commission. He was scheduled to lead one of the units ashore when we invaded Japan. He asked for Schumpeter as his sergeant, but the fat guy said that his luck was used up and he went home. He's a drill sergeant again at Parris Island. When the marines get a good man, they keep him.'

In my opinion, the most surprising fact about Harvey Holt was his ability to quote poetry, for he was not a literary man, nor even one who bothered with the arts, yet in his freshman year at Colorado Aggies a Professor Carrington had asked during one of the first meetings of English 101 how many students could quote an entire poem, regardless of length. When only two hands went up, he cried, 'Disgraceful. Poems are the world's repository of significant experience and you ought to know some of them.' He then said something which impressed Holt as being profound, as if no man prior to Carrington could have entertained such a thought: 'Memorize a poem and you own it for life.' Carrington had then made this proposition to his students: 'For every fourteen lines of poetry you memorize before mid-terms, I will give you five extra points on your examination. Why do I nominate fourteen lines as the measure?'

A smart girl who had gone to high school in Massachusetts said, 'Because that's a sonnet.'

Holt had not heard the word before.

'So there it is! You memorize twenty sonnets—and not only will your grade be one hundred, but you will be immeasurably richer.'

Holt, captivated by this bold proposal, went to Carrington's office that afternoon to ask his advice on what to memorize, and Carrington asked, 'Long or short?' and to his own astonishment Holt replied, 'Maybe something long,' and Carrington said, 'For a young man in an agricultural college, there are only three to consider' and he laid them out: Matthew Arnold's 'The Scholar-Gipsy,' Oliver Goldsmith's 'The Deserted Village' and Thomas Gray's 'Elegy Written in a Country Churchyard.'

The first was quite beyond Holt's comprehension and the second was too long. He said, 'I'll try this one,' and he could still remember those autumn days—when early snow appeared on the Rockies to the west and aspen turned gold along the Cache la Poudre—when he had memorized the simple, exquisite lines.

A curious thing happened. When he came to the last three stanzas, which constituted the epitaph, he found them printed in italic, and these he memorized in funereal tones, as if they were part of a church service. When it came time to recite the poem to Professor Carrington he botched up some of the more difficult central stanzas, but when he reached the italicized stanzas he could see them line by line engraved in heaven, and with profound gravity he delivered the epitaph for this young man who had lived and died unknown in a forgotten village:

> *Here rests his head upon the lap of Earth*
> *A Youth to Fortune and to Fame unknown.*
> *Fair Science frowned not on his humble birth,*
> *And Melancholy marked him for her own.*

Professor Carrington coughed and told the Okinawa veteran, 'You pass.'

In his lonely work at the outposts, Holt had perfected his memorization of this poem and could now recite it practically without error. He had also memorized large chunks of 'Horatius at the Bridge,' and since this was done after his service on Okinawa, he recognized that certain lines of this poem epitomized Sergeant Schumpeter, and now when he recited them in the jungle or along the edge of the desert, he thought of his drill master:

> Then out spake brave Horatius,
>   The Captain of the Gate:
> 'To every man upon this earth
>   Death cometh soon or late;
> And how can man die better
>   Than facing fearful odds
> For the ashes of his fathers,
>   And the temples of his Gods?'

But the two poems which Holt had grown to love best were two that I had not known before I heard him recite them. The first was a rollicking ballad he had picked up from some Australians who worked with him at one of his stations, 'The Man from Snowy River.' It dealt with a wild chase downhill during a stampede of horses, and it was a man's poem, filled with manly images and robust rhymes. When Holt recited its larruping lines he threw his head back, and you could see him upon a horse, galloping down the side of some sunset mountain, disregarding the rocks and crevices. He always made you feel that the poem was better than it was, and I wondered why I had not heard of it. He told me it was a great favorite throughout Australia, and he made a deep impression on tough Aussies in various parts of Asia by standing in the shadows of some bar and slowly beginning the lines which made their pulses quicken:

> He sent the flint-stones flying but the pony kept his feet
>   He cleared the fallen timber in his stride
> And the man from Snowy River never shifted to his feet—
>   It was grand to see that mountain horseman ride.

The other poem was something quite special. I've asked a good many knowledgeable people about this epic of the American west, and so far no one has heard of it. Apparently it has always had

wide circulation in states like Wyoming and Colorado, where almost any campfire will produce at least one man who has memorized it. The rhythm is peculiar in a wild, undisciplined prairie
sort of way. I remember asking Holt several times if he was
quoting the opening lines correctly, so he wrote off to Denver for
a copy—and there it was:

> . . . Lasca used to ride
> On a mouse-gray mustang close to my side.

The poem told of an outlaw cowboy who had only one friend in
the world, a tough Mexican girl named Lasca, who shared his luck
through many adventures in the west, until the day when . . .
Well, the ending is rather sticky, sort of a cowboy epic, but the
power which these lines had to make ranch hands stare into space
was extraordinary, or so Holt said.

I gathered that Harvey loved the poem because it assured him
that occasionally in life lucky men sometimes do find women who
will share the frontier, who will ride side by side. When the Ford
Motor Company brought out a new car and called it the Mustang,
Holt bought one of the first and had it shipped to Sumatra, but
after a while he sold it.

Once as we drove across the semi-desert in Afghanistan he told
me, 'What I'd really like would be to have a couple of horses in
one of the villages along the desert. And some girl who would be
willing to ride . . . you know, she'd have her mustang, I'd have
mine.'

If any base at which he worked had married couples, he went out
of his way to be courtly and proper to the wives. He said that
marriage was by and large a good thing and one should do what he
could to make women feel needed. It was obvious that his own
divorce rankled deeply, a mark of defeat for which he was principally to blame, and whenever he contemplated his failure to find
a faithful woman like Lasca, you could see the disappointment in
his face.

I never heard him speak poorly of his wife, but a man who had
known them both in Turkey said of her, 'A real tramp. Slept with
three different men in Istanbul and shacked up with the steward
on the boat home. Harvey was lucky to get rid of her.'

Harvey did not think so. Frequently he spoke of the excellent care she gave their son, and once when he showed me a photograph of the boy, I saw beside him a very attractive woman in her thirties with blond hair and a movie-star kind of face. I said, 'She's prettier than the girls who used to sing with the bands,' and he agreed.

I never learned all of 'Lasca.' Its broken rhythms were not in my style, but I knew enough lines to throw them at Holt when we were driving from one base to another, and he would pick them up, and soon our car would become a pair of horses and we were riding through the west with a fiery Mexican girl at our side:

> She would hunger that I might eat,
> Would take the bitter and leave me the sweet;
> But once, when I made her jealous for fun,
> At something I'd whispered, or looked or done . . .
> She drew from her garter a dear little dagger,
> And—sting of a wasp!—it made me stagger!
> An inch to the left, or an inch to the right,
> And I shouldn't be maundering here to-night;
> But she sobbed, and sobbing, so swiftly bound
> Her torn *rebosa* about the wound,
> That I quickly forgave her. Scratches don't count
> In Texas, down by the Rio Grande.

The word which best symbolized Harvey Holt was patriotism, both in its ugly sense and in its best. He could not abide living in the United States, yet he loved the country and all it stood for: 'By and large, it's the best nation on earth, and if you can't trust us, you can't trust anybody.' If you had asked him at seventeen why he wanted to enlist in the marines, he would have mumbled something about his country's being in trouble. If you had asked why he acted as he had at Iwo Jima or Okinawa, he would have offered some incoherent answer about his nation and peril. And when I wanted an explanation as to why he was chucking a good job with UniCom to fight in Korea, he told me, 'Who can rest easy if his country's at war?' And now, even though he did not understand the trouble in Vietnam too clearly, he supported our government and felt that Eisenhower and Kennedy had known what they were doing, but he wasn't too sure about Johnson.

It was his opinion that a solid stint with the marines would be good for any young man, and he wished that more of the contemporary generation could spend some time with Sergeant Schumpeter: 'He'd knock some sense into their heads.'

But his patriotism stopped short of blind subservience. It tended that way, but his shattering experience in Korea dispelled any idea he might have had that those who happen to be in command are always right.

The disaster began in late November of 1950 when his marine outfit started a triumphal march north from Hungnam to the Chinese border. The North Korean army was in confusion, and our high command believed that if the marines could compress it against the reservoirs in the north, they could destroy it and the Koreans would have to surrender. There was even confident talk that the war would be cleaned up by Christmas.

But as the march proceeded, Holt became increasingly apprehensive. He was then a full lieutenant, and kept warning his captain, 'You know, Sergeant Schumpeter would be sick if he ever saw this marching order.'

'And who the hell is Sergeant Schumpeter?'

'Boot camp.'

'He probably knew a lot about drill, but this is war.'

'He also knew a lot about war.'

Holt got nowhere with his warning, and this annoyed him, for he could see that his marines had to be headed for trouble. He was so concerned that he insisted upon speaking with the major and then the colonel.

He said, 'I don't want my marines spread so thin that one man can't see the man ahead of him. The enemy could infiltrate us so easy . . .' He was assured that the high command, both in Japan and Korea, knew what it was doing, that this was the final push and that with luck they'd have the North Koreans backed up to the reservoirs within six days.

'What about the Chinese?' he asked. They told him that intelligence had the Chinese problem under control, but when he returned to his men and found them even more strung out than when he left, he remembered Sergeant Schumpeter's dictum that troops had to be kept compact, especially when moving into country that the enemy had recently held, so he tried to bring his front men back and his rear men forward, in order to maintain some semblance of cohesion, but when he had completed this move, a major stormed up and yelled, 'Goddammit, Holt, you're creating big gaps front and back. Now forget your own little problem and get these troops back into position.'

Holt had obeyed, but when he reviewed his men he found that it took him more than thirty minutes to run from the lead man to the tail. Few of his marines could see their buddies fore or aft, and as for enemy infiltration, he told me later, 'Infiltrate? Hell, the Chinese could have marched a company of men right across the heart of our company, if they had spaced themselves. As a matter of fact, that's what they did.'

'How were you sure they were Chinese?'

'Intelligence, of course, were sure they weren't. But if you march straight at a country's border, isn't it natural for that country to send its troops south?'

At dusk on the fifth day, when Holt was numb with anxiety, the Chinese infiltrators struck, precisely as he knew they would, and because the marines were so strung out, so incapable of supporting one another, the slaughter was sickening. If ever in the history of American arms our leadership betrayed our foot soldiers, it was during this march north to the reservoirs. Our marines were thrown blindly against an enemy that had not been identified, located, estimated or prepared against. Our men were forced to march in indefensible dispositions, with inadequate support, inadequate food, inadequate ammunition. It was not a gamble of great dimension which, if it had succeeded, would have led to some great triumph; it was sheer stupidity enforced by blind arrogance, and it collapsed in tragedy as it was destined to do from the first.

Holt once told me at Don Muang, when I met him after an upland trip through Thailand, 'Marines like me were taught to think of the Chinese as skinny, weak-willed little guys from Canton who ate rice and ran laundries. The official doctrine was that one marine was equal to ten gooks. Well, the Chinese we met at the reservoirs were from the north. They ate meat and potatoes. They weren't skinny. They weren't weak-willed. And God knows, they weren't little. In the first fights they kicked the shit out of us. Now grant they had every advantage. They were in compact formations and we were spread all over the landscape, but they licked us . . . they licked us very bad.'

It was against these big, well-fed northern Chinese that Harvey Holt performed one of the gallant acts of the Korean War. In weather that had turned bitter cold, with snow falling and supplies nonexistent, he gathered his shattered company in a low cover of trees, made a brutal assessment of their capacity—'No food, no water, no ammunition, no heavy guns, no captain, no communication with headquarters, no plan'—and by sheer guts led them south for eleven days, holding them together, avoiding combat with the Chinese wherever possible, and inspiring them with the belief that they could make it back to Hungnam and the boats that would evacuate them.

It was an ordeal. A newspaperman, who came upon the unit when it was one day out of Hungnam, wrote a glowing account of the bravery these men were exhibiting even then. He could only guess what it must have been like farther north. When the high command heard what Holt had accomplished they made him a captain on the spot, and every man among the survivors applauded. There was not one who said, 'Aw, he didn't know his ass from his elbow. He was lucky.' They knew that Holt had known. It was of this experience that he once told me, 'I owe my life to Sergeant Schumpeter,' for apparently when the days and nights of retreat became intolerable—truly more than a man could bear—he had recalled the bellowed advice of Schumpeter: 'Keep your men together. Keep to the high ground even if it kills you. In freezing weather wrap a cloth about your breechlock at night. Don't bother to melt snow to drink it. Eat the snow. You'll get the water.' And so on, through that litany of accumulated experience that runs a straight line back to Hannibal and Scipio.

When memory of the disaster had faded, masked as much as possible by clever propaganda releases, the agencies of public opinion swung into action to convert the Hungnam retreat into a victory. The riposte of a marine colonel was widely broadcast: 'Retreat, hell. We're advancing in a new direction.' Even a movie was made with that title, its flamboyant heroism sparking a new faith in the marines. It now became fashionable to speak of the retreat as a glorious feat of arms, planned for in advance and proving the superiority of American troops.

Holt knew different. It was a disaster, a crushing defeat. An ill-led and ill-prepared American army had been overwhelmed by a well-led and well-prepared Chinese army, and if there was glory in the affair, one had to fall back upon strange definitions to substantiate it. Heroism, yes. Glory, no. Unless there is glory in completely botching a job and escaping with more men than chance would have dictated.

In later years Holt tried to get his Korean experience into focus. The fact that it had been so sorely mismanaged did not disqualify the marines. They were following orders, and although they did look pathetic when the Chinese hit, they had quickly reestablished themselves and had even shown a certain grandeur in their ability to absorb defeat and still withdraw in order and not in rout. In Holt's reappraisal the ordinary marines did not suffer.

The high command, both marine in Korea and army in Japan, were subjected to severe criticism at first, for Holt, at the lieutenant's level, had easily foreseen what was going to happen, what had to happen, and he thought it strange that the high-powered intelligence types had been blind to the inevitabilities. He blamed them principally.

General MacArthur came in for no blame whatever: 'He was back in Tokyo and had to rely on what intelligence told him.' I asked whether MacArthur could have known that the marines were marching north into the jaws of three hundred thousand enemy in single-file formation, with thirty yards between men. 'A general can't know everything. I don't fault MacArthur. It was like when Humphrey Bogart guided his boat into those weeds with the leeches. He couldn't be expected to know everything.'

Then, as time passed, Holt looked back upon the Hungnam catastrophe as a minor incident that overtakes armies and nations: 'We pulled out of it.' In fact, when the Vietnam war escalated, he made a great effort to get an active assignment, but was informed that he was too old for his rank. He told me once that he thought of the whole Vietnam war as an overgrown Hungnam miscalculation. 'Something went wrong somewhere, but a few good men could straighten it out.' If he had not had his experience with the incompetence of Hungnam, he would surely have blamed Vietnam solely on the politicians, as did most of the other tech reps. Holt, having seen for himself what could happen with even the best intentions, was not so sure.

———•◆•———

Why, in my travels, did I go out of my way to see Harvey Holt? Why, of all the tech reps I worked with, was he the one who captivated my interest?

The reason was bizarre. I first met Holt, as I have said, at Yesilkoy in 1954, just after his wife had stormed out of Turkey. Since his quarters were empty, he offered me a bedroom while I peddled World Mutual to other technicians in the Constantinople area; and one day when I was about to take my shower, I ran into Holt leaving the bathroom with a towel about his middle. Across his chest I saw a vivid scar. It looked as if a jagged streak of lightning had struck and seared itself into position. Normally one ignores the wounds of others, uncertain as to how the wounded will react to questioning, but this was so conspicuous, so fearsome you might say, that I had to speak.

'You get it in Korea?'

'Nope. Pamplona. Last year.'

This stopped me, and Holt obviously intended saying nothing more, but then a flash of memory came to my assistance. 'Isn't that the town in northern Spain that Hemingway wrote about?'

'Yep.'

'You mean a bull did that?'

'Yep.' And that was all he said that day, but a couple of evenings later, when a friend of his had some Spanish records he wanted transferred to tape, and when the garish trumpets and flourishes had died away, Holt said, 'We were putting in a Big Rally III at Portela, and in late June some of the men who had been in Portugal for a couple of years asked me if I was going up to Pamplona for the running of the bulls. I'd never heard of the place, but they made it sound so interesting that I said I'd like to go along, but I didn't want any part of running in front of bulls. "Hell," they said, "we never touch the bulls. We check in at Bar Vasca and stay drunk for eight days and listen to music and watch other damned fools run with the bulls. That's for idiots."

'So I went to Pamplona, and I checked in at Bar Vasca and listened to the music, and for three mornings I watched others run before the bulls, and on the fourth morning—why, I'll never know —I was there in the narrow street as the bulls thundered past me. On the eighth morning a big Pablo Romero caught me right in the chest. But for horn wounds, Pamplona has the best doctors in the world. They get practice.' Instinctively he pressed his right hand against his shirt to feel the ridges of scar left by the operation.

After that first experience with Pamplona, Holt's contract with UniCom had provided that his vacation begin on July 1. On that day he would report to the nearest airfield and fly to Rome, which he considered the best city in the world. Perched in the lovely square that faces the ancient church of Santa Maria in Trastevere, he would waste two days watching the stately vaudeville show of tourists, priests, cadgers, pretty girls, gigolos and harassed waiters. Late in the afternoon of July 3 he would fly to Madrid, where I would be waiting, for after my initiation in 1958, I, too, became addicted to Pamplona and the ridiculous hilarity of Bar Vasca. On the Fourth of July, Holt would report formally to the American embassy, where he would sign the book and present his respects to the ambassador. That night we would go to bed early, so that on the fifth we could rise before dawn, take our last warm bath for a long time, pack our rented car and be on our way by sunrise.

We planned our arrival in Pamplona for late afternoon, so that we could have our pick of rooms at Bar Vasca—not that any of them were any good—and on the sixth we would sit in the public square and watch the fireworks and meet old friends from all parts of Europe. Five-thirty on the morning of the seventh all hell would break loose from the marching bands assembled in the plaza before Bar Vasca, at which Holt would carefully climb out of bed and stand before the clothes which he had laid out with neat care the night before: tennis shoes, white pants, red belt, white shirt, red scarf. Clad in this historic costume he would go forth to meet the bulls.

For Holt, this compulsive running with wild animals had become a religious ritual, the act which gave his otherwise routine life structure and meaning. When he had first explained the running, I had had no comprehension of what it signified—to him or to others—and even when I saw it for the first time myself, it was nothing more than insanity in the streets, but then someone who knew that I knew Holt said, 'I suppose he's shown you those great photographs from 1953.' When I replied that Holt would never show anyone photographs of himself, the man said, 'They're on display at the Kodak shop around the corner,' and we went over to see them. In 1969 the series was still on display in the same shop, and copies were sold each year, for better than any other these photographs epitomized Pamplona.

I keep a set in Geneva, and strangers who know nothing of Pamplona or Harvey Holt can scarcely credit what the camera shows. They see Holt running a few inches ahead of the stampeding bulls. They see him looking back over his shoulder, laughing, as if this were the apex joy a man could know. They see him stumble in front of the charging bulls. They see five bulls and ten steers run right over him, as if he were a paving block. And most spectacular of all, they see the final bull sink his right horn into Holt's chest and throw him in the air. The last shot shows Holt landing on his head, feet aloft, with blood already staining his white shirt, while the six bulls and their accompanying steers disappear.

Until you see these photographs you cannot understand Pamplona, and until you know that for the following sixteen years the principal actor in the photographs came back to run with the bulls—a total of a hundred and twelve mornings, six hundred and seventy-two bulls, any one of which could have gored him the way the Pablo Romero did—you cannot understand Harvey Holt.

'Why would a man do that . . . voluntarily?' many of my guests in Geneva have asked. When I have explained that he has gone back every year since to repeat, they have been incredulous. 'He was extremely lucky. Look . . . those bulls are running right over him!'

And when I tell them that in addition to this first near-fatal goring, Holt has been hit three other times, so that his torso now looks like a pincushion, they mumble, 'Idiot.'

Finally I show them the photograph of Pamplona which for me best captures the fey quality of the place. It is early morning, of course, and the streets through which the bulls are running are packed with daring men in their white costumes. Harvey Holt has obviously been running like hell right before the horns, but now the moment has come when he can no longer keep ahead of the bulls. He feels their panting breath on his back, so with a superb act of gallantry he draws to one side, rises on his tiptoes, throws his arms high in the air, sucks in his gut, and hangs there poised like the noblest of the Greek statues while the bulls rush by, their horns less than an inch from his waist. Man, the animal, has rarely looked more glorious than in this confrontation with bull, the larger animal; he hangs suspended in time, in space, in meaning. John Keats would have understood this photograph and would not have asked, 'Why would a man do such a thing?' The more pertinent question would be, 'If any man finds such joy in a given act, why would he do anything else?'

X

PAMPLONA

To be young, and in love, and in Pamplona, and in July is heaven itself.

Theoretically, the bullfights at Pamplona are held to honor the bull. Nine fights of six bulls each mean 54 bulls in all. Last year of that number 21 were underweight, 14 had had their horns shaved, 6 especially ferocious ones were served sedatives in their corral water, and the 5 biggest ones had been slowed down by having three-hundred-pound sacks of cement dropped on their kidneys from a height of seven feet.

The fool wanders, the wise man travels.—Thomas Fuller

When J. Edgar Hoover announced that no respectable citizen could trust men who wore long hair and beards, Claude told the local Associated Press man, 'Well, that takes care of Jesus Christ and Ulysses S. Grant.'

Don't put off for tomorrow what you can do today, because if you enjoy it today you can do it again tomorrow.

Lie down, I think I love you.

My old man shouts, 'Goddammit, you should listen to my fifty-eight years of experience,' but what he had was one year of experience repeated fifty-eight times.

Blow in my ear and I'll follow you anywhere.

The only man who propositioned me all night was this old geezer who had reached the age of metal. Silver in his hair, gold in his teeth, and lead in his ass.

Crabbed age and youth cannot live together.—Shakespeare

True courage is to do without witnesses everything that you are capable of doing before all the world.—La Rochefoucauld

> It seems to be an immutable law of human nature that each new generation will dress, speak, make love, and listen to music in the way best calculated to infuriate their elders.

King Kong died for our sins.

St. Paul was certainly a cat who knew
The urge, that demi-urge
To see beyond the last bend in the road.

When Ulysses spoke before the Athens P.T.A.
And told the good Greek ladies of
The wonders he had known, the mighty wonders,
The ladies cried, 'Son, you has been smokin' hash.'

I feel that urge, that demi-urge to give the shaft
To good old Lewis B.
And to escape, my ship will sail beyond the stars
Till it make juncture with Ulysses
And we head outward to the straits.

If you seek martyrdom, St. Paul's your boy,
He knew the way and ended on the block.
If you want ostracism and rejection,
Ulysses is your boy. He gigged them all.
But if you seek yourself, cling to me, baby,
For I am truly lost, lost, lost,
And in the losing we shall find ourselves.

A man who leaves home to mend himself and others is a philosopher; but he who goes from country to country guided by blind impulses of curiosity is only a vagabond.—Oliver Goldsmith

A great country cannot wage a little war.—Duke of Wellington

> Southern Florida is filled with people sixty-eight years old who were going to do something big in their lives but waited till it was safe. Now it's safe and they are sixty-eight years old.

This world has no leaders. Convert the ordinary man on your left.

I N northern Spain, where roads converge, there stands an old Roman bridge of surpassing beauty at a spot called, for historical reasons no one now remembers, Puente La Reina—Queen Bridge, and not Bridge of the Queen, as some would translate it.

When Harvey Holt and I reached this point in the late afternoon of July 5 on our trip north from Madrid, we felt a surge of excitement, even though we had made the trip together eleven times before. Holt looked at the speedometer and said with satisfaction, 'Exactly six miles more,' and we headed into the low hills that lay across the river.

At the end of the six miles we were not in Pamplona, but at the top of a pass which gave a commanding view of the terrain ahead. Puerto del Perdón it was named, Pass of Pardon, and when we reached it Holt stopped the car, as he did each year on this afternoon, and we climbed out to view once more a sight that thrilled us now as it had when we first saw it.

In the foreground, on low hills, stood a group of brown-red square towers that dated back to one of the wars that had ravaged this focal area since Roman times. They were handsome towers, of little use today, but lending the landscape character and even distinction, for they seemed to fix things in place, as if to say, 'We are the protectors around which civilization has coalesced.'

Eight miles beyond the towers, at the edge of the Pyrenees, we could see the white spires of Pamplona, nestling under a sky turned to deep blue by the approaching sunset. Charlemagne must have felt this way when he looked down upon Pamplona on his return to France after having battled the Moors. Ignatius Loyola had stood at this spot in the days before his conversion, when as a lusty brawler from a village to the west he came here to make his fortune. And it was from this spot that Ernest Hemingway saw the city in those pregnant days when he was planning his first significant novel.

It was a remote, peaceful Pamplona we saw that afternoon, and it was difficult to believe that for the next nine days it would be the hell-raising capital of the world.

—•◆•—

Near the center of Pamplona stands the old town hall, and by July 5 each year it looks besieged, as if the Visigoths were about to roar down from the Pyrenees, for all store windows in the area are boarded over, four policemen stand where one stood before, and sedate shops are padlocked with the notation that residents of the city understand: *This Establishment Closed for Nine Days.*

When we arrived in Pamplona, Holt went directly to the town hall to check the plaque embedded in the walls: *Height Above Sea Level at Santander, 443.80 Meters.* Like all tech reps, Holt thought in meters and not feet, and often wondered why the United States did not switch to this sensible system. The altitude, over 1,450 feet, explained why it would be very cold during the festival of San Fermín: 'I always laugh at the Americans who think that because Pamplona is in Spain, it's bound to be hot. They forget it's also in the mountains.'

Behind the town hall lies a small and dirty plaza, one side of which opens onto the public market, the other onto one of the strangest churches in Europe. It is called Iglesia de Santo Domingo and must be very old, for the floor level of the nave lies a good fifteen feet below the present surface of the street, which has been built up through the centuries by the rubble of war and the rubbish of daily living. The façade of the church is something to see, for it has been completely bricked in, so that it looks like an apartment building with fake balustrades, fake windows, fake marble balls and a wonderfully fake bell tower.

In fact, from a distance it would be quite impossible for an un-instructed visitor to detect that a church stood here at all, so completely is it masked by the ridiculous façade and the buildings that encroach upon it. No portion of the nave or apse is visible; centuries ago they were blocked in by little stores and houses. Santo Domingo is a monument submerged by the requirements of the living.

Holt and I headed toward the remarkable building which obscured the western end of the church. It was called Bar Vasca, a rambling arrangement of rooms on five stories, each of which had been added at a different age. The ground floor, opening onto Santo Domingo Street, which ran from the hidden church uphill to the town hall, comprised a dark, low-ceilinged bar which for the next nine days would be the center of our life.

Around the four walls, on platforms eight feet above the floor, were ranged twenty-four great tuns of sherry, cheap red table wine, good white, poorly mixed rosé and powerful cognac. The casks were dark with age, their brass hoops shining bright against the well-polished wood. Beneath these impressive barrels ran a comfortable alcove in which patrons could sit protected from the noise and confusion that filled the central part of the bar, and in the alcoves thus cut off hung ceramic tiles which summarized the rural wisdom of Spain:

> *If Wine Interferes with Your Job,*
> *Quit Your Job.*

> *A Night of Good Drinking*
> *Is Worth a Year's Thinking.*

> *The Worst Thing in the World Is a Drinking*
> *Companion with a Memory.*

> *If You Are Drinking to Forget,*
> *Please Pay Before You Begin.*

> *To an Old Man, Even Musty Wine Is like Mother's Milk.*

> *He Who Eats Well at This Table*
> *And Drinks Well at This Bar*
> *Dies of a Terrible Disease: Old Age.*

Each year, with the approach of feria, Bar Vasca began to fill with disreputable characters from all parts of Europe. There were

Swedes who found great joy in the sun and the bulls, daring Germans who ran a few inches before the horns, American college kids who read of Pamplona in Sophomore English, and a collection of huge Basque woodchoppers.

Holt and I had been returning to this restaurant for the past eleven years, and we came partly for the music—played on strange instruments like the country oboe and the txistula—and partly to renew acquaintance with the woman after whom the bar was named, Raquel La Vasca: The Basque.

She was a big woman, apt mate to the woodchoppers, and of gargantuan appetite. On this evening, when we reached the Plaza de Santo Domingo, Holt parked the car, unloaded his bag and his tape recorder, hurried across the cobbles, reached the door of the bar and shouted, 'Raquel!' From behind the bar she ran to greet us, lifting Holt in the air with her powerful arms and kissing him on both cheeks. She was in her sixties, we judged, but as lively as she had been years ago when her Pamplona husband had bought this bar. Together they had made it a popular place, the head-quarters of all who really loved the feria.

'Is the food ready?' Holt asked, and rarely had I seen him betray excitement so openly.

'Where did you spend this year, little tiger?' the big woman asked.

'Afghanistan.'

She looked at him blankly, knowing nothing of this word. Then she clapped her hands with pleasure at seeing her old friend once more and called the girls to bring in the meal.

The food at Bar Vasca should have been served with a shovel, but it was good. Holt had the same meal three times a day. He tucked his napkin into his collar to prepare for a dish he preferred above all others. 'For our little tiger,' Raquel said approvingly as she helped the maid bring a large tureen to our table. It con-tained a mixture of heavy white beans cooked with ham ends and certain herbs which made it both aromatic and sweet as a nut. It was customary when serving *pochas* for the waitress to keep dish-ing big ladlefuls until the guest said, '*Basta!*'—Enough! With a flourish Raquel herself began serving the delicacy, and Holt merely smiled until his plate was loaded. Finally he called, '*Basta!*' and the meal began.

With his *pochas* he also had a green salad made from the crisp vegetables then coming onto the market in northern Spain and a small helping of bull stew made, when possible, from the bulls that had been fought in the arena the day before. For dessert, vanilla flan; for drink, a strong red wine which Raquel bought from a farm in the Rioja region to the west.

I had reached an age when white beans cooked with ham hocks were more than I could digest, so I contented myself with green salad and bull stew, and this I had twice a day through the feria. It was as good food as I get anywhere in the world, the rough, tough fare of the north, and to have Raquel sitting at your table, sharing the gossip of the past year, while a couple of woodchoppers sing in a corner is an experience I cherish. As I intimated before, the bar was Holt's cathedral.

From the bar, Raquel now called, 'Señor Fairbanks, *los jóvenes* you sent me arrived early this afternoon. They're upstairs.'

'I didn't send you anyone.'

'They said you did. From Algarve.'

'Oh, splendid!' I was pleased to think that I would see my friends again, pleased that they had remembered Bar Vasca. I started upstairs to greet them, but the big woman shouted, 'Finish your supper. Eh, Manolo. Fetch the young Americans,' and soon there was a clatter on the stairs as the six young people rushed down to greet me.

'Didn't you see our car?' Monica cried as she leaned over the table to give me a kiss. They pointed out the window, and there, in the plaza not far from where we had parked, stood the yellow pop-top.

'We were tired of sleeping so cooped up and decided to do the fair in style,' Gretchen explained, and I guessed that she was paying for the rooms.

'I want you to meet my long-time friend,' I said. 'He knows more about Pamplona than anyone you'll meet—Harvey Holt, Afghanistan.'

They moved forward to introduce themselves and shake Holt's hand, and I could see that he was perplexed by the presence of Cato. He didn't actually ask, 'Are you traveling with the group?' but he might just as well have.

'How often have you been to Pamplona?' Monica asked.

'This is my seventeenth year.'

'Groovy!'

Holt looked at the English girl as if asking her to translate, but before he could say anything, the others pressed in with questions, and he alternately stuffed his mouth with bull stew and explained Pamplona.

After dinner they volunteered to show us to our rooms, and Cato took Holt's bag while Joe grabbed mine. They led us to the third floor, where we had stayed for many years, and kicked the doors open for us. There were the dark, small cubicles which had become home to us, the balconies from which we could watch the running of the bulls, the miserable toilet down the hall, the dingy bathroom that never had hot water, the nostalgic odor of bedbug juice, the noise drifting up from the plaza where someone was tuning a guitar.

'We're on this hall too,' Gretchen said, and she led us to a room even smaller than ours in which she and Britta had their gear. Beside it was a room with no window in which Joe and Yigal stayed. That left a third room, extremely small, for Monica and Cato. Their gear was on the bed and it was apparent that they were living together. This was confirmed when Monica said, 'Cato and I use this one.'

When Holt and I were alone in my room, he asked in a whisper, 'Did she mean that she and the black boy were sleeping together?'

'They have been for some months,' I said.

'I should think her mother's heart would break,' Holt said with great intensity.

'Her mother's dead.'

'She must be turning over in her grave.'

———◆·◆·◆———

In recent years Holt and I had developed an affectionate ritual which for us had become as much a part of Pamplona as the halt at Puerto del Perdón and the *pochas* at Bar Vasca, so we asked the young people if they would like to join us.

We walked to the plaza in which the bullring stood, bought a large red handkerchief, and went solemnly to a granite base on which rested a good bronze statue of Ernest Hemingway, bearded and wearing a turtleneck. I made a stirrup of my hands so that Holt could climb up to the neck of the statue, around which he tied the red scarf of Pamplona. When he dropped down we applauded, for now Don Ernesto looked very much a part of the scene. No one thought of anything appropriate to say, so we walked back to the central square and found seats at the Bar Txoco, where habitués from all over Europe came to greet Holt and to talk of past ferias.

One German girl had a set of the famous postcards for Holt to autograph, and Joe asked, 'What are they?' In delightful English the German girl asked, 'You are sitting with this man and you don't know who he is?' She spread the pictures before my young friends, and I watched their jaws drop as they followed the course of the bulls that morning in 1953.

'You mean you did this?' Yigal asked. Holt nodded, and the boy said, 'You must have been out of your mind.'

Monica pointed to the shot in which Holt was landing on his head, and joked, 'You can see that after this he had no brains.'

Britta was fascinated by the picture that showed the bull's horn penetrating Holt's chest, and she asked, 'Did the horn really go in? As deep as it looks here?'

Holt showed no intention of answering, so I said yes and took Britta's hand and placed it over his shirt so that her fingers could feel the ridges of scar tissue left by the wound. She held her hand there for some moments, staring at Holt's rugged face, then said, 'You must have been near death.'

'As a matter of fact,' he said quietly, 'the horn never came within inches of a vital area. Like saber scars in German dueling. Look like hell, but no danger.'

Gretchen picked up the analogy with university dueling and asked, 'Are men like you compelled to run with bulls . . . because of the pressure of your society?'

Holt stared at her. 'What do you mean, men like me?'

'Well,' she said, pointing to the hordes of men shown in the photographs, 'there are a lot of you who do this thing. I meant . . .'

'Lady'—this was a word of contempt Holt saved for such occasions—'there are several thousand men in that street and each one probably had his good reason for being there. Me, I was there because I enjoy it.'

'What she means,' Cato broke in, 'something's bugging you and you feel driven to get down there and do your thing.'

Holt looked from one face to another and said, 'You kids may be driven by the force of your society. I'm having fun. I work my tail off eleven months a year and on the twelfth I come to Pamplona to have fun. You know, even God worked only six days and on the seventh he had fun.'

'You call this fun?' Yigal asked, pointing to the photo in which Holt was standing on his head with the blood gushing from his chest.

Before the tech rep could answer, the German girl gathered up her photos and said, 'You're making it too complicated. Can't you see from the expression on his face in this second photograph that he is experiencing a moment of joy?' She leaned across the table and kissed Holt on the cheek. 'He is the bravest, and if you keep your eye on him the next few days, you'll find out what it means to be a man . . . all of you.'

This did not satisfy Gretchen. 'You mean, Mr. Holt, that so far as you know, you are not driven by any inner compulsion? Any sense of insufficiency?'

Holt shook his head and said, 'Lady, are you here in Pamplona because of any inner sense of insufficiency?'

'Yes.'

The reply startled him and he fumbled for a moment, then said, 'You came to a damned good place to get it satisfied.' He rose, but Gretchen grabbed his arm and pulled him back to his chair. 'Mr. Holt, this is all new to us and we're trying to find out. Please.'

'All right. If you want to understand Pamplona, get up early on the morning of the seventh, go out on your balcony, listen to the noise, wait for the rocket to fire down at the end of our street, then watch as six bulls and ten steers gallop by so fast you'll scarcely see them. Nothing will happen, and when it's done you'll turn to one another and say, "So what's so big about that?" And maybe one of you, maybe this pretty girl'—he put his hand on Britta's for a moment, then quickly took it away—'maybe in that flashing moment when the bulls go past she'll catch a glimpse of one face— of a man running in sheer terror a few inches ahead of a bull who has no intention of touching him—and of you all, she'll be the one who'll remotely understand what has happened.'

This was a long speech for Holt, but he felt the subject deeply, and after a moment's pause he added, 'Of course, if this happens to be a day when some bull goes crazy and pegs a guy right under your balcony, you'll understand a hell of a lot more.'

Yigal moved forward and asked, 'But you do it as compensation for something, don't you?'

I could see that Holt had taken a dislike to Yigal, probably classifying him as a smart-aleck Jew, and now he turned on the wiry fellow. 'Son, I don't know what's eating you—from the worry in your face I'd say plenty—but I'm okay. Now if you'll excuse me . . .'

But he was not to get off so quickly, for Britta asked, 'You said you worked eleven months a year. At what?'

Holt was standing, but as he looked down into the lovely Scandinavian face, he could see that its owner was not trying to badger him. She wanted to know, so he resumed his seat and said, 'I work in places you've never heard of . . . Kemajoran, Don Muang, Mingaladon, Dum-Dum . . . a different place every two years.'

'And when Pamplona is over . . . where?'

'Another place you've never heard of. We start a Big Rally II at Ratmalana . . . and I'll be there two or three years . . . then some other place you wouldn't know where to find.'

'Doing what?'

'I just told you. Installing Big Rallies.'

'Communications centers for airports,' I explained.

'It must be wonderful,' Britta said, 'traveling from place to place like that.' She paused as if savoring the life, then added impulsively, 'Tell me, are these places in the sun?'

'Sure there's sun.'

'I mean, are they hot?'

Holt looked at me and laughed. 'Young lady'—this time it was not a word of contempt—'if you consider thirty-eight degrees centigrade week after week hot, the places I work are hot.'

'What's that in real temperature?' Cato asked.

The question infuriated Holt and he answered it by shrugging his shoulders, as if to say that anyone who mattered these days used centigrade. 'About one hundred,' I told Cato on the side. He whistled. 'That's hot.'

Up to this point Joe had said nothing. Now he leaned across the table and did an extraordinary thing. He slowly unbuttoned Holt's shirt until the scar was exposed. Staring at it, he said, 'You were there.'

Britta, who was sitting beside Holt, turned so that she could see the jagged edges of the wound. She merely looked and said nothing, but Monica ran her fingers along one branch, then stood and bowed. 'You have my respect,' she said.

Holt, astonished by this casual familiarity, rebuttoned his shirt and said, 'If you're really interested, there's also a beauty on the left cheek of my ass.' He started to unbuckle his belt, but Gretchen said, 'We'll take your word for it.' Britta turned to me and asked, 'Is that true?'

'Three others,' I said.

She looked Holt straight in the face and said, 'Now that we've seen, tell us why you do it.'

Holt stared back and said, 'Now that I've seen you young people —Mr. Fairbanks told me about you—you tell me, why do you do it?'

'Do what?' Britta asked.

'Run away from home . . . knock around Europe . . . smoke marijuana . . . sleep with each other.' At this last observation, he stared at Monica.

'It's very simple,' Monica replied. 'We do it because life at home is unutterably boring.'

'And you?' Holt asked Yigal.

'If I told you, you wouldn't believe,' the young Jew replied.

'I'll bet I wouldn't.' His gaze now fell on Joe, who ignored it, so he turned to Gretchen. 'You look intelligent.'

'Police and people,' Gretchen said. 'The police in Patrick Henry. The people in my own family.'

'What does she mean?' Holt asked me.

'The police gave her a bad time.'

'She probably deserved it.'

'And the people,' Gretchen said evenly, 'were the slobs in my own family.'

Holt flushed, as if she had made an attack on him personally. 'A good-looking, well-bred girl like you oughtn't to speak of her parents that way,' he said.

Cato did not wait to be interrogated. He said, 'I'm here, Mr. Holt, because men like you in Philadelphia drove me here.'

Holt nodded, said nothing, then looked at Britta, who said, 'I'm the one who's really escaping. I'm escaping the darkness . . . the cold . . . the beauty of northern Norway.'

'It's pretty cold here right now,' he replied, noticing her flimsy dress.

'But in the daytime there's sun. And if you can see the sun for only an instant each day, that excuses everything.' Her lilting voice with its ingratiating Norwegian accent sounded just right for Pamplona, and Holt smiled. Then he turned back to Joe and said, 'You didn't answer.'

'I'm here to avoid the draft,' Joe said, brushing the end of his beard with his right hand.

Holt froze, stared at the young man, coughed twice, then said, 'Did I understand? You're of draft age?'

'Yes.'

'And they called you?'

'Yes.'

'And you ran away?'

'Yes.'

Holt rose, took three steps away from the table, then turned and said with finality, 'I don't drink with draft dodgers. If you want to, Fairbanks, you can, but I'll be goddamned if I will,' and he stalked off across the central square.

Some hours later, after I led the others on the shortcut to Bar Vasca and we had climbed the stairs to the third floor, we found thumbtacked to Holt's door the Pamplona version of his traditional sign:

You are now in

PAMPLONA, SPAIN

42° 48′ North 1° 37′ West

If you fly along this latitude in an easterly direction, you will look down on Orvieto, Sofia, Tashkent, Sapporo, Milwaukee, Detroit, Santiago de Compostela, Vitoria, Pamplona.

If you fly along this longitude starting north, you will look down on Cherbourg, Leeds, Shetlands, North Pole, Wrangel, Suva, Gisbourne, South Pole, Kumasi, Ouagadougou, Tlemcen, Calatayud, Pamplona.

We looked at the sign with varying degrees of interest, surprised at how far north Pamplona lay, and how nearly on the London meridian. When I left, Britta remained, picking out each of the places with her finger, trying to visualize them in their various climates.

———•••———

In some ways July 6 was the most pleasant day of San Fermín. There was no bullfight, and hence no running of the bulls, but we met for breakfast and while Holt had his *pochas* the rest of us had some of Raquel's semi-solid chocolate drink, so bitter and at the same time so sweet. Old customers, as they took their first sip of the lethal stuff, toasted, 'Goodbye, liver,' but with hot croissants it wasn't bad.

At noon we went to the town hall, where a monstrous crowd had gathered to hear the mayor of Pamplona launch the fair with a cry of *'Viva San Fermín!'*—firing at the same time a rocket which seemed to rip the roof off the administration building. As soon as the echoes had died, the true glory of San Fermín began. It has been said that Pamplona does not have music; it is music, and now Holt and I had a chance to hear again those sounds which had lived with us during the past eleven months.

Most impressive were the bands—huge, clangorous combinations built around the biggest and noisiest drums that men could carry. I don't know what there was about the drums of Pamplona that gave them their power, but they seemed to carry farther than most, and throughout the days to come I would hear them at almost every hour, throbbing in some part of the city.

The txistularis were flute players who carried with them their own drummers. They played shrill music much appreciated by the citizens of Pamplona, and they were hired by the municipality to circulate through the streets for folk dancing. Wherever they went they were attended by young people.

Next came a form of music no stranger would expect to hear but which he would remember as one of the great events of the fair whenever he recalled San Fermín—the bagpipe players, countrymen from the mountain districts who tucked their goatskins under their left arms and played sad music on their chanters until the streets they walked were filled with lament.

The accordionists that followed were delightful, some playing small octagonal instruments with piercing note, others the larger, sweeter kind known in Italy. They played a lovely music, and wherever they appeared, there was dancing.

Finally came that strange instrument which has meant Pamplona to me since that first day I heard it coming at me from an alley near the plaza where they sell the strings of garlic. I can hear it yet, no matter where I am, if I close my eyes and whisper the name Pamplona. It came from the country oboes, ancient ancestors of the reed instrument we know today, played in pairs, accompanied by a drummer who also clanged a pair of tiny cymbals. The music was of haunting simplicity, songs that spoke of medieval days and tourneys; in the crush of this day they were somewhat lost, but in the days to come, when they were met by themselves, in back streets accompanied by teams of dancers, they would be memorable, the best sounds of this echoing week.

In the late afternoon excitement developed, for word circulated that the giants were coming. From various quarters they marched to the town hall, towering figures on stilts accompanied by squatty little mannikins with fantastically large papier-mâché heads. Men who operated the latter carried inflated pig bladders, and whenever they saw a child they dashed at him, belaboring the infant harmlessly but evoking squeals of terror. The giants represented kings and queens and pirates and Moors, and they would stalk among us for the ensuing days, so that when I say later, 'We walked back to Bar Vasca,' you must imagine that as we go we occasionally encounter these giants roaming the streets and the big heads swatting children with their pig bladders; but always we come upon a band, or a group of bagpipers or, if we are lucky, a pair of oboes.

For nine days there will be dancing in the streets, twenty-four hours a day. You will be coming home at two in the morning after drinks in some bar; you will turn a corner and find yourself in the midst of perhaps sixty people of all ages and nationalities, dancing the jota, and they will accompany you for a block or two, and when you leave them you may run into another group, closer to your destination. At dawn, at high noon, after dinner and especially through the night, there will be dancing in the streets. Many visitors to Pamplona will never see a bullfight— they have come merely to hear the music and to dance.

The crowds this year seemed unusually well behaved, and presentable in appearance. Our group was typical. Harvey Holt dressed every day in the same manner: white trousers, white shirt, red scarf, red belt, white canvas shoes with red laces and rope soles. In time the shirt would become stained a pale red from the wine that Harvey spilled as he drank from the many wineskins that were passed to him; he liked to hold them far from his lips, with a small jet of wine leaping into his mouth. I wore rope-soled shoes, a faded navy costume and a beret. Joe, his heavy beard unkempt, wore very tight western slacks, no shirt, a leather vest with a sheepskin lining and Texas-style boots. Cato, with his innate sense of style, kept his beard trimmed and his very modern clothes meticulous; while Yigal wore whipcord pants, army boots, a military jacket and the little Israeli idiot-cap.

The girls had a special problem. They wanted very much to wear their pretty minidresses, but quickly found that to do so in the freewheeling crowd at Pamplona led to adventures they were not ready to pursue. Britta said, 'I never knew a thousand men could have eight thousand hands,' so the girls switched to slacks; but if on some special evening we ate at a restaurant they wore their most modish dresses and, since they were such striking girls to begin with, always created a stir.

When I commented on how clean the crowd looked this year, with a minimum of the rowdy types in filthy clothes that I had anticipated, Joe laughed and said, 'You know why, don't you?' I didn't, so he drove the pop-top some distance out the Zaragoza road and we watched as motorcycle police stopped any incoming car with beatnik types and told them, 'Wash up, dress up, clean up. Or go back.' If the occupants protested that they had no other clothes, or if they refused to cut their hair or comb it, the police turned the car around and sent it in the opposite direction. 'It's the same on the roads from France,' Joe said. I asked, 'How did you get in?' and he said, 'I may look scruffy but I don't smell.'

That night I learned why Pamplona was able to absorb these myriad visitors with so little apparent trouble. At ten-thirty, when we had taken our places in the central square to watch the fireworks, two unusually obnoxious Americans accompanied by a drunk from South Africa began pestering us, and after a while they deduced that Cato must be dating one of our girls, so in spite of all Holt and I could do, they made themselves even more objectionable, but before real trouble could start, the fireworks came on, a lavish display by Caballer of Valencia, and we were able to forget the hecklers, although no sooner had the fireworks ceased than they began once again to badger us.

I wondered why the police did nothing, for they saw the affair, but they merely watched. Monica took Cato's hand and said, 'Let's get out of here,' whereupon the three began to chant, 'Nigger lover, nigger lover!' Holt, who felt as offended as they did about Cato's dating a white girl, nevertheless considered it his obligation to protect any member of his table, and he was about to launch into the trio, having first signaled to Joe and Yigal, when he was stopped by the police, who slowly shook their heads and wagged a forefinger.

Holt and the young people left, but I stayed behind to talk with some old hands from California, a doctor and his wife who often came to San Fermín, and they, having watched the incident, were as irritated as I. 'It's ironic that a colored man should be insulted at the feast of San Fermín,' the doctor said, 'in view of the fact that Fermín himself was a Negro.' I said the Pamplonicos were touchy on this point, and whereas the statue of San Fermín, which would be carried through the streets tomorrow, was coal-black, the legend claimed that the saint was from North Africa and merely sunburned.

I had no more than completed my comment when the three troublemakers spotted me and lurched over to abuse me as 'another of those nigger lovers.' The doctor, a man almost as old as I, was ready to fight, and I supposed I would be drawn in too, but again the police stationed themselves so that we could see them and wagged their fingers.

Then, at three o'clock in the morning, when the crowds had thinned out, a car drove quietly into the square and parked near us. Six policemen moved slowly among the tables, encircled the three bullies, and with sickening effectiveness punched them to the ground, then hauled them off, and we saw them no more.

———•◦•———

On July 7, at five-thirty in the morning, everybody in Bar Vasca woke up. In fact, everybody in Pamplona woke up, for at that hour bands of txistularis began circulating through the city, blowing their pipes and thumping their drums, so that sleep became impossible. And within a matter of minutes we were dressed and headed at a brisk clip for the bullring, as were thousands of others, converging from all directions. 'Do we have to walk so fast?' Monica called petulantly, and I replied, 'To do it right we have to,' and she called back, 'The one thing we insist upon is doing it right, don't we, Girl Guides?'

The reason for my haste became apparent when we reached the bullring, for even at this early hour more than three thousand people jammed the area, waiting for the doors to open at six, and unless we were lucky, we would miss the exciting introduction to Pamplona. By good luck, we were able to elbow our way to a favorable position, so that when the doors finally opened I could scamper up the flights of concrete stairs like a frightened rabbit and dash to a spot not inside the arena but on the stairway overlooking the streets outside.

'Taken, taken!' I shouted to strangers who tried to muscle in, and thus I held seven places until the young people came puffing up to range themselves beside me. Britta and Gretchen were at my elbows, and I explained to them that we would now stand in the cold for one hour.

'Will it be worth it?' Monica asked, and I pointed to the huge crowd that had already formed behind us, eager to glimpse even a portion of what we were to see in perfection.

'We've done this for twenty seconds of excitement,' I explained.

'It better be a good twenty seconds,' Monica retorted, and I assured her it would be.

By seven there were twenty thousand inside the arena, fifteen thousand on the plaza outside, where some had even climbed onto the head of the Hemingway statue. Suddenly, from across the city, a rocket exploded with a roar that could be heard in all parts of Pamplona. Those of us who had seen the run before waited apprehensively, and in a few moments were relieved to hear a second rocket, signifying that the six bulls had left the corrals in a compact group. 'If the second rocket is delayed,' I explained, 'you know that one of the bulls has lagged behind, and that means trouble.'

With the explosion of the rockets many things began to happen in the plaza. First, the police who had been keeping order in the runway which the bulls would follow on their gallop into the arena, left the scene and climbed to safety. Second, everyone in the area grew tense. Third, those who were to do the running began bouncing up and down, knowing that within two minutes the bulls would be upon them. Even blasé Monica grew excited and grabbed Joe's arm, squealing, 'How'd you like to be down there right now?'

The distance from the corrals to the bullring was about a mile, and since a man can run a mile in four minutes and a bull in something over two, it was obvious that anyone running before the bulls must ultimately be overtaken and forced to protect himself in some way as the bulls dashed past. Britta cried, 'Look!' and we saw men dashing furiously into the plaza as if hell were at their heels, and a moment later the first bulls appeared, large dark figures running purposefully ahead, looking from side to side but not chopping with their horns. A mass of runners seemed to clog the way before them, but as the bulls reached any given spot, the crowd mysteriously opened, only to close as the bulls passed.

When the animals reached the plaza they ran straight ahead for about one hundred yards, then, at a large office building called Teléfonos, they turned left to enter the narrow chute which would bring them directly under our feet and into the arena. This morning, as the speeding bulls tried to turn the corner into the chute, the men running before them piled up for a moment, and I heard Monica scream, 'My God! Look at that one in blue!'

A runner had fallen and it seemed inevitable that the bulls must trample him, but miraculously all six maneuvered their hooves so that the fallen one escaped injury. 'His angel was watching,' Monica said limply.

Now the bulls were well into the chute, dashing in our direction, with hundreds of men before them running, falling, struggling, kicking. I think each of us on the balcony caught a sensation of terrible power as the bulls crashed through all obstacles and swept on. 'Oh!' Gretchen gasped as the surge of men and bulls came toward us, blurred in an instant of wild excitement, and passed beneath us into the arena.

'Hurry!' I shouted as the last bull vanished, and we rushed up a long flight of stairs, down a corridor and out into the bright morning sunlight of the arena. We reached our seats just as the last bulls were being herded into the pens from which they would emerge to fight at five-thirty that afternoon.

What we saw next was a kind of divine buffoonery, for the

sand below was jammed with young bodies in white uniforms, red sashes and belts, each with a rolled-up newspaper in his right hand. 'Watch that gate,' I said, and as I spoke, it swung open, and out into that mass of supple bodies catapulted a fighting cow, her sharp horns encased in leather. With a fury that I cannot describe, she threw herself at the multiple targets about her, knocked grown men over with a brush of her head, and created such harmless havoc as to keep the watchers in continuous laughter. I judged that during this cow's eleven minutes in the arena, she must have knocked down about ninety men. At times she looked like a bowling ball, elusive and destructive. The rule was that no runner could grab her in any way, neither by the horns nor by the tail. All he could do was push her away or swat her with his rolled-up newspaper, but if he did the latter, she was likely to turn upon him, drive her head into his gut, and send him spinning.

Five such cows were released each morning—sometimes in pairs—and the last always seemed stronger than the first; or perhaps the runners were tiring. At any rate, it was a raucous way to begin the day and it set the pattern for what was to follow. By eight the arena was empty. As we trailed out, Cato said, 'Them females sure knows how to handle,' and Yigal said, 'The whole thing's ridiculous.' But Joe said nothing. He seemed to be remembering that surge of dark power as the bulls turned into the chute.

Holt disapproved of our three young men: Joe because of his pacifism and his beard, though not necessarily in that order; Yigal because of his outspoken opposition to bullfights and his hesitancy about adopting America as his home; Cato because he spoke ill of religion and was sleeping with a white girl, and again my order is arbitrary.

His reaction to the three girls was more complex. He distrusted Gretchen's attitude toward the police, believing that anybody who got on the bad side of the law, pretty likely had it coming; also, he suspected young people who fought with their parents, even though he had fought with his in order to get into the marines, but that was different. Monica he did not like. He thought she considered herself superior because she was English and spoke with an accent that was popular with far west radio announcers in the 1930s, and he despised her for having an affair with a Negro. Also, her humor was apt to be cynical, an attribute which he prized in elderly people but abhorred in youth. Britta was suspect because how could a girl like that smoke marijuana, and he wasn't pleased that she talked of her father with disrespect, especially if he had been the hero she said he was during the Nazi occupation.

But like all tech reps, he had a difficult time believing that girls as beautiful as these three could have any problems. 'Life is so damned easy for them,' he told me one day, 'no problems at all, and yet they want to make waves. You sort of feel that they ought to be spanked, but I guess even if you are well off and beautiful, things sometimes look confused.' When I said that Gretchen really had a miserable time with the police, he snapped, 'Probably smoking pot and they caught her.'

This day at lunch his reactions to the young people crystallized. Things began well, with various Spaniards stopping by to congratulate him on his running, and Yigal taking pains to be conciliatory, saying, 'You must have shown them something.'

'Just like Humphrey Bogart running his boat out of Cuba,' Holt said reflectively. 'No great sweat if that's your job.'

'I thought it was Errol Flynn who had the boat in Cuba,' Monica said.

'That time he told Lauren Bacall to whistle,' Holt explained.

'Oh, you mean a movie! Never saw it.'

The others hadn't seen it either, and Holt asked, 'You mean to tell me not one of you saw one of the greatest dramatic moments in movie history . . .'

'Bogart didn't make any movies during the last decade,' Gretchen said. 'At least I don't remember any.'

'He's been dead twelve years,' Holt said. 'When was it made?' he asked me. 'That great Hemingway story?'

'I saw it in Libya during the war.'

Holt said he couldn't believe it had been so long ago.

'I saw him in one movie,' Yigal said. 'It was excellent.'

'What was he?' Holt asked.

'You know, that classic—*Beat the Devil*, with Robert Morley and that superb cast.'

'Oh, sure!' Monica cried. 'That wonderfully nutty thing about Tangier.'

'They should all have been arrested,' Holt growled.

'Who? Morley and Bogart?'

'The producer, the director, anyone responsible for such a waste of Bogart's talent. That picture was a disgrace, the only poor one Bogart ever made.'

'Are you talking about the Truman Capote–John Huston classic?' Gretchen asked.

Holt apparently did not recognize the names. 'What I'm talking about,' he said, 'is that miserable picture which somebody threw together and made Bogart look like a fool.'

'It's the only good thing he ever did,' Gretchen said firmly, and the others agreed.

Holt exploded. 'You mean that piece of trash . . .'

'Mr. Holt, it had style, wit.'

'Did you see the time when he and William Holden were both in love with Audrey Hepburn?'

'Who directed?' Gretchen asked.

'Directed? Who the hell cares who directed? Did you see the time when he fought with Leslie Howard in the desert? Or when he was in Europe . . . just like you kids . . . only he was in love with Ava Gardner?'

This last rang a bell with Cato. 'Yeah, I caught it on a late, late show one night. A prime stinker.'

It was obvious that Holt was trying to control himself, and he asked, 'You don't really know any of the great pictures, do you? Like when Spencer Tracy was teaching Freddy Bartholomew to be a man?'

'Please,' Cato broke in. 'Give me names. What was the picture? I think I saw something like that. It was in Death Valley and there was the Gila monster and Spencer Tracy stepped on it with his heel.'

Holt bit his lip, then asked, 'You never saw Mr. Tracy when he fought for the soul . . . the future of Mickey Rooney? That time when Tracy was a priest?'

Gretchen tried to intrude with the statement that for her generation Spencer Tracy never made a picture that related in any way to real life and that girls like her simply dismissed his pathetic old flicks as . . .

'Goddammit!' Holt cried, banging the table. 'You're a bunch of illiterates. You really know nothing. How do you suppose a man gets character? By seeing the great plays and movies and reading the great books. Every one of you young punks would have had more character if you'd seen Spencer Tracy as that Portuguese fisherman . . .'

'It was a Cuban fisherman,' Gretchen corrected, 'and he was trying to catch a big fish . . . and it was a perfectly dreadful picture.'

Holt turned completely around in his chair so that he could stare at Gretchen. 'It's just dawned on me. Sometimes you're stupid. You got fine marks in college, I'm sure, but you're stupid. You know, if you had seen those great pictures in which Mr. Tracy and Miss Hepburn tried to adjust to each other—good man, good woman, but all man and all woman . . .' He hesitated, then said quietly, 'Maybe, Miss Gretchen, you would now know how to get along with men better than you do.'

Gretchen flushed and for a moment it looked as if she would lash back at him, but her natural good manners stopped her, and she said with conciliatory warmth, 'I'm sorry, Mr. Holt. I did see Mr. Tracy once when he was excellent. As the corrupt cop in *It's a Mad, Mad, Mad, Mad World.* He showed a true sense of comedy.'

That did it. Holt slammed down the fork with which he had been eating *pochas* and asked, 'Why is it? Of all the fine work done by these two actors . . . why do you choose the worst picture each of them made? That trashy Bogart film. That ridiculous thing they put Tracy into when he was an old man and needed the money. It was an abuse of talent. Yet that's what you remember.'

'His pictures were mostly corn,' Cato said. 'Some of my white friends took me to see *Guess Who's Coming to Dinner?* What crap.'

Suddenly Holt shot his hand out and grabbed Cato by the arm. 'Don't ridicule what you don't understand,' he said grimly; then, seeming ashamed of himself for having lost his temper, he stomped upstairs and a few minutes later we heard streaming from his tape recorder "The Stars and Stripes Forever" and "From the Halls of Montezuma."

On July 8 the five-thirty serenade outside Bar Vasca consisted of three bass drums of overpowering intensity, thumped for thirty minutes in one extended fugue. The all-night drunks invited the drummers into the bar, from which the hideous hammering could be physically felt in one's stomach, even on the third floor. We assembled downstairs, and since there was no reason to hurry this morning, had coffee in the bar, watching with admiration as the three drummers continued their exercise.

'It's sort of beautiful,' Monica screamed over the noise.

'It feels good in the gut,' Yigal said. 'Like a mortar going off, continuously.'

At about six-thirty we walked slowly up the hill to the town hall, where we started to occupy perches on the barricades, but changed our plans when an attendant in uniform whispered, 'Hsssst! The señoritas like a good spot?' I nodded, and for a few pesetas he led us into a door of the town hall and up a flight of stairs to a balcony that commanded the entire portion of the run. 'We like to please our pretty visitors,' he said in Spanish, and Britta replied, 'And we like to please our courteous friends,' giving him a kiss. Touching his cheek, he responded, 'Today shall be inscribed in the book of gold.'

I explained that what we would see this day would be quite different, more classic in a way, more Spanish. 'The bulls will be charging up the hill we just climbed, and when they reach this spot they must turn sharp left. They will cross directly beneath us, then dash straight down that lovely street called Doña Blanca de Navarra. Who she was I don't know, but now she's famous. At the end, the bulls turn right and enter the greatest of the streets, Estafeta, which we'll see tomorrow.'

Joe asked if we would see Harvey Holt from this spot, but I said, 'No, he runs in a different place. The ones who run here love the openness, the thrill of seeing the bulls come up over that rise, the sudden twists and turns. I used to run here.' Joe looked at me and said nothing.

By quarter to seven the plaza was jammed, and Gretchen said, 'So many people! You'd think there wouldn't be any left over for the bullring. But I suppose it's crowded too.' When I nodded, she asked, 'How many people see the bulls each morning?' I had never tried to calculate, but I guessed, 'A hundred thousand. Maybe more.' And she said, 'In this little town.' She looked to her right at a church that must have been five hundred years old and at the plaza that had known Roman legionnaires. 'Many ghosts run in these streets,' she said, and I thought of those I myself had known in the middle years of this century who were no longer in the streets. They'd had a good run.

At seven the first rocket went off, then promptly, the second. We held our breath, and after a proper interval, saw runners exploding from the street to our right, followed by those dark torpedo-like bodies. Here the bulls were fresher and ran with greater speed, so that the runners before them seemed to fly, and in an instant all was past and men who would never dare to face a bull were leaving the safety of the barricades and climbing into the street so that they could say, 'I ran with the bulls at town hall.'

———•••———

Of course, there were bullfights each afternoon, but the less said about them the better. The fact that the bulls had pounded through the streets in the morning meant that in the afternoon they were tired and excited, which in turn meant that the fights were usually bad . . . and always rowdy.

About an hour and a half before fight time, in various parts of the city, taurine clubs in traditional white trousers and distinctive cotton blazers would begin to assemble behind their individual bands, which contained few musicians but some of the greatest noisemakers in Spain. Members would arrive in pairs, two to a bucket loaded with ice and canned beer. Some would report with their buckets sloshing sangría, an excellent drink made of cheap red wine and fruit juice. In each club a special committee had the responsibility for making forty or fifty sandwiches consisting of huge slabs of cheese and ham slapped between crusty rolls a foot long and wrapped in foil.

An hour before fight time these clubs, marching in wild fashion behind their bands and carrying banners proclaiming their identity, would begin to circulate through the city, each on its own route, and as they progressed they picked up casual followers who would dance along the streets, so that by the time the bands began to converge on the bullring, there would be hundreds of raucous followers behind each one.

Inside the arena, the bands observed one rule: each must play as loudly as possible its own tune in competition with all others, who played their own tunes unceasingly. The result was a cacophony which echoed back and forth across the arena like waves of sound from Krakatau in final explosion. In the interval between the third bull and the fourth, the sandwich committees stood on the top row of the arena and pitched their foil-wrapped rolls far into the air, so that they descended like submarines over the heads of the crowd. If you were lucky enough to catch one, you had lunch for three.

Now drinks were passed, and the beer presented no problem, but the buckets of sangría were something else, because when only a quart or so remained in the bottom of the bucket, it was traditional to pour it over the heads of the crowd sitting below, and if a man came to San Fermín with only one good shirt, it was soon stained an attractive wine color. When the wine was used up, other liquids were thrown on the people below, and whenever the police caught men urinating in paper cups, they frowned.

———·—●—●—·———

At the bullfights, Holt and I had good seats in the shade, across from where the bands played, so we escaped the rowdyism, but the young people sat in the sun and were surrounded by the wine throwers. Joe and Cato and the girls accepted the frenzy as a generic part of San Fermín and even struck up friendships with some of their neighbors—the rowdy element invariably whistled when the girls came down the aisles and threw bits of paper and bread at them—but Yigal grew increasingly irritated and voiced his complaints freely.

This exasperated Holt, who asked at dinner on the fourth night, 'If you don't like bullfights, why bother with Pamplona?'

Yigal, not wanting to get into another argument, said, 'I'm mad because they throw all that wine on me, but never a sandwich.'

This attempt at humor did not placate Holt, who asked, 'Are you afraid of the bulls? Is that it?'

'I'm disturbed by the ridiculous behavior of grown men who seek their thrills this way. That's all.'

'You mean us?'

'It strikes me as silly . . . twenty thousand men in a ring, tormenting a defenseless calf whose horns have been padded.'

'You ever been hit by one of those defenseless calves?'

'Or running down Estafeta with six bulls on your tail. Who needs thrills like that?'

'Have you ever been in danger . . . just for the hell of it?'

I could have warned Holt that he was heading into the wrong alley with that question, but it had been asked, so all of us who knew Yigal's record sat back with smiles on our lips. The young Jew preferred not to answer, so Holt, believing that he had struck the boy on a tender nerve, said, 'You bookish fellows see things very clearly sometimes, but you often miss the main point.'

'What is the main point?' Yigal asked.

'That the male animal, throughout history, has enjoyed testing himself.'

'But what if you don't need a test?'

'No man can be sure of his courage until he has been tested. Everyone requires a test.'

'What I meant was—what if it has been tested?'

'Son,' Holt said expansively, 'I don't mean soccer . . . or climbing some hill.'

Yigal rose and said, 'I'm going to take a leak.'

When he was gone, Cato said, 'Mr. Holt, you ever hear of Qarash?'

Holt thought a minute, repeated the name twice and asked, 'Wasn't that in the Six-Day War?'

'It was.' There was silence around the table, and after a long while Holt asked, 'You mean . . .' He pointed toward the toilet, and Cato nodded.

'He was seventeen,' Monica said, 'and he wasn't even in the army. Just went along for the hell of it.'

'You read about it,' Cato added. 'Surrounded by six tanks and they destroyed four of them.'

'That little jerk?' Holt asked, and Cato replied, 'That's what Nasser said.'

When Yigal returned, Holt stood up out of deference and there was a moment of embarrassment, for he could think of nothing to say, but then he remembered some of the details about Qarash and asked, 'Did you happen to be the guy who worked on the radio?' When Yigal nodded, Holt grew expansive and said, 'You must know a lot about electronics,' and we left them at the table, discussing Big Rallies and tape recorders.

———•◦•———

On July 9 we were wakened at five-thirty by the sweet sound
of oboes playing folk tunes that reached far back into the history
of this region. As I heard them coming slowly down the street,
three countrymen with small drums and those delightful pipes, I
hoped that the big bands would be late in arriving, for we did not
often hear the oboes at Bar Vasca, but soon I heard in the distance
a horrible concentration of sound, two bands converging on our
plaza, each playing its own tune to its own rhythm, and the soft
echo of the oboes was lost.

At six-fifteen I led the way to the barricades where the bulls
leave city hall plaza to enter Estafeta, and as we climbed into position so that we could see both the area we had studied yesterday
and the long reach of Estafeta, we could appreciate the dramatic
significance of this spot, because if you ran at town hall, you had a
limited distance to worry about, with plenty of fences under which
you could duck in emergency. But if you elected to run in
Estafeta, you faced a street of considerable length, extremely
narrow, uphill all the way, and with never a fence to aid you.
When the bulls overtook you, as they must, all you could do was
either press yourself against the wall or throw yourself into the
gutter and hope.

'You mean those men are going to run in there?' Britta asked.
When I nodded, she asked, 'Is this where Mr. Holt runs?' and I
said, 'He runs elsewhere.'

When we had our places atop the fence, our legs hooked around
posts so that we would not be pushed into the street by the crowd
that was forming behind us, I told the young people, 'There are
two things to watch for. The first is very exciting. The second
may surprise you. But when the bulls reach the end of Doña
Blanca de Navarra—right here—they must turn very quickly to get
into Estafeta. Some may fall down . . . right at our feet.'

'That would be exciting,' Monica said.

'The exciting part is when they get up. If they can see the other
bulls heading down Estafeta, they run like mad to catch up and
there's no danger. But if, when they fall, they become disoriented
and can't see the others in Estafeta, watch out.'

'What's the second thing?' Yigal asked.

'When the first rocket sounds, you'll see that mass of men there
at town hall break through the police lines and start to run this
way. One or two in the group will suddenly realize, "My God!

I'm down here where the bulls are going to be!" And they'll try to escape by climbing through the barricades we're sitting on. Watch what happens.'

At seven the first rocket exploded, but the second did not come quickly. 'Some bull has lagged behind,' I called. There was a count of almost thirty before the second rocket sounded.

We waited, and then the crowd of runners surged down upon us, turning into Estafeta so that they could be well down that dangerous street before the bulls came, but as they ran I noticed one fair-haired boy of nineteen or twenty with real panic in his face. He had wanted to run, or he would not have been there. He had even got into the street. But now his courage quite left him, and when he reached the barricade from which Britta's feet dangled, he dove for it and tried to climb to safety, but as he did so a policeman stationed at that point pushed him in the face, throwing him back into the street.

Confused, the boy turned back toward town hall, where the first bulls had already appeared, and they terrified him. Like a wild man he dived for the barricade again, but again the policeman shoved him in the face, shouting in Spanish, 'You wanted to run, run.'

The boy looked up at Britta, at me, at the obdurate policeman. Britta screamed in Norwegian, 'Come this way,' but the policeman intervened. In sheer terror the young man dived for the street and lay huddled on the pavement as the first bulls thundered past, ignoring him. He rose, shaken and unable to speak, when a knowing Spaniard, aware that because of the late start there were still bulls to come, knocked him flat and kept him pressed against the wall as the late bulls arrived.

One slipped and fell, almost on top of the bewildered young man, kicking him twice as his hooves scrambled to regain a footing. Once back on its feet, the irritated bull saw his mates far down Estafeta and set off in pursuit, causing harm to no one.

The young man stayed in the gutter until Britta and I reached him. He was Swedish and kept saying over and over, 'Why did the policeman do that?'—as if the implacable policeman had been more frightening than the thousand-pound bull that had been lying on him.

One of the most enjoyable parts of the day came when the running of the bulls was finished, for then we would convene at Bar Vasca under the wine casks in the alcove that was reserved for us. There, confined by walls on three sides and the low ceiling above, we would find refuge in our private world and talk of what we had just seen. The ceramic tile in our alcove read:

> *How Sweet It Is to Do Nothing All Day Long*
> *And After Having Done So,*
> *To Rest.*

The young people usually got to the alcove first, and after a while Holt would join us, and the girls would ask, 'And how was your run today, Mr. Holt?' and he would reply with that un-equaled Spanish word of contempt, *'Regular,'* with a long-drawn accent on the last syllable. To the initiated, this was the ultimate condemnation: 'Stinking . . . as usual.'

But Britta, who spoke good Spanish, noted that whenever a real old-timer entered the bar he stopped by their table and spoke to Holt in respectful terms: 'That was a great run today, Ameri-cano,' or 'This day the bulls had horns, *verdad?*' Twice she asked Holt further questions about his running and each time he brushed them off. Today, after having listened to the third repeti-tion of the epic about the Swedish youth who had been pushed back into Estafeta just as the bulls were bearing down on him, Holt nodded, said nothing, and walked away. A woodchopper, who had been passing time with Raquel, left the bar and said to our table, 'That one knows!' and he nodded approvingly toward the disappearing figure.

'What does he know?' Britta asked.

Before I could answer, Joe asked, 'He run at any of the places we've seen?'

'No.'

'Tell us about him,' Gretchen said.

Including their interruptions and my repetitions, this is more or less what I told them: 'There are three ways to run the bulls at Pamplona, and you've seen them all. Doña Blanca in the open, Estafeta down the canyon, Teléfonos into the chute.'

'You ever run in Estafeta?' Joe asked.

'Once, and like everyone else who has done so, when I'm in a bar in Amsterdam or Montevideo and someone mentions Pamplona, I let them throw their weight around, then casually say, "I always run in Estafeta," and the conversation halts.'

'I like that,' Yigal said. 'You ran once long ago, but when you speak of it you say, "I always run in Estafeta." '

I laughed and said, 'You've learned the first rule of Pamplona.'

'Why aren't more people hurt?' Joe pressed.

'You ever see the famous photographs of pile-ups at Teléfonos? One man falls, then another, then a hundred. They form a small mountain in the darkness under where we were standing, and if the bulls smashed into them with horns down, there'd be a lot of deaths. But the bulls have this incredible instinct to forge ahead—to keep up with their mates. So they climb right over the men without stopping to gore anyone. This urge to stay with the gang is what makes Pamplona possible.'

'I suppose that goes for the people, too,' Gretchen said.

'But sometimes people must get killed,' Britta said. 'This morning . . . that Swedish boy could easily have been gored.'

'When you come to Pamplona you miss half the excitement if you doubt the rumors. "Three men were killed yesterday, but the Spanish press hushes it up because the government doesn't want bad publicity." '

'But two men were killed yesterday,' Monica protested. 'I heard it at the bar.'

'In every bar men are killed. Strangers solemnly swear that last year eleven runners were wiped out. "But did you read about it in the papers? I'll bet you didn't. The Spanish government isn't dumb." These strangers never see the deaths themselves, but they always know someone who did. "My friend was standing right in Estafeta when this big red bull went crazy and gored three men in the chest. They died before they reached the hospital!" It is always a close friend who saw the deadly events.'

'How many are actually killed?' Cato asked.

I looked about the alcove and invited guesses. Gretchen said, 'What kind of number are we looking for? Hundreds, thousands?'

No one spoke, so I gave them the answer: 'In the last forty years, seven. And always accidents no one could possibly have prevented. In his rush from the corrals to the arena each bull has a chance to gore a thousand targets, but for some inexplicable reason he ignores them, until suddenly, without logic, he drives his horn into some unsuspecting man. If bulls were so minded, they could kill seventy men every year. They've killed seven.'

'How about the accidents?' Cato asked.

'That's something else. Every morning six or eight young men are dragged into the hospital with accidents . . . more or less serious. Some are real gorings, and if Pamplona didn't have sharp doctors, some of these kids would probably die. And if Dr. Fleming hadn't invented penicillin, there would be amputations. But as a matter of fact, even on bad mornings when eleven or twelve are rushed to the operating tables, all of them recover. Some have missing front teeth. Some go out with limps. And a few, like Harvey Holt, wind up with a set of four scars.

'So there are three ways to run with the bulls, and in none are the chances of death excessive. But there is also a fourth way, Holt's way. Only a few foreigners know about this one, for it requires courage of a special character. Cameras don't record this kind of running and those who engage in it are not young men seeking a quick thrill or a one-time challenge. In this running only the tough Pamplona men—the butchers, the woodchoppers, the truck drivers, the men of forty and fifty that you see in this bar—participate. And Harvey Holt, for the Spaniards have accepted him as their brother.

'Holt was invited to this special running in 1954, the year after his bad goring. A big woodchopper here in the bar asked, "Is it true that you're the man in the photographs?" When Holt nodded, the Basque said, "And you came back?" Again Holt nodded, and the woodchopper said, "Tomorrow you run with us." That was how it started. If he had continued to run in Estafeta or Teléfonos, I don't think he'd have returned year after year, but running where he did, and with whom he did, he found himself part of a brotherhood. In time it became the most precious thing in his life. Because Holt runs where the men run.'

This comment was so challenging that the three boys insisted I show them what I was talking about, so, accompanied by the girls, we left Bar Vasca and stood in Santo Domingo Street. 'You've seen that up the hill lies town hall. But if we turn down this way we're headed for the river, and down at the foot of this hill . . .'

'What's this building?' Gretchen asked.

'The military hospital. Very conveniently situated, too, I must say.'

We were now in position to look out past Pamplona toward one of the most interesting views in northern Spain. Far in the distance lay a row of green hills and sunny valleys. To the left rose a congregation of stately towers and the façade of a very old building which now served as an art museum. Its walls ran straight down to the street, a drop of over a hundred feet, and it was this that formed one side of the chute which kept the bulls in line when they first leaped out of the corral.

'To understand how Holt runs, you must understand the corrals,' I said. 'Over there, across the river, lie the large corrals in which many bulls are kept. We have eight fights in the feria . . . plus a couple in the morning. Those corrals can hold a lot of bulls. You see those post holes in the road leading up from the river? Each night around ten o'clock—they shift the hour radically so as to discourage spectators—they build a runway. The bulls come out of the corrals and over that beautiful little stone bridge covered with ivy. They gallop up here and into this small gate. This is the holding corral, where they wait overnight and get acquainted with the steers that will lead them through the streets.

'At seven in the morning the gates of this corral are thrown open and the rocket we heard uptown explodes, startling the animals and starting them on their mad rush up the hill and into the city. For the first hundred yards no runners are allowed in the streets. This permits the bulls to get well started. They run in this chasm formed by the museum walls on one side, building walls on the other.

'Here, where the museum wall ends, this ramp leads up to another level. It's blocked off and filled with hundreds of watchers, who are the first people the bulls see. At this spot the course narrows to only fifteen feet across. Also, it turns sharply to the left and goes uphill to the military hospital, and after that to Bar Vasca, as you can see.

'At six-thirty each morning runners of exceptional bravery are allowed to take position at this point where the course narrows to fifteen feet and turns left for the run uphill. When the rocket explodes, these exceptional men start to run—not uphill toward safety but downhill toward the onrushing bulls. They time themselves exactly, spin on their toes, turn, and race back uphill just in front of the horns. I don't know anything in sport—not even auto racing or skiing—which requires the combination of courage and timing this does, for not only must the runner calculate the relative speeds of himself and the bulls, but when the critical moment comes he must turn and race uphill with absolutely no escape, for as you can see, there are no doors or exits of any kind. In the end he must either dive into the gutter or press himself hopefully against the bare wall, trusting that the bulls will roar past without stopping to gore him!'

'Have you ever run down to meet the bulls?' Cato asked.

'Never had the nerve. But Holt has run here every morning for sixteen years—1954 through 1969—his last three gorings occurred here. Of the seven runners who have been killed, most were pegged on this hill. The charming part is, if a bull does catch you, he knocks you down at the doors of the military hospital. You're on the operating table in less than a minute. When you see Harvey Holt, you see a man who has run into the horns of the bulls more than a hundred times.'

Yigal said, 'He must be completely nuts,' but Cato said, 'He has guts.'

We returned to the bar and waited for Holt to appear. So far, none of the young people had seen him run and therefore had no concept of what he did, but after my explanation they were prepared to speak to him with respect, so when he came in for his *pochas,* Britta asked, 'Did you run down the hill today?'

Holt stared at me reproachfully and said nothing, so Britta continued, 'Could we watch you run tomorrow?'

'No place for girls,' Holt replied, but later that night after the fireworks, as we were coming home to bed, Britta and Gretchen took my arms and said, 'We want to see what Mr. Holt's been up to,' and I told them, 'You ought to see. Be ready at six-thirty.'

———•◦•———

On the morning of July 10 we rose early, fought over the bathroom, went down to greet the singers in the bar, and proceeded down Santo Domingo to the escape ramp leading up to the art museum. Testing several locations, Joe and Yigal finally decided that we should stand not at the end closest to the corrals, but farther up the hill where we could see the men run down the hill, turn, and then run back to the military hospital.

When the girls looked downhill toward the quiet corral and saw the narrowness of the street up which the bulls would charge, they began to appreciate what a powerful scene was about to unfold.

It was not until a quarter to seven that Britta cried, 'Look! There's Mr. Holt.'

In the front ranks at the barrier stood Harvey with his Spanish friends. He was, of course, the only non-Spaniard who would dash downhill toward the bulls. The others were men of approximately his age, with only one or two young fellows in their early twenties who had been accepted by the veterans.

'Watch what he does when the rocket sounds,' I advised, and the girls kept their eyes on Holt in his white outfit with the red sash and scarf.

Whoooosh! With a loud roar the rocket exploded. Deftly the police swung away the barrier and fled to safety on the ramp. At that moment the second rocket exploded. As it did, Holt and his companions raced downhill directly at the oncoming bulls. When it seemed that the horns must catch them, they turned and for some forty yards ran like mad ahead of the pressing animals.

'My God!' Britta screamed as the lead bull gained on Holt, reaching out as if to knock him over or gore him. At that moment Holt dove for the crevice where the high wall and the paved street met, and over him passed the two bulls and three steers who were running wide that morning.

Britta closed her eyes and seemed about to faint, believing that the bull had knocked Holt over with his horn, but Gretchen, who had been watching more closely, saw that he had been neither gored nor stepped upon, and she said, 'He's getting up.' Britta opened her eyes and saw Holt dusting himself off, but now Monica screamed, 'Look!'

Six men came running down Santo Domingo from a spot in front of Bar Vasca where a bull had gored a young boy, whose torso was covered with blood. Across from us the big doors of the military hospital swung open to admit the boy. Before I could assure the girls that he would probably be all right, two other groups of running men dashed down the hill bearing two other young men who had been hit. These men showed no blood. 'Broken ribs,' I said confidently. 'They'll be all right,' but Monica kept shouting, 'Look at them hauling in the corpses!' Yigal, watching Holt, shook his head and said, 'Now I know he's nuts.'

Gretchen now spotted Holt and called down to him, asking him to wait for us, and we descended to the street, where Britta said, 'You were beautiful, running at the bulls.' Holt grunted, then led us to our alcove at Bar Vasca, where a large crowd gathered to discuss the accidents. A total of seven had been hauled to the various hospitals, but nothing serious. One Spaniard stopped by our table to report, 'They didn't even have to call a priest. Very satisfactory run. And with you, Señor Holt?'

'*Regular.*'

———•◆•———

Sleeping arrangements at Bar Vasca were apt to be chaotic and I shall not try to chart a report of who slept in whose bed . . . or more likely, under it. To do so would require one of those transistorized computers, because so many people crowded into Pamplona for San Fermín that there simply were not enough beds to go around, and the luckless ones had to make unusual adjustments. North of town there was a camp on a hillside overlooking a valley, but it was so crowded with tents that not another could be squeezed in. As it was, every tent did quadruple duty, and when you toured the area you had to be careful not to step on feet protruding from the canvas. There were several large fields set aside for trailers but these had been preempted three days before the fair opened. A good many visitors slept on the ground, some in the lee of the Hemingway statue, so that whenever any of our group went into the central square, we were sure to find half a dozen persons who desperately needed sleeping quarters. It was not at all unusual for Joe and Yigal to come back at two in the morning with three or four girls, especially from Canada and Australia, who would pile into the room with them, some sharing the beds with the boys, others sprawled along the floor.

Twice, when I reached home, I found young girls asleep in my bed, so exhausted that they barely wakened when I shifted them to the floor; since it was known that I had a room to myself, Britta and Gretchen were likely to assure any new acquaintances in the square, 'He's a good Joe. Get to the room before one o'clock and don't say anything.' My quarters were frequently littered with sleeping bags in which young men and women, sometimes together, slept, oblivious to me.

Of these strangers who passed through my room, I can say that they were honest, for I never lost anything; they were as clean as life without bath or shower would permit; and a good many of them were as virginal as they would have been under their mother's care back in Australia, Canada or Texas, but an equal number weren't.

As a matter of fact, during San Fermín the word 'sleeping' carried an arbitrary definition: something you rarely did. You got up at five-thirty in the morning, met the gang in the central square at eight, had lunch somewhere, went to the bullfights in the afternoon, had dinner, watched the nightly fireworks, danced in the streets till about three-thirty, and were up fresh two hours later. About the only time that Pamplona was reasonably quiet was from nine o'clock in the morning till twelve, and it was then that most of us slept and did our laundry. Those who failed to do the latter, and there were many, began to smell pretty raunchy by the third day, but since few of us had access to baths, everyone else was smelling rather high too, so it didn't matter.

What happened sexually on the third floor of Bar Vasca, I never clearly understood. About as far as I could safely go would be to say that Cato and Monica were continuing their intense affair, fortified by nightly bouts of marijuana and occasionally LSD, which continued to frighten me. If Joe and Yigal remained continent, they were cast in heroic mold, for the girls I saw them with were among the most attractive at the fair. One morning I had to go into their room for some bullfight tickets and found a girl in bed with each boy and two other girls asleep on the floor. Since that same night two quite attractive girls had slept in my room without incident, I would not have wanted to jump to any conclusions about what might or might not have happened with Joe and Yigal.

The room which Gretchen and Britta occupied was another matter. These girls were careful of their behavior; Britta allowed no one to slip quickly into her bed, and Gretchen was still aloof. Any strangers who shared their room were girls who simply had to have some place to get a night's uninterrupted sleep; but in what I say next I am not speaking of strangers.

At lunch on the day when we first saw Holt run with the bulls, there was a commotion at the bar and I heard Raquel shouting in Spanish, 'You dear little blond bastard, welcome home.' Immediately after, Monica, who was sitting facing the bar, leaped to her feet and rushed out of the alcove to embrace someone. I turned, and it was Clive, with his purple carpetbag, Christ-like beard and gentle smile. He made a tour of the table, kissing everyone, men and all, and I said, 'Clive, this is my long-time friend and Pamplona expert, Harvey Holt,' whereupon Clive kissed him and Harvey almost toppled into his *pochas*. While Holt was still aghast, Clive took Harvey's spoon, exclaiming, 'Delicious! Raquel, you're as glorious as ever. Now get us your turntable, because I have some wonderful music in here for you.'

We made a place for him in the alcove, and while Raquel set up her machine, he regaled us with the sensational news that had rocked London. 'Octopus has broken up! Yes, dissolved. But a powerful new group is coming out of it. You must remember the name, because they're making some of the most fantastic sounds you ever heard. Mauve Alligator, and you're about to hear their magic.' Carefully he unzipped his carpetbag and lifted out a record with a lurid dust jacket. 'This has to last all the way to Marrakech,' he explained, 'and this is the first stop.' With care he placed the needle in the lead-in grooves, turned the volume almost as high as it would go, then sat back with a beatific smile on his face while gigantic, driving sound throbbed from the loudspeakers. The young people pushed away from their *pochas* and surrendered themselves to the flood of emotion that hammered itself upon us. Holt looked at me and shrugged his shoulders, then asked, 'Can we turn the volume down a bit?' But Clive pushed his hand away from the controls.

When the first side of the Mauve Alligator record ended, Clive tucked the precious disk back into his bag and allowed the machine to stand idle for some minutes as he told us, with engaging shyness, of the great thing that had happened to him. 'The Homing Pigeons came to me and said they wanted a new song. They'd dreamed up this staggering theme . . . wait till you hear it. What they had in mind was a set of words that would go on and on. Their lead guitar had heard me in a club one night speaking of Torremolinos and Ibiza and the endless road of music that was uniting us all. He sort of had the idea that this might be a concept . . . well, a concept that would coincide spiritually with the music. I said I'd like to hear their theme again, so they cut a disk for me . . . just a few bars . . . an idea only . . . and I went to Mother's and put it on the machine for three solid days. She went off to her flat in London, And when the whole world was suffused with that beat . . . Listen.'

From his bag he produced the latest Homing Pigeons record, in a psychedelic jacket which pictured two thirds of the Sphinx, a fragment of the Taj Mahal, broken figures from the frieze of the Parthenon, a slum in Liverpool, and Clive's face wreathed in flowers. The title of the album was *St. Paul, Ulysses and Me*.

'You wrote it?' Gretchen asked.

Clive nodded and placed the record on the machine, keeping the volume at its maximum, and for the first time his friends heard the song that was to echo around the world. It started with the driving beat of three guitars, no drums, playing one theme incessantly. It was not monotonous, because the theme was good and the guitars embellished it in various simple ways, but after about a minute of this, an anguished, protesting voice began the words which young people in many countries would find so congenial:

> 'St. Paul was certainly a cat who knew
> The urge, that demi-urge
> To see beyond the last bend in the road.'

It was a song of the disenchanted, the disengaged who threw down a challenge to forces they could not control. One passage attracted my interest because, although it had been written by an Englishman for an English group, it dealt with what one might at first consider a purely American theme:

> 'I feel the urge, that demi-urge
> To give the shaft
> To good old Lewis B.'

'Why such a thought in an English song?' I asked. 'What could listeners over there possibly care about General Hershey?'

'There are two answers to that question, Mr. Fairbanks,' Clive said with exaggerated precision. 'The first is that my listeners are not over there, for as you can see from the sample here, only a few of us are British. And the second is that we care a great deal, because if we can defeat General Hershey and his stupid draft in your country, we may be able to defeat men like him in all countries.'

'There's a third reason,' Gretchen said. 'A crucial one. This song may be much more important in Russia or Brazil than in England. You see, Uncle George, this music really is international.' Then she added quietly, 'As we are international . . . as you are, Mr. Holt.'

Clive played for us until it was time to attend the bullfight. It was a fascinating concert, and I was reminded again of the wide artistic range of modern popular music. On the one hand, he played ultimate noise such as Mauve Alligator in a blast called 'Sunday Excursion,' and on the other, a bittersweet thing like Simon and Garfunkel's 'Dangling Conversation.' For laughs he had a nasal rendition of 'Winchester Cathedral,' but for the most part he held to the newer pieces by Blind Faith, Led Zeppelin, and Crosby, Stills and Nash.

After dinner some Spanish singers came to the bar, and it was surprising how easily their style fitted in to what the young people had been enjoying. Then Gretchen borrowed a guitar and sang some of the old ballads, which prompted one of the woodchoppers to send for his partner, a man who could sing a very high falsetto, and these two entertained us for an hour with the jotas of Navarra and Aragón, and these, we agreed, were the best of all.

About two in the morning we trailed off to bed, and since there were no available rooms in Pamplona, and certainly none in Bar Vasca—some of the singers would sit here all night and we would hear them distantly as we fell asleep—I wondered where Clive would sleep, and as I was about to offer him half of my bed, if someone else had not preempted it, Gretchen subtly interposed herself between us, and by some gesture which I could not see, indicated that Clive was to sleep in her room.

On succeeding nights he kept returning, and what arrangement they made with Britta, I never knew, but I do know that the tension which had till now enveloped Gretchen seemed to dissolve. In the main square when roistering men grabbed at her, she no longer drew back in automatic dismay, and one morning when I saw her and Clive emerge from their room, with Gretchen laughing and a ribbon in her hair, I felt sure that if her sensible father could have seen her at that moment, he would have applauded her recovery.

———•◄►•———

July 11 that year was memorable for two events: Clive's picnic in the morning, Yigal's encounter in the afternoon.

Following the running of the bulls, Clive announced, 'It's going to be a glorious picnic. You can come, Mr. Holt, because we need your tape recorder. And you can come, Mr. Fairbanks, because we need your car.' The boys had struck up an acquaintance with two American college girls who were spending a year overseas, and they brought along a young man from California who kept repeating, 'Boy, do I dig Octopus!' He was desolate when Clive told him, 'Octopus broke up.'

When we had distributed the group between the two cars, Clive asked, 'Where we going?' and since no one had a clue, I suggested, 'Have you ever seen Estella?' and no one had, so we headed for the Puerto del Perdón and the marvelous stone bridge at Puenta la Reina. In less than an hour we were entering Estella, a battle-scarred old town which had withstood a dozen sieges and from which, in medieval days, pilgrim roads had led to shrines in the west. I halted our little caravan at a café overlooking a very old square in which travelers from all parts of Europe used to convene for mutual protection on their trips west.

As we sipped coffee and rested, I asked Gretchen if she knew much about that amazing development in history, and she said, 'To me medieval Spain is a blank,' so I asked, 'Do you know anything about the pilgrimages . . . from the French side, that is?' 'You mean to Compostela?' When I nodded, she said, 'Everyone knows about that. From Chaucer.' 'This is where the road west began,' I said. 'In this little square. It's entertained millions of pilgrims.'

Gretchen rose, walked about the inconspicuous square, rejoined us and said a startling thing: 'Maybe this is what I've been looking for. The Crusaders at Silves proved quite a bust. I find I'm not interested in them, really, because they were bullies—and phonies to boot. But the people who came along this route had faith. Maybe that's what we're lacking today—an appreciation of faith.'

We got back in the cars and I led the way to a historic monastery that had guarded this trail for seven hundred years. It was largely in ruins and had a cloister from which massive oaks grew. Spreading our blankets beneath them, we could look across a broken wall and down a long valley in which it was possible to imagine men in cowls picking their way to sanctuary.

'How these buildings must have looked seven hundred years ago,' Gretchen said quietly as she helped distribute the bread and cheese.

I told her, 'You must imagine thousands of travelers walking along the road we came, lured on by hope of salvation. They come to that ruined door over there, bang on the iron knocker and beg assistance. They've been on the road for months, with a month more to go . . . down that valley and across a score of hills.'

Gretchen stared at the horizon and said, 'What I'd like to write about is what kind of faith enabled them to take such a journey.'

Of those listening to us, the one who seemed to understand best what Gretchen had in mind was Cato. He had a strong sense of pilgrimage. He told us, 'I'm convinced I don't come to a monastery like this by accident. It must be for a purpose . . . but what? I can't even guess.' When I reminded him that all young men of character experience this sense of making a journey to find themselves, he said, 'I don't mean that jazz . . . the old gig about identity. I know damned well who I am. What I mean is that somewhere— down that valley maybe—there has got to be a secret which will make this whole thing come alive . . . give it significance.' I told him that significance could come only from within, but this he would not accept. 'Somebody knows the secret . . . say the mystic word and the mountain opens.'

He said no more and listened as Gretchen continued her speculations while Clive laid out the picnic: 'Perhaps I'll take a family in France . . . it could be Flanders. About a hundred years before Chaucer. I'd study all about it, especially the religion and economics, and I'd bring the father and mother on this pilgrimage. Sometime around the year 1240. I can visualize them now—a man about the age of Mr. Holt, a young wife like Monica.'

I was captivated by her tentative suggestions, and said, 'When your family reaches this monastery door, they meet four young men about to leave for the west. Joe with his beard. Cato with his quick step. Yigal with his books. And Clive the minstrel. They'd be dressed in sackcloth and sandals, and they'd carry staves and wear cockleshells in their hats . . . like him.' I pointed to the ruined door of the monastery, over which stood a carved stone relief of a pilgrim dressed as I had indicated, and its eroded features could have been any one of our four young men.

'Not many blacks came this way,' Cato protested.

'Many,' I said, 'from North Africa.'

'Slaves?'

'Some. And teachers. And merchants. In the cemetery over there I'm sure you'll find the bones of many Negroes.'

'Any Jews?' Yigal asked.

'They owned half Estella,' I said.

As we ate—stout cheese, sausages hefty with garlic, excellent bread—Gretchen nibbled and said, 'I suppose if we knew the facts, we'd find there have always been young people wandering over the face of Europe . . . pretty much as we do today. I don't think of myself as unusual. Or you, either, Monica. You could have been coming down this road and munching this same kind of cheese seven hundred years ago. In fact, I feel much closer to the girls of that age who were on a real pilgrimage of the spirit than to some nitwit in suburban Boston today.'

Joe, sprawled against a tree, said, 'I'll bet most of them came here because they were sent.'

Gretchen stared at him, made her right forefinger into a revolver, and shot him dead. For epitaph she said, 'Joe, you'd have been at the head of the column, fighting off the bandits.'

'And cursing every minute of it,' Joe said from his grave.

'What I'm trying to say is that the motives which brought me to Europe—and you, too—were the same as those which moved the pilgrims. At any rate, it would be a great subject for a book.'

There was a pause as we looked beyond the ruined monastery to the historic route of faith, the difficult hilly path that had lured the pilgrims, and then a strange thing happened. Harvey Holt, who so far as I knew had taken no interest in what Gretchen and Cato were saying, suddenly began quoting from a poem which he had once told me he did not know:

> Come, let me read the oft-read tale again!
> The story of that Oxford scholar poor,
> Of pregnant parts and quick inventive brain,
> Who, tired of knocking at preferment's door,
> One summer-morn forsook
> His friends, and went to learn the gipsy-lore,
> And roamed the world with that wild brotherhood,
> And came, as most men deem'd, to little good,
> But came to Oxford and his friends no more.

'Mr. Holt!' Gretchen cried. 'Those words could have been written about Joe.'

'You know whose they are?'

'Haven't a clue.' None of the others knew and Holt said, ' "The Scholar-Gipsy." A professor wanted me to memorize it once, but

I said it was too long. But one hot spell when I was at Simpang Tiga with no one to talk to . . .'

'I must get a copy,' she said, and for the first time the group felt close to Holt, although what happened next turned them around again.

For Clive said, 'We really must have some music,' and Holt unlimbered his tape recorder, hooking it into the electrical system of our car. His first tape, the one he considered his masterpiece, proved a disaster. It contained the best songs of the big-band era, and when the wispy voices of the male singers and the ultra-cute beepings of the girl soloists came from the machine, like inane ghosts mouthing formal conceits in some courtly age, the young people started to laugh. 'Hey, could we hear that chorus again?' they asked, and when Holt rewound the tape and played 'September in the Rain' a second time, the young people chortled and begged for it a third time. 'It's sensational!' they cried. 'Catch that voice . . . that tremolo.'

All the songs we had loved they abused: 'Just One of Those Things,' 'Don't Sit Under the Apple Tree,' 'I'll Never Smile Again' and 'Symphony' were treated with contempt, but when the tape came to 'My Reverie' the crowd broke up, demanding that it be played again and again.

'They keep telling us, "They don't write lyrics the way they used to." Is this a sample of what you mean, Mr. Fairbanks?'

Defensively, Holt asked, 'What's wrong with "My Reverie"? After all, Bea Wain is singing it,' and Cato asked bluntly, 'Didn't they ever go to bed together in those days?' and Holt snapped, 'Yes, they went to bed, but they didn't sing about it on Victrola records,' and Cato said, 'Frankly, that music is dreadful.'

Holt wanted to know why, and Joe broke in, 'For one thing . . .' but before he could make his point, Gretchen interrupted to say, 'The tunes are dull and regular . . . one, two, three, one, two, three . . . and the lyrics are juvenile . . . intellectual age about nine years old.' When Holt started to defend his favorites, Gretchen cut him short with: 'Mr. Holt, have you ever listened to the lyrics?'

He studied the table of contents for this particular tape, ran it backward and forward a few times, sampling the sounds, until he found what he wanted: Ella Fitzgerald singing Cole Porter's 'Love for Sale.' This bittersweet melody did hold the attention of the young people, and when the lyrics began they did not immediately laugh.

'Clever play on words,' Joe admitted. 'But the rhymes are forced.'

'Don't be so technical,' Holt said. 'Admit it's good.'

'So it's good. One in seven is good.'

'Harvey,' I said, 'I think you have "Night and Day" on that tape. See if you can find it.' While he looked, I told the young people, 'When you hear this I want you to believe that thousands of men my age felt that it summarized their . . . not their attitudes . . . that would be too much. What I mean is, their feelings about how you feel when you're twenty-two . . . or maybe even thirty.'

'You're expressing yourself awkwardly,' Monica said. 'You mean, how you felt about girls?'

'Listen.' Holt had found the famous song, one of the few in which the verse was even better than the chorus, and when it sounded through the cloister, it was all I could do to keep from closing my eyes and imagining—probably with a silly grin on my face—that I was hearing it for the first sentimental time. I knew the young people would laugh at me if I did, and the afternoon was tense enough without that.

As the words unfolded, so handsomely matched to their tune, I asked the critics what they thought of it. 'Same reaction,' Cato said. 'Didn't you cats ever get the girls into bed?'

'Damn it! Listen to the words!'

'I am listening, and it's hogwash. Sentimental hogwash. No wonder the world's in the shape it's in if your generation listened to that slop and if President Kennedy read James Bond thrillers. Preserve me, but that is crap.'

I looked to the others, and they said things like: 'There's no vitality in the music.' 'That beat would drive you to masturbation.' 'Slop isn't the exact word, but it's close.' And: 'Mr. Holt, that music is like the Elizabethan roundelays, whatever in hell they were. Good in their day but . . .' Cato, who was listening to a replay of 'My Reverie,' said simply, 'Oh, brother.'

At this unfortunate point Holt's tape came to Sammy Kaye and the Three Kaydettes in a version of 'Taking a Chance on Love,' and when I heard the beginning I muttered to myself, 'This one we should have skipped,' and when the male voices came on, sounding like a crew of eunuchs at a palace fete, the crowd collapsed. When we got back to sensible talk, I admitted that the worst of our songs were pretty bad, and they were bad for the reason that Joe had so neatly hit on: they all sounded as if the singers and the writers had never gone to bed with anyone. The involuted euphemisms they used were ridiculous, and listening to the songs in this context I wondered how I could ever have taken them seriously.

Surprised at my own conclusions, I asked Clive what he thought, and he said, 'I am much impressed. The artists had to work within such dreadful confinements . . . only a few acceptable rhythms . . . a rigid form for the words . . . all instruments sounding about the same . . . and no beat whatever. I'm amazed they accomplished so much. But I agree with Joe on one thing. The lyrics are really abominable. So fake, so puritan. You can feel the pressure of society in the silly rhymes.' He paused, then added, 'Of course, if you could revive "My Reverie" it might enjoy a smash success . . . ultimate camp.'

Holt turned off his machine in the midst of this pronouncement, but when Clive was through, Harvey began to chuckle, then to laugh outright. Yigal asked him what the joke was, and Harvey said, 'I'm looking forward to that day in July 1998, when some of you wiseacres are here on a picnic with a bunch of young kids from that period. And you try to explain to them how in your youth you got a bang out of the unmitigated slop you call music.' He closed his machine, slamming the cover.

Joe said, 'Wait a minute. You haven't heard the new songs that Clive brought.'

'I heard them last night—at Bar Vasca—and this morning when I went down I asked if they had fumigated the place.'

'You're an old man,' Cato said sharply.

'With trained ears that listen to every note that is played, and I say the slop Mr. Clive was grinding out last night was a fraud on the public.'

'It happens to be the music of this age,' Monica said heatedly.

'Then this age is slop. If you have to listen to music like that for kicks . . . and smoke pot . . .'

'Are you the new Savonarola?' Gretchen asked coldly.

'Is he the guy who burned those things in Florence?'

'Yes.'

'We need him . . . right here.'

'I wouldn't burn your music,' Gretchen said. 'I would keep it in a museum of nostalgia.'

'Yours I would burn,' Holt said. 'It's protest against things you don't understand . . . destruction of things you do.'

'I think this picnic is over,' Monica snapped, but Britta, in her cool Scandinavian composure, took Holt's tape recorder from him and replaced it on the ground, opening the clasps as she did so.

'It's ridiculous for grown people to act this way,' she said. 'I think Mr. Holt should play the tape over again and we should listen to see if there are any songs we can respect. How else can we learn?' She turned to Holt and said, 'How do you start this?'

'Push that button,' he said, accepting no responsibility, but before any music sounded he stopped the machine. 'We'll do it this way,' he said. 'Mr. Fairbanks laid it on the line with you about "Night and Day" and you laughed. I'll take the same risk. There's a piece here that tore me apart when I was a kid. Tell me what you think of it.' He worked the tape till he found what he wanted, then set the machine at good volume and adjusted the speakers.

In a moment we heard Jo Stafford's husky voice singing 'Blues in the Night,' with its haunting vision of youth in an impoverished railroad town and that marvelous pair of lines:

> 'I've seen me some big towns
> And heard me some big talk . . .'

The young people did listen with respect, and I was amused at how apprehensively Holt and I awaited their judgment. At the conclusion Joe said, 'It has a touch of class,' and Gretchen said, 'Tonight, Mr. Holt, when you hear "MacArthur Park" I hope you'll have the same compassion.'

'I've already heard it,' he said. 'It has a touch of class.'

———— •◦• ————

On our return, Holt was driving the lead car when two policemen flagged us down at the outskirts of Pamplona, took one look at Joe's beard, instructed us to pull over to the side of the road, and asked, 'Is this the young man who calls himself Yigal Zmora?'

'In the next car,' I said.

When the police halted the pop-top, I went back to translate. 'Are you the young man who calls himself Yigal Zmora?' they repeated. When Yigal nodded, they told Gretchen, 'Follow us. He's wanted.'

I asked, 'What for?' and they said, 'Don't ask questions.'

We drove into town, but when we reached the fork that led to the police station they turned in the opposite direction, and before I could figure out what was happening, they had hauled up in front of the Hotel Tres Reyes, swankiest in town, where it was practically impossible to get reservations during San Fermín.

They dismounted, leaned their motorcycles in the driveway, and told Yigal, 'Follow us.' As he started to enter the hotel, a small, familiar figure of an elderly gentleman dashed out of the lobby, elbowed the policeman aside, and clutched at Yigal. 'Bruce!' he cried. Yigal, hanging limp and dismayed, called back to us over his shoulder, 'My grandfather.'

It was Marcus Melnikoff, well dressed and alert as ever. When he saw me he ran over to say hello, keeping firm hold of Yigal's hand as he did so. 'I had one hell of a time finding this boy,' he said as we gathered around the pop-top. 'Bruce, your room at the bar . . . it's a disgrace. It was these good officers who tracked you down. Gentlemen, I would like to express my thanks . . .' He took the bewildered policemen aside and handed each a thousand pesetas. 'Spain is well run. You say, "Where's my grandson?" and they find him.'

I asked Melnikoff where he was staying, and he pointed to the Tres Reyes, and I said you couldn't get rooms there, and he said, 'You can if you know the Spanish consul in Chicago and the American ambassador in Madrid. I'm a heavy contributor to the Republican party.'

'What brings you here?' I asked.

Grandly, silently, Melnikoff pointed to his grandson. Then he said, 'I've come to take him home.'

'I'm not going back to Detroit,' Yigal protested.

'Please! In front of so many, it's not necessary to discuss family matters.'

'I will not go home now. I said I might in mid-September.'

'Mid-September is too late to get you into Case Institute of Technology.'

'Who said I wanted to go to Case?'

'Do you know how difficult it is to get in a good school these days? Only because one of the top professors at Case happens to serve as consultant to Pontiac . . .'

'He can give the vacancy to some deserving black,' Yigal said.

This unexpected reply angered Melnikoff, and he snapped, 'I've heard about you at the Technion . . . To waste a talent like yours . . . Please, let's go somewhere. This is a public driveway.'

Yigal said, 'The gang was planning to have dinner together. Join us.'

'I would be honored to meet Bruce's friends,' Melnikoff said graciously. 'But only if I can pick up the check.'

Monica cried, 'You sure can. Free food, gang!' Mr. Melnikoff laughed and asked where a decent restaurant could be found in Pamplona, and Monica had three quick suggestions, concluding, 'But the nicest place is an old castle perched on the city walls. You'd like it, and since we know the food is excellent, so would we.'

'You shall sit at my right,' Mr. Melnikoff said.

The restaurant Monica had recommended was popular in Pamplona, El Caballo Blanco, situated in the old part of town on a cliff overlooking the Río Arga. It was an ancient building, beamed with old chestnut rubbed with oil, and it conveyed a sense of good living. During San Fermín it was crowded, but the manager at Mr. Melnikoff's hotel knew the women who ran it and he had arranged a table for fourteen, which included the two college girls that Joe had picked up and the boy who was grieving over the death of Octopus.

It was a gala evening and Mr. Melnikoff proved a charming host. He told many stories of Detroit's automobile industry, then listened as Clive explained how the musical groups in London operated. He wanted to hear the latest doings of World Mutual and congratulated me on our recent successes, and this led to our serious discussion. 'How could a man of your interest and attainments bother with a cheap Mardi gras like this?'

'Some of us happen to revere Pamplona.'

'Why?'

'As the last evocation of something important.'

He shrugged his shoulders and said, 'I happen to like Miami Beach. My friends in Detroit think I'm crazy.' He hesitated, then asked, 'What kind of boy is Bruce?'

'To begin with, he's Yigal.'

'A phase. Have you heard about his grades? In every science, almost a hundred. Perhaps a genius. We mustn't let that go to waste.'

'Israel produces some very fine scientists. And she needs him.'

'We need him.' He looked down the table to where Yigal was arguing heatedly with one of the new girls. You could see how much the old man cherished the boy. 'Did he tell you that he was a hero in the Arab war? What's a boy his age doing at war?'

'Life everywhere is pretty dangerous, Mr. Melnikoff. Those riots in Detroit . . .'

'A phase. The simple fact is, that boy is needed in the United States.'

'He knows that. I can assure you that as of now his mind isn't made up against America.'

'Then what in hell is he doing in Pamplona? Torremolinos? That no-where place in Portugal? Has some girl got him on the string?'

'Mr. Melnikoff, you see that pretty girl down there, the one they call Gretchen? This morning she took us on a picnic to an old monastery.'

'I know, the policemen here called the policemen there and they said they saw you go in.'

'Good old Spain.'

'What?'

'Anyway, we were discussing the fact that for the last seven hundred years pilgrims have been traveling up and down these roads . . . wanderers in search of meaning. That's what Yigal's engaged in.'

'Some pilgrim! You see the filthy bar he's living in.'

'I'm living there too.'

'You ought to be ashamed.'

'I would guess that in the old days half the pilgrims slept in monasteries, the other half in whorehouses.'

Our conversation was broken at this point by Cato, who came to our end of the table to pay his respects to the host. Monica was with him. 'We have to meet some kids from Denmark at the bandstand,' he explained, and when they were gone, Mr. Melnikoff said, 'Ten years ago I'd have been outraged by such a sight. Now I think it's great. If I were young and had talent, I'd want to be black, and the first thing I'd do would be to marry the boss's daughter . . . for the betterment of everybody.'

Long after midnight I was in my room when a knock came at my door. I supposed it was someone who had been sent to find a place to sleep, but it was Melnikoff; a taxi had brought him from the hotel. He asked softly, 'Can I talk with you, Fairbanks?' I nodded, and he went to the window and signaled the taxi to wait. Sitting on my bed, he said, 'I feel as if I were lost. This dump you're living in. This afternoon when I visited Bruce's room, there was a strange couple in bed. I'm sure they'd been smoking marijuana. What's our boy doing with a crew like this?'

'He's part of a total revolution,' I said, not satisfied with my answer.

'In America the college students burn down buildings. What is it?'

'Mr. Melnikoff, I see these young people over here and I find them some of the finest kids I've ever known.'

'This I cannot accept. I think a sickness has overtaken a whole generation.' Before I could argue otherwise, he took my hands and said earnestly, 'Tell me this. The Negroes. Why can't they work their way up the ladder . . . the way my mother and father did? The way I did?'

'Is that what you ask in Detroit?'

'No. There I keep my mouth shut. I figure there's something going on I don't understand and I don't want to look the fool.'

'I'm glad you haven't preached that in public. It accounts for the bad feeling the blacks have against the Jews.'

'And that's another thing. I've paid my dues to the NAACP for thirty years. Without the leadership of us Jews, the Negroes would still have no civil rights. You look at the record.'

'But don't tell them that because you Jews worked your way up, they could do so, too.'

'Does Bruce feel the way you do?'

'If he has any sense, he does. But let's drop the Jews and blacks for a minute. I happen to know the Irish in Boston. When they came over here they were treated worse than the blacks. Yet they rose by their own power. Why? Because they had at their disposal a ladder of vertical mobility. The older Irish could get nothing from the Protestants in Boston. But those resourceful Irish developed the habit of producing beautiful girls and rugged boys who starred at football in the Boston high schools. So what happened? Whether the Boston Protestants liked it or not, their sons fell in love with the beautiful Irish girls, and Harvard University gave the rugged Irish boys football scholarships, and in time those boys married their roommates' sisters. But the black never had access to this vertical mobility. A white Irish girl can hide the fact that she's Catholic, or she can join the Episcopal Church. But a black never could hide his color, and we allowed him to join nothing. There is no possible comparison between a Jew who got ahead and a black who didn't. They were not even playing in the same ball game.'

'Then you agree with the young people? There is something wrong with America?'

'Much.'

He was silent for a long time, then said abruptly, 'Vietnam. Shouldn't we throw the protesters in jail?'

'I used to live in Saigon. Tell me, has there ever been a worse war?'

'You tell me. If you were a young man, would you burn your draft card?'

Now I was silent. We were engaged in an honest discussion, so I answered honestly. 'It's impossible for me to think as a young man, because I carry the stamp of my education—automatic patriotism, a certain attitude toward women, a belief in contracts, faith in the ideals that were prevalent in 1932 and were proved so dreadfully wrong. I'm an old man, encrusted with all the errors and abuses of age. If, continuing to bear my present stamp, I were suddenly made nineteen again, of course I would respect the draft and go to war. But if I were really nineteen—thinking like today's nineteen-year-old brought up under his own system—I don't know what I'd do . . . probably burn my draft card.'

Mr. Melnikoff rose, paced for some moments, then asked, 'What do you think will happen with Bruce?'

'I think he'll go to the United States, study it carefully, and in the end, decide to cast his lot with Israel.'

He sat down. 'Why do you say that?'

'Because I know him very well, and he is a boy who looks with cold logic at the facts.'

'But the facts are all in favor of the United States.'

'Physical facts, yes. Emotional, no. And this generation is not going to defraud itself where emotions are concerned.'

'Have you advised him to stay in Israel?'

'I've advised him to try the United States . . . but not Detroit.'

'Why not? We have a good life there.'

'I promise you this. If you keep him with you in Detroit, you'll lose him.'

'What can we do to hold him?'

'By doing the only thing that ever holds young people—the good ones, that is—by setting them free.'

'To what?'

'For Yigal it could turn out to be engineering in one of the new Negro republics like Vwarda, or research at Oxford, or teaching at some college in the south. I don't know what it will be, but unless he finds it, for himself, you'll not be able to hold him.'

'You talk very glibly about children. I suppose you have none of your own.'

'I had a son. Much like Yigal. And I lost him.'

'How?'

'By using the same tactics you're using with Bruce . . . as you call him.'

———◆—◆———

I was much agitated by my conversation with Melnikoff. I found that my attitudes were so close to those of Yigal, and Melnikoff's so much like those of Holt, that I wanted to discuss the matter with Harvey to check whether I was on the right course in defending the boy. I was especially keen to get his guess on whether Yigal would choose to remain in the United States, because I didn't want Melnikoff to be swayed by my own somewhat prejudiced opinion.

Before returning to my own room, therefore, I stopped by Holt's. As I started pushing the door open—there were no locks in Bar Vasca and not too many latches that worked—I vaguely thought that he must have a suitcase or something by the door, and it was only when I had the door well opened that I realized it was a chair, propped against the door, purposefully. I started to retreat, but at this moment Holt growled at me from the bed and I, like a fool, stopped to answer. I wish I hadn't.

For the last several days I had noticed—at the picnic this afternoon, for example, when we were discussing music, and the other day when we were arguing motion pictures—that Britta was deferential to Holt's opinions. Politically and socially he was quite unlike the people she preferred, but in his rocklike simplicity he resembled some of the stronger men she had known in Tromsø. There was, she told me once, a certain Norwegian honesty about him. The men of Norway whom she admired had usually been wrong about everything except what mattered most—character. 'With them you felt that if you got into a fight . . . Let's suppose we were in a real fight. I could trust you to decide which side was morally right. I could depend on Cato to make a speech. I could depend on Yigal to know what to do if the going got tough. And I could depend on Joe to give me sympathy if things went wrong. Mr. Holt I could depend upon to do the fighting. In this respect he is much like my father.'

'I thought you said you felt sorry for your father.'

'I feel sorry for Mr. Holt.'

When I saw them together—say, at lunch or if we went out to a restaurant for dinner—well, they weren't together in that sense, but they did usually find chairs at the same end of the table . . . Well, I had the suspicion that pretty little Britta had spotted Holt as her last best chance of escaping Tromsø. Certainly her affair with Joe had permanently ended, and for some years Yigal would have problems larger than girls, and her time was running out, for she had only the money that Gretchen gave her. Under those dismal circumstances, Holt must have appeared the only good bet, and I admired her perspicacity.

Holt, for his part, had never been blind to an attractive girl, and if one flattered him, as Britta had after the run that morning, he was susceptible. I should have caught on when he asked me, 'Are Norwegians pretty much like Swedes?' I began by explaining what I knew of Scandinavian history.

'I don't mean the history,' he interrupted. 'I mean the social customs . . . today. Are the Norwegians as . . . well . . . liberal?'

'Oh, you mean sex? I don't know.'

'You've been there.'

'Yes, and if you want to know about hydroelectric plants, old age pensions, shipping . . .'

'You study the wrong things,' he growled, and I forgot the conversation.

Later I was to learn that after the fireworks one night, Holt and Britta had walked for miles through the darkened city, stopping at one bar after another, till nearly dawn. Britta told me, 'I felt that he was both a little boy and a powerful man, and that's a dangerous way for a girl to feel.' At one of the bars there were some English students who hadn't been to bed for three nights and they were obviously smoking pot, and Holt had asked if she smoked, and she had replied, 'Everybody tries it.' The phrase had struck him oddly; for the first time he vaguely understood that it was a total society in which these young people lived, a society in which it was unlikely that a young person with curiosity would avoid a confrontation with marijuana.

'Have you tried LSD too?' he asked her.

'I'm not that crazy,' she replied. He then asked her if Monica smoked, and she had fenced with him, saying, 'That's each girl's problem. Ask her.'

Holt found her fascinating, a window into a new world, and since it was a world of which he had been contemptuous, he found special pleasure in exploring it with her. The overriding consideration, of course, was the fact that Britta was unusually handsome— a tall, beautifully dimensioned girl, with an enviable complexion, very white teeth, and flaxen hair that shimmered in sunlight and cast flecks of gold by candlelight.

One afternoon I was walking with them back from the bullfight, and I noticed that Britta kept stride with us as if she were our tested companion, and Holt asked suddenly, 'You ever ride a mustang?' and Britta replied, 'American cars are too expensive for us in Norway.'

Now, on this night when Holt growled at me for pushing aside his chair, I saw in the light that entered the room that he had had good reason to block the door, for there was a girl in bed with him. Because of what I had observed in recent days, I assumed it was Britta. I was strangely relieved when I saw it was one of Joe's college girls, wearing nothing and making no effort to draw the sheet over her face. The couple showed no embarrassment, and as I backed out, Holt said, 'Pull the chair back against the door, if you can.'

———— •◦•◦• ————

July 12 produced one of the most dramatic runs in recent years, and this was unfortunate, because standing beside me on the plateau of the art museum was Marcus Melnikoff, who had insisted upon seeing for himself the madness that had captured his grandson. I had advised him not to come, warning him that he would neither understand nor enjoy what he saw, and Yigal had protested that the bulls held no fascination for him: 'In fact, I think the part you're going to see . . . the running . . . it's insane and no rational man would bother with it.'

'Then why are you in Pamplona?' Melnikoff demanded as we had our cups of hot chocolate.

'I'm like the others. I enjoy Pamplona . . . the music . . . the fireworks.'

'I'll see for myself,' Melnikoff said, and now he stationed himself stubbornly on the ramp as if to say, 'Show me.'

I told him, 'What Yigal had to say was right . . .'

'Please don't call him Yigal.'

'Yigal or Bruce, he's a terrific boy and you should accept him as he is.'

'One of the fundamental errors of our age. Anyone who accepts an eighteen-year-old boy as he is . . . he's nuts. The whole purpose of life is to change people into something better.'

I changed the subject to the bulls, and explained, 'They'll come out of that corral down there . . . Look at that man by the wall. That's the fellow we had dinner with last night. Yigal's friend, Harvey Holt.'

'You mean a grown man is going to make an ass of himself? What's he do?'

'Tech rep for UniCom . . . in Afghanistan.'

'That's a strong company. What's an official of UniCom doing in a place like this?'

'He comes every year . . . to run with the bulls.'

'You mean he'll stay down there? When the bulls come?'

'Yes, sir. And what's more, Mr. Melnikoff, he's an intelligent man. And rather wealthy.'

'It beats me.'

There was nothing more I could say, so we stared down the hill to watch the policemen as they slowly moved toward the ramp up which they would shortly escape. The first rocket went off and almost immediately the second, sending the bulls on their vigorous charge up the hill.

'Look at that idiot!' Mr. Melnikoff shouted as Holt started his dash toward the bulls. 'Bruce, Bruce, he's going to be killed!'

'He knows what he's doing,' I assured him, but I was relieved when Holt, spotting some danger I could not see, turned back more quickly than usual and started running faster than I had ever before seen him move. Real fear showed in his face and he dove for the wall.

What had he seen to make him suspect trouble? In the narrowest part of the passage, where jostling among the animals often oc- curred, a steer had bumped into an ill-tempered bull, throwing the latter off stride. The bull had hooked at the steer, missed, and for a fraction of a second had lost his footing. Trying not to stumble, the bull had veered sharply to the left, which brought him close to the wall against which Holt had taken refuge.

Seeing along this wall a mass of forms, some moving, the bull now lowered its head, and like a scythe reaping barley, swept its left horn along the wall, wiping it clean. Three, four, five, six men went down before this savage horn, all punctured in one way or another.

The seventh man to be hooked stood just downhill from Holt, and unfortunately, in place of the traditional sash, he wore a leather belt which caught on the bull's horn, impeding forward motion. Arrested for a moment, the bull savagely chopped its head, goring the man twice more. It then broke loose and for the count of four stood facing Harvey Holt, who remained ice-stiff, with the horn six inches from his gut. The man to Holt's left moved, and the bull drove hard at him, tossing him to the ground and nuzzling at him, first with its nose, and then with its horns.

Mr. Melnikoff screamed, 'For God's sake, take the bull away!'

Britta, standing to my left, prayed aloud, 'Make the bull move on. Make him move on.' But Joe, next to Britta, watched silently, fascinated, as Holt remained motionless while the bull savaged the man at his feet. My breath came in such gasps that I scarcely felt Mr. Melnikoff clutching at my arm. 'This is terrible!' he screamed. 'Get that bull away!'

With sudden force the bull left Holt and scraped his horn once more against the wall, knocking down numbers nine, ten, eleven, the last a man standing in the very door of the hospital. Then, with a kick of his hind legs, the great beast ran straight up Santo Domingo, ignoring everyone.

As soon as he was gone, teams began gathering up the bodies. Some of the gored men had fainted and were dripping blood. Others, not punctured by the horns, shook themselves, felt their bellies and their testicles, and walked off. Eight were carried into the hospital.

Mr. Melnikoff said, 'I want to sit down.' Yigal sat with him and assured him that none of the runners would die, but the old man snapped, 'How can you be so wise? You saw that horn in the man's belly.'

'Believe me, Grandpop, that man is going to live. Ask Mr. Fairbanks.'

'Why should I ask that fool? A grown man who comes here every year to watch such a spectacle. He might as well be back in the days of Nero. Three tickets to the Colosseum, please.' He stopped for breath, then took his grandson's hands and asked, 'Tell me, Bruce, did the war harden you so much that you enjoy this sort of thing . . . look at those pools of blood . . . in a public street?'

'I'm revolted by it.'

'Then why, in the name of God, do you stay?'

'Because there's so much more to Pamplona. Some of the kids don't even go to the bullfights. They never see a bull. Grandfather, they don't go to bed till morning. Why would they bother with this?'

'Tell me, Bruce. Is it a girl? You have a girl here, that's it.'

'Grandfather, I'm just here to enjoy myself.'

'Enjoy! Enjoy! You talk like General Goering. Bruce, you're flying home with me this afternoon.'

And Mr. Melnikoff swung into action. At Bar Vasca, where a huge crowd judged the day's run to have been one of the worst in recent years and congratulated Holt on his miraculous escape, Melnikoff got on the phone, made a reservation on a late TWA flight to New York, hired a taxi to drive him and his grandson to Madrid, and sent a batch of cables to Tel Aviv and Grosse Pointe. Then he asked me to accompany them upstairs to pack Bruce's gear, but when we reached the room and he opened the door, he drew back in disgust, because in Bruce's bed lay two girls from our picnic, with the boy from California who dug Octopus.

'Get them out of there,' he commanded me, as if I were one of his minor employees, so I went in and said to the kids, 'Trouble. Better scram.' All three were naked, and they hastily donned bits of clothing.

'I think that shirt belongs to Yigal,' I told one of the girls.

'He won't care,' she said, and they traipsed through the hall and into Gretchen's room, where they climbed back into bed and went to sleep.

'Your close friends?' Mr. Melnikoff asked his grandson with deep sarcasm.

'I met them yesterday,' Yigal protested.

'They were in your bed.'

'They were in my clothes—but what can I do?'

'You can pack.'

The moment of decision had come. By every sign that I could read, Yigal wanted to stay with the gang, he wanted to continue his exploration of their values, their significance. He was inclined to tell his grandfather to go to hell, but instead he turned to me and asked, 'Mr. Fairbanks, what should I do?'

'Do?' Mr. Melnikoff shouted. 'There's only one thing to do. Pack!'

'Get out of here!' Yigal exploded. 'Go on. Wait out in the hall.' He started to push his grandfather into the hall, but the old man resisted.

I said, 'If you insist on having your way, Mr. Melnikoff, you're going to lose this boy. You wait out in the hall and let me talk with him.' I nudged the old man along—he muttering under his breath about who the hell I thought I was, and I pretending not to hear. When I closed the door I turned to see Yigal sitting on his bed, his head in his hands.

'What should I do?' he asked.

'You're not in love with any of these girls?'

'No. I like Britta, but she doesn't know it.'

'Then there's nothing to lose in that area.'

'There's always something to lose.'

'Sure, but not crucial. It looks to me, Yigal, as if your big problem is exactly like Harvey Holt's . . . and in a sense, mine.'

'I care nothing for the bulls.'

'I don't mean the bulls. I mean America.'

'Oh . . . what do you mean by that?'

'America is the great magnet of our age. It's like the sun exerting its tremendous gravitational pull. Especially if you've ever been touched by America, it becomes the great force which you must maneuver into balance. Holt never succeeded. He's doomed to be an expatriate. I'm a marginal man. I can live in the States. I've proved that. And I can lick the States' economic system . . . just as well as your grandfather has. I've proved that, too. But I'm always content to get away. I'm the way Gretchen and Joe will be when they're fifty. Americans, but quite satisfied to live in Yugoslavia . . . or Israel.'

'You're saying my present duty is to get myself squared away on what I think about the United States?'

'You state things better than I do.'

'Even if it means listening to that old fraud tell me how he made it big in Detroit?'

'I'm an old fraud. One of these days I'll tell you how I made it big in World Mutual.'

'You think I ought to go with him? Fly home tonight?'

'I'm not going to tell you what to do.'

'But goddammit, you are telling me. In your own superior way. No, you won't come right out and say, "Kid, go home for a couple of months and weigh things for yourself." You don't have the guts to come out and say it. You don't want to commit yourself.'

He was shouting, so I shouted back, 'All right, I'm telling you. Go home. Go home this day, unless you're afraid of a test.'

'All right. Don't yell at me,' he bellowed. 'I will go home,' and he started to pack his bag in a way so vicious that you would have thought he hated every piece of clothing. 'Where's my blue shirt?' he raged.

'That girl took it.'

He banged out of his room, stormed past his grandfather, roared into Gretchen's room, pulled down the covers, and ripped his blue shirt off the girl's back before she could properly waken. 'Pigs!' he yelled back into the room.

———— ·•·—

Every summer, as the days of San Fermín drew to a close, Bar Vasca converted itself into an ipso facto tourist agency. At almost any hour of the twenty-four, young people would drop by to ask Raquel if she knew of anyone traveling to Brussels or Istanbul. The most casual arrangements were made, and trips that would require several hundred dollars and eighteen or twenty days were agreed upon within minutes.

But I often wondered what one careful mother from Appleton, Wisconsin, would have thought had she seen how her well-bred nineteen-year-old daughter traveled from Pamplona to Split in Yugoslavia. Joe had met her at the public square only that morning, and when I stopped by their table for a drink, after seeing Yigal and his grandfather off to Madrid, he introduced her as 'Rebecca from Wisconsin.' She was unusually attractive and had had three years at the University of Minnesota. I enjoyed her conversation, for she was majoring in economics and was interested in many of the things that concerned me.

That afternoon Joe brought her down to Bar Vasca to hear Clive's records, and we sat in our alcove passing time till the bullfight began. She asked idly, 'You happen to know anyone heading for Milan? I'd like to look at the industry there.'

We asked around the bar and no one knew of transportation for Italy, but a German, who was having a beer while listening to the new music from London, said, 'I know a Dutchman who's driving to Yugoslavia right after today's fight.' I was looking at Rebecca as he said this, and a reflective cast came into her eye and she said, 'I might as well go to Yugoslavia. Probably never have another chance.' So the German was dispatched to find the Dutchman, and in a little while a very handsome, tall, bronzed young man entered the bar and told us that he was Klaus from Amsterdam, and he was driving a Taunus to Split right after the fight.

I said, 'This is Rebecca from Wisconsin. Economics major.'

'Law.'

Rebecca had had exactly one minute to judge his character, but now she said, 'I'd pay half.'

'You pay for your meals and hotel. I pay for the petrol.'

'How many days do you figure?'

'Can you drive?'

'Four on the floor.'

'We'd probably make it in five days. I don't want to rush, but we'll be deep into France by midnight.'

'I'll get my stuff.'

'Can I help?'

'Thanks. It's out beyond Tres Reyes.'

And they left for Split.

With the departure of Yigal for America, the thoughts of all in

Bar Vasca turned to what to do next. Holt and I would drive back to Madrid. The remaining five in the yellow pop-top had no concrete plans—maybe southern France, although that was rumored to be quite expensive. The two college girls were heading for Rome, and the boy who dug Octopus said he was going to stand on the highway and the first car that picked him up in either direction would determine his future.

So far as I know, at that time not one of my young friends had ever spoken the name Moçambique. It came into the conversation obliquely when Holt said, 'Watching that young lady leave for Split reminded me of how Humphrey Bogart decided to go down the river with Miss Hepburn. It was about the same, only they were much older.'

'What are you talking about?' Joe asked testily.

'One of Bogart's best. I saw it at a movie house at Gago Coutinho.'

'Where the hell is Gago Coutinho?'

'Moçambique,' I explained.

'Where's that?'

'As a matter of fact,' I said, 'it's one of the most exciting places I've worked in. Southern part of Africa, but on the Indian Ocean side. I was doing a feasibility study and fell in love with the place.'

'Ninety-seven per cent Negroes,' Holt replied. 'But the Portuguese are in control,' and he pressed his thumb firmly against the table.

'It would be interesting for you,' I told Cato. 'To the south you have South Africa, where the Negroes are subdued. To the north, Tanzania, where they govern. Moçambique in the middle—geographically and spiritually.'

'Isn't that where they have a stupendous game preserve?' Monica asked. I nodded, and she said, 'Father saw it once and said it was the best in Africa.' She hesitated, for the continent still held unpleasant memories, then snapped her fingers and said, 'I think we should go. Right after Pamplona.'

'Can we drive there?' Gretchen asked.

'No possibility,' I said, 'but boats go down . . . cheap, too . . . car wouldn't cost much.'

'There's a Greek boat which leaves Barcelona on the afternoon of the fifteenth,' Holt said.

'How do you know that?' Monica asked.

'It's my business to know transportation. Sails the fifteenth of every month from Barcelona. Seventeenth from Livorno.'

Excitement began to grow, and Gretchen asked, 'Do we need visas?'

'Yes, but you can apply for them in Barcelona,' Holt said. 'They'll be stamped in your passports at Luanda. That's in Africa . . . on the Atlantic side.' He also knew the cost and the duration of validity.

'What kind of country is it?' Cato asked.

I answered, 'You've heard the phrase "miles of beach?" Well, Moçambique has thousands of miles . . . of the most beautiful vacant beaches in the world. Jungle, huge rivers, fascinating islands, good cities. The more I think about it, the better it sounds. If you can afford the boat fare.'

Without hesitating, Gretchen said, 'If Joe and Britta need funds, I can let them have some. But could we drive our car in Moçambique?'

'Good roads,' I said.

'Not good . . . but roads,' Holt corrected. 'He flies everywhere. I have to go by car.'

'Do you suppose we could call the shipping line in Barcelona?' Gretchen asked.

So Britta got on the phone, spoke to the operator in Spanish, and in a surprisingly short time Gretchen was asking the Greek line if they had any cabins to Moçambique. Then she frowned and shared her disappointment with us. 'All booked,' she reported, and was about to hang up when Monica grabbed my arm and said, 'You know the Greek shipowners. Do something.'

So I took the phone and started to explain that I had some association with their company, whereupon the man on the other end interrupted and I could hear him speaking to someone. Soon a Greek I had met in the Torremolinos negotiations was shouting at me in a tremendous voice, 'Yes, one of our boats does sail from Barcelona on July 15. Yes, it's completely booked. Oh, you're Mr. Fairbanks of World Mutual! Of course I remember, the one who arranged our loan! You need three cabins? Mr. Fairbanks, for you we have just dispossessed an entire Turkish family. Can your people telegraph us five thousand pesetas immediately? They can pay the balance in American traveler's checks when they arrive . . . Yes, we can accommodate a Volkswagen pop-top.'

I pointed to each of the five travelers, and each nodded in agreement. I then told Barcelona, 'It's a deal. They'll see you on the fifteenth.'

While Gretchen went to the telegraph office, the other four remained in the alcove and engaged in the type of discussion that was being conducted in all parts of Pamplona at that moment: 'Shall we stay for the last fight, or shall we duck out a day early?' Prudent people counseled getting out of the city early, for after the last fight the roads, particularly to France and Barcelona, would be jammed; but the more daring, who had paid eight or ten dollars for their tickets to that last fight, argued that it would be shameful to quit San Fermín before it ended. Our young people, with five to share the driving, decided to stay for the fight and ride all night.

That agreed upon, they began asking questions about the adventure to which they had so hastily committed themselves, and Holt and I answered as best we could. When Gretchen returned she had Clive with her, and he said, 'I can go only as far as Barcelona. Then I'll have to duck off to Ibiza, but Moçambique sounds super.'

I said, 'It could prove very important, and for a reason you'd never guess. You've been living in cities . . . and ersatz places like Torremolinos and Pamplona. It would do you good to see nature in a place like Moçambique . . . immense jungles and rivers you've never dreamed of. Before a man's thirty he ought to see for himself what nature is really like.'

'Sounds reasonable,' Joe said.

Then an incident occurred which epitomized those last days at Pamplona. Two young men whom I had not seen before were sitting in the alcove next to us, and they must have heard our conversation, for they excused their impertinence and asked if they could join us. 'Are you heading for Moçambique?' one asked. When Gretchen nodded, they asked, 'Any chance of our going along?' I was amazed when our group seriously weighed the possibility but concluded that there wouldn't be room.

Seeing the dejection on the young men's faces, Clive snapped his fingers as if trying to recall a name or a place. 'Wait a minute! Those three girls at Bar Txoco. Weren't they going to Greece? They wanted some man to go along to sort of look out for them. Cato, you know the ones I mean.'

'Oh, them!'

It was then agreed that Cato would go fetch the girls, and soon they were participating in a conference at our table. The girls were from the American midwest, good-looking kids under twenty, and they seemed to have substantial funds. They looked at the two boys, asked a few questions, and then consulted among themselves, but out loud, so that we could hear. They had wanted just one man, but two might be better. Their caravan slept four easy but five could squeeze in. The boys would have to pay nothing, not even their meals, but they had to promise to stay at least to Greece and back to Italy. The terms were agreed to, then one of the girls, scarcely eighteen, asked, 'You smoke?'

'Of course.'

'Take heavy stuff?'

'No.'

'Do you mind?' She leaned over and rolled up the sleeves of one young fellow to inspect the veins on the inside of his elbows. She did the same with the other, then said to her friends, 'They're clean.' To the table generally she said, 'It's no fun trying to handle a man on heroin.'

One of the other girls said, 'The caravan's over there. We're leaving now . . . skipping the rest of the fights.'

'We didn't bother with the bulls,' one of the young men said.

'Got your gear stashed somewhere?' asked the girl who had made the inspection.

'That pack over there.'

'We're off.'

———— •◦•◦•◦• ————

We came back to the subject of movies once more at Pamplona. A large circle of young people was lolling in the sun at the central square, waiting for the fights to begin, and when Holt and I came past they asked us to join them. They were discussing the flicks, as they called them, and their enthusiasms were quite different from Holt's. They went for directors, for the provocative, half-formed statement, and they were very high on Ingmar Bergman and Antonioni. They agreed that Hollywood had never made a decent movie, whereupon Holt asked, 'What about Spencer Tracy and Fredric March when they had that duel over science?'

None of the young people knew what he was talking about, so

they ignored the question. Later, when they said that the trouble with the American motion picture was that it lacked relevancy, Holt asked if they didn't think that sometimes the good American movies sort of summed up the feeling of a generation, and wasn't that relevant. When they asked him for an example, he said, 'Like at the beginning of World War II, when we fellows were all chopped up about strange lands and death and what courage was and we saw Humphrey Bogart mixed up with all sorts of cross currents, in a strange land, but doing what he could to save Ingrid Bergman . . .'

One of the young men snapped his fingers and said, 'My God! He means *Casablanca*,' and a girl said, 'Like wow! That turkey.'

'It related to the mood . . . well, the mood my friends were in.'

'Mr. Holt,' Gretchen explained, '*Casablanca* was a mishmash of clichés, made solely to earn a lot of money from starry-eyed young fellows like yourself. It succeeded. But don't ask us to take it seriously. The people who made it didn't.'

I expected Holt to blow his stack, but instead he sat back and listened, and after a while he heard a beauty of a statement, an insolent provocation to which he would often refer. A gangling young American with a wispy beard said, 'You forget one basic fact. What Hollywood could do was to come up, at rare intervals, with a confection of ideal camp. It sometimes did just what Mr. Holt suggested—caught an entire era and froze it into motionless motion.' One of the French listeners asked what he had in mind, and he said, 'The greatest movie ever made on our side of the water —one of the greatest, I suppose, made anywhere—*King Kong*.'

Rarely in debate have I heard a thesis so universally accepted. All agreed that *King Kong* was the only really good movie ever made in Hollywood, but I was rather startled when the man with the wispy beard also proposed it as the high-water mark of American culture.

'We'll drink to that,' two of the girls agreed. 'Best single thing we've done. I suppose Fay Wray is the ideal American.' They launched into a discussion of her acting in this picture, and I was surprised at how minutely they remembered the movie. They drank a toast to Miss Wray, who was apparently a huge favorite, but the man with the wispy beard protested, 'Don't forget that without Robert Armstrong's masterful performance, you'd have had no picture.' He imitated Armstrong's musclebound style, and the group had to confess that Armstrong had won immortality.

'The apex of our contribution to world culture,' one of the girls proposed, and they drank to that too.

In a well-controlled voice Holt asked, 'If *King Kong* is the only good thing we've done, where do you put the plays of Eugene O'Neill?'

The crowd laughed, and one girl asked, 'Have you ever tried to sit through one of those turgid things?'

'Don't kid around. What about *Strange Interlude?*'

'Oh my God! Please.'

'What about *A Long Day's Journey into Night*, where his mother is hooked on heroin?'

'Mr. Holt, nobody, but nobody, can take that junk seriously any longer.'

'Then what about Ralph Waldo Emerson?'

'That Sunday School teacher?'

One girl thought that he was merely an apologist for the Establishment, but Holt asked, 'They ever teach you his essay "Compensation"?' No one had heard of it, and he said, 'His idea is that whatever you do, you get a compensatory reaction. Like if you waste your university days without learning anything . . . well, you're really up the creek.'

Holt's idea was brushed aside by a young man who said, 'There's one other American movie that deserves serious consideration. Any of you cats seen this all-time winner *I Was a Teenage Werewolf?*' He added a phrase that one heard often in discussions these days. 'It was so bad it was beautiful. There was this clean-cut high school kid who had only one bad fault. From time to time he changed into a werewolf and killed young girls.'

One of the girls had seen the film and agreed that it was a masterpiece. 'They had one scene that was truly precious. A perfectly wonderful average middle-class American family. Father was a Buick salesman, I think. Serious discussion as to whether it was all right to let their daughter go out with a boy who kept turning into a werewolf.'

Now another girl recalled the film and said, 'It was delicious.'

This is a word that offends me, so before I said something I didn't intend, I judged it best that I walk over to the bullring, but the young critics had one more blockbuster. A Frenchman launched it when he said, 'We've been overlooking a man working today who is certainly the best American of them all. We Europeans look on him as the equal of Fellini.'

'You mean Jerry Lewis?' one of the girls asked.

'Who else? As an actor he's magnificent, but as a director he's a genius. Your only one.'

This brought such unanimous agreement that I had to protest: 'You can't be serious!'

'Ah, but we are!' the Frenchman said, and when the other Europeans nodded, he said, 'Over here we see your country as comic, frenzied, lacking direction and bordering on the psychotic. Mr. Lewis is your only director to catch that quality. A generation from now he'll be recognized throughout the world as your only serious contribution to the cinema.'

'More significant even than *King Kong*,' a German girl said.

This was more than I could take, so I snapped, 'I won't have to wait till the next generation to know that none of you have the slightest critical judgment.' I stalked away from the discussion, but had not gone far when Holt overtook me. 'Thanks,' he said. 'I was speechless.'

——— ·•·•· ———

July 13 brought us a real surprise. When I took the girls down to the museum to watch Holt run, we supposed that the disaster the day before would thin the ranks, but that did not happen. If anything, the number of men who were willing to test the bulls on the slope was somewhat greater than before, as if the carnage of yesterday had whetted their appetites for a true test.

We were commenting on this when Monica suddenly screamed, 'Good God! Look who's down there!'

It was Joe, conspicuous in tight Levis, boots and leather vest, leaning nonchalantly against the wall and looking completely out of place. He had stationed himself not far from the police barrier at the spot where the bull had begun its housecleaning the day before. Fascinated by that catastrophe, he had come down to be part of whatever might happen this day.

Monica called to Holt, 'Guess who's running with you!' and Harvey looked in various directions before he spotted Joe. He started to yell, 'You can't run in those shoes,' but as he did so, the rocket exploded and the bulls came charging up the hill. Serenely

Joe moved to the front rank of the runners, ran easily down the hill, miscalculated his distance, turned back too late and was hit squarely in the rump by a big steer who flattened him and then ran over him. By the time he was able to look up, all he could see was the tails of the disappearing bulls as they rounded the bend for the hospital.

'It happened so damned fast,' he told us at Bar Vasca as we ate breakfast. 'I had seen how Holt did it. But those animals are so big!'

'Did the bull get you with its horns?' Monica asked.

'I wish I could claim it was a bull,' Joe replied, 'but you miserable bastards had to be watching.'

When Holt arrived he said harshly to Joe, 'You should have told me. I'd have warned you not to run in that spot. The steers always take that bend close.'

'I'm telling you now. I'm going to run tomorrow.'

'And so am I,' Cato said, perhaps on the spur of the moment.

'And so am I,' I added, certainly on the spur of the moment.

'Now wait a minute!' Holt protested. 'I will not be responsible for three clowns like you on the slopes of Santo Domingo.'

'I didn't ask for your protection today,' Joe pointed out.

'Yes, and you got knocked on your can . . . because you were stupid.' He rose and stormed about the bar, calling Raquel as his witness. 'They want to run tomorrow . . . Bastille Day . . . biggest crowd of the year. A dumb oaf who runs straight into a steer. A bedroom athlete. And a tired old man with white hair. For Christ sake.'

He sat down, and we assured him that whether he cooperated or not, tomorrow morning we three were going to be in the streets. 'Why?' he asked.

I could explain Joe. He had been indifferent to the running before yesterday, but when he saw the bull sweep the left wall clean he grasped the significance of running. It was something germane to him, something that related. It was as inevitable for him to run as it was for Monica to like men and try LSD. It was his destiny.

Cato was different. Slowly he was beginning to accept the fact that he was a member of the team without any limitations. The one person he had not yet convinced was Harvey Holt, whose prejudices ran deep, so if running with the bulls was Holt's criterion for acceptance, Cato would show him that this was a trivial requirement. Also, he liked and trusted Joe and vaguely wanted to be with him.

As for me, it was quite simple. I was sixty-one years old and might never again be in a group so congenial, men with whom I would so gladly run. Of course, as to why I might want to run in the first place, I am not competent to explain. Psychologists have argued that men in ancient Crete ran with the bulls in order to steal from the animals their virility and courage. Cynics dismiss it as ridiculous, grown men trying to be boys again; and those psychiatrists who explain high-fidelity as a substitute for sexual mastery argue that only those men who are sexually incapable run before the bulls, hoping thus to assuage their incompetence. I'm afraid there is something wrong with this theory, because it raises so many questions about Bar Vasca. If the men I saw there had had one more jot of sex, they wouldn't have been able to stand up in the street, let alone run. Some have argued that it is exhibitionism on the part of old men, yet half the runners are young; and others have reasoned that it is narcissism on the part of the young, but half the runners are old. One American critic of note has claimed that nine tenths of the runners are crazy college kids from America and Germany, whereas in matter of fact, nine tenths of the runners are Spaniards, who may well be crazy but have never seen a college. My own theory is that it is fun—inexplicable fun—like a Turkish bath . . . or anchovies and beer . . . or a Chinese girl in Hong Kong.

Holt gave in. He said, 'All right. Tomorrow the four of us will run. But not in Santo Domingo. You're so dumb you'd get killed.' He then led us into the street and up to town hall, where he blocked out a reasonable program. 'You, Fairbanks, you stand in this corner of the barricade. You don't run, and if a bull should by remote chance happen to hit you, there's not a damned thing we can do about it. The three of us will start here, right in front of town hall, and we'll wait until the bulls pass Fairbanks. We will then run like hell to the next corner, which is about as far as we can make it before the bulls overtake us. Now let's go there and decide more or less what we're going to do. Look the place over and each man makes his own decision.'

We walked slowly down to the corner where the bulls turn into Estafeta, and Cato was the first to speak. He had spotted a shop which sold baby clothes, Los Zamoranos—The Guys from Zamora.

It stood on the corner away from where the bulls sometimes fell down, and under its window was a crevice which provided better than normal protection. 'I'm going to throw myself there, under that window. What do you think?'

'It's each man for himself, but that's a good spot. All right, that's Cato's drill. Joe?'

'I'm going to run right into the barricade and hold fast.'

'And you?' Cato asked me.

'I feel safer in the street. I'll run till they gain on me, then twist away.'

'Is that safer?' Cato asked.

'For me it is. Because I know when to twist . . . and how. You stick to your own plan.'

Holt hesitated, then said, 'Remember, tomorrow's Bastille Day. Hell of a crowd and anything can happen. I want you to see a picture which tells it all.' He led us to a photographer's shop facing the turn into Estafeta, and the proprietor knew what he wanted. It was a dilly. A large black bull had fallen in the street and was about to rise, totally outraged. Its horns were about four feet from a tangle of three men who were taken by surprise and were unable to find protection. They knew that the bull must hit one of them. The first man, nearest the bull, was grabbing the waist of the second man so that he could pull him in front as a shield; the second man had a stranglehold on the third, trying to yank him into position so that the bull would hit him; the third man was twisting so that he could dodge to safety behind the other two.

'This should be labeled "The Spirit of Pamplona,"' Holt said. 'It's every man for himself, because when that bull looks down your throat, you don't know how you will react.' He tapped the photo and said, 'I'll bet each of those men was astonished when he saw what he was doing when the bull came at him.'

'Which one did he hit?' Cato asked.

Holt turned to the photographer. 'Isn't that the time the bull got up, shook himself, and ran placidly down Estafeta?' The photographer nodded.

———•—•———

At dinner that night Holt suggested that Joe and I join him upstairs in a small dining room where we could talk, and after the inevitable chatter about the bullfight, Holt said, 'Joe, I hope you're not serious about dodging the draft.'

'Most serious.'

'It beats me. I know you have courage . . . it's not easy to do what you did this morning.'

'Not a matter of courage.'

'Of course it is. You're afraid to die. We all are. Now let me tell you that when I won my last medal I was as frightened . . .'

'Please, don't ladle out that tired soup.'

Holt kept his temper, for he felt that this boy deserved a hearing. 'If it isn't a problem of courage, what is it?'

'The war's wrong. A decent man can have no part of it.'

'All wars are wrong. But they're forced upon a nation, and the only honorable thing a man can do . . .'

'You're using an old vocabulary, Mr. Holt. We don't accept the definitions you're using.'

'You mean that you're going to place your judgment above that of your President, your Congress . . .'

'Yes and no. As to our last four Presidents, I don't think their judgments have been very good. As to Congress, so far as I know, it hasn't been consulted. So the war's not only wrong. It's also illegal.'

'You don't believe that communism threatens us?'

'Problems at home threaten us a great deal more.'

They stayed on this merry-go-round through the *pochas*, but when Raquel brought up the stew, Holt changed the subject. 'I take it you don't accept the poem I learned in college:

> 'And how can man die better
> Than facing fearful odds,
> For the ashes of his fathers,
> And the temples of his Gods?'

Joe tried not to smile, but failed. 'That seems as ridiculous to me as a Charlie Chan movie.' When he saw the shock on Holt's face, he added, 'That poem was written about the days of spears and shields. I'm talking about the hydrogen bomb.'

Holt flushed, then said, 'Joe, in boot camp I had a powerful drill sergeant, Schumpeter. He wasn't too well educated, but the fundamentals he could see with an eye of crystal clarity. I wish you could spend one month at Parris Island under Schumpeter. You'd see things more honestly.'

Joe slammed down his napkin. 'I might've known it! You're an ex-marine! You got that gung-ho indoctrination when you were a kid and it's the biggest thing that's ever happened in your life. Mr. Holt, to us the marines are an echo of a dead age . . . they and their Schumpeters and their nonsense.'

To my surprise, Holt showed no anger. Carefully placing his fork beside his plate, he thought for a moment, then asked, 'Your friend Yigal is Jewish, isn't he? Do you realize that if it hadn't been for men like Schumpeter, who believed that old poem, or things like it . . . such as justice . . . Well, your friend would have died in an incinerator . . . burned alive . . . along with every other Jew on earth. Does this mean nothing?'

'Under certain circumstances . . .'

'Would you have fought Hitler?'

'That question doesn't face my generation,' Joe said.

'It faces every generation. In different form. And the question of courage faces every life. Ask Mr. Fairbanks.'

I could provide no arguments that Joe had not heard, so I kept my mouth shut, but he said, 'Courage I have. If the government catches me, I go to jail. I've been willing to lay it on the line.'

'You would flee your nation?' Holt asked in disbelief.

Joe laughed. 'Apparently you haven't heard what we're willing to do besides flee. Do you know that we have clinics instructing us in how to beat the physical examination? Eight aspirin an hour before. It's good for five hours in case they pull the delayed buck on you. Go in to the doctors at the end of an LSD trip, and you'll drive the machines crazy. Come to Europe one week before your eighteenth birthday and certify this as your legal residence. I know at least twenty ways to beat the rap, and if they fail, I can fall back on Little Casino and then Big Casino.'

'What are they?' Holt asked.

'Little Casino, you get a doctor to certify that you're a habitual user of LSD and heroin.'

'You'd put that in writing?' Holt asked, appalled at the implications.

'I may have to before the year's out.'

'But, Joe! It would stand there in your record . . . suppose you wanted a job.'

'I wouldn't accept any kind of job in which my military record would be taken into account.'

'But almost any job. A bank, World Mutual that Mr. Fairbanks works for, UniCom . . .'

'I wouldn't take a job with any of those outfits. You don't seem to understand. The system is corrupt and I'm not going to be part of it. If I take Little Casino, I'm not putting anything I'm concerned with in peril. I've done that already.'

'But how about getting married? Suppose you wanted to marry my daughter. Wouldn't I, as her father, naturally look into your background?'

Joe laughed outright. 'Never in a thousand years, Mr. Holt, would you allow your daughter to marry me, Little Casino or no. Nor would I want to marry her. We're living in totally different societies. Look at these chicks around here. You ever see prettier girls? You think I couldn't marry them if I wanted to? You think they're going to ask their parents first, "Is Joe an acceptable young man? Will he fit in at the First National Bank?" Hell, we'd get married and tell them about it on a postcard from Tangier three months later.'

Neither Holt nor I made any response to this, for this radical concept was more than we were able to digest at the moment. We had been reared in a society in which the taking of a man's daughter carried with it a certain commitment which gentlemen discharged in accepted ways. Holt had paid a formal visit to the parents of his girl; I had done the same. It signified nothing, I suppose, and our marriages did not last any longer because of it, but to us, as men, it meant a great deal. Five or six times in my life I've been sworn into office or into a major obligation, and taking the oath meant something, for it confirmed a commitment that I was bound in honor to discharge, and I consider such commitments, voluntarily entered into, as the levees which keep the floods of life within control.

'We reject all the ideas you've been throwing at me, Mr. Holt. But on our own terms we're going to live good and constructive lives.'

'In the long run, the terms have got to be the same. They always have been. You can laugh at Horatius standing firm at his bridge, but unless you identify your bridges and develop the guts to defend them . . .'

'We have defined our first bridge. The Vietnam war is an insult to man's intelligence and we'll have none of it.'

'You keep shying away from my earlier question,' Holt said. 'Was World War II also an insult to man's intelligence?' Joe refused to answer, so Holt continued, 'Then how about Korea?'

'How about it? Isn't that where the trouble really started? America refused to declare war, because she didn't want to upset the internal economy. Nine men made a lot of money and the tenth went to war. We found we could get away with it that time, so in Vietnam we tried the same filthy trick. And it exploded in our faces. It is a corrupt war, Mr. Holt, corrupt in every facet.' There was a pause, and Joe asked, 'How would you like to be drafted into such a war?'

'I volunteered,' Holt said.

Joe looked at his plate, and Holt continued: 'The way I volunteered in World War II and in Korea. I considered the Korean war a noble enterprise. We saved Japan from communism and stabilized that part of Asia. I feel the same about Vietnam. You say our last four Presidents have been dopes. I think they've been excellent men . . . by and large.'

'The gap is wider than I thought,' Joe said, and Holt asked, 'What's Big Casino?' and Joe replied, 'It's very grave. And I may have to take it before January,' whereupon Holt said, 'Joe, you're a valuable human being. You're young and you'll grow older. Don't do anything that would destroy those later years. They're long and you'll need all the character you can muster.'

He placed his knife and fork on his plate and went upstairs to his room, but this time we heard no music.

--- • • • ---

On July 14 Pamplona reached its apex. During the night thousands of Frenchmen had crossed the border in a grand stampede to '*regarder les taureaux.*' They were a handsome lot, neat white trousers and those trim knitted shirts with the crocodile embroidered over the left breast. Many wore berets and all were noisy.

At five-thirty the bands assembled at Bar Vasca, and since this would be their last morning to rouse the city, they played with total abandon, drums crashing like artillery. Holt rose promptly, shaved in cold water, and dressed in his customary uniform, after which he knocked on various doors. By six a varied group of young people assembled in his room, including two very pretty American girls from Wellesley whom Joe had found trying to sleep in the square.

Holt told Clive it was his responsibility to secure places for the girls at the barricades leading into Estafeta: 'Better start right now. All good spots will be gone by six-fifteen.'

When the four of us were left alone, he said, 'Coffee, then up to town hall. We've got to get Fairbanks that safe spot in the corner.'

As we walked up the hill he bought us each a newspaper, and when he had rolled his up, reminded us of our strategy, adding, 'No smart-aleck movements when you think the bulls are safely past. Because they might turn back in one hell of a swipe and rub you out.'

When we reached town hall the plaza was already jammed with men, many of them Bastille Day trippers who had never run before. 'This isn't a good crowd,' Holt said professionally. 'Watch out for yourselves because today anything can happen.' When he had placed me he added quietly, so the others could not hear, 'I don't need to tell you, but resist the temptation to run after the bulls once they've gone by. If a bull should turn back in this plaza, it's got to be trouble, and I don't want to worry about an old coot like you.'

I watched as he led his two young charges into position. At first it looked like a mistake, for they were smothered by the crowd, but when, at two minutes to seven, the police allowed the front men to filter through the barricade, Holt and the boys found themselves precisely where they had planned to be, in the front ranks of those who would run with the bulls in this exciting part of the course.

At seven the rocket exploded and an intense apprehension gripped all of us. I cannot explain why I, who had run often with the bulls in earlier years and had frequently stood my ground along the course, should have been as excited as the newest Frenchman, but I was. I happened to be watching Cato when the second rocket sounded, and I could see that he felt caught up in something from which he could not now retreat.

I turned away from Holt and the boys and looked down the hill toward the corrals, and in a moment I caught my first sight of the bulls, rushing up the slopes, past the military hospital, past Bar

Vasca, and into the narrow alley that would deliver them right into my lap. I found myself praying that each would make the turn and head into Doña Blanca, not into me.

Now they were here, six charging bulls and ten huge steers bearing directly down upon me, and I felt myself grow faint, but at the last moment, as always, they veered left, passed me by with a few feet to spare, and headed into Doña Blanca. Overcome with excitement, I started to run after them because I wanted to see what happened with Holt and the boys, but I had taken only a few steps when a lean Spaniard grabbed me by the arm and jerked me back into the crowd, shouting, '*Señor, otro!*'

In my excitement I had not counted the bulls—indeed, I probably could not have done so had I tried, for they passed me in a blur and my senses were pounding so that I could neither see nor count accurately—and now a last bull, who had strayed behind the others, came roaring up and charged right into the spot I had just vacated. Ignoring me and others like me, he dashed ahead, trying only to catch up with his mates. Again I took up the chase, and was thus able to see fairly close at hand what happened at the turn into Estafeta.

In my first glance I saw with relief that Cato had wedged himself into the crevice beneath the window of the baby shop, while Joe was pressed against the barricade. Holt was safe in the middle of the street, but because he had counted the passing bulls, he knew that one was still to come and that it could be dangerous. Shouting 'Stay down!' at Cato and 'Keep back!' to Joe, he took prudent steps to protect himself. What he could not know was that he was stepping in front of a frightened young Frenchman, who, it developed later, had had a most terrifying morning.

Sashaying into the city hall plaza at about a quarter to seven, he had announced grandiloquently that in order to celebrate Bastille Day he would run with the bulls, and when the rocket had sounded he had moved amiably down Doña Blanca, but when he reached Estafeta and looked down that long, dark thoroughfare where manhood is tested, he quite fell apart and screamed the equivalent of 'What am I doing here?'

In his panic he attempted to crawl under the barricades, but the policeman we had seen in action earlier pushed him back into the runway. He then ran to where the girls were perched, only to be thrust again into the street by a second policeman. In real panic he ran to still a third spot, where he happened to confront a captain of police, who punched him in the face, shouting, 'You wanted to run—run!'

The young man, still terrified by Estafeta, turned back toward town hall, but the bulls had rounded the corner and were coming directly at him. In sheer terror he screamed, 'What shall I do?' and Holt knocked him to the ground and showed him how to lie wedged against the wall of some shop. There the trembling young man had lain while the first five bulls roared by, their hooves striking the pavement not far from his covered head.

When they were past, he got up and started to walk into the middle of the street, but at this moment the final bull appeared . . . and the young man froze. The morning had been simply too much for him. Holt, sensing what had happened, again came to his rescue and pushed him backward toward the wall, then drew himself into a slim, motionless monument as the stray bull rushed past. It was an exciting moment, and all who saw, including myself, applauded.

So all would have gone well, except that when this stray bull tried to turn into Estafeta he was moving too fast and fell down. Then two things happened that changed the course of the morning. When the bull regained its feet it was facing backward, and when it finally peered down Estafeta it could see none of its fellows, so in confusion it began lashing at whatever lay before it.

With a savage swipe of its left horn it ripped at the barricade, striking just below Monica's foot, then leaped across the street at Cato, still huddled beneath the window, knees drawn up to protect his stomach. If the bull were to hit him in that position, with his body already pressed against two solid surfaces, the goring would be terrible, perhaps fatal. Seeing the horns bearing down upon him, he shrieked, but the horns never struck, for at this crucial moment Holt leaped before the bull, waved his arms and jiggled his newspaper, and in this way tricked the bull into ignoring Cato.

It was a magnificent gesture, one of the most heroic in recent years, and a sharp-eyed photographer, alerted to expect drama when the lone bull fell, caught the scene in full beauty: the infuriated animal, a few inches from Cato; Cato cringing on the street; Holt, in an act of voluntary sacrifice, drawing the bull away from the fallen body and onto himself. And this famous photograph shows one more thing: behind Holt there is a terrified Frenchman about to grab him to use him as a shield.

That's what happened. Normally Holt would have pirouetted

out of the bull's reach and the animal would have wound up in position to race harmlessly down Estafeta, but when the Frenchman grabbed Holt, there was nothing the latter could do. Held in a viselike grip from behind, he could not move as the bull lunged directly at him. I was now standing about ten feet from the scene and watched with horror as the bull drove its right horn into Holt's gut, then chopped at him twice more as the Frenchman held him transfixed. Finally a workman with a pole goaded the bull and he ran down Estafeta, causing no more trouble.

I was not the first to reach Holt as he collapsed on the pavement, but I was among the first. I grabbed one leg and saw blood already streaming down it, but my last image of that ugly corner was of Cato punching the bewildered Frenchman. Two Spanish policemen dragged Cato away and then started punching the Frenchman themselves, more savagely.

We ran down Santo Domingo, past Bar Vasca, where Raquel saw us bearing Holt to the hospital. She started screaming, and several woodchoppers ran into the street to follow us. At the military hospital the doors were already opened, and we rushed upstairs to the operating room, where the doctors took one look at the gut wound and said, 'Very deep.' Then they saw the chest scar, which they themselves had made, and one surgeon slipped his hand into Holt's pants to feel the buttock scar. 'Ah, *el Americano*. He will be all right. This one knows how to fight back.' And they began their operation.

When I reached the street I found the three girls waiting at the hospital door. Monica was ashen. Gretchen's lips were drawn tight. And Britta was sobbing. I went instinctively to her, and she pressed her head against my chest. 'I love him so much,' she whispered.

'He'll live.'

'Will he?' the girls asked.

'Another might not, but he will.'

As we stood there, Joe and Cato came up. 'He sacrificed himself to save me,' Cato kept mumbling.

'You're goddamned right he did,' I snapped. 'You remember those words.'

'That was something to see,' Joe said. 'One man and a newspaper.'

'That Frenchman was a beauty, wasn't he?' Monica asked.

'I wanted to kill him,' Cato said.

'Mr. Fairbanks,' Britta whispered, 'I'd like to go to the church.'

So all of us walked away from the hospital and up the hill to the church of Santo Domingo. We pushed open the door and descended the two flights of stairs that took us down to the nave where an early Mass was being said, but before we could take our seats, a runner from the hospital arrived to summon a priest.

'Oh my God!' Britta sobbed as I went to interrogate the runner. He said, 'It's just in case . . . on stomach wounds, you know.'

I returned to Britta and said, 'Just a precaution. Now we'll sit here until we gain control of ourselves.'

And even Cato prayed.

———•-•-•———

That day was miserable. We had no word from the hospital until noon, when a priest came to Bar Vasca to tell me that I could see Holt, who seemed somewhat stronger after his operation. I hurried down the street, with the young people following me, but at the entrance to the military hospital they were stopped by a functionary in a white jacket. I was led to the second floor by a guide, though none was necessary, for I had been there several times before. Propped up in bed was Harvey Holt, very white in the face but smiling.

'A pinprick,' he said.

The attending doctor said, 'No shock. No complications. Extraordinary man, but of course the other scars prove that.'

'Where'd he get you?' I asked.

'In the belly . . . but the safe part. Very considerate.'

'It was quite a save you made.'

'That Frenchman was a sweetheart . . . yes?'

'Cato wanted to kill him. He wants to see you . . . very much.'

'Tell Gretchen I'd like to talk with her.'

When I translated this, the doctor nodded, so I sent the guide down to get Gretchen, and when she arrived, nervous and pale, Holt laughed at her. 'Why the tragedy?' he asked.

'You may not know it, Mr. Holt, but it happened right at my feet. I hated that Frenchman!'

'What I wanted to tell you was . . . catch that boat at Barcelona.'

'Mr. Holt! We couldn't leave while you . . .'

'I'm ordering you. Catch that boat.'

'We're going to stay here . . . we've discussed it and decided . . .'

'Gretchen, the boat is important.'

'You're important.'

'But the boat is important to many people.'

'Do you think Cato could leave until you're well?'

'The last thing I saw before I fainted was Cato punching the Frenchman. That's his exit visa.' He closed his eyes and said in a low voice, 'Tell her, Fairbanks.'

I said, 'Holt's right. He's going to live. There's no sense disrupting everyone's plans.'

Then Holt added, 'One thing, Gretchen. Clive's a dope. You can do better.'

She blushed, started to say something—and I could see tears coming to her eyes. Her instinct must have told her it would be improper for her to cry before this wounded man, so she said nothing, only leaned over his bed and kissed him. Then she turned and left the room.

A moment later there was a scuffling at the door and Cato burst in. The guide followed, trying to grab him, but the doctor said it was all right. Cato came to the bed and said in hesitant manner, 'You're lying there . . . not me. I want you to know . . .'

'Son, I told you that when you run with the bulls, anything can happen.'

'What I wanted to say was that my father . . . in all his life . . . not once has he ever acted like a man. Perhaps if he had . . .'

'Perhaps you people run with tougher bulls.'

The two antagonists looked at each other in silence, then Cato said, 'The bulls I run with, Mr. Holt, have horns as big as this bed.'

'They always look that big . . . always.'

'I'll never forget you risked your life for mine.'

'Who keeps score?' Holt asked, and Cato left.

Holt was weaker than he pretended, the loss of blood having been considerable, and when Cato was gone he fell back on his pillow.

'Was it a rough one?' I asked.

'No. You felt yourself trapped in those powerful arms . . . the poor Frenchman was terrified and totally irrational. What the hell could you do? I remember feeling a sense of satisfaction that the bull wasn't going to hit Cato, pinned against the wall. I remember thinking that it was much better for him to come at me, because I had people behind me who would yield a little when the horn struck. That's what happened.'

'It was sensational to see,' I said.

'It's sensational to be here,' Holt replied. The doctor indicated that I had better go, but as I reached the door, Holt said again, 'Make sure the kids catch their boat.'

At the entrance Britta asked if she could go up, but the guard said, '*Nada más*,' and we walked up to the main square, where all the regulars gathered around us to hear a first-hand report. The German girl whom we had met the first night said, 'They told us the priest had been called and that he was dead.'

'He's sitting up in bed, laughing,' I said.

'Have you seen the photos?' she asked.

Britta, surprised that they should be available so soon, rushed us to the camera store, where we saw the linked series showing the fall of the bull, his charge back toward town hall, and the goring of Holt, but the photograph that would live permanently in the minds of all who had seen the incident showed Harvey Holt, newspaper in hand, citing the bull from a distance of perhaps eight feet. It was a portrait of courage and grace, of a lone man doing what had to be done.

The young people sat in the sun discussing whether they ought to skip the fight that afternoon and give up their plans for Moçambique, out of respect for Holt, but I told them, 'The essence of Pamplona is that you run with the bulls in the morning, then see them fought in the afternoon, and if the doctors at that hospital aren't watchful, you'll see Harvey Holt sitting beside me this afternoon. He's done it before.'

At two o'clock we trailed back to Bar Vasca and had a lunch of *pochas*, in honor of Holt, and after lunch Britta returned to the hospital, but again she was refused entrance.

I insisted that they pack the yellow pop-top so that they could depart immediately after the fight. 'It's a long haul to Barcelona, so if you want to make that boat, get cracking.' Britta had tears in her eyes as she packed her duffel, but I assured her that Holt would be all right and that she could write to him at the military hospital, but later at the arena, when I looked back toward where the young people were sitting, I saw that she had not come to the fight. At one intermission I went back to ask where she was, and

Monica told me, 'She wants to say goodbye to Holt. She'll meet us at the car.' Clive was occupying her seat.

When the fight was over, the last wild fight of this year, and the bands were gathering in the arena for their final march through the city, the young people hurried through the crowd to where the pop-top was parked, and there stood Britta, her duffel bag on the sidewalk. 'I cannot go with you,' she said, and I was astonished at how casually everyone accepted this decision.

'*Poste restante*, Lourenço Marques,' Gretchen said. 'Tell us how he is.'

Cato shook hands with her and said, 'I'll see you in the States . . . or Norway . . . or somewhere.'

'So long, Mr. Fairbanks,' they shouted, and while a huge red sun was still visible in the west, the pop-top headed for the coast.

————·•••·————

Britta and I started for the central square. I offered to carry her duffel, but this she would not permit, and after a few blocks we were mired in an enormous throng of people seeking to march with the bands on this special night. While struggling to free ourselves, we became part of the mob behind one of the noisiest bands and were swept along for a block or more, unable to break free. The noise was tremendous, hypnotic, the glorious end of a feria, and for a moment Britta forgot her anxiety over her own future and Holt's and entered into the abandon.

Then suddenly, on a signal from nowhere except the hearts of those who were saying farewell to a riotous week, the music stopped, the singers fell silent, the noise halted, and even the whispers of the crowd ceased. All in the street fell upon the paving blocks and began knocking their foreheads on the stones. From the silence came one voice, then many, singing the traditional song for this solemn moment:

> 'Poor me, poor me! How sad am I.
> Now the Feria of San Fermín
> Has ended. Woe is me.'

Britta, forced to a prone position by those around her, looked at me as I lay on the stones, and I saw that she was transfigured by this unexpected experience. Grief was walking the streets and giving itself visible form—her grief, and she was part of it. Tears came into her eyes and she pressed her hand over her mouth. She looked away and knocked her forehead against the stones.

Then, again with no visible signal, the bands simultaneously returned to their wild tunes, whereupon the fallen thousands sprang to their feet, and the cacophony resumed, but louder than before. When we had passed through three cycles of lament and exultation, I took the duffel from Britta and told her, 'You should march with the mourners,' and she did.

Toward midnight, as I was lugging her gear back to Bar Vasca, I happened to catch sight of the procession as it passed down a narrow street, and there was Britta, falling to the stones and knocking her head, and I knew it was not in grief for the passing of San Fermín but for that inconsolable anguish that sometimes overtakes young people when they unexpectedly face death, or the loss of their illusions, or a glimpse of the deadly years that lie ahead. She did not see me, nor did she seem to notice those who marched and mourned beside her. She walked like a ghost, eyes blank, through the beloved streets that had brought her so much happiness.

At two o'clock, when the marchers still faced four hours till dawn, she left them and sought me out at Bar Vasca, where I sat with the woodchoppers.

'Mr. Fairbanks, you must take me to the hospital. Now.'

'At this hour!'

'Tell them I'm his wife . . . just in from Madrid.'

I accompanied her down the dark street to the military hospital, where I told the sleepy guard, 'The injured American's wife.'

'Tell her to come in the morning.'

'But she's just arrived from Madrid.'

Protesting, the man in the white smock said, 'All right, if she's his wife I'll go tell him.'

Motioning us to wait, he started upstairs, but I forestalled him by grabbing Britta's hand and leading her along. When we got to Holt's door the guard peeked in to see if he was sleeping, but Harvey was awake, so I pushed the door wider and shoved Britta into the room. '*Su esposa está aquí,*' I said, and the guard departed. I started to leave, but both Britta and Harvey wanted me to stay.

It was an astonishing conversation, and if I had not heard it I would not have believed reports, had any reached me.

Britta went to the bed and took Harvey's hands. 'We prayed for you . . . in the sunken church,' she said.

'I told them you were to catch the boat.'

'The others will.'

'You should have, too.'

'Mr. Holt, I've been walking behind the bands with the marchers. "Poor me, poor me," they've been singing. "Poor Mr. Holt," I've been chanting under my breath.'

'I'm all right.'

'No. You're not all right. You're an unhappy, lonely man. It's ridiculous. A man your age . . . cheap one-night stands with college girls.'

'She was older than you are,' Holt said defensively.

'And when the years go by you're going to be even more unhappy and more lonely. Mr. Holt, I want you to marry me.'

Harvey's mouth dropped open, and I was afraid he might have a relapse of some kind, but it was only his astonishment at her words. All he could do was repeat, 'I told them you were to catch the boat.'

'I'm not catching any boat, Mr. Holt. I'm going to stay here with you. And as soon as you can walk again, you're going to marry me.'

'That's crazy!' Holt finally said.

'I cannot live a life of loneliness, and neither can you.' When she saw the consternation on Holt's face she added softly, 'I can work, Mr. Holt. I can bring in money to help us along, if that's what you're worried about.'

Holt closed his eyes. He had nothing to say. Britta saw him wince and guessed that he was in as much spiritual pain as physical, for she said, 'I'm not going to leave you, Mr. Holt. I'm going with you even to Ratmalana.' She hesitated, then looked at me imploringly. 'Where is Ratmalana, Mr. Fairbanks?'

'It's an airport somewhere.'

'Where is it?' she asked Holt.

'Ceylon.'

The word seemed to explode in the room. Britta started to tremble, put her hand to her forehead as though to steady herself; but she said nothing, only stared into Holt's eyes until tears filled her own. Then she turned away and, addressing a statue of the

Virgin which decorated the wall, said softly, 'All his life my father has dreamed of going to Ceylon. He buys every book about that island. He was a very good man, my father, very brave when the Germans occupied us. He was like you, Mr. Holt, a true hero. But he never got to Ceylon. I am going there with you, Mr. Holt, whether you want me as your wife or not.' She came to the bed and kissed him. 'Get well soon,' she said and left the room.

Holt looked at me in bewilderment, then wiped his cheek and said, 'Seems all you have to do to get kissed by pretty girls is to take a horn six inches in your gut.'

'She means it,' I said.

Trying to get into focus what Britta had said, he made his usual comment, 'It's like the time Signe Hasso watched over Spencer Tracy. She was Scandinavian too.' I didn't get this at all, and he growled, 'When they were hiding from the Nazis.'

When the guard let Britta and me out, he said, 'Your husband is going to be all right.'

As we walked up Santo Domingo, Britta took my hand and pleaded, 'Tell him tomorrow, on your own, that I will not be a financial drag on him. I can type, you know.'

I said, 'Britta, we'd better have some *pochas*, if the fire's still hot.' So we went into the bar, where some men were singing in the corner, the old, sad songs of Navarra, and I asked Raquel for some *pochas*, but when they came they were cold, for the fires were banked.

'You're entitled to know one thing about Holt,' I said. 'He won't need the money you might earn on the side. He has a good salary plus a lot of extras like per diems, hazardous pay for climbing towers in typhoons and a hardship bonus for living in a place like Ceylon. How much do you suppose he totals in a year?' She said she could make no intelligent guess, but when I pressed her, she suggested, 'Maybe as much as six thousand dollars?'

'Over thirty-nine thousand dollars.'

'You mean every year?'

'Some years more, never less. I know, because I save his money for him. And how much do you suppose he has saved?' Again she preferred not to guess, so I told her, 'Almost a million dollars.'

'You don't mean United States dollars?' When I nodded, she stared at the table, then said softly, 'To be a millionaire . . . in dollars . . . and to live so poorly.' She said no more at that moment, but when the singers halted, we could hear in the distance the bands still playing, at four in the morning, and she said, 'Mr. Fairbanks, tonight I'm so lonely I would leap from the window if I tried to sleep. I'm going to join the mourners again.' I took her back to town hall, where I last saw her falling in behind one of the bands that was making a great noise. When the music stopped, Britta fell to the street and began beating her head against the stones. I left her there.

July 15 in Pamplona was hell. The oppression started at five-thirty in the morning, when not a single txistulari blew his flute nor one trumpeter his cornet. At seven no rocket exploded and there were no singers in the cafés. With a speed that seemed impossible, the industrious city obliterated all signs of its preceding debauch, and stores opened at the customary hour. The wooden barricades behind which thousands had viewed the running of the bulls were carted off to storage for another year, and postholes in the streets were filled with wooden blocks and tamped with sand.

The central square showed no preparations for fireworks, and the draperies were gone from the bandstand. Traffic now flowed normally, Estafeta subsided to a minor artery of commerce, and Teléfonos was again a place to make telephone calls and not a scene of adrenalin-bravery. Bar Vasca had four customers at noon, and two of them were Britta and me.

'This town is too lonely to bear,' she said after returning from the hospital, where the new guard would not let her in.

'You miss the others already?' I asked.

'I'd like to hear . . . just once more . . . Clive and his records. Like Octopus beating out a good number.'

'What are you going to do?'

'I don't know. But I will not leave Mr. Holt.'

'If you're going to marry him, shouldn't you call him Harvey?'

'He's afraid of marrying.'

'You think you can change that?'

'It's of no significance. I'm going with him to Ceylon. I must.'

We talked like this through our lunch, and Raquel came to our alcove to tell us that our bull stew was made from the bull that had gored Holt. I asked her how she knew, and she laughed. Britta asked, 'Did you see the photographs?' Raquel pointed to a board beside the bar where four of the photos had been mounted.

'Everybody's surprised Holt acted so brave,' Raquel said. 'What do they think he's been doing these past years?' She sighed and returned to the bar.

At three I went back to the hospital and found Holt deeply disturbed by Britta's visit the preceding night. 'That Norwegian is plain nuts,' he said.

'And you loved it.'

'I've been counting. I can name forty young girls who married old men. But not one of the men was poor.'

'She thought you were. You heard her offer to work.'

'An act. An act. What would I do mixed up with that gang of beatniks?'

'Wrong word.'

'What would you suggest?'

'I don't know. How about individual young people.'

'And Clive? He was a great one.'

'He may be the best of the bunch.'

'Gretchen thought so. Did you know they were sleeping together?'

'As somebody said, "Who keeps score?" How's the stomach?'

'Fine. I get out in a day or two. These doctors are unbelievable.' He showed me the bandages and gave them a hearty slap. I winced.

'When can we drive to Madrid?' I asked.

'Day after tomorrow. You drive.'

'Britta's a good driver too,' I suggested.

'Keep her out of it. She's eighteen and I'm forty-three.'

'She's also in love with you. Walked the streets in anguish all last night.'

'Thousands of people walked the streets last night.'

'Harvey, this one is going to Ceylon with you. Whether you like it or not.'

'I'll buy her a bar in Torremolinos.'

'She knows what I know, Harvey. You need her.'

'Do girls do the proposing these days?'

'The new breed does.'

'I don't like the new breed. And I don't want her in the car. Send her home by train.'

'Harvey, on one thing she's right. This is your last chance. If you throw her out, you're going to wind up a crabbed old man . . . alone.'

Apparently the goring was more serious than he had made it out to be, for he sucked in his breath. I left, and at dusk Britta came to my room and asked, 'Would you walk with me?' so we set out for a very long recapitulation of Pamplona. We walked down the boulevard, past Mr. Melnikoff's hotel, which now had many empty rooms, and out to the railroad station, which stood in the country. 'I suppose he wants me to leave by train,' she said sardonically.

'How did you know I saw him?'

'I was watching the hospital.'

'You haven't convinced him.'

'I will.'

We walked back by paths along the far side of the river and came to that quiet area where the bulls were kept in the early stages of their stay, and as we looked at the bleak corrals, Britta said, 'I understand why men want to run with the bulls. If I were a man I'd run. I was gratified to see so many Scandinavians in the street.'

As we crossed the ivy-covered bridge which delivered the bulls to the holding corral, we could hear the imaginary thunder; in the darkness we could see the vital forms which have challenged men since the beginning of history. And Britta said, 'This is so lonely the heart could break . . . like a twig. God, how can he come back year after year? Don't answer. I know. This is where honor grows. On this steep street.'

We were now at the foot of Santo Domingo, and as she looked into its dark canyon she could visualize what the bulls saw as they leaped clear after the morning rocket. Here were the walls that pinned them in; here the ramp up which the policemen escaped at the last moment; here the spot where Harvey Holt waited to rush down to meet his enemy. In the darkness she could see him come, see the very point at which he made his turn, his gallant charge up the hill. She became a bull and lunged at him with her horns. She stopped and whispered a triad from a song which Clive had composed for Octopus:

> 'Age seems a part of courage,
> But no part of its genesis.
> Father is far more fearful than I.'

We were now in the narrowest part of the passage, and Britta studied the walls which deflected the bulls to the left. She touched them, smelled them, then looked ahead to where Bar Vasca threw its pale light into the empty street.

'And here we are at the hospital . . . where the circle ends,' she said softly. 'Last night I was lonely and thinking only of myself. I felt I had to escape Tromsø at any cost . . . I was scared . . . when he said the word Ceylon, it broke my heart.' She covered her face and mumbled, 'Tonight I am more lonely than I can bear. Thank God, you had the kindness to walk with me. But this night my sorrow is for others . . . the human race . . . all of us . . . you growing old and watching younger men come along with different ideas . . . Mr. Holt afraid of everything except the bulls . . . how he hates Cato and Clive, and they could save him.' She pressed the tears from her eyes and said, 'Now you must take me into the hospital again.'

I was relieved to find that the guard was the one I knew. I told him that the señora was back, and he let us in. As we climbed the stairs I saw that Britta was nervous, but I could hardly have guessed what she had in mind.

When we entered the room she laid her handbag on a chair, and without speaking, kicked off her sandals and proceeded to undress until she was completely naked. She then walked to the bed and said, 'Mr. Holt, you are a man who has been sorely wounded and I am here to care for you.'

Holt, astonished at her beauty and her daring, placed his hand over his bandages, but as she drew down the covers she said, 'I do not mean that wound, Mr. Holt. I mean the terrible wound in your heart.' Placing her hand on his chest, she said, 'This wound I shall cure.' She kissed him on the lips, lay down beside him, pulled up the covers, and motioned to me that I should leave the room.

XI §

MOÇAMBIQUE

God writes straight, but uses a crooked line.

> Men go abroad to admire the heights of mountains, the mighty billows of the sea, the long course of rivers, the vast compass of the ocean, and the circular motion of the stars, and yet pass themselves by.
> —St. Augustine

My old man made a tragic mistake. Took wash-and-wear clothes with him to Europe. After one week Mom said she'd be damned if she had come to Europe to wash his laundry. He started doing it himself, and when she saw how good he was she made him do hers too. When they got home she said that since he was so expert he could do the wash regularly. With the money she saved this way she's going to Asia next summer. Hasn't decided yet whether Pop ought to go along or not.

> Where did non-violence get Martin Luther King? In the end.

If one family of dinosaurs survived on earth, some son-of-a-bitch from west Oklahoma would claim he had a right to shoot the male.

> A barbecue pit in Alabama held this beauty contest and elected a cute colored chick to be Miss Barbecue 1970. So when she got back to her room she said, 'Mirror, mirror on the wall, who is the fairest of us all?' and the mirror snarled, 'Snow White, you black bastard, and don't you forget it.'

Young men should travel, if but to amuse themselves.—Byron

Nature is the balm that will cure all the ills created by those who have abused nature.

> The isle in which we dwell, though it be small,
> Is a safe anchorage for the region round.
> Quilóa and Mombassa here must call,
> Sofála too, when o'er these waters bound.
> And since 'tis necessary to them all,
> We seized the isle for our own stamping-ground,
> And to answer everything of which you speak,
> The name by which it goes is Mozambique . . .
> But it were good a little here to bide
> And take the sweet refreshment of the land.
> What's needful, he who over us holds sway,
> And who himself will greet you, will purvey.
> —Luis de Camões

> I pity the man who can travel from Dan to Beersheba, and cry, 'Tis all barren.'—Laurence Sterne

The elephant came crashing through the trees, standing shoulder-high to the topmost branches, a beast of such magnitude that he stupefied me. I asked myself, 'What right have I to aggrandize myself with a mechanical toy like a rifle so that I can equal this towering beast?' and my folly became apparent, and I could not pull the trigger. 'Fire! Fire!' shouted the hunters, but I could not, so one of them had to do it, and this gigantic element of nature staggered forward a few feet and collapsed like a mountain from which the core of gold has been stolen. At the camp they reported that I had made a very poor showing . . .

> Support mental health or I'll kill you.

> A fox abused a lioness that she brought forth but one whelp at a time, whereas the fox produced seven. 'True,' confessed the lioness, 'but when I produce a whelp it is a lion.'

> Help bring back white slavery.

I was not in Moçambique that August day when the Greek freighter deposited the yellow pop-top on the quayside at Lourenço Marques, but later I heard how each of the new arrivals reacted.

Cato, with his first step ashore, fell to his knees and kissed the stones. When the others said they were surprised that he thought so much of Africa, he said, 'I pay homage to the slaves that were sent in chains from this port.'

Monica threw her dark head back to feel the sweet, warm breeze of late winter. She looked at the flowering trees about to bud, then studied the variety of human beings—African, Portuguese, Indian, Chinese, Greek, Rhodesian—and shivered. It was the same Africa, immense and unforgiving, and it pressed down upon her as heavily as ever.

Joe simply stared. The dockside was more modern than he had anticipated. The presence of a chugging train confused him as did the modern cargo gear and the Mercedes-Benz taxis. What he could see of the surrounding city looked European. 'This isn't what I was led to expect,' he said.

As for Gretchen, she reveled in the exotic beauty and said to the others, 'That was a great decision we made in Pamplona.'

Gretchen wanted to drive, but on the trip in to the city, found it difficult to keep left, and this prevented her from seeing much of Lourenço Marques. The others found it one of the most beautiful capitals they had visited. Its boulevards were wide and ran in straight lines far into the interior, and the buildings that edged them were clean and solid. Joe tried to guide her from a map he had picked up aboard ship, leading her through the residential area to the luxury hotels, huge structures that would have been at home in Nice or Cannes, each with its own swimming pool and tennis courts.

'I keep trying to convince myself this is Africa,' Cato said.

They now got mixed up in a network of concrete superhighways, from which they extricated themselves with difficulty, but ahead they saw that sign which is so reassuring to motorists in Europe and Africa: *Camping.* Swinging off the road, Gretchen stopped the car at a flower-surrounded office and asked, 'Is this where we register?'

'Your passports,' the Portuguese official said. Then he raised a barrier that allowed them entry to a spot which they would remember as a most gracious introduction to a new continent.

When I later caught up with them, Gretchen told me, 'It lay smack on the shore of the Indian Ocean, so that when you got up in the morning you saw the sun rising from the water, and when you went to bed at night you could see the lights of passing ships. There were casuarina trees everywhere and so many flowers that the place must have been run by gardeners.

'In and out among the trees wove a network of paved roads, with places to park at unlikely points. We chose a beauty. We could see a cluster of distant islands. And all this for less than a dollar a day.'

'She hasn't mentioned the best part,' Monica said. 'We'd be leaning against the pop-top, and out of the trees would descend a horde of tame monkeys to chatter about local affairs and beg for food. They were really extraordinary, from grandfathers to babies, and if we didn't feed them they perched out of reach and cursed us, but if we had food they'd come closer and flatter us outrageously. We called them our welcoming committee.'

'The part I liked best,' Gretchen said, 'was the rondavels. If you left the part of the camping reserved for caravans, you came to an area filled with little round huts, each painted a different color. They were patterned after old African-style houses, and when you got tired of sleeping in your car, you could rent a rondavel. It was super.'

The rondavels, I learned later, caused some embarrassment, because after they had slept in the pop-top for two nights, Joe suggested that they needed more room, so they went to the office, where the attendant, seeing from their passports that they were not married, made an elaborate joke out of finding a pink rondavel for the two girls and a blue one for the boys. Gretchen was about to inform him that this wasn't what they had in mind, but Monica interrupted to say, 'That's good.'

When the attendant left, Cato and Monica moved into the pink one, leaving Joe and a self-conscious Gretchen standing before the blue one, uncertain as to what they should do next. On the Greek freighter, life had been simple. Since original plans had called for a party of five, three cabins had been reserved, and when Britta stayed behind, it was logical for Monica and Cato to use one, Gretchen one, and Joe one. This embarrassed nobody, since it was recognized in the group that Gretchen was in some nebulous way attached to Clive, so Joe had paid her normal attention during the long trip and felt neither inclination nor obligation to do more. The two nights spent ashore had presented no problem, since everyone was accustomed to the close quarters in the pop-top and did not interpret them as an invitation to emotional involvement.

But now it seemed as if Gretchen and Joe must share the blue rondavel with its double bed, and Gretchen backed away. In obvious embarrassment she moved to the doorway of the hut and said in a low voice, 'Hadn't you better bring my things from the Volkswagen?'

Joe asked, '*Your* things?' and she nodded. When he trudged back to the pop-top, after having delivered them, he muttered, 'And I was the guy who proposed the rondavels.'

———•••———

On the afternoon of the third day Gretchen surprised the others by saying, 'I'll stake you to dinner at the Trianon.' So that night Cato spruced up and the girls wore their sauciest miniskirts, but Joe appeared in his normal outfit. With a collective 'Oh, brother!' they got him out of his Levis and sheepskin vest, but his boots he insisted upon wearing, and with ordinary trousers, shirt, tie and blazer he didn't look too bad.

When they filed into the posh dining room, everyone stared at them—partly because of the very short miniskirts, partly because of Joe's wild hair and beard, but mostly because Cato was obviously a white girl's escort. Unfortunately, they were seated near a stiff-necked Boer couple from South Africa who took an extremely dim view of everything and muttered audibly about niggers who ought to be kept out of decent places.

Under this provocation, Cato and Monica became completely obnoxious. 'If you please,' Cato said haughtily to the head waiter, 'send us the wine steward.' When the sommelier came, Cato asked in a voice somewhat louder than necessary, 'Have you a really good white Burgundy . . . perhaps a Chablis?' He stroked his beard and said in a confidential tone, 'But it must be very dry . . . very dry indeed.'

The head waiter now started the rumor 'He's a distinguished official from the United Nations,' whereupon Monica said in a clear voice, 'Isn't it amusing that all over the world people use the United Nations as an excuse for being forced to do what they should have done fifty years ago?'

When the wine came, Cato really went into his act. He lifted the sample, looked at it against the light, then carefully sipped a little, swished it about his mouth, and studiously spit it into another glass. Then, reflectively, he leaned back and said, loud enough for the Boer couple to hear, 'There's something . . . something.' He asked for a piece of bread, which he slowly chewed and swallowed. Only then would he try a second taste, which he savored like a connoisseur, finally swallowing it. 'Very just,' he said judiciously. 'You may serve.'

In the kitchen the head waiter said, 'That goddamned monkey knows his wine. His wife must be a millionaire,' but the Boer gentleman whispered to his wife, 'I'd like him to try that on me . . . just once. I'd wring his neck,' and Cato whispered to Gretchen, 'I hope you can pay for this wine . . . whatever the hell it is.' Monica ended the act by saying loudly enough for several tables to hear, 'You clown. You wonderful, stinking clown.'

At another table a distinguished-looking couple—he with white hair and clipped mustache, and she with bluish hair and delicate lace collar—kept staring at Cato, neither in amusement at his buffoonery nor in anger at his presumption, but rather as if they knew him, and after the wine had been served they dispatched a waiter with a note. It was addressed not to Cato but to the young lady in blue, and it read: 'Forgive me, but are you not Sir Charles Braham's daughter? My husband is chief justice of the Vwarda supreme court.' It was signed 'Maud Wenthorne' and carried the postscript, 'Perhaps we can have coffee in the bar.'

Monica read the note with confused emotions: it conjured up memories of pleasant afternoons in Vwarda when the English colony met for tea and talked of schools and summer rains and the most recent outrages of the Labour Government—in London, of course, not Vwarda. Those had been the splendid days, hanging at the edge of change, but swiftly they had turned into tragic days marked by tribal strife, expropriation, loss of jobs that had seemed secure, and the gradual expulsion of the white man. Monica's father and the Wenthornes had seen much of one another, but Monica had been away at school in England and it was understandable that Lady Wenthorne should not recognize her for sure.

Monica felt a strong temptation to send back a note: 'You are mistaken,' for she did not want to reestablish contacts with Africa's British colony, but to reject Lady Wenthorne, after she had been so kind in Vwarda, would be ungracious. Turning toward the other table, she smiled warmly and nodded, then passed the note to her three companions, replying noncommittally to their questions. To tell them all she knew of this distinguished couple would require a backward trip that she was ill-prepared to take; to tell them less than the whole story would be unjust; but her dilemma was solved by Cato, who said, 'Isn't he the cat who's had all that trouble in Vwarda? Handed down a decision the blacks wouldn't tolerate?' Arrogantly he turned to stare at the chief justice in such a way that the latter had to know that this Negro was identifying him with the recent judicial crisis. Sir Victor blushed, then bowed and nodded his head a couple of times as if to say, 'Yes, young man, I'm the one.' At that moment he must have regretted his wife's intemperate invitation to coffee.

The Wenthornes finished their dinner first and were waiting in the bar, where Negro servants in blue uniforms and white gloves moved sedately, serving small cups of very good Angolan coffee accompanied by sugar wafers. The judge and his wife sat in a corner at an ornate cast-iron table whose surfaces were lavish with scrolls and curleycues. A soft light emanated from unseen sources, and Gretchen thought: This must be one of the most civilized spots in the world today; but Monica thought: Here we go again . . . the grandeur of empire . . . this time Portuguese.

Lady Wenthorne acted as if she were presiding over a Victorian soirée, and the judge seemed the epitome of judicial elegance, characterized by that probity and nice regard for proper behavior which marks the best British judges. For example, when Cato asked pointedly, 'Why did the Vwarda decision trigger riots?' Sir Victor rose, excused himself and went ostentatiously to the men's room, leaving his wife to answer the question. 'Because a white judge had to reverse a black judge.'

'Aren't there any blacks on the high bench?' Cato asked.

'How could there be? No natives have studied law.'

'You said the lower judge was black.'

'By courtesy, not by training. My husband was in charge of recruiting a judiciary, and he did wonders in bringing promising young men, even though they were not qualified, onto the bench. But for the superior levels . . . Quite impossible.'

'But I understand that right now the superior judges are black.'

'Yes. Since the riots, all the white judges have been kicked out.'

'Then they did find black judges?'

Lady Wenthorne looked steadily at Cato and said, 'They found black men . . . not black judges.'

Now Sir Victor returned, and this was a signal to drop the subject of the riots, so Monica asked, 'Will you be returning to Vwarda?' and he said with that calm which had characterized him on the bench, 'A mission is arriving tomorrow. The president's brother is in charge, I believe. We're going to explore what might be done, because there's an honest wish in Vwarda that I continue until the various benches have been filled and trained.'

'I thought they were filled,' Cato said.

It was remarkable—Monica made a great point of this when she told me about the affair later—how free of prejudice the Wenthornes were. They liked the black men, had worked with them all their lives, had done all they could to inspire young blacks to study law and medicine, and now they intuitively liked Cato and his imperative questioning. 'I'm afraid the benches are filled, sir,' the judge said, 'but all the leaders in Vwarda acknowledge they are filled with the wrong men—tribalists, corrupt bargainers, men without principle or probity. I doubt if the president and his brother want me to return, but they certainly want someone like me who is capable of cleaning up the mess. And I suppose, for better or worse, it must be a white man.'

This irritated Cato and he asked, 'Suppose that the rioters who threw you out, keep you out? Doesn't the bench continue? Doesn't law continue, but on a different footing? Black justice for blacks?'

'You've hit the nail right on the head, young man,' Sir Victor conceded without rancor. 'Of course the courts can continue without white judges. Why should two Englishmen, two Irishmen and one Australian dispense justice in Vwarda? But what the black judges of this generation will dispense is neither law nor justice, for they know neither. They will dispense tribal revenge. In truth, they are already doing so, and that's why the mission is coming here tomorrow.'

'You condemn the whole legal system of Vwarda?' Cato pressed.

'So long as it steeps itself in mere tribalism, yes.'

'You don't think that tribalism can ultimately work just as well as western legal systems?'

'In a given tribal area, unquestionably it's as good. In a federal area, where many tribes must co-exist or perish, it cannot function.'

'Isn't it possible that Africa may have to experience a long period of tribalism, after which it will evolve its own kind of federalism?'

'Yes!' Sir Victor said enthusiastically. 'That's what we hope for . . . what we plan for. But the steps from tribalism to federalism must be taken honestly and without destroying nations, and this can be accomplished only if all of us observe the universal principles of law. That's where the problem lies.'

'And the law to be followed is of course the white man's law?'

'If you consider Hammurabi, Moses, Muhammad and Solon white men, yes.'

Lady Wenthorne interrupted to steer the conversation away from judges and justice. 'What do you hear from Sir Charles?' she asked Monica.

'He's in London. Totally dreary.'

'What a pity! He should never have left Africa.' She said this as much to her husband as to Monica.

'What are you and Sir Victor planning to do?'

Lady Wenthorne smiled, breathed deeply once or twice, then said, 'I suppose that tomorrow Sir Victor will allow himself to be convinced by the delegation from Vwarda. We shall return to help them establish a bench worthy of respect. One or another of the incompetents that my husband discharges will rally his tribe behind him. There will be new anti-white riots, and in the end we shall both be killed . . . probably with spears.'

———•—•—•———

On the beach next morning the group met five delightful South Africans, sturdy young men who bought a round of beer and were willing to talk about anything. They were bronzed and had the engaging trait of making jokes against themselves and the foibles of their country. They were obviously impressed by the two girls but were more inclined to talk with Cato, whom they interrogated for several hours about conditions in America.

After the swim they congregated at Cato's pink rondavel and bought some more beer, throwing the bottle caps at the monkeys, who reviled them. Their comments on life in South Africa were amazingly blunt: 'It's a police state, and it's bound to get worse. What we're learning is how to keep the blacks under control. Any nation can do it, if you're willing to pay the price.' Cato's responses were equally sharp: 'In America we'll surely have to fight in the streets. Probably by 1972.' But the exchange of ideas was mutually profitable, and when they were gone, Cato said, 'I'm ashamed to confess, but I really dig those cats,' and Monica pointed out, 'Of course, these sensible ones come from the English half of South Africa,' but Gretchen corrected her: 'Of the five, three spoke Afrikaans among themselves. They were pure Boer. I asked them.'

That night we caught a harsher glimpse of South Africa. A

Johannesburg politician, Dr. Christian Vorlanger, arrived at the Trianon on vacation and gave a press conference to advance his peculiar views, which were becoming increasingly popular in the republic. Printed reports of his ideas had created a stir and he volunteered to meet at the hotel with such of his countrymen as might be vacationing in the city, and the five South Africans dropped by Cato's rondavel to invite him and his friends to the meeting.

Dr. Vorlanger was a powerful man, tall, rugged, thick-necked and well tanned from constant life in the sun. He was also attractive, for he spoke persuasively, with no touch of the fanatic. His message was as simple as it was revolutionary:

'What I have to say will be neither popular nor well received, but I speak with the voice of the future and I predict that within five years the position I take today will be adopted by all thinking South Africans.

'It is increasingly clear to anyone who bothers to look honestly at our great nation that when the crunch comes, we shall not be able to depend upon those South Africans of English derivation who have been contaminated by one or another of the liberal philosophies. When the crunch comes, we will be able to trust only those citizens of Boer inheritance who have remained true to the sober teachings of the Dutch Reformed Church. They alone can be relied upon.

'Consequently, my plan is simple. If we know that the English cannot be trusted, and if we know that the Boers can, then in all prudence we must right now—from this moment onward—restrict the ballot to those who can be trusted and deny it to those who cannot. My counselors and I have given much thought as to what criteria would best identify those who can be trusted and those who cannot. Many possibilities were considered. That the person speak Afrikaans as his family tongue rather than English. Or that he have been educated in an Afrikaans rather than an English school. That he have served on an Afrikaans committee in his home community. Or perhaps that he be recognized generally in his home community as a Boer. Serious consideration was given to the proposal that three of his four grandparents had to be Boers. But the deeper we went into the question, the simpler the solution became . . . the more obvious to all of us. We therefore propose that henceforth the ballot be restricted to dues-paying churchgoing members of the Dutch Reformed religion. By this forthright and easily administered rule, we can identify those who will stand with us when the crunch comes—those we can trust to defend the South Africa we love and keep it the South Africa we love.

'Now before I entertain questions, I want to assure three groups of people that they have nothing to fear from our proposed program. First, the natives. They will not be persecuted in any way. They will live their own lives separated from ours and they will enjoy a standard of living and justice not found in any black republic in Africa. They will have good homes, good jobs, good education and good law courts. There will be an honored place in South Africa for them. They will be with us but not among us.

'Second, the English. We acknowledge in all we do, even in the language that I am using tonight, that our debt to the English is enormous. We will continue to acknowledge that debt, but we will no longer allow our government to be contaminated by sentimental English liberals to its own inevitable destruction. We promise you that we will govern wisely and well and that your liberties will be preserved and protected. But the government of the nation must be kept in the hands of those who wish to preserve it as it is, and the persons we can depend upon are those who have been reared in our great traditions, the Boers who speak Afrikaans and who attend our church.

'And that brings me to the third group I wish to reassure, those who belong to other churches. I am mindful that tonight I am speaking in a Catholic country. This is the right religion for this Catholic nation. I am also mindful that many of you may belong to the Church of England. That is the right religion for Englishmen who live in England. And if there are Baptists from America here, or Lutherans from Germany, I assure you that we believe that those great religions are right for your nations, and we will grant freedom of worship throughout South Africa. But our government must be in the hands of the only religion that speaks to our historic heritage, the Dutch Reformed. Into its keeping must be given the salvation of our nation.'

He threw the meeting open for questions, and speaker after

speaker rose to report: 'I happen to be from South Africa and I want the people in this audience to know that I and most of my friends support the ideas put forth so ably by Dr. Vorlanger tonight.' Others assured the audience: 'We promise that the English-speaking South Africans will be in no way discriminated against. The courts will continue to be scrupulously fair, but when the crunch comes we must have the reins of government in hands that we know and can trust.'

Later that night, as they sat together in one of the clubs, Gretchen asked her South African companions what this phrase 'when the crunch comes' meant, and one of them explained, 'It hides at the back of every waking moment and determines thought on every problem. "When the crunch comes," when the blacks finally rise in armed rebellion and we have to shoot them down with machine guns.'

Cato said, 'It's an idea which fascinates Americans. "When the crunch comes. When we have to shoot down the niggers." I must remember it.'

'Blacks have their own version,' Monica warned. 'You meet it in countries like Vwarda and Tanzania. "When the crunch comes." On the night we slaughter the whites. Which of our neighbors can we trust to do the slashing? It's what Lady Wenthorne referred to the other evening when she said that she and Sir Victor would be killed . . . by spears.'

It was on this night, Joe told me later, that Monica and Cato began that alternation of euphoria and depression that would characterize the rest of their stay in Africa. They knew that the course laid out by whites and blacks could end only in collision and escalating bloodshed. 'From then on,' Joe told me, 'they were like two doomed souls. They found consolation in the rondavel, smoking dagga with their South African friends, but you could see that something was gnawing at them. I couldn't guess what until that day I saw Monica coming out of the Indian store. From there on, it was mostly downhill.'

Monica's gloom was deepened the next afternoon when the judiciary mission from Vwarda arrived at the Trianon to try to persuade Sir Victor to return to the supreme court, for in the mission, which was completely black, were many old friends from the good days. The president's brother, dressed in formal clothes with pin stripes and piping down his trousers, had been chauffeur to her family for eighteen years, a good and dignified man who had watched over her when Sir Charles was absent in the jungle. Secretary to the mission was a fine man from one of the interior tribes, illiterate till the age of eighteen, then educated by Monica's mother until he qualified for school in England. In the group were former storekeepers, bricklayers and runners for the big estates, some dressed in African costume, but most, like rural undertakers from the south of England.

They did not come begging. As Lady Wenthorne told the Americans later that night, 'They want Sir Victor to supervise the courts for a three-year period—not the decisions, mind you, only the orderly progress of cases . . . the distribution of the workload.'

'Will he accept?' Monica asked.

'What can we do? Who wants to go back to England at our age and sit around like dotty old fools?' She suddenly realized what she had said and seemed to consider apologizing for any unintended insult to Monica's father, but she had spoken the truth and there it lay. 'Sir Victor is making only one demand, that the three worst judges be disqualified. Trouble is, one of them happens to be the president's nephew. So perhaps we'll be going back to Devon. They're telephoning Vwarda and we'll know tomorrow.'

Cato asked if he might be allowed to interview the mission, and Lady Wenthorne said, 'I should think it might be arranged, but what can we tell them is your reason?' and Monica suggested, 'He's a scholar.' Shortly thereafter a member of the mission came to the Wenthorne's room to report that Mr. Jackson would be granted half an hour with the chairman and three other members who would like to talk with an American Negro, so Cato went down to their quarters. He told me later what happened.

'The four men were very proper, three in formal dress, one in African. They asked me questions for fifteen minutes, then I laughed and said, "I'm here to interview you," and they were very gracious. I launched right in with the best questions I had. "Why do you need help from white judges at all?" and they said, "Our black judges are quite capable in administering tribal law. But they have no sense of overall organization—appeals and such—so for some years we'll need a practiced hand." Then I asked if they thought Sir Victor could be effective if he were in an advisory position only, and they said, "With an ordinary man it wouldn't work, but Sir Victor is no ordinary man." So then I asked, "But isn't the time at hand when you'll want to get rid of all the whites?" and the president's brother said, "That time will never come. It would be fatal if Vwarda were to become black racist the way South Africa is white racist. We blacks are going to prove that we can rule without hatreds." I asked if there hadn't been a lot of hatred when the white judges were thrown out, and he said, "There was. And our whole society was ashamed. That's why we're here." I asked if Vwarda would accept Sir Victor's conditions and fire the unsatisfactory judges, and he said, "That's what I'm talking to my brother about on the phone this evening. We want Sir Victor enough to make certain concessions." So finally I asked, "Will the nation be able to hold together against the pull of tribalism?" and he said he was sure it would, that every day the breakaway forces grew weaker and the central tendency stronger.

'And when I left the meeting, I was sick at heart, because every one of the commissioners looked and talked and acted just like my father. To me the whole damned lot were Uncle Toms on the international level, and the people Sir Victor ought to have been talking with were the young hotheads who had been yelling "Death to the white judges," because I'll bet they weren't conciliatory. You know what I did? I went to Monica and told her, "You advise the Wenthornes not to go back to Vwarda, because they're in a no-win position," and she asked how I could say that, and I told her, "By looking at the president's brother," and she asked how I could tell anything by looking at a man, and I told her, "Because he looks so damned much like my father," and she knew what I meant.

'She went to Lady Wenthorne and warned her against going back to Vwarda, but while she was there the telephone call came through from the president, and he accepted all of Sir Victor's conditions, so the Wenthornes accepted, and Monica said, "Because men look alike, it doesn't mean that they are alike."

'Of course, when Sir Victor got back to Vwarda he found that strong tribal pressures had been brought to bear upon the president, who did not find it possible to fire any of the judges, especially his nephew. So Sir Victor, being a man of character, said to hell with it and prepared to leave, but this was interpreted as an insult to Vwarda, and the black rebels started a rampage under the motto "Death to the white judge!" and in the melee, which the president's own tribesmen led, Lady Wenthorne was shot dead, but not her husband.'

———•◦•———

At the pink rondavel one evening nine young people—four from the pop-top plus five from South Africa—were in a placid mood from smoking dagga when one of the South Africans suggested, 'We've accepted your hospitality so often, tonight you're coming with us to the night clubs,' and they roared off to introduce Monica and the Americans to that garish strip near the waterfront where entertainment flourished: Bar Luso, featuring an exotic Negro stripper; Aquario, with a Negro band; Pinguim, with a bevy of Negro hostesses; and of course Bar Texas, marked by a five-pointed tin badge.

The patrons were mostly South African whites, and the fascinating fact about them, as Cato spotted immediately, was that they preferred black girls as dates, as if their policy of apartheid at home drove them to contrary behavior abroad. When Cato pointed this out to Joe, the two watched more closely, and the theory was confirmed: South African men did constantly approach the colored hostesses, did buy them expensive drinks, and did try to get them to leave the clubs with them.

At Bar Texas the group met a clever chap from the American consulate, and Cato asked him bluntly, 'In your experience do South African men prefer sleeping with black girls?' and the man replied, 'Standard. I'd have been surprised, except that I served in Japan.'

And he went on to explain: 'In Japan I was given the job, with a couple of smart psychologists, of unraveling this bit about GI–Japanese marriages. And what we found after much study was this. In Japan thirty-eight per cent of the troops were from the deep south. I forget now how we categorized what the deep south was, but at any rate, it contained Mississippi, Alabama, South Carolina and Georgia, and if I remember correctly, certain others. So

the soldiers we were studying contained thirty-eight per cent deep
south, which meant that the men who married oriental girls should
have come thirty-eight per cent from the deep south. What percentage do you suppose actually did come from there? Go ahead.'

The South Africans guessed figures like eighteen and twenty.
Gretchen said, 'Thirty-eight, the normal behavior.' Only Cato
guessed a higher number, fifty. The young official smiled and said,
'Seventy-eight per cent. More than twice what the normal expectancy should have been.'

There was some hot discussion of this, but the young man held
to his figures. 'Same in Korea as Japan, and I suppose same in
Vietnam today. We spent a lot of time on this startling fact, talked
to a lot of GIs, and derived one clear generalization. When they
first hit Japan, northern boys and southern boys were impressed
about equally with Japanese girls, but the southern boys, because
they had been told so many things about race, had an inner compulsion to date these girls, then to marry them.

'Extrapolating, I would suppose that you fellows from South
Africa would have an inner compulsion to date black girls . . . just
for the hell of it . . . to see if what everybody said was true.'

'And because it's forbidden at home,' one South African said.
'Don't forget that.'

'I was coming around to that. From our interviews with a couple
of thousand GIs who had married oriental girls, we got the strong
feeling that a lot of the fellows had done it principally to irritate
their fathers—not their mothers so much . . . we didn't get that
reading. But, boy, they sure wanted to throw the shaft at their
old man.

'And we discovered one final thing, which perhaps was the most
significant of all. When the GIs got their Japanese brides back
home, which part of the States accepted them most easily?'

Gretchen asked tentatively, 'The south?'

'Yep. Adjustments were much easier in the south, resentment
much less. We also looked into this, and found that when a society
has rejected one race, as the south rejects the Negro, it bends over
backward to be congenial with other races, as if to say, "See. We
have no prejudice. It's just that Negroes really are inferior. Decent
races we can accept and do accept." So extrapolating again, I

would guess that the South African, behaving as he does at home, experiences this same compulsion to be gracious toward all other races when he goes abroad and becomes, as it were, a man set free. He wants to say, "See I really have no ingrained prejudice. It's just that our blacks really are impossible." '

Cato kept his beer mug close to his lips, almost masking his eyes, then brought it down with a bang. 'Too ingenious. The simple fact is that white men have always had one hell of an urge to mate with black girls, and black men feel the same urge about white women. For what reason? Simply for the hell of it.' Then, to everyone's astonishment, he burst into raucous laughter.

'What gives?' one of the South Africans asked.

'I was thinking of this cat. One night he tell me, "Cato, I just as much white as them white cats you knows. I figured it out. I'm one third black, one third German, and one third Episcopalian." ' Cato slapped his hand on the table and looked from one white face to the next. No one laughed, and after a moment he said, 'I didn't catch it either till I went to bed that night and stayed awake till morning trying to figure out how a man could be thirds. Try it.' Gradually, around the table, one face after another broke into a grin as minds grappled with the problem and saw its ridiculous aspect.

'Thirds a man can't be,' Cato said, and one of the South Africans said, 'Damn it all, I still don't see what the joke is,' and Cato said, 'Go back to your four grandparents. How you gonna cut them into thirds?' and the South African asked, 'Yes, but what about the generations way back?' and Cato said, 'Even you South African cats has got to march by fours,' and suddenly the man saw it and burst into laughter, which prompted him to order a round of drinks, and it was this camaraderie which encouraged him to confide in the American the terrible fear that was gnawing at him.

'I'm a newspaperman. I work for one of the finest papers in South Africa . . . or anywhere, for that matter. And the government is determined to silence both the paper and me. Have you heard about the new bill they introduced yesterday? Proposed by Dr. Vorlanger and supported by his group and others. We're to have a new secret police called BOSS, Bureau of State Security, and they are to have unlimited powers. If they arrest you, no habeas corpus. At your trial, if any member of the cabinet comes into court and states that evidence which you might produce to defend yourself might be prejudicial to the state, it cannot be given. You cannot testify in your own behalf if they say no. But the really terrifying part is that if BOSS searches your home, which they can do without a warrant, and finds there any notes or photographs or sketches or even random ideas in any form which might be used to write an article which might be offensive to the state, they can lock you up totally incommunicado for six months without producing their evidence, such as it might be.'

Cato said, 'In America they laugh at us when we say, "Don't do it to the blacks because next week you'll be doing it to yourselves." '

And late that night, when Monica and Cato were sleeping in the pink rondavel, with Gretchen in the blue and Joe in the pop-top, there was a soft knocking at Cato's door, and when he opened it a crack, there stood the South African journalist asking to be let in, and in the darkness he sat on the bed and asked Cato to summon the other two, and when they were assembled, like conspirators on some dark night, he said, 'After you left the bar a friend slipped me word that a most evil woman has arrived in Lourenço Marques. Her name is Margaret Villinger. She's attractive, intelligent. You'll like her. She writes for a good newspaper in J'burg and she's going to interview Cato tomorrow. What the American Negro thinks of South Africa . . . and she'll print what you say. But her real job is to get the goods on me. She's an agent of state security, and they're determined to wipe me out . . . and my paper. She'll use every trick to make you confess you know me. She'll try to discover what I've said, so I beg you. Don't mention my name . . . not under any circumstances.'

'Is it that bad?' Gretchen asked.

'It's worse. That's the real reason we seek vacations in Lourenço Marques. To breathe.'

'The other night,' Cato said, 'Joe asked me why I fooled around with South Africans. It's because I'm so sorry for you. You think you're doing it to us blacks. Really, you're doing it to yourselves.'

———•—•—•———

When the four wanderers left Lourenço Marques for the long trek north, they entered upon an adventure for which neither Harvey Holt nor I had prepared them: they came upon boundless physical beauty, and at the same time encountered insoluble social problems. And two of them achieved an unexplainable emotional repose.

The beauty consisted of unbroken miles of beach, flawless as it lay vacant beside the Indian Ocean. I had told them, in Pamplona, that the beaches were there, but they could not envision that they would stand day after day at the center of some sweeping reach of sand and be able to gaze miles to the north and south without seeing one human being or even the evidence that one had ever stepped on this beach. True, there were seaside resorts—some of them quite attractive—but these they avoided, preferring the lonely stretches of unbroken sand and ocean.

When they reached the first one, not far north of Lourenço Marques, they established the rather daring pattern they were to follow throughout Moçambique, whenever opportunity permitted. Gretchen was spelling Joe and was driving along the main road, and this in itself was something of an adventure, for Moçambique was so vast and its taxes so inadequate that good roads were a luxury; therefore, only a narrow strip, one car wide, was paved, which meant that when you drove at fifty or sixty miles an hour, you had constantly to be on the alert for someone thundering at you at the same speed from the opposite direction and on the same strip of road. The deadly game you played was to come head-on at the other car, refusing to yield a millimeter, while he did the same, and at the very last moment, swerve aside ever so slightly, holding onto your half of the paved surface. If you were really tough, you bluffed the other man completely and kept your car in the middle, forcing him to leave the macadam completely, but the game grew really sticky when two such drivers approached head-on, each refusing to give way, so that at the last possible moment they both veered at the same instant, passing with their tires squealing only inches apart.

What made the game hellish for an American was the driving on the left, for at each moment of crisis you had to behave contrary to every instinct and veer your car to the left in what always seemed like certain disaster.

After about an hour of this, in which she lost every war of nerves and failed to keep her car even once on the macadam, Gretchen said, 'I'm cracking up. One of you fellows take over,' and Joe took the wheel.

As each of the first four cars approached, he slowed down, drove well off the macadam, and gritted his teeth as the victor flashed by, grinning at his discomfort. For the next four he maintained his speed and kept his right wheels on the pavement, and after that he became an ornery bulldog, fighting for every inch of the macadam, driving people completely off the road when possible, and behaving exactly like a Portuguese.

'This is William James's moral equivalent of war,' he chortled at one point, and Gretchen thought how ironic it was that so combative a young man, one who so obviously loved the challenge of a running bull or a careening car, should have become a conscientious objector. She realized that he was objecting not to war, but to the immorality of the particular war in which our nation was involved.

They now came to a crossroads with a sign pointing to the right indicating that a beach was not far off. On the spur of the moment Joe swung the car down this road, and after about ten miles, came upon a small resort hotel. Beyond it lay the first of the majestic beaches, vast, empty and untouched.

Joe stopped the car. For a few moments no one spoke, for the sight of this almost primeval beach was overwhelming; one had to contrast it with the crowded beaches of England and America and to reflect that they, too, had once looked like this. It was Monica who broke the spell. 'I'm going for a swim,' she said, tossing off her clothes and running lightly to the water. Cato also stripped and followed, his handsome black body outlined against the white sand. This left Joe and Gretchen sitting in silent embarrassment in the pop-top, and it was her responsibility to decide what course they would follow. She blushed, tried to think of something casual to say, then quickly undressed and skipped across the sand to join Monica, but as she did so, Cato ran up also, and the three of them stood there naked and Cato yelled to Joe, 'Hurry up!' So he kicked off his boots and climbed out of his skin-tight trousers and joined them.

They spent the better part of a week this way, naked children cavorting on the endless beaches—the girls very pale to begin with and gradually tanning, Joe bronzed from the start and becoming quite dark, and Cato the handsomest of the lot, a lithe, well-proportioned young male whose blackness lent a noble accent to the scene. There seems to be something in young people the world around that inspires them toward nude bathing; personally, I have reached the age when I am grateful for whatever cosmetic help a well-designed bathing suit can provide. When Monica told me of the great joy they found in such bathing, I had to ask, 'Does this mean that Joe and Gretchen . . .' and she interrupted by saying, 'Not at all! I think it was really a struggle for Gretchen to strip. She certainly didn't want any part of Joe. Also, she was still fond of Clive and . . .' I interrupted to ask, 'Then you mean that these two went swimming nude every day and that was all?' and she snapped, 'Hell, I've gone swimming naked with lots of men I haven't wanted to sleep with.' I suppose she was telling the truth, but with my upbringing I found it hard to believe.

The sociological confusions presented by the journey were profound. Moçambique had a population of about eight million, of whom nearly ninety-eight per cent were black, yet it was totally controlled by whites. In Lourenço Marques, where the power lay, white men clustered, giving the impression that the division was something like eighty per cent white, twenty per cent black, but in the country the true situation could not be masked. The blacks did not live in small towns; they lived in tiny kraals, consisting of a clearing in the jungle surrounded by three or four rondavels, and here life continued much the same as it had for two thousand years, altered now and then by a discarded rubber tire or an empty gasoline drum. The major possession of any family was a large wooden cask for lugging water from the government well, which was usually far away. This meant that the women of the huts had to spend most of their day hauling empty barrels to the well and drawing filled ones home. They did this by an ingenious means: they simply laid the barrel flat on the ground, and with ropes secured to the two ends, dragged it along behind them, the barrel itself forming a kind of wheel which rolled endlessly, bumping over tree stumps and almost shattering when it struck rocks. In Moçambique the wheel proper had not yet been accepted.

These kraals had an ugly effect on Cato. In Philadelphia he had ridiculed African dress and felt no desire to learn Swahili, which was spoken by so few in Africa, but he had nevertheless believed that if the white man could be kicked out, the blacks would be able to run Africa at least as well as nations like Belgium and Portugal, and probably better. But the blacks he was now seeing made him wonder, for in all Moçambique he saw no evidence to indicate that they were ready for self-government, or even for effective minor participation in government dominated by white men.

'There must be a literate leadership here that they don't let us see,' he reasoned. 'The Portuguese stifle it, I suppose, but it exists underground. It stands to reason that eight million people must have an intellectual culture of some sort.'

He was never to find it. If it did exist, it was so submerged that its effect had to be minimal. Whenever the pop-top needed gas, he would poke into the areas back of the filling station, would talk with everyone who spoke English, would look with his keen eye, and what he learned depressed him. His vision of an African renaissance vanished like a shimmering mirage. Since he was a young man of intelligence, he did his best to bring this new evidence into focus, and during the long trek north he would often harangue on this gloomy topic.

'You have three patterns in southern Africa,' he always began, as if this were the basic truth upon which to build an analysis. 'You have white-dominated repressive societies in South Africa and Rhodesia. You have black-dominated in Vwarda, Zambia and Tanzania. And you have the white-dominated cooperative societies in the Portuguese territories, Angola and Moçambique. What's going to evolve out of these patterns?'

In his judgment on South Africa he was surprisingly generous, influenced by the likable qualities of the South Africans he had met in Lourenço Marques. 'They're hurting themselves as much as they're hurting us,' he said, but he could no longer support the theory that within a decade the blacks would rise up and take control of that country. He had seen too many stiff-necked Boers, too many men like Dr. Vorlanger, to ignore the terrible staying power of their society. 'I used to think we could drive them out within ten years . . . in a horrifying blood bath. Now I see that if there's to be a blood bath, we'll be the ones supplying the blood.'

He was also fairly clear in his thinking on Moçambique. 'The whites here will eventually have to side with South Africa and Rhodesia. I wouldn't be surprised to see homeland Portugal slough the colonies off . . . they must be a heavy burden . . . men and money. And when that happens, the local whites will take over, just as they did in Rhodesia, and I suppose there'll be a kind of federation. South Africa, Rhodesia, Angola, Moçambique, with South Africa supplying the money and the brains and most of the arms. The sad part is that each step of that development will radicalize the white men more and more, and in the end the whole southern part of the continent will be just like South Africa. Moçambique will have to have its BOSS, because two per cent of the population will be dictating to ninety-eight per cent, and you can do that only if you install a police state, not to govern the blacks but to keep check on the whites . . . to see they remain loyal.' Whenever he reached this part of his analysis he always added, 'But I suppose the same thing will have to happen in the United States. We blacks will require something like the Black Panthers to keep us loyal, and you whites will have to have a super-FBI to keep you in line . . . when the crunch comes.'

It was when Cato reflected on the all-black states that he became unsure of himself. 'I look at Moçambique and say, "These blacks couldn't possibly govern themselves," but just over the border to the north is Tanzania, where the same kinds of blacks *are* governing themselves, and over the border to the west the Zambian blacks govern themselves, and up in Vwarda other blacks of about the same level of development govern themselves. So I guess that if tomorrow you kicked every Portuguese out of Moçambique, the land would govern itself somehow. Airplanes would still fly into Lourenço Marques, and someone would see to it that the electric-light plant produced electricity, and dinner at the Trianon would still cost five bucks. It might be a lousy government, but it would govern.

'So I'm tempted to say, "Let the blacks govern. They won't do much worse than the whites have done." And then I hear about Nigeria and Biafra and the tribalism in Vwarda and the Chinese taking over in Tanzania, and I wonder if that's the answer either.'

They were now approaching the Zambeze River and saw repeated convoys of armed white troops moving toward the Tanzanian border, where a minor but persistent revolution was under way. Cato said, 'I'm damned sure guns aren't the way to solve the Moçambique problem,' but what the way was he did not care at this moment to guess, nor did he come back to the matter later, because waiting for him at a place called Moçambique Island, their destination in the far north, was a confrontation of an entirely different nature, one that would shatter all his preconceptions and move him into new turmoils.

Obviously, the emotional repose of which I spoke when the young people were launching their tour north did not involve Cato, for he was to find little peace in Africa; nor did it concern Monica, who was increasingly depressed by the recollections forced upon her. When she was in Beira, the big middle city of Moçambique, she read of the assassination of Lady Wenthorne. She sought out some vacationing Rhodesians—their railroad had its terminal in Beira—finding several who remembered her parents, and together they lamented the death of Lady Wenthorne.

'What changes have occurred in Vwarda!' they said. 'All whites are being expelled. Properties are expropriated, bank accounts confiscated. Of course, they've murdered many of the Indians. We see refugees stepping off the planes in Salisbury with only the clothes they wear.'

One man said, 'I consider it fortunate that your father got kicked out when he did. Probably protested, but he did get his money out. You hear about poor Sir Victor? Wasn't even allowed to bury his wife. Plopped him on a plane for England, and three hundred screaming blacks stood outside the door, shouting, "Throw us the white judge!" He barely escaped.

It was to Joe and Gretchen that emotional ease came. They were on one of the vast beaches north of Beira, where inland swamps prevented the shore from being developed—so that two centuries from now, when bridges have been built over the swamps, a splendid recreation area will be waiting for the crowded population that will need it—and were lazily wandering along the beach, naked, when they happened to turn toward each other. You could say it took place in a millisecond. They had been together for seven months but had never really seen each other. Gretchen had watched Joe in his love affair with Britta, and Joe had seen Gretchen fall half in love with Clive. But now each saw what the other was. Gretchen saw Joe as a tough, inhibited, uncertain man with courage to spare, and Joe saw Gretchen as the gentle girl she was, apart from her brilliance at school and her many hang-ups.

They were standing about eight yards apart at this moment of recognition, and slowly they walked toward each other, and who led whom behind the sand dune, it would be difficult to say, but Cato and Monica went down the beach and swam for a couple of hours, and after that the sleeping arrangements in the yellow pop-top were much different.

When I heard this story from Monica, with Gretchen confirming it later in her own hesitant way, I thought how curious love was among this new breed. A boy and a girl live in the same Torremolinos apartment for four months, sleep side by side in a pop-top for two months, go swimming nude for a month, and finally discover that they like each other. It was a style of courtship I did not comprehend, but as I reflected on it, I began for some bizarre reason to think of Jane Austen and her delicate novel *Northanger Abbey*, in which two English girls at a resort are thrown into a tizzy by the fact that two soldiers are following them at a respectful distance, and I reflected that Miss Austen's fiercely proper young ladies must have experienced the same flood of emotion—precisely the same—as Gretchen did when she walked naked to Joe and took him by the hand, and I felt sure that if Miss Austen were writing today, she would not be particularly outraged by what had happened on the beach, and neither was I.

———•—•—•———

One afternoon, when they had been lying on the sand, observing the crested waves move slowly, subsiding before they reached the shore, as if too tired to make further effort, Gretchen watched as Monica pulled Cato to his feet and led him down the beach, her slim tanned body a lovely counterpart to his black. Gretchen lowered her voice, although there could have been no stranger within five miles, and asked, 'Joe, have you noticed anything odd about Monica these last days?'

Joe said no, but she persisted: 'Are you sure? Or about Cato? Is he different?'

'They seem to want to be alone a little more than they used to. But so do we.'

'Joe, I hate to say this, and if I'm wrong, forgive me. But I want you to look very closely at the inside of Monica's left elbow.'

'What's up?'

'I'm sure I saw needle marks.'

'You must be kidding!'

'No. They're needle marks. And just where you'd expect them to be . . . where the veins show. What I want you to do is to look at Cato's arm. I can't see marks on his skin . . . supposing there are any.'

'What am I to do? Grab his arm the way that American girl did in Pamplona? "Excuse me, but are you on heroin?" '

'I think they both are, and I think that accounts for a lot of things recently . . . their euphoria and depression coming so close together.' She sat on a small sandbank, her trim knees drawn up to her well-tanned breasts, and dropped her head upon her knees, saying half to herself, 'That's all she needs . . . heroin.'

When Monica and Cato returned, the marks on her left arm showed so clearly that even Joe detected them. However, when he tried to study Cato's arm he was able to see nothing, since if there were scars, they were camouflaged by the black skin.

For the next several hours Joe and Gretchen found no opportunity to compare notes, but each stared with such fascination at Monica's arm that they were afraid she must notice, but she was in a state of such exaltation that she saw nothing. It was not until the two couples went to bed, with Monica and Cato thrashing around, that Joe and Gretchen found themselves alone, but they were so close to the others that normal talk was impossible, so Gretchen whispered, 'Like I said, the marks were there,' and Joe whispered back, 'I looked at Cato's arm but didn't see anything. You'd have to get real close,' and Gretchen said very softly, 'What should we do about this, Joe? I don't mean only about the kids. We could lose this car if the police caught us. You know Monica . . . she probably has a gallon of the stuff stowed away somewhere. Does it come in gallons?'

'What's the big whispering about down there?' Monica asked abruptly.

In the darkness Gretchen drew in her breath, squeezed Joe's hand, then said quietly, 'Joe and I were trying to decide whether you were using a hypodermic needle on your left arm.'

Silence, then: 'I am.'

'You, too, Cato?'

'Not technically.'

'But it is heroin?'

'Yep.'

The four young people lay in silence for some minutes, each trying to think of what ought to be said next. It was Monica who finally spoke: 'Kids, it's super. It's really super. All the things they've told you. No matter how you take it . . . *zing*, it goes right into the mainstream and it's perpetual spring. You think LSD expands the consciousness . . .' For some minutes she spoke in these extended bursts, proclaiming the superiority of heroin, and her euphoria was so marked, Gretchen and Joe were now certain that at some point that afternoon Monica and Cato must have given themselves shots.

Joe asked, 'You started with that Indian store in Lourenço Marques, didn't you?'

'We were also able to get some in Beira, and I have the name of a man who is highly recommended on Moçambique Island.'

'If you wanted to stop right now,' Gretchen asked, 'could you?'

'Stop? Are you kidding? All my yesterdays were preludes, as the poet says. I was building up to this all along, and now I'm home safe.'

'Tell me, Monica, you aren't inserting the needle into your veins, are you?'

'No. I'm just popping it under my skin. But when I do decide to mainline, it'll be none of your business.'

Comment seemed superfluous, and silence filled the pop-top, but after a long interval Joe asked, 'Cato, what's with you?'

Apparently he had given himself a smaller dose than Monica's or it had had a different effect, for he was deeply morose: 'As Holt used to say in Pamplona . . . *regular*.'

'I mean, could you stop now if we decided . . .'

'If you decided? Who the hell are you to decide?' Cato paused, then his voice grew louder and higher. 'You think that because you're the Man you just say, "Cato, little black brother, lay off the stuff" and I lay off. Well, who the fuck do you think you are? You subside, buster, or somebody's gonna subside you.' He began throwing words and phrases from his alley days, so that Gretchen covered her face with her hands and wondered what she had got into.

Then suddenly the lights switched on and Monica was climbing down out of her bed and crawling in with Joe and Gretchen. 'Kids, it's really the most. It's what you've been looking for without knowing it. It's so beautiful, you'll simply never be satisfied with anything less. Joe, you particularly. If you'd only join up you'd see everything so clearly. You'd have a power . . .'

She spoke in this agitated manner for nearly an hour, assuring her bedmates that if only they would take a good hypodermic full— she'd show them how it worked—they would end their hang-ups and everything would become clear. 'You see so far into the distance that you seem like an eagle,' she said. 'For example, I see very clearly now why I started this liaison with Cato. Father had been badly hurt by the niggers . . .'

Joe gasped at her use of this word, expecting Cato to explode, but on Cato the heroin had acted as a depressant and he was asleep, twisting convulsively now and then in the bed above. 'As I was explaining,' Monica continued, 'Father's ego had been diminished at the hands of the niggers, and as a loyal daughter I assumed the burden of his conscience, so actually I hate niggers. But I wanted to humiliate myself the way Father had been humiliated, and the best way to do this—in fact, the only way, if you look at it—was for me to take a nigger lover, repulsive though it was.'

'Monica!' Gretchen protested. 'Cato's up there.'

'Forget Cato. He was an instrument of my self-abasement.' She continued with an analysis so turgid that her listeners could not understand any of it.

'I think you ought to go to sleep,' Gretchen said, and Joe helped lift the girl back into her own bed, where, as soon as she felt Cato's body, she began mumbling, 'Wake up, you dark Greek god, and humiliate me.' She pestered him until he wakened, and for a long time Joe and Gretchen, lying a few feet below, could hear them making impassioned and athletic love.

—————•—•—•—•—————

Target of the trip north was an unusual island. For five centuries it had stood less than a mile offshore from an area that had remained nothing but a primitive hinterland, populated with savage animals and Stone Age blacks, while the island had flourished as a center of government, sophistication and culture. It was famous as one of the world's most beautiful islands, not because of its physical attributes but because it contained, over almost every square foot, buildings dating far back into history, spacious squares dedicated to the heroes of Portuguese navigation, and broad avenues lined with flowering trees. At the end nearest the mainland stood an ancient church which St. Francis Xavier had known, and at the opposite end, a forbidding fortress set inside massive walls which had been constructed as long ago as 1545. Repeatedly foreign troops had tried to wrest this fortress from Portugal, but always a bare handful of resolute Portuguese had withstood the invaders for a year, or two, or three. The sieges were fearful, no quarter given, and often Dutch invaders would control ninety-five per cent of the island, but invariably when the siege ended, the fortress would still be occupied by Portuguese troops who would move out cautiously from the walls to reconstruct the rest of the island.

Ilha de Moçambique with its fortress was a shrine in Portuguese history, the most sacred overseas possession, and the roster of great Lusitanians who had served here was endless, led by that one-eyed seaman who had sat on a stone bench at the south end of the island scribbling the verses which were later to be issued as the epic of Portugal, The Lusiads of Luis Vaz de Camões.

The wanderers first saw the island from a slight rise on the road that had been cut through long miles of mainland bush. They saw the great gray fortress, the long straight bridge erected recently, and the flowering trees. 'It was worth the trip,' Joe said, and Monica agreed: 'All my life I've heard of Moçambique Island. It stands like a sentinel in African history, but I never thought I'd see it.'

Joe was surprised that a girl on heroin could be as lucid as

Monica. With Cato it was different. The drug had a decidedly depressing effect on him, and even when he had just popped a shot, the effect was down rather than up. But the major surprise was that the drug, for all its powerful properties, still left them both in apparent control of their capabilities most of the time.

'The beginning user,' Gretchen pointed out when Joe discussed his observations. 'These kids are just starting, and we don't know how much they're taking or what the final effect is going to be.'

'We know that it permits some pretty torrid love-making.'

'Who needs that?' Gretchen asked. 'I mean, who needs the extra stimulus?' During the last week there had been little evidence of heroin in the pop-top, but twice Monica had spoken of the Indian pusher who controlled the traffic on the island, so Gretchen feared they would have trouble now that they had arrived.

The drive across the long bridge, whose pilings were sunk deep in ocean water, was exciting, for now the young people could see the island clearly and could guess what it held in store for them. 'Look at those beaches!' Cato cried. They bordered both sides of the island and ran practically into the center of town. 'And the trees!' Monica added. 'Nobody ever told me they had so many trees on Moçambique.'

Then they were on the island itself, driving along a handsome boulevard lined with casuarina trees and overlooking the Indian Ocean. At a corner they met a black policeman, and Gretchen asked in English, 'Have you a camping?' and the policeman, who could speak no English, caught the key word, left his post and walked beside the car for a block, pointed finally to a large and handsome public park.

'Camping,' he said.

'For automobile?' Gretchen asked, and the man nodded. 'For sleeping?' she asked, making a pillow of her hands and resting her head upon it. Again he nodded, pointing to where they would find water.

Even though the camping at Lourenço Marques had been ideal, in some ways this surpassed it, not because it fronted on the Indian Ocean, nor because of the flowers, but because it was situated right in the heart of the city. You lay in your bed and around you passed the wild and varied life of a strange community. Joe maneuvered the pop-top under a huge flowering tree, and a crowd of residents —black and white—gathered to make them welcome. Speaking no English, they showed the girls where the markets were and the stores that gave good bargains. Children explained the beach and the best locations for bathing. Another policeman stopped by to show the men how to buy gasoline and where city hall was, in case of trouble. Then, to the amazement of the group, a rotund Portuguese businessman came by in freshly pressed whites to invite them to a nearby bar for a welcoming drink.

'This is Bar Africa,' he said in patois—part Portuguese, part French, part English. 'Over there, the hospital. Down there, the Catholic church. A little more, the mosque.'

'Is the island Muslim?' Gretchen asked.

'Eighty per cent,' the Portuguese said. He paid for the drinks and was about to leave, when Cato said unexpectedly, 'A lot of my friends in Philadelphia are Black Muslims. Could I see the mosque?'

'I wouldn't be the best guide,' the Portuguese said. 'I'm Catholic. But I know who would be.'

He dispatched a black boy to run to the post office, and within a few minutes the child returned leading a tall elderly Arab dressed in gray caftan and turban. He wore a small beard, had a deeply lined face and compelling eyes, with which he now studied the young people, paying particular attention to Cato.

'This is Hajj',' the fat Portuguese said, placing his hand affectionately on the arm of the old man. 'He is our saint.'

'Hajj' what?' Gretchen asked.

'Just Hajj',' the Portuguese said. 'He had an Arabian name, of course, but for the past fifty years he's been just Hajj' . . . the holy one who made the pilgrimage to Mecca . . . only man of his generation to get there.'

Two Arabs, passing the bar, saw Hajj' and stopped, asking his blessing, which he gave with a bow of his turbaned head. 'And now I leave you in his hands,' the Portuguese said in French, after which he disappeared.

At first the young people were uncomfortable to be with an Arab, for they did not know his language, but Hajj' smiled and said, 'I speak English. And even though I am a Muslim, I will have a little of your wine, which is something else I learned from the English.'

He told them of his hajj: 'In those days it was not easy to get to Mecca. We took a small boat north to Zanzibar. It's always been a center of Islam, a great center. And we waited there for several weeks till a pilgrimage was arranged and we sailed together to Mogadiscio, which was terribly hot, and we waited there for a couple of weeks, then sailed up to Djibouti for some more pilgrims, and from there to Jidda, where there was almost no water. We walked on foot to Mecca, so many miles that older people died along the way and younger people thought they would die. It was just after the war—the big war—and I remember the automobiles that whizzed past us, throwing dust in our faces, and one broke down, and as we overtook it we laughed at the rich people sitting inside, but pretty soon it was fixed, and when they drove past us again they not only laughed, their tires also kicked pebbles at us, but when we got to Mecca we saw them again, and the car was broken again, so we could not decide who had the best of it.'

'Was it worth it?' Cato asked.

The old man turned, studied Cato's dark face, and said, 'Worth it? For me it's been the difference between living and dying. When I returned, everyone knew me as the hajji, the pilgrim who had made the great hajj. Later two other men tried to reach Mecca, but they died. I was the hajji. Ship captains knew me as Hajj' and brought me business, but so did God. Mecca inspired me to be a saint, and although I fell short, I have borne testimony to saintliness.'

As he spoke, other visitors came for his blessing, which he gave with his hands together and his fingers pointed downward. Gretchen asked if this was the custom of his church, and he said, 'It's a habit I fell into. There is no one else on this island now who is a hajji, so I remind them that Mecca is still there . . . at the end of a very long and dangerous journey. This is what pilgrimage accomplishes. Now shall we see the mosque?'

He led them to the waterfront and along the bay to a handsome green building topped by a minaret. At the door the Americans started to kick off their shoes, but he restrained them, saying, 'You do that inside,' and he showed them the racks for shoes and the line of eight basins for washing hands. He took them to the prayer room, a large, clean area with its mihrab indicating Mecca. Then they climbed to the roof, from which he explained the island's structure. 'There by the bridge that you crossed, six or seven native compounds looking exactly as they did when my forefathers came here more than a thousand years ago. Grass huts with grass roofs and a thousand people jammed together where a hundred ought to be. In this area around the mosque, our middle class, mainly Arab. Up toward the fort, the big homes of the Portuguese Catholics. And see how narrow the island is. From one waterfront to the other, not more than three city blocks. We are living on a precious little jewel, one of the treasures of this earth.'

'Is that a rickshaw?' Gretchen asked as a black man hurried past toward the center of town pulling a two-wheeled vehicle containing a Portuguese woman.

'For five hundred years that's how we traveled . . . before the bridge brought us the automobiles. People still prefer rickshaws, so we allow no taxis.'

In succeeding days, Cato often sought out this agreeable Arab, who kept a small home overlooking the harbor where he had worked for sixty years. Every day people concerned with shipping stopped by to chat with him, but he always found time for Cato. 'You ought to attend services at the mosque,' he said, 'because Islam has been the salvation of your people. Look at the map of Africa. Wherever the blacks of a nation have a strong attachment to Islam, they have good government. Where they are ignorant of Islam, they are powerless to stand up against the white man. In America you will be powerless, too, until you embrace Islam.'

He had many beliefs about the good that Islam could bring to black people, for he held that Muhammad had expressed a special concern for blacks and had constructed in his religion a special home for them. 'There have been many Muslim leaders who were black,' Hajj' said, 'and there will be more. When I was at Mecca it seemed that half the pilgrims were black. I am told that in America your finest Negroes are followers of Muhammad.'

He invited Cato to attend the Friday services and to see for himself the companionship that existed on this island between the black Muslims and the white, so on Friday noon Cato had lunch with the old man, at the home of a family of Muslims who had come to the island from Pakistan, and Cato observed that all the other guests were Caucasian—either Arab like Hajj', or Indian like the host—but when he got to the mosque, he saw that most of the worshipers were black. It was a pregnant moment when all in the mosque knelt shoulder to shoulder, regardless of color, and prayed with their faces directed toward Mecca, which lay so far away and across such rough and burning waters.

After prayer a visitor harangued the meeting in a mixture of Arabic, Portuguese and the local bush language, and he became quite excited with the news he had to report. He was a short, florid man, apparently half Arabic, half native, and his dark face grew flushed as he repeated certain phrases with great fury. Cato asked Hajj' what the topic was, and he replied gravely, 'He says that we may have to send men and money to Arabia for the great jihad against the Jews who burned the Al-Aqsa Mosque. He says that black Africa can never know freedom until the Jews have been driven out. He says that a holy war is inevitable, and we must all play our part.' It was a heady broth the visitor brewed, and the good Muslims of Moçambique listened with many noddings of the head as he explained how Islam was on the verge of greatness again and was deterred by only one thing, the presence of Jews in the holy places.

During the next week Cato visited Hajj' often, and with the aid of old maps, retraced the pilgrimage to Mecca seven or eight times, until he could visualize the harbor at Zanzibar, the customs officials at Mogadiscio, the automobiles abandoned on the desert route to Mecca, and the fellowship as thousands marched around the Kaaba, that ebony monument at the heart of Islam. And the more Hajj' expounded his religion, the more clearly Cato understood its appeal to the black people of America. It was a religion of universal brotherhood, as much at home in Africa as in Arabia, and it spoke directly to the problems of the black man, in that it was above all else a religion that made revenge respectable. Dozens of passages in the Koran justified the man who bided his time to correct a wrong, so that gradually Cato came to see Islam as a movement specifically created for blacks who had old scores to settle. He was not drawn to the religion himself, for he supposed it to be as bad a racket as

Christianity, but he did perceive that it might be an agency of terrible power for his people, and for this reason he kept returning to Hajj's quarters near the mosque to talk about the number of black people throughout Africa who had enlisted under the green banner of Islam. Once Hajj' showed him a magazine article displaying the new flags of Africa and proudly pointed out the new states that showed the crescent—nations like Algeria, Tunisia, Libya, Mauritania—or the bright green, which appeared in almost a score of flags. 'We are the new force in the world,' the old man said, 'and in our parade there is a noble place for you.'

Gretchen, watching the effect of the new religion on Cato, thought it strange that he had been able to reject his father's Christianity and immediately accept old Hajj's Islam, for although it was true that Christianity had defrauded the black man totally in one of the great deceptions of history—almost as if Christianity had been devised and held in reserve for this peculiar purpose—Islam had treated him worse, and it was ironic that this religion should now be thought of as the savior of the Negro race when for so long it was the principal destroyer through its sponsorship of slavery.

It was in this very field of slavery that Hajj' had his deepest influence on Cato and generated those emotional storms of which I spoke earlier. Cato himself told me how this happened. 'I had gone to the mosque one Friday with Hajj', and after services he invited me to his quarters, where we sat on the veranda looking over the bay in which ships were docked for the night, and he used a word I had never heard before. He said, "In the old days—well, in fact, even when I was a little boy—the barracoons were over there," and he pointed toward the dark jungle opposite the island. I asked him what they were, and he looked at me in surprise. 'You don't know what barracoons were? Your ancestors did, of that we may be sure." And he explained how in the days of slavery, which lasted on this island till the early 1900s, blacks were caught in the center of Africa and driven in herds to the port areas, which ships would visit periodically in order to load up with the precious cargo. In the waiting period between the time when the slaves arrived at the shore and the boats sailed in to pick them up, they were kept in large stockades guarded by riflemen and fierce dogs, and these were the barracoons." I suppose the word *coon* came from this. The man from the barracoon.

'Well, Hajj' was so surprised that I hadn't known about this that he showed me several books he thought I should read. He'd gotten them from ship captains or from visitors who had studied about Moçambique on the long trip out from Europe, and I used to leave the pop-top right after breakfast and go over to his place and sit on the veranda all day long, reading those terrifying books. They dealt with slavery.'

As he told me this, he shivered, for although like any schooled Negro he had known of slavery, its full horror had been blanked from his consciousness, as if it were too heavy a burden for the mind to bear. 'But now I became steeped in it. In Hajj's books I would read: "From Moçambique Island so many slaves were loaded into the ships that a marble seat was erected on the shore in front of the palace, and here, when the slaves were assembled in their chains, the bishop would come and with a wave of his hand convert them all to Christianity, so that if they died on the Middle Passage their souls would go to heaven, and this was prudent, because the ships were packed so tightly that thirty or forty per cent of the slaves would perish before the ships cleared the island, and their bodies would be thrown into the sea, but all died as good Christians."

'I remember one phrase I'll never be able to erase from my mind. It hides there like a cancer. I came upon it by accident, and the author was not trying to make any special point. Just trying to be complete in his reporting. He said, "The Jesuits kept their barracoon on the mainland opposite the island and hauled their slaves to the ships by barge." Ponder that one.'

But the passage that Cato remembered most often, he never mentioned. I think he knew he could not trust himself to speak of this lest his voice break, but he had copied it on an old typewriter owned by Hajj', and it was this copy he showed me:

In one of the great houses on Moçambique Island there lived in these years the Portuguese wife of a wealthy official. Unfortunately, her body had gone to fat and her face became so large and ugly that she was known universally as The Lioness. It was reported that she knew she was so called, for her disposition grew worse each year, and since she had no children and her husband consorted with others, she was able to vent her displeasure only on her slaves, and it became her custom to tie to the ground any female slave who promised to be of such beauty as to attract her husband and then to knock out her front teeth. She carried with her a palmado, a club with a head about the size of a small saucer, cut through with many holes and attached to a bamboo handle which was most resilient, and if any of her seamstresses made even so much as one mistake in the dresses they sewed for her, she would make the girl hold out her right hand and she would strike it seventy or eighty times with the palmado, swinging it with full force so that the holes raised blisters on the seamstress's hand, after which the girl was required to return immediately to her sewing and make her next stitches without error, lest she be visited with the palmado for another six or seven dozen strokes.

The more Cato read in Hajj's books, the more grisly became the true story of Africa, and no part had been more bloody and terrible than that played by this benevolent island, for it had been the *entrepôt* where the market value of slaves was determined for the east coast; it was here that slavers from all the civilized nations of the world convened to pick up their valuable cargoes. How many slaves had been transferred from the barracoons on the mainland to the ships at anchor off the island? Two or three million, perhaps, so that many Negroes in Brazil and Cuba and the United States had known the profile of this marvelous island, had known its slave market, its barracoons, its chains and, at the end, the benevolence of its bishop's blessing as he sat in his marble chair, dispatching his new Christians into the holds of the waiting ships.

Cato told me, 'While the others were exploring the fort or getting to know the Portuguese traders or arguing under the awning at Bar Africa, I was either reading at Hajj's or walking along the waterfront, visualizing those endless streams of black people being marched out of the jungle. I could see them being thrown into the holds while the rich Portuguese watched from the shore, from right where I was standing, and I began to feel a kind of bitterness in those days that will simply never leave me. It was your economic system, your church that did this, and I doubt that the debt can ever be repaid.'

So during that long and peaceful stay on Moçambique Island, Cato Jackson underwent a spiritual upheaval composed of one part Islam, one part history, one part racial memory, and he began to formulate the ideas that would motivate him as a man. His instructor was Hajj', an Arab who had seen a vision in his twenty-fifth year and had found it sufficient to guide him the rest of his life. He explained many things to Cato, admiring the young black's quick intelligence and keen desire, but when all the lessons were finished, and Cato thought he now comprehended what before had been obscure, Gretchen heard him railing one day against the Christian church which had permitted the system of slavery, and she grew irritated and said, 'You know, of course, that almost every slave delivered to Moçambique Island was brought here by Arab slavers who were devout Muslims?' When Cato stared at her, she added, 'The last big batch smuggled out of here was in 1902, and was handled by Hajj's father. The last big group to hit the coast anywhere was in 1952. More than three hundred slaves herded together by Arabs and sold to Arab dealers who smuggled them across the straits to Arabia.'

'Who told you that?' the black man stormed.

'I can read, too.'

Of course there was an Indian trader rumored to be selling drugs and of course Monica tracked him down within an hour, but in a whining Irish-type voice he said, 'Heroin? Who ever heard of heroin on Moçambique? I would be insane if I touched heroin. Please go away.'

Joe and Gretchen then witnessed for the first time the panic that overcomes a heroin user when his supply is threatened. Monica became a woman with a single purpose, for the Beira stock was almost gone and she could foresee that morning when she would awaken to an empty purse. She had to locate a source on the island, but even after repeated visits to the Indian, he put her off in his lilting, singsong way: 'It's all very well for you rich women to come here asking a poor Indian to help you out, but do you ever stop to think about my problems?'

'Who sells it?' Monica demanded desperately.

'It's all very well for you to stamp your foot and make demands
. . .' This continued for some time, until finally he said, 'You go
along the waterfront to the garage run by João Ferreira Dos Santos'
—he pronounced this in the Portuguese manner, *Jow Fer Shantzh*,
which Monica could not understand—'and in the small house beyond you'll find a half-caste seaman. Give him my name.'

She picked her way along the waterfront, unusually conspicuous if anyone had been tracking her, and came to a garage whose
name she could equate to Jow Fer Shantzh, and beyond it she saw
with expanding relief the small house, and in it she found a fat seaman who spoke no English. Reciting the Indian's name, she waited,
and after a moment's inspection, the seaman produced a medium-
sized bundle of untreated marijuana. In despair Monica whispered,
'No, no!' using the thumb and fingers of her right hand to make the
sign of a working hypodermic. Unperturbed, the half-caste took
back the grass and went into a back room. Much later, with Monica
fidgeting the while, he returned with a small packet of heroin.
'More, more,' Monica pleaded, but on this day he would allow her
only the minimum ration. It was priced at nine dollars, more than
twice what she had paid in the south.

Six more times she came back to the half-caste, until she had put
together a satisfactory cache, but when she felt herself secure, there
rose the question of Cato. What about his needs? She asked him
one afternoon as he returned from Hajj's, and he said, 'Don't worry
about me. I think I've about had it.'

This abrupt information shocked Monica and she began challenging him: 'You discover something as big as snow and you reject it?
Haven't you any self-respect?' This seemed ridiculously irrelevant, and Cato tried to explain that he had not been impressed with
heroin: 'Also, I don't know whether I could handle it in the long
run.'

This so infuriated Monica that her questions turned to accusations, and it was at this point that Joe and Gretchen returned from
a swim. Joe told me what happened next: 'Monica became enraged
to think that a black man would dare to tell her what she should or
should not do, and when Cato tried to explain that he was judging his own character, not hers, she flew into a rage and began

shouting so loud she could be heard throughout the park. Gretchen tried to quiet her, and after a while Monica and Cato had a big reconciliation. They made love and she persuaded him that if a person kept his head—if you stayed in the driver's seat—heroin could produce an endless rainbow. In the end she gave him a brutal ultimatum: "If you want to sleep in my bed, buster, stay with me."

'Next day he sought me out to talk it over. He was so damned unsure of himself. "Joe," he said, "twice I've had the feeling that maybe it was going to prove too big for me to handle. Real premonitions." So I said, "If there's even a possibility of that danger, why not stop?" and he said, "But I'm in love with her. You can't even imagine what it's like to be in bed with her." I figured that this was a topic on which he was the expert, so I said nothing, but then he grabbed my arm and said with his old-time cockiness, "I'm the guy who's gonna keep his head. I'm sure that if I stay in the driver's seat, I can handle the stuff." So I told him, "You do that, son, and they'll write you up in the medical books," at which he got mad, growling, "All right! When we were just sniffing, she tried it every day and I sniffed maybe once in three. Now that she's popping, I use the needle only every fourth or fifth time. And if she starts to mainline, I get off the train. I call that keeping things under control."

'But Monica kept the pressure on. She even applied the heat again to Gret and me. "It really is super," she assured us. Said she'd picked up an extra supply from the half-caste. Her main argument was that until you'd tried it, you'd never discover your true potential. She said your perception of beauty was enhanced and that you could never understand sex without heroin. Then Gretchen said, "That's what you told us about LSD," and Monica said, "Revelation comes in steps, darling," and Gretchen asked, "So what's your next big step?" and for a minute Monica stared off into space, as if she had caught an unwanted glimpse of some dark corridor she might not wish to travel.'

Of the various books that Hajj' loaned Cato, one was to have a lasting impact on all the Americans. It was a history of Portuguese exploration and had been brought to the island as a summary of events in Moçambique, and after Cato had read that dreary account of how the Portuguese had seduced and bullied the original black inhabitants and had sold a large part of them into slavery, he looked by chance at the section dealing with the Atlantic Ocean side of Africa, and there he came upon the story of King Afonso I, who had ruled the Congo basin from 1505 until his death in 1542.

It was a story of gripping force, the equal of anything that had unfolded in Europe or Asia during that period. It told of how Afonso's wily father, ruling an area larger than most European countries, had reacted to the arrival of the white men, how he had fenced with them and tried to select from their confusing ways the good while rejecting the bad. The old man had turned his favorite son, Afonso, over to the care of a group of Catholic priests, who then spent ten years instructing him in what was best in European culture. They had been remarkable men, devoted servants of God and the Congo, and in Afonso they produced a black man who would have both the knowledge and the sophistication to guide his people from primitivism to a place of equality in the world's councils.

They showed him how to trade the untouched riches of the Congo for the skills of Europe, how to protect his nation by judicious alliances between the powers that would one day want to absorb it, and above all, how to make the transition from tribal gods to Christianity, so that the civilized nations of the world would accept the Congo as an equal. They taught him much more, and at the age of twenty-two he was well prepared to govern his huge kingdom.

Apart from his fortunate education, Afonso was a man of unusual abilities, for he possessed the gift of charismatic leadership and a clear perception of where he and his people stood in history. He was also an honest man, brave in battle, and with a keen sense of strategy. He was, in short, the finest leader that the black people of Africa were to produce over a five-hundred-year period, and if ever the African Negro had a chance to establish a secure position vis-à-vis Europe, it was through Afonso; his letters to the King of Portugal in Lisbon were documents of prime historical importance, for in them he asked not for cannon or gold but for teachers and priests who would show his black subjects how to govern themselves.

When Cato reached this point in the history he felt that he had to share his discovery with the others, so he asked Hajj' if he might take the book to the pop-top, but when he got there, a little boy told him, 'They go Bar Africa,' so he joined them, and under the awning, while the fan droned noisily, disturbing the air hardly at all, he read them portions of the record. His white listeners were impressed, and Monica said, 'I never heard of this man.' Nor had the others.

It was Gretchen who introduced the subject that would occupy them for several hours: 'If black people comprise such an important segment of the world population, and especially if they are so crucial to the United States right now, why don't we study about men like King Afonso? At college I had a course in Belgian history. How big is Belgium? I don't know, eight or nine million people? Maybe a third as many people as we have Negroes in the United States. Yet it's academically respectable to have a course in Belgian history because Belgium happens to be white and a part of Europe. But it would be ridiculous to have a course in Congo history, even though the Congo has one and a half times the population of Belgium, because it's black and is not a part of Europe. Crazy world.'

'That's it!' Cato cried with some excitement. 'That's why we blacks demand that we be given courses in black history. God knows it's more important to the world today than Belgian history. And for America it's fantastically more important.'

Gretchen had a subtle point: 'I don't agree with you, Cato, that only blacks should be given the course in black history. It's us whites who ought to take it . . . so that we can see you and ourselves in different perspective.'

But shrewd Monica saw the flaw in this argument: 'You can rationalize all you wish, and you can daydream about what might have happened, but the cold fact remains that the history of the world is and apparently always will be the history of what white men have accomplished. The history of Belgium is at least fifty times as significant as the history of the Congo if only because Jan van Eyck invented oil painting there and Maurice Maeterlinck wrote his books. When somebody in the Congo accomplishes something like that, it'll be worth our while to study how his culture enabled him to do so. Until then . . .'

Cato grew angry, and demanded, 'What about the Benin sculptures?' and Monica, who had heard this question a hundred times in Vwarda and London, snapped, 'What about the giant heads on Easter Island? Do they make history? Does one lucky break build a culture? You saw the cultural history of Africa . . . when that commission came down to talk with Sir Victor . . . then went back and slaughtered his wife. That's Africa.'

Cato said, 'I happen to think that tribal groups murdering a white woman in Vwarda is neither better nor worse than Protestants slaughtering Catholics in Ireland. Neither country is fit to govern itself, but we're stuck with both of them.'

Gretchen, always unhappy when Cato and Monica argued, tried to conciliate their points of view by asking, 'What happened to King Afonso?' and Cato replied, 'I haven't got to that part yet,' and Monica said, 'Pounds to sixpence he sold his people out.' When Joe told me of the argument later, I asked what part he had played, and he said, 'I sat there nursing a beer, listening and trying to decide what I thought.' I asked him what he had concluded, and he said, 'Like on so many things, I was mostly confused.'

When Cato returned with the book to Hajj's veranda, he settled down to follow the history of Afonso I, and as he read, a grief of great magnitude enveloped him as he learned how Afonso's reign had ended in disaster. The missionaries that Portugal sent to help him found that they could make a fortune by rounding up slaves for European ships that were starting to anchor at the mouth of the Congo; the first of the terrible chain gangs leading from the interior to the beach were shepherded by priests. Traders who were to guide the king became buccaneers waging war against him. White counselors who were supposed to help bring the Congo into the concert of nations perverted everything they touched and defeated each effort of the king to civilize his domain. Worst of all, the Portuguese who had opened the kingdom to trade and Christianity saw quickly that it was not to their interest to have the area governed by a strong central power, so they supported any insurgency that came along and initiated their own when native rebellions flagged. Afonso's attempts at leadership were frustrated. Savages who stood to gain a little gold by selling other savages into slavery were encouraged to overthrow the king, and in the end, betrayed by the God he had accepted, by that God's representatives, by his tutors the Portuguese, and by his own people, he fled his homeland, unable to comprehend the collapse that had engulfed him.

Cato closed the book, and when Hajj' asked him a question about it, he merely stared at the tall saint and walked out into the evening cool. Without seeing the people who passed him on the boulevard, he wandered toward the fort and came to that attractive plaza which stood between the sea and the governor's palace, and there he saw the familiar statue of Vasco da Gama looking toward India, with the inscription which Cato had always disliked but which now infuriated him:

VASCO DA GAMA

1469–1524

Descobriador

de

Moçambique

en

1496

'Just like the arrogant bastards,' he muttered to himself, thinking not of the Portuguese but of all white men. 'They stumble upon this island in 1496 and announce to the world that they've discovered it. The damned thing had been known by Arabs for a thousand years and by blacks for two thousand years. But until white men got here it didn't exist. When they set their sacred feet ashore it became a part of the known world. Known to whom? Goddammit, the Queen of Sheba knew this island. Regular boats were sailing from here to Arabia when Portugal was still a pigpen.'

He stared at the metal explorer and cursed him: 'A savage murderer, that's what he was. That's what they all were.' And then, as he stood on this historic spot, where trading ships had tied to the shore for two thousand years, he seemed to see in the shadows the endless procession of slaves, reaching back to the beginning of time, shuffling silently from jungle to barracoon to ship. Among those naked women heading for the slave markets in Lisbon or Pernambuco or Charleston was one who could have been his great-great-great-great-grandmother. Among the men, weighted with wooden yokes, walked his spiritual father, and over all the passage there was a smell of death.

He covered his face with his hands, as if he were ashamed to have the white captains of the slave ships see him weep; his anguish was deep. But then his pride took over. Wheeling away from the shore and its hideous scene, he faced the metal statue and in a loud voice, shouted, 'Fuck you, Vasco da Gama.'

——— · • · · ———

And then one day the letters arrived! In Lourenço Marques, in Beira and here on the island, Gretchen had gone often—but in vain—to the poste restante; finally, this day, there was a batch of mail sent north by the young man from the consulate. There was a letter from her mother and one from a former escort, both of which she tucked into her handbag. With joy she saw that Yigal had written to Cato, from Detroit, and that Mr. Holt had written to Joe, from Lausanne, and it required much self-restraint to keep from ripping open the envelopes, so eager was she to know what was happening to her friends. But what pleased her most was a letter addressed to her, also from Lausanne, and in Britta's precise European hand.

Hurrying to Bar Africa, she ordered a glass of white wine and ripped open her precious letter. Then, unfolding the sheets with care, she spread them before her and began to read.

> Hotel Splendide
> Lausanne, Switzerland
> 2 September, 1969

Dearest Gretchen,

Not a day goes by but what Harvey and I ask ourselves, 'How are the kids doing in Moçambique?' I have read three books on the area and probably know it better than you do, because Harvey adds to the reading with strange bits of information. Did you know that Lourenço Marques was almost the cause of a war between the French and Germans and English and Portuguese, and not too long ago, either?

How did I get here? Well, after you left Pamplona that night to catch the boat in Barcelona, I went back to the military hospital, told the guide I was Mrs. Harvey Holt just in from Madrid, broke into the room and told Harvey that I was going with him to Ceylon whether he married me or not. Both he and Mr. Fairbanks wanted me to leave Pamplona, but I saw very clearly what was right for Harvey, and I refused to leave.

We drove to Madrid . . . Harvey got well so soon you'd never believe it. The doctors said he must have been raised on tiger milk. There's a real hole in his belly, but the doctors said it would fill in as the muscle grew back into place, and before we left Pamplona something terribly nice happened which I think you kids, and especially Cato, ought to know. The young Frenchman who grabbed Harvey from behind and caused the accident came to the hospital and apologized and wanted to pay the entire hospital bill because he had been told that Harvey was a poor man who worked in the oil fields all year and saved just enough money to run with the bulls at Pamplona each summer. I had tears in my eyes and Mr. Fairbanks coughed and Harvey embraced the young man, the way they do in French movies, and then what do you think happened? He—the Frenchman, I mean—brings out a big photograph of the scene where he is grabbing Harvey and the bull is goring him, and would you believe it, he wants Harvey to sign it, and when Harvey does, he brings out another copy which he has signed and he gives this to Harvey as a present! When he left, the young man said, 'I'll see you next Bastille Day,' and Harvey said, 'That would be just my luck.'

I suppose you want the big news. Harvey refuses to marry me but I am going to Ceylon with him . . . that much I insist on and I think he rather likes the idea because I do many things to help him. I'm sort of unhappy that he doesn't want to get married, but not too much. Between you and me, I think he'll gradually get used to the idea, and if the gradually doesn't string out till I get wrinkles, I have a feeling it will work out all right. For the present, though, no babies. Every time we have a quarrel, which is not too often, he says, 'Damn it all, I'll set you up in a bar in Torremolinos,' as if that were the greatest thing a girl could want. So maybe years from now when you and Clive come back to Torremolinos, there I'll be. He got the idea in Japan, where if a man lives with a woman for a certain number of years, when they break up he's obligated to buy her a bar. I told him that if that was my destiny, the least he could do was give me a book on how to mix drinks, and the other night he brought one home wrapped in silver foil.

How did we wind up in Lausanne? Dear Mr. Fairbanks persuaded

Harvey, when we got to Madrid, that he ought to have a recuperation. Besides, all his savings are invested in World Mutual here in Geneva and he ought to see the head office. What I think it really was was that Mr. Fairbanks likes Harvey very much and wanted to encourage him to marry me. So we came to Geneva, which was very busy, and then came right down here, which is lovely—Lake Leman, which I used to read about in school, and a super art museum and the mountains not far off. I was so happy the other night I said, 'This is like a honeymoon,' and Harvey said, 'This is your honeymoon,' so I guess that's that.

Of course, Harvey was worried about getting back to work, but Mr. Fairbanks said, 'You're entitled to sick leave, take it,' but Harvey was afraid UniCom might think he was only playing sick, so Mr. Fairbanks had his company physician examine Harvey so that he could write a letter and certify that Harvey had really been injured, and when the doctor saw that first big scar across the chest, and the latest one in the belly, and the big one on the rump and the two shrapnel wounds from Okinawa when Harvey got one of his medals, the doctor said, 'Hell, this man should *never* go back to work,' and they spent the rest of the day drinking and talking about war and bulls and far-off places.

Gretchen, I want you to do something very important. Harvey is going to write Joe a letter. He thinks of Joe all the time. Some days he mentions his name four or five times, almost as if Joe were his son. Something Joe said in Pamplona has worried Harvey very much and he thinks that maybe when they were talking he didn't express himself very well, so he's going to write this letter in which he hopes to express his ideas more clearly. He's afraid that Joe won't take the letter seriously. Joe will listen to you. As a matter of fact, I think he is in love with you, in his sweat-shirt sort of way, so please see to it that he takes the letter seriously. It will mean a great deal to Harvey.

Give my love to Monica. She is a girl who needs a great deal of love, Gretchen, and I don't mean from men. Stay close to her. I miss her sadly, as if she were my little sister, although I am no older than she is. And give sweet little Cato a kiss for me. I like to hear him arguing about things he knows nothing about. He's marvelous fun, but I often wonder what'll happen when Monica breaks it off.

And to you, as we Spaniards say, *un abrazo grande*. I would stain the page with tears if I told you how indebted to you I am, not for the kindness—anyone can give kindness—but for the money. Without it I'd never have met Harvey and I'd never have gone to Ceylon and my life would have been frustrated and barren. We shall meet somewhere and I will try to tell you, but I'm sure you know.

Love,
Britta

P.S. When you live with Holt you live with music, but his tape recorder is so complicated he won't let me touch it. I made him get me one I could play. It cost $50 and I tell him it sounds better than his.

Gretchen finished her drink, folded the letter, and smiled as she visualized dour Mr. Holt trying to remain indifferent to Britta while she wove about him an increasingly intricate web of love. Raising her empty glass, she toasted aloud, 'To Britta,' then walked back in the fragrant shade to the pop-top, where she distributed the mail, telling the others that they could share her letter from Britta when they had finished their own. Joe's letter read:

Hotel Splendide
Lausanne, Switzerland
September 3, 1969

Dear Joe,

That night we discussed the draft in Pamplona, I didn't express myself clearly. What I wanted to say was that a young man twenty-one years old or whatever you are is a very precious thing, and the older a man like me gets, the more he appreciates this. Almost every good thing that will be done in the world from now on will have to be done by young fellows like you, and to lose even one would be a tragedy.

I don't want the world to lose you, Joe. If I am anywhere around when you decide to take Little Casino or Big Casino, I'm going to do everything in my power to stop you. I will have you arrested, or beaten up, or thrown into jail, but I will not allow you to make an error which would scar you for life . . . and I don't mean scar you on my terms, which you laugh at, but on your own terms, which you take seriously. I think I know what Big Casino is, and if you smear yourself with that brush, it will not be me who will reject you in later life, it will be your own people, because they will not dare to risk contaminating whatever good thing they have going at the moment.

Joe, I'm going to be in Lausanne for a few weeks and after that I'll be on the job at Ratmalana. There will always be a home for you.

There will always be someone to talk with, even if he is, as you once said, another goddamned marine.

What I have to say next is not easy, as you will guess. If at the end you need some place to hide from the draft, you can come to Ratmalana. I still think you're dead wrong about evading the draft, but I am now willing to grant that you may be sincere in your position. But your other idea of rejecting life itself I could never understand. Please think this over before you do something that you would regret the rest of your days.

If you need money, let me know. Britta happens to be in town and sends her love.

> Yours,
> Harvey Holt

Yigal's letter to Cato had been mailed to the Alamo in Torremolinos and had been forwarded from there. It read:

> At My Grandfather's
> 1188 Esplanade
> Grosse Pointe, Michigan
> August 12, 1969

Dear Cato and Gang,

When my grandfather hauled me away from Pamplona, I was so mad I could have strangled him, but now that we're home, Mr. Holt and his god-awful music and those wild times at Bar Vasca seem very far away. I'm beginning to appreciate something Mr. Fairbanks said when he was arguing with me that last miserable day. He said that America was the lodestone of the world right now, the magnet against which you had to test your strength. He was right. This is where it's happening and I suppose my biggest job is to get it into focus, because until I do I won't be able to judge England and Israel, and as I told you that night in Alte, one of these days I've got to make up my mind.

Actually, I suppose I'm making it up each day. I see now that this is one hell of a country, and I respect it. You'd be interested in the one thing that holds me back. Television. I don't mean the programs, which I can take or leave, but the advertisements. No matter what's happening in the world, even the moon walk, which was something, believe me, the ads come on and show illiterate men and stupid women all excited about the most trivial aspects of living, and you honestly begin to wonder if that isn't the real America.

You wouldn't believe my grandfather. He's a wonderful old geezer and I hope I have at fifty the vitality he has at seventy. He gets wildly excited over what General Motors has done during the last sales year, and he isn't even with the company any more. You'd think he was president or general or something and the fact that GM sold more cars than Ford or Chrysler was a staggering victory, surpassing Waterloo and Zama combined. But that isn't all. What gives him a real lift is that within GM it was Pontiac that accounted for the big success. He calls all the Pontiac men and says, 'By God, Harry, you're doing even better than we used to in the old days. I knew you had it in you when I picked you out of Replacement Parts.'

I report to Case next month, and from what I've been hearing, it must be a drag. They seem to teach science like we taught it in Israel six years ago, so you wonder where this great technology that America boasts about is coming from. Don't be surprised if you see me on your doorstep one of these days. I've had Detroit and I doubt if Cleveland will be much better.

I'm not much impressed with the Negroes in Detroit, and if your boys don't pull up their socks they're going to be behind the eight-ball throughout eternity. I've concluded they need about a dozen guys like you, and sooner or later you ought to come back here and do some stirring up, because you had constructive ideas. The big idea at present among the Negroes is to eliminate Jews, which seems to be so screwy it doesn't merit consideration, but grown men keep saying that if they can only eliminate Jews, everything will be all right. I'd like to talk to you about this some more, because I can't believe the Negroes have swallowed the Goebbels pill so long after it was exposed.

Big news right now is a Swedish movie called *I Am Curious (Yellow)*. I haven't seen it, but some of the fellows told me it featured a Swedish bombshell who is crazy about sex, and sometimes I tell them that I knew a Norwegian bombshell. Give her my best and tell her to watch those GIs in the bar.

Yours,
Yigal

P.S. Christ, am I tired of being Bruce!

———•◆•———

The finest thing that happened to them during their visit to Moçambique occurred, as was so often the case with this generation of young people, because of their love for music.

The opening of the school year in America had come and gone without creating apprehension among the drifters. The autumn season, when jobs ought to be pinned down in England and the States, was upon them, but they were in Moçambique, where spring was just beginning, and mentally they looked forward to an endless summer. No one had to bother about money so long as Monica's father continued her allowance, Gretchen's inheritance arrived on time, and Mister Wister sent Cato his regular checks. It was an age of pilgrimage, and they intended to enjoy it.

And Ilha de Moçambique exceeded their hopes. It was nepenthe-land, an enclave in history where days drifted by under a flawless sun, beside a controlled sea. The camping grew more interesting every day, for the people who stopped by to talk with them, or to bring fruit, seemed an evocation of all who had lived on this fortunate island since the beginning of history—not Vasco da Gama's truncated history, which had begun only when the island was already two thousand years old, but the true history which ran back to aboriginal times.

For Cato this daily procession posed a dilemma, because among the blacks who came to stare at the pop-top and to wonder how four grown people slept inside, and in what arrangements, appeared a special group of Negro women. They were big, handsome black women, true African types, not intermixed with white blood, as was so often the case in America. Cato once calculated that he was at least three eighths white, and in Philadelphia he knew almost no pure-blooded blacks, but on Moçambique Island he was seeing the unspoiled African. Unspoiled, that is, except for one thing! In woman's eternal quest for beauty, these handsome blacks covered their faces with paste made from the chewed root of a leafy plant, which, when it dried, became a white mask. Throughout the community he would spot black women of unusual dignity and physical charm, dressed in lovely gold and yellow cloth, but when they turned, their faces would be a ghastly white.

'They're not dumb,' Monica teased. 'They know that to be really beautiful you've got to be white.' It seemed that way. Once, seeking refuge from Monica's goading, he left the pop-top to find Hajj', and asked the tall Arab to serve as interpreter while he questioned a group of black women. Why did they smear the paste on their faces? . . . To be beautiful. Why did they use white? . . . Because it was beautiful. Could a black woman be beautiful without the paste? . . . She might be attractive, but to be beautiful she had to take pains. Did they think that this black woman coming down the street was beautiful? . . . She was attractive but it was a shame she hadn't whitened her face. He tried repeatedly to find out why they had chosen white for their ghostly makeup, and the best they could tell him was that their tribe had always known that white made a woman beautiful, and as they said this, Cato pointed to a Portuguese woman who was fat, dumpy and ill-complexioned. Did they think she was beautiful? . . . Not like us, but she is white.

'I don't think Africa will make it,' he grumbled to himself when Hajj' and the women had gone. 'Unless Islam saves the black race.' He continued to feel that in this religion Africa would find its salvation, but again this assessment had its teeth pulled when Gretchen, in her usual straightforward way of searching for evidence on her own, pointed out that the Muslims of Moçambique maintained two cemeteries, one for white men on the island, another for blacks well hidden on the mainland.

Among the citizens of Ilha de Moçambique who developed the habit of stopping by the pop-top to watch the young visitors and to talk with them occasionally was the rotund Portuguese businessman in the white suit who had welcomed them that first night and introduced them to Hajj'. In idle conversation one evening he discovered that they had been to Silves, and he cried joyously, 'I come from Portimão!' and they spent some time just reciting the well-remembered names of Algarve: Albufeira, Lagos, Faro and, with a certain reverence, Alte; and Gretchen, nostalgic for that village in the mountains with its plaza watched over by the stone poet, brought out her guitar. And the plaza quickly filled with Negro women, their white faces glowing in the sunset.

Gretchen sang for nearly an hour to an audience which appreciated every note she offered, and when she put down the guitar, the Portuguese businessman said, in his fearful patois, 'How good it is to have music at the end of the day,' and he insisted that they accompany him to Bar Africa for drinks, and as they were chatting idly, he said, 'Of course, you plan to visit our great game sanctuary at Zambela.' When they replied that they hadn't considered it, he summoned a man who could speak English and together they told of the extraordinary game refuge that lay about three days' travel to the west.

'You must see it,' the two Portuguese agreed, the fat man adding, 'We know you've heard of Kruger Park in South Africa and Serengeti in Tanzania, but Zambela is something quite special, because there you have a concentration of wildlife that is unbelievable. I don't mean that you'll see some Cape buffalo. I mean that you'll see five thousand of them, perhaps at one time. Can you imagine five hundred hippopotamuses crowding one small island?'

The two men were so persuasive that the travelers decided that night to make a detour to Zambela, and next day they reluctantly packed the pop-top and said their goodbyes to some of the kindest people they had encountered in their travels. When the white-faced Negro women realized that the campers were about to leave, they wept, and several came to kiss Monica and Gretchen farewell. The fat businessman in his white suit reported, 'Zambela will be my gift to you for the music you made.' When old Hajj' came to give them his final blessing, as if they were pilgrims departing for Mecca, they felt a sense of sorrow, for it was apparent that he and they would not meet again. He took Cato aside for some last-minute instructions on Islam, but the others were impatient to depart, so he had to be content with placing his hands on Cato's shoulders and saying, 'Remember, the answer to your problems lies within reach of your hand,' and he said a prayer in Arabic.

The vast, unfenced park to which the pop-top headed lay along the western border of Moçambique on the shores of Lake Nyasa, and the road they now chose took them along no curving beaches, but inland through bush country, where for whole days they saw only the dusty kraals and Stone Age blacks. For these near-savages there was no Portugal, no United Nations, not even an Africa.

At evening on the third day, while Joe was driving, they came to a pair of wooden pillars that marked the entrance to Zambela, and as soon as they had crossed into the sanctuary they felt that they had exchanged the world of reality for a dream. On the side of the road stood the painted sign: *Beware of Elephants*, and in the middle of the road lay an even more pragmatic sign: an enormous ball of brownish-black manure dropped a few minutes earlier by one of the elephants, whose tread they could hear not far off.

At the camp, which lay ten miles inside the gates, they saw something which caused them to shout with pleasure: a set of rondavels, well constructed and located amidst flowers; and they had barely checked into the two assigned them—one for the girls, one for the boys, an arrangement that would be honored only in the official register—when a lean, ruggedly handsome man, in his mid-sixties and dressed in khaki, knocked on one of the doors and said, 'I understand that Sir Charles Braham's daughter is here.' When Monica appeared, he introduced himself, 'John Gridley, Salisbury. I used to work with Sir Charles in Vwarda, and now I'm here on loan from the Rhodesian government.' He was punctilious in acknowledging each of the young people, even though Cato's blackness and Joe's scraggly beard must have disconcerted him.

He said, 'Government in Lourenço Marques sent us a signal that you'd be coming and to look you out. They also forwarded this letter to you, sir,' and he handed Joe an official envelope from the American consul in the capital.

'Final draft notice,' Joe said, handling the envelope as if it were a time bomb, which it was.

'Then you'll be joining up at the end of this visit?'

'No, sir. I'll be running.'

This confession brought an uneasy silence, broken by Monica, who asked, 'Couldn't you take the letter back and make believe it hadn't been delivered?' She said it so sweetly that the ranger assumed she was joking, and the pending unpleasantness passed.

Mr. Gridley was the kind of capable man you hope you will meet on your travels but rarely do. He had worked in all of the parks in Rhodesia and knew more about big game than most of the men now operating, for he had learned from the old hunters who had penetrated the jungle at the end of the last century, in addition to which he had an innate sense of what the animal reaction to most situations would be. He enjoyed instructing young people and appreciated his good fortune in being able to work in Africa.

He spoke with stately charm, derived from his education in England, but although his name and his manner were British, and although as an English partisan he found the extreme ideas of Dr. Vorlanger in South Africa rather comical, he was a convinced supporter of the present Rhodesian government.

'At seven tomorrow morning the gates to the inner park will open and I'll have a bush car to show you what we have hiding out there. In the meantime, Mrs. Gridley would be honored if you'd stop by our house after dinner.'

A hot shower and fresh clothes converted the travelers into social beings again, and after a good meal at the mess hall, featuring fresh fruit, they wandered across the well-kept grounds till they reached the set of cottages in which the staff lived. Mrs. Gridley was waiting for them, a steel-gray Scottish woman in her early fifties, well known throughout Africa for her habit of bringing to her fenced-in garden all baby animals who had been afflicted or abandoned, so that it was possible to look from her back door, no matter in what park her husband was serving, and see a small Cape buffalo, a baby elephant, some zebras, and even a small hippo soaking himself in the pond she maintained. She felt no discomfort in entertaining Cato, but the girls were her chief pleasure. 'Is there anything you need?' she asked them solicitously. 'I've all sorts of medicines and things that one requires in this sort of life.' She noticed a small abscess on Monica's left arm and said, 'I've just the thing for that. You shouldn't let it go, you know, not in this climate,' and when she applied her salve she noticed, without commenting upon it, the cluster of marks against the fair skin and knew immediately what had caused them.

Joe told me later, 'I was watching her face, to see what she'd do when she saw the hypodermic marks, and she knew I was watching. What do you suppose she did? After satisfying herself that Monica's sore was an ulcer which came from popping heroin, she looked carefully at my arm, and I left it extended so that she could see it, and then she looked at Gretchen's and at Cato's. Only then did she serve tea.'

The Gridleys were a surprising pair, Rhodesians who were totally loyal to their government yet willing to discuss its policies with anyone, even an American Negro, whom they told, 'We believe the white man can hold on without much trouble for at least thirty more years. We possess all the ammunition, all the power. There might be pressures moving down from the north, but we think we can control them. Of course, after these thirty years great changes will probably take place throughout the entire world. Who knows what the relationship between nations and races will be then?'

'You don't fear an uprising?' Cato asked, astonished at their willingness to talk, because these were not young marijuana-experiment people such as he had met in Lourenço Marques. These two were close to the heart of Rhodesia, and what they had to say was significant.

'Yes, there's always a fear of insurrection,' Mrs. Gridley confessed. 'Just as you face insurrection in the United States. But does anyone doubt that when the crunch comes in America, the white man will be able to hold on . . . at least for the duration of this century?'

'Is there any doubt of that?' Mr. Gridley repeated.

Cato said, 'Four years ago people like you in America were asking, "Is there any doubt that the great United States can defeat little Vietnam?" A lot of us doubted. We didn't know how it would happen or what dreadful thing would go wrong, but we honestly doubted that America could win. And do you know why? Because the war was historically wrong, and things which are historically wrong tend to be righted . . . how, no one can predict.'

Normally, at this point the discussion should have become heated, but it didn't. With scientific precision the Gridleys considered the views that Cato had presented and countered with arguments of their own. 'I agree with you,' Gridley said with real enthusiasm. 'Things that are historically wrong do not persist. But in this case, Mr. Jackson, I'm afraid you've misinterpreted what it is in Africa that is historically wrong. I'm a technologist—an ecologist, to be exact—and we look at man as an animal. He has precisely the same problems of survival that the elephant has . . . or the sable antelope.' He paused to ask if any of them had ever seen a sable antelope. 'Ah, it will be my pleasure to show you one of the superb sights of creation. But to get back to my point. It seems to me, as an ecologist, that man's supreme problem today is finding a way by which he can live with technical advances. Really, if he doesn't, he's lost. And it is the white man who is grappling with this problem. I don't mean that it was white scientists and a white nation that put a man on the moon. I mean that it is the white man who is struggling with the matter of automation, of air pollution, of urban control, of whatever is significant in the world today.'

'What about Japan?' Cato asked.

'They are allied with us. The blacks are not. And there's the terrifying difference.'

'How about India?'

'Historically they're whites. Actually they're blacks.' He then spoke with the deep distrust that Rhodesians seemed to hold for the Indians: it was as if the Rhodesian reserved his harshest feelings not for the black, whom he understood, but for the Indian, whom he would never understand. Gridley said, 'India is a potentially powerful nation that could direct its energies to the problems I'm talking about, but for the rest of this century and no doubt throughout the next, they'll be preoccupied with religious struggles and a crushing overpopulation. They can't even decide on a common language. And the failure is primarily a matter of religion. So I think we can dismiss India as of no consequence.'

'That's a fairly large dismissal,' Gretchen said. Like most girls who have gone to good colleges in the United States, she had been indoctrinated with the idea that India owned a culture that was at least equal to America's and probably superior, and now she was astonished to hear a man of wide knowledge dismissing the whole subcontinent as not worthy of serious discussion where the ultimates of contemporary life were concerned.

'I don't dismiss it because of spite,' Gridley said. 'It's just that the nation is incapable of organizing itself and therefore of making any serious contribution.'

'But what about her moral leadership?' Gretchen persisted.

Gridley smiled indulgently. 'Ask the Portuguese about that. Ask them about the rape of Goa.'

'The important point,' Mrs. Gridley said, addressing herself to Cato, 'is that the white nations are concerned with the future. The black nations are absorbed in arranging the present, and until they catch up, the drift of history has to be with us.'

Cato laughed. 'On the long drive north to Moçambique Island, I came to the same conclusion. I told my white friends that Rhodesia could hold out for the rest of this century. History was on your side. So then the problem becomes—how can we change history?' The room grew quiet, and he said, 'Tanzania is doing it by throwing in her lot with China. Suppose that Russia occupies the Middle East countries like Jordan and Israel . . .'

'Do you think Israel is going under?' Gridley asked.

'The Muslims are determined,' Cato said, expressing for the first time in public his newly acquired conviction. 'Even the Muslims in Moçambique are talking about a holy war.'

'Muslims everywhere have been talking about a holy war for the last thousand years. I understand that many blacks in America have turned Muslim. Watch. Within ten years Muslims all over the world will be talking about a holy war to rescue their brothers in America.'

Cato almost grew angry, but instead returned to his main argument: 'So let's suppose that Russia, having absorbed the Middle East, decides to drop down into Africa. Let's suppose that Communist China applies pressure on Moçambique via Tanzania, and Communist Russia applies pressure on Rhodesia from the Congo. Then what?'

'Within a year they'd be fighting each other, and we'd be down here consolidating our position,' Gridley said.

'You don't believe that the drift of the future is black pressure from the north?'

'Oh yes! Pressure, agitation, threats. We shall have to live with them for the rest of our lives. But my point is that there isn't a damned thing the blacks can do about it. Not for this century at least.'

'You sound just like an American general discussing Vietnam . . . four years ago.' The group laughed, and Gretchen asked, 'What does a sable antelope look alike?' and the Gridleys searched their books until they found a color photograph, but before they showed it, Mr. Gridley said, 'You still haven't allowed me to make my point. I think that for the rest of this century the white man can hold on, and in that time he'll have established certain big principles. And by then the black nations will have produced many citizens as able and as well educated as Mr. Jackson here. Then there may be a totally different symbiosis between the races in which Rhodesia's addiction to her present solution may be of little importance, because larger solutions will be afoot. However, I feel sure that Rhodesia will be a partner in the larger solutions. But of course, I'm speaking as a man interested in how elephants solve their problems. They do so within the determinations of water, forage, security and a mysterious something called life force, that is, the will to survive. Among the whites in Rhodesia today, the life force is extremely strong.'

'Show them the antelope,' Mrs. Gridley said, but before her husband could do so, Cato placed his hand on the cover of the book and said, 'The life force of the black is also terribly strong,' to which Mr. Gridley replied, 'Good! Self-respect demands it. But the difference is that for the rest of this century the white man has not only life force but the guns and the airplanes.'

'Like in Vietnam,' Cato said.

———•—•—•———

For some months I had been intending to review our investments in Lourenço Marques, with an eye to extending them into Swaziland, a nearby Negro kingdom, and the presence of the four young people in Moçambique gave me an added incentive to make the trip now. It was an easy jet trip from the capital to Beira, where the government offered me a small plane for the flight to the game preserve.

It was always hazardous to land at Zambela, for although the sanctuary maintained a sizable airstrip, well mowed, the grass there was so clean and fresh that wild animals could not be prevented from breaking through the fences to browse, and as we approached I saw with apprehension that it was populated with seventeen Cape buffalo, each weighing nearly a ton, a couple of dozen blue hartebeest, a substantial herd of zebra, numerous giraffe and three elephants. I raised my hands in a gesture of futility, but the pilot showed no worry. He simply buzzed the field three times and drove the animals away, but by the time we had taxied to the administrative buildings, the zebras and buffalo were again grazing.

The young people had been notified by Lourenço Marques that I was arriving and were on the field waiting, profuse in their gratitude for my having suggested Moçambique, and they spent the first hour talking about their letters from Britta and Yigal and telling me what they had been doing with Mr. Gridley. I judged that he had given them a solid introduction to Africa, and even though he was Rhodesian, Cato spoke of him with respect. Next day's plans called for an expedition far into the bush to see if they could spot a fugitive herd of sable antelope, which had so far eluded them, and I was invited to go along . . . 'if you can get up at six,' Gretchen added.

When I retired to my rondavel to unpack, I was visited by the three Americans, in turn. Joe showed me a letter which the American consul in Lourenço Marques had sent him. It was from his draft board in California and was a coldly stated announcement that Joe was now considered a draft evader, that his passport was to be confiscated by any American official, and that he could be sentenced to a long term in jail if he did not immediately return to the jurisdiction of the board. Attached was a legal opinion from a government solicitor stating that Joe, for his own good, had better return promptly to California.

'What should I do?' he asked.

'What else? Go back.'

'But if the war is illegal and therefore indefensible?'

'No individual is big enough to make this judgment.'

'Who else?'

We kicked this around for some time, then Joe said, 'I'd better get to Marrakech. I have the name of a guy there who handles these things.'

'I'd stay clear of Marrakech. I'd head for California.'

'For you California would be right. For me it would be reverse gear. Absolutely wrong.' And he tore up the letter from his draft board.

A short time after he left, Gretchen dropped in, a girl who had obviously discovered in her life a spaciousness she had not known before. When she spoke of Zambela, her face was radiant: 'You were so right that day in Pamplona when you told us to reestablish contact with nature. I had never dreamed that places like this existed. We spent all yesterday afternoon just looking at the lions as they stalked a zebra.' Then the look of contentment vanished and she said, 'Mr. Fairbanks, it's Monica. I'm dreadfully worried about her. She's started taking heroin. Sniffing it at first. Now she's popping it under her skin and has developed a lovely abscess. I suppose she'll be mainlining next, and I really don't know what's going to happen to her.'

I asked how she had got started, and Gretchen said, 'By herself. No pressure from anyone that I know of. She did meet some sailors in Lourenço Marques who told her about an Indian there who did a little peddling on the side. But I'm sure it was she who pressured him.'

She then added that Cato was also using the stuff but was only sniffing it. I asked her where she had learned such a term, and she said, 'All the kids know about Big-H. That is, we know what we need to know.' I told her I doubted that, then asked how she was so sure that Cato was merely sniffing, and she said simply, 'I asked him. And I looked at his arms. For a while he was popping, but he seems afraid of that now.'

She asked if I would talk to Monica, try to reason with her, and I said, 'What can I do? She's a grown girl over whom I have no control,' but she corrected me: 'She's only seventeen and she's got to have help.' I told her that where heroin was concerned, I was powerless, but she said she was going to send Cato to talk with me.

He arrived wearing only shorts, and I hoped, from seeing his unscarred arms, that he had not progressed far in his use of heroin. I found him much subdued by his experiences in Africa, but I was ill at ease and found it hard to bring up the subject of drugs. He solved that quickly: 'With me heroin is no longer a problem. I've tried the stuff and at first I thought it was a breeze. But one day it terrified me. So I quit cold turkey.' I said this sounded like an arrogant boast, but he said, 'You don't believe those fairy stories about the man in the hospital who gets one shot of morphine and is hooked for life? I've sniffed it and I've popped it and I've quit for life.'

'You feel cocky enough to play around with heroin and walk away?'

'I've done it. I will never be hooked because I won't allow it. So let's drop that.'

'I hope you're right,' I said.

Abruptly he said, 'Monica's in trouble, not me. She likes heroin. Needs it. She's taking it regularly, and I'm pretty sure she's mainlining. Anyway, she keeps her gear with her all the time—the bottle cap for heating the stuff, that hypodermic she bought in Pamplona.'

'Were you two using heroin at Bar Vasca?'

'No. She bought the needle . . . just for the hell of it. Then, since she had it, she figured she might as well use it. Some American sailors got her started in Lourenço Marques. And she kept pestering me to try. And she eats practically nothing. And when we go to bed, mostly she sleeps. She's lost a lot of weight.' He continued his classic description of a young girl in the first stages of addiction, and from listening to him, I was ready to accept his assurance that he had indeed been able to move toward the brink of that precipice and voluntarily retreat. I was glad for him.

At dinner that night I had my first chance to study Monica, and outwardly she was more appealing than before, an enchanting young lady of seventeen with an ethereal beauty. Her exaggerated slimness made her additionally attractive, for now her pale face was more exotic. She wore a miniskirt with such style that everyone visiting the sanctuary was forced to stare at her. The only sign that betrayed her new explorations was a small skin-colored adhesive that Mrs. Gridley had insisted upon applying to the abscessed spot.

Monica sat on my right and took pains to charm me, keeping in rein the quick wit that sometimes offended older people. She ate sparingly, and during dessert, which she merely toyed with, I realized that she was quiet because she was at a low point in her cycle of euphoria-depression.

Later we visited the Gridleys, whom I had known in the parks in Rhodesia, and after he warned us that we must all get to bed soon, for we were starting at six to hunt for the sable antelope, Mrs. Gridley found occasion to maneuver me into the kitchen, where she said bluntly, 'If you know Sir Charles Braham, you'd better cable him to get his daughter out of Africa and into a sanitarium.'

'Sir Charles has no influence over her.'

'But she's suffering from dreadful malnutrition . . . because of the heroin. At seventeen. I could weep.'

'Have you discussed this with her?'

'I didn't have to. When I treated her abscess, she knew I knew. Do you realize, Mr. Fairbanks, that she could have lost her arm? She has absolutely no resistance and was giving it no treatment.' She paused, then asked me directly, 'The young Negro boy. He seems a decent sort. He hasn't led her into this, has he?'

'It was the other way around.'

'He's stronger. He can absorb such an experience. She can't. Are they planning to marry?'

'I don't think so.'

'Thank God. She'd destroy him, and he'd think she did it because he was a Negro. Fact is, she'll destroy any man she marries.'

'Why do you say that?'

'Because she's one of the sick of this generation. Don't you think we see them in Rhodesia? Our world has become too much for them to handle. They're doomed, and speaking as a geneticist, the sooner they're removed from society, the better.' She returned to her guests, a stalwart woman who saw people precisely as they were.

———•◆•———

At six next morning we gathered at the gate which separated the rondavels from the areas where the wild animals roamed, and I was pleased to see how lively Monica was, as if breakfast had rebuilt her spirits, but Gretchen told me, 'We've brought some sandwiches, because Monica hasn't eaten a thing.' Later, when we were well into the trip, Cato confided that she had taken heroin before going to bed and was now high. I looked for signs which would indicate this, but detected none.

In two cars we set out across the normal grazing areas, those to which tourists were admitted, along dirt roads that provided one spectacular panorama after another. 'Keep your eye out at this next turn,' Gretchen warned me. 'Elephants.'

We were in a land of low trees spaced at twenty-yard intervals with high grass in between, and as we turned a corner the lead car, driven by Gridley, came to a slow halt. Ahead, in the middle of the road, stood three very large elephants. 'They're the ones that were on the airstrip yesterday,' Gridley called back as the huge beasts stared at us without moving. We drove to within a dozen yards of them, our cars side by side, and Gridley said, 'A couple of weeks ago they picked a small Volkswagen up and turned it over. Keep your gears in reverse.'

For about fifteen minutes we were blocked by the big gray animals, but finally they ambled off; we were in an area where animals were kings, as in the old days. This feeling was enhanced when we left the forested area and came upon a series of large plains, where we saw before us a herd of nearly a thousand Cape buffalo, those dark beasts whose curious draped horns give them the appearance of wearing cloche hats of the late twenties. As we drove past, the males formed a protective ring, shoulder to shoulder, with their massive armament lowered as if prepared to charge.

In fields closer to the river we found immense herds of zebra, antelope and wildebeest, intermixed. I particularly remember Joe's and Cato's reactions. Joe said, 'A thousand Cape buffalo make more of a dent on the landscape than a thousand human beings,' and Cato, seeing the converging groups of animals, said, 'I always thought of Africa as people . . . always black . . . always naked. Lourenço Marques and this place sure change images. The people who matter are white, and the permanent life is the animal.' I did not ride with the girls, so I don't know how the herds affected them, but certainly the young men were jolted by the sight. When we came upon our first pride of lions tearing a buffalo apart, with the vultures and the hyenas standing by, Cato, after watching two lions battle for a preferred position, cried, 'How does that grab you?' I could see that he was deeply moved by the savagery of the animals and their lack of consideration for anything but a full belly.

As we approached the river, along whose banks we would travel for an hour or more until we reached a ford which would throw us into the higher hills, I learned that the young people had not yet seen a hippopotamus island, and when I got a chance I called to Gridley, 'Let's go by the hippos,' and we took a fairly long detour, which was one of the best things we did that day, for it led us through a veritable fairyland populated with all the birds one could imagine: large vultures, superb fishing eagles, flamingos, crested cranes of rare delicacy, and hundreds of low-flying birds of brilliant plumage. Among them moved large herds of impala, leaping and twisting as we approached, their fawn bodies gleaming in the sun. We saw that morning a combination of color and motion that nature sometimes provides the lucky viewer; anyone who liked music or painting or dance would intuitively feel that he was in the world of another art. When we halted the cars for a cold drink, Gretchen said, 'It's like having your brain geared to slow motion and your eyes to a kaleidoscope. I could watch impalas all day.'

I told them that a few miles beyond waited an image of opposite quality, one they would never forget, and as the two cars approached a low, swampy area, the two girls spotted something which they supposed was what I had been talking about: a group of five large crocodiles sunning themselves on the riverbank. They looked like logs that had floated downstream from the mountains, hideous creatures covered with knobs and oozing malevolence.

'Stay well back,' Gridley warned as he and the black rangers who drove our cars unlimbered their rifles. The massive crocodiles watched us approach, saw the sun glistening on the rifle barrels, and slipped quietly into the river. That is, it looked as if they had disappeared; one, so well camouflaged it could not be detected, remained on shore, a tactic which the reptiles had found effective, and as Monica, elated by what she had been seeing, got out of the car and ran across the grassy bank, this great beast allowed her to come parallel to him, then with a mighty sweep of its long, fleshy tail, knocked her nearly into the water, from which two other animals leapt with their massive jaws open, while the one who had knocked her down came at her from the land.

She screamed, seeing the gaping jaws closing in upon her from three sides, but Gridley and the rangers, followed almost immediately by Joe, sped to the scene and began battling the crocs. 'Don't fire!' Gridley shouted to the rangers as they clubbed at the beasts with their rifles while Joe, with his stout Texas boots, kicked at their heads. As quickly as they had attacked, the crocs retreated, disappearing into the waters they had churned to a muddy brown.

Of us all, Monica was the least perturbed. Apart from her first warning scream, she had behaved with marked composure, and now brushed herself off and bowed to the four men who had saved her. 'Lots of girls are attacked by wolves,' she said, 'but damned few by crocodiles.'

'It was no joke,' Gridley said. 'If Joe hadn't kicked that one in the head you'd be minus a leg . . . or worse.' We were all badly shaken by the affair, and Gretchen said, 'It was quite a surprise you had for us, Mr. Fairbanks,' and I said, 'That isn't what I had in mind,' whereupon Monica cried, 'Let's go,' and we continued through the swampy area until we came to a slight rise overlooking the river. I waited to see who would be the first to spot what lay ahead, and finally Gretchen cried, 'Oh my God!'

There, on a rather small island in the middle of the river, clustered together in one heap, lay not less than a hundred and fifty giant hippopotamuses, a mountain of heaving flesh and one of the most extraordinary sights to be seen in Africa. It was really unbelievable, this massive assembly of beasts, one lying atop the other in a sprawled-out community. From time to time some hippo would detach himself from the group and splash clumsily into the river, while others, satisfied with their morning swim, would slowly lumber out of the water and find a place for themselves in the pile.

After we had studied them for some time, we became aware of the fact that far more hippos lay submerged in the river—only their eyes and nostrils showing above water—than we saw on land, and the girls tried to estimate how many animals were there. 'Four or five hundred?' Monica asked, and Gridley nodded.

We returned through the swamps and started our long drive to the hills, arriving there about noon. We spread our picnic lunch and ate under some leafy trees, while Gridley with his binoculars surveyed the vast extent of sanctuary lying below us and pointed out one herd after another of animals we could not see with our naked eye. Passing the glasses from hand to hand, we were enjoying this long-distance tour, when Gridley grabbed the glasses, studied a wooded area much closer to us, and said, 'Here are some beauties. Who knows what they are?'

One at a time we peered through the glasses at a herd of some forty large animals which, had I seen them in the American Rockies, I would have said were elk. Gretchen asked, 'Are they the sables?' and Gridley said, 'The antelope will be much more beautiful. These are elands and we rarely see so many.' Then, as if they were as curious about us as we were about them, the large animals came slowly toward us, over thirty handsome beasts sniffing the air and testing the terrain cautiously. They came very close, almost in single file, then froze in position for at least five minutes, while we finished our lunch and enjoyed this strange floor show. Finally the lead buck sensed something he did not like, and with a flash of white tails the animals vanished.

'Oh, I wish we had some music!' Monica cried. 'It would make our day perfect,' and the three young Americans agreed that what they really needed on this picnic was Harvey Holt's tape recorder. 'I'd even settle for his sappy songs,' Cato said, but Monica protested: 'Not that goo. I'd give anything to have Clive ride up here on an eland's back, bringing his records so we could hear Octopus again, or Cream or Blind Faith. You know, something real gutsy, with a beat you can feel.'

Each of the four spoke of the hunger he or she felt for some strong music; and Gretchen, remembering how I had liked 'MacArthur Park,' made believe she was playing her guitar, and sang: 'Someone left the cake out in the rain . . .'

They formed a band of imaginary instruments and ran through a repertoire of numbers I had come to know, and as I listened to them, I realized anew how this music sustained them. Gridley watched in bewilderment, but when Cato began to sing 'Sic 'Em, Pigs,' in which the police were ridiculed with grunts and other swinish noises, provided by Joe, he stiffened. In Rhodesia police were essential, and to denigrate them was to align oneself against the constructive forces of society. He said nothing, and a little while later, when the four were lying back in the shady heat of noon, still talking about music, he winked at me, an act whose significance I did not then comprehend.

The songs made Monica talkative, and she said, 'I keep remembering what Gretchen told us at our picnic at the monastery . . . that there have always been people like us on pilgrimage. The songs we were singing that Mr. Gridley didn't like . . . oh, I saw you wincing. I'll bet respectable people in the castles didn't approve of the troubadours either. You know, the other night I was thinking about the way my family carried on at the beginning of the last century. Lady Wenthorne, rest her dear dead soul, had been reprimanding me for wasting my life bumming around Africa. But my ancestors wasted their lives bumming around Europe. There was Christopher Braham, friend of Keats and Shelley. He knocked around Europe for eleven years. Lived in that house at the Spanish Steps in Rome. And Pittenweem Braham, named after an uncle in Scotland. Pronounced his name *Pinnim* and toured Europe with a covey of homosexuals. And the great Braham, Fitzwilliam, who served in Gladstone's cabinet. He was a total loss till the age of thirty-seven, but then, with his wild experiences in Spain and Germany behind him, he became invaluable to government. I suppose it's always been the same. The good people survive and are better for the experience. The weak go under. No, that's not my point. It was the experiences that made them good people. You lose Pittenweem to the fairies. You save Fitzwilliam for the cabinet.'

She looked fondly at Cato, as if to suggest that one day he might be in the cabinet, then added, 'I still haven't made the point I had in mind. In the last century it was only the rich who could afford the grand tour of Europe. Now everybody can do it. And what galls a hell of a lot of people is that then only the young men went. Now girls go, too.' She started to laugh, just a bit hysterically, and said, 'And wasn't that a glorious euphemism? The grand tour of the capitals of Europe? The low-life tour of the whorehouses of Europe. More than half my ancestors came back to England with syphilis. Today we come back with other things.'

'We'd better get back in the cars, it's getting late,' Gridley said, and we started the rough part of our exploration, across open brush where no roads ran. So long as we kept to areas where elephants and buffalo had not foraged during the wet season, the ground was fairly flat, but when we struck areas which the feet of these beasts had churned into potholes, the going was so uneven that we were almost jolted from our seats. It was a trying hour, made bearable only by Gridley's repeated assurances, 'Any moment now!'

At last we broke onto a smooth meadowland, along whose border stood a line of trees, and when we had approached to within a hundred yards of them we halted and Gridley slowly looked the terrain over with his glasses. Then, silently, he raised his right arm and pointed, and ahead of us, standing half in sunlight, half in shadow, half in meadowland, half in forest, stood twenty of the most handsome beasts I had ever seen. Joe looked at Gridley as if to ask, 'Sable antelope?' The Rhodesian nodded.

They were something to see, worth every bump we had absorbed, the elegant jewels of Africa. They were about the size of a large horse, and as they moved in and out of the shadows, we could see that their coats ranged from a light tawny color to deep purple, but what made them memorable was their facial marking: blazing white stripes cutting across an almost black field. When he saw these extraordinary faces Cato whispered, 'That's where every mask of Africa came from,' and he was right. Their horns were enormous scimitars sweeping backward in breathtaking curves. To use them, the animal would have to drop its face parallel to the ground. Gridley whispered, 'With those horns an antelope can kill even a lion.'

We watched the beasts for about half an hour, praying that they would move out into full sunlight, but perhaps they were aware of us, for they kept in half-cover, and possibly that was best, for we had to use our imagination to fill in the shadowy outlines. For Gridley the sight was a sad one. 'The last time I shall see them this year,' he said, pointing to the clouds that had begun to form in the west. 'Soon the rains.'

'Do they make the roads impassable?' Gretchen asked. He laughed, then said, 'Impassable? Almost every road we've been on today will be under five or six feet of water . . . for five or six months. When it rains here, it rains.'

The antelope now moved closer, though they still remained in their half-half world, and never did they emerge into sunlight. We saw them as ghosts, with masks of white and black, with gleaming swords curved backward, with coats of fawn and blue and purple. They were startling in their grace and beauty, the animals of elegance, and after a while they vanished imperceptibly, one by one, with no sudden motion, into the forest.

They vanished—that is, for all of us except Joe. Apparently captivated by this glimpse into the heart of Africa as it had been a thousand years ago, and reluctant to relinquish its spell, he left us and moved like a native stalker through the edge of trees, where some of the antelope still lingered, and after a while he froze, staring into the shadows, and he remained in this position for nearly half an hour, studying the sables while they studied him.

'Isn't that dangerous?' I asked.

'Very,' Gridley said. 'Where you see sable, you see lion.'

'What are we going to do?'

'For a young man, there are some things more important than lions.' With his thumb he indicated something that none of us had noticed: the two Negro rangers had moved out quietly and were on guard with rifles.

When Joe returned he asked Gridley, 'Will they survive?' and the ecologist said, 'They're numbered. But the population is of a magnitude that will permit survival . . . if we do things right.' With visible emotion Joe said, 'If they disappeared, it would be criminal.'

'Must get going,' Gridley warned, pointing to the dark western sky where rains were about to conclude one cycle and begin the next. By the time we reached camp our cars were covered with mud.

———•••———

We had intended that this night be the farewell party for Zambela, but were so exhausted by the day's excursion that there was talk of skipping it and going to bed. 'We've got to drive out of here at dawn tomorrow,' Gretchen said. 'That Greek freighter won't wait. We'd better get some sleep.'

But Monica, who needed rest more than any of us, protested: 'Mrs. Gridley's gone to a lot of trouble. We'll take a hot shower and a nap and start fresh.' As I entered my shower I heard a small plane fly over, then buzz the field to scare away the animals, but by the time I popped into bed I had forgotten about it.

I was wakened an hour later by Monica, who was touring the rondavels to gather us for the party. As she came into my room, practically naked, she seemed a sprite of the forest, as much at home there as the antelope had been. 'Time to frolic!' she said, ripping away my bedclothes and giving me a kiss. As she was about to dart away, I grabbed her by the arm, deciding, suddenly, to try to talk rationally with her, and for a brief moment she must have thought I intended to make love to her, for her eyes brightened as if to say, 'This is crazy, but it could be fun.' I ended such thoughts by wrapping her in my bathrobe and sitting her on my bed.

Determined to make her face up to the danger of drugs, I said, abruptly, 'Monica, you've got to drop this heroin bit.'

'What right have you to give me orders?'

'I was your father's friend. I'm your friend.'

Drawing my robe snugly about her, she shrugged petulantly and said, 'I didn't request your friendship . . . or your lectures. And certainly not if you're going to talk like Father.'

'Someone must.' I grabbed her left arm and shook it free of the robe. Pointing to the adhesive, I said, 'Do you realize that if you had allowed that to fester two more days you could have lost your arm?'

'Who said?'

'Mrs. Gridley. She takes care of wounded animals, remember? And you're a sorely wounded little animal, Monica.'

'Nothing wrong with me Marrakech can't cure.'

'I forbid you to go to Marrakech.'

'I go where I want to go,' she said insolently.

This so infuriated me that I twisted her arm, and my eye caught what I was certain would be there—the pale purple nick left by a needle as it entered a vein. 'You crazy child!' I cried. 'You've been mainlining!'

'What if I have?' she asked defiantly.

I slapped her across the face, unable to control my sick fury. 'You're killing yourself—for God's sake, can't you see that!'

Tearing loose from my grip and dropping the robe, she shouted, 'Oh, go to hell!' and stormed out of the rondavel, but when we were assembled for dinner, she ran up impulsively, took my arm, and whispered, 'I'm sorry, you dear worried old man. I'll take care. Promise.'

When we reached the Gridley house I found the explanation for the airplane: waiting in the living room were two good-looking young Portuguese officers, Captain Teixeira and Lieutenant Costa Silva, from the barracks at Vila Gonçalo, and I watched their eyes pop when our two girls appeared in their miniskirts. Immediately the excitement of the evening escalated, but the presence of the officers was not only social; it was also a tribute to the thoughtfulness of the Gridleys, who had listened at various times as the young people lamented the lack of music. Mrs. Gridley had called the barracks that afternoon to ask if any of the men had modern phonograph records, and Captain Teixeira said, 'I have some, but Costa Silva has the good ones.' He also had the airplane, and the record player, and now, before dinner, he piled a stack of records, placed his speakers the proper distance apart, and smiled.

'Guess what the first one will be,' he said in good English. I could see apprehension on the faces of the young people, as though they expected Glenn Miller or Benny Goodman. When 'Aquarius' burst forth, in crisp tones and heavy rhythm, they cheered and Monica grabbed Costa Silva by the hands and did a little dance with him, shouting above the music, 'You're promoted to general!' Soon the blended voices of the Fifth Dimension were shouting, 'Let the sunshine in!' and we settled down to a musical session that duplicated what we had heard in Torremolinos four months before, except that the records were newer.

I asked Captain Teixeira how he had got them, since he was stuck away in one of the remotest parts of Africa, and he said, 'In one of the musical papers from London we see lists of what's popular, so whenever we fly strangers into the sanctuary or down to the dam at Cabora Bassa and they ask, "What can we send you from New York?" we hand them a list of records and the address of Sam Goody. Look!' He shuffled through the albums and I saw Octopus, Cream, Led Zeppelin and The Mamas and the Papas. To the astonishment of the Gridleys, who had no ear for this kind of music, I asked Silva Costa if he would play 'Creeque Alley' from the last album, and as its familiar strains filled the small living room I again thought how contemporary the song was: unpretty, undistinguished, it offered nothing first-rate except its totality, and that depicted what was happening with the young people I knew.

The next record provided a burlesque interlude. The incident began when Cato announced, 'This is our theme song.' When the first chords sounded, Monica leaped in front of the record player to defend it in the way a mother lioness is supposed to defend her cubs. I failed to understand what she was up to, but the other young people knew, for they recognized the music and burst into taunting laughter. Obviously the joke was on me, and finally I caught on. The song was 'Lucy in the Sky with Diamonds,' and it sounded just as innocent as when I had first enjoyed it.

'Our Savonarola smashes this one,' Monica warned Costa Silva. Then, as if we had not quarreled in the rondavel, she pirouetted over to me and kissed me on the cheek, and despite my earlier anger, I still wanted to keep her in my care.

With only a short time out for dinner, we played music till midnight, when I said, 'These officers have to get home, and we must get some sleep,' but Captain Teixeira said, 'We can't fly out of here in this rain,' and the girls cried, 'Who needs sleep?' I looked at Mrs. Gridley, and she shrugged her shoulders, saying, 'Nobody will work much tomorrow,' so we stayed on, with Joe searching through Gridley's books for information about the sable antelope, and it was about three in the morning when Costa Silva happened to put on his machine a new song about how the housewives of Pompeii behaved in the days before the volcano—'The Yard Went On Forever,' it was called—and suddenly the Gridleys were listening, and when the music ended, Mrs. Gridley asked, 'Could you play that one again?' and we sat there, nine of us, and for the first time that night all of us understood a common tune. 'That one's very good,' Mrs. Gridley said.

'They're all good,' Monica said.

'I suppose they are,' Mrs. Gridley said. 'I suppose if I could take all that shrieking, I'd find them fairly good.' She was a tough woman, accustomed to jungle and desert, and where Africa was concerned she had a seventh sense. Looking at Cato, she said, 'I suppose we two could hear the same music, if our ears ever became attuned.'

'Not in this century,' Cato said.

'I wasn't thinking of this century,' she said. 'I'm fifty-two and in twenty years I'll be dead. You're twenty-two and in fifty years you'll be dead. We seem to have made a hash of our generations, but we can hope that by the year 2050 something sensible will have been worked out.'

'Do you think it will be?' Cato asked.

'No. That's too soon. But we can use it as our target.'

She had tears in her eyes when the time came to kiss Monica good-bye. The two Portuguese officers had fallen asleep on the couch and a pair of chairs when we left, and on the airfield their plane stood in the rain. 'There will be few visitors from now on,' Mrs. Gridley said, surveying the dark sky. She asked where we would be going. I said, 'Back to Geneva,' and Gretchen said, 'The Greek boat stops at Casablanca and we decided the other night that we ought to try Marrakech.'

'That's no place for Monica,' Mrs. Gridley said, but Gretchen said, 'Joe has some draft-board problems he must settle there.'

When Cato left he shook hands with the Gridleys and said, 'This was the best stop in Africa,' and Mrs. Gridley said, 'It was instructive, talking with a young man who can express himself so well. Perhaps by the time you die, things will be a little clearer . . . not much . . . but a little.'

Cato said, 'It's curious. In Africa I've met Portuguese, and Boers, and English judges, and Arab saints, and American sailors, and Chinese cooks. But I haven't met one damned black . . . socially, that is.'

'They're not yet visible,' Mrs. Gridley said.

'They will be,' he predicted.

Moçambique should have ended with the beauty of the sable antelope or the friendliness of the night music at the Gridley's, but it didn't.

About five in the morning I was awakened by rough shaking and Joe's frightened voice. 'Mr. Fairbanks! We need you! It's Cato.'

'What's he done?'

'He mainlined. I think he's going to die.'

I pulled on a pair of pants and dashed across the grass to the rondavel. I rushed past Monica, who was standing in the doorway, wringing her hands and staring vacuously into space. Gretchen, weeping, was leaning over the bed, applying cold towels to Cato's sweating forehead. 'My God, he's going to die!' she said, and I could see the terrible convulsions that racked his body.

First thing I did was to grab his left arm and look at the veins, and the evidence was clear. Even on his dark skin a raised dot showed the mark of a hypodermic needle. In spite of his promises to Joe and his arrogant assurance to me, he had done exactly what he had sworn never to do. I glanced up, and Gretchen said, 'She pestered him for more than an hour. She told him there'd be no more sex if he didn't keep up with her. We could hear her screaming in our rondavel.'

I looked back at Monica, shivering by the door, incapable of comprehending what was happening. I wanted to shake her, bring her back from that awful shadowy world, make her acknowledge the hideous thing she had done.

I turned again to Cato, who had begun a series of tremendous contractions, any one of which might end in his death. It seemed probable that he had got a poisoned dose, and I grew as frightened as the young people. Beckoning to Joe, I said, 'You'd better get Mrs. Gridley. This is too much for us to handle.'

Joe ran to the warden's cottage and returned with Mrs. Gridley, who brought with her a doctor's kit. She went directly to the bed and started examining Cato. 'He's nearly dead!' she cried in horror. 'What in hell has he been doing?' She looked at his arm and saw the mainline nick.

'Let's walk him around,' she directed Joe and me. 'This may be just the wrong thing to do, but this boy's about to die. It might at least restore circulation.'

So we hoisted him from the bed, and with his arms slung around our necks, we walked him back and forth. He was no burden, for he carried no excess weight, and after a while he began to breathe deeply.

By dawn it was apparent that he would survive, so we laid him gently back on the bed. Only then did we notice that Monica had gone peacefully to sleep on the floor. She looked like a little kitten, tired from playing, and Joe helped Mrs. Gridley lift her and place her next to Cato. But as the Scottish woman tucked the sheet about the beautiful and pallid face, she said, 'It's a shame she wasn't the one to catch the lethal dose.'

XII §

MARRAKECH

Tunis is a beautiful mare, Algeria a proud stallion, Morocco a lion.

When one of the editors of *The New Yorker* retired, he told about the time they had this fabulous
story but wasted three weeks trying to think up
something funny to say about it. Seems a New York
bank clerk absconded with $100,000. and blew it all
in riotous living in Philadelphia. No comment you
make is funnier than the fact itself. I feel the same
way about Algeria announcing that it is firing 1,200
teachers trained at the Sorbonne and replacing them
with 1,200 trained at the University of Cairo.

So there was this mighty conclave of the leaders of
Islam in these parts . . . distinguished-looking kings
and philosophers all in turbans . . . enough gold
cloth to found a bank. And when the Arabs had left
the lobby, this Texas GI comes up to me and says,
'Hey, bub, who was all them rag-heads?'

Koutoubia, Koutoubia!
Land of keef and hash and honey,
Where brotherhood is a bond of love
And who gives a damn about money.

Koutoubia, Koutoubia!
Bring me home from across the oceans,
I must return, I must return
To the scene of my devotions.

That guy in the corner of the fort is a sorry case. There's
so much noise in here he can't remember what it was he joined
the Foreign Legion to forget.

Before the war I used to see this Arab striding down
the road followed by his three wives carrying the
bundles. After the war I see him coming down the
same road, with the same three wives carrying the
same bundles, but this time they are in front and he
is in the rear. I stop and tell him, 'Abou, this is
progress.' He looks at me with contempt and says,
'Not progress. Land mines.'

> In the end, there'll be only one thing
> that'll bridge the generation gap: Money.

> The *I-Ching* is the Bible without its
> capitalistic moralizing.

> Old boys have their playthings as well as young ones; the
> difference is only in the price.—Franklin

> As late as 1941, when travelers from the desert ar-
> rived in Marrakech without their harems, they stayed
> at this hotel, and in every room there was a little
> Arab boy to satisfy their accustomed sexual needs.
> I have some of the old bills. 'Boy, thirty-six piasters.'

The trouble with television is that it is like a sword rusting
in the scabbard during a battle for survival.—Edward R. Murrow

> The happiest women, like the happiest nations,
> have no history.—George Eliot

> Death is nature's way of suggesting
> that you slow down.

For the Negro to hate the Jew is like a left half-
back hating a right end, or a merchant hating a
fireman, or a lieutenant in the army hating a sergeant, or an older brother hating a younger; for in
each of these instances, cooperation is unavoidable
and joint action to a common end makes each partner
markedly stronger than he could be alone.

> Being educated means to prefer the best not only to the worst
> but to the second best.—William Lyon Phelps

> Youth is truth.

*W*HEN the Greek freighter docked at Casablanca, Joe suffered traumatic shock. The customs official, after having checked the young people's luggage, pointed a forefinger at Joe and said, gruffly, 'In that door.'

Wondering what could have been found in his gear, Joe went through the door and found himself in an unexpected situation. An obese Moroccan official, wearing a fez, sat stuffed in a chair before a cluttered desk, while a short, wizened barber in a long white gown stood by an old-fashioned barber's chair. The official said briefly, 'If you want to land in Morocco . . . no beard, no long hair.'

Joe started to protest that as a free citizen . . . but the official cut him short: 'Don't shave and stay out.'

'But . . .' Joe's protest was halted peremptorily when the official plopped a cheap watch on his desk and said, 'You have three minutes. Shave or no shave.'

Joe felt the blood rising to his brain. He wanted to kick that office apart and punch the fat official in the nose, but the man merely stared at him and pointed to the watch: 'Two more minutes and out you go.'

'Can I speak to the others?' Joe pleaded.

'Ninety seconds left. Better get in that chair.'

The little barber, who needed a shave himself, waited unperturbed as the decision was being made. He did not exactly invite

Joe into the chair, but he did stand at the ready, so at the last moment Joe shrugged his shoulders and climbed into the chair, whereupon the little fellow sprang into hectic action.

'I cut hair for three years . . . Boston. Fine city, Boston. Red Sox. Ted Williams.' He spoke like a machine gun, but his hands were even faster. With a creaking electric clipper he started at Joe's right ear and plowed steadily down through his chin, then up the other side. When he reached the left ear he did not stop, but continued right across the back of Joe's head until he returned to the right ear. Three more times he completed this circuit, zipping away all of Joe's beard and the long hair at the back of his head.

Then, switching rapidly to a pair of scissors, he cut huge swatches of hair from the top of the head and within a few minutes had Joe in a condition from which it was possible to proceed with a rational haircut. 'You gonna like Morocco,' he said. 'Marvelous country . . . good food . . . first time you taste couscous, remember me. I recommended it.'

He was employed by the government to whisk off the hair of every hippie seeking entrance to Morocco, and he would have carried out his responsibility if he had merely hacked off the offending hair, but he was an artist, so as soon as he finished his brutal preliminary shearing he became a polished barber, giving each young man his personal judgment as to how the new hair should look. 'I see you cowboy type, maybe,' he told Joe. 'Or maybe bicycle champion touring France for glory. Very manly . . . big chest. I want you to have good hair about your ears . . . not shaved. And maybe brush type on top. Your physique you could stand brush type . . . very manly.'

As he lathered Joe's face he whispered, so that the official at the desk could not hear, 'They don't give me money for good razors. You not gonna like this, but I rub your beard a long time, make it soft.' At the first swipe of the razor Joe winced, and the little fellow said, 'I sympathize. I sharpen this goddamned thing one more time,' and he stropped it furiously, producing a tolerable blade.

After he had washed Joe's face and combed his hair he stood back to admire his handiwork. 'You a very handsome man . . .

when you allow us to see you. Such a perfect haircut. The young ladies outside will applaud.' He then took a small bellows whose handles were decorated with copper rivets, and with a quick twist of his wrists, applied a generous helping of powder to Joe's head.

'Please!' Joe protested, reaching for a towel. 'I don't use talcum powder.'

'Not talcum powder,' the barber said. 'Flea powder,' and with another puff of his bellows he gave Joe a snootful, adding, 'Welcome to Morocco.'

When Joe stepped back into the customs shed and started walking toward his waiting companions, he got almost to them before they recognized him. Then Monica screamed, 'My God! It's alive!' and Cato shouted, 'That's our boy!' As they clustered around him he said, 'I feel naked,' but Gretchen whispered, 'You're really very handsome,' but when she tried to give him a kiss, he pushed her away and muttered, 'This white stuff . . . flea powder.'

———— · ◆ · ————

From the moment the yellow pop-top entered the broad highway to Marrakech the occupants were aware that they were approaching a very special city, one that had become a magnet for adventurous young people around the world. They spotted Swedes and Germans and Americans in small cars or hitchhiking. Whenever they passed a bus, they could see hanging from it an assortment that would have terrified the sheriff of an Iowa town or a mayor in Massachusetts awaiting a rock festival. There was a sense of excitement in the air, and when they stopped for gasoline at the halfway point they talked eagerly with a couple returning to Casablanca.

'How come the long hair?' Joe asked the man.

'No problem. Big deal about cutting it off when you land. After that, who cares?'

'Is it as much fun as they say?' Monica asked.

The girl closed her eyes and blew a kiss. That was all, but the man said, 'We were there for six months. Going back to the States is like committing suicide.'

They introduced one another: 'This is Jeanette from Liverpool . . . Joe from California . . . Gretchen from Boston . . .'

Then Gretchen asked, 'When we get there . . . how . . . well . . . what do we do?'

The departing couple laughed at her naïveté, and the girl said, 'You drive right through town, past the Koutoubia—that's the marvelous minaret—and go to the Djemaá el Fna.' This was the first time the newcomers had heard the name that was to form the center of their life for the ensuing months.

'What's that?' Gretchen asked.

'The hub of the universe,' the man said. 'The big public square.'

'You go to the Djemaá,' the girl from Liverpool continued, 'and you stand there for one minute looking like a foreigner, and so many things will happen that you'll be dizzy for a week. You don't look for things in Marrakech. They look for you.'

'Warn them about Jemail,' the man said.

'Oh, yes! Jemail you must be careful of. He's a little Arab boy about eleven years old. He lives in the Djemaá. Speaks six or seven languages. And is the most evil human being since the Marquis de Sade.'

The man told Gretchen, 'Within one minute of the time you step out of your car, Jemail will tell you that he can get you up to fifty dollars a night if you want to sleep with the local merchants. If you're brave enough to go to a town behind the mountains, he'll get you more.'

Cato asked, 'Grass?'

'Best in the world.'

'Better than Nepal?'

'I've been in Nepal. This is twice as good.'

'They sell it in cellophane sacks like a supermarket,' the girl from Liverpool said.

'But where do you get it?' Cato asked.

The man said, 'Jemail will have four sacks waiting for you. Watch. You'll take four sacks whether you want them or not. But be careful of the little green cookies he peddles. Almost pure hash. I ate a whole one on an empty stomach and was flat for twenty-one hours.'

'Yes, he was,' the girl confirmed. 'He was damned near as green as the cookies.'

Gretchen asked, 'Where's a good place to stay?' and the girl replied, 'Jemail will try to put you in the Rouen, but don't touch it. What a stink! We lived at the Bordeaux most of the time and it was super. Great crowd of kids.'

Tentatively, Joe asked the man, 'You ever hear of a fellow called Big Loomis?' whereupon the couple started talking excitedly, recalling various experiences with a man who had become a legend in Marrakech.

'Big Loomis! If you meet Jemail within one minute, you'll meet Big Loomis within six.'

'Can he be trusted?' Joe asked.

'In Marrakech nobody can be trusted,' the girl said. 'Even at the Bordeaux, they would steal the last eight crackers from a stack and fill the space with crumpled newspaper. Big Loomis lives there, on a small check from home and what he can scrounge from people like you. But he's worth every dirham. And let me assure you of this. If you get into trouble—I mean real trouble— Big Loomis will stand by you with the police, the municipality, the American embassy. He'll take on the world.'

Gretchen had one final question. 'We could sleep in the Volks. Would you stay at the camping if you were us?'

'To hell with the camping,' the girl said. 'One look at the Djemaá and you'll know that this is where the action is. I'd go without meals in order to be near the scene.'

And so the couples parted, one toward Tangier and a resumption of their normal life in England and the United States, two toward Marrakech and the apotheosis of change.

———•—•—•———

It was late afternoon when they first saw the towering mountains that guarded Marrakech. They stood in ranges, one behind the other, and stretched so far north and south that they seemed a barrier which no man could pass. This was the High Atlas, home of the Berber and the sheep, and it provided a majestic backdrop for the city which nestled at its feet.

The mountains were visible for a good hour before there was any sign of Marrakech, but when the sun was beginning to show red upon the highest peaks, Cato spotted a tower rising from the plain. 'Look!' he cried, and as Joe drove south, the outlines of this remarkable structure became clearer. It was the Koutoubia, a massive square minaret over two hundred feet high, built sometime around 1150 and historically important as the archetype of the famous Giralda in Sevilla; although the same Muslim architect designed both, the Koutoubia is superior, and well worth the attention that has been bestowed upon it. For the next months it would be the permanent reference point for the travelers.

As it grew larger, vast groves of palm trees became visible, probably the most extensive concentration of such trees in the world, and while the passengers were admiring them, Joe jammed on the brakes and said, 'There they are!' and ahead lay the great red walls of Marrakech. They formed a tremendous square, miles on each side, and they were high and very thick. It is difficult to describe these walls to someone who has not seen them; I know, for I've tried, but you are not to think of a large wall that runs in a straight line for perhaps half a mile. You are to visualize a wall of staggering size that runs for forty or fifty miles, twisting in and about, dull red and glowing in the sunlight, one of the most massive structures made by man. These are the walls of Marrakech.

The four young people entered the walls as strangers have always done in coming to this brick-red city, with quiet respect. For centuries armies and pilgrims had come to Marrakech, and always with apprehension when they saw these formidable barriers.

A representative incident occurred in this region some decades ago when a large army from Marrakech, fed up with dictation from the central government, marched north to sack the city of Fez at the same time that an army from Fez was marching south to discipline Marrakech. Scouts advised each general of the enemy's approach, so the Marrakech army kept to the eastern valleys and roared unimpeded to Fez, where they wreaked havoc, while the Fez army kept to the western valleys and arrived unscathed at Marrakech, where they tore the place apart. Then the two armies retreated, each keeping to its own valley system, and the honor of everyone was satisfied. Of course, a lot of people were dead in both Fez and Marrakech, but they were civilians, and the walls that had been torn down in each city could be rebuilt.

'Look at that!' Cato cried as they breasted the Koutoubia. Tall and brutal and rugged, with its top crenelated like a fort, it was a stirring sight and a reassuring one, for whenever they came upon it unexpectedly, they knew that the Djemaá el Fna was just down the street.

Suddenly, there it was, an enormous rhomboidal expanse of macadam so vast it could accommodate a million people, hemmed in on three sides by low souks and crisscrossed by stalls at which all kinds of kabobs and baklavas and honeyed breads were sold. Joe parked the pop-top along an edge of the huge plaza, and they started to walk slowly toward the center, where large crowds were seated in various circles, but as they walked they were met by an extraordinary man. He was dressed like an elf from some distant mountain, with pointed hat, loose jacket studded with brass, tight knee breeches of green felt, handsome, heavy leather shoes. Over his shoulder he carried a goatskin bag to which were attached four small brass cups, but the mark of his trade was a leather pouch adorned with very old silver and gold coins. He immediately began pestering the new arrivals, who could not understand what he was saying. Finally he squeezed his goatskin bag and sent a small jet of water into one of his cups and handed it to Monica. He was a water-seller, and the first purchase the four made in Marrakech was from him, but as they were drinking, Cato felt a tug at his left arm, and he looked down to see an urchin who was saying in good English, 'You looking for a place to stay, pardner?'

'Are you Jemail?' Cato asked, and the boy drew back, as if afraid.

'You know Jemail?' he asked warily.

'He's my friend,' Cato said, whereupon the boy fled.

And then they saw what must surely be Jemail. Coming toward them with an insinuating shuffle was an Arab boy of eleven or twelve dressed in a unique mixture of clothing obviously stolen from previous visitors: German leather pants cut down to size, a high-sheen rayon bowling jacket labeled *Mildred's Diner*, army boots, and a Little League baseball cap from the Waco Tigers. He had an alert, foxlike face and he flashed an ingratiating smile as he addressed his prospective customers in a make-believe deep voice: 'Hiya, buster! Come wiz me to ze casbah!' Laughing at his own joke, he asked, 'You like place to stay, eh? You got Volkswagen pop-top 1969 automatic shift. You could afford the best hotel if you liked. But you want to be near Djemaá, eh? I have just hotel you want, not too expensive. Rouen, very classy, you smoke marijuana in the lobby, you like.'

'We're looking for the Bordeaux,' Gretchen said.

'You won't like it,' Jemail warned her. 'Fleas . . . very low type of people.'

'You take us to the Bordeaux,' Gretchen said.

Jemail stood back, stared at her, and said, 'You so fucking goddamned smart, you find Bordeaux yourself.'

Joe took a hefty swipe at the boy, who had anticipated the move and had jumped back, whipping out a knife. 'You lay a hand on me, you stinking draft dodger, I cut your balls off.' He continued a vile outpouring of profanity, including much instruction as to what the two girls could do sexually, either with each other or with their goddamned nigger friend. When this explosion subsided, the boy calmly put away his knife and said, 'Now we understand each other. I think Rouen is best for you . . . more class.'

'We're going to the Bordeaux,' Gretchen repeated.

'Okay. But when rats run over your face at night . . . nibble your tits . . . don't scream for me.'

Cato said, 'How's the grass?' and Jemail said, 'My boy bring you four bags,' and putting his fingers to his mouth, he gave a shrill whistle, at which the boy who had first spoken to them returned respectfully and listened as Jemail barked out a set of orders. When the boy had gone, Monica took Jemail aside and asked, 'How about heroin?' and he said, 'The best. This I handle myself. I bring it to your room Rouen.'

'Bordeaux,' Monica corrected.

'You let her order you about?' he asked, jerking his thumb at Gretchen. 'She a lesbian? Got you under her thumb?'

'Let's keep the discussion on the heroin,' Monica said.

'All right. Four dollars a packet, guaranteed not to be lactose.'

As Gretchen studied the child, wondering how a mere infant could have become so totally corrupted, he sidled up to her and said, 'You look damned good. You ever want to earn some real money, let me know.' Gretchen shook her head, but the boy, undaunted, continued his sales talk. 'Respectable Europeans at Mamounia Hotel, fifty dollars. If they like you, even more. But black men other side of the mountains, you name your price.'

'We'll go to the hotel now,' she said.

'Rouen?'

'Bordeaux.'

'Find another boy. I not take a dog to the Bordeaux,' and he stalked off, but when he saw them being approached by yet another boy, Jemail returned and drove him away. 'Follow me,' he said, and he led them across the Djemaá, explaining in various languages to passers-by the sexual habits and parentage of the four he had in tow.

They were a long time getting to the hotel, because when they reached the center of the Djemaá they found large circles of men and children gathered around storytellers who were giving them impassioned accounts of Moroccan history and such world events as the conquests of Alexander the Great and the landing on the moon. Some had acquired old music stands on which were hung large sheets of oilcloth containing a series of little squares depicting the adventures of Hercules, which the storyteller would point to as he recounted the miracles. The most theatrical storytellers used tripods from which were suspended numerous sheets of painted oilcloth, one on top the other, so that as the narrator progressed, he could quickly flip the sheets over and illustrate each lurid incident.

How powerful the voices of the storytellers were when the hero was in danger, how dulcet in the love scenes. Blood was a feature of almost every painted scene, and there was so much depiction of death that history seemed an unbroken succession of treachery, ambuscade and strangulation; indeed, in these parts it had been.

Within other circles, acrobats performed, holy men expounded the Koran, clowns put on crazy acts, and three men from the hills who could have performed in any theater of the absurd in Paris or New York had as props a bicycle pump, a German saber, a baby carriage and one long-tailed black frock coat. By swiftly changing into and out of the coat and leaping into the baby carriage, and by using the saber and bicycle pump in a wild variety of ways, they created a half hour of hilarity, their faces grave and their personalities constantly affronted by what was happening to them. Every so often one of the members of the troop tried to swallow the saber, and actually got a substantial length of it down his esophagus when his two partners rammed the bicycle pump up his anus and blew so much air into him that the saber kept popping back out of his mouth.

At the conclusion of each segment of a performance, a brass bowl was passed through the crowd, and occasionally someone put in a small coin, but the large majority of the audience sat on the macadam and watched for nothing. Gretchen was so delighted with the sword-swallowing trio that she gave them two dirhams, whereupon the clown working the bicycle pump produced from it a fanfare that sounded like trumpets.

It was now well past sunset, and as darkness fell over the great square, kerosene tapers appeared in brass holders, giving the open-air theater a ghostly aspect, with caftaned Berbers moving silently from one circle to the other while wide-eyed newcomers from the southern deserts looked upon a metropolis for the first time. More than fifty circles were now operating: snake charmers, dancers, orchestras, balancing acts, haranguers, and always the enchanting storytellers dragging their hundreds of listeners back into past ages, back to the glories of Islam.

'You seen goddamned near everything,' Jamail said impatiently. 'That boy got your keef. I got your heroin. Now we go to Rouen.'

With a sudden movement, Joe grabbed the boy by the throat and said, 'Listen, you punk, you stay away from us with your heroin. Now take us to the Bordeaux.'

'I gonna castrate you yet, buster,' the little Arab said, calmly pulling Joe's fingers away.

He led them away from the Djemaá and into a dark alley that zigzagged its way through the most ancient part of Marrakech. They would have been afraid to go down this forbidding lane alone, for it was an evocation of every cheap film about the casbah.

And then, coming toward them out of the shadows, they saw a startling sight: a man of about three hundred and fifty pounds moving in slow rhythms, attended by three scrawny, long-haired types, one of whom could have been an adolescent girl. His heavy ankle-high boots of gigantic size were made of yak skin. For trousers he had a South Pacific lava-lava cut from finely woven gray-brown cloth. He wore an immense Nehru jacket, but no hat, for his beard and hair comprised an enormous circle which no headgear could encompass. The jacket was virtually covered with strings of beads, and above his left ear he wore a woman's comb with a long, straight handle. As he talked rapidly with his disciples, the newcomers noticed that he moved with a delicate grace, lifting and dropping his immense feet in the competent way an elephant does when moving through high grass. Then, as he was upon them, his face clear of shadow, they saw that he was a Negro with a countenance of almost childlike simplicity.

'That's got to be Big Loomis,' Joe said, moving forward to introduce himself.

At this moment, however, the Negro's manner changed, for he spotted Jemail, and the two faced each other in the narrow passageway, screaming curses. With big swipes the huge Negro tried to cuff the little Arab, who deftly avoided the blows and returned infuriating epithets.

Jemail, taunting the fat man, screamed, 'Motherfucking fat slob, why you don't pay your bills, shit-heel, blubber-gut?' to which the fat man shouted, at the very top of his voice, 'Listen here, you miserable little cork in the asshole of progress, if I get my hands on you I'll barbecue you,' whereupon the child screamed, 'Bloody likely you get your hands on me. You find your own little boys.' And here he descended to new depths of depravity, describing the fat man's presumed sexual life.

It was a staggering performance, one that the young people frequently referred to when I met up with them later. Gretchen told me, 'They stood there in the night, cursing each other, a great obese black man and a skinny little Arab boy, as if the elephant and the mouse we used to read about had come to Marrakech. The

fat man accused the boy of trying to trick us for a few miserable
dirhams into the Rouen, the vilest sink in town and no place for a
lady. Here he bowed to Monica and me, a mountain of flesh and
flowers bending in the middle. The boy countered with the charge
that the fat man was trying to lure us to the Bordeaux so that he
could make money by selling us drugs. There were more unprint-
able curses, then the black man moved majestically on, like an ocean
liner steaming past a tug. I won't repeat what the boy said of him
as he disappeared. And that was our introduction to Big Loomis.'

Jemail did finally take them to the Bordeaux, a hotel of marked
squalor perched at the edge of the alley they had been traversing.
An ancient door admitted them to a central courtyard, around
which ranged four stories of rooms, with a rickety interior stair-
case leading from one level to the next. Each floor had its own
wooden balcony, so that if anything exciting happened in the hotel,
all residents could be on the balcony of their respective floors
within a few seconds. Also, each sound from a given floor was
magnified many times as it reverberated up and down the central
shaft.

To the left of the door stood the concierge's room, its walls
covered with colored scenes from airline calendars and festooned
with cobwebs. The office was occupied by a man known only as
Léon; what nationality or race, no one cared to guess. He was a
patient man, much harassed yet always willing to listen when stray
Europeans or Americans came to his door seeking help. He was able
to be generous partly because Big Loomis occupied the whole top
floor; if any traveler was really broke, Léon simply shunted him up
to Big Loomis, who invariably found a place for him to sleep.
There were eight rooms on the top floor, and some nights they
contained as many as forty vagabonds in a confusion that could
not be unraveled.

Léon led Jemail and his charges up the wooden stairs to the top
floor, where he kicked open one after another of the six doors until
he found a room that was more or less empty. 'You sleep here tonight,' he said, and Jemail added, 'My boy be here soon with keef.
But to give you welcome to Marrakech . . . here!' And from his
jacket he produced a greasy piece of brown paper containing four

greenish cookies. 'Four dirhams. Be careful, they knock you flat on your ass.' Gingerly the girls placed the cookies in their luggage, saying they would try them later.

Jemail now came up with another proposition. He snapped his fingers and cried, 'We go back to Djemaá and see it in moonlight?' They considered this, and were so enchanted with Marrakech that they agreed, but Jemail said, 'First we arrange money. I gonna take care of everything. I guard your car. I got a boy there now. So what's it worth?' Gretchen proposed a figure, which he rejected with scorn, pointing out: 'I take care of you . . . no trouble. Police . . . nobody. No little boys bothering you in Djemaá. Good prices in the souks. I interpret. I do everything. You lose your passport? I know the man who prints new ones.' He proposed a fee of six dollars a week, and they agreed.

He led them back to the square, where a transformation had taken place. The storytellers and actors had vanished. In their places had risen a multitude of transportable kiosks offering all kinds of food and tier upon tier of handsome oriental cakes and candies. 'Don't touch!' Jemail warned. 'Cholera catchers.' He was about to explain what he meant by this when a tourist asked the candy seller a question, and in a flash Jemail took over the negotiation in German, which he spoke as well as he did English. Pocketing his tip, he returned to his charges and said, 'See the moon . . . resting on the Koutoubia,' and there it was, a half-moon standing tiptoe on the minaret.

———— • • • ————

In the morning they had a chance to inspect their hotel, and found it even dirtier than they had expected, but also more interesting. It had been built sometime in the last century and left untouched since then. Heavy deposits of grime discolored doorways and bathrooms, but Léon did sweep the floors weekly, so they were fairly clean. What attracted the newcomers was the social warmth of the place, the easy movement of many young people from room to room and up and down the flights of exposed stairs.

Each of the four floors contained eight rooms, and each room an average of three people, excepting the top floor where Big Loomis crowded large numbers into his quarters. There were thus more than a hundred residents, with Canadians, Australians and Swedes in the majority. The average age could have been no more than twenty, and girls slightly outnumbered boys. They were a clean lot, not too well dressed or coiffured, but presentable; the fact that it took considerable money to reach Marrakech meant that a natural weeding-out had taken place.

The principal characteristic of the Hotel Bordeaux was the heavy, sweetish smell of marijuana; practically all the young people were smoking it, laced half the time with hashish, which was in some ways easier to buy in Marrakech than grass. To take a casual look at the inhabitants of the hotel, one would not detect that they were smoking marijuana, but upon closer inspection, one could see a fair number of vacant expressions that betrayed the recent user of hash.

The Americans in the hotel were an especially congenial group: two girls from Wellesley College, one of whom played the guitar; four or five kids from California universities who had persuaded their parents to send them abroad for a year to study European history and languages; the standard contingent from the midwest, most of them from some college or other along the Mississippi basin; and a quiet group of three from the south, including a pallid, sensitive boy from Mississippi.

Of all the young people from other countries, the Canadians and Australians were the most adventuresome and well heeled. Gretchen said, after meeting a score of them, 'Those countries must be rolling in money. The kids are sure spending it.' Joe found the Australian girls great fun: outspoken, brash, extremely active and courageous. With a knapsack and some bread they would go anywhere; most of them had been abroad for two years or more, working in England part of the time or taking ill-paid jobs in France, and almost every girl said sooner or later, 'Six months more of this, then back to Australia and the long drag . . . marriage to some cattle-man . . . yearly visits to the Melbourne Cup.' They were a marvelous, roistering lot and several indicated to Joe that they would not be unhappy if he would do his sleeping in their room, but he always pointed to Gretchen, as if to ask, 'What can I do?'

The generalizations I have just made applied to the first three floors. The fourth was somewhat different. Here Big Loomis offered refuge to those who had come unprepared to Marrakech and had found themselves unequal to its demands: the high school girl from Minneapolis who in the souks had slept with dozens and become pregnant by one, but which one she could not say; the boy from Tucson who had dropped out of freshman year at Arizona State, who had discovered marijuana, hashish and heroin in one explosive week, and who would probably never recover—his main problem now was to master a sense of balance so that he could at least walk through Djemaá; the schoolteacher from London who had found the homosexuality of Marrakech overpowering; the three young men from California who were trying to avoid the draft; the terribly muddle-minded philosopher from a Catholic college who was determined to reconcile St. Thomas Aquinas, Herbert Marcuse and the *I-Ching*, the joining cement being marijuana.

It was a mixed lot, over which Big Loomis presided with tenderness and understanding; some of his clientele, such as the Catholic philosopher, he provided with free lodging for months on end; others he asked to leave when he felt they had more or less stabilized themselves. The residents of the fourth floor did not mix much with those of the three lower floors; in fact, some of Big Loomis's patients, to give them their proper description, did not leave the top floor for weeks at a time, content to lie in their rooms, smoking hash and dreaming of the better world they were supposed to be making.

To the average newcomer the principal advantage of the Bordeaux was its ready supply of hashish and heroin. One did not even have to search for these exotic temptations, because little Jemail knocked on the door each day, soliciting orders: 'Cheapest prices Marrakech. Merchandise guaranteed.' He made only three hundred per cent on each transaction.

Only three residents in the hotel were foolish enough to dabble with heroin—four, after Monica checked in—and two of them were sniffing, with only an occasional popping under their skins; there was a good chance that these two might withdraw, because Big

Loomis kept them under his care on the fourth floor, trying to break them of the habit. The third user was the pallid young man from a good family in Mississippi, whom Gretchen saw one day leaning languidly against the door of his room on the third floor. She doubted that he would ever make it back home, for it was clear that he was taking heroin into his veins and had not eaten for some days. His drawn face, slack body and emaciated arms betrayed a man who had passed into a walking coma—a frightening vision that should have been enough to keep any witness from heroin. But of course, Monica was already taking it intravenously . . . and secretly.

The three Americans now assumed the responsibility of trying to keep watch over Monica, and whenever they caught Jemail sneaking his packets into her room, drove him off, but it was on Cato that the principal burden fell, and his faithful attention won the respect not only of Joe and Gretchen but of Loomis as well. The big Negro told him, 'You're doing the only helpful thing, son. Stay with her, because she can fight her way back only with your help.'

It was a difficult assignment. After his terrifying experience that last night in Moçambique, Cato refused even to sniff the deadly white powder, and for this decision, suffered much abuse from Monica. Frequently she denied him the right to sleep with her, screaming at him, 'You climb in my bed, you climb all the way.'

He tried to speak with Joe about this one day, but broke into tears. After controlling himself, he mumbled, 'How could I ever leave her? Christ, I love that girl in ways you couldn't even guess. I need her. She's tearing my heart out.' When Joe tried to comfort him, he said, 'But I will not touch Big-H. Not ever again.'

Often the other guests on the third floor could hear him, when Monica was being difficult, imploring her to quit what could only destroy her. 'If something's bound to kill you, why mess around with it?' He did his best to divert her to hashish, which he felt she could handle, but she laughed at him tauntingly. 'That's for kids, and I'm a woman now.'

In one respect his efforts to rescue Monica were misdirected; hashish was a more powerful concoction than he supposed. As purveyed by Jemail, it was a cube of compressed resin extracted from the mature marijuana plant and ten times as strong as a joint. It was thus a concentrate of marijuana and could be used in two ways: smoked, or eaten in the form of the hideous green cookies common on the Djemaá. Cato had learned about the cookies from the Swedes.

On the ground floor of the Bordeaux, to the left of the entrance, stood a room somewhat larger than the others. In recent years it had been occupied by an engaging couple from Stockholm who stayed on from June through November. Rolf worked the rest of the year in Sweden as male nurse in an asylum for the insane, and Inger taught kindergarten. Their room was known throughout Marrakech as Inger's and it served as a mail drop for Scandinavians passing through and as the social center for all other Europeans. Inger's, when the Swedes were in residence, was one of the most civilized rooms in Africa, a place where you could get a drink of cold gingerale, a kind of rude smorgasbord, back copies of the *London Times*, and conversation that had wings. Rolf and Inger were in their late twenties, unmarried and quietly attractive. When on the first morning, they heard that three new Americans and a lovely English girl had checked in, they climbed the stairs to introduce themselves and to offer the hospitality of their quarters. They assumed responsibility for locating empty rooms—Cato and Monica on the third floor, Joe and Gretchen on the second—and then assembled the group in their room.

'Music!' Monica cried as she spied a gramophone, which she quickly activated, closing her eyes to the heavy beat of the latest recording by Blind Faith. 'It's like rain in the desert,' she said, but after a few moments she opened her purse and asked, 'What about these green cookies Jemail sold us last night?'

'Rather potent,' Rolf warned. 'They brew an infusion of concentrated hash and rancid butter. Then bake these sticky macaroons.'

'How do you eat them?'

'With care. Girl your size could handle about an eighth of a cookie. If you were heavier, you could eat more. Big Loomis, I suppose, could eat a whole one, but you couldn't.'

'You don't know me,' Monica replied, plopping the entire

cookie into her mouth and chewing while she grinned at the others. Rolf watched apprehensively, and Inger started to clear a section of her bed, but Monica showed no immediate adverse reaction.

Cato and Joe took small nibbles of their cookies. Gretchen refused any but did accept a cigarette that Rolf had been rolling, half marijuana, half hashish. 'It's certainly different,' Monica said as she began to feel the authority of the hash. As Gretchen was about to take a second puff of her cigarette she yelled, 'Oh my God!' Monica, as if struck by an axe, had dropped unconscious to the floor; Cato, who had not seen her fall, turned and stood with his mouth open, an unswallowed cookie fragment visible on his tongue. Joe stooped down to pick her up, but Rolf and Inger had anticipated him and stretched Monica out on the bed. She remained there, motionless, for eighteen hours, watched over by Cato.

During this time a constant flow of young people from all parts of Europe visited the room. They would see Monica stone-cold and say casually, 'Ah, hah! Tried one of our cookies.' No one seemed particularly disturbed; they sat on the edge of a bed and on the floor and talked about Sweden and Germany and Australia. Toward evening one of the Wellesley girls produced her guitar, which encouraged Gretchen to get hers, and they sang ballads, with the group joining in when they knew the words—and through all these hours of chatter and song, Monica did not move once. Occasionally Cato would shake her and try to get her to speak, but she remained totally immobile, and Rolf said professionally, 'Only thing to do is let her sleep it off.'

It was almost dawn when Monica finally made a movement. Half an hour later she opened her eyes, looked about the unfamiliar room and said, 'Next time only half a cookie.'

———•◆•———

'The beauty of this letterhead,' Big Loomis explained to Joe in his office on the top floor, 'is that it confuses a draft board for at least two months. In that time, a smart man can be in Nepal . . . or Shinjuku.' He produced a formal-looking sheet of high-quality paper, at the head of which appeared:

Office: Telephones:
1283 Cadwallader   Tuscarora 4–1286
                                                         1287
                                                         1288

DR. J. LOOMIS CARGILL
Practice limited to the treatment
of psychiatric disabilities.
By appointment only

'First of all, no city is named, so they can't send an investigator. Now 1283 Cadwallader sounds especially impressive. You notice that for both the address and the telephone I use four-syllable names. In America a ringing four-syllable name is as good as money in the bank. But I'm told by fellows I've helped that what really makes them pause is those three telephone numbers. In America, a sure signal of success. They see that and they think, "This guy must be important. Better not try to push him around." But I personally think it's the name J. Loomis Cargill that does the trick. Because every town in the United States has its Joe This or Jim That, who was born a very ordinary fellow and continued to be very ordinary until that pregnant day when he had the brilliant idea of calling himself J. Worthington Scaller. This single act puts the entire community on notice: "I intend to be taken seriously!" And since we tend to accept a man on his own terms, we help him to become J. Worthington Scaller, man of substance. America is full of appalling drips who would have remained that way if they'd been known in their community as plain Jim Scaller, but let that good old J. Worthington step forth, and the drip is transformed into a community leader, if you like. I figure that as J. Loomis Cargill, I've kept more than a hundred young fellows out of the draft. If I'd submitted my letters as Joe Cargill the draft boards would have snorted, "Get his ass in here."

'The real clincher is that notice in smaller type. *Practice limited.* Magic words. They mean you're not just some family dope, working sixteen hours a day, making house calls, saving lives. Once you put that sign in your window, you escalate into a whole new orbit. You have arrived, son. You are in. You sit on your fat tail and haul in big fees without doing disagreeable things like delivering babies. Now what draft board would dare to ignore a letter that comes from a man whose practice is limited, whose name is J. Loomis, and who has three phones?'

'How about the doctor bit?' Joe asked.

'I am a doctor,' Big Loomis replied. 'Physical education, Central Texas State Teachers. That's a Negro football college. A professional outfit in Chicago wrote my thesis for me. I played guard . . . for seven years . . . under three different names. We played a different set of teams each three years so they wouldn't recognize me . . . or the other clowns on our team.'

'Were you any good?'

'Pretty good. Weighed in at two-forty and could have played with the pros . . . the Rams drafted me. I told our coach I'd been in the pros for the past seven years, but he didn't think that was funny. I objected to the draft, but my family were all atheists, so I couldn't plead conscientious objection. So I got out the hard way.'

'How?' Joe asked.

'Eating. In a few months I put on a hundred pounds.'

'How?'

'On your frame you couldn't hack it. I did it by eating bananas and cheese cake and gallons of milkshakes.'

'Hurt your health?'

'I suppose so. Doctors tell me I'll die a couple of years earlier than I would have otherwise. But that's better than dying age twenty-two in Vietnam.' He hesitated, then added, 'Of course, once I've got this draft thing licked, I'm gonna slice this weight off as fast as I put it on. That's why I live on the top floor. Good exercise going up and down. You know, I used to do the hundred in ten-three, and when this craziness is over, I'll do it in ten-four. Now your problem.'

He listened carefully as Joe outlined his various confrontations with the draft board in California and told about the letter of warning in Moçambique and his discussions with Harvey Holt. 'A classic case,' Loomis said. 'No religious excuse. No disabling infirmity. No cowardice. No mental derangement. Just another clean-cut man who doesn't want to louse up his life in Southeast Asia. I think we better try Little Casino. Have you considered what it means?'

'Yes.'

'You engaged to that attractive girl in your room?'

'No, no!' Joe spoke as if being engaged to the girl you were living with was unthinkable. 'I think she's in favor of Little Casino. She had a rough time with the fuzz.'

Big Loomis went to his typewriter and after a while handed Joe a crisp sheet of paper, accurately spaced and typed, which said among other things:

> It would be folly to induct this patient into the armed services because he has for some years been addicted to drugs. Starting at age fourteen, he smoked marijuana cigarettes under the tutelage of a Mexican girl who was working for his parents. He quickly escalated to hashish, LSD and now heroin, which he requires daily. It would take eight months of intensive hospital care to break him of the habit. Under the influence of drugs he has developed such a manifest schizoid behavior that it would be criminal to place him in any position involving guns or the safety of others. In a normal case I would recommend immediate hospitalization under guard, but his physical condition is so emaciated that I am advising his parents to keep him under their strict surveillance until he puts some flesh on his bones and can withstand the hospital treatments I have in mind. Under these circumstances, it would be a waste of public funds to take this pathetic individual into the armed services, since you would have to hospitalize him immediately, with little hope of reaching a point at which his participation in military life would be of any help to you or to his fellow soldiers.
>
> Professionally,
> J. Loomis Cargill

———•—•—•———

I was working in Geneva when Gretchen's letter arrived telling me that they had reached Marrakech. I had some apprehension as I visualized them exploring the Djemaá. I wished that Monica could have avoided a place like that, but being too busy with my own affairs, dismissed the matter. Then Holt and Britta stopped by on their way from Lausanne to the airport for their flight to Ceylon, and when I showed them the letter, Harvey scowled and said, 'Last place in the world Joe should be is Marrakech,' and on the spur of the moment he decided to fly to Ceylon via Morocco. Britta, of course, was delighted at the prospect of seeing Gretchen and Monica again, so the detour was quickly arranged.

Holt then said, 'Fairbanks, your company has big holdings in Morocco. Why not join us?' and I proved as mercurial as they: 'Sounds like a good idea.' And within an hour we had picked up a Lufthansa plane and were on our way. I'm sure there must be people in this world who plan trips in advance and then have to obtain their passports, but I know none of them; the people I know keep their passports viable at all times and leave for the airport within the hour of deciding to visit Asia or Africa or Australia.

We landed in Marrakech in the late afternoon and caught a taxi to the Mamounia Hotel, one of those fine old palaces like the Raffles in Singapore or the old Shepheard's in Cairo. It stood not far from the Koutoubia in the center of gardens that would have graced a palace. Since I was well known from earlier visits during which I had explored the economy preparatory to our extensive investments, the manager had good rooms waiting for us. I telephoned the three government engineers in Casablanca with whom I would be working, then asked the doorman how to get to the Hotel Bordeaux. He shrugged his shoulders and asked the taxi drivers, but they said a taxi couldn't manage the alleys. 'What you do,' he then suggested, 'is walk down to the Djemaá. Someone there will surely know.' He sniffed as if the Bordeaux were a hovel.

So Holt and Britta and I set out for the Djemaá, and we had scarcely entered the vast plaza when I was accosted by the young Arab of whom Gretchen had written. He was everything she had described: fox-faced ragamuffin in a baseball cap from Waco, Texas. He came directly to me and said, 'Mr. Fairbanks, World Mutual, Geneva, Switzerland.' Bowing to Holt, he said, 'This got to be Harvey Holt, builds airports. And this the Norwegian girl.' I asked him how he knew our names, and he said, 'I mail their letters. If you need anything Mamounia . . .'

'How did you know I was at the Mamounia?'

'Where else?' he asked. Then dropping his voice to a low basso, he leered at Britta and said, 'Come wiz me to ze casbah.'

'To the Bordeaux,' I said, and he started across the Djemaá, but our progress was slow, for Britta wanted to stop at every circle to watch the clowns or listen to the storytellers, so after a much retarded transit we reached the area where the autobuses parked—scores of them headed to all parts of the High Atlas—and after negotiating the alleys we reached the doorway to the Bordeaux. It was now night, and for a moment as we stood there in the darkness, with light shining from the interior of the hotel, and the sound of guitars coming from one of the rooms to the left where voices harmonized an old ballad, I could appreciate what such an adventure must mean to a young girl from Brisbane, Australia, or a young man from Moose Jaw, Saskatchewan, and I noticed the flush of excitement on Britta's face as it emerged from shadow.

'The action is over here,' Jemail said, but before he could lead us to the big room where the Swedish couple stayed, he whistled and cried, 'I better be going,' for he saw coming down the stairs the gigantic form of Big Loomis, moving like a black mountain covered with flowers, and it was apparent to us that the boy and the man were enemies, for the former fled and the latter growled in a deep voice as he rumbled past, 'That little bastard is a good one to keep clear of.'

We went to the door that Jemail had headed for, knocked, and were admitted by a soft-spoken Swede who introduced himself as Rolf, but he had barely spoken his name when Gretchen, who was playing her guitar, spotted us and leaped across the room, followed by Cato and Joe. There were warm greetings and many kisses and much admiration of Joe's handsome new appearance, but the enthusiasm was marred by Holt, who sniffed the heavy air and asked, 'What in God's name is that smell?' Gretchen gave his arm a little hug and whispered, 'Pot. Most of the kids are smoking, but there are no problems.'

'Smells like a problem to me,' Holt said as we met the crowd, but soon we were seated on one of the beds, and Gretchen resumed singing a Child ballad which told of a girl who had been saved from the gallows just as the rope was being put about her throat. 'Child 95,' she called it, and the chorus was so winsome and so simple that by the end of the second verse we were all singing.

Britta kept looking around for Monica, and after the ballad Cato explained, 'She's upstairs. I think she's sleeping.' Britta suggested that we new arrivals go up to surprise her, and it seemed to me that Cato was against the idea and that Gretchen, strumming her guitar, looked apprehensive, but I wasn't sure, so with Cato leading the way, we left the room and climbed the stairs. Pushing open a door, we walked into darkness, but in the shadows we could see a bed on which lay the figure of a young girl. It was Monica, and even when we entered the room and turned on the light, she did not move. Completely stoned, she lay with her lovely mouth agape, her eyes rolled far back into their sockets.

Britta ran to the bed to embrace her, but Monica was incapable of recognizing us. When Britta shook her, she mumbled something, then lapsed into total unconsciousness. We looked at Cato, standing against the wall, saying nothing. 'What the hell is this?' Holt demanded.

Cato pointed to her arm and said, 'The needle. And she insists on eating those goddamned cookies.'

'What cookies?' Holt asked. Cato kicked at a greasy bag made of folded newspaper, and Holt stooped to pick it up, feeling the greenish crumbs and smelling them. 'Is this hashish?' he asked, and Cato nodded.

'She looks dreadfully sick,' Britta said, looking sick herself at the appearance of her friend.

Cato offered no comment; the anguish in his eyes spoke for him. I sat on the side of the bed to check the unconscious girl more closely, and noticed something which I was often afterward to recall, but which at the time I dismissed: Monica's complexion was noticeably sallow. This should have forewarned me, but it didn't, because I was even more struck by her extreme loss of weight. 'She must have dropped fifteen pounds since the last time I saw her,' I said.

'Maybe more,' Cato agreed. 'She won't eat. But when she comes to see you tomorrow, she'll be as bright as ever.'

'You mean she'll be able to get up?' Holt asked.

'Sure,' Cato said, and next morning about eleven o'clock when I was standing in the lobby of the Mamounia with the three engineers from Casablanca, the oldest, who had graduated from Yale, cried, 'Whew! Who's that dish?' and we turned to see that Monica had come to greet us.

I can see her now—slim, very black hair, very pale face, radiant with a remnant of childhood charm, yet as enticing as a grown woman, she moved toward us with that subtle grace which such women command and which reverberates in a room like a sound of flutes. I forgot her appearance of the night before and hurried across the lobby to accept her kiss. The three Moroccans were close behind me, for they saw the same exquisite quality that I did, so I introduced them before they regretfully left the hotel, pausing frequently to stare back at Monica.

We talked of Moçambique and Marrakech, and Monica was so witty in her observations about Cato and the love affair between Joe and Gretchen, so utterly amiable, that I found it impossible to visualize her as the same girl I had seen only a few hours before; then slowly I realized that within the hour she must have given herself a booster shot of heroin, brought to her by Jemail, and we were seeing the apex of her euphoria. It was, I suppose, the apex of her loveliness too, and my heart expanded, as a man's should, when I saw how charming she was.

That night Holt and I invited our five young people and the Swedish couple to dinner at one of the French cafés in the business district. I suggested that we include Big Loomis, but Holt objected: 'I don't trust any fat slob that advises young men how to beat the draft.' I argued, 'He understands young people. We may need his help with Monica.' Grudgingly Holt assented, but during the meal he kept a close eye on Loomis and listened closely any time the fat man spoke to Joe.

Later we trailed down to the Djemaá, where the night cast was putting on its show, then on to the Bordeaux, where Rolf and Inger introduced me to hash. We were seated on the beds, some twenty of us, with fine guitar music filling the room. Gretchen had announced, 'Child 12,' and there had been applause. This was a ballad she had taught me, and when other guitars joined in, the effect was powerful, and I noticed especially a verse I must have heard before but had not listened to, for the words, although they referred to a young man, seemed painfully applicable to Monica, and as they rose in soft echoes from a dozen voices, I had to believe that they referred to my beautiful English girl, and I took her hand, and when the verse was ended:

> ' "What gat ye to your dinner, Lord Randal, my son?
> What gat ye to your dinner, my handsome young man?"

"I gat eels boild in broo; mother, make my bed soon,
  For I'm weary wi hunting, and fain wald lie down." '

I whispered, 'Why don't you quit taking eels in broo?' and she reproved me, 'Don't talk like my father,' and I said, 'I am your father, and I am heartsick when I see how you are destroying yourself,' but she put her fingers to her lips and said, 'Listen to the music,' and we listened as Gretchen sang:

' "O I fear ye are poisond, Lord Randal, my son!
  O I fear ye are poisond, my handsome young man!"
  "O yes! I am poisond; mother, make my bed soon,
  For I'm sick at the heart, and I fain wald lie down." '

'Nobody need bother about making my bed,' Monica whispered, 'because I don't intend to lie down.'

It was now that Rolf, with Inger's help, rolled a blockbuster cigarette, about as long as a commercial one but at least three times as thick; indeed, it looked more like a cigar. It was made first of marijuana leaves, arranged lengthwise, but when these were in place, Inger sprinkled over them a generous helping of crumbled hash, so that the brownish stuff filtered through all parts of the cigarette. When it was lit, it flamed like a torch for a moment, then subsided to an ordinary cigarette glow, emitting a heavy coil of smoke which hung in the air, yellowish and pungent. 'We call this the Winston Churchill,' Rolf said, referring to a man who had once lived in Marrakech and loved it.

Inger took a deep draw, allowed the freighted smoke to circulate through her lungs, and blew it out. She took another, then passed the joint to Rolf, who puffed and handed it to Gretchen. She was preoccupied with her guitar, so passed the cigarette unused to one of the girls from Wellesley, who took a deep drag and handed it along until it reached Monica, who took three tremendous puffs, which seemed to have no effect. She handed the joint to me, and since I had never tasted hash I thought I might as well try it under these favorable circumstances, so I took a token drag, feeling the smoke enter deep into my throat and lungs; even that small quantity carried an authority which I perceived immediately. I tasted the smoke, then blew it out. 'I can see how this might become popular . . . but not with me,' I said as I handed the cigarette to Holt, who passed it immediately to Britta. She took two deep puffs and said, 'It's been a long time since the last one,' and Harvey said, 'It's gonna be a long time till the next one,' and she patted his hand. Holt asked me, 'Is it pretty strong?' and I said, 'So far I feel no effects, but I'm sure they're there.' When the mighty Winston Churchill made its subsequent rounds, Monica tried to shame me into keeping up with the crowd, but I, not being a teenager, felt that I could survive the accusation 'chicken,' and as the night progressed I observed that those who continued smoking hash grew more lethargic and poetic and amenable and drowsy, and when familiar ballads were sung they tended to sing about half a bar behind Holt and me, and one of the girls from Australia said, 'Isn't this beautiful? Just sitting here and singing and not being mad at anybody?' But her singing kept no pace with ours.

Early next morning Cato was at my hotel. He was most distraught and said he felt powerless, unable any longer to try to help Monica, who was now alternating heroin and hashish cookies in a way that kept her unconscious much of the time. She was not eating at all and occasionally had hallucinations in which her father and I were oppressing her in a London hotel.

He brought me her handbag: passport proving that she was seventeen years old . . . British citizen . . . notify Sir Charles Braham in case of trouble . . . and other items of ugly import—cap from a Danish beer bottle, cork liner scraped away so that the cap could be filled with water and held over a match for the dissolving of heroin powder; a good German hypodermic needle, not too clean and with marks of blood on the interior, indicating that she had stuck the needle into her vein, then aspirated it to be sure of its location; a small square packet of paper containing remains of a whitish powder; and finally a letter seven months old addressed to her in Torremolinos. 'Should I throw the needle away?' Cato asked.

'I don't know,' I said. 'I feel as powerless as you. But she looks terribly sick . . . maybe we'd better talk to Big Loomis.'

When we climbed the stairs to his quarters we had to pass

Monica's door, and as we peered inside we could see that she was unconscious and would remain so for many hours. 'What ought we to do with this child?' I asked Loomis. 'She ought to be in a hospital . . . but not in Morocco,' he said. I said I wished I had the authority to ship her out to England, then asked how far gone he thought she was in her addiction, and he said, 'It boils down to this: will she give herself an o-d and kill herself, or won't she?' I asked what an o-d was, and he said, 'Over-dose. It happens by accident—her accident in taking too much, or the seller's accident in making his mix too strong. In the first case, suicide. In the second, murder.'

'Does this happen often?'

'Yes. We've had three young people die in this hotel of o-d. That skinny drink of water from Mississippi better watch out, or he'll be next.' He spoke with the professional detachment of one who had seen much tragedy from the use of drugs, and I asked, 'Are you on heroin?'

'Me?' he asked in astonishment. 'On Big-H? I'm here to beat the draft . . . not to wreck my life. When this is over I expect to lose a hundred and fifty pounds and coach football in some college. But recently I've been thinking maybe I ought to go into counseling.'

'We have Monica's outfit here,' I said. 'Should Cato throw the hypodermic away?'

Big Loomis reflected on this for some moments. 'With Monica I'd have to say no. There's still a chance you can bring her back. But not cold turkey. She'd rebel and you'd lose her.' From the authoritative way he spoke, I judged he had handled several such cases. He concluded, 'One thing you can do is keep that filthy little Jemail away from her.'

'Why do you hate him so?'

'Because people like you think he's cute. Actually he's a depraved little monster—the creation of his society, yes, but he kills much of what he touches. You might call him the curse of Marrakech . . . and only eleven years old.'

As we descended the stairs we spotted Jemail sneaking out of Monica's room; we were sure he had brought her a new supply of green cookies, which she had been too unconscious to accept, so he had probably slipped them under her pillow, on credit, then moved on to deliver his daily ration of heroin to the young man from Mississippi.

Ever since that night when Cato nearly died from an injection of heroin, I had been preoccupied with the problems raised by this destructive drug, and now Jemail seemed to provide an opportunity to find out more about it, so while Cato stopped off to see if he could make Monica eat something, I purposefully followed the little Arab into the alley, but as soon as he detected me, he stopped abruptly, turned to face me, and asked, 'What you want, buster? Nice young girl, very clean?'

'Where do you get the heroin you peddle to these people?'

Instantly he became a businessman and I could see his shrewd brain clicking like a computer. 'Maybe you like to buy a load . . . fly back to Switzerland? You smuggle a lot of good stuff into Geneva . . . you make a million.'

'I'd like to see where you get it . . . how good it is.'

'Why not?' he asked, shrugging his shoulders. Then remembering that I came from Geneva, he continued our discussion in very good German, switching to French when we reached the Djemaá; this he spoke idiomatically.

We left the plaza and entered the low-covered souks, where he spoke a flippant Arabic to the shopowners. We passed the goldsmiths, the rug merchants, the metalworkers, the shoemakers, with all of whom he maintained a running conversation. I judged that he was saying, 'No business with this one, Gamal. But later today I'll bring you someone.' The merchants nodded as he passed and some even greeted him with respect, acknowledging the fact that he was an important cog in their operation.

Our first stop was an apothecary's stall, where a serious-looking Moroccan in red fez was parceling onto paper squares minute portions of heroin, weighing each on a bronze balance whose index arm wavered back and forth like a butterfly preparing to land on a flower. When the papers were prepared, sixteen of them lined up carefully in rows, he placed on each a spatula full of dextrose, which formed the bulk and body of the package. With a different spatula, carefully cleaned, he mixed the powders on each of the papers, then folded the edges to make neat packages, which he would sell to runners like Jemail.

'Very scientific,' Jemail said proudly. 'With this you never catch an o-d.' For some minutes he spoke to the chemist in Arabic, then informed me, 'He says that for a large order . . . he puts everything together for you . . . very small package . . . two American dollars each one. In Geneva you sell each one for thirty dollars . . . in New York, fifty dollars.' I said I would think about this, and the red fez nodded.

'Don't try to buy lower,' Jemail warned me as we left the shop. 'You pick up some boy on the Djemaá . . . one of the others . . . sure he sell a little cheaper. But what you get?' He led me past a kiosk whose door was barred and said, 'This is where they bring you . . . cheap heroin to begin with . . . no scales for weighing . . . some here, some there . . . who knows what you're getting? One dose very weak, one dose very strong. This man known as the killer. Don't go.'

He now led me to a much different section; indeed, I wondered if it was technically a part of the souk, for it seemed more like a warehouse area, and even before I was well into it I could detect the rich, clean smell of new-mown hay. This had to be the marijuana center, and Jemail led me to his two principal hashish suppliers. The first was a small nervous man who kept cleaning his fingernails with a silver penknife. He greeted Jemail affectionately, and when the boy told him that I was interested in a large order of hash for Switzerland, he became businesslike and told me in French, 'Jemail has probably warned you that I make only the cheap quality, and he's right. If you had to sell my product in Morocco you might have trouble. But in a foreign country, where they don't know, you could make a lot of money on my stuff.'

He led us inside his warehouse, whose floors were piled with cannabis which he said he got from plateaus in the High Atlas. Two men were sorting and packing it raw into the cellophane bags that Jemail sold on the Djemaá. In a shed nearby, a substantial fire burned, over which hung a large cast-iron cauldron in which huge quantities of marijuana were being boiled in order to extract the resin which, when drained and compressed, would form hashish. It was a crude process, uncontrolled and accidental—more than six hundred kilos of marijuana to produce one kilo of hash—and the hash which did result was undependable, but as the proprietor said while working on his nails, 'Very reasonably priced.' I said I would consider his offer.

It was the second warehouse that produced top-quality hash, and Jemail recommended strongly that I establish a long-time business relationship with its proprietor. 'You could become rich,' he assured me. What he said next betrayed his self-interest in this matter: 'Maybe next year I bring you your supplies. Fly Air France to Geneva . . . Paris.' I nodded, as if to encourage his delusions.

The proprietor of this establishment looked like an old-fashioned miller; he could have come from the Canterbury Tales or from Shakespeare, for his face was round and covered with dust, as were his shoes and clothes. He had several teeth missing in front and was most amiable as he approached to do business with me. He spoke French and assured me, 'Here you get the best hashish in Morocco . . . probably in the world. Now if you want to be our representative in Geneva, I can guarantee top quality. Come inside.'

He led me to one of the strangest industrial rooms I had seen in long years of inspecting the unusual. It was small and completely lined—the floor, the walls and the ceiling—with a coarse burlap. In the center lay a pile of dried marijuana, from which two workmen lifted small bundles to place on heavy boards, where they beat the leaves and stalks with whips, each consisting of a handle from which sprang ten or twelve heavy reeds. There was a constant flurry of dust, which, as it rose above the beating blocks, deposited its burden of resin on the waiting burlap. When Jemail explained what was happening, I could detect tiny globules of grayish stuff.

'From the ceiling,' the proprietor told me, 'we scrape the very finest hashish. From the walls a good grade indeed. From the floor . . . well, not such high quality but infinitely better than the boiled stuff.' Then he made his little joke: 'Since you are a tall man, Monsieur Fairbanks, the dust on your clothes right now would be worth five hundred dollars.'

He said he mixed his hash with no adulterants and promised me that as his agent for Central Europe, I would receive only the best. 'For your personal use,' he confided, 'I shall lift your hash only from the highest point in this special room.' He pushed open a door to another burlap-lined room which contained no workmen or pile of cannabis. 'Here, once in a while, we beat specially selected female plants. They yield the best.'

I spent some time with him, discussing the trade, and he assured me that smoking hashish carried no ill effects. He had heard about the assassins of ancient Syria and the oft-told fable that they murdered only when lost in hash-induced stupors. 'This never happened,' he insisted, and his manner was so cocksure that I had to say, 'But I know of an English girl who ate one of your cookies and went stone-cold for eighteen hours.' He raised his hands, causing precious dust to fly from his sleeves. 'Cookies . . . those damned green cookies. They are something else. A wise man never eats hashish. He smokes it.'

We parted with the understanding that he would make a careful estimate of the best price he could offer me when I became his representative in Europe: 'It will be a price, I assure you, on which we can both become very rich. Because there's a lot of money to be made in this business.'

———————•◦•———————

In some ways the most interesting section of the Djemaá was the area adjacent to the souks, for not only was the covered market visible but also one found here the focus of various interesting activities. There was the bicycle stand, filled with hundreds of vehicles throughout the day, a lounging place at night. There was the Sportif, the dark and grimy café in which one could buy a plate of greasy stew for fifteen cents and meet people from various parts of the world. The Sportif sold doughnuts, caked with chewy sugar, and poorer travelers sometimes lived on them for days. Nearby stood the stall of a woman who made hashish cookies, and beyond her was the kiosk which sold fruit during the day and served as a flophouse for Jemail and other gamins during the night.

But the lodestone which drew all foreigners to this end of the Djemaá was an extraordinary restaurant perched on the second floor of a building much damaged by the violent earthquake of February 1969. Huge wooden poles positioned throughout the ground floor supported the upper, which contained the eating areas, so that waiters—a seedy lot of men in filthy clothes—had to dodge in and out among the poles as they carried the food upstairs on a set of stairs so tenuous that visitors climbing aloft to dine sometimes grew queasy even before the food was placed before them.

At each meal this typically Moroccan dining hall served only one main dish, usually some kind of heavy stew, with large chunks of crusty bread and a sickly sweet orange drink, but if one could grab a table on the balcony and then squeeze himself into the narrow space allowed each customer, he found before him a panorama of unforgettable grandeur: the snow-covered Atlas, the solitary minaret of the Koutoubia, the vast expanse of wall, and the broad unfolding of the Djemaá with its constantly changing cast of characters. The restaurant was called the Terrace and from it one saw the tragi-comedy of Marrakech: an ancient city founded by Berbers who had wandered down from the mountains, a city which still retained the confusion and character of a frontier hideout.

I was sitting on the balcony of the Terrace one lunchtime with Gretchen and Britta when we spotted Jemail coming across the Djemaá. He had a young man in tow, and we were watching idly to see what the little devil was up to, when Britta suddenly leaped to her feet and started waving frantically. Soon Gretchen did the same.

'It's Yigal!' Britta cried, and now the oncoming figure began waving to us, and I saw that it was our friend, in an expensive suit and looking the perfect tourist from Detroit.

The girls started to run down the rickety stairs to greet him, but waiters were ascending at that moment, so Jemail shouted, 'I'll bring him up!' and soon the two were standing before us, with Jemail grinning benignly as Yigal kissed the two girls.

'Yigal!' Gretchen cried in delight, but he stopped her, whispering, 'In Morocco I'm Bruce . . . my American passport,' and now it was Gretchen who whispered, 'Shhhh! Don't let the boy hear. He'd turn you in to the police for a penny.' And Jemail moved closer to try to catch whatever new thing was developing.

Yigal took Britta's hands and said, 'You're even prettier than I remembered,' and Gretchen, eager to forestall embarrassments, interrupted: 'Did they tell you in Torremolinos?'

'I wasn't there,' Yigal said. 'Tell me what?'

'Britta and Mr. Holt are married . . . well, sort of.'

'Oh . . .' If Yigal was hurt by this news, he masked his feelings and said, 'Then you'll be going to wherever he's going,' and she nodded, with Gretchen explaining, 'This time it's Ceylon.'

'Great place,' he said. Then, in a new voice, pitched higher, he asked, 'So where is the gang living?' and the girls explained that they were in the Bordeaux, where he must stay, and Britta was in the expensive hotel, along with Harvey and Mr. Fairbanks. But what they really wanted to know was why he had come to Marrakech and what he was going to do about his citizenship.

'America is difficult to take . . . if you take it seriously,' he said.

'What does that mean?' Gretchen asked.

'I think you know,' he said.

After lunch we led him through the alleys to the Bordeaux, and found Joe and Cato in Inger's, listening to records.

'Hey, you look great!' Yigal cried when he saw the new-shaven Joe. He turned the tall fellow around, admired him, then said to Gretchen, 'You ought to fall in love with this one.' In the embarrassed silence that followed, Yigal deduced that this was what had already taken place, so he said, 'A lot must have happened when I wasn't looking.'

They sat him on one of the beds and offered him a smoke, but he refused. They then interrogated him about his life in Detroit, and he said, 'I liked Case Institute in some ways, but it seemed so immature after the schools in Israel. The courses were quite simple and the professors didn't seem dedicated to their work, but what really put me off was the kind of thing the kids were excited about —the draft, for example—things that we had settled in Israel six years ago. In the end I found it quite unbearable.'

'I know what you mean,' Gretchen said. 'But after a spell with us . . . you'll go back to the States, won't you?'

'I think so. I just got fed up with college . . . and in a way, Detroit. But that is one helluva country.'

'Do you think you'll go back to college?' Britta asked.

'I suppose so. But not to Case. I might like Harvard. Something to bite into.'

'Then you've decided to become an American?' Gretchen asked approvingly.

'I think so.' He paused, then added, 'The country is so big, no matter what you want to do, you can find the space to do it in. It makes Israel look very small. I suppose I was so preoccupied with Israel's small problems that I couldn't appreciate America's larger ones.'

'Your grandfather will be happy,' Britta said.

'Right now he's probably tearing his hair out. Thinks I've gone back to Israel. He'd never be able to understand that I simply had to talk with you kids. That I'd throw over my admission to Case to compare notes with you in Marrakech.'

'But he'll be relieved you've given up on Israel,' Gretchen said.

'Very. Out of fairness to the old geezer, I'm going to write him tonight.'

Up to this point Cato had been silent, but now he looked soberly at Yigal and said, 'I'd go slow on what I write the old man.'

'What do you mean?'

'It might be better if you elected Israel.'

'How so?'

'Because from what I learned in Moçambique—and here—well, things aren't going to be too easy for the Jew in America.'

'What do you have in mind?'

'The blacks will have to drive the Jews out of American life. There has got to be open warfare.'

'What are you saying?' Yigal's small, tight face had hardened, and he leaned forward so as to confront the Negro directly.

'I'm saying what I learned. That the American blacks are going to reject Christianity.'

'The Jews did that two thousand years ago.'

'But the blacks are converting to Islam. And that'll make them part of a great confederation—Arabs in Egypt against the Jews of Israel . . . blacks in the United States against the Jews of America.'

'Are you out of your mind?' Yigal asked.

'You saw the beginnings in Detroit,' Cato said quietly. 'It'll happen across America.'

Yigal moved closer and said, 'For a black man to talk like that to a Jew is insanity. You better go home and sort your ideas out, because if you can't make an alliance with me—and with Jews like me—you are finished, Brother Cato. You are dead.'

Cato did not draw back, but at the same time he did not speak so forcefully as to make his next statement a challenge. He said simply, 'The Jew has got to be removed. For one clear reason. He holds all the positions the blacks are entitled to.'

Yigal was about to respond when he saw, standing in the doorway, a figure he scarcely recognized. It was Monica, risen from a heroin hangover, shaking and painfully thin. He rose from the bed, hurried to her and took her hands in his. 'Monica, what's happened? You look so yellow.'

'No sun,' she said, kissing him on the cheek.

'I didn't say sallow. I said yellow.'

'Who the hell are you? Dr. Schweitzer?' She pushed him away and asked if anyone had a joint going. Rolf offered her a smoke, and she inhaled deeply, the soporific quality of the marijuana quieting her nerves. After the fifth deep drag she came back to Yigal and asked, 'How was the land of the Big PX?'

———•◆•———

At periodic intervals the American residents of Hotel Bordeaux found it necessary to leave the old section of Marrakech and venture into the new. At such times they left the security of the ancient red walls and wandered like invading Visigoths into the spacious business district on whose borders stood the elegant homes erected in the days of French occupation. This part of Marrakech resembled any substantial suburban community of Paris or Los Angeles, and the beatniks looked ridiculously out of place. They sensed this, for they moved uneasily, aware that the police were watching, but the sorties, unpleasant though they might be, were unavoidable.

On this particular Thursday my presence in the expedition was required, so it was agreed that all concerned would assemble at the Terrace at eleven in the morning, and I was there having a cup of coffee when I saw the motley gang entering the Djemaá in single file, Big Loomis in the lead, a pachyderm with beads, jangling bracelets, flapping yak boots and an embroidered woman's bag slung over his left shoulder. He was followed by three scrawny girls I had only vaguely seen before; they came from various parts of the United States, and so far as their parents knew, were studying

French at the university in Besançon. Behind them came two boys from New England with heads of hair as big as watermelons, followed by Monica and Gretchen in miniskirts, with Yigal and Cato bringing up the rear, the latter dressed in a weird half-African, half-University of Pennsylvania costume.

As they came slowly across the Djemaá, Big Loomis had to bear the insults of Jemail and his militia, but the others were greeted pleasantly. Merchants familiar with the group nodded approvingly as the entourage passed and the crowds at the bicycle stand parted to let them by. Finally Big Loomis stood below me, raised his massive face to the balcony where I sat, and cried, 'Alert, up there! Today we resume communication with the little old lady in Dubuque.'

I joined them and we walked up the broad Avenue Mohammad V, past the Koutoubia, as beautiful in sunlight as it had been at midnight, and into the business section. We stopped at a well-constructed building with bars over the windows and a modestly placed bronze sign: *American Banking Corporation, New York*. Pushing apart the heavy doors, Big Loomis stalked into the foyer and headed with homing instinct to the cage marked *Incoming Drafts Overseas*. Rapping smartly on the counter, he demanded, 'Any good news from Petroleum, Texas?' The clerk shuffled through a stack of papers and said, 'It's arrived, Mr. Cargill,' and he brought to the window a bank draft for two hundred dollars sent some days ago by the big man's mother in Petroleum. With a flourish, Loomis signed the necessary papers and took his money in Moroccan bills, kissing each one as he stuffed it into his embroidered shoulder bag.

After he concluded his business the three scrawny girls moved to the window, asking in turn whether their bank drafts had arrived, and two were lucky. As they accepted their money they told the third girl they'd stake her till her parents forwarded her check. The two New England boys were disappointed, but the lucky girls assured them, too, that there would be money and not to worry.

Now I was needed. I accompanied Cato and Yigal to the window and told the clerk, whom I knew from the varied transactions I had conducted with him during previous trips, 'This young man is Cato Jackson, from Philadelphia, and I think he may have a cable here from a man named John Wister. What specific bank it will be coming through, I wouldn't know, but I can vouch for him.' The clerk shuffled his stack and found a draft from the Fidelity Bank in Philadelphia.

I then introduced Yigal as 'Bruce Clifton, Grosse Pointe, Michigan. It was named by French explorers.' The clerk smiled and bowed. 'The draft will probably be from some Detroit bank,' I said.

'Detroit's also French, isn't it?' the clerk asked, and when I nodded, he smiled and produced Yigal's draft. Finally it was Monica's turn, and I introduced her as the daughter of the distinguished British diplomat Sir Charles Braham, at which the clerk bowed very low before handing her a draft for sixty pounds from a Canadian bank—an arrangement whereby the stiff British regulations against exportation of currency could be evaded. There was some hitch in the paper work, so we lounged in the lobby and idly watched as another group of seven Americans arrived to pick up their allowances from home.

They were the usual lot—long hair, ragged clothes, unwashed—and they came from all parts of the United States. The four girls must have been beautiful in the days when they bathed, and one was still special. She was a honey-blonde, well proportioned, vivacious and quite talkative. She was remarkable in that her general conversation consisted almost exclusively of 'Like wow!' and 'You know.' To pass the time she started talking with Gretchen: 'You're with Big Loomis. Like wow! You know, he's well, you know. Like wow, we heard of Big Loomis in Tangier and they said, you know, he's well, you know, like wow!' At this point Gretchen didn't know anything, but the newcomer went on to explain: 'You know, you can trust him, you know, on all sorts of things, you know, like wow!'

'Where you from?' Gretchen asked.

'Claire from Sacramento. My father's with the space center in Houston, like wow. You know men on the moon, like wow. I hope he sent me a check. Wow, I got exactly one American dollar, like wow, who's gonna eat on one American dollar, you know, like wow?'

As the girl rattled on, Gretchen unraveled the fact that her mother and older sister had refused to move to Houston when their father was assigned there, 'because you know who wants to live in Texas, like wow, I'm no cowboy and you know when a man makes love to me I don't want spurs up my tail, like wow.'

Gretchen noticed that the girl seemed to have a wide circle of friends, because any American who entered the bank to pick up money from home knew her, and spoke to her on familiar terms, as if he had been doing business with her. When one pair of especially unkempt girls, who may well have been stoned from too many green cookies, reminded her of an important date, Gretchen asked, 'Are you selling something?' and Claire threw back her head and laughed heartily. 'I read the, you know, the Tarot.'

'The what?'

'Like wow, the cards. I read the Tarot, you know.'

Vaguely Gretchen remembered something about a gypsy deck of playing cards with special designs. The Hanged Man, swinging insouciantly upside down from a holly tree, had been used in an advertisement she had once seen and it had inspired her to look into it further. The only other cards she remembered now were the Hierophant on his throne with the two cardinals kneeling in obeisance and the Hermit in gray robes carrying a lantern. As she recalled these three striking images, Claire kept talking: 'Like wow, I give maybe, you know, twenty readings a day, you know. If I charged money I'd be rich, like wow, twenty times a buck, like wow, that would keep you in hash for weeks.'

On the spur of the moment Claire threw herself prone on the lobby floor and took from her bag a pack of slightly oversized cards, shuffled them, asked Gretchen to cut, then laid ten of them out in diamond form, chanting as she did, 'This covers her. This crosses her. This is behind her. This crowns her.' When this was completed, she looked up at Gretchen with a beatific smile and said, 'Like wow, if I'm gonna read your Tarot, come down to my level,' and she tugged at Gretchen's miniskirt till the latter was sprawled on the floor beside her. Big Loomis and the others, familiar with Claire's skill in reading the Tarot, gathered about the two recumbent figures, and the reading began, but Claire had made only a few preliminary observations when a bank guard hurried up and said petulantly in French, 'I've warned you before, you cannot lie on the floor of this bank.' Claire beamed up at him, patted his shoe, and kept on reading her cards. Gretchen, not particularly interested in what Claire was saying, smiled at the guard and said in French, 'Officer, she'll only be a minute. Please excuse her,' but the guard remained where he was and kept tapping his toe. This annoyed Claire, who gently placed her hand on his shoe, smiled at him and said, 'Like wow, I need all the concentration, you know, I can get,' and she proceeded to ramble on about Gretchen's future, much of which the latter did not hear. Then suddenly Claire was saying, 'In the last election you backed Senator McCarthy and were beaten up by the police.' Gretchen stiffened, looked at Cato and Big Loomis, but they were staring down at Claire, who had now passed on to other inconsequentialities, but just before the impatient guard reached down to pick up the cards and clean his bank of this rabble, Claire said, 'You were in love with a man who makes music, rather excellent music, but that's ended.'

The guard tapped Gretchen on the shoulder and said, 'Your paper is ready,' and she replaced Monica at the window, where her regular check for four hundred dollars was waiting. When our group left the bank, eleven other young people were in line for their drafts from home.

As we walked back to the Djemaá, Claire from Sacramento stayed with us, and her conversation, under open skies, seemed even more bizarre than it had within the confines of a well-organized bank. I shall not try to indicate all the 'like wows' and 'you knows' she used; once when she told me of her family she must have uttered each phrase a hundred times. Her father was a space-age scientist, who, while working at Lockheed in Southern California, had married a girl from western Oklahoma who was in the secretarial pool. They had had two daughters, after which the mother took up astrology—'Like wow, she gives, you know, the best readings in all California. Wow!'—while the older daughter specialized in numerology—'Like wow, did you know that everything you do has a number, and every number a meaning?'—which left the Tarot to Claire.

Between them the three women pretty well blanketed the occult universe, and when Claire at age seventeen wanted to leave home and travel alone to Marrakech, her older sister gave a reading of this city and found that it would be perfectly safe for Claire to visit, but after Claire's departure the sister discovered that she had been using the old spelling, *Marrakesh,* and that if you substituted a *c* for the *s,* everything turned quite ominous. But then her mother read the stars for a blonde like Claire in Marrakesh with an *s,* and things were clearly favorable, so mother and older daughter drafted a letter of advice: 'When you are there you must always think of yourself in a city spelled with an *s,* and if you ever write the name down, be sure to spell it with an *s,* because then all confluences will be favorable.'

Claire explained that the women in her family had decided not to move to Houston because it gave off very bad vibrations in numbers, was poor in the Tarot and only fair in the stars, but what was more important, her mother was making a nice piece of change in California as an astrologist and she doubted that the people of Texas were as far advanced as those in California; that is, they weren't used to laying out real money to have their horoscopes read, whereas in California it was as much a part of a family budget as bread or milk.

Claire said she was staying at a place called Casino Royale, but she accompanied us to the Bordeaux, where she gave Cato a solid reading of his Tarot, in which she displayed considerable native cunning plus a shrewd sense of practical psychology. When she was immersed in the cards, she drew upon a whole new vocabulary, as if she existed on two levels—that of the flower people with their abbreviated speech and that of the occult with its arcane overtones. At times this girl with the bovine face, now eighteen years old, quite astonished her listeners; for example, she told Cato, 'If I told you the full meaning of this card the Hierophant, you would understand when I say that you have lived in a world torn apart by religious factionalism, and you've failed to bring the two halves of your sphere into harmony. I see the left lobe of your brain totally compressed as a result of this failure, and you will be prevented from achieving what is within your power until you bring the two halves into balance. But when you accomplish that, you will find untold energies unleashed.' At this point she looked at Cato as simple Claire of Sacramento and cried, 'Like wow! A new Thomas Aquinas.'

'Where did you learn about Thomas Aquinas?' Gretchen asked.

'Like wow, everybody knows the greatest, you know, the father of the church. Like wow, could you consider yourself educated if you'd never heard, you know, of Thomas Aquinas?'

I was constantly astonished by the reliance these young people placed on the occult. A group of serious students would lead a rebellion against the antiquated methods of a university, and one of their first demands would be that the updated curriculum initiate courses in astrology. I had often sat in gatherings of otherwise intelligent students who had worked hard to make their society a better place but who fell apart when coming under the influence of some guru who had a cursory acquaintance with the Bollingen edition of the *I-Ching*. In India I met one California girl who was convinced that if only she could determine the exact sequence in which the various chapters of the Pentateuch had been written, she would have at her command the secrets of the universe, and I remember with amusement the Ph.D. in philosophy from the University of Chicago who refused to leave Marrakech for his new job in Massachusetts until his readings in the *I-Ching* were favorable.

It was because of this frightening rebellion against intelligence that I learned so much from Claire, for she represented the assault against the smug self-satisfaction of science. If scientists could control space ships 186,000 miles distant, it became imperative to prove that they could not control the inner space ships of the human mind. In an age when science dominated all universities, these young people found it necessary to proclaim their faith in the least scientific of human endeavors: astrology, the Tarot, witchcraft, numerology and palmistry.

I once calculated that of the roughly three hundred young people I had met in Marrakech, all but a few believed in astrology and at least two hundred and seventy were convinced that flying saucers were arriving from outer space. They believed not on the basis of recurrent reports from our southern states of people who had actually made trips in the saucers, but because such belief infuriated their parents and confounded their professors.

As Claire said, 'Like wow, my father is unbelievable. He's a scientist but he has the vision of a mole. Like wow, he doesn't believe in astrology, or the Tarot, or the *I-Ching*, or practically nothing. The only thing he's, you know, good for is sending me my monthly check.'

After she finished her reading of Cato's Tarot she announced that she had decided to move her gear from the Casino Royale to the Bordeaux, and her reasoning was interesting: 'Like wow, on his floor Big Loomis attracts all the kooks in Marrakech, and if you lived up there you'd see the craziest, and you'd find the answers to everything.' When Big Loomis came klop-klopping into the hotel, she asked him, 'Like wow, could I move into one of your rooms? Like wow, it would be the greatest.' He nodded benignly and klomped upstairs. 'Besides,' she added as she prepared to leave for her gear, 'like wow, he has the best supply of grass in Marrakech.'

The others were busy, so I walked with her through the alleys, which were now more familiar to her than the streets of Sacramento, and after many turns into tight little passageways and with many greetings to tradesmen who had come to know her blond hair, she brought me at last to a dead end, and I saw a sign scrawled on a once-white wall: *Casino Royale*. 'Home,' she said.

The Casino, named by some hopeful Arab in the days of French occupation, was a one-story, mud-walled affair with a central courtyard around which were ranged sixteen of the smallest cubicles I had ever seen offered for rent. Not one had a window, so doors had to be left open, and as I stood in the court, almost overcome by the stench from the one inoperative latrine, I could look in upon any of the sixteen rooms, each of which contained up to six sleeping or dozing forms, not in beds—for the Casino Royale contained not one stick of furniture of any kind, neither bed, nor chair, nor table—but in sleeping bags or, in some cases, on wafer-thin blankets spread directly on the earth. This was Marrakech at its worst, a sleeping area renting at forty American cents a night, supervised by a miserable one-eyed Arab whose sole responsibility was to collect money, if he could, and keep the foul bathroom functioning, if he could. He performed his two tasks with equal incompetence.

Claire went directly to her cubicle, which she shared with four young men she had met in the Djemaá, and when they heard she was leaving they showed much apprehension, for like most American girls in Marrakech, she was supporting the men, since it was easier for a girl to get money from home than for a man. She told them not to worry, that she would look out for them for the rest of this month, after which they would probably be leaving anyway. 'But we have nothing to eat,' one of the boys complained, so she gave him half the money her father had sent her that morning. They thought that would enable them to get by. At this point she introduced them: Harold from Detroit; Cliff from New Mexico; Max from Portland, Maine; Bucky from Philadelphia. I spoke with the boys briefly and found that all had been to college for one or two years, had dropped out, might return at some future date. I didn't ask, but I judged that none had had a bath during the last three or four months, and the only luggage I could see was four sleeping bags. They probably had toothbrushes and passports, but I doubted that they had razors or soap. There was, of course, a communal bag of marijuana and a newspaper cornucopia of green cookies.

When word of Claire's departure drifted through the other cubicles, their occupants streamed out to bid her goodbye, and there was a show of real affection for this good-spirited, convivial girl with the limited vocabulary, but I noticed that from the room next to hers no one appeared. I peeked in and saw six young people, boys and girls, lying on their sleeping bags completely unconscious, as if dead. For a moment I was frightened, thinking that some disaster had happened with poisoned heroin, but Claire, noting my apprehension, looked in the room, kicked one of the girls, got a groan in reply, and assured me, 'Nothing wrong here. They're in good shape.' I must have betrayed surprise at this evaluation, for she added, 'Well, last night they did want to see how strong the cookies, you know, were—and, you know, like wow, they each ate two and went all numb. But you can see for yourself that they're all right now. Another ten hours and they'll start to move.'

As Claire went about saying her farewells, I was left with the six immobile bodies and knelt to tap the shoulder of one of the girls. Slowly her eyelids opened, but only the whites were visible. She groaned, rolled over and returned to total unconsciousness. One of the boys—Claire told me later he was an honor student from the University of Michigan—seemed to be slowly working off the effects of his two cookies, but when he tried to raise himself on one arm, he collapsed and again fell into his deep sleep.

I thought, as I surveyed this filthy room with its extraordinary freight, that these busted students represented a significant portion of the new world that was evolving. They stood for that legion of lost young souls in Paris and London and Tokyo and Berlin who had rejected their societies. It was they who populated the communes in the hills above Taos, the colonies in Nepal and the caves of Crete. They were a new breed, most difficult to understand, and as I looked at this selection I thought of the homes from which they had come. They must have been little different from the home that I had left when young; their parents surely had the same hopes for them that mine had had for me. Each of these sleeping six had probably gone to college and had busted out, forfeiting the tuition his parents had provided, and I wondered what those parents would have felt had they been able to stand where I was standing. This was the new part of the world, and the reverberations it was arousing would echo for many decades.

Then I visualized that familiar other part, those millions of young people throughout the United States and all nations who had entered college on the same terms as these six but who had found it possible to accommodate themselves to traditional demands, and I knew that the future work of society—the factories, the hospitals, the art museums the city councils—would be accomplished by those who were back home learning and working in the way most young people have done throughout history. The drop-outs of California and derelicts of Marrakech were spectacular; the stable young people working at their education were reassuring. It was inspiriting to remember that Harvard and Michigan and Tulane were producing just as many well trained graduates as ever, and that by and large it would be these students who would ensure the continuance of our society. Young men who had to learn calculus were learning it; girls who required chemistry were mastering it.

But then I had the nagging suspicion that the spiritual leadership of the society—whose physical continuance was assured by the standard students who stayed on the job—would probably be provided by those more adventurous ones who had picked up a vital part of their education in such unlikely dormitories as the Casino Royale in Marrakech or the pads in Greenwich Village. I thought of St. Paul, who gave the Christian church its greatest impetus; he came not from the conservative yeshiva but from the sinks and alleys of his day. The singers who would best express the spirit of this age would come not from Harvard or Stanford or Tulane, but from less-structured centers of learning like Pamplona or Copenhagen or Conakry, for the true education of a probing mind occurs unexpectedly and in surroundings that could have been neither anticipated nor provided.

I thought that perhaps the most creative mix for a society would be nine parts solid worker from institutions like Massachusetts Institute of Technology to one part poet from Marrakech, but in spite of the fact that I myself had been trained to be one of the solid workers, which meant that all my sympathies lay with that group, I would not surrender the poet. The problem was to find him.

Standing in this mud-floored cubicle, with the stench of the latrine filling my nostrils and six unconscious scholars at my feet, I judged that of the young people then occupying the Casino, a good ninety per cent were already ruined for creative work. Of these doomed ones, a handful would escalate to heroin and become totally incompetent. Others would be content to move lazily from one marijuana session to the next, never completely incapacitated but never fully in control of their capacities. Some would acquire sex habits which they could not accommodate, and I would see them a decade from now haunting the Torremolinos bars or living in Algarve with some rich widow from London. And there would be others among the lost ninety per cent who would be stained by a terrible disease from which there was no recovery—memory—and these would repeat endlessly to the irritation of their friends, 'You should have been with us that year in Marrakech.' They would recall it as the high-water mark of their lives.

That left a group of about ten per cent from which would rise the survivors, the one or two who would come to see the world whole, who would comprehend life as a terrifying reality, a combination of accomplishment and failure, and who might provide some degree of spiritual guidance to the world. The education of such leaders is never easy, nor is it cheap or safe. No man with a precious son would educate him in the baleful way that Saul was educated, on the dicey chance that as an adult he might mature into St. Paul; no logical planner would require a crocodile to hatch a hundred eggs a hundred yards from water in hopes that one new-born reptile might make it to the river before hyenas and storks devoured him as they had his ninety-nine brothers and sisters, but that is the way nature has ordained it. The system is prodigal and tragic, but it functions.

As I looked at the disheveled crowd saying farewell to Claire and her Tarot cards, I would not have wanted to gamble that even one of that unkempt mob would ever produce anything, for apparently they were among the doomed; but I also knew that if I were given the job of finding the charismatic leader who could speak to the coming generation, I would stand a much better chance of finding him not in the antiseptic Mamounia where I slept, but here in the Casino Royale where they slept.

However, no sooner had I thought this than I realized that I was using the word *leader* in two senses. From the hard-working young people at home, who were completing their education in traditional fashion, would come constructive leaders like Aristotle, Pericles, Maimonides, Martin Luther, Thomas Jefferson and Winston Churchill, while from the Marrakech gang would rise meteoric figures like Saint Paul and Augustine, who had confessed to living in similar conditions, Byron and Dostoievsky, who had absorbed equivalent experiences, and Josef Stalin and Adolf Hitler, who had been nurtured on the same kind of confused political thinking. I suspected that for all centuries to come the world would continue to produce and follow this same kind of dualism in its leadership and that history would be the record of interaction between the two worlds of Michigan and Marrakech.

As I carried Claire's malodorous bedroll out of the Casino, she clutched my arm and said, 'Like wow, this place, you know, I can never forget it. Even the smell. The long discussions we had.'

But when we reached the Bordeaux we found excitement of a different kind, for everyone seemed to be crowding the balconies. 'What's happening?' I asked, and one of the Wellesley girls pointed to the third floor toward Monica's room. I dropped Claire's bedroll and started running up the stairs, but before I got very far, I saw Monica in her doorway, watching as Big Loomis and Cato carried an object from another room.

'What is it?' I asked.

'That skinny kid from Mississippi,' a girl whispered.

'What about him?'

'Stiff.'

Big Loomis and Cato had moved to the head of the stairs. As they carried their rigid bundle down, the balconies grew silent. Scores of young men and women watched the procession, and not until it had passed me in solemn quiet did the second Wellesley girl whisper, 'We went into his room . . . to give him some food. He was real stoned. We shook him but he didn't respond . . . not even in the unconscious way he usually did. We got scared and called Big Loomis and he came down. We said, "Hadn't we better call a doctor?" and he said, "Why?" Then we knew he was dead.'

There was now a commotion in the courtyard. It was Jemail rushing in to defend himself: 'Not my fault, not my fault!'

'Get out of here, you miserable son-of-a-bitch,' Loomis growled. 'You brought him heroin this morning. The girls saw you.'

'He always buy cheapest stuff. Never pay for safe stuff. So he catch o-d. Not my fault.'

'Why don't you get the hell out of here?' Cato asked, taking one hand from the corpse and pushing Jemail in the face.

The little Arab drew back and shouted venemously, 'Goddamn nigger! Don't touch me! Your girl up there, she not your girl much longer, goddamn nigger!'

We all turned and looked up to the third floor, where Monica was standing. Realizing that Jemail was speaking of her, she put the back of her left hand to her lips and retreated into the shadows. Cato, aware that she had been hurt by what Jemail had cried, tried to strike the boy, but Jemail easily evaded him, shouting, 'Stinkin' nigger, you ain't got white girl much longer. I know.'

The pallbearers edged the corpse out the door, for Big Loomis had learned from involvement in earlier heroin deaths that it was best to carry the dead to the police station, where paper work was easier to complete, and as the impromptu cortege disappeared,

Claire, in a hushed voice, delivered the funeral oration: 'Like wow, that one is stoned, you know, for keeps!'

————— • • • —————

After the funeral was over, the Bordeaux echoed to happier sounds, for Clive flew into town on one of his periodic tours, his purple carpetbag crammed with new releases. As in Pamplona, his most popular disk was one he had written, 'Koutoubia,' consisting of two contrasting parts, a verse built around an oriental wail and a driving chorus which pictured young people cavorting across the Djemaá:

> Koutoubia, Koutoubia!
> Finger of Allah, pointing to Marrakech.
> Koutoubia, Koutoubia!
> Symbol of my desire.
>
> In Djemaá and in the souks
>   I find a world apart.
> Beatniks, flower boys and kooks,
> Weirdos, singing girls and spooks.
> Squares prefer to call them gooks . . .
>   I take them to my heart.

The song captured the lyric quality of Marrakech, while at the same time, in its broken and naïve rhythms, depicting the darker side of the city:

> In Djemaá snake-charmers tame the serpents
>   While the souls of men stay free,
> Inhabiting the edges of my mind
>   In smoke-dreams that become reality.

Listening to the childish sentiment of the song, I doubted that the poetry of this generation was much better than the sickly-sweet junk of my youth. Once I heard Clive play five successive songs, each of which happened to feature the word *reality*, partly because it contained four crisp syllables and an easy rhyme, but mostly because its philosophical concept was a teasing one: 'Our generation had found reality.' The misty smoke-dreams so often alluded to in the new songs had little to do with reality; they referred specifically to marijuana and hashish, and this constant indoctrination explained in part why so many young people wanted to try the two experiences.

In spite of these lugubrious reflections I found that I liked Clive's new song and I asked him to airmail a copy to Lieutenant Costa Silva at Vila Gonçalo, certain that he and Captain Teixeira would enjoy it. In fact, I was somewhat embarrassed to find that the heavy beat of Clive's new records made me somewhat nostalgic for the ones I had grown to know in Torremolinos. These sounds were endemic to the age and appropriate to the young people who lived in it; so I lay back on Inger's bed and allowed the heavy beat to reverberate against my stomach, thinking that if it had such an effect on me, how much more powerful its effect must be on young people. The tentative understanding I had glimpsed that evening in Brookline when Gretchen first sang ballads for me was now enlarged many times, and I knew without doubt that the music was revolutionary; the lyrics, when comprehensible, were intended to destroy the old order of morality and family life; the hammering beat was a bugle call to rebellion against established norms.

Clive brought us sad news regarding one consequence of the rebellion. 'Two of our finest record companies in London decided last month to quit issuing classical disks. No market for them. How pitiful! I'd have known nothing about music if I hadn't been weaned on Mozart. What will the following generations do for understanding if they don't have Beethoven?'

But when I asked if this demise had not been caused by the kind of music he wrote, he had a firm reply. 'Each generation must defend its own values. If your group requires classical music and patriotism and the family, defend them. It's your job to see that your values survive. Our job is to see that our type of music goes forward . . . our style of life.'

About midnight Joe and Gretchen walked in and Clive languidly moved toward her as if to resume their love affair, but with the mysterious power of communication that young people have, Joe interposed himself between them in such a way that Clive had to know that a change had occurred. To verify his interpretation, he tried twice more to sit with Gretchen, but Joe stayed in command and he retreated. Then, with the good grace that characterized all he did, he said, 'Why don't we hear some songs from Gretchen,' and several of the gang went for their guitars and soon we had four singers who were able to join with Gretchen when she called out the Child numbers, but the surprise of the night, for me, was a song which did not come from Child. Gretchen announced it quietly between puffs on a passing cigarette: 'Moorman and I are going to try something that ought to have two good voices. We haven't practiced much and crave your indulgence.' She struck a few chords, whereupon the honor student from the University of Michigan, whom I had last seen unconscious on the floor of the Casino Royale, cleared his throat and began strumming his guitar. 'It's called "Greenland Whale Fisheries,"' Gretchen said, and I wondered anew why the songs they liked best bore such strange titles. But when the pair began singing in a gently blended duet, I as well as the others in the room were caught up in its beauty.

> 'O Greenland is a dreadful place,
> It's a land that's seldom green,
> Where there's ice and snow
> And the whale fishes blow,
> And daylight seldom seen, brave boys, seldom seen.'

Then came a passage that might have been fashioned from leaping whale spume, or the shadows cast by a fleeting sun in northern latitudes, an authentic cry of women whose men followed the sea. When it ended we sat in silence:

> 'No more, no more Greenland for you, brave boys!
> No more, no more Greenland for you.'

When Gretchen repeated these words, she directed them to Clive, and he smiled. Then as a gesture of deference to her he suggested, 'How about Child 173?' and the others applauded, so after a few preliminary strummings on her guitar and a nodded invitation to the others to join her, either in the playing or the singing, she led with her delicate clear voice in the ballad of the four Marys, and when she came to the much-cherished verses in which the doomed serving lady reviews her tragic life, the two other girls joined in the words, and it seemed they were singing a lament for many of their generation, one verse in particular being especially appropriate for the audience in this city:

'O little did my mother think,
  The day she cradled me,
What lands I was to travel through,
What death I was to dee.'

The singing continued for some time, after which the crowd was eager to hear Clive's new records again, and this time when he played 'Koutoubia' they joined in the chorus, improvising the words they had not yet mastered. At one point Big Loomis filled the doorway, keeping time with his shaggy head, and later we could hear him plodding up the long flights of stairs. About four in the morning the singing ended, and Clive, who would sleep on the floor at Inger's, went to the door of the room and watched as Joe led Gretchen upstairs to their quarters and closed the door behind them. He then looked at me and shrugged his shoulders, and I thought how casually these young people handled their love affairs. On succeeding nights he played music for us, always insisting that Gretchen sing, and after a while he quietly drifted north to Tangier and from there to Torremolinos, where they were waiting for him at the Alamo.

———•—•—•———

Often as I walked back to my hotel at night I reflected on the discussions I had heard in Inger's and I was amazed at how vocal the young people were in stating their opinions and how little they read to support them. This was a generation without books. Of course, everyone had handled volumes by Herbert Marcuse and Frantz Fanon, but I found no one who had actually read even the more easily understood works like *Essay on Liberation* or *Toward the African Revolution* or *The Wretched of the Earth*. It was also true that most of the travelers had read newspaper reports of Marshall McLuhan's theories, and hardly a day passed but someone would proclaim, 'After all, the medium is the massage,' but I met no one who had read the book of which this taut summary was the title or who knew what it meant.

There was always a dog-eared copy of the *I-Ching* somewhere in the hotel, and many had dipped into it, but no one had read it, not even Claire from Sacramento. The strong books of the age were unknown to this group, and I often wondered how they had got as far along in college as they had. On the other hand, their verbal knowledge was considerable and they could expatiate on almost any topic. Six pronouncements I noted one night were typical of the conclusions reached every night:

'We have entered what Walter Lippmann terms the New Dark Age.'

'Before 1976 an armed showdown between races will be inevitable in American cities.'

'The military-industrial complex rules our nation and dictates a continuance of the Vietnam war.'

'A permanent unemployment cadre of seven million must be anticipated.'

'By the year 2000 we will have seven billion people on earth.'

'Universities are prisoners of the Establishment.'

But in spite of these statements, I found that most Americans overseas were hard-line conservatives; of the many in Marrakech, the majority had supported the Republican party in 1968 and would do so again in 1972. I took the trouble to check the six young people I had seen unconscious on the floor of the Casino Royale; Claire took me back one morning, and I found that four were solid Republicans, one was a neo-Nazi, and Moorman, the honor student from Michigan who sang ballads with Gretchen, said, 'I don't know what I am.'

I found more than a few supporters of George Wallace, and Constitutionalists, and crypto-fascists, and backers of other ill-defined movements. The basic ideas of the John Birch Society were often voiced, but I met no one who admitted membership.

Most older people who visited Marrakech were surprised to find that among the young Americans, there were practically no old-style American liberals. This was true for obvious reasons. To get as far as Marrakech required real money, so that those who made it had to come from well-to-do families of a conservative bent, and throughout the world children tend to follow the political attitudes of their fathers. A boy of nineteen might rebel against Harvard University, country-club weekends and the dress of his father, and run away to Marrakech to prove it, but his fundamental political and social attitudes would continue to be those his father had taught him at age eleven. In my work I constantly met conservative adult Americans who, when they saw the young people with long hair and beards, expected them to be revolutionaries; they were pleasantly gratified to find that the young people were as reactionary as they were.

Harvey Holt exemplified this response. When he first met the gang at Pamplona he was positive they must be revolutionaries, but after several long discussions involving politics, he told me, 'You know, apart from Vietnam and this nonsense about brotherhood between the races, these kids are pretty solid.' Later he said, 'You could be misled if you listened to their songs. You'd think they were going out to burn down New York. But when you talk to them about economics and voting, you find they're just as conservative as you or me . . . but they do it in their own way.' I asked him how he thought I voted, and he said, 'Oh, you sympathize a lot with the young people, but I'm sure that in a pinch you can be trusted.'

'To vote Republican?'

'How else can a sensible man vote?' he asked.

I was constantly appalled also by the poverty of language exhibited by many of the young people, and these from our better colleges. Claire, as I have said, sometimes talked for a whole hour saying little but 'you know' and 'like wow,' but this had a certain cute illiteracy. More intolerable was the girl from Ohio who said at least once every paragraph, 'You better believe it.' Whenever one of the boys from the south agreed with one of my opinions, he said, 'You ain't just whistlin' "Dixie," bub.' A college girl from Missouri introduced every statement with: 'I just want you to know,' while a young man from Brooklyn related everything to André Gide—he seemed quite incapable of any other comparison.

Two aspects of the intellectual life of these young Americans surprised me. The first was politics. Not one person I knew ever mentioned the name Richard Nixon; they rejected Lyndon Johnson and ridiculed Hubert Humphrey, charging these men with having betrayed youth, but Nixon they dismissed. They would have voted for him, had they bothered to vote, and would vote for him in 1972, if they happened to be registered, but he played no role in their lives. A whole segment of American history was simply expunged by these people; they had opted out with a vengeance.

I say that they would vote Republican in 1972, if they voted, and by this I mean that of all the young Americans I met over the age of twenty-one, not one had ever bothered to vote, and it seemed unlikely to me that any would do so much before the age of thirty-two or thirty-three. To hear them talk, you would think they were battering down the barricades of the Establishment, and some few I suppose would have been willing to try, but they were not willing to vote; in fact, I met none who were even registered.

In spite of this seeming indifference, there were those few I reflected upon that morning when I stood in the Casino Royale amid the stenches and the fallen forms, the few who were painfully carving out an understanding of their world, and their place in it. Because they came from families with income and advantage, they tended to be Republican, and when they settled down, they were going to be good Republicans. Some, like Gretchen, had worked for Senator Eugene McCarthy, but not because he was a Democrat; they would quickly return to creative Republicanism and the nation would profit from the forging process they had gone through.

But when I have said this about politics, I have still not touched upon the mighty chasm that separated them from me: they honestly believed that their generation lived under the threat of the hydrogen bomb and that consequently their lives would be different from what mine had been. They were convinced that no man my age could comprehend what the bomb meant to them, and even when I pointed out that a man of sixty-one like me had been forced to spend nearly half his adult life under the shadow of nuclear bombs and had adjusted to it, they cried, 'Ah, there it is! You'd enjoyed about half your life before the bomb fell. We haven't.' It seemed there could be no bridge of understanding on this point, and after several futile attempts to build one, I concluded that on this topic we could not talk together meaningfully.

The second surprising aspect was religion. It was rarely mentioned. Occasionally Cato referred to his hatred of what Christianity had done to the Negro, but he was speaking sociologically; Yigal sometimes spoke of the problems faced by the Jews in

Israel, but only their political problems, never their theological. I would go for a month without hearing God mentioned, not even as a curse word. With this generation He had become an expletive, used primarily by girls, as when Monica or Britta cried, 'My God, look!' He was used to draw attention to camels or especially beautiful mosques, but His ancient relationship to eschatology or morality was not referred to. I think if some college girl from our midwest, sitting on the bed at Inger's, had asked, 'Do you believe in God?' the crowd would have passed out stone-cold, as if hit by an extra strong cookie. About half the young people, especially those from Australia and Canada, were Catholic, but they were as indifferent as the others.

There was talk of morality, but only in the form of ethical conduct; the old problems of sexual morality that had plagued us so much when I was young no longer existed. If someone in the night sessions happened to tell a friend that 'Margot moved in with Jack from Glasgow,' it was descriptive and not pejorative. In fact, the news was disseminated principally so that others might know where to find Margot without wasting a trip to the third floor.

I found myself becoming more and more irritated by the casual assumptions of these young people concerning their easy matings and unmatings. Margot would move her gear down to Jack's room, and he would accept it and her as if no obligations were involved; she did not have to pass muster with his mother, and he did not have to support her. They seemed unaware that over a period of ten thousand years, mankind had evolved other patterns of mating which in all societies and all climates had more or less worked. I found it presumptuous that they should think they had discovered an escape from the involvements that human beings had traditionally engaged in, but apparently they had, for the ebb and flow of matings throughout the various rooms of the Bordeaux were as difficult to keep track of as those in Pamplona had been.

I was amused at my own conservatism on this matter and once or twice tried to analyze my reactions. I supposed I was a lot like the fundamentalist in Texas who railed, 'I am agin' the new morality for three reasons. It's contrary to the law of nature. It's destructive of the family. And I ain't gettin' none of it.' What complicated my

reasoning was the fact that I in no way resented Gretchen's successive affairs with Clive and Joe, nor Britta's with Joe and Holt, but
I did object to Monica's involvement with Cato, when she was only
seventeen. At first it was easy to rationalize this as a result of an
intuitive anti-Negro prejudice, and I so dismissed it; but beginning
in Moçambique and now in Marrakech, it was becoming evident
to me that I had a special interest in this frail girl. Part of my feeling stemmed naturally from my long association with her family;
I had often referred to her as my daughter and in a sense she was.
But in addition, there was the inescapable attraction she held for
me. I never, so far as I could judge myself, loved her in the traditional way; I would have been embarrassed had there been any
physical relationship between us, but I did love her. She had become a symbol of the unfolding of youth, its headstrong will, its
perpetual skirting of the edge of doom. Even her addiction to
heroin was part of her allure, for in this she represented the temptation of her age and showed it in high relief. She was a remarkable
girl, uneducated in the formalities, profoundly learned in the es-
sentials. If I could have summed up my feeling about her in Marrakech, it would have been: 'I wish her well.'

I wished her very well, and when I saw her lying inert from
green cookies or falsely exalted from heroin, it was as if my own
daughter were lying there, or some girl I had loved forty years
earlier.

———•◆•———

My working days were occupied by the three government
engineers from Casablanca, capable men who understood Morocco's
economic needs. They interposed no objections to plans I had for a
big new hotel in Marrakech, supported by a chain of farms throughout the lower slopes of the Atlas to ensure a constant food supply,
but they did have a plan of their own which they wanted World
Mutual to finance, and from the first moment they proposed it I
was excited about the possibilities.

To the north of Marrakech, but so close to the walls of the city
that one could drive there in a few minutes, lay one of the gems of

Africa, a vast palm-tree plantation that covered thousands of acres. It had accounted for the wealth that had built the walls of Marrakech.

Some years ago someone in the government had had a clever idea, and I often wondered how he had sold it to his superiors, for basically it was preposterous. A single-track macadam road had been built, running in great meanders through the grove, going nowhere and serving no visible purpose except to carry visitors through the palm plantation. Thousands who had come to Marrakech, attracted by the Djemaá and the mountains, would find that their most vivid memories were of the red walls and the palm trees, and any who had an appreciation of natural poetry would discover to their surprise that it was the palm trees which dominated.

When I found that Gretchen and her companions had not visited the grove, I proposed a way by which we could combine two obligations into one, so I invited the troupe to breakfast at my hotel and had the three engineers join us. The latter were delighted, since they wanted to talk with an American Negro and to see what our notorious hippies looked like at close quarters. I reserved a corner of the dining room; and when the three Moroccans arrived, I handed them slips of paper I had prepared, telling them who the Americans were. I indicated that Britta was Norwegian and Monica English, but I listed Bruce as an American, for if it became known that an Israeli national—and a soldier to boot—was in Morocco, he might find himself in trouble.

Holt and Britta were first to join us, and she was stunning in blue miniskirt and yellow band through her hair. The engineers were much taken with her, and she spoke with such frankness and in such an attractive accent that they hammered her with questions about her homeland, but I noticed that even though they were impressed with her as a beautiful girl, this did not prevent them from posing practical questions, such as: 'Do you think many Norwegians would fly to Moroccan cities . . . along our Mediterranean or Atlantic . . . for vacations?'

After breakfast half the crowd piled into the yellow pop-top, the other half into a long black limousine driven by the engineers, and we started our tour of the palm plantation. Monica, Cato and I rode in the black car with the engineers, who peppered Cato with ques-

tions: Were American Negroes serious about Islam? Would they
enlist in a jihad against the Jews? Would they ever have enough
political power to force the American government away from its
pro-Israel position? If the Jews were driven out of American life,
would the Negroes take their place as financial leaders? Would the
Negroes one day own the *New York Times* and what changes
would they make in its policies?

We were barely through Cato's first tentative replies when we
reached the entrance to the palm drive, where our lead car stopped
to allow one of the engineers to move back into the other car and
serve as guide. The interrogation of Cato ended, but a conversation
of even more interest began. The Yale graduate, oldest and most
intelligent of the engineers, said rhapsodically, 'Once we have
settled the Israel question, the Arab nations will enter a period of
great flowering. All things will be possible to us. We shall make
the desert flower like a garden, our ships will sail to all the seas. We
will take Islam to all continents. Poets will flourish as of old, and
there will be a new Damascus in every nation, a center leading the
world in science and art. In Morocco it will probably be Fez.
Learned men from all over the world will have to travel to Fez to
acquire the understanding they need for modern life. Once again
our philosophers will lead the universe. All will be disclosed to
them.'

He continued expounding his vision of the future, which included a peaceful Muslim hegemony in Africa, the expansion of
Islam throughout Russia-in-Asia, and the quick union of all Arab
states bordering the Mediterranean. 'As soon as the Israel question
is settled, we will have enduring peace and harmony among our
nations,' he assured Cato, with whom he was most concerned. 'And
when we are a united and powerful people we will be able to give
you much aid in your struggles in America.' He spoke thus for the
hour we traveled among the palm trees, and he came back repeatedly to the poetry that would flourish in those happy days and
the brilliance of the philosophy, but never once did he allude to
social justice, or the distribution of oil revenues, or the establishment of a civil service that could be trusted. Cato, so far as I could
judge from his questions, did not notice these omissions.

Deep in the palm plantation, our little caravan halted, and as we stood among the bending trees, the engineers held an impromptu seminar in which they explained their plans for a complex of hotels, swimming pools, belvederes and golf courses set within the majestic grove: 'It will be an oasis of the spirit, surrounded in all directions by impenetrable forests of palm trees. On one side you will see the High Atlas . . . well, imagine it for yourselves. As soon as we solve the Israel problem we shall start building.'

'Is Israel a problem for you?' Yigal asked quietly.

'Oh, yes! That nasty little thorn is distant . . . but it remains in our flesh and festers.'

'I can't see what Morocco has to fear from Israel.'

'Fear? We don't fear her. In the next battle we shall send a hundred thousand armed men to the army which will gather to annihilate her. Then we can get on with our plans.'

'Did you send any men the last time?' Yigal asked.

'Oh, yes! We assembled eighty thousand . . . maybe more.'

'Did they reach Israel?'

'No. Gamal Nasser and King Hussein granted the Jews a truce before our men could join the fighting. But next time . . .'

'I still don't understand what business it is of Morocco's,' Yigal persisted, and one of the engineers said sharply, 'You sound as if you favored Israel,' and Yigal said quietly, 'As of now I don't know,' and Britta said something irrelevant, and the crowd laughed.

The oldest engineer turned to Holt and asked, 'Well, would it make a good vacation spot?' and Harvey said, 'The noisier the world gets, the more we'll appreciate escapes like this,' and the engineer said, 'That's exactly our vision. Now if Mr. Fairbanks will put up the money and if we can force Israel to leave us alone, we can go ahead with a project that will be fantastic. I see beautiful pools . . . not the ordinary swimming pools . . . with reflections of palm trees . . . and great music . . . Beethoven, Wagner . . .' His narcotic dreams mesmerized the group, and Monica expressed our general approval when she cried, 'Wow!'

On the way back to town the Yale graduate said, 'This afternoon there's something at the big field west of your hotel that you must see,' and since we had had big breakfasts, we skipped lunch and drove directly to an immense drill field in the center of the city, where Berber tribesmen on handsome Arab horses and armed with mountain rifles from the past century were engaging in a sport with which they had terrified the city dwellers of Marrakech for countless years.

Assembled in rows of forty or fifty, their steeds champing at the bit as if posing for Eugène Delacroix, their brightly colored robes flashing in the breeze, the Berbers would give a wild shriek, spur their horses, and come riding headlong down a field some three hundred yards long. Then, at some signal I could not detect, they would throw themselves forward, almost leaving their saddles, turn backward, and manipulating their rifles with their right arms, fire blasts into the air. Recovering their position, they would continue their charge right at us, fire again, and rein up with their foam-flecked horses a few inches from our faces.

They were terrifying, primitive, untamed by a century of French occupation, the scourge of the High Atlas, the devastation of the plains. No matter how brave a man might be, when those shrieking horsemen lunged at him over those last few yards of ground, with rifles crackling in the sun, he drew back.

The Yale graduate, thrilled by a sight he had first seen as a boy, grabbed Cato's shoulder and cried, 'I guess that will teach the Jews something, eh?' And his nostrils flared with excitement.

———•—•—•———

When we tried to figure out what had happened, we agreed that Yigal had started the conversation. We were listening to music in Inger's when he said, 'I'm amazed at the Arab's capacity for self-delusion. Did those engineers really believe that if they defeated Israel, some kind of benevolent peace would settle over their lands?'

Cato not only took objection to the question, but responded to it in an ugly manner: 'Look, Mr. Goldberg, when them Arabs and us blacks join forces on you, you gonna be ee-lim-eye-nated.'

'What the hell's hit you, Cato?'

'I seen the light, Mr. Goldberg. I seen what your people done been doin' to my people.'

'All we did was lead your battles for you . . . in every area.'

'Don't you condescend to me, white boy. Your people move into every goddamned ghetto I ever seen and bleed us white.' He laughed nervously at his inept metaphor, then added, 'And it's gonna stop, Mr. Goldberg, I'm tellin' you, it's gonna stop.'

'I don't like that name Mr. Goldberg,' Yigal said.

'Well, it's your name, and you gonna learn to like it when the crunch comes.'

'What do you mean, when the crunch comes?'

'Ask them. They know.'

Yigal was openly pained by Cato's line of reasoning and for some moments we could see he was trying to judge the best way to counter it. Then he said, 'Cato, your people have been in a losing position all your lives. Now, in your first moments of freedom, you choose a losing religion. Islam isn't going to save the Negroes. You know what I think? When Cassius Clay and all those others made the conspicuous move to Mecca, you experienced a surge of hope. The new religion. The new day. And what happened? Right after that your new-found champions challenged the Jews and got their blocks knocked off. You're suffering traumatic shock. And you'll go on suffering it till you shake yourselves awake.'

'Listen, Jew-boy,' Cato snapped, 'don't you try none of that psychology on me.'

Yigal looked at his opponent with compassion, then said, 'This morning when the engineer was spinning his poetic fancies, you enjoyed it, didn't you? His wild flights of rhetoric were exactly to your taste, weren't they? That was the wild way you talked with your street pals when you were together, wasn't it? Great flights of words?'

Cato, aware that Yigal had touched upon the fundamental bond that attracted the Arab and the Negro—their love of soaring rhetoric—grew angry and would probably have struck Yigal had not Monica entered the room at this time, looking very pale but extremely beautiful. She sought a place for herself between Cato and Yigal and patted each on the knee. 'It's good to see you two arguing again,' she said, unaware of how tense that argument had become. 'Cato tells me you've decided to opt for America,' she said to Yigal. 'I think it's a good idea.'

'Is that final?' Holt asked.

'I think so. America is a nation you can be proud of,' Yigal said.

'It has a hundred faults, but it tries. And, Cato, that trying is worth a great deal.'

'Goddammit, Jew-boy, don't patronize me!'

'I'm sorry,' Yigal apologized.

'You should be,' Cato growled, little disposed to accept the apology.

'Doesn't anybody have a smoke?' Monica asked, and as a large cigarette loaded with hash circulated, the tension eased and the talk turned to the palm grove and the charge of the Berber tribesmen.

'They're from another century,' Britta said. 'You do business here, Mr. Fairbanks. Don't you find it archaic?'

'I find every nation peculiar in its own way . . . therefore attractive in its own way.'

'But some you like better than others?' Britta persisted.

'If you want me to compare Morocco with Norway, I find nothing in your country as exciting as the Djemaá.'

'So you like the Djemaá?' she asked.

'One of my favorite spots in the world,' I confessed. 'Because when I'm here, I never think I'm in England or Norway. This is unique. I appreciate the reasons why Inger and Rolf come back every year.'

The Swedish couple bowed and Rolf said, 'When you're through work in Stockholm and fog is drifting in from the Baltic, it's most reassuring to know that in Marrakech the vaudeville is still playing the Djemaá.'

'You've made a song,' Britta said.

'It is a song,' Rolf replied. 'A song that keeps me going in the cold days.'

'And that's not a trivial contribution,' Yigal said with force. 'I like Marrakech. If only the Arabs would learn to govern themselves . . . to live with others.'

'They'll never live with the Jews,' Cato broke in.

'They must learn to,' Yigal said stubbornly.

'They'll push you into the sea,' Cato said. 'Just as we'll push you into the sea in America.'

'Are you insane?' Yigal asked.

'I can see the future,' Cato said, 'and your kind is doomed.'

'You're smoking hash,' Yigal said contemptuously, turning his back and starting to rise from the bed.

This dismissal infuriated Cato, and he reached across Monica and grabbed Yigal around the neck, throwing him down. With startling speed he then leaped from the bed and began pummeling Yigal, who was badly tangled on the floor. With swift blows Cato kept knocking the Jew back onto the floor, hurting him badly with fists to the head. Yigal struggled to get a footing, but whenever it seemed that he was about to succeed, Cato kicked his feet away and Yigal sprawled once more to the floor, where Cato kept hammering at him. Before any of us could stop the punishment, Cato drove a conclusive blow to Yigal's unprotected chin and knocked him out.

Suddenly, while Holt and Joe were trying to minister to the unconscious boy, Monica rose from the bed, stood precariously erect, and screamed at Cato, 'Don't you strike a white man, you filthy nigger. I've been ashamed of myself ever since you laid your hands on me, you monkey. Get away from me, nigger, nigger!'

When Cato went toward her, she struck at him, screaming, 'Take your filthy black hands off me. Get away, you goddamned nigger. You destroyed Africa. You destroyed my father. So get away, you savage beast!'

She retreated to a corner of the room and stood there, castigating herself for ever having lived with Cato. When Gretchen and Britta tried to quieten her, she thrust them away, shouting, 'He's your friend, not mine. Go kiss the nigger and make love to him. He's your type, not mine.'

Cato just stood there, dazed. At his feet he saw Yigal, still unconscious, with Holt and Joe trying to revive him and casting accusing glances. In the corner he saw Monica, looking as if she would kill him if he moved a step closer.

'Inger,' Rolf directed, calling upon his experience in the asylum, 'take Monica to her room. Mr. Fairbanks, give Yigal some of this ammonia.' Rolf gave Cato a bottle of orange drink and sat him on the bed. Inger started to lead Monica away, but the English girl fought her off, so Joe grabbed her in his arms and carried her roughly upstairs, but when he tried to throw her on the bed, she resumed her obscenities. She began tossing Cato's gear into the central well, shouting as she did so, 'No goddamned nigger will ever again put his hands on me—filthy animals!'

———•-•-•———

Next morning I was in the Hotel Mamounia, typing out my report to Geneva—I told them I liked the concept of a recreational hotel among the palm trees, provided water could be found for the various pools—when a soft knocking came at my door. It sounded like a girl's, and I wondered who could be wanting me at this early hour, but when I opened the door it was Jemail. 'Sssssssh!' he cautioned as he slipped into my room. 'Doorman not allow me in hotel.'

'What's up?' I asked suspiciously.

'Cato Jackson,' he said.

'What about him?'

'Terrace Café. Drunk maybe. Talking very loud about Bruce.' There was a long pause, during which the little criminal studied me carefully, after which he said slowly, 'Of course, I know Bruce an Israeli soldier.' When I caught my breath, he said, 'That first day you acted suspicious. I searched his baggage. Saw the two passports.' He waited for this to sink in, then said, 'But you know me. I never speak of such things. Maybe forty dollars.' Then, as if dropping the subject, he said briskly, 'Cato Jackson talking a lot. Somebody bound to hear.'

I looked down at my little blackmailer and said, 'And if Cato talks too much, then your chance to earn forty dollars . . .'

'Go *ppphhhttt!*' He shot his arm into the air like a rocket and added, 'But Yigal Zmora also go to jail . . . or maybe get shot . . . I think better we talk with Cato.'

He persuaded me to accompany him to the Djemaá, and we were leaving the hotel when the doorman spotted him and tried to grab him, but having anticipated the move, Jemail evaded him and stood at a safe distance, cursing in Arabic. The doorman bellowed back his own set of curses, listing what he was going to do if he ever caught Jemail, and in this barrage of noise and profanity we made our escape. Jemail hurried me across the Djemaá to the terraced café, where Cato was indeed drunk and was indeed talking in a loud voice. When he saw me he started to become abusive, stood up as if he wanted to slug me, then sort of fell apart and clutched my arms, crying, 'What can I do about Monica?'

I gave Jemail a few coins and sent him away. Then I said harshly, 'Cato, keep your mouth shut about Yigal.'

'Have I said too much?' he asked apologetically.

'Too damned much. That kid heard you blabbing, and now Yigal's in trouble.'

'I didn't mean to do that,' he protested. 'We had a fight, but I wouldn't . . .' There could be no doubt of his sincerity, and he returned to his earlier concern. 'What can we do about Monica?'

I sat him in a chair, ordered an orange drink, and listened to his rambling analysis of himself. He was sentimental over the benevolence of Mister Wister, angry over the Negro-Jewish confrontation, euphoric when he thought of Islam, bewildered over Monica's behavior. He was an appealing young man, that sunny morning in Marrakech, a confused human being, not a black robot reacting to stimuli: white girl, sex; Jew, resentment; older person, contempt; Christianity, abhorrence. He asked me, 'Do you think I could patch it up with Monica?' and I said, 'Why would you want to?'

'Because she's my woman and I want to help her.' He said this so simply, so much like any young man caught up in a perplexing love, that I wanted to assist him in winning her back, but I knew it was impossible, so I said, 'Cato, it's over and I think you knew that someday it would be over.'

He looked at me with narrowing eyes and said brusquely, 'And you're glad.'

'That's a silly statement.'

'Oh no!' he said. 'I've been on to you ever since Moçambique. You're in love with her, too. And you're jealous as hell of me.'

'Quit talking such crud.'

'I know. You'd just love to get me out of here so you could move in.'

'Cato, we see a girl in deep trouble. We both want to help her. Let's let it go at that.'

'No, we won't let it go at that. You're trying to edge me out so that you can move in.'

'Cato, she moved you out.'

Faced by this harsh reality, he sobered, and asked, almost humbly, 'What can I do?' and I said, 'You can suffer. Like every young man before you who has lost a beautiful girl. Join the human race, Cato. You're one of us.'

'What do you mean by that?'

'Just this. You arrogant young punks go around as if you'd discovered sex. You think that because you can slip into bed so easily with a beautiful girl that you can slip out just as easily when it's all over . . . without being touched by the experience. I got news for you, bub. You bleed exactly like the rest of us. Good men begin to grow up on the morning they find that some girl has thrown them over. Then, by God, they've got to face up to themselves. You're not the superman you visualized. Sex is not so simple as you thought. It's the terrible, mixed-up, complex thing it's always been.'

'What can I do?'

'Squirm, goddamn you. The way I did when I was twenty and lost a girl. The way young men have been doing for ten thousand years.'

Very quietly he said, 'But, Mr. Fairbanks, with me it's different. I'm black.'

'Bullshit! Yigal's Jewish. You read his letter from Detroit . . . about Britta. Don't you suppose he bled the other day when he found out she was hooked up with Holt? Clive is English. Don't you think he bled too when he discovered that Gretchen was now Joe's girl? Talk with Holt sometime about how his wife walked out. Join the brotherhood. You're mortal like the rest of us.'

'But when a black man is ridiculed by a white girl, everything's different,' he insisted.

'The relevant words are man and girl. All men, all girls. And whenever there's a savage rupture, we all bleed, Cato. We all bleed.'

'You sound as if you were pleased.'

'I am. You've been acting as if you were some sacred black god. You've really been a drip. I'm glad that life has chopped you down to size. You're much more likable.'

'But mostly it's because you love Monica, isn't it?'

'All right. We both love her. We both want to see her well again.'

'We'll have to get her off heroin. That's the big thing.'

'Have you quit?'

'After that night in Moçambique . . . I've quit.'

'Can Monica?'

'Not by herself. I've tried to help but I can't. Big Loomis is about the only man who could swing it. He understands these things.'

'We've got to talk to him—get him to try,' I said.

He extended his hand, and as we walked down the rickety stairs together, we saw the waiting Jemail, and I said, 'But right now we've got to protect Yigal.'

'From what?' he asked.

'From the damage you've done . . . from that little bastard over there. Jews are like Negroes. On all sides they have enemies.'

———•◆•———

I deemed it obligatory to warn Yigal that Jemail was onto his secret and would remain silent—he said—for forty dollars, but when we started to leave the Terrace to find Yigal, the canny little Arab was at our heels, having anticipated what I would want to do and determined that he participate to protect his financial interests. 'I go along,' he said softly, 'to be sure no one betrays your friend, Yigal Zmora.'

'How do I know that if I pay the forty dollars you will not betray him?'

'Could I stay in business a week . . . suppose word leaked out . . . I dishonest?' He smiled at me self-deprecatingly, but kept close behind us.

At the Bordeaux I did not enter, for it was essential that Cato and Yigal be alone to restore their friendship, so I said, 'Cato, go in and fetch Yigal,' and by a look I indicated that he was to alert the Jew to the trouble that threatened. A few minutes later they appeared, with Yigal nodding at me in such a way as to assure me that Cato had informed him of the blackmail. They shook hands and I set off with them to get the money.

To my surprise, when we were crossing the Djemaá, Yigal patted the little Arab on the shoulder and said, 'You're clever. How did you find out?'

'That first afternoon at the Terrace. When two grown people whisper . . . I listen.'

At the Mamounia, Jemail asked if we could slip in by a side door, since he did not wish to confront the doorman, and when we were in my room I asked if Yigal would fetch Holt, whereupon the four of us entered into serious negotiation. Jemail put his cards on the table, and I could almost visualize his shifting them about with his small, adept fingers. 'He's an Israeli soldier . . . could be shot.'

'He's also an American citizen,' I said, 'and he's decided to surrender his Israeli passport.'

'No matter. If our government knows . . . they shoot him.'

'Suppose we pay you the forty dollars,' Holt broke in. 'What guarantee would we have that you wouldn't go right out and talk?'

'I'm an Arab,' the boy said haughtily, 'a man of honor. Don't you think my government give me a reward . . . if I told them? Why didn't I? Because you people good to me. Because Mr. Fairbanks and I going to be partners . . . heroin business . . . Geneva. Our association a long-term deal. I got to treat him like a gentleman.'

The other two looked at me, but I stared straight ahead, whereupon Jemail made us this proposition: 'You give me forty dollars. I stay in this room under your guard twenty-four hours. In that time Yigal Zmora fly out of here and catch Air France plane Casablanca for Rome, where he catch El Al plane for Tel Aviv.'

'When he is safely out of the country, why couldn't we club you on the head and take back our money?' Holt asked.

'Because you also gentlemen. I got to trust you.'

There was a long silence, after which I said, 'Yigal, you better fly out of here on the early morning plane. If the Moroccan government finds out about your second passport, things could become sticky.'

'Is there a plane?'

Jemail broke in with the full schedule, so I went to the phone and asked if we could get a confirmed ticket to Rome. It was arranged, but when I proceeded to ask for a continuation to New York, Yigal put his hand over the phone and said, 'I've decided to go back to Israel.' This so surprised me that I terminated the phone call abruptly and turned to ask what had happened, only to find that Holt had leaped from his chair to grab him.

'What in hell did you just say?' Holt demanded.

'That I've made up my mind.'

'To give up your American citizenship?'

'Yes.'

Holt looked at me as if only I could explain what he was hearing, but I was as shocked as he, because nothing in recent weeks had indicated that Yigal was going to opt for Israel. In fact, all indications had pointed to the opposite. 'What happened?' I asked.

'So he is Israeli soldier?' Jemail asked smugly.

'You keep your goddamned mouth shut,' Holt snapped, pushing the little Arab into a chair. Then, as a precaution, he locked the doors and windows, slamming onto the table two twenty-dollar traveler's checks. 'When the plane takes off, I sign them,' he said. Then, turning to Yigal, he asked, 'Son, what's confused you?'

Yigal thought for a moment, then said, 'These last days have showed me so much. Cato and his attitudes. I suppose they're universal. The Jew really does bear a stigma. And that amazing exhibition yesterday. Those horsemen charging and firing their old rifles . . . as if it meant anything.'

'One good Israel machine gun,' Jemail broke in. 'Yat-tat-tat-tat-tat. There go the horsemen.'

Yigal turned to look at the Arab and said, 'That's what I mean. He sees so clearly. The engineers were so blind. Maybe his generation and mine can come to some kind of understanding.'

'Son, you can't fight everybody's battle,' Holt pleaded.

'But only the Jew fights the Jewish battle,' Yigal said. 'My place is . . .' I thought he was going to say that his place was with his people, but he ended his sentence, 'with those who trained me.'

'Israel can get along without you,' Holt argued. 'But America needs every good man we can produce. You've got to go back.'

'There's another thing that makes me wonder about America,' he said. 'Television.'

'Oh, for Christ's sake!' Holt exploded. 'That's like those damned-fool kids at Pamplona saying that the only good thing America ever produced was *King Kong*.'

'No, I mean it,' Yigal said. 'A stranger like me looks at America, and if he has any sense he sees much that's good, much that's bad. On the average the good wins out . . . by far. You really do some wonderful things in America. I used to laugh at my grandfather and his devotion to General Motors. But I found he was just as devoted to the Detroit Art Museum. And the man who had been under him was just as devoted to Case Institute. But when you're alone, trying to get everything in balance, you turn on the television, and you see that the people who really run America, the men who make the commercials, believe that all American men are dopes and all American women so stupid they can hardly count to seven. And the suspicion grows that these wise men writing the advertisements know better than you do. They even know how to sell you a President.'

'You believe what you're saying?' Holt asked.

'I sure do,' Yigal said. 'In Israel we know that we couldn't exist if our people were dopes . . . so we don't treat them that way.'

'What worries you is merely a style,' Holt argued. 'It can change. What the hell is television?'

'A mirror,' Yigal said. 'It mirrors the empty silliness of American life. With all your vast problems, your pattern of life is essentially silly. In Israel, because we are under the hammer, we can't afford that luxury.'

'Why not work with us and change the silliness?' Holt asked.

'I watched you with Joe—the pressure you put on about Vietnam. Joe is trying to change one of the silliest wars men ever engaged in.'

'Are you siding with him, too?' Holt asked.

'Yes. His war in Vietnam is totally unjustified. Mine in Israel was totally justified. We young people are going to make these distinctions. And you've got to go along with us, even if it requires juggling the ideas of a lifetime.'

'Do you think you can do anything to help Israel . . . really?' Holt asked.

'I'm not doing it to help Israel. I'm doing it to help myself. Mr. Holt, I'm going to live only once. Not too many years if the hydrogen bomb goes off. And I am not going to spend my life in absurdities.'

We talked all night. Jemail dozed during the parts of our debate he could not fully understand, wakened whenever Jews or Arabs were mentioned. Holt used every argument in his arsenal—Korea, Sergeant Schumpeter, an international citizenship, patriotism that goes beyond religion, the manly life, the destiny of the United States—but young Yigal Zmora countered with a stubborn realism. He was a Jew who would have to fight his battle somewhere, and he did not propose to fight it for economic reasons against Cato Jackson in the streets of some American city; he would fight it in Israel where the enemy was known and where the survival of a people was at stake. He was a young man who had acquired that terrible burden—a clear vision of what ought to be done—and he was committed to doing it.

At dawn, when the plane to the north was being rolled out onto the Marrakech airstrip, Jemail wakened and said, 'You better get going,' and Holt insisted upon accompanying Yigal to the plane, hoping that he might convince him at the last moment to stay with his American citizenship. This meant that I was left to guard Jemail until such time as the Air France plane left for Casablanca. The last thing Yigal said to me was, 'Monica is very sick. There must be some way . . .'

But that was not the last thing said among the four of us, for as Holt left the room, Jemail grabbed his arm and said, 'Suppose you don't come back sign traveler's checks . . . you know what I do?' When Holt asked, the little Arab said, 'I go to police . . . charge you with smuggling spies out of the country.'

———•◆•———

Yigal's rejection of America had a demoralizing effect upon Holt. We would sit in his meticulously ordered room in the hotel and stare at the current sign which told us that we were at the same latitude as Jerusalem, Lahore, Shanghai, Kagoshima, Waco, the same longitude as Alte, Santiago de Compostela, Donegal, Samoa, Christchurch—and he would pound his knee and ask, 'How in God's name could a self-respecting boy choose a dump like Israel over the United States?' Even as we listened to Glenn Miller playing 'A

String of Pearls,' he would growl, 'They call this the Age of Anxiety. It ought to be the Age of Insanity.' Several times at meals he put aside his fork and told me, 'If I had any sense I'd get the hell out of here.'

He lingered on because of Joe. He suspected that Joe was planning some new, hideous move to escape the draft, and he even went so far as to interrogate Gretchen, who forestalled his questions by stating, 'I approve whatever he decides to do in this stupid business,' so Holt found no ally there, but still he hung around, maintaining an uneasy surveillance of Big Loomis and telling Britta each day, 'We ought to get out of here.'

His indecision reminded me of two notable passages in literature. In *The Eve of St. Agnes*, the best story-poem I know, Keats has that wonderful sentence, 'So purposing each moment to retire, she lingered still.' In *Death in Venice*, Thomas Mann had elaborated this concept with those telling scenes in which the learned narrator, even though aware of the impending plague, tarries in the doomed city in order to remain close to the golden boy, Pribislav Hippe. Why would Pribislav Hippe sweep into my consciousness in Marrakech, especially since the relationship involving Holt was entirely different? I suppose because educated men are doomed to carry burdens like this, depending upon them for illumination in times of crisis. Keats and Mann would have understood Holt, even if I could not, and the little comprehension I did acquire stemmed from them.

Holt's confusion mounted when the United States embassy in Rabat forwarded a cable to its consulate in Casablanca, which dispatched a special messenger to deliver it in Marrakech. The messenger, looking for Americans, came naturally to the Mamounia Hotel, where he inquired how he might best locate Joe. The desk clerk grabbed at Holt, who happened to be in the lobby. He signed for the cable, and when he had it in his hands, became suspicious, ripped it open and read it—then stalked through the alleys to the Bordeaux.

The cable said that the California draft board was determined to make a test case of Joe's refusal to cooperate. The board had rejected the opinion of Dr. J. Loomis Cargill, whose name they could find on no medical roster, that Joe was a drug addict. Let

Joe present himself to a convenient United States military base—
in this case Wheelus in Libya or Morón in Spain—for their doctors
to inspect him, and then let him report for immediate induction,
it being assumed that the military doctors must find Cargill's
diagnosis fraudulent.

At the Bordeaux, Holt demanded crisply, 'Where's Joe?' and was
told, 'Up in his room with Gretchen.' Bounding up the stairs, he
kicked opened the door, snapped Joe to his feet, and said, 'Cable from
the government.'

'I know what it is,' Joe grumbled, rubbing the sleep from his
eyes with one hand and trying to fasten a towel around his middle
with the other.

'What the hell were you thinking of when you announced yourself as a dope addict?'

'Give me the cable and get out of here.' He grabbed for the
torn envelope, but Holt evaded him.

'How dare you imperil your whole career with such an admission?
Thank God, the government had sense enough to know it was a
phony. Joe, you've got to come to your senses.'

Now Joe got angry: 'Why don't you get out of here? I don't
need you and Gretchen doesn't want you.'

Holt directed his attention to the girl, and said, 'You have some
influence on him. Keep him from doing these shameless things.'

But Gretchen said, 'You forget. I happen to agree with him
about Vietnam.'

'Who's talking about Vietnam?' Holt thundered. 'I'm talking
about a human life—a precious human life—and if you had any
womanly instinct, you'd want to protect it too.'

'I do want to. I want him to stay out of Vietnam.'

'Damn it all, life is something more than shacking up with some
broad! Life is also self-protection . . . and honor.'

'Please,' Gretchen said, 'go away. We'll never understand each
other.'

'You can say that again. How a woman in love can allow her man
to do the things this miserable son-of-a-bitch is contemplating is
beyond my understanding. Lady, for me you represent a new low.'
He had started stomping from the room when Gretchen said
quietly, 'If you had read Aristophanes, Mr. Holt, you would know

that the revolt of women against war is very old—one of the oldest themes in history.'

Holt went to the bed, grabbed her by the shoulders, and said, 'I read Aristophanes when you were sucking a bottle . . . and not a gin bottle either. For your information, Aristophanes was writing comedy . . . anything for a laugh. I'm talking deadly serious. Joe, I'm not going to let you do what you have in mind.'

He stormed from the room and they could hear him rampaging down the stairs, an ex-marine on fire. He left the hotel, and as soon as he got out of sight of the Bordeaux, ducked into a doorway and signaled to one of the numerous boys who infested that part of the city, hoping to pick up a tip here or there. 'Get me Jemail,' he said, giving the boy two dirhams.

It was a long time before the boy could find the little gangster, for Jemail was in the business section of town trying to unload his two twenty-dollar traveler's checks in the black market for more than their face value. When he did arrive he asked in a whisper, 'What's up, bud?'

'When Big Loomis has a special job with a draft dodger . . .'

'You mean, the photograph?'

'Yes, who does he use?'

'You ever seen Ugly Abdullah?'

When Holt shook his head, Jemail said, 'Well, I know him,' and it was agreed that for a price Jemail would wait with Holt to see if Abdullah was summoned to the Bordeaux.

He was. After Holt stormed out of the hotel, Joe had immediately climbed the stairs to consult with Big Loomis. 'They didn't buy the dope addict bit,' Joe reported.

'I didn't think they would, but it gave us time.'

'The cable said they were sure you were a fake.'

'Sometimes I think so myself.' There was an embarrassed pause during which Big Loomis was obviously reluctant to speak, but when the silence became prolonged he said, 'So you've decided to take Big Casino?' When Joe nodded, Loomis asked, 'You know what it entails? It'll be in your file for a long time.'

'I know.'

During this conversation Big Loomis had been furtively whipping through his papers, and now, with a quick thrust of his huge right hand, he pushed a photograph at Joe. It was intended to shock, and he watched Joe's face closely to see the effect. It showed two nude male figures—one a young American boy on his knees, the other a large, muscular Arab standing with his legs apart in order to display a huge erect penis which the boy was about to take into his open mouth. Joe, expressionless, said nothing. Big Loomis said, 'When they get this through the mail, they drop you from the draft rolls. It's very final.'

'I'm ready,' Joe said, and the big man directed one of his tenants to go fetch Ugly Abdullah.

When the Arab came down the alley, ready to be photographed again, Jemail whispered to Holt, 'That's our man.' It was a phrase he must had learned in the movies.

They trailed the big Arab into the Bordeaux, waited till he ascended the stairs, then dashed up the four flights to where Joe waited while Big Loomis prepared his camera. There was a moment of shocked dismay, broken when Holt dived headfirst at the huge Negro, butting him hard in the belly with his head and knocking him backward. 'You bastard,' Holt shouted. 'Not with this boy!'

A silent, grunting brawl ensued, with Holt lashing out indiscriminately at Big Loomis, at Joe and at Ugly Abdullah. As occasion permitted, Jemail darted in like a viper to attack his permanent enemy, Big Loomis, who took ineffectual swings at his little tormentor.

At first rush it looked as if Holt would subdue all three, for he quickly immobilized Joe and Ugly Abdullah, but he had sorely underestimated flabby Loomis, whose football training now manifested itself. With deft footwork and ham-handed swipes from left and right, he first defended himself, then started driving Holt back. Two effective wallops to the side of the head stunned Holt momentarily, but he recovered and swarmed over Loomis like a one-man typhoon.

The preliminaries over, the main bout now began, with the fat Negro dancing about the room on his toes, seizing every opening to slam Holt against the wall. Occasionally Loomis would shake one leg or another to drive away Jemail, who was kicking at his shins.

Now Joe and the big Arab regained control of themselves and vectored in on Holt, the former trying to grab his arms, the latter to knee him in the testicles. Surrounded by three such able adversaries, one might have expected Holt to call it quits, but the idea never entered his mind. Swinging with silent and dreadful force, he put into practice all the low tricks Sergeant Schumpeter had taught him in boot camp, clubbing first one, then the other of his three enemies until blood began to appear on their faces. One powerful blow rocked Big Loomis, who retaliated with a vicious swipe at Holt, knocking him clear across the room, but the engineer was up swiftly, butting his head into Ugly Abdullah's gut and knocking him out of the fight momentarily. Then he turned to face Joe, launching a violent blow which caught him on the side of the head, spreading him on the floor.

Loomis used this diversion as an opportunity to assault Holt from the blind side, and with a powerful slap of his open hand, knocked Holt down, but the ex-marine did not stay down. He was up and flailing in all directions, taking a moment's time out to knee fallen Abdullah in the face as he tried to rise. Two teeth splattered to the floor and for the first time one of the brawlers spoke. 'Get his photograph with no front teeth,' Holt gasped.

The end was inevitable. Big Loomis gave Holt a mighty cuff on the side of the head, and Joe, stung by the pain from Holt's knock-down blow, staggered up and swung with all his force and caught Holt's head as it was being snapped back. As if struck dead, Holt fell in a lump, and Big Loomis cried, 'You next, you little bastard.' He launched a blow at Jemail, but the little Arab was well down the stairs.

I did not enter the scene until two hours later. Jemail had run from the Bordeaux to the Mamounia, shouting, 'Mr. Fairbanks! They going to kill each other!' I hurried to the Bordeaux, but the battlers were gone and I surrendered my search. Late that afternoon Jemail came to inform me that they were all having hot soup together at the Terrace and sharing a bottle of whiskey which he had bought for them on the black market.

Where had they been? In a Turkish bath, salving their bruises and relaxing their muscles. When I reached the Terrace, they were drinking like old buddies and Big Loomis was explaining that in a brawl, he rarely used his fists: 'I prefer that good old-fashioned football swipe. You get your arm swinging, you can knock a man clear across a room.'

'I know,' said Holt, and there was no more nonsense about Big Casino.

———·◆◆◆·———

We stayed together most of that night, talking football and war and gang fights in Marrakech. Holt asked how an apparently decent man like Big Loomis, a man you could get to like when you saw him in action, could involve himself in a filthy deal like the photograph with Ugly Abdullah, and Loomis said, 'Some of us believe the war in Vietnam is indefensible. We're willing to do anything to escape it.'

'But you and Joe are born brawlers,' Holt said. 'You obviously love fighting, yet you claim conscientious objection.'

'I never claimed it,' Joe said.

'What I mean—how can you take a high moral stand against war and smear yourself with Big Casino?'

'Anything's permissible,' Joe said.

'But don't you realize a photograph like that could ruin your life?'

'With whom?' Big Loomis interrupted. 'Maybe years from now a photo like that dated 1970 will be a badge of honor. Certainly the people of our generation will understand and the others don't count.' He took a long swig of whiskey and pointed at Holt with the bottle: 'Take Gretchen. Suppose next year Joe wanted to marry her. A photo like that would rip her old man's head off. He'd go right up the wall and zoom around the ceiling like a dead chicken. But would it matter a damn to Gretchen? Wouldn't she love Joe even more for his guts?'

This was a line of argument I did not want to follow, so I left them and wandered across the Djemaá to the Bordeaux and as usual drifted into the big room, where I found twenty-odd young people submerged in the sweet, heavy smell of marijuana and captives of the gentle lassitude which prolonged smoking of that weed induced, and this was one of the most instructive things I was to do in Marrakech, for late that night I was given a view of the future which I have never forgotten.

The crowd was indulging in their usual sport of how they would settle the world's problems, and no one showed any rancor or strong conviction as he passed idly from one gigantic confrontation to the next. Vietnam, Cuba, revolution in South America, the Sino-Russian conflict, the folly of having wasted billions of dollars on the moon shot, the California report proving that Negroes are genetically inferior—all these were discussed with charming sincerity, and dismissed in a cloud of marijuana.

After midnight, when the crowd thinned a bit, conversation centered on the hydrogen bomb, and again I witnessed the deep confusion produced by this ever-present threat, but with irresponsible grace the conversationalists drifted away from this hovering topic and went on to talk about the fact that in all nations a new breed was rising which simply would not go to war: 'They'll have to machine-gun us in the streets,' one boy of nineteen said, and I suspected that this conclusion had not been idly reached; I regretted that Harvey Holt was not there to argue with him, for I was beginning to believe that the larger group of young Americans—the ones back home—would retain views somewhat like Holt's and would support war if it was presented to them within the historical tradition. Consequently, between these two groups of war-resisters and war-supporters there would have to be a conflict.

It was not then, however, that I caught my glimpse of the future. During most of the evening Rolf and Inger had served merely as hosts, supplying marijuana for the various pipes that were being passed and going to the Djemaá for bread and cheese for their smorgasbord. Toward three in the morning, when the last of the crowd was departing, Rolf stopped me as I was about to leave and asked, 'What do you think of the conclusions tonight?' and I replied, 'They reached a major conclusion every four minutes, and frankly, I'm dizzy.' He laughed and asked, 'I mean about the war bit?'

I said, 'I find it mildly offensive that a generation whose very existence was saved by the men who opposed Hitler before they were born should tonight be applauding when The Beatles make fun of that effort.'

Inger said, 'Not the effort. The wrong uses to which memories of that effort are being put today. We are truly fed up.'

I saw there was no use in my trying to discuss a theme on which so many had made up their minds so firmly, so I thanked Inger for her hospitality and started out the door, but again Rolf stopped me. 'Don't go,' he said, and I realized that he wished to talk with someone older, someone with a more combative mind than those he had been listening to that night, so I sat on the bed and he began, 'You seem to miss the big point about our generation. You get hung up on war or sex or drugs, and we don't. Inger and I, for example, we have a whole new thing going.' I asked him what it was.

'It's this. We are really cutting out from society. Whole segments of us are simply not going to have anything to do with the values that have motivated you. Take Inger and me. We see no reason to get married. We're sure it's an honorable estate for those who need it, but we don't. We see no reason to get educated in formal schools for formal degrees. If you want to be an engineer or a doctor, I grant that you need such degrees, but we don't. We educate ourselves . . . perhaps to a high level . . . but it's for us, not for some examining board.'

Inger, who now sat down on the bed beside me, holding between her fingers the fag end of a cigarette which one of the departed guests had rolled, broke in to say, 'We try to do everything as inoffensively as possible. Even our dress and the way we wear our hair is temperate. On those points, which society takes so seriously, we'll make concessions. But on the big issues, we won't. Honestly, we would die rather than submit to the old forms.'

She was so sincere, so attractive, with the yellowish smoke drifting past her head, that I asked, 'That's quite satisfactory, I'm sure, when you're twenty-eight. But how are you going to adjust later on?'

Rolf snapped his fingers and cried, 'That's precisely it! This is later on.'

'What do you mean?' I asked. 'I'm referring to a home . . . children . . . reliable income.'

The two Swedes winked at each other and broke into open

laughter. She grabbed my arm and said, 'You dear man! Don't you realize what we're saying? This is the future. This is our home . . . for six months every year.'

'Who's supporting you?'

Rolf shook his finger back and forth under my nose. 'You are missing the whole point, Mr. Fairbanks.' He opened an orange soda, poured me half a glass, kept the bottle for himself. 'In two weeks Inger and I fly back to Stockholm. We take no hash or keef with us. In those suitcases over there we have normal clothing, and before we go we cut our hair a little shorter. When we leave the airport at Stockholm we catch a bus that takes us to a flat just like thousands of others, and if you were to see us the day after we get home, you wouldn't be able to tell us from millions of others who look just like us. At noon that first day Inger will start to visit kindergartens, and by the time she's seen three, she'll have a good job at a good salary. She's a wonderful teacher and is in great demand.'

Inger interrupted to offer me her cigarette, which I declined, so she took several drags and said, 'As soon as Rolf lands, he reports to almost any asylum for the insane, and they're so happy to find someone who can cope—who will report to work faithfully—that he lands a good job even faster than I do.'

'For six months we work most diligently,' Rolf explained.

'Then what?'

'Then we quit.'

'Just like that?'

'Of course. It's time for Marrakech. Our real life is down here and we've saved enough bread to swing it. So Inger quits at the kindergarten and I quit at the asylum, and we're on our way.'

'And there's no problem when you get back?'

'I've been telling you. Within two or three hours after we land we have good jobs again.' He reached for Inger's cigarette, took a few puffs and returned it. 'It's a new world. Look at Inger. Can't you see that she's really very competent? Don't you suppose that if she wanted to apply herself to the rat-race of a school system, she could become headmistress in short time? There'll always be a place for Inger. And do you know why? Mainly because she's found a contentment that others haven't. She doesn't fight or elbow.

She has no aggressions. She is truly one of the beautiful people. If she went to America, she'd land a well-paid job within one day.'

'But I would never work more than six months a year,' Inger said. 'Then it would have to be back to Marrakech . . . for the real life.'

'You find this so gratifying?'

'Don't you?' she asked.

For a long time I could not answer, for I was trying to judge this mysterious life on its own terms—the Djemaá, the fellowship, the surcease the young found in marijuana, the benevolent indifference of the local society, the narcotic suspension of real life, the Arabian Nights milieu, the endless conversations, the music, the irresponsibility—and I had to confess its lure; but against it I had to weigh the tough gratifications of the other world, from which I also derived so much pleasure in hard work, competitive triumphs, art museums, tall buildings well designed, Beethoven symphonies, and homes with growing children. Finally I said, 'It could be gratifying . . . as a vacation.'

'Enough!' Rolf cried. 'That's all I want you to admit. As a vacation it has merit. You see, the difference between us is only the length of the vacation. Inger and I insist that it last at least six months, the work no more than six.'

'In Stockholm we work intensively,' Inger assured me, and I could believe her. 'Rolf usually takes over the most difficult ward of the asylum and ends the problems. He'd make a superb director. So we pay our way in society. But from society we demand a much better life than our parents had.'

'We thought of splitting the year, five months' work, seven months' vacation,' Rolf said, 'but you'll appreciate the reason we didn't. Inger found that in five months she couldn't train her children. I found I couldn't really clean up a ward in less than six. And we do like to do a good job.'

'Children?' I asked.

'We have a little girl,' Inger said, passing the cigarette to Rolf. 'When we get back, she's overjoyed to be with us. When we're down here, she's quite content to be with her grandmother.'

Rolf said, 'She's growing up rather better than those we see around her,' and Inger said, 'Don't look so surprised, Mr. Fairbanks.

In Israel thousands of children are brought up in the kibbutz. And they seem to turn out better than those who are brought up in the traditional ways. In the next generation it'll be standard across the world. The family is vastly overrated.'

'Will you ever get married?' I asked.

Rolf shrugged his shoulders. 'I've suggested it once or twice . . . not very strongly. Inger says she has all the children she wants. Also, when you work in an asylum, marriage looks somewhat less enchanting than it does when you're twenty and hopeful.'

'I doubt we'll need marriage,' Inger said, blowing the black bangs out of her eyes. 'Of course, we don't know how we'll feel when we're forty.'

'How about your daughter?'

'You mean . . . does our not being married affect her adversely? The only case in which our not being married might have harmful consequences would be if she wanted to marry the son of some traditional middle-class family, but we'd do anything within our power to prevent that anyway, and not being married ourselves seems an effective tactic.'

Then a new idea struck me. 'What you're doing is gambling that the economic system which men like me organize and keep going will be elastic enough—secure enough, if you wish—to enable you to enter it on your own terms, grab off a little cash, and return to your six-month vacation? In other words, you exist because we pay the bill?'

'Exactly,' Rolf agreed. 'With this correction. The system exists primarily for your benefit. You don't run the system for us. You run it for yourself. But in order to keep it functioning, you need our work and our consuming. You need us as much as we need you. And the price you're going to have to pay us in the future is one year's wages for six months' work.'

'And the promise of a secure job each time you come back?'

'Definitely. But not for our sake. For your sake. When I clean up the mess in the asylum—and I work very hard for the money you pay me—I'm not doing it for myself primarily. I'm doing it for you—to keep your system going.'

'Isn't it everybody's system? How many couples like you can it support . . . on half production?'

'Obviously it can support us,' Rolf said, 'and we're not concerned about the others.'

'Why not make your contributions over the whole year?' I asked in some irritation.

'Because that's too long a spell to work at other people's tasks.'

'Why not make them your tasks?'

'What you really mean is, "Aren't you interested in promotion and higher salary?" Inger would find no satisfaction in being head-mistress. I'd get none from being an asylum director. That kind of career gratification we've eliminated from our thinking, and so have millions of others. As for the money, we frankly don't want any more.'

'Has it been marijuana that's killed your drive?' I asked.

'In Stockholm we never touch it. Our police make it too risky . . . for the present. So abstinence is the price we have to pay for being eligible to work in your system. It's not particularly onerous.'

Inger said, 'You mustn't think of us as getting off the plane at Marrakech every six months and panting into the Djemaá, "Give me some keef, quick!" '

'What we do,' Rolf said, 'is what any sensitive person would do. We take one look at that kaleidoscope . . . then we hear Jemail shouting from the entrance to the souks . . . and we see Big Loomis paddling along . . . and tears come into our eyes . . . and we come through the alleys to this hotel . . . and Léon says, "Your room is waiting," and when everything is unpacked and the kids have dropped by to welcome us back and we've read our mail, we send Jemail out for some real fine grass and we roll a joint, and as we hand it back and forth we say, "We've come home." This is the reality. Stockholm is where we go into exile to help you run your asylums.'

It was nearly morning. As the last cigarette passed between the two, I asked, 'But doesn't it dull your energies?'

'Life does that,' she said.

'Then you admit they are dulled?'

'Yes. I can no longer take war or promotion or big income or a large house seriously. I reject empire and Vietnam and placing a man on the moon. I deny time payments and looking like the girl next door and church weddings and a great deal more. If you want to blame such rejection on grass, you can do so. I charge it to awakening.'

———— •·•·• ————

After Monica rejected Cato, she stayed alone for a while, but she was so sick that someone had to care for her, so, at Cato's and my urging, Big Loomis agreed to take her up to his quarters for a crash effort at persuading her to kick the heroin habit, and at first he made some progress, although whenever she could sneak a shot from Jemail she would feel exalted and would stand on the balcony and fill the central well with obscene accusations against the fat man, usually ending with the charge that he and Cato were sleeping together.

In spite of this accusation, the two Negroes drew closer together. At first Cato had been wary of the huge Texan, whose ideas showed none of the racial animosity that animated the Negroes of Philadelphia, even suspecting him of being an Uncle Tom. But as he came to know him better, he recognized that Loomis, through a conspicuous success in football, had acquired something denied to many blacks: a gratifying sense of personal achievement. Loomis knew he was as good a guard as any white man in Texas, and he had the offer of a contract from the Los Angeles Rams to prove it. He felt quite secure in the belief that if he returned to the States and got a degree in medicine he'd be as good a psychiatrist as any white man in New York, and maybe better, because he'd have a broader human experience.

So Cato had gradually developed a wary respect for Loomis and would have liked to be more friendly, but did nothing about it, fearful lest the Texan make fun of the phobias he had acquired in Philadelphia. But now that Monica had turned away from him, he felt desperately alone and unable to accept solace from any of the whites he knew. He moved more and more, therefore, into the orbit of the big man and often climbed to the top floor to talk with Loomis. He was surprised at the man's stability and breadth of vision.

'Staying alive in the United States is a game,' Loomis argued, 'and any smart boy should be able to lick it.'

'But you got to play white man's rules.'

'Man, white men face plenty of problems.' Loomis laughed. 'You think they're exempt from the pressures just because they're white? You see any Negroes killing themselves with heroin on this floor?'

And sooner or later, Cato always brought the discussion around to Monica. 'What can we do for her?' he asked one day after she had been even more hysterical than usual.

'You love her, don't you?' Loomis asked.

'Not that way, not any more. She took care of that . . . but good. But she is worth saving, Loomis.'

'You're beginning to show intelligence, son,' the huge football player said. 'The secret of life really is to love . . . and not only when someone else loves you back, and even when there's no obvious reason. That's when you grow up. We'll think of something to save this wounded chick.'

As Cato was descending the stairs he ran into Holt, who said, 'I'm looking for Gretchen.' Cato just nodded and kept going down.

Holt went on up to Gretchen's room, but she was out. Joe, lying in bed dressed only in skin-tight Levis, turned sleepily as Holt entered, and asked, 'What's up?'

'Britta and I are flying on to Ratmalana,' Holt said, 'and before we go I'd sort of like . . . well . . . I'd hate to be so close to Casablanca without seeing it.'

'It's a real drag,' Joe said. 'Sort of like Pittsburgh.'

Holt coughed, looked at his shoes and said, 'Well, being so close to where Humphrey Bogart saved Ingrid Bergman . . .'

'What are you talking about?' Joe asked.

'You know . . . that great song . . . "As Time Goes By." I'd sort of like to see where Claude Rains had his office . . . Peter Lorre . . . the whole bit . . .'

At last Joe realized that Harvey was referring to one of his old films, something made no doubt before Joe was born, so he asked, 'You speaking of a movie?' and Holt said, 'We discussed it in Pamplona,' and Joe said, 'We discussed a lot of that old-time crap in Pamplona. Was one of the films you liked shot in Casablanca?' and Holt said, 'That was the name of the film. Didn't you ever see it?' and Joe said, 'I never went to the movies much.'

They heard Gretchen coming up the stairs, and Joe called, 'Mr. Holt's here to see you,' but when she came into the room, Holt, not wishing to risk further embarrassment, said no more about the movie, but Joe said, 'He wants to drive to Casablanca,' and Gretchen cried, 'Of course! That's where the famous Bogart movie was laid. You told us in Pamplona you liked it. Want to borrow the pop-top?'

'Yes, but we want you and Joe to join us. Fairbanks is waiting at the hotel.'

Joe said that if you'd once seen Casablanca, there was no reason to double back, but Gretchen said she'd enjoy seeing the Moroccan plains and insisted that Joe come along, but as they were about to leave for the pop-top they saw Cato at the foot of the stairs, looking quite bereft, and Gretchen ran to him and took his hands and said, 'You've got to come with us.'

Cato came, but Britta did not. At the last minute she decided to stay at the Bordeaux, saying, 'I don't think Monica should be left alone,' and she remained to look after her. So our expedition consisted of four men and Gretchen, and we agreed that Casablanca was a bore, with little of the excitement that marked Marrakech and none of the mystery that had made the movie so popular. Holt said, 'Sometimes it helps to see the facts,' and he treated us to a good couscous, after which we prepared for the drive back to Marrakech.

But I said, 'Since we've come so far, let's go home by way of Meknès,' and with this adventuresome crowd, no further persuasion was necessary. I had suggested Meknès because I wanted Cato to see this royal city which had been rebuilt in its present form in the late 1600s by a remarkable king of Morocco, Moulay Ismail. I particularly wanted him to meet Moulay Ismail.

But on the trip to Meknès a diversion occurred which I could not have anticipated. As we were riding past fields now barren and abandoned, Joe stopped the car and got out to inspect some unimportant ruin that had been defending itself against the weather for some hundred years. He kicked at it with his shoe, inspected how the stones had been joined together, then knelt down and pulverized some of the soil in his hands. He asked, 'Is it true that what we now see as the deserts of North Africa were once the gardens and wheat fields of Rome?'

'No doubt of it,' I said.

'What happened?'

'You ever hear of Leptis Magna? Up on the coast?' He said he hadn't, so I told him, 'You ought to see it sometime. Or go way into the Libyan hills at Germa.'

'What do I see there?'

'Enormous cities which used to control some of the richest land in the world. Now it's a desert.'

'Climate change? Rainfall?'

'We think it happened because men misused the land. Destroyed one of the best agricultural areas Rome ever possessed.'

Joe stayed at the ruins for some time, standing there and looking around as if he were trying to imagine what this part of Africa must have been like in the good days. When he returned to the car he asked, 'What was the name of that place?' and I told him, 'Leptis Magna. Once you see it, you don't forget it.'

As we came in sight of Meknès, I asked Joe to stop the car for a moment so that I could point out something to Cato: 'Look at those enormous walls. They hide one of the most remarkable cities ever built by one man. Of course, there had been an earlier city, but he tore most of that down and started fresh. He worked on the job about fifty years, but in the end, had himself a masterpiece."

We circled the walls for some time so that my companions could savor the massive undertaking Moulay Ismail had attempted. Then we entered by a magnificent gate of many arches and drove through gardens and past palaces almost endless in extent, after which we parked the car and started to walk through the souk, with evidences of Moulay Ismail's megalomaniacal building urge always at hand.

At a café overlooking one of his grandest constructions, a nest of palaces, each big enough to house all the royal families of Europe, we found a table, and as we sat with our wine, I said, 'He was the cruelest man in African history.' Gretchen asked what kind of administrator he had been, and I said, 'Rather good. He had something over a hundred wives, and at one point asked King Louis XIV of France for an alliance with one of his daughters. He ruled with terrible severity and there is solid proof that he killed more than thirty thousand slaves with his own hand. Contemporary records tell how he held daily inspections of the construction, and if he detected even the slightest flaw or tardiness, he would personally isolate the blame, then with his left hand in the culprit's hair, he would jerk the head back and with his right hand slit the man's throat. More than thirty thousand . . . all Negroes.'

I was watching Cato's face as I said all this, but he gave no sign that he was even listening.

Gretchen took up the discussion: 'I was reading a book by a Scotsman who told about Bou Hamara. He operated in Meknès around 1908. Led a revolt against the government, so they threw him into a cage of lions, but they ate only one arm. So he was put into an iron cage and hauled around the country till he died. He had gathered his following with a magician's trick which made him notorious throughout Morocco—talking with the dead. In the early morning—now this was in 1908, remember—he would bury alive a slave and leave a tube projecting through the soil so the man could breathe. Then, when a crowd gathered in the afternoon, he would announce that he could talk with the dead, and he would stand near the tube and ask questions, which the buried slave would answer. After this continued for eight or ten minutes, with the man's voice giving good clear replies, to the astonishment of the mob, Bou Hamara would grind his heel into the tube and bury it. The slave, of course, would suffocate, and after about an hour, when he knew the corpse was well dead, Bou Hamara would spirit away the tube and invite his audience to dig up the dead body. He performed this trick over five hundred times.'

'And the slaves, of course, were always Negroes?' I suggested.

'The book said so.'

'Goddammit, Gretchen, you're always throwing history at me,' Cato finally burst out. 'What are you trying to prove?'

'American Negroes are making some historic decisions about Islam,' she said. 'I thought you ought to know what the traditional position of the Negro has been in Islam.'

'It's a bunch of fairy tales,' he snorted. 'Thirty thousand killed by one man. Five hundred buried alive by another. Ghost tales.'

'Exactly the right description,' I said. 'This city is populated with ghosts—thousands upon thousands that I haven't even referred to. An enormous percentage of them were slaves, and they were Negroes.'

'Why are you telling me this?' he cried in anger. 'Did you set this up on purpose for my benefit?'

'The trip to Casablanca was Holt's idea. But I thought: If we're going so far to see nothing, we might as well go a little farther to see something.'

'And you wanted to be damned sure I saw it?'

'I did. Ever since Moçambique, I've heard you spout a lot of nonsense about the historic relationship of Islam and the Negro. You ought to look carefully at what that relationship really was.'

'I have been looking,' he said quietly, 'and I get a constant feeling that with Islam we have a future. With Christianity, none.'

I pointed to the towering walls and structures of Meknès and asked him to try to re-create what had actually happened in the fifty years of Moulay Ismail's reign: the tortures, the slavery terminated only by death, the cruelty, the starvation, the warm corpses tossed by Moulay Ismail into the rising walls, the endless, timeless agony of slavery in those days, but at the end he said, persistently, 'In the United States it was the same,' and I said, 'If you think that, you're an idiot.'

The conversation ended there. Cato bought me a drink and we joked for a while, until he broke the mood by bringing us back to the subject that lurked in all our minds: 'We've talked and we've talked. But now we can't put it off any longer—we've got to do something drastic about Monica.' Harvey, who had kept out of the previous conversation, said, 'I think she ought to go into a hospital . . . right now,' and Cato said, 'I do too, but have you tried to argue with her . . .' His voice trailed off and I could see that he was biting his lip. Gretchen must have seen this too, for she leaned across the table and kissed him on the cheek. 'As soon as we get back to Marrakech, we'll drive her to the hospital.'

Holt said, 'Britta's very sensible on such matters. She located a hospital yesterday. That's why she wanted to stay with Monica.' He hesitated, then said, 'She's a very strong girl, Britta.'

Then, for no reason that I could explain, I said, 'When I saw Monica this morning, shouting down into the stairwell, I had the strange feeling that she could have been one of the young girls from Germany or France in the thirteenth century who had set out with the Children's Crusade, only to end as a slave in Meknès or Marrakech . . . endless sexual abuse . . . death at eighteen or nineteen.'

Very quietly Gretchen asked, 'What did you say?'

'I was thinking of the young people of all centuries whose destiny it has been to die in Marrakech.'

Gretchen rose, left our table, walked to the great wall that had been built by the anguish of so many, and pressed her back against it, keeping her palms extended against the stones. Facing us, she asked with excitement in her voice, 'You say that children from the Crusade got this far?'

'You must know the story. Their Crusade reached Marseilles, where Christian ship captains took them on board, promising to take them to the Holy Land . . .'

'I know. And sold them to the Moors as slaves. You mean they got this far south?'

'Where do you think they were sold? In Algeria and Morocco . . . many shiploads . . . they were lashed together in caravans and marched south to the good markets. Many of them must have died right here and in Marrakech. Boys and girls alike were sold as prostitutes and few of them lived into their twenties.'

Holt said, 'A hell of a lot of crusades end like that.'

Gretchen, keeping her place against the wall, said, 'This is what I was looking for . . . Portugal . . . Pamplona . . . Moçambique. It was this idea that kept eluding me. Of course! The Children's Crusade! It's been there all the time—and I couldn't see it.'

One of the most exciting things that can happen to a man past the age of sixty is to see a young person of talent and character stumble upon a concept big enough to occupy him in his first absorbing test of strength. Such moments are the building blocks of meaning. Now I watched as Gretchen reacted to the sudden explosion of an idea whose ramifications were extensive enough to encompass all that she had been inchoately dreaming of; it is quite possible that in those few minutes against the wall of Moulay Ismail she saw the total structure of the extraordinary book she was to write. I am sure she saw its interrelationships, its significance for our day, its heavy thrust of meaning for our young people. For the children of each generation enlist in their own crusade; it is only the banners that change.

We should have started back, but Gretchen and Cato wanted to wander through the souks of Meknès, and as we did so we often came upon evidence of the vast city that Moulay Ismail had built, and these two young people took from the stones and the crowds whatever evidence they required for the concepts they were building. For example, it could have been mere caprice when Cato stopped before the shop of a man selling hats; more likely it was the logical next step in an as yet unplanned but surely developing pattern of life. At any rate, he took Gretchen with him into the store and enlisted her advice in selecting the red fez which was to become his trademark in Philadelphia and the east. Wearing the fez for the first time, he led us through a nest of alleyways, walking in silence beside Gretchen, and long after I was exhausted, they kept on looking and probing.

Joe walked with Harvey, and from time to time I could hear snatches of conversation as they discussed Vietnam and ways whereby we could extricate ourselves from that imbroglio. It seemed as if they had reached some kind of understanding; Holt no longer rebuffed Joe's arguments as idiotic, and Joe listened to Harvey's stubborn logic.

This left me trailing, excluded from each of the dialogues, which gave me an opportunity to reflect upon the six young people I had come to know so well during the past year. As of this day Gretchen was settled; she saw ahead of her the long years of work and their fulfillment. As to what would happen emotionally from her involvement with Joe and Clive, no one could foretell, but at least a solid groundwork of self-understanding had been accomplished. Britta, God bless her open face, was locked into a course which, whether correct or not, was at least satisfying to her. Cato was on the verge of concretizing his concepts, and although I did not agree with many of them, I appreciated the fact that for him they were both necessary and inevitable. I hoped he could handle them. I had great faith in tough little Yigal and suspected that he had made the right decision on what was perhaps the gravest of all the problems faced by the six, but I doubted that I would have opted that way.

Joe remained as unsettled, as insecure, as he had been on that first day I met him at the Alamo. His love affair with Gretchen impressed me as immature, and his inability to solve his draft problem bespoke a character that was alien to mine, yet he remained the most likable of the three men, the one with whom I felt the most solid sense of identification. I felt like a father when I found myself thinking: I wish to hell he would make up his mind about things.

And there was Monica. As I thought of her my pace slowed and I fell behind in the crowded souk; for she was the one with whose previous life I had had the closest contact; she was, in a very real sense, my daughter, but as Cato had detected, I loved her also in another way. It had been no idle conceit when I had said that she stood for me as a summary of all those tragic European girls who had through a dozen centuries found their way to Meknès and Marrakech. Now, still relying on her youth and resiliency, I shook off my lugubrious thoughts, and hurried through the crowds to overtake the other four. When I caught up with them I said, 'We'd better be driving back,' and on the trip Gretchen chose a seat beside me and whispered, 'Thank you.'

When I asked for what, she said, 'You handed me the key.' To the others she said, 'This sounds ridiculous, but at the café when Mr. Fairbanks said "Children's Crusade," my whole book flashed before me. Within three seconds I saw the entire outline . . . each detail in order.'

The pop-top was filled with argument as to whether such a thing was possible, and my opinion was, 'It's not ridiculous. You've been brooding on this general topic—preparing yourself to receive such a flash of inspiration. Don't be surprised that it finally came.'

'But in three seconds!'

'It would be ridiculous only if it happened without your having done the spadework. In Portugal you devoted a lot of time to rejecting the Crusades. At Pamplona you were apparently wasting your time on the religious pilgrimages. In Moçambique it was probably something else. And your long preoccupation with ballads. All this made you eligible to receive what might seem like a sudden idea.'

We agreed that a young person's years of indecision were not wasted if they provided thinking space fortified by relevant data, even though some of the latter might not be understood at the moment, so that when the lucky moment of inspiration struck, it found tinder to ignite, but Joe asked, 'What if you just keep on drifting, not knowing what tinder to collect because you don't know what's going to ignite you?'

'You go on long enough,' Holt growled, 'you become a bum.'

Now there was extended discussion of what the term 'long enough' meant, and someone asked me what I thought, and I said, 'I don't know much about girls, but for a man it's almost impossible to waste a year before the age of thirty-five. Now if he wants to enter some field with a highly defined training period—say, medicine or engineering—he'd obviously lose time and relative advantage if he dropped out for five years, so if he wants to be a doctor or scientist he'd better get to it, even though his prescribed course might leave him narrow or even uneducated. But for everyone else, no year can be wasted. Knocking around Europe may be the very best thing a young man can do if he wants to become a great lawyer. Working in a lumber camp may be the real road to a vocation for the ministry. Suppose you want to be a fine dramatist. Maybe the route lies through Marrakech. I think a man has till the age of thirty-five for exploration.'

'By thirty he's a bum,' Holt said.

Again the talk became heated, with Cato and Gretchen agreeing with Holt that thirty-five was much too late, and finally I was challenged to prove my point, so I said, 'I graduated from the University of Virginia in 1930 . . . high marks and not a clue as to what it was all about. My uncle put up the money for a summer in Europe . . . kind of graduation present. So I came over, and it was totally confusing. A man in my uncle's office had scheduled me into Belgium, Italy and Spain, keeping me out of London and Paris as too dangerous. Every hotel was arranged for, and along with my letter of credit I carried introductions to specific gentlemen in Antwerp, Milan and Sevilla.'

'Why those three?' Gretchen asked.

'Because those were the bankers my uncle's firm knew. And they were the salvation of my life . . . those accidental cities.'

'How?'

'It happened in Sevilla.'

'Sounds like a song,' Cato said.

'It was one of those three-second bolts of lightning that Gretchen spoke of. I was standing in the nave of the cathedral at Sevilla and was comparing it with the cathedrals I had seen at Antwerp and Milan.'

'So what happened?' Joe asked.

'So in a flash of revelation I realized that I had a capacity which I guessed most men did not have. I could keep in mind an intricate series of data on these three cathedrals, and from that data, reach value judgments.'

'What do you mean?' Joe asked.

'Their length, their breadth—pure statistics. The beauty of their design, the quality of their light—aesthetics. Their location in the city, their relationships to their surroundings—comparatives. The enormous gloom of Sevilla versus the tracery of Milan versus that staggering Rubens altarpiece at Antwerp. I even had an evaluation of the French language in Antwerp, the Italian in Milan, the Spanish in Sevilla. In other words, I could crank into my cranium an immense volume of confused data and sort it out into a concise summary. One which encouraged the making of value judgments.

'In World War II I served on Admiral Halsey's staff, keeping conflicting purposes in balance. When I joined World Mutual it took them only a little while to discover that they could send me into a place like Morocco and ask me to decide whether to invest in Marrakech or Tangier or even jump the border into Algeria.'

'You keep all the data in your mind?' Joe asked.

'I'm a kind of IBM,' I said.

'Do they ever bend, staple or tear you?' Cato asked.

'Worse. They blow the fuse.'

'Could you crank me into your system?' Joe asked.

'It works only when value judgments are to be derived from facts,' I said. 'And I don't know the facts about you.'

'The fact is,' Holt broke in, 'he's a bum.'

'Not at twenty-two.'

'But at thirty-two he will be a bum, and at forty-two,' Holt said, but you could tell he hoped his prediction was wrong.

———•◦•———

When we reached Hotel Bordeaux at one that morning, Britta rushed out to throw her arms about Gretchen, crying, 'Monica's run off. With three young Moroccans.' Then she added irrelevantly, 'In expensive western clothes, Léon said.'

As we entered the hotel we could hear Big Loomis thrashing about the top floor, cursing Jemail. We ran up the stairs to find him issuing orders that the little bastard must be found . . . that he had the answer to this. When he saw us he exploded, 'Why in hell did you leave a mortally sick girl alone in a dump like this?'

Holt snapped, 'Why didn't you look after her? She was living up here,' and the big man said, almost tearfully, 'That filthy little pimp has been propositioning her for weeks. As soon as Britta went out for food, I saw him sneaking about my floor and I kicked him down the stairs. I thought that was the end of him.'

Now Britta burst into tears, explaining, 'I was gone only a few minutes. To the Terrace for some stew. When I came back she was gone. Léon said something about some Moroccans.'

We hurried down to find Léon, and he gave us our first substantial information: 'Jemail waited for Britta to leave. As soon as she was gone he rushed upstairs, but Loomis kicked him back down. So he whistled . . .'

'I heard that whistle!' Loomis cried, striking his forehead. 'My God, I thought it was a bird.'

'Right away Monica slipped down the stairs with her suitcase, and Jemail led her to the Djemaá,' Léon said. 'I followed to see what he was up to, and he led her to a car where three young men were waiting. *Whhhhhst!* They were gone.'

'We'll find Jemail and strangle him,' Loomis said, and with this he led us clop-clopping up the alley toward the Djemaá, asking all he passed whether they had seen that filthy little swine. At the great square we spotted some of Jemail's gang, and Loomis managed to grab one of the boys, demanding to know where Jemail was hiding. The boy called in Arabic to his companions, and within a minute Jemail came swaggering across the Djemaá, a stick of barbecued meat in his left hand.

'You want me?' he asked, striding right up to Big Loomis, who tried to grab him by the throat.

'What have you done with Monica?' Loomis roared.

'Monica gone,' Jemail said firmly, like an ambassador conducting negotiations with a sovereign he knows to be his enemy.

'Where is she?'

'Right now probably in bed with three clean young men.'

'Where?' Again Loomis lunged at the slippery little fellow, who danced away to safety.

'Why should I tell you?' he asked.

'Because within one minute I'm going to call the police.' Loomis fumbled for the chain from which his watch was suspended, located it, and started counting the seconds.

Jemail saw that the big Negro really intended to turn him over to the authorities, so he began to temporize: 'I do nothing wrong. I tell her these nice gentlemen like to sleep with her . . . pay her well. She want to. What police care about that?'

'Where did they take her?' Holt asked, trembling with anger.

This Jemail refused to answer, and, enraged, Holt reached out and caught the sleazy bowling jacket. 'Now, you little bastard, talk.' As Holt said this, Big Loomis grabbed for the boy, and Jemail screamed, 'Keep him away!' and Holt hauled the boy out of reach, cuffing him enough to let him know that he would receive no gentler attention from him than from Loomis. Then, as he shook the boy, he realized with loathing what the child was up to, for Jemail grinned at Holt and asked, 'How much you pay I tell you?' Holt was so repelled by the little pimp, he thrust him over to Loomis, who began coldly strangling him, so Holt had to grab him back again. 'Hold it, Loomis,' Holt said. 'Not till we find out where they took her.'

'What's it worth to you?' the boy insisted.

'Do you know where she is?' Holt asked.

'I know.'

'Where?'

'How much?' the boy repeated, whereupon Holt, to my astonishment, began beating the child about the head with blows of real force.

'You little son-of-a-bitch,' he whispered, 'you tell me where she is or I'm going to knock you unconscious.'

Jemail twisted partially free, turned to face his captor, and spit square in his face, an act which so surprised Holt that he relaxed his grasp, allowing Jemail to spring free. From a safe distance he reviled us in English, with a flow of such hideous indecency that we wondered anew how he could have acquired the words. There was no hope of catching him again that night, and we last saw him surrounded by his gang, obviously describing his exploits in getting the English girl out of the hotel and himself out of Holt's strong grasp.

We returned to the Bordeaux, distraught, and after an inconclusive conference as to what we might do next, Holt and Britta and I walked gloomily back to our hotel, and as we went upstairs, Britta said, 'Just as I was going to take her to a hospital.'

The next day was miserable. We convened at the Bordeaux in the morning, and in the daylight, its grubbiness was inescapable. In our speculations no one referred to the fables always current in Morocco of beautiful white girls surreptitiously fed hashish cookies, then abducted into a life of prostitution and slavery; these were tales used to frighten newcomers. Inger made the common-sense suggestion that Monica had voluntarily run off with the Moroccans for a sexual adventure and that after two or three days, would show up as though nothing had happened.

Two days passed with no Monica, and on the morning of the third we were not surprised to see Jemail, smiling, cheerful as ever, entering the Bordeaux to offer us another chance. 'I not talk with the fat one, or him or him,' he said, indicating Joe and Holt. 'But if you want to find your girl,' he said to Cato, 'we talk.'

They went out into the alley, and after a while Cato came back and said, 'For ten dollars he'll tell us where she is. I think we'd better pay.'

'Did he give you any clue?'

'No, but I got the idea she's not in Marrakech.'

'Not a dime to that monster,' Big Loomis protested so loudly that Jemail heard him. The boy popped his head through the door and warned, 'That fat prick makes one move, I never tell you.'

We concluded that we'd better give the little blackmailer his ten dollars, so we sent Cato back to negotiate. The agreement was: Jemail and I would hold the money till he told where Monica was, and I would guarantee that no one would hit him. Like a little pirate, he countered with a demand that we not start to chase him until he reached the end of the alley, and to this we agreed.

With the bill held half by me, half by him, and with his feet turned toward his escape route, he smiled up at me sweetly and said, 'Your friends the three engineers . . . they see her your hotel . . . on ride to the palms. They take her Casablanca, Hotel Miramar. That her idea, not theirs. She send me to arrange it.' Grabbing the money out of my hand, he darted up the alley.

I was too stunned to say anything, appalled that the engineers should have used me in this way, but Big Loomis swung into action. 'We'll call them from your hotel,' he said, and en route he arranged for two airplane tickets to Casablanca. The phone call was a disaster. I reached the Yale man at his office, and when he heard what I had to say, he started laughing. 'Please, Fairbanks. She was just a little tart. We took her to the hotel and had a good time with her . . . Yes, three of us . . . We gave her some money and sent her on to Tangier with two other men . . . It was her idea . . . She was in good shape . . . Hotel Splendide, Tangier.'

Quickly Big Loomis got three tickets to Tangier, saying, 'I'd better fly up with you and Cato. The others can leave by car right away.' He was not hopeful of finding Monica in Tangier: 'So many things can happen in that city.' Then he called the Splendide: 'Yes, two men did check in with Monica Braham—two days ago—but they checked out this morning . . . No, not engineers from Casablanca—two rather ugly types from Tangier, who could be traced if you were here.' Loomis said he would be, within a couple of hours. As soon as this disturbing call was completed, he phoned the Tangier police, asking for an officer he had known favorably for some years: 'Ahmed, we're in trouble. Name is Monica Braham, eighteen years old . . .'

'Seventeen,' Britta corrected.

'Seventeen, beautiful, fair-skinned, dark-haired English girl. Daughter of an important family. Using heroin daily. Checked into the Splendide two nights ago. Left this morning. We've got to find her.'

He hurried us back to the Bordeaux, but as we crossed the Djemaá, he stopped in anger and looked to the far side of the square, where Jemail lounged against a kiosk, watching our progress. As we approached, he met us with a new proposal: 'You fly to Casablanca, right? How about I get you the very best taxicab to the airport?' I shook my head no, and he countered, 'Then how about a limousine? Drive you non-stop right to Hotel Miramar, Casablanca?' Again I said no, and he replied, 'Hope you find her.' Then nonchalantly he waved goodbye and moved to the part of the Djemaá at which tourists were beginning to unload.

———— • • • ————

Police Inspector Ahmed was a large-boned, dark-complexioned officer who had served on the local force when Tangier was a free city belonging to no nation. It was then the roughest spot in the world, cynically governed by a commission of foreign consuls; it had been easier to arrange a murder in Tangier than to fix a traffic ticket in Chicago. Dope, forgery, blackmail, forced prostitution and the printing of false passports had been openly acknowledged specialties, and Inspector Ahmed had done what he could to keep the corruption within bounds.

Now Tangier was part of Morocco, and his job was easier, but not much. 'In the old days,' he said as we sat in his office, 'she'd probably be smuggled over the border into some well-run whorehouse. Today that sort of thing doesn't happen. Here's what we've found out. She hasn't left Tangier by plane and was not seen on the ferry to Algeciras or to Málaga. She's got to be here somewhere. So don't worry.' He was not a bland man, assuring us that everything would be all right, but he did convince us that if Monica could be found, he would find her.

The first day he accomplished nothing, and most of the effective searching was done by Big Loomis, who had a remarkable knowledge of Tangier and a host of friends. From one bar to the next we plodded, interrogating any habitués who had seen the English girl, and we established that she had spent her first night in the city touring the smaller bars with a man who had not driven her to Tangier. Apparently she had picked him up in this city, but none who had seen him recognized him.

We scoured the Zoco Grande, finding no trace of her, and passed down the narrow passageways to Zoco Chico, a small square surrounded by bars which served as headquarters for the hippies of Tangier. We asked young people of all nationalities and in all costumes if they had seen Monica, and two Swedish girls who looked as if they hadn't bathed for months said they'd seen her at a miserable flophouse called the Lion of Morocco. For fifty cents they took us down a series of filthy alleys to a ramshackle building. Its upstairs windows overlooked the harbor, and as we stood staring down at the scene which had excited so many travelers in past ages, an asthmatic Arab climbed the stairs to greet us. 'Yes,' he admitted, 'I had the English lady as a guest. One night. Yes, she was with several young Moroccan gentlemen and they left after only one day.'

That was all. We hurried back to police headquarters to inform Inspector Ahmed, but it was he who had news for us. 'We've found her,' he said, 'but I must warn you that she's in dreadful shape.'

'What happened?' Cato asked.

'Nothing unusual. Malnutrition, dope. She's in our hospital.'

He led us to the edge of town, where, on a cliff overlooking the incomparable bay of Tangier, a group of Catholic sisters still remained to run a hospital for a country which had more or less kicked out their church. The mother superior who met us was as gracious as nuns always seem to be when dealing with men of other religions, but she was not optimistic about Monica.

'This girl is gravely ill,' she warned us as we approached the ward. 'Only one of you had better enter.'

We looked at each other and by common agreement chose Cato to see her, but before he could enter, Inspector Ahmed produced a British passport: 'This is the girl, I assume.' Cato took it, opened its cover, and gave a deep sigh when he saw Monica's slim patrician face smiling back at him.

'It's her,' he said, and the nun led him into the room, but within a few seconds he was back, his face contorted: 'It's not Monica!'

Ahmed and I brushed past the mother superior and hurried into the room, where there on a bed lay a blond girl of about twenty who looked not at all like Monica. We guessed she was a Swede, but it was apparent from her appalling condition that we were not going to be able to question her. In fact, from my brief glimpse of her slack-jawed face I wondered if she would live much longer.

We piled into Ahmed's car and drove hurriedly back to the Lion of Morocco, where the asthmatic innkeeper told us that there had been several Swedish girls staying with him over the past week, but he knew nothing of them. One of them could have stolen the English girl's passport, but that was unlikely, because he ran a clean establishment, as the police would verify.

Cato suggested doubling back to the Zoco Chico to see if we could spot the two Swedish girls who had first told us Monica had stayed at the Lion of Morocco, and we found them there, lounging in the sun outside one of the bars. 'Are any of your gang missing?' Ahmed asked professionally, and in a slap-happy way the two girls began to cast up their friends, but they had apparently been eating hash and could not focus on anything, so Ahmed pushed them into his car and drove them to the hospital, but when we got there, the mother superior told us, 'She's dead.'

Ahmed dismissed this information as irrelevant and took us all into the morgue, where the young girl we had seen less than an hour ago lay stiffly under a sheet that left her face exposed: emaciated, debauched, dead. The girls required only a brief glimpse: 'It's Birgit.'

'Birgit who?'

'From Uppsala.'

'But what's her name?'

'Birgit from Uppsala.'

Inspector Ahmed jerked the sheet away, inspected the veins in her arms, rubbed the abused scar tissue, looked at us impassively, and replaced the sheet. 'Heroin,' he said.

On our ride back to the center of town I saw that Cato was trembling, and I turned as though to comfort him, but he kept his eyes averted and shrank away from me. When we reached our hotel room he fell into a chair and held his head between his hands, staring at the floor and mumbling, 'Oh God, let us find her . . . quick.'

'Any ideas, Loomis?' I asked.

'One. At the Zoco Chico, I know a waiter in one of the bars. He works only at night and he's the most corrupt human being in North Africa. Let's get a little sleep now, because he's our last chance.'

It was ten o'clock that night when we trailed down the hill to the Zoco Chico, to find it brightly lit and filled with tourists. It could have been a square in ancient Baghdad, or modern Damascus, or Cairo of a hundred years ago, except that this year it was crowded with drifters from all parts of the world, most of them young students who had vaguely wanted to see Marrakech but who would never get beyond Tangier. They were not an attractive lot, for most of them were sodden-eyed, unkempt, and shuffling of gait, as if they were hopeless men in their sixties instead of hopeful people in their teens.

Big Loomis headed directly to the principal bar, went to the inside office, and shortly returned with a waiter of indefinite age; he was probably no more than thirty-five but looked to be in his seventies, for he was totally debauched, and I was astonished that he could still hold a job. When he spoke, however, he was alert and persuasive: 'Gentlemen, you come to me highly recommended. My friend Big Loomis can be trusted and I have good news for his associates.' He dropped his voice, sidled up to us, and through black teeth whispered, 'The flowers were never sweeter in Lebanon.'

'What?' Cato asked.

'From Lebanon, riches beyond compare,' he said with a sly wink.

'What?' Cato asked again.

'Marijuana!' he snapped. 'Damned good marijuana from Beirut.'

'Kasim,' Big Loomis said, placing his arm about the waiter's shoulders, 'what we're interested in tonight is what happened to the English girl, Monica Braham.' Kasim showed no sign of recognition, but Loomis continued, 'She's a most important young lady. Seventeen. Daughter of Sir Charles Braham, London.'

'And Vwarda,' Kasim said, not changing his expression.

'The same,' Loomis said. 'And we're phoning Sir Charles tonight. He'll be deeply concerned about the whereabouts of his daughter.'

'He'll pay for helpful information?' Kasim asked.

'I will pay,' I interrupted.

Kasim, relieved to find that an American with funds was accepting responsibility, said, 'I know nothing of this girl. English girls? Look for yourself. There are hundreds. But I'll ask.'

'That's all we could hope for,' Loomis said reassuringly.

We sat down at a sidewalk table, and with Kasim standing over us as if he were only a waiter, we told him all we knew, giving him the names of the two places where Monica had slept and the name of the dead Swedish girl who had been using her passport. With this information, Kasim disappeared.

As we waited for his return, Big Loomis tried his best to divert us by saying he could calculate within a few months how long each passing foreigner had been in Tangier. Germans with quick step and keen searching eyes had come in this week. Englishmen with dragging feet and glazed expressions had been here upwards of a month. Americans shuffling along, looking furtively this way and that, uncombed and unwashed, had been here for half a year. And a few nondescript types from almost anywhere—California, Sweden, Sydney, Vancouver—were habitués who would never leave as long as they could collect money from some relative. A goodly number of this latter group, Loomis said, were remittance men from England or France, and some of them recognized the big Negro, who was himself technically a remittance man, and these sat down to inform us that things in Tangier were not so good as they had been four years ago.

When they heard why we were there, they expressed no interest at all in the disappearance of an English girl; it happened all the time and they had found it wisest to keep clear of such messes, because if you didn't, the damned girl was certain to wind up in your flat, with her parents accusing you of having seduced her. Cato, furious at such indifference, said, 'Don't be so goddamn casual,' and the Englishman said, 'She your girl?' and when Cato nodded, he said, 'Unquestionably she's shacked up with someone else, and what can you do about it?' Cato said, 'You son-of-a-bitch, she may be dying,' and the Englishman said, 'Aren't we all, really?' Cato wanted to clout him, but Big Loomis said, 'Cool it. We may be here for days.' As if to support this conclusion, Kasim returned about two in the morning with sorrowful news: 'No one knows where she is.'

———•◦•—

Our phone call to Sir Charles Braham in Sussex proved abortive. He was not at home . . . had gone off to some kind of agricultural meeting; and as I waited while the telephone girl tried unsuccessfully to track him down, I reflected that during each crisis in his daughter's life he had been absent. We could expect no help from him.

We spent the next day running down futile leads and at night we again went to the Zoco Chico, but Kasim was not on duty. Loomis asked where he was, and the proprietor said, hopelessly, 'With Kasim, who knows?' Fortunately we waited, for after midnight the clever fellow appeared with a big smile on his face. 'I have found her! The police could do nothing, but I have found her.'

We leaned forward, and he said, 'It's been most expensive. I had to send a boy to Chechaouèn.' At the mention of this ancient hill town, Big Loomis whistled, for it was a considerable distance southeast of Tangier, and that an English girl would go there was inexplicable.

Cato spoke first. 'Can we drive there?'

'I think you should,' Kasim said.

'What do you mean?'

Kasim looked at Cato, then at me. 'Maybe it's better I speak with this gentleman,' he suggested, leading me to the rear of the café. 'The news is not pleasant,' he whispered. 'Two boys from here made her acquaintance . . . rented her out to seven of their friends . . . one after the other. Then they took her to a country place in Chechaouèn. She became very sick, so they ran away.' He paused, then added a scrap of information which he knew summarized the case but which was too strong to share with Cato. 'My boy told me over the phone, "They screwed her eight or nine times a day but wouldn't give her anything to eat." '

When we reported her whereabouts to Inspector Ahmed, he commandeered an official limousine, loaded the three of us in, and sped eastward toward Tétouan, the city which Spain had renamed grandiloquently Tetuán-de-las-Victorias in commemoration of some minor skirmish. It was dawn when we got there and turned south along a winding road that carried us high into the foothills of the Atlas. The day was well begun by the time we reached Chechaouèn, a very old caravan stop nestled within a rim of hills. We drove to a spot near the square and were met by local police, who set out to find Kasim's boy. He was located at a booth in the square, and as we crossed this irregular-shaped market we could have been in any Biblical city two thousand years ago. Even the costumes of the

Arabs who were opening their stalls were unchanged, their habits untouched by the modern world, for this was a city with very old religious interests, and modernism was not welcome.

Our guide was a boy of fifteen, trained by Kasim in the intrigue of Tangier, and knowledgeable in those vices which could be turned to profit. As he led us past the market and into an ancient quarter of the town, one that for centuries had been forbidden to infidels, he selected me as the probable leader of the group and confided, 'Your daughter is very sick. Maybe we should get a doctor.'

I started to say that I was not her father, but decided not to complicate things. 'Fetch a doctor, if one is available,' I said, and he took us on a short detour to the home of a young medic who had been trained in Casablanca and was now posted to Chechaouèn for public service. He spoke excellent French and asked which of us was ill. When the boy explained that my daughter had fallen upon bad days, he nodded gravely and told me, 'We saw a good deal of this in Casablanca. Swedish girls mostly.'

The boy took us down some extremely narrow alleys, and I said to the doctor, 'Things haven't changed much here in two thousand years, have they?' He shook his head sadly. 'This is the backland of Morocco. And things won't change for another two thousand years.' We stopped at the door of a small mud-walled house that must have been at least two hundred years old, and I experienced a sense of tragic drama when I thought that it was to such a hovel that Monica had come. I was about to enter when the doctor said, 'I'd better go first,' and he allowed the boy to lead him inside.

As we waited apprehensively, I could see that Cato was tense to the breaking point. To Inspector Ahmed, of course, Monica was merely another European girl to be traced; if he did find her today, tomorrow he would be looking for someone else.

Now the doctor came out, very grave, saying, 'One of you had better join me.' I stepped forward, but Cato in his red fez elbowed his way ahead of me and disappeared through the small door. In a moment we heard a terrible cry—a shriek of mortal anguish. Ahmed darted into the house, but before I could follow, Cato appeared in the dark hallway, bearing in his arms the dead body of Monica.

She was a ghost, her arms and legs hanging like withered twigs, her black hair a tangle about her once-beautiful face. Her left arm showed the hideous and familiar sore which I supposed had finally caused her death.

The doctor shook his head in professional disgust. 'That abscess could easily have been cured.' He looked at Cato and me and said, 'Didn't any of you notice her face? Her color? That's what killed her. Serum hepatitis. For weeks it must have been incubating in her body and was able to break out with terrible force because of her malnutrition.'

'She died?' Inspector Ahmed asked professionally. 'She wasn't killed?'

'She died.'

'Then we face no legal problem,' Ahmed said, evincing no further interest in the case.

'How did she catch hepatitis?' I asked.

'Infected hypodermic. Lots of young people kill themselves that way.' The doctor turned to face us: 'Any of you use her needle six weeks ago . . . seven weeks?'

Cato, still holding the dead girl, shook his head numbly.

The doctor spit in the dust and said, 'The tragedy is that if any of you had made one sensible move, she could so easily have been saved.'

———◦•••◦———

When it came time for us to drive back to Tangier, the question arose as to what we should do with Monica's body, and Inspector Ahmed suggested, 'We'll put her in the trunk,' but when that dark receptacle was opened, Cato rebelled. 'No! She rides with us.' Ahmed shrugged his shoulders and said, 'It's going to be damned uncomfortable.'

Cato pulled off his shirt and wrapped it around Monica, and we climbed into the car, placing her body across our knees, her head resting against Cato's chest.

As we picked up speed along the road that would take us into Tangier, I affected not to notice that Cato, drawn deep within his corner, his arms about Monica's shoulders, was weeping silently. Occasional convulsions of his sagging shoulders betrayed his passion, and I thought of how bitter his experiences with love had been: Vilma kicked to death, meaninglessly, on the streets of Philadelphia; Monica dead of a dirty hypodermic needle in Morocco, when even the most routine attention would have prevented it. As I maintained surveillance of him I felt that he represented his generation, courageous in building new modes of behavior, defenseless when overtaken by the ancient tragedies that no man escapes.

In my compassion I reached out to touch him, but he reacted as if I had struck him. 'Keep your hands off me!' he cried. 'I want no sympathy from white men,' and I told him, 'I didn't offer it as a white man.' From the front, Big Loomis growled, 'Cool it back there.'

Cato half-turned to look at me, his red fez cocked to one side, his dark eyes brimmed with tears. He wanted to say something conciliatory, of that I am sure. He wanted to return my gesture, for his hand left Monica's shoulder and started to reach for mine, but at this moment his grief overcame him and he collapsed in shaking sobs which he no longer tried to hide. In this manner, sharing the burden of the dead girl we had loved, we returned to Tangier.

As we drove up to the police station, I spotted the yellow pop-top. Gretchen and Joe ran out to greet us, and before they could see what Cato and I were holding, Gretchen asked eagerly, 'Did you find her?'

'We did,' Loomis said.

'Britt! They've found her,' Gretchen cried as Holt and Britta came up.

They saw Cato and me, grim and silent, and then, looking down, saw the motionless form on our laps.

'Oh my God!' Gretchen cried. 'What's happened?'

'She's dead,' Cato said.

Gretchen put her hand to her lips and watched, stunned, as we climbed out of the car, leaving the body stretched across the seat. Cato and I had brought Monica home; we could do no more, and so we stood aside.

Inspector Ahmed and another policeman came back and routinely started to unload the body, but as they did so, the shirt pulled away from Monica's head and disclosed it to all who were watching.

'Jesus!' Joe cried at the awful sight.

Quickly Inspector Ahmed replaced the shirt. But Britta, walking stolidly to where Ahmed held the dead girl by the shoulders, carefully drew it back and gazed down at her friend. She was hideous, terrifying, staring at us, her mouth ajar, her tongue protruding. This was not death; it was an indecent mockery.

'Cover her,' Holt said, but Britta put an arm around Monica's head. Tenderly she closed the eyelids and straightened the wild strands of hair. She bent to kiss the sunken cheeks, then turned to us, crying, and said, 'We gave her so little help.' Holt started to say that nothing would have helped Monica, but Britta placed her hand over his mouth, and Ahmed and his man carried the dead girl to the plain wooden box that awaited her.

———————

Morocco was used up.

We sat at our sidewalk table in Zoco Chico and found the parade of young drifters frightening and ugly. Each stringy-haired girl reminded us of what had happened to Monica.

No one proposed going back to Marrakech, and to remain in Tangier was unthinkable. Nor was there any need of us. The authorities showed no inclination to track down, let alone prosecute, the young Moroccans who had taken Monica to Chechaouèn, because she had accompanied them willingly. As for their maltreatment of her, it would be impossible to prove that they had collected money from the friends they had called in to use her, and Inspector Ahmed shrewdly guessed that her father, Sir Charles, would not be eager to fly to Tangier to press charges that could only reflect on him. He told us, 'Last year we had twenty-nine girls die. Much like your friend. From all parts of the world. And in only two or three cases did the parents wish us to delay the burial so they could come. The case is closed.'

Not with us. It never would be. I could see that Gretchen and Britta considered themselves fortunate that they had associated with men who had protected them, and I noticed that each drew closer to her man. The men, for their part, were filled with helpless outrage that a girl as fragile as Monica had been so abused. A wandering pimp, seeing Joe momentarily detached from our group, sidled up to him and asked, 'You like to spend one whole night my sister? Very young, very clean.' Joe punched him viciously in the gut, doubling him with pain. It was then that I said, 'We'd better get out of this town.'

Now Gretchen sprang her surprise. Leaning across the table, she reached for Joe's hands and said, 'It's time for us to do what must be done. I'm giving you the pop-top. Go where you have to go, then sell it.'

There was a protracted silence. Joe reddened and was speechless, confused by the transparent revelation contained in her impulsive act. Britta smiled approvingly. It was practical Holt who spoke: 'How are you going to transfer the papers?' I suggested the American consul, but Kasim, monitoring our conversation, hurried up to suggest, 'I have a friend who is a printer. For ten dollars he'll forge you a complete bill of sale . . . all documents in order.'

'What country to what country?' Big Loomis asked.

'You name it. Germany to Sweden, Egypt to Tanzania. To him it's all the same.'

To my surprise Holt agreed. 'Probably the best way. You get mixed up with an American consul . . . there aren't that many months in the year.' So Gretchen unloaded her purse and produced a series of papers which Kasim stuffed into his inside pocket.

'How long?' Gretchen asked.

'With my friend, every case is an emergency,' Kasim said reassuringly. 'Forty minutes.'

'So fast?' Gretchen asked.

'In Tangier . . . yes,' Big Loomis said, but Kasim did not depart immediately. Going to Joe, he asked, 'How about a passport? Maybe a special passport?'

'How much?' Joe asked cautiously.

'Depends upon what ones we happen to have on hand. By the way, any of you like to sell your passports? Good money.'

Holt, afraid that Joe might be seriously considering exchanging his American passport for some other in order to escape detection by American officials, said firmly, 'We'll get along with the pass-ports we have.'

'If problems should arise,' Kasim said unctuously, 'I'll be back in forty minutes.'

'Are you serious about the car?' Joe asked.

'Yes. It's a present . . . to an extraordinary young man.' Quietly Gretchen added, 'A young man with dignity.'

'Where will you go, Joe?' Holt asked.

'I heard these kids at the Bordeaux the other night. They said the big scene was Shinjuku.'

'It's very good,' Holt said. 'Lot of girls . . . lot of action.'

'Where's Shinjuku?' Britta asked, insistent as ever upon iden-tifying places.

'Tokyo,' Holt said. 'The most exciting part of Tokyo.'

Gretchen suggested, 'Why don't you try India? A lot of people find the answers . . . the illumination . . . in India.'

Now Big Loomis broke in: 'You would be out of your mind to waste one minute in that country. No fable of our time is more ridiculous than the one which says that India has the answer to anything.'

'I was speaking of the spirituality,' Gretchen replied.

'So was I,' Loomis said. 'I lived in India for the better part of a year . . . also Sikkim and Nepal . . . good grass . . . good con-versation among the Europeans. But the illumination referred to by starry-eyed kids in Greenwich Village and Bloomsbury . . . it's not there. That's an illusion sponsored by half-ass professors in half-ass American colleges.'

Holt confirmed the big man's thesis: 'It's like Tyrone Power wandering through Europe and finally winding up in India. He didn't learn anything.'

We turned in our chairs to look at Harvey, who refused any further elaboration. Joe started to ask what Tyrone Power had to do with this conversation, but shrugged his shoulders and turned back to Loomis, who said, 'I appreciate the fact that you girls have had a rough time . . . Monica's death . . . and I apologize for what I'm about to say, but from the nonsense that Gretchen's been spouting, I suppose you have to hear it. When I landed in Calcutta —God forbid that such a thing should happen to any man—I was in search of illumination. I spent three days in that cesspool of horror, with starving children mocking my fat, with men and women dying in the streets, with whole families living off one garbage can, but I was able to forgive it all on the principle that it is from such squalor that we sometimes gain illumination. Great spiritual leaders simply do not arise from banks or university faculty clubs. I made every concession, and in time I began to revel in the death and terror of Calcutta. I also established contact with a great sadhu who volunteered to explain the world's mysteries to me. He was six feet two inches tall and weighed ninety-one pounds, including his beard. He had once stared at the sun for forty-eight uninterrupted days, and he had about him a certain modesty, because he felt that in my case he ought to consult with two other sadhus, built a lot like himself and with equally long beards. These three holy men—who conducted office hours in a village close to Calcutta, and charged stiff fees—told me many things, and occasionally they said something about equal to what a fifth-grade teacher in a good elementary school might say. Offhand I can't give you an illustration, because the teaching of these holy men was more or less nullified by what they were caught doing two days before I completed my course.'

He paused, looked only at the girls and waited for Gretchen to ask what they had done. 'In conformance to the ritual of their particular school of sadhus, they dug up the grave of a five-year-old girl, dead for three days, and ate her.'

For a moment no one spoke; then Britta said, 'I think I'm going to be sick,' and she disappeared. Gretchen sat tapping her fingers on the table, then said, 'Now I know it's time I went home and got to work. What are you going to do, Cato?'

He waited till Britta returned, pale and embarrassed, then said in hard syllables, 'I haven't known what I wanted to do . . . exactly. Now I do. I'm going to leave here and bum my way to Egypt. Then I'm going down the Red Sea and cross over to Jiddah. From there I'm walking every step of the way to Mecca, where I shall run six times around the great black stone, and when I get back to Philadelphia, I shall put on my fez and announce myself as Hajj' Cato. I'm going to start a movement, and it's going to be just as great a racket in favor of blacks as Christianity was against them.

And when it's securely launched, you sons-of-bitches better beware.'

With that he rose, adjusted his fez, and left us.

When he had gone, Big Loomis said reflectively, 'Three years ago I wore a fez. But don't worry about that kid. He has staying power. When he gets back to Philadelphia he's going to be difficult for you whites to handle, but he's the kind of Negro we all need.'

Gretchen said, 'I notice you use *Negro*,' and Loomis replied, 'Three years ago I used *Afro-American*. And to me it was important.'

I asked the huge man what he proposed doing, and he said, 'I'll probably stay in Marrakech as long as my mother can send me a little money. I've a lot of work to do down there. Sometimes I'm able to help kids like Monica and Cato.' He rose in full regalia of beads and hand-woven fabrics and Tibetan boots and stalked up the hill toward Zoco Grande, where he would catch a bus back to Marrakech.

'You think what he said about India was true?' Britta asked.

'I saw things like it,' Holt said.

'How would I get to Shinjuku?' Joe asked.

'Well, you'd drive from here to Egypt. Then you'd have to take a boat to Beirut, because you couldn't transit Israel. From there you'd head for Damascus and Teheran and then across the desert to Afghanistan and down into Pakistan and through Lahore to India. It's easy to drive across India and you'd go through Burma and Thailand. You wouldn't be able to transit Vietnam, so you'd ship your car on a Japanese freighter . . . they cost practically nothing . . . and you'd be in Shinjuku.'

I listened with admiration. It was like telling a neighbor how to get to the new grocery: 'You go to Afghanistan and turn left.'

'Could I make it on two hundred and eighty bucks?' Joe asked.

'Why not?'

There was now an awkward silence as Joe and Gretchen looked at each other—one preparing to head for Tokyo, one for Boston—and out of natural respect for her feelings, he extended her an invitation: 'How about coming to Japan with me?' and she said, 'Thanks, but no thanks. I heard a man say that taking your wife to Tokyo was like taking a ham sandwich to a banquet.'

'You're not his wife,' Britta pointed out.

'I know, but I don't want to spoil his fun with those almond-eyed chicks.' This fell flat, and there was another awkward silence.

Impulsively Gretchen opened her handbag and fumbled around for her traveler's checks. 'You were the best driver in Africa,' she said, 'and you merit a bonus.' Hastily she signed a batch of checks—whether they were fifties or hundreds I couldn't see—and with acute embarrassment shoved them at Joe. He took them, mumbling his thanks. She then looked up at him with a radiant face, free of fears and tensions. 'We'll meet somewhere,' she said, and they shook hands.

What Joe said next must have been difficult for him, for he knew it was likely that Holt was aware of his former interest in Britta. Sucking in his breath, he said, 'You know, Holt, since you're heading for Ceylon and I'm heading for Japan, why don't we drive across Asia together? The three of us, I mean.'

'I'd like that,' Holt said evenly. 'We could talk.'

'That's what I had in mind.'

'And we could share expenses,' Britta suggested.

'There's one thing,' Joe said. 'I'd want to stop at Leptis Magna.'

'Why not?' Holt said. 'We go right through it.'

'What's to see in Leptis Magna?' Britta asked.

'Ruins. I want to see one of those Roman cities that vanished because they misused the land. Maybe—when I'm through with jail, that is—I might like to work in land use. Mr. Gridley said I ought to think about getting a job in a national park. Keeping the earth alive.'

'We could look at the irrigation in Egypt, too,' Holt suggested, but I noticed that as he said this, Britta frowned and was about to speak, but she was forestalled by the return of Kasim with the forged title. Gretchen paid him the ten dollars, but he whined, 'That's for the printer. What about me?' So I threw him another two and Joe started stowing his gear in the pop-top.

Now Britta spoke. 'We can stop at Leptis Magna,' she said cautiously, 'but not a lot of other places, because we have to be in Ceylon by December 23.'

'No we don't,' Holt assured her. 'It's true, I'm due back. But the company isn't going to get itchy about a week here or there.'

'What I meant to say,' Britta explained, 'is *I* have to be there on the twenty-third.'

'Why?'

She blushed and said in a low voice, 'Because I've sent my father an airplane ticket to visit us in Ceylon.'

Holt was startled. 'Where'd you get the money?' he asked.

Britta put her hand on his and said, 'Whenever you gave me money for anything, I put a little aside.'

I was looking at Holt when she said this, and he cocked his head and stared at her in astonishment, and across his deeply lined face came that look of loving bewilderment which husbands sometimes cast at wives with whom they have lived for many years but are only now discovering.

But Gretchen remembered: 'In Alte you told us that if your father was ever forced to see Ceylon as it actually was, he'd collapse.'

'I said so then,' Britta confessed, 'but now I believe that men ought to inspect their dreams. And know them for what they are.'